SAY GOODBYE

Titles by Karen Rose

DIRTY SECRETS
(enovella)

Baltimore Novels

YOU BELONG TO ME
NO ONE LEFT TO TELL
DID YOU MISS ME?
BROKEN SILENCE
(enovella)
WATCH YOUR BACK
MONSTER IN THE CLOSET
DEATH IS NOT ENOUGH

Cincinnati Novels

CLOSER THAN YOU THINK
ALONE IN THE DARK
EVERY DARK CORNER
EDGE OF DARKNESS
INTO THE DARK

Sacramento Novels

SAY YOU'RE SORRY
SAY NO MORE
SAY GOODBYE

SAY GOODBYE

KAREN ROSE

BERKLEY

NEW YORK

BERKLEY
An imprint of Penguin Random House LLC
penguinrandomhouse.com

Copyright © 2021 by Karen Rose Books, Inc.
Penguin Random House supports copyright. Copyright fuels creativity, encourages
diverse voices, promotes free speech, and creates a vibrant culture. Thank you for buying
an authorized edition of this book and for complying with copyright laws by not
reproducing, scanning, or distributing any part of it in any form without permission.
You are supporting writers and allowing Penguin Random House to continue
to publish books for every reader.

BERKLEY and the BERKLEY & B colophon are registered trademarks of
Penguin Random House LLC.

Library of Congress Cataloging-in-Publication Data

Names: Rose, Karen, 1964- author.
Title: Say goodbye / Karen Rose.
Description: New York: Berkley, [2021] | Series: Sacramento novels; 3
Identifiers: LCCN 2020047400 (print) | LCCN 2020047401 (ebook) |
ISBN 9781984805331 (hardcover) | ISBN 9781984805355 (ebook)
Subjects: GSAFD: Suspense fiction.
Classification: LCC PS3618.O7844 S28 2021 (print) |
LCC PS3618.O7844 (ebook) | DDC 813/.6—dc23
LC record available at https://lccn.loc.gov/2020047400
LC ebook record available at https://lccn.loc.gov/2020047401

Printed in the United States of America
1st Printing

To Sheila. I'm so very lucky to have your friendship. Much love always.

To Canadian Sarah. Our door is always open, especially on Thanksgiving. I wasn't able to slide your idea into the book, so I hope this is the next best thing.

To Martin, as always. There's no one I'd rather quarantine with than you. I love you.

SAY GOODBYE

PROLOGUE

EDEN, CALIFORNIA
WEDNESDAY, APRIL 19, 10:30 P.M.

Hayley Gibbs winced as her belly scraped against the doorjamb lead-ing into the clinic. *Dammit.* She'd underestimated her current—and increasing—size yet again. Damn pregnancy.

She gave her stomach a soothing pat. *Not you*, she silently told her unborn child. Her daughter. *I'm not mad at you, Jellybean. Never you.*

She was mad, however, at her mother. She was beyond furious with the woman. And scared of her at the same time. The fury was nothing new. The fear . . . well, that was new. At least this kind of fear. It had always been the fear of not having enough to eat, or of where they'd live the next week, or what her mother would do if she learned that Hayley was having sex with her high school boyfriend Cameron, or that her little brother Graham was shoplifting electronics.

Then she'd found out what her mother would do if she found out.

Move us here. To this hellhole in the middle of fucking nowhere.

From which Hayley was going to escape or die trying.

She just needed to get into the clinic's office.

Drawing a breath, she eased her way through the clinic door and quietly closed it behind her. She stood statue-still, listening for the sound of anyone else. But it was silent.

Thank you, she mouthed, not sure whom she was thanking. Probably not God, or not her mother's God, at least. The God Hayley wanted to thank would help her keep her baby safe. The God she wanted to thank definitely wouldn't approve of these . . . monsters.

Eden was full of monsters and her mother had dragged Hayley and her brother here, kicking and screaming.

Hayley rubbed her fingertips over the thick chain welded around her neck.

Welded. Around. My. Neck.

It wasn't jewelry, despite the locket that dangled from it. It was a collar. It was ownership.

It was also empty, at the moment. The locket. But after the baby came, her locket would be filled with her wedding photo. She was technically married now—and had been since the day they'd arrived in this awful place. Luckily her "husband" didn't want to "consummate" their union with another man's bastard in her belly, so she hadn't been forced into sex. Yet.

He didn't want their wedding photo sullied with the evidence of her sin. He'd have the photo taken after the "bastard" was born. Which gave her a little more than six weeks.

Hayley's gut churned at the thought of being the fourth wife Brother Joshua would have—at the same time. Polygamy abounded in Eden, and Hayley wanted no part of it.

She hadn't wanted any of it. She just wanted to be with her boyfriend and live their lives the way they'd always planned since their first homecoming dance in the ninth grade.

No, this baby wasn't what she and Cameron had planned, at least not now. They were only seventeen, after all. But Cam's parents had stepped up and said that they could live with them once the baby came, that they could still go to college.

But her mother hadn't agreed. The next thing Hayley had known, she and Graham had been forced into the back of some guy's truck. *And now I'm here.*

Here in Eden. Here in the clinic, closed at the moment. If she got caught . . . She shuddered at the very thought. But she had to try. She was more afraid to stay in Eden than she was of any punishment. And Pastor—the creepy leader of this creepy cult in the mountains—he terrified her. The people here obeyed him like robots.

She rubbed her stomach as it lurched again. *Come on now. Don't worry, Jellybean. I'll get us out of here before you arrive. I promise.*

So now she had to. She'd just promised her daughter.

Her daughter. She was going to have a daughter. She and Cameron had seen the baby on the ultrasound back at the ob-gyn's office in San Francisco, had heard her heartbeat. Cam had cried, his hand clutching hers as they'd stared at the small screen.

I love you, Cam, she whispered inside her own mind. *I love you both.*

They hadn't chosen a name yet, so they called her Jellybean for now.

Her daughter didn't even have a name, but Hayley would have given up everything to protect her. Which meant getting them out of this place, with its clinic that would have been considered medieval even in *Little House on the Prairie* days.

She looked around the dark room, shrouded in shadow. There was no ultrasound here. No oxygen if the baby needed it. No painkillers. At all. Just a bed with stirrups and straps.

Hayley didn't want to know what the straps were used for.

She did know that women died in childbirth here. She'd heard the whispers.

It would be God's punishment for her sin, one woman had said.

She's a whore, another had added.

And then one old crone had whispered words that had chilled her to the bone: *Sister Rebecca will take the baby and raise it as her own.*

Even if she lives? the first woman had asked.

Even if the whore lives, the crone had confirmed. *God wouldn't want any baby to be raised by that Jezebel.*

Hayley cradled her stomach with both arms. *No fucking way in hell.* Even if Sister Rebecca had been a good person, which she was not. She was Brother Joshua's "first" wife—the highest-ranking of all the sister-wives. Brother Joshua had a total of four wives and Hayley was at the bottom of the list, which meant she had to obey the other wives as well as her "husband."

Hayley wanted to spit the word out of her mouth. *He is* not *my husband.*

He was a horrible person, snide and cruel. Unfortunately, Sister Rebecca was also a horrible person as well as being barren. That was the word the other women had used. *Barren.*

It was like living in a costume drama from the 1800s.

Sister Rebecca had three children, all taken from other women in the compound. Two of the women had apparently died in childbirth. The third had been birthed by an unwed mother. *Like me.* No one had mentioned what had happened to the unwed mother and Hayley wondered who she was.

Nobody's taking my daughter from me. Nobody. They'll have to kill me first.

Which . . . if she was caught in the clinic was a real possibility.

So get moving, Hayley. Get into the office and—

She stifled a shriek when the outer door opened and closed quickly. Spinning to see who'd entered, she let out a harsh breath of relief. "Graham," she hissed. "What are you doing here?"

Her brother Graham crept across the room, reminding her of a spider, all gangly, skinny limbs. He was taller than she was, even though he was only twelve.

He'd be thirteen soon. Which meant he'd be apprenticed to one of the tradesmen in the community. Which, in a place other than Eden, might not be so bad.

But people whispered. "Bad things" happened to some of the boys.

Bad things. The words were whispered in the same way that the women whispered about the sex their husbands forced on them or the "fallen" who'd tried to flee this hellhole.

Hayley had an idea of what those bad things were. And there was no fucking way she'd let that happen to Graham. Not while she drew breath.

"What are *you* doing here?" he hissed back. "I followed you because you got that look on your face like when you're planning something. You're going to get us thrown in the box."

The box. It was basically an outhouse, with little ventilation. One got locked inside for a period of time that suited the crime. Whatever the hell that meant.

"I'm trying to get into the office," Hayley whispered.

Graham's brows lifted. "Why? There aren't any drugs in there."

She rolled her eyes. "Like I'd use while I'm pregnant? There's a computer in there, assface. I'm sure of it."

Graham's eyes widened. "Here? In Nowheresville?"

"Here, in hell." She gestured to the locked door that led to the healer's office. "I was in here yesterday for my appointment." Which was a joke. The healer basically weighed her and told her to eat more vegetables. "I heard a printer. I know it. This door was cracked open and the healer went real still, like she heard it and was afraid I'd heard it, too. I pretended I didn't, but there is *something* in there. If it's a printer, there has to be a computer."

Graham frowned. "How is it running? There's no electricity here. How is it connected? There's no cable, no Wi-Fi."

Hayley wanted to scream. Graham was all about the *why* of things. "I don't know. I don't care. If there's a computer, I can get a message to Cam. He can get us out of here." She swallowed hard. "I can't have my baby here, Graham. They'll take her from me. I heard the women talking. Even if I live through it, they're going to give my baby to Sister Rebecca."

Graham's mouth set in a firm line that Hayley recognized all too well. It was his stubborn face, which meant he was about to dig in—one way or the other.

"I need your help," she whispered pleadingly. "Please, Graham. Don't tell anyone."

He nodded once. "Move away from the door."

She warily obeyed, blinking in surprise when her brother dropped to his knees in front of the door, squinting at the lock. "Piece of cake," he muttered, then slipped off his shoe, revealing . . .

"Is that a lock-picking kit?" she asked, already knowing the answer was yes.

He glanced up, mid eye roll, before selecting one of the slim tools. "Duh."

Hayley shook her head. "I don't want to know." Graham had gotten involved with a rough group of kids back home and had spent a month in juvie for shoplifting. Turned out that their mother had been planning and plotting to bring them here the entire time Graham was locked up. Now they were both locked up, just in a different place.

"You really don't," Graham agreed amicably.

"Thank you," she said quietly. "I didn't know how I was going to get into the office."

"How'd you get into the clinic?"

"It wasn't locked," Hayley said with a shrug.

In seconds he rose to his feet, pushing the door open. "Ta-da!" He slipped into the office, letting out a breath at the sight of the computer on the healer's desk. "It's old," he murmured, "but not that old. Son-of-a-fucking-bitch. They take our phones, but have something like this here? Assholes!"

"*Shhh*. Be *quiet*. And stop swearing. They'll throw you in the box for that, too."

He lifted one shoulder. "If they catch us here, swearing will be the least of our worries."

He was right. "Leave now. Go back to Mom. I'll figure out the computer."

"Right," he said with a shake of his head. "Shut up and let me work. Better yet, go back to your hut before Joshua or one of his wives realizes you're gone."

"They're all at the prayer meeting. They won't be back for another twenty minutes."

Graham made a face. "Don't know why they're all pretending to pray for DJ. There's not one person in this compound that wouldn't be happier if he'd bled to death."

"Graham," she chided, but her brother was right. Brother DJ was the only one allowed to leave the compound for supplies. And, apparently, to track down missing Founding Elders. One of the old guys, Brother Ephraim, had gone missing. So far no one knew what had happened to him, only that DJ had barely made it back to the compound earlier that evening. He'd left the compound a few days before in Eden's pickup truck, but had returned in a bigger delivery truck before collapsing. He'd been shot at least twice.

At least that was the gossip. The prayer meeting was for DJ's recovery, although Graham was right. Nobody liked DJ, Hayley included. He was handsome enough—on the outside, anyway. At least six feet tall with bright blond hair and deep dimples when he smiled. But his smile always seemed . . . off. There was something oily about the man that gave Hayley the creeps. He had pretty, dark eyes, but they watched everyone with a detachment that felt like he was sizing a person up, trying to figure out what he or she could do for him.

Graham sighed. "Password protected. I was hoping they'd be too dumb for that."

So had she. "Now what?"

"Now we try to guess. Or . . ." He lifted the large calendar that covered most of the healer's desk, then grinned. "Or we hope that the healer's memory is going and she has to write passwords down." He pointed to the Post-it Note on the underside of the calendar and snorted softly. "Password is 'Eden89.' I could have guessed that."

The community had been founded in 1989, so that made sense.

"And . . . I'm in," he pronounced. A few keystrokes later and he'd opened a browser window. "This would have been so much easier if they hadn't taken our damn phones. You can't text. You're gonna have to go old-school and e-mail him."

He tapped a few more keys and Hayley found herself looking at her own Gmail account. There were dozens of unopened e-mails, ninety percent of which were from Cameron.

She gaped. "How did you . . . Graham Gibbs, you hacked me."

He huffed a quiet laugh. "I didn't read your love messages. I just wanted to see if I could break in. Yours was my first hack. You really shouldn't use Cam's name as part of your password. You made it way too easy. What do you want to say to your baby daddy?"

"Besides 'HELP ME' in all caps?"

He smirked and began to type. "'Subject: HELP ME' in all caps. 'Dear Cam,'" he murmured as he typed, "'we are in a place called Eden.'" He clicked out of the e-mail tab to Google Maps and squinted at the screen. "There's a way to get coordinates. Oh, yeah. I remember now." He right-clicked on the flashing blue dot that was in the middle of a forest and entered the numbers into the e-mail to Cam. "We are at these coordinates," he continued to type. "Please come ASAP and bring the cops. This place is insane and we are being held against our will."

"We could just e-mail the police directly," Hayley said quietly. "Or even the FBI."

"And we will. But Cam can go to the cops in person, and that might get better attention than our e-mail, which sounds like we're crackpots." He hit send, then opened a new e-mail. "I'll send the e-mail to the cops now. According to the map, the closest town is—"

A voice outside had them freezing in place.

"I need to pack up the clinic," the healer was saying.

"You will have time to do that," a male voice said evenly. "Get back to the prayer meeting."

Shit. Panicked, Hayley met Graham's wide eyes. "Joshua," she mouthed.

If her so-called husband found them here . . . *He'll kill me. He'll kill Graham.* "We need to get out of here," she mouthed to Graham.

He nodded once, then began closing windows on the computer. He clicked the history and erased their activity before shutting it down. Quietly he rose from the chair and joined her at the office door.

"Pastor wants you at his side when he tells everyone that we're leaving," Joshua told the healer.

Leaving. *Leaving?*

Hayley glanced at the computer, her heart racing faster than was good for her baby. They'd just told Cameron where to find them and now they were leaving?

She took a step toward the computer, but Graham grabbed her arm, shaking his head.

"I'll be there in a few minutes," Joshua was saying. "I need to find the new girl. She was asleep when we left for the prayer meeting, but Rebecca says she isn't there now."

The new girl. *That would be me. They know I'm missing. I need to get out of here.*

"She might run," the healer said hesitantly. "She seems the type. She hasn't fit in well."

"I know." Joshua sounded grim. "I swear to God, I'll kill her and rip that baby out of her if she tries. I promised Rebecca the kid would be hers."

Hayley covered her mouth to silence her gasp. Graham's grip intensified until tears burned her eyes. Her brother looked absolutely livid.

Livid and terrified. *For me. Hurry, Cam. Get here before we're gone.* Or before Graham did something foolish and got himself killed.

The voices trailed off and Graham opened the office door, gesturing for Hayley to follow. With a final frantic look back at the computer, she complied. It didn't matter. She didn't know where they were going, so she couldn't tell Cam. When they got to the outer door, Graham pointed to himself, then to the left. He pointed to Hayley, then the right.

They no longer lived in the same hut, so it made sense that they'd come from different directions. *Thank you, little brother*, she thought. *For having your shit together better than me.*

She looked both ways when she left the healer's hut, relieved that everyone was in the square already, looking away from her and toward where Pastor stood on a raised platform. He was an average-looking man, maybe five-eight. On the surface, he seemed unremarkable in every way. His brown hair was graying, his face almost always smiling benignly. He wore round glasses that gave him a professorial air. He shouldn't have been a leader of anything, but there was something about him that drew the people of Eden like moths to a flame. They trusted him implicitly.

He was, however, holding Hayley captive against her will, and so she would never trust him. She slipped out and made it to the back of the group in the square, then gasped again when bony fingers grabbed her arm, in the same place Graham had.

"Where were you?" Rebecca asked, her tone low and ominous. The woman was older, though her age was hard to tell. Hayley thought she might be younger than her own mother, but years of living in this hellhole had made her haggard, her skin wrinkled. More important at the moment was her size and strength. She was much taller and stronger than Hayley. She wouldn't stand a chance if the woman tried to seriously hurt her. "You weren't in your bed, where I left you." She squeezed harder, giving Hayley a shake that rattled her teeth. "Do not lie to me, girl."

She spoke quietly enough that no one around them heard, or at least didn't appear to. All eyes were closed as Pastor led them in prayer.

Hayley's mouth opened, then closed. "I was here," she stammered. "On my way here."

Rebecca's eyes narrowed. "You're lying. You can't even lie well."

"She was with me," a soft voice said from behind them.

Both Hayley and Rebecca twisted around to see Sister Tamar, who was smiling sweetly. "I went to wake her up, Sister Rebecca. I knew she'd stayed behind to sleep. It's taxing, being pregnant." Her smile grew brittle. "But I guess you wouldn't know that, would you?"

Rebecca's jaw grew tight; the muscles in her neck corded as she controlled the rage that flashed in her eyes. She shoved Hayley away with a glare. "Stay out of my way. Both of you."

Hayley turned to Tamar with wide eyes and a hammering heart. *Why?* she wanted to ask. *Why did you cover for me?*

The woman was young, maybe twenty, and was one of the weavers. That was all Hayley knew about her. She wasn't one of Joshua's wives and she and Hayley had never spoken one-on-one. Hayley wasn't even sure who the woman was married to, although she had a husband.

That was a given in Eden. All females over twelve were married.

Tamar shook her head, the movement so slight that Hayley would have missed it had she not been staring. Then, shoulders sagging, Tamar folded her hands and lowered her head as Pastor prayed that the good Lord would bless them in their upcoming move, that he would protect them in these "treacherous times" when the government was trying to "steal their religious freedoms." He prayed that everyone would make the trip to the new site safely and that Brother DJ would heal from his "grievous wounds" inflicted by the FBI just hours before. He asked God to "shield them" from the evil men who'd killed so many at Waco.

The FBI's failed takeover attempt of the Branch Davidians was mentioned often by the Eden authorities. It was a fear tactic that worked, several of the men murmuring, "Amen."

After Pastor's final amen, everyone looked up as one. Hayley still hadn't gotten used to the synchronized movement. It was as if the crowd were a well-choreographed chorus line.

"We leave at dawn," Pastor announced. "Pack what you can easily carry. Do not be tardy. This is not a drill. Anyone who isn't ready at dawn will be cast out."

The group gasped, again as one.

Cast out. That was bad, Hayley knew that much. She glanced at Tamar, who whispered, "Left in the woods for the wolves."

Hayley shuddered. This was a nightmare. Worse than a nightmare. Worse than hell could ever be. *God, please get me out of here. Help me save my baby.*

"Our new home won't be as nice as this one," Pastor continued. "There will be some adjustments, but I promise you'll be happy there. We'll be together, and with God's help and protection, we will prevail. Now go and prepare. We have only a few hours before dawn."

Not as nice as this place? This was . . . hell. She met Graham's gaze across the square. He looked taller, somehow. More grown up. And grimly determined.

As the crowd dispersed, Tamar darted back to her own hut without giving Hayley a chance to ask her a single question. She began to walk back to the hut she shared with Joshua and his three other wives and their seven children, trying to control the panic in her gut.

They were leaving. Cameron would get here with the cops and they'd be gone. She'd have to have her baby in a place even worse than this. And then Sister Rebecca would steal her.

Graham came to her side, taking her arm as if to guide her across the uneven ground. "You shouldn't fall in your condition," he said, loudly enough that anyone around them would hear. Then he whispered, "It'll be okay. We'll get away."

Hayley nodded, her heart in her throat. Her twelve-year-old brother was telling her it would be okay, but it wouldn't be. It couldn't be.

They were leaving this place for somewhere even worse. She couldn't imagine what that would be like.

I'll find out soon enough. She smoothed her free hand over her stomach. *Don't worry, Jellybean. Your dad will find us. He has to.*

ONE

DJ Belmont looked over the list in his hand. "It'll take me forever to get all this shit."

Sister Coleen shrugged in apology, unconcerned about the swear word he'd let drop. They were alone in the clinic—he, Coleen, and Pastor—so Eden rules did not apply.

Rules he'd grown up with. Rules he intended to shred the moment he took over Eden. He was one step closer to his goal, having killed Brother Ephraim a month before. He'd have taken care of all of his problems had he not been shot himself. After a month, his left shoulder still ached and the arm remained basically useless.

The first shot to his shoulder had hurt like fire, and for that he planned to hunt down the bitch who'd pulled the trigger. Her name was Daisy Dawson and her death would serve a dual purpose—payback for the injury and heartbreak for the man who shared her bed.

Gideon Reynolds. The very name had DJ seething with rage. He banked it, unwilling to have to explain it to Coleen and Pastor. Because Gideon was supposed to be dead. Supposed to be dead at DJ's father's hand, in fact.

Except now he knew that Waylon Belmont—DJ's own father—had let Gideon go. He'd set Gideon free from Eden. Lied to everyone when he returned, saying that Gideon had died for the sin of murdering the Founding Elder Edward McPhearson as he'd attempted to flee. Everyone had believed him.

Even me. The banked rage flared anew and he shoved it back. He hadn't realized the extent of his father's betrayal until last month when he'd learned that Gideon was still alive.

His father had been punished, though. It had been DJ's first killing and it had felt so damn good, watching the light dim in that bastard's eyes. He'd been seventeen years old and had finally understood that true power lay in the ability to grant life. Or death.

DJ granted a lot of death.

"It's been a month since your last trip," Coleen said, unaware of his mounting anger. "And you came back wounded, so you couldn't bring back the supplies you'd gone to buy. We had emergency rations, but they're gone. The women stretched the rations as far as they could, but a hundred and fifteen people require a lot of food. We've run out of most of our essentials."

"Yeah, yeah. I get it." They were scraping the bottom of the supply barrels, and DJ was already tired of the jerky that seemed to be their remaining source of protein. "I'll pick up the supplies and scout out a new place for us to live."

That was the plan, anyway. The compound was freezing and hungry, huddling in the caves as they were. The caves had never been intended to be a long-term location, but DJ's injury had forced them to remain far longer than was healthy for any of them. *Especially me.*

He had other priorities for this trip, however. He'd search for another location if he had time.

She studied his left arm, resting in a sling. "You're sure you're okay to drive?" A tiny brunette in her early fifties, she was Eden's healer, their only medical "expert." To his knowledge, she'd had no formal training, but she'd done the best she could with his wounds.

At least he wasn't dead, although he'd apparently come pretty damn close.

"I'm fine," DJ grunted. He flexed his left shoulder, then moved that arm around, swallowing the pain. "See? Full range of motion."

Which wasn't nearly true. Fortunately, he'd trained for years to shoot with either hand. He wouldn't be completely helpless when he left the compound, but the pain was still excruciating. Sleeping on a pallet on a cold, damp stone floor wasn't helping matters any. He couldn't wait to get to civilization so that he could sleep in a real bed for a change.

"Not quite," Coleen murmured, "but I gave up trying to tell you what to do years ago."

Because she was not stupid and she valued her life. DJ didn't suffer fools, nor did he allow anyone to give him orders.

No one except the elderly man in the chair. Pastor was the shepherd of Eden's flock. He was the leader, and he gave the orders. DJ disobeyed him frequently, but Pastor never found out.

Like his father before him, DJ was the only person permitted to leave the compound—at least the only person the community knew about. The Founding Elders had taken leaves of absence four times a year, ostensibly to "pray on the mountain." In reality, they went to the nearest city and fucked, drank, and gambled like sailors on shore leave.

Now DJ and Pastor were the only remaining elders. Pastor himself was the only remaining Founding Elder. DJ had taken his father's place after Waylon's untimely demise. To this day no one suspected he'd killed his father.

Because I'm damn good. He didn't leave loose ends.

At least none that he'd known about until a month before, when he'd learned that the woman he'd thought he'd killed thirteen years ago was still alive. He could have sworn Mercy had been dead when he'd left her bleeding in front of a bus station.

Mercy Callahan. Gideon's sister. Except that she'd been Mercy

Burton when she'd lived in Eden. She'd been Ephraim's wife until DJ had let her and her mother believe he was helping them escape. He'd wanted them to hope.

He should have shot both women in the woods outside Eden, but he'd been young and stupid and focused on his cartoon-villain revenge plot. Mercy's mother was definitely dead, and he'd brought her body back, but he'd been interrupted in the middle of killing Mercy. Someone had come and he'd run, leaving her behind. He didn't see how she could have survived the two bullets he'd put into her body, but she had.

Which left him a huge mess to clean up now. He'd told Pastor that he'd buried Mercy himself. If Pastor ever found out that she'd survived, DJ would lose everything.

So he had loose ends to take care of. He'd almost done so a month ago, but a second shot had damaged the nerves in his left arm, leaving him unable to shoot and bleeding profusely. He didn't know who'd fired the shot, but when he found out, the fucker was dead. He'd barely made it back to the compound alive. He'd barely managed to stay conscious long enough to tell Pastor they had to move. Immediately.

Luckily Pastor trusted him implicitly. *The old fool.*

DJ had only let him live this long because the old fool was also a crafty fucker. He'd memorized the account numbers and passwords to the online bank accounts that held Eden's fifty million bucks.

DJ needed those passwords before Pastor kicked the bucket. The old man was still in decent shape, though, goddammit. He was seventy-two, but his heart still beat soundly in his chest.

Coleen glanced at Pastor, technically her husband. Coleen had gone through three husbands in the thirty years she'd been at Eden. Two had died of natural causes. One had been murdered.

Not by my hand. Although DJ had longed to kill Ephraim's brother, Edward, more times than he could count. No, the thanks for Edward's death had to go to Gideon Reynolds. Gideon had claimed it was an accident, and DJ had believed it. At thirteen, Gideon had been a goody-goody. And strong enough even then to best Edward McPhearson in a fight.

When DJ met Gideon again, he'd kill him slowly, making sure it hurt especially badly. Partly for denying DJ the satisfaction of killing McPhearson himself, but mostly for escaping. For having a life, when DJ had been stuck in this hellhole, serving a narcissist with a god complex.

Even putting all of those reasons aside, Gideon would have had to die, simply for becoming a goddamn FBI agent who had apparently been searching for Eden since the day he escaped.

Pastor cleared his throat gently. "You seem agitated, DJ. Are you not healed enough to take this excursion?"

"I'm fine," DJ snapped, then blew out a breath at the unamused look on Pastor's face. It was never a good idea to make Pastor angry. "I'm sorry. It does hurt, but we need supplies."

And I have loose ends to snip.

He needed to find Gideon and put him down like the dog he was. He needed to find Mercy and make her suffer the way she should have suffered thirteen years ago.

And then he'd find Amos Terrill, Eden's former carpenter and Gideon and Mercy's stepfather. The month before, that bastard had smuggled himself and his young daughter out of Eden in the back of DJ's pickup truck. Which Amos had then stolen. *Asshole.*

Hopefully he'd find Amos in a graveyard somewhere, because one of DJ's bullets had struck the man in the throat. He'd need to die eventually, because he'd found Gideon and Mercy and had probably updated them on everything about Eden since they had left. For that, if he was still alive, he'd pay.

And then I'll come back, force Pastor to give me those damn account numbers once and for all. He'd stayed in the same toxic pattern, serving Pastor for far too long. He hadn't realized how much time had passed until he'd been shot.

Nothing like a near-death experience to reset one's priorities.

"It's all right," Pastor said evenly, making it clear that DJ's outburst *wasn't* all right. The fucker. "Will you locate little Abigail? She may have been taken into the foster care system."

Because he'd told Pastor that he'd killed and buried Amos after finding him hiding in the back of his pickup when he'd stopped in the next town. He hadn't mentioned Abigail at all. He wasn't sure why. Maybe it was because she was a child and he hadn't considered her a threat. Pastor had assumed she'd escaped.

"I'll try," he said.

Pastor's lips pursed, a sign of his displeasure. "She'll tell someone about us. Luckily she's so young that no one will believe her, and luckily she's the only one to have gotten away."

For a career criminal, Pastor was damn gullible. He actually believed that all the escapees had been rounded up over the past few years. To be fair, DJ had used surrogate bodies, like his father had before him. When the escapee couldn't be found, he found a random person—usually homeless or a runaway—about the same size and coloring, then killed them, mutilating the body so that it couldn't be identified.

Pastor believed that no one had ever escaped Eden.

Pastor was an idiot.

"Luckily," DJ agreed. "I'll get the supplies, scout out a new location, and search for Abigail Terrill. Is there anything you'd like to add?"

Pastor shook his head. "No, but I would like you to fix the satellite dish before you go. I haven't been able to get online since we moved here to the caves."

A move that had been necessary because Amos Terrill had been thick as thieves with the FBI. If Ephraim hadn't spilled his guts, it was almost certain that Amos had. So they'd moved the community to their ultimate safe space, a series of caves just outside the border of the Lassen National Forest.

It had been DJ's storage spot for their drug harvest for years and his father's before that, the rock shielding their stash from government eyes in the sky. Neither conventional satellite imagery nor infrared cameras could find them here.

"I'll try," DJ promised, but he was lying through his teeth. There was no way he was fixing the Internet. He hadn't allowed Pastor online while his wounds were healing, claiming he was too weak to manage it. But the truth was that Pastor could not know that Mercy and Gideon were alive, and, given the shoot-out the month before, they could still be in the news. "But the dish was damaged in the last move." DJ threw an accusatory glance at Coleen. "She didn't pack it correctly."

Coleen looked down, her jaw clenched. "I did my best, considering how heavy it was, and that I had to move it into the truck by myself. I couldn't ask for help, because you were hurt and Ephraim was dead and nobody else is supposed to know we have a satellite dish."

She actually had done well. There was nothing wrong with their dish, but he couldn't let them know it.

"We need to bring in another elder," Pastor said thoughtfully. "One young and strong enough to help with things like that, but old enough to bring some wisdom."

"Also one who won't go crazy with rage, knowing we lied to them all these years," Coleen added carefully.

Pastor chuckled, because Coleen was the only person allowed to be candid with him. She'd earned the right through thirty years of being Pastor's lapdog, but even she tiptoed around the man. One never knew what mood he'd be in at any given time, on any given day.

"True." Pastor studied his manicured nails, a sure sign that whatever he was about to say would not be what DJ wanted to hear. "I'm considering Brother Joshua. He was extremely helpful in coordinating our move, and considering we only had the one truck you brought back, DJ, this move was one of our most stressful. We packed the congregation into the truck like cattle, but with over a hundred people, plus the heavy equipment, he made at least ten trips."

"And I had to keep everyone calm, because no one wanted to live in these caves," Coleen added. "There was an unusual amount of unrest. It took us four days to get everyone settled. You don't recall because you were unconscious."

"Brother Joshua behaved admirably under pressure," Pastor finished. "He would make an excellent elder."

To an untrained observer, it might have seemed that Pastor was asking for input. DJ knew better. He exchanged a glance with Coleen, long enough to see her slight grimace, because she didn't like Joshua. Well, mostly she didn't like Joshua's first wife, and if he was chosen as an elder, his first wife would be elevated in status as well. But Coleen's expression was wiped clean by the time Pastor lifted his gaze from his hands. That was the purpose of him looking at his hands—to give the receiver of orders time to appear okay with his edicts.

"I'll be ready to brief him when I return," DJ promised. Like that was ever going to happen. Once he had control of Eden's money, he'd leave Joshua and Coleen and all the other Edenites to do whatever the fuck they wanted.

Pastor stared at him through narrowed eyes. "Find Amos's child. Bring her to me. I will not allow her to become a symbol of concern or discontent in my flock. Make it your priority."

DJ gritted his teeth. The "or else" was always left unsaid. "Yes, sir. If she's in foster care, it might take a while to find her and, once I do, extracting her will be a delicate operation."

But DJ knew that the child wasn't in foster care. Her father, Amos, had reconnected with Mercy and Gideon, and there was no way those two would allow Abigail to go into the system. Once he found Mercy, Abigail wouldn't be far. It would, however, buy him more time to snip off all of his loose ends.

Pastor sighed, visibly irritated. "I suppose that's true. How much time will you need?"

DJ pretended to ponder. "A week? Maybe more."

Pastor looked to Coleen with a frown. "Do we have enough supplies to last us a week?"

Coleen shifted uncomfortably. "It's going to be tight. We have the chickens that we've been using for eggs. We can slaughter them if we must. We're running out of feed, so they'd starve soon, anyway. But we need fresh vegetables and milk. The children haven't had milk in weeks."

Pastor nodded grimly. "One week, DJ. And then you'll return with supplies and news of Abigail. At least whether she's alive or dead."

"And a new location," Coleen added meekly.

Pastor nodded again. "That, as well. Goodbye, Brother DJ. May God be with you."

DJ managed not to roll his eyes. Pastor didn't believe in God. He only believed in himself. The blessing was Pastor's way of donning his pastoral persona, his signal that their business was completed.

DJ inclined his head wordlessly. Waiting until he was back in his quarters, he whispered, "Goodbye, Pastor." Because this was the beginning of the old man's end. Once Mercy and Gideon were no more, DJ would return to claim leadership of Eden.

He only wanted the money. The others could have the rest.

It would be the first time in a month that he'd left the compound. With any luck, Mercy Callahan would have let her guard down.

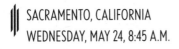 SACRAMENTO, CALIFORNIA
WEDNESDAY, MAY 24, 8:45 A.M.

"Well?"

Special Agent Tom Hunter looked over his shoulder, unsurprised to see Special Agent in Charge Molina standing in the doorway of his office. He'd expected the visit from the SAC of the FBI's Sacramento field office. Today was her first day back after the attack that had left her injured and several other agents dead. She looked paler than normal and tired. But determined.

He automatically rose, because his mother had raised him right.

This put him more than a foot taller than his boss, which made her look up with an irritated glare. At six-six, he towered over almost everyone in the Bureau, which was a new experience. He'd been average height during his three years with the NBA. Shorter, in fact, than many of the men he'd met on the court. He hunched his shoulders a bit to offset the difference, but Molina's glare did not soften.

As her chin lifted, her dark eyes bored into him. "What do you know?" she demanded.

Tom gave her a warm smile. "Good morning." The woman wasn't the coldhearted beast she wanted everyone to think she was. He'd watched her manage two crises in the past few months, and while she was quick-witted, with razor-sharp focus and an even sharper tongue, she did care. He suspected she might care too much and fought not to let it show.

He knew the type. He'd been raised by a wickedly smart group of women. His mother's friends were cops, social workers, and attorneys. When pressure was high and risk to humans they cared for even higher, they'd pasted on the same face Molina wore right now.

He held out the chair next to his desk, motioning her to sit.

She shot him a dark scowl but took the seat, tugging at the jacket of her suit unnecessarily. No fabric worn by Tara Molina would have the nerve to wrinkle.

"I know a lot of things about a lot of things," he said, retaking his seat as he answered her question. "But I'm assuming you're specifically referring to Eden."

The cult he'd been actively seeking since mid-April. The cult that'd provided a hiding place for vicious killers for the past thirty years. Vicious killers who had abused two of the people who, in a short period of time, had become Tom's friends. Both Gideon Reynolds and his sister Mercy Callahan had been children when they'd escaped Eden, but both were scarred for life, physically and emotionally.

Because the killers hadn't simply hidden in Eden. They'd thrived there, starting a cult that condoned—no, *encouraged*—the rape of twelve-year-old girls by middle-aged men, calling it "marriage." They condoned the rape of thirteen-year-old boys, calling it an "apprenticeship."

Gideon and Mercy had been only two of their victims.

"Yes. I'm talking about Eden." Molina rolled her eyes. "And here everyone said you were some wunderkind," she drawled, but her tone was light. Almost teasing.

"I don't know about that," Tom muttered, his cheeks heating. He was good at what he did—specifically hacking. He was *very* good at what he did, in fact.

The fact that he still hadn't found the cult's compound after months of searching left him thoroughly irked. But they had made progress.

"I got into their offshore bank account," Tom stated. Which, under most circumstances, would have been cause for congratulations and maybe even a promotion. Or a prison sentence, if he hadn't been working for the good guys. Either way, it had been damn difficult to do.

"You did that three weeks ago," Molina stated flatly, popping any hope he might have had for an attaboy. "My temporary replacement briefed me weekly. What have you learned about Eden *recently*?"

Tom could only imagine what Molina's temporary replacement had told her. He and Agent Raeburn had not gotten along well at all. "From their bank account, not much," he admitted. "No money's been moved either in or out, not since they pulled all of Ephraim's money out of his personal account and back into the main Eden coffers, three days before he was killed."

It was Molina's turn to grimace. "I must say that I hate the sound of that man's name. All of his names," she added bitterly.

Ephraim Burton, a Founding Elder of the Eden cult, had been born Harry Franklin, under which name he'd earned a record as a bank robber and murderer, before going into hiding thirty years ago. Burton had other aliases that had allowed him to mingle in the real world during the times he left Eden.

Which wouldn't be happening ever again, because Burton was

dead. Tom wished that he'd been the one to do the honors, but one of the other cult elders had killed Ephraim Burton, possibly to keep him from telling the FBI of Eden's whereabouts. A lot of people had died in connection to Eden. The stakes were high. Its bank accounts held in excess of fifty million dollars.

It was more likely, though, that the other elder had killed Ephraim to keep him from spilling the biggest secret—that two of the cult's runaways hadn't died trying to escape but had been living free for more than ten years.

Gideon and his sister, Mercy, had been abused by Eden in their youth but were fighting back now, helping the FBI track down Eden and end it, once and for all. Tom respected the siblings more than he could say.

"I put an alert on the offshore accounts," Tom said. "If they move any money, we'll know."

"But they haven't yet."

"Not yet. However, someone resembling DJ Belmont did withdraw some cash from a different bank account outside Mt. Shasta an hour after Ephraim Burton was shot."

"Belmont?" Molina hissed, anger flashing in her eyes.

Belmont was second-in-command to Eden's leader, a charismatic man known only as "Pastor" to his followers. Luckily the FBI had learned a bit more than that. Pastor's name prior to his starting the Eden cult had been Herbert Hampton. Prior to that he'd been Benton Travis, serving a sentence in a federal penitentiary for forgery and bank fraud.

They knew the identities of the cult leaders. They just didn't know where the cult was. It was a small community that moved around remote sections of Northern California, and they were clever at evading detection.

Belmont was more than Pastor's second-in-command, though—assuming he was still alive. He was a dangerous, ruthless, alarmingly competent killer who'd taken out five federal agents, most of them

SWAT. He'd also fired the bullet that had taken Molina out of commission for the past month, so her reaction to his name was understandable.

Tom pulled up a file on his computer, then turned the screen to show her the photos taken from surveillance cameras. "The resolution of the bank's drive-through camera is good, but he was wearing a bandana over his face, sunglasses, and a cap with a wide brim. Facial recognition couldn't pick up anything useful. The body type and size fit Belmont's description, though."

"If he didn't withdraw cash from Eden's offshore account, which account was it?"

Tom gave her a sideways glance. "I thought you got weekly briefings from Agent Raeburn."

Molina's eyes narrowed. "I did. I want to hear your version."

Tom managed to hide his wince. "My version?"

"Yes," Molina said coolly. "Agent Raeburn's version was less than satisfactory."

Well, damn. "I figured as much," Tom muttered. "He's . . . well, he's not very flexible."

Her brows lifted. "He is a damn good agent."

Careful, careful. "Never said he wasn't."

"You thought it."

Tom pursed his lips, unsure if Molina was amused or upset. It was often hard to tell. But of course he'd thought it. Raeburn was by-the-book to a fault and left no wiggle room for the humanity of any situation. He wasn't going to say that out loud, though. He was aware that Molina knew he bent the rules now and then.

He had, in fact, bent the rules often since his first day on the job. Which seemed like it had been a year ago, even though it had only been five months. There was something about Gideon Reynolds and Mercy Callahan that made him want to help them, to ease their fears—even when he technically wasn't supposed to. But the brother and sister had been through too much abuse.

Tom knew abuse. He still bore the scars from his own biological father's cruelty. He knew heartache, far more recently. He knew that sometimes rules needed to be bent or even broken in order to do the right thing.

But he also knew that if he wanted to continue helping Gideon and Mercy, he'd need to toe Molina's line. Or appear to, at least. Which meant not badmouthing her temporary replacement, who was still technically his direct supervisor.

He bent his mouth into a smile that was convincing because he'd practiced making it so—a side benefit of heartache. People didn't ask you questions if you smiled and looked happy.

"The account Belmont withdrew money from at the ATM was an individual checking account in the name of John Smith," he said, shifting them back on topic. "Assuming this is him in the photo, he withdrew the cash about ninety minutes after he fled the scene at Dunsmuir."

DJ Belmont's shooting spree in the forest two hundred miles to the north had left five bodies on the ground that day—the FBI SWAT members and a special agent named Schumacher. Molina had been lucky. Her injuries at Belmont's hand had "only" hospitalized her for a week and required physical therapy for three more.

Unfortunately, Belmont had also taken out Ephraim Burton that day. They'd hoped that Burton might have led them to Eden, to the people who lived under Pastor's authoritarian rule.

The adults who'd followed Pastor had perhaps been misled, but they'd made their choice. The children of Eden, however, had not chosen and many were being abused every single day.

But federal agents hadn't been Belmont's only victims that day. Tom pointed at the ATM photo. "Belmont was driving an old box truck that was later reported stolen by the surviving family of an itinerant farm picker. He was shot in the head twice with Agent Schumacher's service weapon."

"So he didn't shoot Schumacher from afar, like he did us." From a tree, far enough away that the SWAT team hadn't been able to locate him before he'd shot them all. Far enough away to reveal Belmont's impressive, albeit terrifying, sniper skills. "He took her weapon after he killed her." Molina swallowed hard. "She was a good agent. A good person."

"I know. He killed the picker, stole his truck, and hasn't been seen or heard from since."

"Maybe Belmont's dead," Molina said hopefully.

"Maybe."

She studied him. "You don't think so, though."

"I don't know," Tom said truthfully. "We can't assume it, though. He wanted to kill Mercy and Gideon that day. If he is alive, he has too much at stake not to try again."

"You're right that we can't assume. Did the picker's truck have GPS?"

"It didn't. It was twenty-five years old." Tom had to draw a breath, the memory of the man's grieving family still clear enough to make his chest ache. He'd accompanied Agent Raeburn to inform the victim's wife and five kids. It had been his first time delivering such news, and Raeburn hadn't been overly sympathetic. Tom figured that was how the man coped, which might be better than the nightmares that still plagued his own sleep. "The family was poor. The truck was all they owned."

Molina was quiet a beat longer than necessary. "Agent Raeburn said that the family received a gift from an anonymous benefactor a few days later, through their parish priest."

Tom didn't blink. That the money had come from his own bank account was a fact he was not prepared to admit. "I hadn't heard that," he said mildly. And he hadn't actually *heard* it, so technically he wasn't lying.

"Raeburn said the amount was enough for them to live on for several months, plus a bit more than their funeral expenses."

He could feel his skin itching, like Molina could see his every secret. But still he didn't blink. He knew he couldn't replace every victim's losses, but he could help that family. So he had. It hadn't made a dent in his bank account, flush after his three years in the NBA. Being able to help people like that was one of the best things his time as a professional basketball player had done for him. He'd never planned to make the NBA a career, always knowing he'd join the Bureau, but he'd been young and better than decent on the court. It had seemed a shame to waste the talent he'd been given—or his earnings. He'd donated a fair bit and saved the rest.

He was grateful for those years, even if after his fiancée's death he hadn't had the heart for it anymore and had retired early. Now he kept his tone bland. "That was a nice thing for someone to do."

Molina rolled her eyes, but her tone was almost sweet. "Don't make it a habit, Tom."

He blinked, unprepared for her use of his first name. "Make what a habit?"

She shook her head. "You know, when I was told I was getting a hacker rookie, straight out of the Academy, I was not happy. When I found out you were a former pro athlete, I was unhappier still. I didn't have the time to train an agent wet behind the ears. Or one with an ego the size of Texas."

Tom frowned. "I have an ego the size of Texas?"

"No. I assumed that you would, but I was pleasantly surprised on that score." One side of her mouth lifted. "I'm glad you're here. If only so I can toughen up that soft heart of yours so you make it to retirement. I'm not kidding, Agent Hunter."

Tom bit back his own smile. "So noted, ma'am." His watch buzzed, reminding him of the time. "Morning meeting," he said. "You coming?"

She scowled at him. "I called the meeting."

He grinned. He couldn't help it. If she was taking over morning briefings, it meant that Agent Raeburn was history. Which meant his own life would be a lot less stressful going forward. "You're back, all the way?"

"Most of the way," she said cryptically. "But Raeburn is still your direct supervisor."

Fuck. Tom's grin disappeared, his expression becoming grim.

She gave him a careful once-over. "Agent Raeburn reported that you've been feeding information about this case to Agent Reynolds and his sister. That stops now. Are we clear?"

Tom considered his words. Of course he'd been feeding information to Gideon and Mercy. Gideon had been recused from the case because of his personal involvement, but that shouldn't mean he got cut off from updates.

"They have a right to know the facts, Agent Molina. It's their lives Belmont is targeting. Agent Raeburn has been keeping them in the dark." Which wasn't only unfair, it was cruel and dangerous. Raeburn was taking criminal chances with the lives of Tom's friends—and everyone they loved, because anyone around them was also in danger.

"We've provided Mercy Callahan protection," Molina snapped. This wasn't playful banter. She was reining him in, and he didn't like it. At all. "Agent Reynolds can take care of himself. If you can't agree, perhaps the Bureau isn't a good fit for you after all."

There it was, then. The choice.

He could hear his aunt Dana's voice in his mind. *Keep your friends close and your enemies closer, Tom.* And then his mother. *Do the right thing, even when it's the hard thing.*

He gave a curt nod, knowing he'd continue doing what needed to be done. "I understand."

"I have your word?" Molina asked, her jaw taut.

He was tempted to cross his fingers behind his back, but that was childish. "I will not feed Gideon and Mercy information in the future. You have my word."

Molina narrowed her eyes at him. "Why don't I believe you?"

He managed a thin smile. "I gave you my word. Ma'am."

There were, of course, so many other ways to get vital information to them. If it was a matter of life and death, if Gideon and Mercy's safety was on the line, he'd find another way.

"All right, then." She gave him a sideways glance, sharp as a knife. "What else do you know, Agent Hunter? I take it that you've checked out all of the former Eden sites."

"Of course. The notebook we found in Ephraim's safe-deposit box had a very accurate map. None of the locations are currently occupied, though it was still valuable to find that map. We learned that their earlier locations are obvious from the sky, but the more recent ones are not. They've effectively utilized ground cover, building earth homes. We thought we might locate them through infrared, checking for heat signatures, but so far that's been a bust."

Ephraim Burton had left a veritable Eden playbook in his safe-deposit box, with detailed descriptions of all of the Founding Elders' sins, meticulous records of the cash stored in the offshore accounts, and the map of previous Eden locations. Tom assumed that it was some kind of dead man's switch, that if he was killed mysteriously, the contents of his box would somehow be made public. And indeed, it had ended up in the hands of the FBI.

"You found the most recent location?"

"Yes, ma'am. But there wasn't anything there. Nothing living, anyway. We found evidence of animals—a lot of very fresh shit in a variety of sizes. It was still fresh, maybe a few days old. We also found a lot of animal blood. It appears they slaughtered at least some of their farm animals. Maybe they couldn't take them all. We didn't miss them by much."

"Did you tell Miss Callahan and Agent Reynolds that you have a list of the old sites?"

"I told them we'd found the very first Eden, but not the other sites. That would have made them want to explore each one, and I didn't want them to be seen there in case Pastor and DJ returned for some reason."

"Why did you tell them about the first site?"

It had been an impulse decision, but he didn't regret it. "I thought visiting it might provide them some closure." He'd had personal experience with closure. "The site was cleared of trees and easily spotted by satellite surveillance. I didn't think Pastor would bring Eden back there."

"Did they go for closure?"

"Not to my knowledge, ma'am."

"Anything else?"

"Not really. Mostly I've checked off potential suspects. What I know is right here." He pointed to the bulletin board next to his desk, on which he'd attached photos and maps and documents relating to his Eden search. He had an identical one in the office at his house. "I tracked down DJ Belmont's surviving family on the off chance he'd hide with them. His uncle Merle Belmont lives about an hour from here in Benicia. He and his wife filed the missing-person report when DJ and his mother went missing when he was four years old. They claim that they haven't seen him, though, and thought that he'd been dead all these years."

"You believed them?"

"I did, but you're welcome to interview them yourself."

"I might. What else?"

Tom wasn't offended. He was new. He expected others to check his work, especially on a case as important as this one. "I've interviewed a number of people who knew Pastor when he was the minister at the church in L.A. The one he embezzled from and defrauded." The one he'd fled to hide in Eden to escape a criminal investigation. "Those people told us what we already knew—Pastor was a sociopath who could charm the bark from a tree. We have the rifle that Belmont used last month. We've pulled prints, but they don't match anything in the system. Other than that, we haven't had any new leads. Raeburn's had me working on a few other projects until we do."

Which was a waste of valuable time. But if they had no leads . . . Tom knew all they could do was wait for a break, but he hated it.

Molina examined the board. "What is the significance of the key?"

Tom glanced at the photo of a key bearing the GM logo. "It was in Ephraim's pocket when he was killed. It's old and didn't belong to any of the vehicles that Ephraim stole last month." Of which there'd been quite a few. "That's all I know."

"All right, then." She rose abruptly. "Let's go to my morning meeting."

Exiting his office, they walked in silence until she said, "How is Miss Barkley?"

Surprised, Tom almost stumbled. He smoothed his gait and his voice. "She's doing well."

Liza Barkley was indeed doing well. Deep irritation blossomed within him at just how well his best friend was doing. The memory of her arriving home way too late the night before grated. She'd been holding the hand of the ass who'd believed that paying for her dinner entitled him to a whole lot more.

She'd called him Mike. *Mike* had been too familiar, too handsy. It had taken nearly all of Tom's self-control not to throttle him when he'd groped Liza's butt like she was some kind of . . .

He had to take a deep breath, conscious of Molina watching him.

Liza hadn't objected, though, so he'd remained silent. At least Mike hadn't stayed long enough to do anything more than groping. Because, yes, Tom had stood at the window watching until the man drove away.

"I'm glad," Molina said. "I enjoyed her visits."

Tom stared down at his boss, and she had to crane her neck to look up. In heels, Liza could look him in the eye comfortably.

And he wasn't sure why he thought about that now. "Liza Barkley? *My* Liza Barkley?"

Except she wasn't his. She was Mike's.

Molina looked amused. "Tall? Long auburn hair that she wears in a Heidi braid? About five-ten, but likes heels? Always smiling? She's your Liza Barkley, is she not?"

Yes, she always smiled. Yes, she wore her hair up in a braid, a habit she'd picked up during her years in the army. He preferred her hair down, but his preferences didn't count. Because she wasn't his. "Liza visited you?"

"Both in the hospital and after I went home. She brought me crime thrillers and lasagna and homemade caramel brownies. She even did my laundry a few times. I appreciated her kindness."

"I didn't know," Tom murmured. Because Liza hadn't mentioned it. His best friend hadn't mentioned a lot of things lately. She'd been steadily pulling away from him for the last month and he didn't like it one bit.

Molina frowned. "I figured you'd asked her to come."

"No. I didn't." He recovered his composure and cleared his expression, because they were nearly at the meeting room. "She's good at caregiving. She's going to make an amazing nurse."

"She told me that she's starting nursing school in July. UC Davis is one of the best nursing schools in the country."

"Yes, it is." He'd been stunned when he'd learned that she was headed to Sacramento. She'd told him about her acceptance to UC Davis at his parents' house over Christmas dinner six months ago, having just arrived back from Afghanistan. He'd been working up the nerve to tell his mother that he'd been posted to the Sacramento field office, knowing she'd be disappointed. His mother had been so hopeful that he'd get assigned to Chicago so they could live in the same city again. That Liza would be joining him in Sacramento had taken some of the sting out of the announcement.

He'd been happy. As happy as he'd been able to get, anyway. He'd still been numb with grief over Tory, and seeing Liza had . . . he wasn't sure, but it had been like a kick in the gut. He'd been so glad to see her, but sad at the same time. She'd known that he'd fallen in love with Tory. She'd known that Tory was pregnant. But he hadn't told her that Tory had died, and she'd been so shocked. She'd tried to hide it, but he'd been able to tell.

The past five months of having her just next door in the duplex he'd bought had been . . . nice. More than nice. Her very presence had helped him heal.

Molina cleared her throat, yanking him back. "You must be very proud of her."

"I am," he said fervently. "So damn proud."

Liza had overcome so much to get where she was in life. It was too bad she was too proud to accept his help when he offered it.

He wondered if she allowed the butt-groping *Mike* to help her.

Molina paused in the doorway, giving him a calculated look. "I think that might come as a surprise to her." And then she entered the meeting room, leaving him gaping at her.

Why would Liza be surprised to learn that he was proud of her? They'd been best friends for seven freaking years. She *had* to know.

"Agent Hunter." Raeburn's voice cut into his thoughts. "Are you planning to join us or not?"

Tom jerked to attention, realizing too late that he'd been standing in the doorway while the others took their seats. Seven of Raeburn's agents, most of whom worked on cases other than Eden, watched him curiously, and he had to fight to keep his cheeks from heating.

Gideon Reynolds wasn't in attendance, which meant Eden would be on the agenda. Gideon had been his trainer for the last few months, but Raeburn had assigned him to someone new after Gideon had been recused from the investigation.

His new trainer was Ricki Croft. She was in her late thirties and could be abrupt, especially before she'd had her morning coffee. She was a good agent, though, her career on a trajectory to make Special Agent in Charge one day. She was more by-the-book than Gideon had been, but far less than Raeburn, so Tom liked her well enough. She eyed him now, travel mug clutched in her hands, one brow lifted. She indicated the empty chair to her left, which Tom took, still feeling off balance.

Raeburn welcomed Molina back, then ceded the meeting to her. She allowed each agent to give an update on their cases, and Tom found his attention wandering for the first time during a briefing of any kind. He was known for his laser focus and his ability to remember nearly every-thing he heard, even the assignments that had nothing to do with Eden.

But his thoughts were on Liza now, on Molina's startling disclosure. He needed to talk to Liza, as soon as possible. He needed to mend this rift between them. He needed to make sure she knew he was proud of her. She needed to know what she meant to him.

She wasn't his oldest friend, but she was the one whom he trusted above all others. Liza knew his deepest secrets. For a long time, she'd been the only person in his life who'd known about Tory, about what she'd meant to him. About the life Tory had carried.

She understood what he'd lost.

His attention was brought back to the room by the buzzing of the cell phone in his pocket. It was his work phone—not the burner he never left home without—so he peeked at the text.

It was from Jeff Bunker, a sixteen-year-old budding journalist who, despite authoring a trash piece on Mercy Callahan that had hurt her deeply, had since made amends. Now Tom considered the kid a friend and ally.

Call me. Please. It's important.

Tom glanced up to see Croft frowning at him. He winced and slid his phone back in his pocket.

Only to have it buzz again.

Again, he peeked. Again it was from Jeff. **PLS CALL ME! About Eden. CRITICAL.**

Jeff knew the buttons to push. He knew that anything "Eden" would bring Tom running. Wincing again, he pushed his chair back, grateful it didn't squeak.

Raeburn still whipped around to glare at him. "You are not dismissed, Agent Hunter."

Tom held up his phone. "An informant. It's about Eden."

Molina held up her hand, silencing the retort poised on Raeburn's lips. "Hurry back."

Tom nodded and left the room, dialing Jeff Bunker as soon as his ass cleared the doorway. "What is it?" he asked when Jeff answered.

"I put an alert on any news articles about Eden," Jeff said. "Last night I got a hit from an article by a guy named Cameron Cook. His pregnant girlfriend disappeared two months ago. He got an e-mail from her, saying she'd been taken to Eden and she needed him to bring the cops to spring her. He said she sounded scared. She's due in two weeks."

Tom sucked in a breath, both excited and dismayed. Eden's conditions were primitive at best. Many women died in childbirth. "How did she get an e-mail out?"

"He doesn't know. He told the police and they went to the coordinates in the e-mail but the place was just forest."

Tom stood straighter. "She sent him *coordinates?*"

"Yes, but they were bogus. The cops got mad at him, threatened to have him arrested if he kept bugging them, because he kept calling. He finally went to the newspaper. He's desperate. He's been searching the area around the coordinates for weeks all by himself."

"Where is he?" Tom asked, his pulse ratcheting up. This could be the break they'd been hoping for.

"With me, in the lobby of your building. I drove to San Francisco to get him. I figured you'd want him to stop talking to the newspaper."

A grin pulled at his mouth, so wide it hurt his cheeks. "You thought right. I'll be down to get you both as soon as I can." He started back for the meeting room. "Don't let him leave."

Jeff whooshed out a relieved breath. "Thank God you believe me. I told him that he could trust you."

Tom paused, his hand on the doorknob. "Thank you," he said, then ended the call, reentered the meeting room, and smiled at Molina when she stopped talking to meet his gaze.

"Well?" she asked.

"We may have someone on the inside. Of Eden."

Molina's eyes sparkled. *"Yes."*

Raeburn looked reluctantly impressed. "Explain." Then pointed to Agent Croft when Tom had finished giving them the details. "Check it out."

Tom held up his hand. "The kid came to see me. He was told to trust me. I don't know that he'll be as forthcoming with Agent Croft." He glanced at Croft. "No offense."

Croft's lips twitched. "None taken." She turned to Raeburn. "I'll take Tom with me. It'll be good training for him."

Raeburn glared. "*I* want regular updates. Report back directly to *me*. Go."

Tom looked at Molina questioningly, because Raeburn's orders excluded her.

"Come on," Croft muttered. "I'll fill you in."

With a last look over his shoulder at Molina, he followed Croft.

TWO

Liza Barkley looked up at the security camera over the Sokolovs' front door, wondering if anyone else had been watching her standing on the porch, psyching herself up to enter. The FBI agent standing guard by the door certainly had, although he hadn't said a single word.

Just go in, she told herself. *You can paste on a smile. You do it every day.*

But she wasn't certain that she could pull it off today. She'd tossed and turned, trying to forget the six-six blond, blue-eyed Adonis whom she'd loved for seven years but who'd unknowingly stomped on her heart the evening before. Tom was completely unaware of her feelings— as he'd shown last evening by making friends with her date. *I should have known better than to try to move on with anyone new.* Her own reaction to Tom's lack of reaction was proof that she had no business trying to date other men. She wasn't ready. She wasn't over Tom.

She'd wanted to stay in bed today with the blankets pulled over her head.

She had, however, made promises to the stepsisters—one a little girl and the other a grown woman only a few years older than Liza. Both deserved a lot more than life had given them so far, so she knocked, taking a surprised step back when the front door flew open before she could rap the second time.

"Liza! You're here!"

Liza barely had time to lift the cake plate she held out of the way before she was tackled by the seven-year-old who wrapped her in an impressive bear hug. "Hey, Shrimpkin," Liza said, hugging back with one arm while balancing the plate on the other palm. Without making it obvious, she angled her body so that Abigail Terrill was shielded from both prying eyes and any other dangers that might be lurking.

Yes, there was an FBI agent standing guard, but Liza had sharp eyes, trained eyes, and she intended to use them. Because no one in this house was safe. Yet. "Careful. I've got cake."

Abigail pulled back, her gray eyes wide. "You brought me cake?"

Liza tapped the end of Abigail's nose while nudging her backward into the house, still protecting her. "I brought everyone cake. You can have your portion after lunch, *if* I don't drop it on the floor by accident. Your puppy will eat it and then he'll puke. Remember last time?"

Abigail's sigh was long-suffering. "That was disgusting. Did you bring Pebbles?"

"I did not. She'd destroy everything in Miss Irina's house." Shuddering at the thought of the young Great Dane running loose in the Sokolov house, Liza closed the door securely behind them. Habit had her ruffling Abigail's hair, but her finger caught in a tangle. "Where's your brush? You have snarls." She flexed her fingers. "Let me at 'em. Snarls flee from me in terror."

Abigail's childish giggles were like music to Liza's ears, and suddenly her weariness abated. "Will you do the fancy braid thing?" Abigail asked, looking hopeful. "Like a princess's crown? Papa can't make a crown. He tried."

"Of course I'll braid your hair." Liza had grown so fond of Abigail over the last month, gladly taking her to visit her father in the hospital as he recovered from a gunshot wound. A single father, Amos Terrill had always braided Abigail's hair, so Liza had taken up the job until Amos was discharged. Abigail, however, liked Liza's "fancy braids" better, so her daddy had been demoted to backup stylist. Liza had thought that Amos would be upset by this, but he loved seeing his little girl settling in with people who made her happiness a priority. Liza patted her pocket, having come prepared. "I brought a bunch of hair ribbons, so you can choose the color I braid in. But I need your brush."

"I'll get it." Abigail ran, her long dark hair flying back behind her like a cape, but stopped abruptly when she nearly crashed into the woman standing in the foyer. "I'm sorry, Miss Irina."

"It's fine, Abigail." Irina Sokolov tilted her head, her blond hair streaked with silver. She was somewhere close to sixty, about four inches shorter than Liza's five-ten, and huggably round, her brown eyes sparkling with humor and love. She was also a retired nurse, and Liza was about to start nursing school, so they'd clicked right away. "But what are the house rules?"

"No running."

"And?" Irina prompted, throwing a look at the front door.

Abigail's shoulders slumped. "And no opening the front door, because it's not safe." She peered up at Irina. "I'm sorry. I forgot," she added meekly. "And I thought it would be Liza."

Irina nodded, her smile warm. "It's okay, *lubimaya*. I don't mean to make you sad, just safe. The front-door rule will not last forever. I promise. Now, did you finish your math?"

Abigail nodded. "I left it on my desk for you to check."

"Perfect." Irina ran a loving hand over Abigail's hair, making Liza's heart squeeze with affection for them both. "Go get your brush for Miss Liza." She stepped back to let the little girl pass, then tugged Liza into a hard hug.

Liza never got tired of Irina's hugs. The Sokolov family matriarch had pulled Liza into her nest, fussing over her like she was one of her chicks and making Liza miss her own mother so much that it hurt.

"How are you this morning?" Irina asked once she'd let her go.

"Not bad," Liza lied.

Irina studied her face, her expression dubious. "Why don't you go upstairs and take a nap?"

"Nah." It wasn't like she'd be able to sleep there, either. Not with her thoughts whirling like a tornado. "I promised Abigail I'd take her to the eye doctor."

"I can do it."

Liza smiled at the older woman. "But you're with her all day, homeschooling." Catching Abigail up so that when she started public school in the fall, she'd fit in with her peer group. Abigail had lived in a repressive cult her entire life, and her education was just one of the things that had suffered. Basic medical care had also been neglected and, although Abigail seemed healthy, she'd never had an eye exam. Irina had been the first to notice how the child held her books too close to her face, squinting at the print. "Besides, Mercy is supposed to come with us. I cleared the trip through Agent Rodriguez, and he's vetted the optometrist's office and even an ice cream store for afterward. Is Mercy here yet?"

Liza and Mercy Callahan had also become close in the month that they'd known each other. Most of the times Liza had accompanied Abigail to the hospital to see her father, Mercy had already been in his room. The bullet Amos had taken had been intended for Mercy, and the man who'd fired the shot was still out there. Still a threat.

Thus, the rules about Abigail not opening the front door.

Thus, the FBI agent standing watch outside, assigned to protect Mercy.

Thus, at least a portion of Liza's trouble sleeping. Her new friend was careful, but this level of vigilance wasn't sustainable—not even by the military. Liza knew that from experience.

That experience had been responsible for more than a few sleepless nights as well. She and her team had been highly trained combat soldiers, and they'd still been caught in a single unguarded moment. People had died. People Liza had cared for.

Civilians would be far quicker to make a mistake, which could cost Mercy her life. Liza wasn't going to let that happen.

Irina looked up the stairs, growing more concerned. "Mercy's here. She's on the phone."

Liza frowned. "Is everything okay?"

"Well, nothing new is wrong. Mercy is on a video call with her therapist."

Liza sighed. "Oh. That's good, at least. I imagine they have much to discuss."

If anyone in this world needed therapy, it was Mercy Callahan. That the woman had made it through her life with her heart and soul intact was testament to her personal strength.

Unfortunately, Liza knew about that from personal experience, too. She wondered if Mercy's therapist was taking new clients. Giving herself a little shake, she held the cake plate out to Irina. "For the family."

Irina peeked under the aluminum foil and grinned wolfishly. "Chocolate. Did you make it?"

"No, ma'am. One of the nurses at the veterans' home did, for my last day."

Irina motioned Liza to follow her into the kitchen. "Your last day, it was good, yes?"

"It was very good," Liza said, dropping into a kitchen chair while Irina put the cake plate on top of the refrigerator, where Abigail wouldn't see it. Her job as a nursing assistant in the veterans' home had ended the evening before. "The nurses signed a card and we had goodbye cake, which is yummy, by the way. Lucky for us, most of the nurses were on diets and only ate tiny pieces, so there's a lot left. It's not as good as yours, of course," she added hastily, because nobody's cake was better than Irina's, "but I figure you can make use of it."

Irina busied herself making tea. "Oh, I'm sure we can find someone to eat it." With eight children and nine grandchildren, plus Abigail and all the others Irina and her husband Karl had enveloped into their brood, there was never a shortage of mouths to feed. "That person might even be me. Chocolate cake is my stress food. Did your manager give you a good reference?"

"He did," Liza confirmed. "He said he wished he could keep me on, but the woman who I was filling in for returned from maternity leave. At least the reference he wrote is glowing."

"As it should be," Irina declared, sliding a cup in front of Liza before settling into the chair beside her with her own cup. "You being a veteran and all. And a medic with a smart brain, quick hands, and a good heart. He was lucky to have you."

Liza's eyes burned and she widened her eyes to keep the tears from falling. "Thank you," she said quietly. "I think I needed to hear that today."

Irina's hand covered hers, warm and comforting. "What is it, Liza? I've sensed your unhappiness lately and I want to help if I can. You can tell me anything, you know."

Liza studied the older woman's face for a long moment before smiling ruefully. "Probably hormones," she deflected, unwilling to tell Irina what was really bothering her, because there wasn't anything anyone could do to help with that, not even the indefatigable Irina Sokolov.

The heart wants who the heart wants, Liza's mother used to say. Which was true, sadly. "Sadly" because what her heart wanted wasn't attainable.

It's my own fault. She hadn't agreed to the date with Mike last night to make Tom jealous, although now she had to admit that she'd hoped deep down that he would be. At the same time, she'd really hoped she'd find a spark with Mike. Even a tiny one. Anything to help her forget about her obsession with the man she'd loved for seven long years.

But the only spark she'd felt the night before was when Tom had appeared on the doorstep of the duplex they shared. Only when Tom had smiled at Mike and talked about the current baseball season and the basketball season that had just ended. He'd even signed an autograph for Mike, once her date realized who Tom was. Or who he'd been, anyway.

An NBA star. Now an FBI agent. There was little Tom Hunter couldn't do.

Except love me.

Irina was staring at her, evidently not having bought her hormone excuse. Probably because Liza had used it a couple weeks before. "Liza."

Liza searched her mind for something she could share. "You make me miss my mom." Which was the unvarnished truth. Irina and Liza's mother would have been fast friends.

"You lost her," Irina murmured, allowing the redirected conversation. "How old were you?"

"Sixteen. She had cancer and . . ." Liza sighed. "We didn't have insurance, so she waited to see a doctor. And then it was too late."

"Is that why you're going to nursing school?"

"Partly. My sister was murdered. Did you know that?"

"Yes." Irina didn't break eye contact, but her gaze was sad. "I looked you up." One side of her mouth lifted. "I'm nosy, in case you hadn't noticed."

Liza laughed, surprising herself. "I'm shocked, Irina. Shocked, I tell you."

Irina had the good grace to look a little shamefaced. "But not angry?"

"Of course not. You welcomed me into your home on the invite of another. I would have checked me out, too. Just to be sure I wasn't a threat. Especially now."

Irina's blond brows lifted and Liza's heart sank. The expression the older woman wore was too knowing and Liza mentally backtracked, trying to figure out what she'd said.

Of another.

Shit. She should have said Tom's name. But it hurt to even think it. Saying it aloud . . .

Still. *Shit.* Irina started to open her mouth, but Liza raced on, unable to change the subject fast enough.

"Anyway, Lindsay, my sister, she sacrificed a lot for me to stay in school. She wasn't much older than I was and she'd quit school to take care of our mom. Mom hated it, but . . ." It hurt to think of her mother and sister, too, but it had been eight years since her mother's death and seven years since Lindsay's murder. Her grief had softened over time. "Mom was too sick to fight Lindsay, and Lindsay was stubborn. More than me, even," she added lightly, then swallowed hard when tears clogged her throat. *I guess it hasn't been long enough after all.*

"She was murdered by a killer who preyed on prostitutes," Irina said. "I read about it online."

"She was. She worked the streets to pay our rent and buy food. I wanted to get a part-time job, but she wouldn't let me. Said she wanted me to stay in school, to become a doctor or a nurse to help other people's mothers. After Mom died, Lin got a job cleaning office buildings at night. She never told me that she'd lost her job, so when she didn't come home one night . . ."

"You were still in high school."

"A senior. I thought my worst problem was keeping my A in AP English. Then she didn't come home and I didn't know what to do. When I called the cleaning company, they told me that she'd been laid off months before."

"How did you find out about the prostitution?" Irina asked, her voice so incredibly gentle.

Liza closed her eyes, not wanting to think about those days. "I went to file a missing-person report at the police department. They pulled up her arrest record." She drained the rest of her tea and let out a harsh breath. "So I went looking for her."

Irina's eyes widened. "You went looking for prostitutes? How did you know where to go?"

A chuckle tickled her throat as a memory resurfaced, unexpected yet welcome. "That's what Tom said. I met him during that time. He got his friends involved in searching for Lindsay."

Irina's brows drew down in a frown. "You met Tom Hunter while looking for prostitutes?"

The chuckle became a belly laugh, long and loud and far more cathartic than it should have been. "Oh no," she said when she caught her breath. The very idea of straitlaced, Dudley Do-Right FBI Special Agent Tom Hunter looking for a hooker . . .

She wiped the tears from her eyes. "God, that's too funny. No, he wasn't out looking for a hookup. It was the next day. He'd come to my school to tell the jocks to stay in school. He was already a college basketball star by then, so I guess the administration hoped the kids would listen to him." She sobered and sighed. "I was skipping the stay-in-school assembly to go back to the police station, because no one on the street had seen Lindsay. Tom left the assembly, literally ran into me, and my school papers went everywhere."

"He helped you pick them up." There wasn't even a question in Irina's voice. Tom Hunter was a gentleman. A truly good man.

"Of course he did," Liza said, unable to keep the trace of bitterness from her voice and hating herself for it. It wasn't Tom's fault that she'd developed an impossible crush. Nor was it Tom's fault that he didn't feel the same way. "He saw the police report on Lindsay. He took me to a detective friend of his, and she was instrumental in finding Lindsay's killer."

Irina was studying her too closely. "That's how you became friends? You and Tom?"

"Yep." And Liza was finished talking about Tom Hunter. "But back to your original question. Lindsay is the main reason I'm going to nursing school. She sacrificed too much for me not to." She checked the time on her phone, abruptly realizing that Abigail should have been back with her brush several minutes ago. "Where is Abigail? I hope she's all right." She started to get up, but Irina motioned at her to stay put.

"I'll go find her. Have some more tea." Irina pulled a muffin from a basket on the table and plated it for Liza. "Eat. It's got no raisins. I made the batch especially for you."

"Thank you, Irina," Liza murmured, touched. She thought she'd managed to hide her aversion to raisins from the woman, but she should have known that Irina missed very little.

"You're important to us, too, Liza," Irina told her. "And at some point, when you're ready to talk about what Tom Hunter did to hurt you, I'll be ready to listen."

Then she was gone, calling Abigail's name a split second before there was a shout and the thunder of running feet above Liza's head. Liza ran from the kitchen, ready to do whatever needed to be done to help, but ran into Mercy Callahan as she came down the stairs.

Mercy's face was puffy, her eyes red and swollen. Liza took one look at her, then opened her arms. Mercy immediately accepted, huddling close as she shuddered out a harsh breath.

"Hey," Liza murmured, stroking Mercy's sleek hair. "What's going on?"

She'd seen this woman under the most stressful of situations for a month, but she'd never seen her cry. Not like this.

"I scared her," Mercy sobbed. "Abigail, I mean. I was on a call with my therapist and when I finished, I just sat there and cried. But I heard you come in and knew I needed to hurry to get Abigail to the eye doctor, but then I heard someone else crying. I opened the door and she was sitting on the floor."

"Oh no," Liza breathed. "What did she hear?" Because the horrors that Mercy had experienced were nothing that anyone else should ever hear, especially not a child Abigail's age.

"That was what I first thought—that she'd been listening in. I . . ." Mercy's body shuddered as she sucked in great, gulping breaths. "I yelled at her. Asked her what she was doing there. Accused her of spying on me."

"I don't think she was," Liza said, trying to think logically. "If you heard me come in after your call was over, she didn't hear anything. Except maybe you crying."

"That was what she heard," Mercy confessed. "She went sheet white, like I was going to hit her. She ran to her room."

"Should we go after her?"

"Irina already did." Mercy pulled back, wiping her eyes with the sleeves of her sweater. "I'm a mess. I need to apologize to her. She didn't do anything wrong."

"Not intentionally," Liza reasoned. "But she has to understand that she can't listen at doors. What if she had heard what you were telling your therapist?"

Mercy looked sick at the thought. "I'd never forgive myself."

Liza cupped Mercy's cheek in her palm, cooling her heated skin. "You need to stop that. Abigail knows you were hurt in Eden."

Eden. The very name was an abomination. It was a cult, its leaders criminals hiding from the law. They'd harbored pedophiles who'd abused Mercy and tried to assault her brother, Gideon. One of the cult leaders had killed their mother for helping them to escape.

And these evil men still, after thirty years, managed to elude the authorities. Except now the FBI was rigorously searching. And at least one of the agents on the case would not give up until he found them.

Tom Hunter would never love her, but he was a good man who wouldn't stop until he'd avenged Mercy and Gideon and saved the remaining innocents who were trapped in the cult.

"I think she understands more than we give her credit for," Liza went on. "But at this point she doesn't understand that it was sexual. She doesn't understand the concept yet." *I hope.* "Her therapist checked, because we were all worried about what Abigail knew."

Mercy knew this. She'd talked to the therapist herself. But Liza knew that hearing it again, calmly stated, would do more to soothe Mercy's anguish than all the platitudes in the world.

"You're right." Mercy drew a deep breath. "I need to apologize for shouting at her."

"You want me to come with you?" Liza asked, brushing Mercy's damp hair from her face.

"No." Mercy managed a small smile. "I'll tell her I'm sorry, then I'll get cleaned up and we can go."

"Tell Abigail that I still need to brush her hair. That's why she went upstairs, to retrieve her hairbrush. She probably heard you crying and didn't know what to do."

Mercy's nod was shaky. "Which means I really need to apologize now."

Liza watched her go up the stairs, then returned to the kitchen, retrieved the cake from atop the refrigerator, and cut a generous slice for Abigail.

"Stress food, indeed," she muttered, cutting an even larger piece for herself, leaving enough for Irina and Mercy. The day had to get better from here. It just had to.

Except she could hear Abigail crying upstairs and it ripped at her heart. The child had experienced enough fear and heartache for a lifetime. A particularly shrill wail pierced the air and Liza found herself gripping the edge of Irina's counter, her knuckles white.

She'd heard wails like that before, not nearly long enough ago. From terrified and dying children. From wounded mothers clutching babies to their breasts, praying for a miracle to save their lives. The memory triggered what the army therapist had labeled PTSD. All Liza knew were the images crowding her mind, the ones that normally waited until sleep to torment her.

She glanced at the kitchen door, tempted to run. Run where, she wasn't sure. Just . . . run. Away. As far and as fast as she could. She dropped her chin to her chest and focused on breathing. She'd promised Abigail that she'd go with them today, and the child needed a distraction. Some sense of normalcy.

No running. Not today.

Upstairs, Abigail wailed again, not at the same intensity or decibel level, thankfully. But it was enough to make Liza's heart beat faster. Desperately she looked around Irina's kitchen, then spied the mixer on the countertop, clean and ready to work. Irina had allowed her to bake in her kitchen in the past, so Liza knew where everything was.

Stuffing her mouth full of chocolate cake, Liza gathered the ingredients for her favorite stress recipe: Caramel-Pecan Dream Bars. Or brownies, as everyone not from Minnesota called them. She wouldn't have time to finish them, but she could get the batter in the oven. Irina wouldn't mind taking them out when the timer dinged.

Her mother had taught her to bake, and it was one of Liza's most precious memories. Re-creating her mother's recipe step-by-step would replace the bad images with good ones. This she knew from experience.

Plus the whir of the mixer would drown out the sound of Abigail's tears.

 SACRAMENTO, CALIFORNIA
WEDNESDAY, MAY 24, 9:30 A.M.

"What's going on between Raeburn and Molina?" Tom asked as he and Croft walked toward the lobby where Jeff waited with the boy whose pregnant girlfriend had managed to send an e-mail from Eden.

"Molina's been recused from the Eden investigation because Belmont shot her," Croft said. "The edict came down this morning, according to Raeburn. He told me before morning meeting. I think he had something to do with it, though. He was entirely too pleased that he was still leading the investigation."

"Son of a—" Tom cut himself off before he was publicly disrespectful to his boss.

Croft's lips twitched at his near curse. "So that's why Raeburn demanded we report straight back to him when we get back."

Tom was irritated, yet a half chuckle escaped when Molina's words sank in. She'd said that Raeburn's version was "less than satisfactory." Tom had assumed she'd meant Raeburn's assessment of his performance, not that the ass was withholding information from Molina.

She was pumping me for information. He'd appreciated Molina before, but he really appreciated her now.

"Tell me about this contact of yours," Croft said, increasing her pace to keep up with Tom's long stride. The woman was only about five-two, but her bearing made her seem so much taller.

"Jeff Bunker is a sixteen-year-old going to Sac State, majoring in journalism."

Croft made a face. "He wrote that awful article about Mercy Callahan, didn't he?"

"He did, but his version wasn't the same as the one that was published. His boss added material Jeff had deleted." Making Mercy look like a slut, when really she was a victim of sexual assault. It still made Tom furious. "Jeff issued a retraction and used his platform to give victims a chance to tell their stories. He wanted to make amends. Helping Cameron Cook is most likely part of his making amends. He set up an alert for articles about Eden."

Croft gave him a side-eye. "So did we. Why haven't we seen this Cameron guy's article?"

"Good question. I already planned to ask Jeff."

Croft was quiet for a minute. "So Jeff Bunker knows about Eden?"

She asked the question with care, like she'd been instructed to find out who else Tom had given information to. But like she wasn't happy about it. Tom trusted her, to a point.

"He does, but I didn't tell him."

Croft visibly relaxed. "Who did?"

"Probably Zoya, the Sokolovs' youngest daughter. She and Jeff have been getting friendly. Zoya knew about Eden because she's known Gideon nearly all her life, and she was in the room when Mercy told her story. Zoya's a good kid. So is Jeff, actually. Even though his relationship with the Sokolovs started out on the wrong foot because of the story about Mercy, Jeff's redeemed himself in the family's eyes."

Croft nodded thoughtfully. "So you trust him."

"I don't *not* trust him," Tom replied truthfully.

"All right, then." Croft pointed as they approached the lobby where two young men sat waiting. Both looked ready to fall asleep in their chairs. "That them?"

Jeff Bunker's head jerked up, his body relaxing when he saw Tom. "You came."

"I said I would." Tom shook Jeff's hand, then extended his hand to the young man at Jeff's side. He looked about the same age, but scared. "I'm Special Agent Hunter. You are?"

Wiping his palms on his jeans nervously, the kid came to his feet, all gangly limbs. "Cameron Cook." His handshake was as nervous as the rest of him. "Will you help me?"

"I'll do what I can," Tom promised, then gestured to Croft. "This is Special Agent Croft. We're going to an interview room so we can talk. Do you need anything? A soda, some food?"

Cameron shook his head. "We ate on the way."

Jeff was texting rapidly, then looked up. "Needed to tell Zoya that we found you so she can get to school."

Tom blinked. "Zoya Sokolov drove you to San Francisco?"

Jeff's cheeks turned pink. "I don't have my driver's license yet." He grimaced. "Or a car."

"I see," Tom murmured. "Do her parents know?"

"Maybe? I didn't ask, she didn't tell. She's on her way to school now, so if they didn't miss her yet, they won't. And we didn't get any phone calls on the road, so I think we're clear."

Tom held Jeff's gaze. "You and Zoya will tell her parents. Got it?"

Jeff sighed. "Yeah, yeah. Or you will. Got it. I hate being sixteen."

"Seventeen isn't much better," Cameron muttered. "Nobody listens to you."

"Come with us," Croft said. "We'll listen."

The young men were quiet as they signed into the building and followed Tom and Croft to an interview room. Once they were seated at the table, Cameron looked at the two-way mirror. "Is anyone back there watching?"

"No," Tom assured them. "But we will be recording this. It's standard operating procedure." He turned on the video camera and recited the date and the participants.

Croft leaned forward, concerned. "Cameron, do your parents know where you are?"

The boy sighed. "Kind of. I texted them that I'd left the house early to meet a friend at school. But I'll tell them the truth when we're finished here. They know about Hayley's e-mail and they know I've been trying to get someone to listen to me. They've been really supportive, taking me to the police station and to the coordinates Hayley sent me. They won't be too mad that I'm here. I hope," he added under his breath.

Croft shot Tom a look. "We should have a guardian here."

"I'll be eighteen in two weeks," Cameron protested. "I need to make sure someone is looking for Hayley." He swallowed. "She's pregnant and due soon. She's got to be so scared."

"He's not being accused of anything," Jeff inserted. "You can talk to him without a guardian. The law allows it."

Croft frowned at Jeff. "I'm aware of what the law allows, Mr. Bunker."

Jeff didn't back down. "Then you know you don't need a guardian."

Croft rolled her eyes. "It's to protect him. But . . ." She waved her hand. "Mr. Cook, please start from the beginning."

Cameron folded his hands on the table and drew a breath. "Hayley has been my girlfriend since we were fourteen." His cheeks darkened with embarrassment. "She got pregnant. We . . . well, we weren't careful once, but that was enough, I guess."

Croft's expression softened. "I guess. How far along is she?"

"Eight and a half months. We . . . we saw the ultrasound. It's a girl. We call her Jellybean for now."

Croft smiled. "Cute. What about your folks? How did they feel about the pregnancy?"

"They weren't thrilled, of course. We're too young. But we always planned to get married as soon as we could, and my folks knew that. So when we told them, they took a day to cool off, then brought us into Dad's office and told us that we would go to college and live with them. That they'd help us as much as they could. I expected them to be supportive, but Hayley . . . She cried. She was so sure that my folks would throw her out, that she'd have to be homeless."

"Her folks weren't as supportive, I take it," Croft murmured.

"No. Her mom isn't married. Divorced when Hayley was ten and Graham was five. Graham's her little brother. Kid is wicked smart. Her mom is very . . ." Cameron paused, searching for the right words. "Old-fashioned?"

"Judgmental," Jeff muttered.

"That too," Cameron admitted. "I don't want to be cruel about her mom, because it was a shock. Mrs. Gibbs believed Hayley was a virgin. That she was pregnant didn't go over well. She screamed and threw a fit." His expression darkened in anger. "She called Hayley names, like 'whore' and 'slut.' And that's not true."

"Did she throw Hayley out?" Tom asked, already feeling sorry for these kids.

"She didn't throw Hayley out. We told my parents first, because I knew we'd have a safe place to fall, you know? When we told her mother, she threw *me* out. Like, dragged me out by my hair, screaming at me. I wish I'd taken Hayley with me, but I didn't want to make it worse."

"And then?" Croft prompted.

Cameron shoved his hands through his hair. "Then they were gone. The next day. All of them—Mrs. Gibbs, Hayley, and Graham. Just gone. The house was put up for sale, with all the contents included. They disappeared. I've been crazy with worry."

"But you heard from Hayley," Tom said quietly. "When was that?"

"A month ago." He pulled a folded piece of paper from his pocket and gave it to Croft. The paper was limp from handling and falling apart at the creases. "I got this e-mail."

Croft read it silently, then passed it to Tom.

"April nineteenth," he said quietly, and Croft nodded her understanding. The date was the exact day that DJ Belmont had murdered Ephraim Burton, destroying any link the FBI had to Eden. Until now.

"'Dear Cam,'" Tom read aloud, noticing Cameron mouthing the words. He'd obviously memorized the e-mail. "'We are in a place called Eden. We are at these coordinates. Please come ASAP and bring the cops. This place is insane and we are being held against our will.'" Tom put the paper down. "What did you do next?"

"I went to the police station closest to the coordinates. My dad took me, but when the cops got there, it was forest. No houses, no signs of life at all. Nobody lived there."

"You didn't find anything?" Tom probed, because he'd seen Eden's most recent compound, now deserted by the cult. It had been populated with earth shelters and camouflaged with branches to hide the settlement from any satellite cameras.

"No. There was no evidence that any people had been there, ever. It was just forest. After the cops told us that they hadn't found anything, Dad and I checked an area about a mile square around the coordinates. That day, anyway. We've been back several times and expanded the search. Every weekend, my dad and I looked for Hayley, but there's nothing there but forest."

Tom checked the coordinates on his phone. The location was twenty miles from the closest of the known Eden settlements—that the FBI knew of. The position of the coordinates in Hayley's e-mail was over *a hundred miles* from the most recent Eden site. That was not a small error. Someone or something had altered the coordinates, probably using a proxy program.

"How did Hayley get these coordinates?" he asked.

Cameron shrugged miserably. "I don't know. I've waited for another e-mail from her, but I haven't gotten anything. If they caught her sending me a message . . ." His eyes filled with tears. "They might hurt her," he whispered. "She's scared. I know it." He clenched his fists. "Her mother dragged her to that place. I don't know if she left Hayley there by herself, or if she and Graham are there, too. And I don't know *why*."

Jeff squeezed Cameron's shoulder. "The place is a cult, Cam, like Zoya and I told you. They live like they're in the nineteenth century, and they're super fundie. Someone probably told her mother that they'd fix Hayley's sin. Make her repent."

Croft gave Jeff a dry look. "You know a lot about Eden, Mr. Bunker."

Jeff glanced quickly at Tom before returning his attention to Croft. "I haven't told anyone. Only Cameron."

Croft turned back to Cameron. "We can't promise you that we will find her, Mr. Cook, but we will do our best. The good news is that finding this cult is a priority of this office."

Cameron's lips twisted in a grimace. "And the bad news?"

"You're one of our first leads," she admitted. "But the other good news is that Agent Hunter is one of our best cyber experts. If you'll give him access to your e-mail account, he might be able to trace the e-mail."

Tom smiled at Cameron. "It's a fact. I'm good at what I do. You okay with giving me some passwords and access?"

Cameron's pent-up breath rushed out of him. "Of course. I don't have anything to hide."

"I do have a few more questions, though," Tom said. "For both of you. Cameron, you said no one listened to you. Who did you ask for help? Who else has seen this e-mail?"

"Dad and I went to the local sheriff nearest to the coordinates first," Cameron said, his expression showing only desperate truth. "Once he and his deputies searched and didn't find anything, he said he didn't have any more time for 'teenage drama.' I was so mad, but my dad dragged me out of there before I could give the man a piece of my mind. Dad said I wasn't doing Hayley any good by getting myself arrested."

"He was right about that," Tom said. "Who else?"

"I went to San Francisco PD and tried to file a missing-person report, but they said they couldn't take it because Hayley left with her mother, who had custody of her. But one of the detectives talked to their old neighbors. Nobody knew anything about them. They kept to themselves. They heard screaming sometimes, but the kids didn't look abused, so they never said anything to Mrs. Gibbs. The detective asked the real estate agent who was selling their house and the woman said that Mrs. Gibbs claimed she was moving to be closer to family. That her kids were 'troubled' and she needed help in getting them back on the straight and narrow."

Croft tilted her head. "Both kids were troubled? Or just Hayley for getting pregnant?"

"Both. Graham went to juvie right after the holidays. He got caught shoplifting." Cameron shook his head. "I tried to be a big brother to him, but he fell in with a rough crowd. He's amazing with tech, though. He can hack into websites. He might be the one who figured out how to send the e-mail from Eden. If that's the case, at least Hayley isn't alone."

"How old is Graham?" Croft asked.

"Twelve. But he's a genius, for real."

Tom tapped the printed e-mail. "Who else knows about this?"

"We live outside San Francisco and our town has a dinky paper, so

I asked if they'd print something. I figured I could link to it on social media and maybe it'd go viral. If someone had seen Hayley, they'd call. The article went up last night."

"We'll need to take it down," Croft said to Tom, then looked at Cameron. "We don't want the Eden leadership knowing that we're getting close. They tend to move around, especially if they fear being found out."

"I'll ask them to take it down," Cameron said. "Or should you do it?"

"If we do it, they'll know they have a story," Tom said. "Best you do it. Or we can do it together."

"Because you want to make sure I'm not going to say anything stupid," Cameron muttered.

"Partly," Tom admitted. "Mostly because I need to be able to trace every piece of Eden information out there."

Cameron nodded once, mollified. "Jeff says you're all right. I'm going to have to believe that, because I don't have another choice."

Jeff had gone very still. "Are you worried that someone from Eden will come after Cameron if they see the article in the paper?"

Cameron's face drained of color. "Me?"

Tom sighed, wishing Jeff weren't quite so quick on the draw. "Well, yes. I might have approached that more delicately later, but since you've let the cat out of the bag—yes. Cameron could be in danger if Eden learns that he knows about them."

Cameron's Adam's apple bobbed nervously. "They're that bad?" he asked hoarsely.

"Yes," Croft said. "They're that bad. Not trying to scare you, kid. Just want to keep you safe so that your Jellybean will have a mom *and* a dad."

Cameron's lips lifted at the mention of his daughter. It had been the exact right thing to say and Tom was grateful that Croft had said it. "Thank you," Cameron whispered.

Tom turned to Jeff. "How did you find Cameron's article? I have alerts set for Eden articles as well, and nothing pinged for me."

Jeff looked a little proud. And smug. "You might only be getting feeds from the big-city newspapers, or if you've got a broad enough net, you're getting too many hits. I'll show you how to set up your search to be more inclusive and discerning."

Tom had to laugh. The kid reminded him of himself at that age. "You little—" He cut himself off, but not before Jeff's eyes sparkled.

"Admit it, Big T," Jeff said, using Tom's nickname from when he'd played professional basketball. "I am the master."

"Gentlemen," Croft warned, but she looked amused as well. She sobered as she met Cameron's gaze. "We will make it our top priority to find Eden and bring Hayley and her family home. Thank you for coming in this morning. I know you must be exhausted. Can we drive you somewhere to rest before you start for home?"

Jeff and Cameron exchanged weary glances. "We can't go back until Zoya gets home from school," Jeff said. "And she's going to be tired, too. She'll need a nap. If her parents let her take us back," he added when Tom lifted his brows.

"I can call my father," Cameron said. "He'll come get me when he gets off work. He won't be happy to make the drive, but he will be happy that someone is finally looking for Hayley. Jellybean's gonna be his first grandchild."

Croft patted the boy's hand. "Call your dad. We'll get you a ride to Jeff's house and you can sleep till your dad arrives. For now, sit tight here. I need to confer with Agent Hunter, but we'll just be out in the hall."

"Well?" Tom asked as soon as they left the room and closed the door behind them.

"If this Graham kid is as tech savvy as Cameron says, he would know how to find their coordinates if he'd managed to hack into their computer to send a message."

Tom nodded. "But Cameron only found forest. The coordinates in the e-mail aren't anywhere close to any of the Eden sites. Eden could have set up a VPN or anonymity software like Tor to redirect their ISP and mask their location."

"To hide," Croft translated dryly.

"Exactly. We know DJ Belmont is the runner for the cult. We also know he sells drugs for a living, because we found traces of psychedelic mushrooms in the truck that Amos Terrill stole when he escaped." They'd also found evidence of the cult's drug operation when they'd searched their most recent location. "If he was using the computer to communicate with customers, it's likely he's using Tor to get on the dark web. He could easily fake his location that way. He wouldn't want customers to know where he was. I wouldn't, if I were him."

"We know where the cult was when Hayley sent the message, because it was their most recent site, most recently vacated. Can you back-extrapolate or triangulate or whatever to find them?" Croft blew out a frustrated breath. "Does that make sense?"

"It does. It's not triangulation—that's only possible if you have at least three locations. Or two locations and the nearest cell tower. VPN software bounces the data from server to server, all over the world sometimes. It's not simple to trace communications that have been relayed thousands of times, but it's not impossible. If Hayley can send another e-mail, I'll have another data point."

"That's what I was thinking," Croft said. "What about Bunker and Cook? Do we trust them not to talk? We need to keep this as need-to-know only. The wrong person could expose Eden to the press and then we'll never find them."

"I don't think either of the boys will talk," Tom said. "Cameron has already talked and no one believed him. He wants his girlfriend and their baby back, so I think we can trust him. Jeff has known about Eden for a month. If he hasn't talked by now, I don't think he will."

"Agreed. Let's get photos of Hayley and Graham if we can, so that we can show them around if we need to."

"Eden isn't all that big a settlement," Tom mused. "I bet Amos Terrill can positively identify Hayley and her brother. That way we can be certain that we're not chasing our tails."

"Good idea. Let's get a photo array and talk to Mr. Terrill. Do you know where he is?"

"I do. He's working on my friend's house, renovating it."

"Of course they'd be your friends," Croft said dryly. "Whose house?"

"Rafe Sokolov. He bought a fixer-upper so that he and Mercy could have a place of their own. Amos is a master carpenter and has been helping him, usually just in the mornings. Amos is still recovering from being shot by DJ Belmont last month, so he's only working part-time."

"Right," Croft murmured. "Your friends have suffered at the hands of this Eden group."

"They have," Tom agreed grimly. "And they're trying to get on with their lives, but it's hard, knowing that DJ might be back."

"So let's find DJ and Eden," Croft said, making it sound so simple.

Tom smiled down at her. "Yes, ma'am. Cameron needs to request that his article be taken down and I need to get his e-mail password, then we can go to see Amos."

THREE

Y ou didn't have to come with us today," Mercy murmured, her gaze locked on the small girl who was dubiously gazing up at the rows of eyeglasses on the wall. "It's your first day of vacation before nursing school."

"Of course I did. I promised Abigail that I'd be here to help her pick her new glasses." But also to help protect Mercy and the little girl, because their lives were in danger every time they left the safety of their house. "Besides, I need a new pair of frames." She dug her glasses from her handbag and held them up. "These are . . ."

"Ugly?" Abigail offered over her shoulder, an impish grin on her face.

"Abigail!" Mercy scolded, but Liza laughed.

"Very ugly," she agreed. "Military issue. I can't believe I waited this long to replace them."

"Because you can wear contact lenses," Abigail groused. "I wish I could have contacts, too."

"When you're older," Mercy promised. "Which I hope doesn't happen for a while."

Abigail shot her stepsister a look that was far too wise for a girl of seven. "Because you want me to be a normal kid."

Liza's heart contracted painfully, but before she could say a word, Mercy was on her knees in front of Abigail, hands on the little girl's shoulders. Amos had been a stepfather to Mercy and was Abigail's father in fact. Liza didn't think Mercy could have loved the child any more if they had been sisters by blood.

"You *are* a normal kid," Mercy assured her. "I want you to be a happy kid. And a safe kid."

"I am happy." Abigail's eyes brightened. "I'd be happier with contact lenses."

Mercy chuckled and pulled her close for a hug. "The doctor said to wait until you're ten."

"But you have them. And so does Liza."

"We're older than ten," Liza said. "By quite a bit."

Abigail sighed heavily. "But ten . . . That's *forever*."

"I hope so," Mercy murmured. "You have a lot of fun to catch up on." She rose to her feet. "But right now, we're shopping for new glasses. I can't believe you managed as well as you have without them all this time."

Abigail shrugged. "Nobody back home had glasses except for the really old people."

Back home. Eden.

Liza could see the sudden tension in Mercy's shoulders. And, apparently, so could Abigail, because the child flinched. "I mean back *there*, Mercy. Home is here. With Papa and you and Rafe and Miss Irina and Mr. Karl." She lowered her eyes, studying the floor. "I'm sorry."

Mercy's sigh was quiet as she tilted Abigail's chin up, cupping the child's cheek in her palm. "You have nothing to be sorry about. I'm just so very glad you're here with me, and that your papa is here, too. I hate to think about the people you left behind, that's all."

"But you'll find them, right?" She glanced over at Liza. "Right?"

"Agent Hunter will," Liza said confidently. She'd given up hope on her own relationship with Tom, but when it came to his single-minded focus in finding Eden, she had no doubts. "Come on. Let's pick out some kicka—um, kickbutt glasses. I need your fashion sense, Shrimpkin."

Abigail snickered. "You can say 'kickass' around me, Liza. I'm seven."

"I think I can't." Liza chuckled. "Miss Irina would send me to bed without dessert."

Abigail exaggerated a shudder. "That would be awful! We'll get kick*butt* glasses." She returned to her study of the kids' frames.

Liza followed, looking over her shoulder to the optometrist's glass door. The Fed who'd been assigned to protect Mercy was standing guard outside. Rodriguez was armed and experienced and took his duty very seriously.

He'd chosen this optometrist because it wasn't in the mall, which offered too many points of egress to cover adequately. This office had only two doors—the front door and one in the back, which was locked and alarmed. Liza wasn't crazy about the wall of plate glass windows in the front, but it was covered by promotional displays, so that would have to be good enough.

"Molina says that Rodriguez is a good agent," Mercy murmured.

"I know. She told me." Liza trusted Special Agent in Charge Molina more than she trusted most people, which still wasn't a lot.

Mercy's lips twitched. "I forgot you two were besties now."

Liza rolled her eyes. "We are far from besties. I just looked in on her a few times when she was on disability."

"You cooked her meals, changed her dressings, and did her laundry," Mercy said. "She told me that you did, so no use trying to deny it. Molina doesn't warm up to just anyone, you know."

Liza shrugged uncomfortably. "She doesn't have any family in the area. Her daughter lives out east and had to go back to work, so she was alone. I was glad to help her."

"Which makes you a nice person. I wish I'd visited her more while she was laid up."

Liza patted Mercy's shoulder. "You were a little busy taking care of Amos."

Abigail's father still had a ways to go before he fully recovered, but he was improving daily, and Mercy's care during his recovery in the hospital was one of the reasons.

Abigail turned at the mention of her father's name. "I helped!"

"And he's getting better faster because you did," Mercy agreed.

Abigail beamed, choosing a pair of purple frames, sliding them onto her face. "I like these."

Mercy leaned down until their faces were side by side in the mirror. "I like them, too. They make you look smart and very pretty."

Abigail shifted and bit her lip, but nodded.

"It's okay to look smart and pretty," Liza said gently. The slump of Abigail's shoulders told her that she'd guessed right. "It's also okay to *want* to look smart and pretty. There is nothing wrong or sinful about that."

"It's vanity," Abigail whispered.

Mercy shot Liza a grateful glance in the mirror. "Maybe," she allowed. "But as long as you understand that it's not the most important thing in life, a little vanity is okay. I'm a little vain."

Abigail's eyes widened. "You are?"

"I am," Mercy said, her eyes twinkling now. "I like to look good for Rafe."

Abigail's sigh was wistful. "You're beautiful."

Mercy kissed the child's temple. "So are you. And these glasses make you even more so. I say we get them."

"Now me," Liza said. "I think that purple will clash with my hair, though."

"I like your hair," Abigail insisted. "It's brown and red together."

"I like it, too. But it's got a little too much red to go with that purple. What color do you think I should go for?"

For the next ten minutes, Abigail considered the choices before picking out a pair of hot pink glasses in a retro cat-eye style. The corners were covered in rhinestones, sparkling in the overhead lights.

"These," Abigail announced. "They're perfect."

"Perfect" might not have been the word Liza would have chosen. They were . . . "Wow," Liza managed. "They're about as far from military-issue specs as I could possibly get."

Abigail bounced on her toes while Mercy visibly struggled to swallow a grin. "Try them, Liza!" Abigail urged.

"Yes, Liza," Mercy said, her lips curving. "Try them."

Biting back a wince, Liza slid them on, then stared at her reflection, barely recognizing the woman staring back. She liked the frames. She actually loved them. "They really are perfect." She hugged Abigail to her side. "You are a genius, Shrimpkin."

Abigail preened. "Agent Tom will like them, too."

Liza stiffened. Agent Tom couldn't care less what she wore or how she looked. "Why do you say that?"

"Because you're friends," Abigail said simply.

Liza's throat tightened and she barely managed to smile. "Yes, we are." *And that's all we are. All we will ever be.*

It was high time to move on. Time to stop pining for what and who she couldn't have.

Mercy tapped Abigail's nose. "Now me. Pick a pair for me. I've worn the same style since college. I'm ready for something different."

Still wearing the rhinestone frames, Liza turned away, needing to process the sudden swell of grief that had solidified in her chest, making it hard to breathe. She closed her eyes, telling herself that she'd get over Tom Hunter. She'd done it before.

Which was a lie. She'd never gotten over him. She'd simply found an . . . adequate replacement. The memory of Fritz had another wave of grief hitting harder than the last. She pressed the heel of her hand against her breastbone, trying to give herself room to draw a breath.

One breath. Then another.

I am not a nice person. A nice person wouldn't have allowed Fritz to fall in love with her. A nice person wouldn't have convinced herself that she loved him back.

A nice person wouldn't have married him in front of his family.

But Tom had been with Tory at the time. Engaged. Taken forever. Tory was gone now. So was Fritz.

Tom still grieved his lost love and had no room in his heart for anyone else.

Liza grieved Fritz, but mostly the fact that, while she'd loved him, it hadn't been as he'd loved her. She could only hope that he hadn't known the truth.

Time to move on. Mike, the nurse from the VA facility, was a nice guy, and they'd had a good time at dinner the night before. Hell, Tom had even liked him. Liza had felt guilty, though, the entire time. Like she was using Mike.

Because you are. Like you used Fritz. But she had to do something. Sitting around crying about Tom Hunter was not going to be her life. Maybe she needed a new hobby. Maybe another part-time job until she started nursing school. She'd planned this gap between her job and school, foolishly thinking she might take a vacation.

The idea of a vacation itself hadn't been so foolish. That she'd daydreamed about taking it with Tom had been colossally stupid, and there was no way she was taking one alone. Not now.

So a new job it would be. She'd start looking tonight.

Opening her eyes, she lowered the hot pink frames so that her vision wasn't obscured by the display lenses. She scanned the buildings across the street through the plate glass wall of windows, an act more habit than intentional. She'd learned the hard way to scan rooftops, searching for the enemy in Afghanistan.

But there was nothing up there. Just rooftops and a few pigeons. Nothing . . . nothing . . .

Something. She froze, recognizing the flash of light on a visceral, instinctive level. She'd seen it before.

A scope. Of a rifle. In her mind she heard the sharp crack of gunfire, the screams of the women and children in the marketplace. The shouts of the men. The bleating of the animals who knew something was wrong but didn't know what. She smelled the blood.

And saw the lifeless eyes staring up at her from what was left of her husband's face.

Go. Run. Those had been his last words, and they echoed in her memory.

Go. Run.

Abruptly she turned to the sisters, who were giggling over the pair of glasses Abigail had chosen for Mercy. *Get them out of here.* Without scaring Abigail.

"Abigail," Liza said, hoping the tension in her voice wasn't obvious to the seven-year-old, "we need to be going now. Do you need to go to the bathroom before we leave?"

Abigail blinked, then tilted her head, evaluating. "Yes, I do."

Mercy's eyes narrowed, but she didn't question. "Let's find the bathroom, sweetheart."

Liza followed them to the restroom at the rear of the optometrist's office, keeping her body between the sisters and the glass door. When they were safely inside, Liza speed-walked to the front and opened the door.

"Agent Rodriguez. Top of that building, twelve o'clock. I saw a scope."

Rodriguez gave her a disbelieving look. "*You* saw a scope?"

Liza met his gaze unflinchingly, keeping her tone level when she wanted to snarl. He was a good agent, she reminded herself. "Half my unit was killed by a rooftop sniper in Afghanistan. The rest of us got down in time because I saw the flash of a scope. I saw a flash. Just now."

Agent Rodriguez turned to scan the roofline. "I don't see—" He stopped abruptly. "Fuck," he muttered, one hand going to his firearm, the other to his phone. "I'm calling it in."

"You saw it?"

"I saw a person," Rodriguez said grimly, dialing his phone. "Just a glimpse. Where are Miss Callahan and Abigail?"

"I sent them to the bathroom. It's secure with no windows. Please bring the car to the back. I'll escort them out through the rear door."

Moving his body in front of the door, Agent Rodriguez gave her a nod. "I'll get the car, you get the ladies." Through the door she heard him giving their location to whoever he'd called.

Taking off the pink glasses she still wore, Liza quickly gathered the frames the sisters had chosen and took them to the counter, stepping far enough away that both she and the woman tending the store were out of the line of fire. "Can you make a note of these frames? You have the little girl's prescription because she just saw the doctor. My friend and I will have our prescriptions faxed and we'll call back with a credit card this afternoon. Something's come up and we need to leave. We may need to have someone else pick them up for us."

The woman behind the counter nodded uncertainly. "Is everything all right?"

Liza debated telling the woman the truth. If she didn't and the woman got hurt . . . *No more blood on my hands.* "Can you take your lunch break in the back? Away from that glass door?"

The woman paled. "Yes. Of course."

Liza tried to smile. "Thank you. And if you could make sure anyone else stays away from the door as well? Is the doctor still here?"

"No. He went to lunch. It's just me right now."

"Then take care of just you," Liza said, making sure the words came out like a warm request and not a barked order. "My group needs to go out the back."

The woman managed a nod. "Of course. I'll walk you out, then take my break."

Liza put her arm around the woman's shoulders and guided her to the back. When she was standing outside the restroom, no longer in front of the window, she got out her phone and fired off a text to Tom.

With Mercy and Abigail at eye dr. Agent Rodriguez on duty. I saw flash of a scope on roof across street. Taking Mercy and Abigail to Soko's. Rodriguez calling 4 backup. Advise.

She began to pace, wishing for her sidearm as she waited for Tom's reply. It came ten seconds later. *Send address of eye dr. On my way. Keep your head down.*

There was a pause, then a final text from Tom. *Be careful. Call me as soon as you're back at Sokolovs'.*

Liza finished texting him the address as the restroom door opened. "We're going out the back," she told the sisters with a smile that she hoped was carefree. "Let's go, Shrimpkin."

Abigail regarded her with her old-soul eyes. "He's back, isn't he? Brother DJ. He's back."

Yes, Liza thought, *this child knows a lot more than anyone gives her credit for.*

Mercy's mouth fell open in surprise. They'd all taken great pains not to discuss DJ Belmont or any of the Eden founders in front of Abigail.

Liza took a moment to choose her words and decided to go with the truth rather than sugarcoating it. The child's life could depend on her obedience, so she needed to understand at least some of the danger. "I don't know, baby girl. I saw something outside. I could be wrong, but we're not taking any chances, okay?"

"Go and chase him," Abigail whispered fiercely.

It was almost a certainty that DJ Belmont—or whoever Liza had seen on the roof—was already long gone. "Agent Rodriguez is calling for backup."

Abigail's eyes filled with tears. "But he'll get away. He'll come back."

Liza let out a careful breath. "Maybe. Probably, even. But the FBI will not let him win, Abigail. I need you to believe that. For now, I really need you to get into Agent Rodriguez's SUV and lie down on the floor with Mercy and me."

Abigail swallowed hard. "Yes, ma'am."

Mercy put a protective arm around Abigail's shoulders. "It'll be all right, honey." Her voice shook and her eyes held fear, but her jaw was firmly set. "I promise." She looked at Liza. "Thank you."

Liza gave her a nod, then shepherded them out. "Let's go."

FOLSOM, CALIFORNIA
WEDNESDAY, MAY 24, 11:30 A.M.

Fucking hell. DJ scrambled to put his rifle in the guitar case he'd modified to carry it. He fumbled the buckles on the case and pulled his gloves back on, cursing that his clumsy right hand couldn't feel the trigger with them on.

So much for Mercy Callahan letting her guard down. He'd been made. He jogged down the stairs from the roof of the office building across the street from the eye doctor.

He'd had Mercy in his sights. *In my goddamn sights.* Not only Mercy, but the little girl who was with her. He could have dragged Abigail Terrill back to Pastor after taking Mercy out.

He could have. If he hadn't been made. *Goddammit.*

He'd taken too long to set up his shot. *Goddamn bum arm.* His finger had been on the trigger when the woman with Mercy had turned and . . . somehow spotted him. She had to be a Fed. The guy waiting outside certainly was.

I should have taken him out first, but that would have alerted Mercy to run. Now I'm *running away. Again.*

Exiting the office building, he looked both ways before calmly walking to his truck. Stowing the guitar case on the passenger-side floorboard, he drove away with no one the wiser.

Things had been going so well. It hadn't taken much work to figure out where Mercy was hiding out. Several news stories about her in the past month had been videotaped in front of a house in Granite Bay, owned by Karl and Irina Sokolov.

DJ had started at the Sokolovs' house, parking far enough down the street that no one would give him a hard time. He hadn't been worried about interference. The magnetic sign on his truck identifying him as a plumber allowed him to operate under the radar. He was largely ignored wherever he went.

He was glad he'd kept an extra magnetic sign and extra license plates in his backpack. It had saved him a trip to the house he used during his time away from Eden, which was where he kept his supplies. He always had an extra rifle in his quarters in Eden. Coleen had made sure that it had been securely packed when they'd moved to the caves, which was good, because he'd lost the one he'd used the month before when he'd taken out five Feds and Ephraim Burton.

Which meant his prints were now in a federal database. That sucked.

Which also meant he had to be ultra careful now about avoiding any law enforcement of any kind. He would have done so anyway, but now the stakes were higher. Because now Mercy and Gideon were trying to find Eden. If they succeeded before he got the millions, he'd have to go to ground. No Caribbean. No white-sand beaches.

To say that he was motivated to stay under the radar was putting it mildly.

He'd gotten lucky that morning when an SUV that screamed "FED" had driven by, coming from the direction of the Sokolovs' house while he'd been waiting. He knew how to follow a vehicle without arousing suspicion. He'd had a very good teacher.

Roland Kowalski had taught him nearly everything he knew about the outside world, specifically everything about making easy money and not getting caught. Kowalski was going to be pissed off that DJ's prints were now on file.

He was unlikely to fire him, though. *I know too much.* DJ had closely watched Kowalski's rise within their gang, listening and learning. *He'll either kill me or deal me in from the periphery.* Either way, DJ's days of enjoying favored status within the gang were probably over.

He pulled into an alley and got out, changing the plumber's sign for an electrician's. Then he pointed his truck toward the interstate. He'd end up back at the Sokolovs' sooner versus later, but not today. They'd be looking for him now.

He needed to regroup and take care of some other business.

He'd already set the expectation with Pastor that he wouldn't be back for a week. He could afford to wait and watch. Mercy Callahan would have to lower her guard sooner or later, and next time he had her in his sights, she wouldn't have bodyguards.

Because the next time he had her in his sights, he'd take the bodyguards out first. He'd gotten a good look at the man's face. Unfortunately, he'd only gotten a quick look at the female bodyguard, but he thought he'd recognize her if he ever saw her again.

MIDTOWN SACRAMENTO, CALIFORNIA
WEDNESDAY, MAY 24, 11:30 A.M.

Shit, shit, shit. Liza's texts had Tom's heart pounding. Thanks to her sharp eye, a disaster had been narrowly avoided.

A sniper on a rooftop. Aiming at Mercy Callahan.

And Liza. Because he knew his friend. She'd protect Mercy and Abigail, even if it meant putting her own life on the line.

He wasn't sure who his heart was pounding harder for, Liza, Mercy, or Abigail.

Dammit, Liza, don't get yourself shot before I can tell you I'm proud of you. Because Molina's casual observation still weighed heavily on his mind. *Don't get yourself shot, period.*

He checked the time and wanted to groan aloud. He and Ricki Croft were in Midtown, at the house Amos Terrill was helping to renovate. They were at least forty-five minutes from the eye doctor where Liza had taken Mercy and Abigail. The sniper was likely long gone already, but they could at least look at the scene.

That DJ Belmont had returned was Tom's first assumption. The man was a skilled sniper. He was not to be underestimated.

Tom silently swore, wondering how to tell Amos that his child had been at the scene of a thwarted shooting. The man was going to freak out, and he'd be perfectly right to do so.

He looked up from his phone to see Croft showing Amos the photo array they'd made, including the picture Cameron Cook had provided of his missing, pregnant girlfriend.

"Yes," Amos Terrill was saying with a brisk nod. His voice was raspy and hoarse, a lingering effect of the gunshot wound to his throat the month before. He leaned forward to tap the photo of Hayley. "That's her in the bottom row, middle picture. Sister Magdalena."

"You're certain?" Croft asked him.

Amos pushed the laminated sheet of photos over the blueprints that covered the makeshift table to Croft, who'd led the interview. "One hundred percent, Agent Croft. It's only been a month since I saw her. She was clearly unhappy to be in Eden. I worried for her. She wasn't fitting in very well."

Croft frowned at the photo. "Her name is Hayley Gibbs."

Amos shrugged. "Not in Eden. Most in the community have biblical names. My parents named me Amos, so I was good to go when I got there. A few get to keep their old names, but that's generally up to Pastor."

"But why Magdalena?" Croft asked. "Wasn't Mary Magdalene a fallen woman?"

"So is Hayley." The caustic reply came from Rafe Sokolov, who was sitting next to Amos. Rafe had given Amos and Abigail an apartment in the house he owned in exchange for the help Amos was giving him on the renovations for his new place.

Tom liked Rafe, having felt an instant kinship with the man who'd also lost someone important to him to violence. That kind of loss changed a person. Made him open to . . . alternate means of ensuring justice was done, something Tom understood too well. It was one of the reasons he'd first gotten into hacking. Information was power.

Croft's brows rose. "Explain?"

"Hayley's pregnant out of wedlock," Rafe said. "They gave her the name of a prostitute to make sure everyone reminded her every time they said hello."

"My first wife—Mercy's mother," Amos specified, "was named Selena, but I knew her as Rhoda. She told me much later that she'd been given that name on her first day in Eden because she hadn't wanted to stay once she got there and found out the rules, especially those requiring women to be married. Rhoda was a servant in the early church. My Rhoda said that Eden's elders wanted her to know her place."

"I see," Croft murmured.

Amos sighed. "There are quite a few people in Eden who are as desperate to escape as Hayley is. Is there anything I can do to help?"

"You just did," Croft said with a smile. "For now, you can help the most by staying safe."

"And not interfering in your investigation," Rafe added dryly.

Croft shot him a quick grin. "That too."

One of the things Tom liked about working with Croft was that she genuinely cared about people. But the clock was ticking and he wanted to get to the building across the street from Abigail's eye doctor.

He cleared his throat. "Agent Croft, something's come up. If you've got everything you need, we should be going."

Rafe's brow immediately furrowed as he studied Tom's face. He was a SacPD homicide detective on disability leave, and his instincts were still perfectly sharp. "Why? What's wrong? Is it Mercy?"

Croft didn't question Tom's cue to leave. She rose from the table and gave both men her card. "Call me if you think of anything else. Agent Hunter? I'm ready when you are."

Rafe lurched to his feet, his face now pale. "Tom?"

Tom hesitated, then shot Croft a look of apology. "She's okay, Rafe," he assured him. "She and Abigail are with Liza and Agent Rodriguez, on their way back to your parents' house."

"But something happened," Amos said, his voice growing raspier. "Tell us."

"I don't know the details," Tom said, which was mostly true. "When I do, I'll let you know. For now, know that they're all right. You can call Mercy if you need to make sure."

Rafe was already dialing her number, Amos watching his every move.

"We'll see ourselves out," Croft said quietly.

When she and Tom were on the street, she turned to him. "Well?"

"Liza texted me. She spotted the flash of a scope on a rooftop across the street from the eye doctor where they took Abigail this morning."

"A scope?"

"She thought so. Rodriguez has reported it and called for a team. He remained with Mercy, Abigail, and Liza, getting them away from what, at that point, they believed to be an active shooter scene."

"He followed protocol. Good man. You got the eye doctor's address from your girlfriend?"

Tom blinked. "Liza isn't my girlfriend." Although it was a common mistake. Everyone assumed they were more than friends. But Liza knew the score, so Tom didn't worry over the label too much.

It was Croft's turn to blink. "Oh. I thought you lived together."

Tom felt his face heat, because he'd recently found himself wishing that they did. Not *actively* wishing, of course. Just the stray thought every now and then. It didn't mean anything. It *couldn't* mean anything. Because Liza was his best friend. Period.

"I own a duplex." It was basically two town houses stuck together. *Perfect for our needs.* "Separate doors. She rents the other side from me. It was a mutually beneficial solution," he added defensively when Croft continued to stare at him in confusion. "I needed a house and so did she. We were both new to town and didn't know the area or anyone else. This way I get rental income and a tenant I know I can trust."

"Oh," Croft repeated. "So . . . you just happened to move to Sacramento at the same time?"

"Pretty much. I got my first assignment here when I graduated from Quantico and she'd already been accepted to school here." He shrugged. "Serendipity, I guess."

"I guess." She shook her head. "Okay. Sorry. I just . . . never mind. Let's go."

FOUR

Liza huddled on the floorboard in the back seat of Agent Rodriguez's SUV, a pale Abigail on her lap. Mercy was on the opposite floorboard, still trying to calm Rafe down over her phone.

"My papa must be worried, too," Abigail whispered.

Liza rubbed her back. "You want to talk to him?"

"Yes, please."

Even terrified, this child was polite. Liza wasn't sure if that was a good thing or not, but she motioned to Mercy, then pointed at Abigail.

Mercy nodded, her expression weary. "We're okay," she said to Rafe for the tenth time. She'd described the situation at least three times. "I promise. Look, Abigail wants to talk to Amos. He must be as freaked out as you are." A moment later, she handed the phone to Abigail.

"Papa?" Abigail said softly. "I'm here."

Liza could hear Amos's voice because Abigail's hold on the phone was tentative. After growing up without technology in Eden, phones still made her nervous. "Are you all right?" Amos asked, his voice calm but with an underlying urgency. "Agent Tom said you were fine."

"I am, Papa. Liza was there. She saw a gun and got us out of the eye doctor's." Abigail snuggled more firmly into Liza's hold. "She was brave, Papa."

"So were you," Liza told her. "Very brave."

Abigail rested her head on Liza's shoulder. "I was brave, too."

"I heard her say so," Amos said thickly. "I'm proud of you, Abigirl. I'm always proud of you, though. You're a good girl and *very* brave. Remember that."

Abigail sniffled. "I will, Papa."

"That's all I can ask. Can I talk to Liza for a minute?"

"Yes." But Abigail hesitated. "Agent Rodriguez is taking us to Miss Irina's house. Will you be there soon?"

"I will. We're on our way now, but we're stuck in traffic. Mr. Rafe is saying it might take us an hour to get there. Give the phone to Miss Liza now."

Liza took the phone and kissed Abigail on the top of her head. "Very brave," she murmured, then spoke to Amos. "She's okay, Amos. Really okay."

"I know. I wanted to thank you. You likely saved my baby's life."

Liza's cheeks heated. "No need. I did what anyone would do."

Amos made an impatient noise. "Stop it. I heard Mercy tell Rafe what happened. How many people would have seen a flash of light and acted so quickly? Not many. So let me thank you, then tell me 'You're welcome.'"

Liza laughed softly. She'd come to care for and respect the older man during his convalescence. He exuded a paternal steadiness that calmed her. "You're welcome."

"That's better. Now put Abigail back on. I want to tell her I love her before I hang up."

Abigail told her papa that she loved him, too, then squinted at the screen. "I push the red circle to hang up, right?"

"Right," Liza said, then handed the phone to Mercy. "Your papa is a nice man."

"I know," Abigail said. "He loves us. Me and Mercy. And Gideon, too," she added, then pulled away enough to stare up at Liza. "Do you have a papa?"

"Abigail," Mercy chided gently. "Liza may not be comfortable talking about her family."

Abigail frowned. "Why not? What's wrong with your family? Are they . . ." Her frown deepened. "Are they mean to you?"

Liza tapped the end of the little girl's nose, charmed by the protective look in Abigail's eyes. "No, they weren't mean to me. Mercy is concerned because my family is all gone. It was always just me and my mother and my sister. My father wasn't in our lives. He . . . well, he left when I was a baby. We heard later that he died."

Abigail's eyes widened. "He just left? On *purpose*?"

"On purpose," Liza confirmed. "He wasn't a nice man like your papa. He sometimes hit, so I think my mother was happier once he left. But my mother died. She got sick with cancer."

"And your sister?" Abigail asked.

"She died, too." Liza glanced at Mercy, who looked sad but gave her a nod of approval. "She was killed. A very bad man killed her."

Abigail sucked in a startled breath. "Oh no. I'm sorry."

Liza smiled down at her. "Thank you. I miss her, every day."

Abigail's eyes filled with tears and they spilled down her cheeks. "Then you were all alone?"

Her sorrow was like a punch to the gut. This child saw, heard, and felt too much. "Yes and no." Taking the tissue Mercy offered, Liza dabbed at Abigail's wet face. "I met Agent Tom about that time and he introduced me to his family. I was only seventeen then, so I went to live with a friend of his mother. Her name is Dana and she's like my new big sister."

"Like Mercy is to me?"

"Very much like that. She let me live with her and her husband. They had a lot of kids, so I wasn't alone anymore, and that was nice. Some of the kids were hers, and—Well, that's not true. All of the kids were hers. Some were permanently hers and some were temporary. They lived with her while their own families fixed the problems they were having. That's called foster care. But Dana loved every child that came through her house."

"How long did you live with them?" Mercy asked. "I've been curious, but didn't want to pry. Don't answer if you don't want to."

"It's okay. I don't mind." And it was true. That phase of her life was one she didn't mind remembering. "I stayed with them until I was eighteen. I'd already decided—even before my sister Lindsay died—that I'd go into the military. Lindsay and I didn't have any money, and, at the time, I thought Lindsay was cleaning office buildings at night to put food on the table. I didn't want to be a burden to her when I was old enough to carry my own weight. I'd already discussed my plans with an army recruiting officer in Minneapolis."

Abigail's eyes were wide. "You were a soldier?"

"I was," Liza said soberly.

"Did you kill people?" Abigail whispered.

"Abigail!" Mercy hissed.

Abigail stiffened. "I'm sorry."

But Liza could see that she didn't understand why she'd been scolded. "It's a fair question, Mercy," Liza said, giving Abigail a hug. "It's all right, Abs. Yes. I did. And . . . well, that's hard to talk about."

"Why?" It was asked with such innocence that Liza's heart hurt. She remembered being that innocent, so many years ago. Before her mother died. Before Lindsay was taken.

Before she'd made decisions that still haunted her.

"Because my job was taking care of people, not shooting. But one day we were attacked and I had to jump in and help." Changing the subject, she gave the child what she hoped was a warm smile. "I was a medic. Do you know that is?"

Abigail mouthed the word, testing it. "Like a doctor?"

"A little like that. I'm not a doctor, though. Someday I'll be a nurse, but medics do . . ." She faltered, trying to figure out how to explain it to a seven-year-old. "We took care of soldiers who got hurt on the battlefield. Emergency fixes, until they could get to a surgeon."

Abigail looked doubtful. "Emergency fixes?"

Liza hesitated. "Soldiers get hurt sometimes."

"Like Papa did." Abigail lifted her chin. "He got hurt saving Mercy, because Brother DJ wanted to shoot her. Because he's bad."

"You're right," Liza agreed. "DJ is—"

"Evil," Abigail interrupted angrily, her jaw clenched. "He is going to *hell*."

Mercy blinked, taken aback at the little girl's vehemence. "That sounds about right."

Abigail seemed to relax at Mercy's confirmation. "Gideon's girl-friend took care of Papa until the para—" She pursed her lips. "What are they called again?"

"The paramedics?" Liza asked.

"Yes. Daisy made his bleeding stop until the paramedics came. That's what Miss Irina told me. Then they put bandages on Papa and took him to the hospital. In a helicopter. Is that what you did when you were a medic?"

"Pretty much. Lots of bandaging."

"Did you go in helicopters?"

"Sometimes. It depended on where we were and how close the enemy was."

"Who was your enemy?"

Liza blew out a breath. "I'll get a map and show you, okay? I'm not ignoring your question," she said when Abigail frowned. "It will be easier to explain with a book and a map."

"And a miracle, maybe," Mercy muttered.

Liza had to agree. After years in the army, she knew who they'd been fighting, but that knowledge was clouded with memories of the civilians who'd been caught in the cross fire.

Women, children. Little girls who'd been Abigail's age. Until they died. In her arms.

She swallowed hard, pushing that memory back as well. She was not going there now.

Or ever, if she had her way. Unfortunately, her subconscious didn't play by the rules. She'd probably dream of the children tonight.

Mercy was watching her, concern in her eyes. "Are you all right, Liza?"

No, not really. "Yeah." She turned back to Abigail. "Is that okay? Waiting till later?"

"Yes. Thank you." The child went silent and Liza wished she'd start talking again. It was unnerving, hunkering down on the floor of an FBI SUV as a grim-faced agent drove them back to Granite Bay, where Karl and Irina lived.

In fact, they should have arrived by now.

"Agent Rodriguez?" Liza said quietly. "ETA?"

"Ten," Rodriguez said, tone clipped. "Thought we had a tail, so I took the next exit."

"The tail is gone?" Mercy asked.

Abigail went still on Liza's lap, hearing the tension in their voices.

"Yes. They exited already. Just being careful, Miss Callahan."

"Thank you," Mercy said sincerely.

A grunt was her answer and Liza's lips twitched unexpectedly when Abigail piped up. "You should say 'You're welcome,' Agent Rodriguez. It's not polite to say—" She imitated Rodriguez's grunt.

Agent Rodriguez coughed, probably hiding a laugh. "You're right, Abigail. You're welcome, Miss Callahan."

Liza hugged Abigail hard. "Nice job," she whispered loudly, tickling Abigail's ribs.

Abigail giggled and wriggled, then froze, staring at the vee of Liza's blouse. A button had come loose, revealing more cleavage than Liza normally did.

"You have a tattoo," Abigail said with a mix of awe and horror.

"Yes," Liza said slowly. "I do. Is that bad?"

"They made Papa get a tattoo. They made all of the boys get one when they turned thirteen. Even the grown-up men had to get one if they joined the congregation."

"Oh." Liza sighed. Abigail sounded too grown-up herself as she parroted the words she'd undoubtedly heard from Eden's adults. She'd known that Eden marked the males in the community by tattooing their chests with the cult's symbol—two children kneeling in prayer beneath an olive tree, all under the wings of an angel holding a flaming sword. "Well," she said, stalling for time as she considered her response.

Mercy's brother Gideon had gotten his tattooed over, choosing a phoenix to cover the symbol of the cult's cruelty. Liza had seen Amos's tattoo when a hospital physician had pulled his gown aside to listen to his heart. She hadn't realized that Abigail would associate all tattoos with oppression.

"Well," she said again, "not all tattoos are bad. Not like in Eden when the boys were forced to get them. I got mine because I chose to."

"But why?" Abigail pressed.

Liza tugged her blouse a little farther down so that Abigail could see more of the tattoo. "It's a rose and a musical note, twined together. For my mother and sister. Mom loved roses. Lindsay played the piano. So I got their favorite things inked over my heart."

"Oh." Abigail seemed to consider this. "Did it hurt?"

"A little. But it was worth it to me."

"Do you have any tattoos, Mercy?" Abigail asked.

"No," Mercy answered. "I'm kind of like you, kiddo. For me, a tattoo is a bad memory of Eden. But you remember my friend Miss Farrah? The one who lives in New Orleans?"

Abigail nodded. "Does she have one?"

"She does. Hers is a shield with her fiancé's name. He's a police officer, so that's why the shield. Like the shape of a badge. Mr. Karl has a tattoo, too."

Abigail's eyes widened comically. "He does?"

Mercy nodded. "From when he was in the army. So not every tattoo is bad."

Abigail bit her lip. "But what if the person is bad? Are all their tattoos bad?"

Liza lifted Abigail's chin so that their eyes met. "Who do you mean?"

"Brother DJ. He had another tattoo that wasn't of the Eden tree."

The hairs on the back of Liza's neck lifted, her intuition shouting that this was important. "What did it look like?"

"It was letters. A long word." Abigail moved her hand in the shape of a rainbow. "Across his back. I saw it once," she admitted in a small voice that sounded guilty.

"How did you see it?" Liza asked. "Were you guys swimming or something?" She hoped it was something that innocent. She hadn't considered that DJ Belmont might have touched her Abigail. Fury flared at the very notion.

Abigail shook her head hard and fast. "No. We didn't swim. At least we girls didn't."

"It wasn't proper for women and girls to show any skin," Mercy said. "Luckily we were usually living up high enough that it didn't get terribly hot in the summer."

"Oh. Wow." That shouldn't have surprised Liza, based on what she'd heard about the fanatical restrictions in Eden. "So how did you see his tattoo, Abs?"

She kept the question casual, but Abigail wasn't fooled. Her eyes narrowed and she clamped her lips shut.

"Nobody's going to be angry with you," Mercy said quietly. "You're safe with us."

Abigail swallowed hard. "I saw a bunny and I wanted to pet it. But it ran away."

"So you chased it?" Liza prompted when Abigail said no more.

She nodded miserably. "It ran into the smithy."

"DJ was the blacksmith," Mercy offered. "He was Edward Mc-Phearson's apprentice before Edward took on Gideon."

Liza knew how that story ended. McPhearson had been a sexual predator and had tried to rape Gideon. Gideon had fought back and killed the man accidentally. The community had nearly beaten Gideon to death as a result. They might have, had his mother not smuggled him out of Eden that very night. He'd been thirteen, his Eden tattoo still raw from the artist's needle.

Liza wondered if DJ had been molested by Edward during his apprenticeship, but that was a question that was definitely inappropriate for Abigail's ears.

"Did you chase the bunny into the smithy?" Liza asked.

Abigail's face went pink as a peony. "I started to, but I saw Brother DJ in there. He was standing at the forge and the fire was hot. Kids weren't allowed in there. He took off his . . ." Her face flushed even darker.

"He took his shirt off," Mercy said softly.

Abigail nodded. "I wasn't supposed to look. Not at a . . ."

"A man," Mercy supplied. She glanced at Liza. "The genders were kept very separate. Women weren't supposed to speak to or even look at men unless they'd been spoken to."

Liza swallowed her sigh. Abigail's information was more important than any indignation over Eden's repression of women—including little girls. "Do you remember any of the letters in the word you saw? In his tattoo," she specified.

Abigail's forehead wrinkled. "There was a 'Z' at the beginning. It was bigger than the other letters and"—she made a face—"it looked like a snake. Fangs and everything."

"Sounds scary," Liza said, keeping her excitement tamped down. Tom would need this information, she was sure of it.

"Just yucky," Abigail said. "And mean. The snake was trying to bite a bat."

Liza heard Agent Rodriguez suck in a breath. She was about to ask what the significance of the tattoo was when the SUV slowed.

"Almost there," Rodriguez said. "I'm going to pull into the garage. I don't want to see anybody's heads until the garage door comes down. Okay?"

"Okay," Abigail agreed. She looked up at Liza. "Can we have cake when we get inside?"

Liza nodded, lifting her eyebrows. "Cake or bars?"

"Bars?" Abigail asked, then recognition sparked in her eyes. "You made Dream Bars?"

"I did. Mixed them up when you guys were talking this morning." Because she'd needed something to do with her hands, and clanging the pots and pans had covered the sound of crying from the bedroom upstairs. "Miss Irina promised to take them out of the oven for me."

Abigail's eyes went sly. "I think it's been a really hard morning, Liza."

"Oh?" Liza couldn't hold back her smile, because she could see where the child was headed. "I suppose it has, at that. But what does that have to do with my bars?"

"I think we need both."

"Bars *and* cake?" Mercy asked, chuckling. "I don't know. What do you think, Liza?"

Liza could see Rodriguez's shoulders shaking in the front seat, laughing at Abigail's soft-sell approach. "I don't know, either," she said. "Agent Rodriguez, what do you think?"

He brought the SUV to a gentle stop in the Sokolovs' garage and Liza felt her own shoulders slump in relief at the sound of the door lowering. They were back. Safe. No bullets. No blood. No dead eyes staring up at her.

He turned around, leaning over the seat to look down at them. "I think cake, bars, and milk are in order. Small pieces, of course."

"Of course," Abigail agreed, grinning. "Can I pop my head up now, Agent Rodriguez?"

He smiled at her. "You can. You were very brave, Abigail. And very well-behaved. Your papa will be pleased."

Abigail beamed, carefully climbing from Liza's lap to perch on the back seat. "You'll be sure to tell him?"

"You bet. Give me a second and I'll let you out." He helped Abigail out, then extended a hand, first to Liza, then to Mercy. "It's a gang sign," he murmured, so low that only they could hear. Abigail had already skipped into the house, going for the sweets.

Mercy had started to stretch her back but went stock-still. "DJ Belmont is in a gang?"

"It makes sense," Liza said slowly. "The cult makes money selling drugs, right?"

Mercy nodded. "Pot and opioids in the past. Shrooms more recently."

"I guess he was more deeply involved than just as a supplier," Liza said.

"He shot both Ephraim and Amos with a long-range rifle," Mercy said, then turned to Agent Rodriguez. "He must have learned to shoot from the gangs."

"It fits," Rodriguez said. "I'll report it to my boss. Do I need to tell Agent Hunter?"

Or will you?

Liza shrugged. "You can call him, or wait until he gets here." Although she knew she'd be contacting Tom. She was weak when it came to Tom Hunter. "He'll be here soon enough. He'll be worried about Mercy and Abigail."

"And you," Mercy said meaningfully. "He'll be worried about you."

Sure, Liza thought bitterly. *Because I'm his* friend. She forced a smile. "And me."

Agent Rodriguez started to say something, then shook his head. "I think Miss Abigail has the right idea. I'm gonna have some chocolate while I make my report. After you, ladies." He gestured to the door into the house, following them into the laundry room.

Irina was waiting in the door to the kitchen. She hugged both

Mercy and Liza at the same time, her body trembling. "Rafe called me," she whispered. "I was so afraid for you." She let them go, then discreetly swiped under her eyes. "Come. Let me fuss over you."

That was an offer too tempting for Liza to pass up. She'd get fussed over now and text Tom in a bit. He was probably busy at the scene anyway.

FOLSOM, CALIFORNIA
WEDNESDAY, MAY 24, 12:00 P.M.

Tom stepped off the stairs they'd taken to the office building's roof, Croft right behind. They paused to study the scene on the roof. The first responders had cordoned off the entire stairwell and the crime scene unit had already constructed an evidence grid. Twine crisscrossed the roof, blocking off search areas, each a square foot.

A man in white coveralls approached and Tom flashed his badge. "Agents Hunter and Croft."

"Sergeant Howell, SacPD CSU." He offered them both protective booties.

"Report, please," Croft ordered quietly, as they slipped the covers over their shoes.

"Someone was here," Howell said. "Latent is taking prints from the stairwell and the railing around the perimeter of the roof. We've got a boot print in the dirt close to the railing."

"Camera feed?" Tom asked, looking around them. He'd seen several cameras in the building's lobby and in the stairwell. There was another one mounted to the outside wall enclosing the stairs, but it had been painted over.

"One of my techs is getting the feed from the building's security."

Croft picked her way to the edge of the roof. "Entry and exit points?"

"We can't be completely certain until we get the security footage, but it appears he used the stairwell exclusively. There's a brick off to the side of the ground-floor door." Howell grimaced. "The security chief wasn't happy to see the brick or the butts on the ground. Apparently, employees use the brick to prop the door open while they slip out for a smoke."

Tom sighed. The best security systems were often ruined by a single human trying to circumvent the rules. "I'll need copies of the footage, as soon as possible."

Howell nodded. "Of course."

Tom followed Croft to the edge of the rooftop. She was staring down, examining three depressions in the sandy dirt on the roof. "He had a tripod," she said. "Set himself up here."

Tom crouched down to simulate the shooter's viewpoint. He could see through the glass door of the optometrist, but the signs in the windows blocked his view of the eye doctor's interior. "He had only a narrow window of opportunity to get Mercy Callahan," he noted. Or Liza, because he had not a single doubt that she would have protected Mercy and Abigail with her own body.

His chest constricted when he realized how close she'd come to being hurt. He drew a breath that physically hurt. *Liza. Dammit.* This was how he'd felt when she'd joined the army without telling him first. Like a sledgehammer to his heart. Worry and hurt and helplessness.

Howell crouched next to him. "Agent Rodriguez called it in after the woman accompanying the presumed target noticed a flash of light from this spot on the roof. The woman was standing in front of the door, but she must have a hell of an eye. I don't know that I would have noticed it from there. Rodriguez said that once she'd pointed it out, he briefly glimpsed someone, and got them out of there."

Tom's jaw tightened and it was suddenly important that she be acknowledged as more than *the woman* who'd accompanied Mercy Callahan. "Liza Barkley. She spotted the shooter."

She'd been standing in the direct line of fire. He wondered if she'd been scared. He knew he was scared at the thought of her in the path of a sniper's bullet.

The Liza he'd known before the army would have been terrified, but she would have done the right thing anyway. Trouble was, he didn't recognize parts of the Liza who'd returned from combat duty. That needed to change. He'd asked about her experiences in the military, but she'd always evaded his questions, and he'd respected her need for privacy.

He wondered if he should have. Maybe he'd left her alone with her memories for too long.

"Well, she's got one hell of an eye," Howell stated again. "Rodriguez said she was as cool as a cucumber. Just pointed it out and told him to bring the car. She got Callahan and the little girl to safety and made sure the optometrist's receptionist was away from the window as well. She handled everything so calmly that no one panicked."

"She served in Afghanistan," Tom said quietly. "I think she's seen much worse."

He was going to get the specifics this time. Something had been bothering her for months and he was going to get to the bottom of it. He knew that she had PTSD, but she would never talk to him about what had happened to her over there, and that sent another sharp pain into his heart. He didn't want Liza to suffer anything. She'd already had a hard enough time, with the losses of her mother and sister.

Slowly he rose, not taking his eyes from the glass door of the optometrist's office. "Were any shots actually fired?"

"Not that we can find," Howell replied. "Nobody reported any gunshots and there are no spent cartridges here."

"We need to know where Agent Rodriguez was standing," Croft said, taking out her cell phone. "I'm going to call him now."

"He included that in his report when he called it in," Howell said. "He was standing off to the side, against the plate glass window. He'd lit a cigarette and pretended to be taking a break. He also said that he didn't see the shooter until Miss Barkley pointed him out."

"It was a man, then?" Croft asked.

"Rodriguez thought so, but his glimpse was too brief for him to be certain."

It was DJ Belmont. Of that Tom was *completely* certain. But they needed actual proof. "We'll need access to any prints Latent lifts," he said. "We think we know who this was, and we have his prints on file."

"I'll make sure you get everything we gather," Howell promised.

They exchanged business cards and, after thanking the man politely, Tom and Croft walked back to the stairwell.

"I want to see that security footage right now," Tom said as soon as the door closed.

"I agree. If this is Belmont, we need to know." She angled him a look. "Miss Barkley does have a damn good eye. What did she do in the military?"

"Army medic," Tom said.

Croft winced. "She *did* see a lot worse, I'm afraid. What's she doing now?"

Tom lifted his brows. "You trying to recruit her?"

Croft shrugged. "You never know."

"She's starting on her master's in nursing in July," Tom said, "at UC Davis."

Croft whistled softly as the doors opened. "Good school. She must be smart."

"She is," Tom said, and he could hear the pride in his voice. Then he remembered what Molina had said that morning, that Liza might be surprised to learn that he was proud of her.

That had to change, too.

They found the security manager's office on the first floor near the lobby. A CSU tech wearing white coveralls sat next to a man in a black suit like Tom wore.

"Excuse us," Croft said after knocking on the open door. "Special Agents Croft and Hunter. Can we have a moment?"

The CSU tech gestured to the monitor he was watching. "My boss just texted that you'd probably be by." One brow lifted. "Even though he promised to share everything with you."

Tom's lips curved. "Busted." He sobered, crossing the room to stand behind the tech's chair. "You are?"

"I'm James Gray, head of security for the building." The man in the suit rose from his chair, offering it to Croft. "Ma'am?"

Croft's smile was tight. "Thank you, Mr. Gray." Sitting, she peered at the image on the monitor, then looked over her shoulder at Tom.

The footage was paused, freezing on a man wearing jeans and a gray hoodie on the staircase. They'd found an angle that showed his face clearly. Tall and rangy with shaggy blond hair, the man looked like he could be a cowboy, despite wearing a baseball cap without a logo. He matched the descriptions of DJ Belmont given by Gideon, Mercy, and Amos.

Tom nodded curtly, unwilling to say Belmont's name aloud. "Can you zoom in on his hands?" he asked.

Gray leaned over Croft to manipulate a mouse, bringing the man's hands into prominence. "Gloves," he said, anticipating what he was looking for.

"He had them on when he entered the building," the CSU tech added.

"Dammit," Croft cursed softly. "We still want Latent to process prints from the roof on the off chance that he took them off when he was setting up his shot."

"I'll let the sergeant know," the tech said dryly, clearly unimpressed with taking orders from Croft. Tom wasn't sure if it was a Fed thing or a woman thing, but neither was acceptable.

He directed his next question to the head of security. "Do you have a camera outside to show how he got away?"

Once again Gray leaned in to tap his keyboard, then stepped back, letting the video play. "He wasn't trying too hard to hide his face," the man observed as Belmont ran out the back door, then kicked the brick away.

Tom had noticed that. Of course, Belmont had operated under the radar for years. He probably thought it didn't matter even if they did see his face. He probably figured that once he got rid of Mercy Callahan he'd disappear back under the Eden rock from where he'd crawled.

Squaring his shoulders, Belmont slowed his pace. In one hand, he carried a guitar case, which he slid across the floorboards of a box truck with a sign proclaiming him to be a plumber.

Tom's throat thickened as he recognized the truck despite the bogus plumbing sign. It had belonged to the man Belmont had murdered a month ago as he'd fled the scene at Dunsmuir. Where he'd murdered five FBI agents, executed Ephraim Burton, and shot Amos.

The surveillance camera caught the license plates as the truck peeled out of the parking lot, kicking up gravel and dust. "Pause it, please," Tom requested. He then took a photo of the monitor with his phone, capturing the license plate number. "Thank you," he said. "I'll still need a copy of the footage. Sergeant Howell has my contact info."

The CSU tech gave him a little salute. "Of course."

Croft relinquished Gray's chair. "Thank you, gentlemen."

"Should we be watching for this man to return?" Gray asked. "My clients in the building are understandably shaken at hearing that a gunman was on the roof."

"Probably not," Croft said. "He was aiming at a specific target. It's unlikely that the person he wanted to shoot will return."

Gray nodded grimly. "Thanks. I'll let my clients know."

"Tell them that we said your surveillance system is excellent," Tom said. "So many cameras get a grainy feed that's all but useless. Yours is crystal clear."

Gray dipped his head, his expression appreciative. "Now if I can only get the employees to stop propping that door open to take a smoke, my life would be peachy."

Tom frowned. "Was the door alarmed?"

"It was supposed to have been," Gray said with a scowl. "That door is entry by key card only. The alarm should have alerted everyone when it remained unsecured. Someone deactivated it, and I'm going to find out who."

"I don't think it was your guy, though," the CSU tech offered. "He just walked in and didn't seem to touch anything but that guitar case."

"Unless he planned it," Gray mused. "He could have come earlier and set everything up."

It was possible, although unlikely unless they had a mole in the field office who had alerted him that the women were visiting this optometrist. The security footage would reveal if Belmont had been there earlier. Tom gave both men his business card. "Let me know if you think of anything else."

This time Croft opened the door for him, waiting until they were alone in the Bureau SUV before sighing. "Definitely Belmont. How did he know where they'd be this morning?"

"I don't know," Tom said grimly, starting the engine. "Either he followed them—which means he has a view of the Sokolovs' house—or we have a leak."

Croft shook her head. "Rodriguez is a good agent. He's careful to a fault, but we'll check his vetting process. I'm more inclined to believe Belmont has eyes on the Sokolovs' house."

"Me too." He pulled the SUV out of the parking lot, looking for the stolen truck even though he knew it was long gone. "That was the truck he stole a month ago."

"The one he killed that farmer over." Croft's expression said that she, too, knew exactly what he'd done for the farmer's family. "Whose family someone anonymously donated money to."

"I don't know anything about that," Tom lied.

She shook her head. "I'm afraid for you, Hunter. This job will chew you up and spit you out, especially if you wear your heart on your sleeve like you do."

"Have no idea what you're talking about. Can you call in the truck's license plate?"

Her eye roll said that she was unimpressed with his very clumsy subject change. "Sure. Send me that photo you took with your phone."

Tom unlocked his phone and handed it to Croft. "Check my photos."

She lifted one eyebrow. "You're just handing me your phone," she said, her disbelief clear. "I thought you hacker types were a lot more paranoid."

"I'm driving. But that's my work phone," he told her. "Everything on there is stuff you already know."

She flashed him a delighted grin. "I knew you'd have multiple phones. How many?"

He debated answering, then shrugged. "I carry at least three at all times. My work phone, my personal phone, and a burner."

"Huh. So if I need a burner . . . You got extras?"

Tom chuckled. "Of course. You can choose any color as long as it's black."

"Then I guess I'll take a black one. Is it okay if I text myself this photo?"

"Sure. Text away. Like I said, nothing on that phone that you don't already know."

"Kind of takes the fun out of it," Croft grumbled, but she was smiling as she called dispatch to get the plate traced. A minute later her smile fell. "What? Where?" She scribbled something on the notepad she carried. "Can you have someone do a drive-by and see if it's where it's supposed to be? I'd like a photo of the vehicle. Thanks." Ending the call, she sighed. "This plate doesn't come up as lost or stolen. It belongs to a guy in San Dimas with a food truck business." She typed something into her cell phone. "According to the guy's Facebook, he was open today and had long lines. Ran out of Cronuts before lunch."

Tom frowned, taking his eyes off the road for a moment to glance over at her. "So . . . what does that mean? I mean, either the food truck guy hasn't reported his plates stolen yet or they were switched, right? Or—"

Abruptly he pulled the SUV to the curb and took his phone back, enlarging the photo with a frown.

"Or what?" Croft asked, seeming unperturbed by his abrupt stop.

He stared hard at the license plate in the photo, wishing it were an actual picture of the plate instead of a picture of another picture. "Or it could be a duplicate."

Croft's brows flew up. "A duplicate? How?"

"3D printer."

Croft frowned. "Shit. I hate those things."

"They certainly have their place for legit projects, but they do muck things up." Guns were a particular concern, but license plates were also becoming a problem.

"Can a 3D printer really make a plate that looks real? Because that one looks real."

"Google it. Include 'toy' and 'custom' in your search field. You should find a tutorial or two with no—"

"Shit," she interrupted, having immediately done the search.

"No trouble," he finished. Tom put his phone in his breast pocket as his personal phone buzzed in the pocket of his trousers, announcing an incoming text. "Give me a second."

Croft watched him retrieve his personal phone. "Not the burner because it's blue. Personal, I'm guessing."

"Yeah. I'd normally let it go, but . . ." He didn't want to admit it, but he was still unsteady at the thought of Liza standing in front of that glass door. He knew she was all right, but still.

The text was, indeed, from Liza. But not to tell him that she'd arrived safely at the Sokolovs', as he'd asked her to do. No, this message was curt and to the point.

Abigail saw DJ's *second* tattoo. Rodriguez says it's a gang design. Thought u should know.

Oh wow. First Cameron Cook, and now this. Two leads in the same day after weeks of nothing. He showed the text to Croft. "Next stop, the Sokolovs'?"

She nodded, her eyes sparkling with excitement. "Absolutely."

FIVE

A nything?" Hayley whispered when Graham sidled up behind where she sat on the makeshift bench.

Pastor had designated the largest of the caves to be the church. Because of course he would. Most of the parishioners would sit on the stone floor during services, but she, as a pregnant woman, was allowed to sit on a half-rotten plank balanced on two large rocks.

If the last site was primitive, this place was prehistoric. *Please, don't make me have my baby here. Please.*

Graham palmed her shoulders, giving her a massage that nearly had her crying where she sat. Everything hurt. "Nothing that'll help us get out," he murmured. "I still can't find the computer or the dish."

Hayley had used her pregnancy as an excuse to visit the clinic as often as she could, and each time she attempted a peek into the office. There was no longer a door keeping everyone out of the office. Only a curtain. The outer entrance to the clinic was secured by a sliding wooden door, bolted into the rock itself.

They could only hope that the computer had been brought with them to the caves, because it wasn't on the healer's desk. Hayley had finally managed a glimpse of the clean desk when Sister Coleen had emerged from her office a few days ago. The older woman had looked pale and was coughing, like she needed a healer herself.

The caves were damp and cold. Only the areas near the entrance had ventilation, so fires were only allowed there. Most Edenites had no heat and had quietly grumbled—when no one in authority was there to hear them—and wrapped themselves up in handwoven blankets to stay warm.

Hayley had grown up in San Francisco, so the damp cold wasn't anything new. Still, this was a miserable way to live. Pastor had promised it wouldn't be much longer, that they were waiting for the roads to clear of snow so that they could move to an actual settlement site.

Snow. In freaking *May.* It was crazy, but it was their reality. She'd had a vague notion of areas in California where the snow lingered this late in the year, but that was up in Lassen National Park. Her class had been forced to cancel an end-of-year field trip to Lassen's volcanic fields because the roads hadn't been cleared in June.

She assumed they were somewhere near that now because of the snow and the caves, but she had no way to be certain. Especially since Graham had been unable to find the computer. He'd even risked being sentenced to the box by leaving the caves to search the surrounding area.

Fortunately, he hadn't been caught. Graham was good at not getting caught. Except for the shoplifting arrest, of course, but he'd informed her that he hadn't been caught at least a hundred other times. He'd also met some colorful characters in juvie and learned "ever so much."

Hayley would have to do something about that when they got out. Graham would *not* become a criminal. Or at least a worse criminal, she thought with a wince. But first, they had to actually get out of Eden.

Unfortunately, even if Graham found the computer, it was useless without an Internet connection. Graham figured there had to be a satellite dish of some kind, but he hadn't been able to find that, either. They couldn't send out another message for help or use Google Maps to figure out where the hell they were.

Cameron had not come to help her. She didn't even know if he'd received the e-mail she'd sent. Part of her mind taunted that he'd found someone new, that he didn't love her anymore. But Cameron *did* love her. Of this she was certain, just as she knew that he wanted their baby.

We're running out of time. Little Jellybean kicked, both a welcome sensation and one that filled Hayley with dread. This baby was coming soon.

She'd feared giving birth at the last Eden settlement, but at least the clinic there had been warm and somewhat clean. The thought of going into labor here was terrifying.

The fact that Brother Joshua had promised her baby to that awful Rebecca . . . The knowledge nearly brought her to her knees, every single time.

Graham stalled her anxiety attack by tightening his grip on her shoulders, leaning close to mutter in her ear. "Stick with me here, Hayley. I did find something else."

The room was beginning to fill with worshippers, so their little bubble of privacy was coming to an end.

"So tell me," Hayley said, speaking through her teeth while keeping her lips still.

"Drugs," Graham whispered. "A lot. Some pot and what looked like coke. And shrooms."

Hayley opened her mouth in surprise, forgetting the danger for a moment. She snapped her mouth closed when Sister Tamar slid onto the pew beside her.

"People are watching you," Tamar said, also speaking through her teeth. Her lips curved up in a placid smile and she folded her hands on her lap. She was the picture of serenity, resembling a painting of the Madonna that Hayley had seen in one of her textbooks.

Hayley had been trying to corner Sister Tamar for weeks. She needed to know why this woman had helped her when Rebecca had nearly caught her breaking into the clinic the night they'd moved. But Sister Tamar always managed to be somewhere that Hayley was not. Hayley hadn't taken it personally at first, but it had become apparent that Tamar was avoiding her.

And now, here she was. Smiling like absolutely nothing was wrong.

Graham leaned forward, digging his thumbs into the stiff muscles inside Hayley's shoulder blades. Again she bit back a moan as Graham whispered, "Meaning?"

"Meaning you need to stop wandering around the caves," Tamar replied sweetly, her smile never faltering. "They've been watching you both."

"Why do you care?" Graham asked in a near-silent growl.

"Because you're trying to get out," Tamar said, still speaking through her teeth. Her gaze was fixed on the pulpit, where Pastor was arranging a stack of hymnals. "I want to go with you."

Hayley stiffened. Should she deny it? Refuse to allow Tamar entry into their club of two?

"It's all right," Tamar said, speaking normally, then turned to smile at Hayley. "I'd be happy to attend you at the birth. I've already cleared it with Sister Coleen. I'm also happy to answer any questions you might have about the birthing process."

Fighting a blink at the rapid topic change, Hayley glanced over her shoulder at Graham, who'd pursed his lips like he'd just eaten a lemon, still trying to process having been spotted as he'd searched for the computer. Her brother prided himself on being nearly invisible when he wished to be.

"Are you a midwife or something?" she asked the other woman.

Tamar's shuttered expression cleared for a moment, exposing a sadness and rage that made Hayley suck in a breath. And then it was gone, hidden behind her serene smile. "Or something," Tamar replied sweetly. "I have . . . experience."

Hayley frowned. Then straightened as Tamar's words made sense and something else clicked into place. Tamar had vivid blue eyes, just like Rebecca's youngest child.

Oh my God. The child that Rebecca had stolen from another woman because she'd been barren, unable to conceive her own children. Rebecca's other two children had come from mothers who'd died in childbirth, but the youngest had been taken. *Rebecca stole Tamar's baby.*

"Okay," Hayley breathed, her hands cradling her belly of their own volition. "I understand. Thank you. I welcome your help. *All* your help."

Tamar patted Hayley's hand lightly. "It's my Christian duty to provide it. I need to go now. My husband and his family await me." She rose and glided across the stone floor with such grace she might have been an angel, joining the family belonging to Brother Caleb. He was an older man and not cruel like Joshua was, at least not that Hayley had been able to see.

Pastor rapped on the pulpit with his fist, silencing the quiet murmurs of the assembled group. "Please stand for prayer."

Hayley struggled to stand, shooting Graham an appreciative glance when he helped her up. Bowing her head, she stared up through her lashes at Graham, who now stood beside her, one hand on her elbow to steady her. *Be careful,* she mouthed, and her little brother nodded grimly.

Someone was watching them. Someone was watching Graham.

This place kept getting worse. It wasn't simply a prison, although that would have been bad enough. Now someone here was dealing drugs?

Cameron, please find us. Please.

GRANITE BAY, CALIFORNIA
WEDNESDAY, MAY 24, 12:35 P.M.

"These are so good," Abigail moaned around a mouthful of the Caramel-Pecan Dream Bars that Liza had made that morning. She'd had three already, without dropping a single crumb—much to the dismay of her puppy, who lay beneath her chair, ever hopeful.

Liza nodded, her mouth too full to speak her thanks aloud.

"They are," Irina agreed. "I want this recipe, Liza."

"Anytime. It was my mother's."

Mercy gently tapped Abigail's hand when she went for a fourth helping. "First, you're going to get sick. Second, save some for your papa, Rafe, and Mr. Karl."

Abigail's sigh was long-suffering. "And Zoya, too. She likes a sweet treat when she comes home from school. When will that be, Miss Irina?"

Irina's mouth tightened. "In three hours, but I don't think Zoya will be having any treats."

Recognizing the look on Irina's face as one her own mother had worn too often, Liza's brows lifted. "What did she do?"

Irina looked away, then huffed. "She decided it would be prudent to take her car and drive to San Francisco this morning."

Mercy's eyes widened. "Why? Is she all right?"

"She is fine," Irina said with a wave of her hand. "I got a call from the school saying that she hadn't been present in homeroom this morning. I was busy"—her gaze flitted to Abigail—"so I let the call go to voice mail. I listened to it after you all left for the eye doctor's."

"That doesn't sound like Zoya," Mercy murmured. "She's so responsible. What happened?"

Irina rolled her eyes. "By the time I called the school, she'd appeared, claiming 'car trouble' made her late. Then I remembered that she'd already left when I came downstairs this morning. She does that sometimes when she has a club meeting or needs to get study help from a teacher, so I didn't worry at the time. But it was not car trouble that made her late."

"How did you know she went to San Francisco?" Liza asked, suspecting the answer.

Irina's chin lifted. "I can track her car," she said without apology.

Liza held out both hands in a stop gesture. "You get no judgment from me. My mom would have done the same if we'd had a car to track."

"Why did she go to San Francisco?" Mercy asked, then turned to Agent Rodriguez, who suddenly was very interested in the chocolate drizzled atop Liza's bars. "Agent Rodriguez?"

Irina had also turned to stare at the agent. "What do you know?" she demanded.

He shook his head, then shoved a bar in his mouth. He shrugged, pointing to his lips as if to say he couldn't talk with his mouth full.

"Oh, for heaven's sake," Irina muttered. She took out her cell phone and tapped a number. "Geri? Hi, this is Irina. Is Jeffrey home?" She listened to whatever Jeff Bunker's mother was saying, her brows rising again. "I thought he might be involved. May I speak with him? Thank you." She looked at Mercy and Liza. "He wasn't home when she woke up this morning, but was recently returned *by the FBI* with a guest in tow. One Cameron Cook from San Francisco."

Agent Rodriguez rose from the table. "I'll wait outside."

Irina pointed at him, then the chair. "I'd appreciate it if you would stay." She nodded at him when he complied, then cocked her head, listening to her call. "Yes, Jeffrey. This is Mrs. Sokolov. Why did Zoya take you to San Francisco this morning?"

Right to the point. That was just one of the things that Liza loved about Irina Sokolov. Liza pursed her lips to keep from smiling. It wasn't funny, but . . . it kind of was.

Abigail tugged on Liza's sleeve. "What's happening?"

"I don't know," Liza whispered, "but I think Zoya is about to get grounded."

Abigail's eyes widened, then narrowed contemplatively. "Then she won't want her brownie."

Liza snorted, covering her mouth with her hand, then let the chuckle escape when Irina pushed the plate in front of Abigail.

Abigail's grin was triumphant. "Yes!"

"No," a voice said from the kitchen doorway.

Abigail slumped as her father strode across the room. Pushing the plate away, he sank to his knees and pulled her into a bear hug. Abigail patted Amos's hair. "I'm okay, Papa. See?" She opened her arms wide. "Not a scratch."

Amos pretended to examine her arms, tilting her face one way, then the other. "Not a scratch," he agreed, but his voice trembled. He looked to Mercy. "And you?"

Mercy held her arms wide, just as Abigail had. "Not a scratch." Then she stood up when Rafe rushed into the kitchen, letting herself be swept up into his arms.

Swallowing hard, Liza looked away. She was so happy for Mercy— her friend absolutely deserved all the good things life could bring. But at the same time, it was hard to watch when she knew she'd never have that.

"Thank you, Jeffrey," Irina said into the phone. "You will put your mother back on the phone now." She waited, rolling her eyes when Liza met her gaze. "Geri, I think we're going to have to sit our children down for a little talk. Can you come for dinner and bring Jeffrey?" She smiled. "Of course Cameron is welcome, too. Tell his father he can pick him up here." She ended the call and grimaced. "Zoya has some explaining to do."

Rafe derailed Liza's thoughts by sitting next to her, engulfing her in a huge hug before she could say a word.

"Thank you," he whispered fiercely. "Thank you so much."

"I didn't do anything," Liza said, patting his back.

"Yeah, she did," Agent Rodriguez butted in. "And we'll hear all the details in three, two, one—"

"Hello?" Tom called from the front door. "Anybody here?"

Liza stiffened. He was here already. She hadn't expected him so soon. They must have used the flashing lights to beat traffic.

"In the kitchen, Tom," Irina called back. She stood up and put the kettle on. "Who wants tea?"

Liza raised her hand immediately. "Special tea?"

Irina laughed. "You got someone to drive you home?" Because Irina's "special tea" was infused with cannabis.

"I'll take her," Tom said. "She's on my way," he added jokingly.

His entry was as different from Rafe's as day from night. There were no hugs. No comfort. He hadn't even asked Liza if she was all right. He'd just breezed into the kitchen with his partner, Agent Croft, a woman who was somewhere in her late thirties or early forties. She was supposedly good at her job, which meant she'd watch Tom's back.

She was also single. Liza had asked.

Liza hoped that Tom's back was all the woman was watching, but it didn't really matter, did it? *He's not yours. And I'm not going to let him take me home.* She didn't want to be trapped in a car with him right now, not after watching Rafe and Mercy together. It hurt enough knowing she'd never have that. Not with Tom, anyway. "Just Earl Grey, then," she amended.

Irina glanced from her to Tom, then shrugged. "As you wish. Liza, if you want to stay here tonight, you're welcome."

"Thanks, but no," Liza told her. "It's my turn to walk Pebbles."

The young Great Dane was the only decision Liza had known Tom to make on impulse. The pup had needed a home, having grown too big for the family who'd originally adopted her.

Tom had taken one look at the Dane's big brown eyes and was a goner, but he'd worried that he might not be home enough to care for a dog. Liza had pledged her help and now their schedules were synchronized around Pebbles's meals and walks. The dog was a big slobbery pain in the butt with whom Liza had fallen into insta-love.

Also, Pebbles was the perfect excuse to flee.

Tom frowned at her, then turned to Irina. "Have you met Agent Croft?"

Irina held out her hand to the other woman. "Welcome, Agent Croft."

"Call me Ricki," Croft said with an easy smile. She looked at Liza, her smile not faltering. "Miss Barkley, it's always a pleasure to see you. I understand you had a busy morning."

Liza could feel all eyes on her now and, to her dismay, felt her own eyes begin to burn. *I need to get out of here.* "Just a bit." She stood up, leaning over to kiss Abigail's forehead. "I'll see you tomorrow, okay, Shrimpkin?"

Abigail seemed disappointed. "You're leaving?"

"Gotta go. Pebbles needs to be walked." *And I'm about to cry. Not here.*

"But why can't you bring her here?" Abigail asked, a whine edging into her tone.

"Because she'll tear up Irina's pretty house, not to mention stomping on poor Sally." Sally was Abigail's Maltese puppy, named for astronaut Sally Ride, over whom the little girl obsessed. Denied in Eden, the idea of space travel had quickly caught—and held—Abigail's attention.

"Oh yeah," Abigail grumbled. "I remember now."

Amos chuckled. "I think someone has earned a nap."

"Don't wanna nap." Abigail's whine was at full power.

"Sugar crash," Liza said. "These bars pack a powerful punch. I'm feeling tired myself." Which was no lie. Her sleepless nights had abruptly caught up to her. "I'll see you tomorrow, Abs. And then we can finish the book we started reading last week."

"Thank you," Amos murmured when Liza began gathering her things. "You spend so much time with her."

"She's a good kid," Liza said, ruffling Abigail's bangs. "She did all the right things today. I'm proud of her."

Abigail grinned. "'Cause I'm awesome."

Amos winced. "And humble. Come on, Abi-girl. You have a nap with your name on it."

"That doesn't make sense, Papa," Abigail said as Amos started to lead her from the room.

"Um, can we talk to Abigail, Amos?" Tom asked, gesturing to his partner. "Before she goes down for a nap?"

Amos narrowed his eyes. "Why?"

Right. The tattoo. How quickly Liza had forgotten. She leaned in to whisper in Amos's ear. "Abigail may have seen DJ Belmont's tattoo. The one he didn't get in Eden," she added when the older man frowned, clearly confused.

"All right. But make it quick, okay? She's fading fast," Amos told Tom.

Amos, Tom, and Agent Croft were gone for only a few minutes, during which Rafe got a rundown from Mercy and Irina set the table for afternoon tea.

When they returned, Croft and Amos sat down with Abigail and a sketchpad, and Tom approached Liza the way a zoo handler might approach a wounded animal.

It was fair, Liza decided. Being in the same room with Tom Hunter left her feeling wounded.

"Can we talk for a moment?" Tom asked quietly.

"I really need to go," she said, trying not to sound as whiny as Abigail had. "Pebbles has probably eaten your sofa again."

"Liza," Tom said urgently. "Please."

There was something in his tone that gave her pause. "Fine. But just for a minute."

I need to get out of here. Now.

Tom pointed to the laundry room, then followed her in and closed the door. It wasn't a small room, but Tom filled it like no other man could. It wasn't just that he was big, because he was. Six-six and solid muscle. Or that he was handsome, because he was that, too. He had a presence that filled her mind, and she couldn't look anywhere else. He was her true north and she'd been in love with him since she was seventeen years old.

Fritz had caught her staring at Tom's NBA team photo once, before they'd first started dating. Luckily, he'd been more interested in the fact that she knew *the* Tom Hunter than that she'd been mooning over another man.

Guilt filled her at the thought of Fritz. He deserved more than she'd been able to give him. He deserved to at least be claimed verbally as the man she'd married. So far, she hadn't told anyone about him. Not stateside anyway. His family knew, as did their friends in the army. And they'd grieved with her, not knowing that most of her grief was guilt for not loving him enough.

Closing her eyes, she leaned against the wall as far from Tom as she could get. "What's up?"

There was silence. Long, long silence.

Finally, she opened her eyes to find Tom staring at her as if she were a stranger. "What is up?" she asked again, enunciating every word.

He swallowed audibly. "What the fuck, Liza? What were you thinking?"

GRANITE BAY, CALIFORNIA
WEDNESDAY, MAY 24, 12:55 P.M.

Tom closed his eyes. Of all the things he'd wanted to say, that hadn't been on the list. "Shit," he muttered. "I'm sorry."

"It's fine," Liza said. "Now, if you're finished, I need to go home and walk your dog."

He opened his eyes to see her holding herself rigidly. She was a tall woman, five-ten without her boots. With her boots, she could meet his eyes with a chin lift that, at the moment, seemed more vulnerable than defiant.

Fuck. Now he'd hurt her feelings. "That's not what I meant to say," he whispered, taking a step closer. She backed up a step—or would have if she hadn't already been up against the wall.

Something stirred within him, a desire he'd tamped down years ago, right after they'd met, in fact. It still reared its head from time to time, but he was usually able to smack it back down.

She'd been too young, only seventeen to his twenty. Then she'd been deployed. Then . . . Tory had come along and he'd thought he'd found his forever. But . . .

She's not too young anymore. She's not deployed anymore. She's here. And Tory is not.

That last one had him taking a step back. His Victoria was dead. It had only been a year.

What am I thinking? Nothing smart, that was for damn sure. "Are you all right?"

Her smile was brittle. "Of course. Now, if you'll excuse me."

He frowned, having no idea what to say next. Then he remembered Molina's words from that morning. "You know I'm proud of you, don't you?" And if the words sounded a little desperate coming from his mouth, that was understandable, because he *was* desperate.

She blinked, her lips parting in surprise. Then her eyes narrowed. "Why?"

He stared at her, at a loss for words. "What do you mean, why?" he finally asked.

"Because when you start with 'What the fuck were you thinking?' and progress to you being proud of me, you have to admit it sounds a little suspicious."

"Fair enough," he acknowledged. The slight relaxation of her rigid shoulders made him relax a little as well. He'd been genuinely afraid there for a moment. "I was worried."

The rigidity returned, and with it the brittle smile. "Mercy and Abigail are fine."

He blew out a frustrated breath. It was like she was turning his words upside down and inside out. He hadn't meant just Mercy and Abigail, and she knew it. "What's *wrong* with you?"

Which was the exact *wrong* thing to say.

Because she swallowed hard and tears welled in her usually warm brown eyes. "Clearly too many things to count," she whispered. "Tell Irina I'll be back tomorrow."

And with that, she fled from the laundry room into the Sokolovs' garage. *Follow her, you idiot.* But his feet wouldn't move, his body frozen in place at the sight of her tears. What had he done? Why was she crying?

A moment later, the rumble of the garage door going up finally got his feet moving. He made it into the garage in time to see her back as she retreated to her car, parked at the curb. She paused a split second to wave at Irina's husband Karl, who was pulling into the driveway.

Tom stood there, completely at sea. Liza wasn't a crier. Well, sure, she cried at sad movies, but so did he. They often spent the evenings on his sofa watching movies, sometimes sharing a box of tissues between them before she retreated to her own side of the duplex for the night.

But *he* had never made her cry. He was frowning when Karl parked his Tesla and hit the button to bring the garage door down. Karl was also frowning as he got out of his car.

"What the hell did you do to her?" Karl demanded.

Tom's mouth fell open. "What?"

"She's crying," Karl said, as if Tom's guilt was obvious. "What did you say?"

"Nothing!" Tom protested. Which wasn't exactly true. "Well, I did tell her I was proud of her. She probably saved Mercy and Abigail's lives today."

Karl Sokolov looked unconvinced. "What *else* did you say?"

"Why do you think it was me who said something to her?"

Karl tilted his head, studying him. "For real?"

Tom threw up his hands. "Yes. For real. I just *got* here. I didn't *do* anything."

Which wasn't true, either. *What's* wrong *with you? You fucked up big-time.*

"Kid, I've been married for nearly forty years, and if there's one thing I've learned, it's that you've *always* done something."

Tom huffed. "Maybe she's . . . y'know . . . hormonal."

Karl winced. "Oh my God. Are you stupid? Do not ever say that to her."

"I'm not! I'm saying it to you."

Karl shook his head, chuckling. "How old are you, again?"

"Twenty-seven," Tom answered stiffly.

Karl patted Tom's arm as he headed for the laundry room. "You've still got time, then."

Tom turned to stare at the man. "Time for what?"

"Time to get it right."

Tom gritted his teeth. "Time to get *what* right? No offense, sir, but the sooner you stop talking in riddles, the sooner I might understand what you're saying."

Karl shot him a pitying look. "Never mind, Tom." He opened the door to the kitchen and called, "Where is my lovely bride?"

Tom pinched the bridge of his nose, feeling a headache coming on. Slowly he followed Karl into the kitchen, feeling addled and irritated about it.

Irina looked behind him. "Where is Liza?"

"She left," Tom said brusquely.

"I passed her in the driveway," Karl said, then leaned in to whisper something in Irina's ear.

Irina's back straightened as she turned to Tom, glaring daggers. "You let her *leave*? *Alone?*"

"Shit," Tom whispered, his blood running cold. She'd witnessed the sniper on that rooftop. If he saw her . . . "She needs protection."

"Which I was providing," Rodriguez said very slowly. "Until you let her leave. Alone."

Tom's temper boiled. "I didn't *let* her do anything. She's a grown woman, for God's sake."

Who he'd made cry. And he still didn't know why.

He clenched his eyes shut, giving in to the need to rub his temples. "Dammit," he whispered.

"I can't go after her," Rodriguez said. "I'm on Callahan detail until she's safe at home."

"Rafe can take me home," Mercy offered. "He can take Amos and Abigail, too."

Because they all lived in apartments within the same house until Amos and Rafe finished renovating the new house.

Rodriguez shook his head. "I'd need to get that cleared, Miss Callahan."

Irina made a noise. "All this talk, all while Liza is unprotected." She took out her cell phone and pressed a button. "Damien, this is your mother." Her lips pursed. "Do not sass me, young man. I am not in the mood."

Damien Sokolov was one of Irina's sons, a uniformed cop with the Russian division in West Sacramento. Tom had thought at first the division dealt with Russian organized crime, but instead it served the large Russian-speaking population of West Sac.

"I need you to go to Liza's house," Irina was saying to her son. "To make sure she gets home safely." Irina smiled. "You're a good boy, Damien. I will send the address."

Tom's head fell back to hit the laundry room door. "Tell him not to worry about it. I'll go."

Irina's smile was smug as she slipped her phone into her pocket without saying goodbye. "Good."

Tom scowled. "Did you even call him?"

Irina just chuckled. "Go and make sure she is okay, Tom. You know you want to."

Hell of it was . . . he did.

Which was not a big deal. At all. *It's what friends do for each other.* Like she'd taken care of him when he had the flu in January when they'd first arrived in California and knew no one but each other. Or like he held her every time he heard her cry out in the night through the duplex wall they shared, her nightmares making her shudder and tremble in his arms.

Or like she took care of "his dog." Except that before today, Pebbles had been "our dog."

Today she'd said "his dog." He'd just realized that, and his heart hurt. Something had happened. Something new. *Something that I did.* He needed to figure out what that was.

He looked to Croft, noting that Abigail no longer sat at the table. Amos was gone as well. "Did you get what you needed from Abigail?" he asked.

She nodded. "I'm about ninety-five percent sure it's a Chicos tat. I don't think there're many tattoo artists in the area who'd ink that design. They don't want negative gang attention. Mr. Terrill said he hadn't seen the tattoo, because he hadn't seen DJ without his shirt in a very long time. Abigail must have caught DJ at the right moment. Terrill said he knew that DJ has an Eden tattoo because he was there the night they tattooed him."

"On DJ's thirteenth birthday," Tom said, recalling Mercy's brother Gideon talking about the night he got his Eden tattoo.

"If not many artists would do the tattoo," Mercy said, "do you know who would?"

"I have a few ideas," was all Croft would say as she put her sketchbook into her briefcase and locked it. "Agent Hunter, let's make sure Miss Barkley made it home all right, and then you can drop me off at the field office so I can get my car."

Mercy frowned and Tom wanted to sigh. This was an example of information civilians didn't need to have, so Croft was right not to share. He also knew Mercy would be looking before he and Croft had left the Sokolovs' driveway.

It wasn't Mercy that was bothering him, though. It was Rafe. He looked like he wanted to say something but was holding his tongue. Maybe because Croft was there. Or Rodriguez.

Or even me. Tom would ask him later. Once he knew that Liza was all right, he'd call Rafe. And then he'd get to work doing what he did best—hacking. He still had Cameron Cook's e-mail to trace.

Karl followed them to the door, tugging on Tom's sleeve to hold him back when Croft jogged to the Bureau's SUV.

"Talk to her, Tom," Karl said quietly.

"I talk to Agent Croft all the time," Tom said lightly, but he knew what Karl meant.

Karl looked disappointed with him. "Liza's become important to us. Her happiness is important. It should be to you, too."

Tom sighed. "Of course it is. Something's been bothering her for a while now, but I've let her be. I figured she'd tell me when she was ready, but I'll push harder."

Karl shook his head. "See that you do."

SIX

DJ pulled the truck around the back of his house, into the detached garage. He wanted a hot shower, a decent meal, and a nap, in that order.

Forcing himself to climb from the cab, he retrieved the guitar case that held his rifle from the floorboard, then removed the electrician signs from the doors and the license plate from the holder and stuck them in his backpack. Pulling the garage door down, he made sure it was locked.

His regular printer would be fine to make a new magnetic sign, but he'd use his 3D printer to produce a license plate that could fool cops with even the sharpest eyes. His 3D printer had been dirt cheap, and even if it hadn't been, he considered it a necessary business expense. Staying one step in front of the cops really was too easy with the right technology.

Again, Kowalski had taught him well, guiding him to buy the best tech for the best price. Printing his boss's fake plates had been one of his first jobs when he'd joined up with Kowalski's crew. Now he could do it for himself practically in his sleep.

But first he had to actually get some sleep. He'd thought he was mostly recovered from getting shot, but taking the stairs up to that roof and down again had left him fatigued.

"Johnny!" a trembly voice called out.

DJ bit back a curse. Damn meddling woman. He wished he'd bought a house farther out in the country. That woman next door was the nosiest gossip.

He glanced at her over the fence between their properties. "Mrs. Ellis."

Minnie Ellis was about seventy-five years old and resembled a prune. She was a pain in his ass, but she made amazing pies and she liked to bake for him, so he made nice.

"It's been a while since we've seen you," she said, concerned. "I was worried."

He'd been away for more than a month, courtesy of Mercy Callahan's friends. "I had a family thing. I'm so sorry. I should have told you. But everything's fine now."

Like hell he would have told her anything.

"Your grass is getting high," she noted. "You want my grandson to mow it for you?"

"Maybe when I go out of town again." Mrs. Ellis thought he was a traveling electronics salesman and that the boxes she'd seen him bringing into his house were filled with inventory.

In reality, the boxes in his basement were filled with vacuum-packed weed, none from Eden. DJ had learned to diversify. He rented the house next door and a third house in the next neighborhood, both converted into grow houses. Tons of dirt covered the old 1970s lino-leum and he'd added another set of fuses on both houses to carry the current for the grow lamps inside.

He grew a lot more pot this way than Eden ever had, and the profits belonged solely to him. But he'd still earned only a pittance compared to what Pastor controlled in Eden's offshore bank accounts. And a good chunk of the revenue he earned from the grow houses was due back to the man who'd given him a start-up loan.

Kowalski had taught DJ more than Pastor ever had. DJ usually spent time in Eden during the week, venturing down the mountain to tend his plants the rest of the time. He'd learned to pad the estimates for how long his trips would take so that he could spend more time away from the compound than was required. He'd started out taking only the weekends, but was able to sell Pastor on the need for more time to sell Eden's illegal products—the drugs they'd grown since he'd arrived at the compound when he was four years old.

He'd argued that allowing him more time away enabled Pastor to continue sending just one person from the compound each week, which kept their secrets safer.

He also shopped for supplies and sold Eden's completely legit handmade goods, claiming that he had to travel far away to keep from raising any suspicion. In reality, he shopped and sold the legit stuff wherever the hell he wanted, used cash, and no one was the wiser. But his precautions—and the money he brought in—made Pastor happy and in return, Pastor would eventually make him very rich.

Until then, he cared for his plants, turned the harvest over to Kowalski, and deposited his cut of the proceeds into a bank account of his own.

"You look tired, dear," Mrs. Ellis said. "I've got chicken soup that will fix what ails you."

"Thank you, but I've got dinner plans." Pizza sounded amazing. "You have a good evening."

"Thank you, dear." The top of her head disappeared abruptly as she climbed down from whatever stool she'd gotten up on to see over the fence. She was only four foot nine. Still, he didn't want her angry with him. She was the de facto neighborhood watch queen, and had he known that, he would have bought a house literally anywhere else.

"Wait!" Her head reappeared. "There's been someone in your

house for the past few weeks. He said he was your friend and was watering your plants. He had a key and nothing seemed amiss when I checked, so I didn't make a fuss." Her lip curled in a pout. "I could have watered your plants. You didn't have to ask someone else."

DJ knew that Kowalski had been in and out of his place. Since Kowalski was his direct boss, it was his right. In a way it was Kowalski's house, since he'd footed the start-up costs.

"He's my cousin, ma'am. Family." He shrugged. "You know how it is." He waited for her to climb down from the step stool, then jolted when her words sank in. "Hold on a moment. What do you mean, when you 'checked'?"

"I looked in your windows, silly boy. How else was I to check? I don't have a key."

And she never would. DJ managed a smile. "Thank you, ma'am. It's a relief to know I have good neighbors."

"Who should have a key," the old woman pushed.

"I'll try to remember." *Over my dead body.* Because if she did have a key, she'd snoop, she'd report, and his dead body would be all that was left of him when Kowalski found out.

He rounded the house, unlocking the front door with one of only two keys to exist.

"She's a peach," Kowalski said sarcastically from his seat in front of the television. Middle-aged, white, and nondescript, he'd been the gang's local front man for quite some time. His appearance was wholly unremarkable, and he had a masterful ability to blend in to any crowd. "I don't know how you've managed not to kill her."

Schooling his expression against the surprise of finding Kowalski here—and why hadn't Mrs. Ellis warned him about *that?*—DJ closed the door and twisted the dead bolts. "It's a constant trial," he said dryly. "Where's your car?"

"Not your concern," Kowalski said mildly.

DJ wanted to swear. Kowalski was exactly like Pastor—both wore a mask to hide any annoyance they might feel. The trouble was that the annoyance could become explosive rage in the blink of an eye without warning.

Kowalski was more dangerous than Pastor, though. Pastor didn't have any other muscle now that Ephraim was dead. The old man had no one to take DJ out. Kowalski, however, carried a gun wherever he went. DJ thought the man even slept with it. And DJ knew full well that Kowalski would have no qualms about snuffing him out like a candle. There were plenty of other guys out there who'd jump at the opportunity to make the kind of cash Kowalski offered.

Like DJ's predecessor, who now lived at the bottom of a lake outside Oroville. Dumping him there had been DJ's first test of loyalty. The threat of joining the dead man was always present.

So DJ bit his tongue, stowing his irritation at seeing Kowalski sprawled on his sofa. "I wasn't expecting you," he said instead. "I don't have any food to offer you."

Kowalski tipped the foot he rested on the coffee table, motioning to a pizza box. "I saved you a slice."

Sitting in the chair adjacent to the sofa, DJ dumped his backpack and the guitar case on the floor and pulled the box to him. "Thanks, but I'll need more than a slice. I'm starving."

Kowalski tilted his head, making no secret of the fact that he was assessing DJ's physical condition. There was nothing sexual about his perusal. It was one hundred percent business with Kowalski. He was assessing the strength and fitness of one of his many minions.

DJ was getting tired of being a minion. "Well?" he asked around a mouthful of pizza. "What's the verdict?"

"You look like shit," Kowalski said baldly. "You should have called me when you got shot."

"I did," DJ said, sounding petulant. "I told you I'd be laid up for a while."

Kowalski's brows lowered in a warning frown. "I meant right *after* you'd gotten yourself shot. Not days later, once that 'healer' of yours had gotten you in her clutches."

"I wasn't thinking straight," DJ admitted.

Because revealing the existence of Sister Coleen had been a mistake. DJ hadn't given her name, but he'd called her their "healer" when he'd phoned Kowalski to tell him that he'd been shot. He hadn't wanted Kowalski to know he was hurt—weakest member of the pack gets eaten first—but he'd had no choice. When he'd regained consciousness, he'd been on a pallet in the back of the box truck, bumping over the mountain roads, surrounded by packing crates, alone and burning with fever from his wounds. He'd been with it enough to know this might be his only opportunity to talk to Kowalski without Pastor or one of the others overhearing.

But the fever had loosened his tongue, giving Kowalski glimpses into the community that the man hadn't had before. Because Eden itself was a liability and DJ wasn't about to give the Chicos any ammunition against him. He needed them to stay out of Eden, because that fifty million was his, goddammit. He wasn't going to share it.

At least his satellite phone couldn't be tracked, so Kowalski still didn't know where the community was hiding. That sat phone had saved him, though. If he hadn't informed Kowalski of his injury and probable recovery time, he would have been declared AWOL and shot on sight when he resurfaced.

Which could be why Kowalski sat in his living room right now, he realized, a shiver running down his back. Of all the people in his life, only Kowalski truly scared him.

"No, you weren't thinking straight," Kowalski agreed, his tone still mild. "I'll forgive it this time, but only because you regularly reported in."

I'll forgive it this time. The words stung even as they relieved DJ. He didn't want to be beholden to anyone for anything, but he was in with Kowalski up to his eyeballs.

Regular reporting was nonnegotiable, and for this reason, the sat phone was a godsend. Pastor only knew about the cell phones, which operated off Wi-Fi generated by Eden's satellite dish. The sat phone, which connected directly to an orbiting satellite, had become DJ's only link to the outside world, because Pastor couldn't be allowed online for any reason right now. There was too much media coverage of Mercy and Gideon. So far they weren't mentioning Eden, but Ephraim had murdered too many people for the Feds to completely hide his killing spree from the general public. Mercy and Gideon had been news for weeks.

DJ closed the now-empty pizza box and frowned. He must have been tired because, like Mrs. Ellis's words, Kowalski's had just sunk in.

"How did you know what Mrs. Ellis said to me? We were in the backyard."

Kowalski hit a few buttons on the TV remote, bringing up a camera feed. Of the rooms of this house, his backyard, and the basement—which was empty of the boxes he'd left there.

That the pot was gone—and with it, his cut—was infuriating, but not all that surprising. That Kowalski had cameras was a greater concern.

"How long have the cameras been here?" DJ asked.

"I had them installed before you bought the place." Kowalski cranked up the volume on one of the frames, picking up Mrs. Ellis's voice from the backyard. "I get audio, too. This mic is mounted on Mrs. Ellis's side of the fence. She worries me."

"If I kill her, the cops will come snooping," DJ said, anticipating Kowalski's next order.

"Find a way so that they don't snoop. She's seventy-five, for fuck's sake. Make it look like she died in her sleep."

"I can do that."

"Have you done it before?" Kowalski pressed.

"Yes. Once." To his own father, as a matter of fact.

No one in Eden had questioned his father's death, when they should have. Waylon Belmont had died in his own bed, two days after returning to Eden with a sobbing, repentant Rhoda, along with the remains of a young man whom he'd claimed was Gideon Reynolds.

Gideon had deserved to die. He'd murdered Edward McPhearson, who was not a good man. Actually a really bad man, but Gideon *had* killed him.

Waylon had also deserved to die, and DJ hadn't even known the full extent of his father's betrayal. Now that he did, he wished he could kill Waylon all over again.

Or, at least, that he'd made his father's death more painful.

"How did you do it before?" Kowalski asked, yanking DJ from the pain of the memory.

"Pillow. Looked like a heart attack." He smiled, picturing the look on Waylon's face as he'd struggled to breathe. *Mine was the last face he saw.* That Waylon knew who had killed him had been important to DJ then.

That Mrs. Ellis would know who killed her wasn't important at all. He hadn't killed anyone so up close and personal in a while, but he imagined it'd be like riding a bike.

Kowalski dug in his pocket, producing a syringe and a small vial, placing them on the coffee table. "If you're gonna do it that way, go with the injection. MEs can detect pillow smothering. This'll make it look like a heart attack because it will *be* a heart attack." He pressed the TV remote again and a different set of camera feeds appeared.

Mrs. Ellis was sitting in an easy chair, speaking on a phone with an honest-to-God cord. "He's weird," she was saying. "So antisocial. Never smiles, never talks to me unless I talk first." She paused, listening, winding the curly cord around one finger. "Well, he's handsome enough, I guess. Gives me the willies, though." She shuddered. "He's only here part of the time. I wonder what he gets up to when he's not here." Another pause. "Of course I asked! He says he's a traveling salesman. I bet a lot of serial killers say that." Her face hardened with resolve. "There is something odd about that man and I'm going to find out what."

Fucking hell. Several things occurred to DJ, in no particular order:

Kowalski had cameras inside the woman's house. *He'll know when I've killed her.*

This is a damn test.

Mrs. Ellis is talking about me. And it was dark outside her window, but the sun hadn't set yet. It was barely one in the afternoon.

"Wait." DJ held up a hand. "Is this prerecorded video?"

Kowalski hit the pause button and the screen froze. "It is. This conversation happened last night. She was peeking in your windows this morning."

"What about whoever she was talking to? That phone she's using is ancient. It won't have caller ID."

"She has a cordless phone in the kitchen. It will."

"What about the cameras? Once she's dead, her family will be all over the house. They'll see the cameras."

"They're the size of a pencil eraser. You're good with your hands. Cover them up."

"Fine." DJ waved at the syringe and vial. "You knew you were going to tell me to kill her."

"Yep. You really should have had the cameras installed the first time she pushed you for information. Little old ladies often get ignored, but they are fonts of knowledge. All it takes is her telling the wrong person that you're weird and antisocial and people will start to wonder."

The man spoke truth. "I'll do it today, but I'm going to eat first. She won't go to sleep for a while yet." He pulled his own cell phone out. "Want some more pizza?"

Kowalski stood, stretching until bones creaked and joints popped. "No, I have to get going. My son has a recital after school. He's amazing, but I have to sit through the rest of those little brats and it makes me cranky. So I'll be looking for good news tomorrow."

He walked to the door to the basement, turning back to look at DJ. "By the way, where are the fifteen kilos of coke I gave you to distribute? I reviewed the accounts this week and realized that money never came in."

Shit. He should have known this was coming. "This is my first time out of the compound since I got shot."

"So you have it with you?"

DJ knew exactly where it was. It was stored in a box labeled *Smithy Tools* in the cave farthest from the main entrance. "No. It would have raised questions if I'd hauled it out." The truth was that he hadn't been able to lift the boxes that had been stacked atop it. His arm was still useless. He'd barely managed to get his rifle off that rooftop this morning.

Kowalski's smile thinned. "Figure out how to 'haul it out.' That's my money. I've been very patient during your recovery. In the meantime, I want a full report on the old lady. I also want to see a hearse outside her house, taking her body straight to a funeral home."

Translation: *Make it look like a natural death or else.*

DJ nodded tightly. "What about my pot? I couldn't help but notice my basement is empty."

"I 'hauled it out' the day you called me to tell me you were out of commission for a few weeks. I've been tending the plants in your grow houses, too. They're ready for harvest."

Translation: *Get busy or else.*

He disappeared into the stairwell to the basement and a moment later, DJ heard the muffled sound of a door closing. His house had a walkout basement, and that was the way Kowalski generally came and went. It let out on the side of the house opposite Mrs. Ellis, so she wouldn't see him.

DJ rubbed his temples. Food, then sleep. He also needed to make a few new license plates and signs for the truck. He figured he'd been caught on surveillance at the office building that morning. His own face wasn't as important as the identifiers on the vehicle he was using.

Mercy and Gideon had likely described him to law enforcement, and if they hadn't, Amos Terrill had. But nobody knew where Eden was, so he'd been safe there. Would be again once Mercy and Gideon were dead.

His vehicle was another story, though. That was more easily tracked. If they were able to identify his vehicle through street and toll cameras, he wouldn't be safe anywhere.

Still, Kowalski was the more immediate threat. He'd be pissed off if he found out that DJ's face and fingerprints were known to the FBI. He'd decide that DJ's usefulness was over and . . . well, that would be bad. So he wouldn't get caught. It was that simple.

He called in an order for pizza delivery, then went back to his home office and powered up the 3D printer. Using an "unauthorized" searchable database of vehicle registrations, he found the list of license plate numbers that belonged to trucks most closely matching his. None of the vehicles with these plates had been reported stolen, so no cops would be looking for them. He typed the next number on the list into the template he'd developed and set it to print.

The resulting plate would be indistinguishable from an actual California DMV-issued plate.

Technology was so cool.

ROCKLIN, CALIFORNIA
WEDNESDAY, MAY 24, 1:05 P.M.

"Well, hell," Croft muttered as Tom drove them from the Sokolovs' house to his duplex in Rocklin. It was a tidy two-story, split down the middle into two separate units. They shared the garage and the backyard. He'd bought it after his first visit with the real estate agent partly because it would allow him to live close to the field office. But mostly because Liza had loved the backyard and a duplex allowed him to keep her close without stomping on her privacy.

She could come and go as she pleased. An image of Mike the Groper flitted across his mind and he wanted to snarl. But he didn't, because she could also date as she pleased.

I don't own her, he told himself firmly.

But you could. The sly whisper was barely a blip of a thought but was enough to steal his breath. *No. God, no.* He'd never *own* her. He'd never own *anyone.* His own father had tried to own his mother, using violence to get his own way.

No, not his father. The man named Rob Winters was his sperm donor only, and when he'd died in prison, Tom had been so damn glad. Max Hunter was his father in every way that counted. A good man never *owned* anyone.

Max Hunter was the kind of man Tom had always aspired to be.

Thinking of Max sent a pang of homesickness straight to Tom's heart. *I need to call home.*

"Hey, Hunter." Croft reached across the console to snap her fingers next to his face.

Tom startled, his hands clenching on the steering wheel until he realized she'd been trying to get his attention for at least a minute.

"I'm sorry," he said. "My mind was wandering."

"I'll bet it was," Croft said dryly. "I've been saying your name for a whole *hour.*"

He laughed. "We've only been driving for five minutes."

"Fine. So maybe I exaggerated a little."

Tom shook his head good-naturedly. "So what did you find out?"

"The food truck with Belmont's license plates still has them. They are standard DMV issue. You were right about Belmont making a copy."

"Not a shock," Tom murmured. "The sign was a fake, too. 'Adam and Eve's Plumbing' is just an Eden pun."

Croft made a face. "And a bad one at that. The bastard is cocky, isn't he?"

"He's operated under the radar for his whole life. Never had to worry about consequences. But he will," Tom vowed.

"Your mouth to God's ears." Croft was quiet for a moment, studying her phone. "You're going to trace Cameron Cook's e-mail this afternoon?"

"I'm going to try. I'm assuming they're using a VPN and proxy servers, which makes it more complicated. Amos saw a satellite dish at the last Eden settlement, right before he escaped with Abigail, so that adds additional network parameters I have to take into account. But if I can dig through the layers of proxy servers, I'll be able to find their IP address, which—as long as their computer is connected—will give me their actual location even if Hayley Gibbs isn't able to e-mail Cameron again."

Croft's brows lifted. "I'm surprised that Amos knew what a satellite dish was. He'd been in Eden from the beginning, right?"

"Yes, he joined a few months after the community was founded by Pastor. But there were personal satellite dishes back then, mostly in rural areas for TV reception."

"Amos was so young back then," she said sadly. "He lost a huge portion of his adult life."

"Also his family legacy. He sold the land he'd inherited and donated the proceeds to Pastor's church. It was a sizable chunk of change. Just one of many donations that Eden's grown into a buttload of cash."

"Fifty million bucks," Croft said softly. "But why does DJ need to kill Mercy Callahan? I mean, if he doesn't want to share the cash, why not simply kill Pastor to get the money?"

"Good question. We do know that DJ tried to kill Mercy once before, but failed."

"When her mother smuggled her out of Eden. DJ killed her mother."

Tom nodded. "Right. But we assumed that DJ thought Mercy was dead, or he would have come looking for her years ago to keep her from spilling the beans about Eden. If Pastor finds out that Mercy isn't dead . . ." He shrugged.

"Then DJ has a lot of explaining to do and Pastor might punish him somehow."

"From what we know of Eden, punishments are severe, especially for betrayal. It's likely DJ would be killed and the congregation told that he'd met with an accident. Either way, it's unlikely he'd get any of the fifty million."

"No wonder Belmont wants Mercy dead. That's a lot to lose."

"Yeah," Tom said grimly, once again thinking of Liza in the monster's sights. "This morning Molina asked if Belmont might be dead. I've wished it a thousand times in the month since he disappeared, but I didn't think we'd be that lucky."

Croft hesitated. "It was Gideon's girlfriend who shot Belmont, wasn't it?"

Tom nodded. "One of the shots, yes. Daisy Dawson is a sharpshooter. She climbed a tree to get the shot." He glanced at his trainer. "Why?"

"Because he probably has a grudge against her, too," Croft said. "Did you tell Gideon?"

"Nope." He feigned innocence. "I told Molina that I wouldn't feed them information."

Croft snorted. "You didn't have to tell Gideon. Rafe Sokolov has already filled him in."

Tom grinned. "But I didn't tell Gideon."

She was quiet for a few beats. "I think I like you, Hunter."

"I'm glad," he said sincerely. "I'd hate to be stuck with someone who doesn't. Tell me about the tattoo on Belmont's back. Which gang is it?"

"It's a gang out of San Fran called Zhonghua Yanjingshe, which translates to 'Chinese Cobra.' It was originally managed by one of the crime syndicates in mainland China, but a few years ago the gang was hit hard by the Bureau. The syndicate had purchased about a hundred houses in Northern California and turned them into grow houses. If you want more info, ask Rodriguez. He was part of the task force that took them out. They seized over four hundred pounds of pot, plus cash and weapons. Grow houses are still a problem around here, but it's not as organized as it was."

"I read about that when I knew I was coming to Sacramento," Tom said, slowing to stop at a red light. "Folks think that illegal pot isn't a thing in California anymore because it's legal to buy, but the product seized by the task force was going to states where it's still illegal."

"Exactly. Homeowners who rent their houses continue to worry about grow houses. Renters look legit, some even show up with a prop family, then they trash the house, fill it with dirt, and grow weed until they're caught. By then, they're usually in the wind, and the home-owner is left with a ruined house."

"I'm glad I know my renter," Tom said lightly, turning left when the light changed.

Croft chuckled. "I guess so. Liza doesn't seem the type to grow illegal weed."

"I'd be shocked if she's ever even tried it."

Croft shot him an incredulous look. "Hunter. She was asking Irina for cannabis tea when we walked into the Sokolovs' kitchen today."

Oh. "That's true, but I'm sure that was a onetime thing. Not that there would be anything wrong with her drinking Irina's tea, especially now that she's in between her job and school."

"Or maybe you don't know her as well as you think," Croft suggested softly.

Tom's head swiveled to stare at her. "What?"

"How long have you known her?"

He refocused on the road. "Seven years."

"But most of that time she was in the military, wasn't she?"

Tom shrugged, suddenly uncomfortable. "We e-mailed and Skyped at least once a week, whenever she could get screen time." *Until I met Tory.* Then he'd forgotten about their calls, too wrapped up in Tory to pay attention to anyone else. And after Tory had died, he'd been too wrapped up in his grief. He'd left Liza with no one to talk to. *God, I'm an asshole.*

Maybe that's why she's upset with me. She certainly has a right to be.

Croft sighed. "All I'm saying is that you seem convinced that you know her. Maybe she's changed." She shifted in her seat, seeming as uncomfortable with this tangent as Tom was. "Anyway, the gang was hurt in the raids, but not destroyed. The management structure has changed, though."

Tom was simultaneously grateful to Croft for getting them back on track and tempted to ask her what she saw in Liza that had driven her comments. Something was wrong with his friend, but he was either too close or too thick to see what everyone else did.

"Changed how?" he asked, pushing worries about Liza aside for the moment. "Like an internal shake-up, or someone came in from the outside?"

"Both. The gang has become more local, with fewer international ties. The letters tattooed on DJ's back are part of the original name. Now they call themselves the Chicos."

"Meaning 'boys'? They jumped languages?"

"No. It's short for Chinese Cobras. I guess there were too many gangs called the Cobras, so they got creative. The 'chai' became 'chee.' It was probably easier for them to say."

"Yeah. And because 'chai-co' sounds stupid."

"Truth." Croft smiled at the sight of two kids playing in a neighbor's front yard. "This is a nice neighborhood."

"It is. I see those kids sometimes when I jog. They're very sweet. They did a lemonade stand last month to raise money for a sick classmate."

Croft turned her smile his direction. "Did you buy any?"

"Of course." He chuckled. "It was awful. They added ten times more sugar than they should have. But they looked so hopeful, so I drank it and bought more. Which I poured out as soon as I got around the corner. I was worried about a sugar coma, but Liza assured me I'd be fine."

Croft was quiet for so long that he glanced over, only to see her shaking her head. "We don't know a lot about the Chicos' current management, but it's thought that lower-tiered workers rose up through the ranks. Not a coup, really. More that they filled a power vacuum when the old bosses were arrested and deported."

"And DJ Belmont is one of theirs?" he asked.

"That's what I'm going to find out while you're tracing Cameron Cook's e-mail. It would help if I had a photo of Belmont. Can you send me a still from the video once you get it from Mr. Gray at the office building?"

"He sent it already. It's in my inbox. I'll forward it to you as soon as I check on—"

He slowed in front of his house, frowning at the Jeep sitting in his driveway. He'd seen it before—the night before, when Mike the Groper had brought her home. From their date.

"She's got company?" Croft asked casually.

Tom swallowed the growl that rose from his chest a split second before Croft would have heard it. *Keep it together, Hunter. Liza is a grown woman and can see who she wants to.* But it felt wrong. Really wrong. "It would appear so." He pulled behind the Jeep and put their Bureau SUV into park, leaving the engine running. "I'll just be a moment."

Not waiting to hear Croft's reply, he jogged up the front walk. But when he'd gotten to Liza's front door, he hesitated. What if she was . . . busy?

The very thought made his gut hurt, but he needed to know that she was okay, so he lifted his fist to knock.

The door opened before his knuckles hit, startling him into taking a step back. Then a very deep breath, because Mike the Groper stood there, smiling congenially.

"Tom! We didn't expect you."

"I . . ." *I what? Didn't expect to see you, either?* "I'd like to speak with Liza for a moment."

Mike leaned forward, his brows crunching. "She's resting," he whispered. "I put her to bed when she got home. She looked a little shocky to me. I think this morning's close call shook her more than she wanted to admit. But I'm sure she'll be fine. I'll tell her you stopped by." He started to close the door.

She told you what happened?

No. No way. That wasn't possible. Liza knew the Eden investigation was under wraps. He shoved his foot over the threshold just in time to stop the door.

"It's official business." Which was mostly a lie, but at this point, he didn't care. "I need to talk to her myself." He shouldered the front door open, Mike too surprised to give him any resistance. "I know my way around."

Mike opened his mouth to argue, then snapped it closed. "Fine. I'll wait down here."

Yeah, buddy. You do that.

Tom took the stairs two at a time, slowing when he reached the hall upstairs. He'd helped her move in, so he knew where her bedroom was. He'd even been in it a few times, when she had woken screaming from a nightmare that she wouldn't discuss, no matter how many times he'd asked.

That Mike the Groper had been here, too, even if only to tuck Liza safely into bed . . . Well, he didn't like it. At all.

He started to knock on her door, then stilled. He could hear her, and she was crying. Still.

Goddammit. He felt horrible, made worse because he didn't know what to apologize for. Carefully he knocked.

"I'm *fine*, Mike," he heard her say. "I already told you that. You can go home now."

That made Tom stand up straighter, and the tension released its grip on his chest. "It's me, Liza. Can I come in?"

Silence met his ears. Complete and suffocating.

"Liza?" He rested his forehead on the door, suddenly weary. "Please?"

She huffed out a breath. "Suit yourself."

He opened the door enough to make sure that she was decent before entering the room. A smile tugged at his lips at the sight of Pebbles curled up against Liza's back, her head on the spare pillow. Pebbles lifted her head enough to see that it was him, then slumped back down with a doggy sigh.

Liza was curled up as well, facing the window. She'd pulled the shade down, casting the room into semidarkness. "You can tell Irina that I'm fine. I know she told you to check on me."

Tom frowned, not sure what to say to that. If he acknowledged the statement, it made him look like he hadn't cared enough to check himself. But it was true, so he couldn't deny it, either.

Instead he took a step forward, then another, until his knees were up against the mattress. "Why did you run from me?" he asked instead, because that was really what he wanted to know.

"Why did you come here?"

Her voice was hoarse, her nose stuffy. And he didn't know how to help her.

"I was worried today." He wasn't certain where the words came from, but once he'd said them, he realized this was where things had started to go wrong. "Not about Mercy and Abigail, because I knew you'd have shielded them with your own body if the bullets started flying. I knew they'd be fine." A teensy exaggeration, but he figured no one would fault him. "I was worried about *you*. I was on that roof, Liza. I saw what that gunman would have seen, looking through that glass door. He would have seen you, wouldn't he?"

Another long silence, then, "Yeah. Probably."

Now she sounded small and vulnerable. He took a chance and rounded the bed, sitting on the edge of the mattress near her knees. He stared at his hands. In the past he would have gathered her in his arms for a reassuring hug, but right now that seemed like a colossally poor idea.

Her hair covered her face and he gently pushed it aside so that he could see her features. She was beautiful, but she always had been, from the moment he'd laid eyes on her when she'd only been seventeen. *She's not seventeen anymore.* She really, really wasn't.

He shoved the thought aside because it felt so wrong. She was his *friend.* "Why did you run from me? What did I do?"

Her eyes remained tightly closed. "Nothing," she said in a tone that meant he'd done something. He hadn't been born yesterday. He knew that women usually meant "something" when they said "nothing." He also knew that pushing her was a bad plan.

But *not* pushing hadn't worked, either. "Something's been bothering you," he murmured, stroking her hair.

For a moment she seemed to relax into his hand, but then she lurched back several inches, putting her out of his reach. "I'm all right," she said through clenched teeth. "Why did you come here?"

Tom recoiled as if she'd slapped him. She'd never pulled away from his touch. Not ever. His brain stalled and no words would come. "What did I do?" he whispered.

Her face fell and she pursed her lips the same way she had in the Sokolovs' laundry room, like she was holding her emotions in tight check. Finally, she opened her eyes and gave him such a sad smile that his heart hurt. "Nothing, Tom. You didn't do anything wrong. Now, if there's nothing else, you need to go."

He opened his mouth, then closed it. He started to rise, then sat back down. "Mike the—" He barely stopped himself from saying *the Groper.* "The guy downstairs," he improvised. "He said you were shocky from your ordeal this morning."

Her jaw tightened. "I told him that I'd nearly hit a kid on a bike."

"I knew you hadn't told him anything important. He took me by surprise, that's all."

"You and me both," she muttered.

The aching of his heart lessened, just a bit. "You didn't call him?"

She rolled her eyes before closing them. "No. He was here when I got back and I told him to go home, but he's a nurse, too. He wouldn't leave until he'd taken care of me."

I should have been taking care of you.

The thought was as clear as the blue sky beyond her closed window shades, and it stunned him into a moment of silence. Then his brain caught up and he cleared his throat. "The shooter was DJ Belmont. We saw his face on the surveillance tape."

"What a shock," she muttered sarcastically. "I figured that this morning, without fancy tech."

He nearly smiled at her snark, but the gravity of the situation kept him sober. "So did I, but I have to prove my theories with evidence. He may have seen you. You could be in danger."

Her expression didn't change. "And?"

He wanted to force her to open her eyes so that he could truly *see* her. But he kept his hands on his thighs and his voice steady. "And you need to take appropriate precautions. You shouldn't go running off alone. Anywhere. With *anyone*." He added that last sentence with Mike the Groper in mind. "Not until we catch him."

She opened one eye. "If I run off *with* someone, then I'm not running off *alone*."

He wanted to snarl at her. She wasn't taking him seriously. "You know what I mean."

"Fine, Tom. I'll be careful. I won't even walk Pebbles without an escort."

"A cop escort," he insisted. Which eliminated Mike the Groper.

"Fine." She closed her eye and tugged at the blankets. "I'm going to nap now. You can see yourself out. Tell Mike that I just need some quiet and that I'll be okay by tomorrow."

Tom stood uncertainly. "What happens tomorrow?"

Her lips thinned, her expression changing to one of determination. "We're going out to dinner. Do I need a bodyguard?"

He stood silently, words failing him once again. He watched her swallow, then brace herself before opening her eyes. She stared up at him, brown eyes full of challenge. "Do I need a bodyguard?" she repeated. "Or should I cancel on him? I will if you tell me to."

Cancel, dammit. Cancel.

But that wasn't fair. It wasn't right.

Neither is Mike the Groper!

But he knew what he needed to say. "Don't cancel. But don't leave the house until I can ask Agent Raeburn how we can handle your protection."

She visibly flinched. "All right," she murmured. "I look forward to hearing from your boss. If I don't hear by tomorrow morning, I'll call him myself."

It was his turn to flinch. She'd not-so-subtly bypass him, going straight to Raeburn for information. "All right." He turned to go, but paused, hand on the doorknob, when she called his name. "Yes?"

"Tell Mike that I'll be down in a few minutes and that I'll make him supper."

He nodded once, then left without looking back. Passing her message on to Mike the Groper was harder than he thought it would be, especially when the man became smugly pleased.

"I hadn't planned to go anywhere," Mike said. "Don't worry. She's safe with me."

Tom managed not to slam the front door on his way out. He did, however, slam the SUV door when he got in.

Croft shot him a look. He glared back at her, daring her to ask him anything. "She's fine," he snapped. "She's got someone with her for now. I'll ask Raeburn for a protection detail."

"He won't agree," Croft said very carefully. "She's not the primary target and he's down a man with Mercy's protection detail. Just preparing you."

"Then I'll set up drive-bys." *Or I'll hire someone to guard her.*

Until then, he'd watch over her himself. Whatever he did, she'd be safe. "I'll take you back to the field office now."

"And where will you be?"

"My home computer setup is better than the piece of shit machine they gave me." He gritted his teeth. "Is there a problem with me working from home?"

"Not at all. I'm going to talk to my tattoo artist friend about the Chicos design."

Immediately Tom was contrite. "Is it safe? Should I go with you?"

One of Croft's brows lifted in warning. "I graduated Quantico when you were still in middle school. I think I'm capable of taking care of myself."

Face flaming, Tom put the SUV in reverse and backed out of his driveway. "I'm sorry."

She patted his arm. "It's okay. You're a little raw today. I get it. Thanks for offering to have my back. I'd prefer you use your time to track that e-mail, though."

"Will do."

SEVEN

It has to be DJ," Graham muttered, leaning in to drag his thumbs down either side of Hayley's spine.

She barely heard the words, which had been Graham's intent. He'd been permitted to escort her from the prayer service to the quarters assigned to Joshua's wives. Right now the room was empty because the wives were off doing whatever jobs they'd been assigned to. There was a schedule among the other three wives dictating who slept with Joshua and on which night. Hayley would be added into the rotation once the baby was born.

For now she was on "light duty" since she was two weeks away from giving birth.

Which scared her to death.

"Hayley?" Graham whispered. "Listen to me. This is important."

"I know," Hayley whispered back. "Tell me." Focusing on Graham would help her keep her growing dread in check.

"DJ's the only one who leaves the compound. The drugs have to be his."

"Makes sense. But how does that help us?" She flinched when Graham dug too deep into her sore muscles. "Not quite so hard, please."

"Sorry," Graham said. "I didn't mean to hurt you."

She reached back to pat his arm. "I know, Cookie." She'd started calling him the nickname when he'd developed a love for graham crackers at age four because he believed they'd been named after him. He'd been such a cute kid. Now he was a serious preteen, saddled with a lot more responsibility than any kid his age should have to bear.

He snorted softly. "I prefer that to Achan."

Achan was the biblical name given to him when they'd arrived in Eden. "A whore and a thief," Hayley said softly. "That's us."

"That's me," Graham corrected. "You are no whore."

Her heart melted. "Aw. You say the sweetest things."

He huffed. "Shut up. You're not paying attention."

"I am. I just don't see how finding DJ's stash is going to help us get out of here."

"It's not a stash," Graham said. "A stash is a baggie or two of weed. This is a *shipment*. There had to be thirty pounds of coke in that box that was labeled *Smithy Tools*. It was under a stack of other boxes."

"DJ's hiding it if he's labeled the box as something else," Hayley murmured. "The others don't know he's dealing."

"I bet Pastor knows." Graham started massaging her back again.

She nearly moaned because it felt so good. "That's a sucker bet. Pastor knows everything that happens here. What are you thinking about?"

He leaned in again, whispering in her ear. "Using that coke to buy our way out of here."

Hayley jerked out of his reach, staring at him. He wasn't joking. In fact, he looked grimly sober. "What the hell, Graham?" she hissed.

"Shhh," he admonished. "You're going to get us both thrown in the box."

She covered her mouth, but her eyes were filling with tears. "You can't. You'll get caught."

"And if I don't, that bitch is going to steal your baby."

Hayley blinked, sending tears down her cheeks. Quickly she wiped at them with the scratchy woolen sleeve of her homespun dress. "I don't want you hurt."

"If I do it right, I won't be."

"You heard Tamar. People are watching you. They know you've been exploring."

"We need a diversion." He glanced down at her stomach. "Tonight you're going to pretend to go into labor. If I get caught, I'll say I was trying to get blankets or towels or something."

"No," she whispered. "I can't let you take that risk."

"You can't tell me what to do. Technically—here in this hellhole— I outrank you."

He smirked, but Hayley didn't think it was funny. "You're going to get killed."

"We need to get out of here," Graham said stubbornly. "And we're running out of time."

She closed her eyes. "I know."

"Then you'll pretend?"

"Yes," she breathed wearily. "Of course I will."

He squeezed her shoulders. "Good girl."

She leaned into him, resting her head on his shoulder. "I'm scared, Graham."

"I know." He slid his arm around her, giving her a quick hug. "I'm going to fix this."

Hayley's tears kept falling, because she wasn't sure if this situation could be fixed. She was trading the safety of her brother for the safety of her baby. Graham thought he was tough stuff, but he'd never be able to defend himself if all the men of Eden decided to teach him a lesson.

He pressed a kiss to her temple, something he hadn't done in so long that she was momentarily stunned. "You'll have to name Jelly-bean 'Grahamina.' Like Wilhelmina, but not."

She laughed, a watery sound. "You're insane. And I love you."

His answer was another hug and then he was on his feet. "Lie down and rest. I'll get you something to eat. What do you want? Jerky, jerky, or jerky?"

Jerky had been a staple for the last week. Luckily, the women had put up canned goods last fall, so they weren't starving yet, but she was really getting tired of jerky. "Jerky."

He exaggerated a bow. "Your wish is my—" Then he straightened abruptly at the shout from somewhere toward the front of the cave system. "What the . . . ?"

Hayley struggled to stand, but Graham motioned for her to stay put. Worried, but unable to stand on her own, she complied.

"I'll see what's up," he said, then disappeared around the curtain that provided all the privacy they were allowed.

A minute later he was back. "It's Pastor. He fell down and he's not getting up. The healer's with him now. So's most of the community."

Hayley frowned at him. "Graham . . ." she warned.

"This is our diversion." He grinned. "Ask me no questions, I'll tell you no lies." And then he was gone.

Hayley bit back the swear words that she wanted to shout at him. *Don't get caught. Please.*

ROCKLIN, CALIFORNIA
WEDNESDAY, MAY 24, 5:05 P.M.

This is wrong.

Liza sat rigidly on her sofa, Mike at her side. He'd stretched his arm across the back of the sofa and was playing with her hair.

This is wrong. It was the thought that kept circling through her mind, drowning out the movie they'd been watching. She'd been thinking about Tom the entire time. And fighting the urge to run next door because she'd heard the garage door go up when he'd come home.

You're hopeless. You're just pathetic.

And then there was Mike. He was chuckling at the movie, having no idea about all the thoughts churning in her mind.

You're using him. You just want to show yourself that you can walk away from Tom Hunter, but you're being unfair to Mike. Just like you were to Fritz. Don't make the same mistake again.

Liza despised herself for making this man think that there could be anything between them. *Tell him the truth, then.*

She drew a deep breath, turning to face him. "Mike?"

"Hm?"

"Can you pause the movie? I need to talk to you."

He immediately hit the remote, and the movie stopped. "What's wrong?"

She huffed a mirthless laugh. "So many things, I'm not sure where to start. But the biggest is that I don't think I'm ready for a relationship."

He froze. "Why not?" he asked cautiously.

Because I'm in love with a man who doesn't want me and you're second fiddle. She closed her eyes, unwilling to utter the truth aloud. "Um . . . I was married."

Mike pulled away, his shock evident. "What? When? To who?"

"More than a year ago. He . . . he died."

Mike sucked in a breath. "Oh my God, Liza. I'm sorry."

"Thank you." *I'm sorry, too. Sorry that I'm giving you such a bastardization of the actual truth.* Because her inability to be with Mike had nothing to do with Fritz and everything to do with Tom. "He was killed by a sniper outside Kabul."

"Oh my God," he said softly. Kindly.

"I was there."

This time his gasp was completely silent. Then he let out a breath. "Liza, I had no idea," he whispered. "I'm so sorry."

"So . . ." She waved her hands in a vague gesture. "I'm not ready.

I don't want to hurt you." That was true. So true. "I don't want you to think this is more than it's going to be."

Mike was quiet for a moment, then pulled her close for a hug. "I'm sorry you lost him. I'm sorry you couldn't save him."

Also a nurse, he understood that part, at least. "He bled out before I could," she said hoarsely.

"Were you hurt?"

"Not really." The bullet she'd taken in her hip had been so meaningless in comparison.

"Was he the only one who died?"

"No," she whispered. "Several others."

"I'm sorry."

"Me too."

He let her go, a crooked smile tilting his lips. "So this is where I exit stage right, huh?"

"I'm sorry," she whispered.

He laid a finger over her lips. "I get it. I don't like it for a lot of reasons, obviously, because I like you a lot. I think we could have been good together."

She swallowed hard, saying nothing. What could she say? *It's unlikely we'd ever have been good together, because I can't seem to get over my seven-year crush on my best friend.*

That was too much truth.

He sighed. "Well, if I have to bow out gracefully, at least it's because of a combat hero and not a basketball star."

Liza blinked. "What?"

"Your neighbor Tom. I thought it might have been because of him."

Her eyes burned. "No. We're just—"

"Just friends," Mike finished. "I hear you. Not sure he does. He nearly bit my head off when I wouldn't let him in earlier."

Liza could only stare. *What if Mike was right?*

You are stupid. Stupid, stupid, stupid. She'd already gotten her hopes up, and it would hurt worse the next time.

"He knows about your husband?"

She shook her head. "No. It was too painful to tell anyone when I got back, and then . . ." She shrugged. "You're the first person I've told."

The crooked smile reappeared. "Well, that's something, I guess." He leaned in to kiss her forehead. "You call me when you're ready, okay?"

She somehow found a smile of her own. "Okay. But I hope you're happily with someone wonderful before then. You're too nice a guy to be alone."

"I'd say ditto, but I think we've covered that." He rose and stumbled over Pebbles, who'd been lying at their feet.

Pebbles lifted her head to stare at him, then went back to sleep. Mike reached down to scratch behind her ears. "Walk me out so I know you've locked your door."

Liza did as he asked, then slumped against her front door. She was not going over to see Tom. She was not. She'd keep busy.

Step one was checking the want ads to see if anyone wanted to hire an ex–army medic for a month. The decision to take a break before she started nursing school had been based on dreams anyway. She'd had hopes that things would be different once she and Tom were in the same city. Living next to each other. Tory was gone. Fritz was gone. They were both single and . . . together. Except they weren't.

She'd hoped this month's break would be spent with him. That they'd both ended up in Sacramento had seemed like fate was finally smiling her way.

She sighed. "I am so damn stupid."

Pebbles lifted her head, then tilted it curiously. Tom usually came to get the dog when he got home from work, but after the conversation in her bedroom, either he must have figured she needed Pebbles for comfort or he was giving her a wide berth. Maybe both. Whatever the reason, she was glad for the company.

"But no more," she told Pebbles firmly. "Plans have changed. I'm going back to work. But first, I'm going to get your dinner."

Pebbles bounded to her feet excitedly, prancing in place as Liza pushed away from the door. She stopped next to the big dog and planted a kiss on her muzzle. "You love me, don't you?"

Pebbles licked her face and Liza laughed. "Come on. Kibble first, then playtime in the backyard. And then I'll take you home."

She'd slip the dog into Tom's house through his kitchen door, hopefully avoiding him. Because she wasn't sure she'd make it through another conversation with the man today.

ROCKLIN, CALIFORNIA
WEDNESDAY, MAY 24, 7:35 P.M.

Tom jumped when something cold and wet burrowed under the hand he had resting on his keyboard. Then settled when he realized it was Pebbles. He'd been so deep in his work that he hadn't heard Liza bring her over.

Giving her an ear scratch, he got up to look for Liza, then remembered that she had company. Mike the Groper had stayed and he'd heard them watching a movie when he'd come home from the field office.

That he'd had to press his ear to the wall to get that tidbit of information wasn't anything he'd admit to anyone. Even to Pebbles, although she'd never tell.

He peeked through the blinds, relieved to see his driveway clear. He hadn't heard the garage door open, so Liza's car was still in there, parked next to his own. Mike the Groper was gone.

Going to the door, he called for her. "Liza! Where are you?" Because she always came in with Pebbles. They'd have dinner together and settle in to watch some TV.

Tom needed that. He'd been staring at his computer screen for far too long and was becoming frustrated. He'd been unsuccessful in tracking Cameron Cook's e-mail. He'd traced it through several proxy servers, then hit a wall.

Either their network person was really good, or their server was no longer active. He hoped Croft was having better luck with tracking the Chicos' tattoo artist.

"Liza!" he called again, then sighed when his phone buzzed with an incoming text.

I just put Pebbles in your house. She's been fed.

That was all. No *See you later* or *How's it going* or *What's for dinner.* He wondered if she and Mike were still going out tomorrow. He wondered if he should have told her not to go.

She'd almost seemed like she'd wanted him to.

He started to call her, then stopped himself. He didn't know what to say. They'd been friends for years. Liza had been the only person he'd trusted with knowledge of Tory while they'd dated. They'd shared secrets and hopes. He'd even told her when Tory got pregnant.

But not so much after that. Tom had been in love, blind to the rest of the world. And then he'd been in shock, grieving. And then he'd been focused on getting justice for his love and their unborn child.

He'd shut Liza out, albeit unintentionally. He'd never even told her that Tory was dead. She'd found out when she'd arrived home from Afghanistan last Christmas Day. She'd come fully expecting to meet the woman he'd wanted to spend his life with.

He still remembered the shock in her eyes when he'd told her that Tory was dead. Then the hurt that he'd kept it from her.

"But she seemed fine after that," he told Pebbles, who stared up at him. "She was happy." Until she wasn't. And when did that really start? Now he couldn't seem to remember. Distracted by the danger Mercy and Gideon were in, he hadn't been paying attention. "I don't know what to do," he confided. "What do you think is wrong?"

Pebbles simply wagged her whip of a tail, her tongue lolling to the side.

"You're no help at all." He leaned down to rub her ears. "But you're still a good girl."

She licked his face and he abruptly straightened, grimacing. He'd nearly broken her of that habit, but Liza let her do it.

He sank back into his chair, glumly staring at his screen. He'd created a project file for Eden a month ago, when Ephraim had been intent on kidnapping Mercy Callahan. It was still pathetically thin.

He heard the car engine a second before Pebbles began to bark. She sounded fierce, even though she'd most likely just lick a burglar's face.

He shushed her, then checked the window again, frowning when Rafe Sokolov and Mercy Callahan emerged from the Subaru parked in his drive. Leaning on his cane, Rafe escorted Mercy up the front walk, keeping his body between hers and the street every step of the way.

A glance across the street revealed a black SUV with Agent Rodriguez behind the wheel. His shift would be over soon and his replacement would take over guard duty. For now, the man was watchful, giving Tom a slight salute before resuming his surveillance of the street.

Mercy quickly disappeared into Liza's side of the duplex, as if Liza had been holding the door open. This made him want to march down there and remind her that she'd witnessed an attempted murder only hours before.

He'd be giving her a lecture on proper security when her guests left. For now, Rafe was with them, and that was more than good enough in Tom's eyes. The homicide detective was savvy and knew his way around firearms. He wasn't a sharpshooter like Gideon's girlfriend, Daisy, but he was more than capable of protecting Liza.

Except Rafe didn't go inside. Blowing a kiss to Mercy, he stepped back from Liza's doorstep, aiming a look up at Tom's window before crossing the grassy patch between their two front doors. His knock had Pebbles barking again and Tom went downstairs to open the door.

"Hey," Rafe said, his eyes taking Tom in. "No offense, dude, but you look like shit."

Tom smoothed his hair, which had to be standing every which direction. "I've been working," he said stiffly.

"I figured as much." Rafe pointed inside. "Can I come in or do I need to tell you stuff standing on your front porch?"

"Oh. Sorry." Cheeks heating, Tom stepped back to allow Rafe to come inside. "My mother would be very upset with me. Can I offer you something to drink? I have beer, water, and pop."

"How about a beer? Mercy and Liza will be busy for a while, so I don't need to drive for a few hours. I can have one."

Tom walked to the kitchen, Rafe following behind him. "Busy doing what?" he asked.

"Talking." He smiled. "And talking, and talking some more. I'm thankful for Liza. Mercy needed a friend. She misses Farrah."

Farrah was Mercy's best friend from New Orleans. Tom liked Farrah. She was funny and smart and had a heart like his mother's. "I guess she does."

Rafe perched on a stool at Tom's kitchen island. "Liza seemed . . . off today. Mercy was worried. I told her it was probably the shock of seeing a sniper, but Mercy had to check for herself to make sure Liza is all right."

"She seemed fine when I saw her," Tom said, then winced. He could hear the acid in his own voice and wasn't foolish enough to think that Rafe hadn't. Sure enough, when he turned from the fridge with two beers, Rafe's brows were lifted.

"Do I want to know?" Rafe asked.

Tom shrugged. "Nothing to know." He rummaged in the drawer for a bottle opener, then flipped the caps off the bottles. "She had company when I got home."

Rafe looked way too interested. "Company?"

Tom handed Rafe a bottle and drained half of his own in one gulp. It had been a long day and technically he was off the clock, so he wasn't going to feel guilty about drinking a beer.

He stared at the bottle in his hand, glaring. Yeah, he was going to feel guilty, because he hadn't yet traced Cameron Cook's e-mail. He set the bottle aside and pulled some cheese from the refrigerator. "I didn't have lunch. Want some?"

"It's dinnertime," Rafe said mildly. "Who was her company?"

Tom took his annoyance out on the cheese, stabbing at the block with more force than needed. "Mike." *The Groper.* "Some nurse she knew at the veterans' home."

"Mike," Rafe said slowly. "Well, he wasn't there just now."

"Because he left." He finished slicing the cheese and put a plate on the kitchen island between them. *Time to change the subject.* "Today, at your parents' house? You looked like you wanted to say something before I left, but you didn't."

"That's why I'm here. The gang, the one whose tattoo Belmont has on his back?"

"The Chicos? What about them?"

"I know them."

Tom went still. "How?"

"I was Narcotics before Homicide. I worked with the Gangs division."

Tom nodded. "I knew that. You went undercover. Took down a local crime boss." That was no small feat. Undercover work could be emotionally debilitating, on top of being dangerous. Especially for a man as social as Rafe seemed to be. "How long were you under?"

"Two years." And from his expression, those had been very difficult years.

"And you met someone from the Chicos?"

He nodded again. "They didn't call themselves that then. They were still Yanjingshe. Going by 'Chicos' was a smart move on the new leadership's part. They were a supplier to the organization where I was embedded. This was before the big raids."

"Agent Croft told me about them. She also said the management had changed."

"True. Many of the lower-level guys moved up to take over when the bosses were hauled in by the Feds. The lower-level guys would have been the guys we worked with, so . . ."

Tom felt a small spurt of hope. "Excellent. Croft is checking with tattoo artists. If she can track the one who did their tats and they point us to DJ's fellow gang members, maybe you can do an ID from a photo array."

Rafe's expression went wry. "I get to be a civilian witness. Oh goody."

Tom winced. Rafe was on DB from the police force because of an injury he'd sustained months before. Last he'd heard, Rafe's return to the force wasn't a given. "I'm sorry. I didn't—"

"It's fine," Rafe interrupted firmly. "I didn't take offense. Seriously. It'll just be weird, being on the other side of the process."

Tom thought about Tory. He hadn't been interviewed by the cops when she'd been killed, because no one knew they were a thing. He hadn't come forward, either. He'd tracked down her killer on his own. And . . . well, he wasn't proud of the outcome, but the asshole was dead, and that was what was really important. The monster would never hurt another innocent woman.

"Yo. Hunter."

Tom blinked, suddenly aware that Rafe was snapping his fingers. "Sorry."

"Where did you go?"

"Somewhere I don't like to talk about."

Rafe lifted his brows. "Fair enough. Anyway, I'm happy to help you take down some of those Chicos bastards if I can. Full disclosure—it's personal for me."

Tom sat on a stool, leaning an elbow on the counter. "How so?"

Rafe's expression was a combination of grim determination and banked sadness. "You once told me that you left the NBA for the FBI because you lost someone. That you'd always planned to make the change, but that the loss spurred you."

Tom remembered the conversation. It was the first time he'd met the Sokolov clan, the first time Irina had sent him home with cake and a motherly hug, making him miss his own mother so much that he'd called her as soon as he'd gotten to his car. "You said you'd also lost someone, that that was why you moved from Gangs to Homicide."

Rafe's nod was sober. "You told me not to do anything that would get me into trouble with Molina, but then you said that you'd have done anything to protect your fiancée. I figured that's who you lost. Am I right?"

Tom's throat tightened, making it hard to force the words out. "Yeah."

"What was her name?"

"Victoria. I called her Tory." He swallowed, the movement painful. "She was murdered." As was the baby she'd carried. *Our baby.* But it hurt too much to think about their unborn child, much less to talk about them.

Rafe blinked. "I didn't know that. My fiancée was Bella. She was killed by the mob boss's men. She was the prosecutor working our case." He hesitated. "Our relationship wasn't public."

Wow. Helluva thing to have in common. "One of you would have had to recuse yourself."

"Yes. And neither of us wanted the other to have to do it, so we kept our relationship secret. I wouldn't have been able to make it public anyway, not when I was UC, but I wanted to."

Tom dropped his gaze to the plate of cheese, absently fiddling with one of the slices. "I get it. Tory was our team's physical therapist. It probably would have been okay, but she was adamant that we not tell anyone. She was afraid she'd lose her job."

"I didn't realize we had so much in common. I'm sorry you lost your Tory."

"Likewise." He looked up. "Did you get the guys who killed Bella?"

"I did. Had to kill a few of them. Was able to take a few in alive. I didn't lose a wink of sleep over the ones who chose to fight me, though. They shot first, but my trigger finger was ready, willing, and able."

Tom thought about what he'd done to take down Tory's killer. He wasn't sorry. Well, maybe about one or two details, but not about the end result. "Does Mercy know?"

"She does. I wasn't sure what she'd think of me, but she was happy I'd taken them out. Said that I'd made it possible for my partner to go home to his family by having his back. That I'd survived and seen justice done."

"I'm glad." Tom's voice was rough, and he had to clear his throat. He wondered what Liza would think if she knew what he'd done and immediately relaxed, knowing that she'd be happy about the end result as well. His Liza was fierce and unafraid and wired to protect. *Tory would have liked her.*

Wait. What? His breath stuttered in his chest, making him cough. *His Liza?* She was not his. And if he wanted her to be? She wouldn't be happy with that. Especially not given their most recent conversations. And even if she were happy with it . . . Just thinking of her and Tory in the same breath seemed like betrayal.

"You okay?" Rafe asked blandly.

Tom took a gulp of beer. "Yeah. Just swallowed wrong." He cleared his throat again and waited for his breathing to even out. What were they even talking about? *Oh. Right.* "Did the Chicos have a hand in Bella's murder? Is that why it's personal?"

"Indirectly. They were one of our target's biggest suppliers. The Chicos had a reason to keep the city's organized crime alive and well. Supply and demand and all that. I remember a few of the midlevel thugs. DJ wasn't one of the ones I worked with. I can tell you that."

"Good to know." Tom pushed the cheese plate away, no longer hungry. "I hope Croft is more successful with her search than I've been with mine."

"You've been trying to track that kid's e-mail."

Tom just looked at him. "Jeff Bunker told you?" Because of course he would have.

"Yeah. It all came out over dinner when his mom and mine teamed up to make sure Zoya and Jeff know never to drive to San Francisco alone again. You weren't able to track it?"

"Not to the source. I think they've pulled their server offline. Or maybe they only hook it up when they want to use it."

"Before this morning, I'd hoped that they'd gone quiet because DJ was dead."

"Yeah. Asshole," Tom muttered. The picture of Liza standing in front of that glass door would not vacate his mind. "How are Mercy and Abigail doing?"

"Abigail is okay but Mercy is wrecked. She held it together for Abigail, but once we were alone, she fell apart. After a month of watching her every move she'd grown a little complacent. Her word, not mine. She knew he'd never give up, but, like the rest of us, she hoped he was dead. She was worried about Liza because of the way she left this afternoon."

Tom felt his cheeks heat at the question in Rafe's direct gaze, but there was no way he was going there. Especially when he didn't understand it himself. "She was upset for a while, but I think her friend helped cheer her up."

"Her friend?"

"Mike." The groper. Smug bastard.

"Right." Rafe shook his head again. "If the e-mail trace is a bust, what else do you have?"

Tom opened his mouth, then closed it again. "I can't talk about those things."

Rafe pulled a notepad from his pocket. "Good thing that I *can* talk about it."

"What?"

Rafe waved the notepad. "A summary of my own Eden project file."

"You're not—"

"Supposed to be working on it. Whatever. If you can't talk to me, you can listen."

Tom settled on his stool. "I wondered what you'd been doing for the last month. I figured you wouldn't sit idle when it came to Mercy's safety. Hit me."

EIGHT

Mercy dipped her spoon into the carton of rocky road. "Why don't you just talk to him?"

Liza rolled her very sore eyes. Because as soon as she and Mercy had been alone, Mercy had opened her arms and patted Liza's back while she cried. "He had a fiancée. Her name was Tory."

"Oh." Mercy winced. "Was?"

"She was killed. Murdered, actually. It was a little more than a year ago, when I was still in Afghanistan. He went dark, wouldn't talk to me, wouldn't answer any of my e-mails."

"A year isn't all that long, is it?"

"No." That Liza had lost her own husband wasn't something she wanted to discuss, even with Mercy. So she added the one fact that would ensure Mercy understood. "She was pregnant."

Mercy paled. "Oh no."

"Yeah. So I get it. I do. He's not ready. And when he is, it won't be for me."

"So what are you gonna do?" Mercy asked practically. "Avoid him forever? Move out and share custody of the dog?"

"Maybe. I'm going to try to get a room in the dorms for this semester. It might be too late, but I'll get one for next year. That'll give Tom time to find a new renter."

"I was being sarcastic," Mercy said.

"I wasn't." She ate some ice cream, then sat back to study her friend. "You're not okay."

Mercy laughed, the sound harsh. "No, I'm not. I figured we could be not okay together."

"Is Rodriguez still outside?"

"For another hour. They do the shift change and Agent Fisher comes on. She's a fan of Irina's cooking, so I always save her a snack for later. It's in a cooler in the back of Rafe's Subaru, along with a late-night snack for Rodriguez to take home."

Liza smiled. "Those guys are going to miss guarding you when this is over. I bet they've never eaten so well."

Mercy's smile was strained, but real. "They've fallen in love with Irina."

"I have, too. She makes me miss my mom."

"Me too. Oh, I nearly forgot." She pulled a baggie from her pocket, filled with loose tea. "Special tea," she said, waggling her brows. "Irina set you up. She sent dinner for you, too. I forgot it in the car, but Rafe can get it before we leave."

Liza chuckled, and it made her feel so much better. "That woman," she said fondly. "I'm going to miss her."

Mercy's brows flew up. "Why would you miss her? You're going to nursing school in Davis, not Timbuktu. She'll still expect you to come to Sunday dinner." Her brows lowered, a frown furrowing her forehead. "You *are* still planning to come to Sunday dinner, aren't you?"

Fuck no. Tom will be there. "I'll probably be busy," she managed stiffly.

"Bull*shit*." Mercy shook her spoon before digging back into the ice cream. "You are not going to dump us because Tom Hunter is a clueless dick."

Liza choked. "He's not a dick."

"He made you cry," Mercy said stubbornly. "And he is clueless."

"Totally clueless," Liza agreed. "But not a dick. He's a good man."

"You are hopeless. If he's such a good man, then grab him and talk to him."

Liza started to reply, then glared. "Hey. I see what you did there. I said that you're not okay and you—quite deftly, I have to say—turned the conversation back to me."

Mercy sighed. "What do you want me to say? Yes, I'm scared. I'm always scared. And I'm tired of being scared. I'm kind of glad DJ made a move today, as crazy as that sounds."

"Not crazy at all. At least you know where he is. Or where he was at that moment."

"Pointing a gun at us. At you, actually. Don't ever do that again. He could have shot you."

"He *would* have shot you. And Abigail."

Mercy shuddered. "Don't even go there. I'm going to have nightmares about that forever. It makes me afraid to go anywhere with anyone."

"It's a terrorist tactic," Liza said. "Makes you afraid to live your life."

"It works," Mercy said grimly. "Makes me want to buy a bull's-eye costume and yell, 'Come and get me, asshole.'"

Liza sucked in a breath. "But you won't."

"No." But even Mercy's smirk looked scared. "I don't know where to buy a bull's-eye costume. Although I bet Amazon would have one."

"*Mercy.*"

Mercy focused on the ice cream. "I'm not going to do it. But I want to. I want this to be over." She looked up, her green eyes filled with tears. "I want my life back. I found Rafe and Gideon and Amos and Abigail and all of you. I don't want them to get hurt. Or you. Especially when you make yourself a target because you're protecting me. This is between DJ Belmont and me. Nobody else should get hurt."

"This is between DJ Belmont and the FBI. Promise me that you know that."

Mercy only shook her head. "They can't find him. Eden has stayed hidden for thirty years for a reason. They are good at hiding. DJ will crawl back under his rock and it could be another month before he comes back out. Or a year. I can't keep this up, this living in fear. I can't ask the Sokolovs to do it, either. I'm liking the bull's-eye costume idea more and more."

Liza's blood went cold. "Promise me," she whispered. "Goddammit, Mercy."

Mercy blinked, wiping the tears from her cheeks. "No. I can't promise I won't. Luring him out makes the most sense and I'm the only bait." Her brow lifted in challenge. "And if you mention this to Rafe, I'll say you were drunk on vodka."

"I'll tell Tom," Liza threatened.

"Vodka," she repeated.

"He knows I don't drink that stuff."

Mercy's chin lifted. "Then I'll tell him that he's a clueless dick and he should notice you."

Liza's mouth fell open. "You wouldn't."

Mercy rolled her eyes. "No, I wouldn't. But I'd think of something else to discredit your dirty lies."

"Dirty lies that are the goddamn truth."

"Potayto, potahto."

Liza exhaled. "Please don't do anything stupid. Please."

Mercy looked away. "Did you know that Rafe is planning a surprise party for me?"

Liza blinked, thrown by the abrupt change in subject. "No. When is it?"

"Sunday. He's doesn't know that I know. It's going to be held at Irina and Karl's. You're invited, of course."

"Okay," Liza said slowly. "What can I bring?"

"Yourself." One side of her mouth lifted wryly. "Maybe some of those Dream Bars."

"Done and done. But why are you telling me this?"

"Because Rafe has hired six of his old SacPD buddies to be bodyguards. Six, Liza. They'll be armed and will have the house surrounded."

"That's . . . good?"

"No," Mercy snapped. "That's bad. Six men will be put in harm's way because DJ Belmont won't give up trying to kill me. And we won't even go into what Rafe is paying them, out of his own pocket. How long can we do this? How long before he decides I'm not worth it?"

"Never," Liza said sharply. "That man loves you."

Mercy's gaze met hers once again, this time beseeching and afraid. "That's why I have to do something. He loves me. I know he does. He's going to get himself killed—or someone he's hired—and it'll be on me. I *cannot* live with that. Do you understand?"

"Yeah," Liza said softly, covering Mercy's hand with her own. "I really do. It's like you're in a combat situation, always prepared, always ready. It grates at you, makes you jumpy. Sometimes it makes you throw caution to the wind just to feel normal for a day. An hour."

Mercy's throat worked as she tried to swallow. "Thank you," she whispered. "That's exactly it. You sound like you know this from experience."

It was Liza's turn to look away. "Yeah. You spend weeks, months, in uniform, and gunfire is like . . . background noise." So were the screams and moans of the wounded she cared for until the surgeons could work their miracles. "And you want just one day to be . . . normal."

"And then?" Mercy asked quietly.

"And then a sniper on a rooftop starts shooting and . . ." She shrugged. "People die."

"Oh, Liza." Mercy looked as if she'd start crying again.

Liza hoped that wouldn't happen, because she didn't think she could keep from crying, too, and her eyes hurt too much. "It happens. I mean, it's combat. A war zone. Shit happens."

"That's how you recognized the sniper's scope this morning."

"Yeah."

"Who died?"

Liza smiled bitterly. "People I liked. People I loved. People I'd never met before that day. *People died* and I couldn't save them. I have to live with that, every goddamn day. So please, *please*, do not make me have to mourn you, too."

Mercy exhaled. "I don't want you to have to mourn anyone. But something has to give, Liza. We can't go on like this forever."

"Don't do anything impulsive. Can you at least promise me that?"

Mercy nodded. "I can promise you that."

Liza's heart settled. "Thank you." Forcing a grin, she rose from her dining room table. "You wanna watch TV until Rafe comes back? I've been bingeing old *Amazing Race* episodes."

Mercy put the lid on the ice cream. "That sounds really nice."

‖ YUBA CITY, CALIFORNIA
WEDNESDAY, MAY 24, 8:15 P.M.

DJ crept through the semidarkness of Mrs. Ellis's house, patting his pocket for the tenth time. Yes, the used syringe and empty vial were there. No, he hadn't left them behind.

He'd watched the surveillance feed from the cameras that Kowalski had mounted throughout the old woman's house until he'd seen her get into bed with a novel to read, then had donned his leather gloves and broken in through her back door. He'd be fixing that before he left her house, along with covering the cameras.

She was dead. He'd stayed to make sure, ignoring the tug of remorse at the sight of her facial muscles going slack, her mouth falling open. She'd been a pain in his ass, but she had baked the most amazing cherry pies.

No more pies, he thought with a silent sigh. He'd watched the camera feed, mouth watering, as she'd filled three plastic containers with cookies and taken two pies from the oven to cool.

He paused now as he passed the pies in the kitchen, his stomach growling loudly. His name was written on one of the pie pans, and he was tempted to take it, but he left all the baked goods behind. He wouldn't do anything that might alert investigators to an intruder in her home. He wasn't so certain the ME would buy that she'd had a heart attack.

The needle had left a mark on the inside of her elbow. It might get missed in the crepey folds of her skin. But if it didn't? He wanted nothing to point to him.

No more pies, he thought again, stifling a sigh as he picked up the cordless phone. He'd reviewed the video of her talking on the phone the night before, the conversation in which she'd called him "weird and antisocial." She'd picked up the receiver of the ancient phone in the living room and begun speaking, so it had been an incoming call.

He pulled up the call log, then took out his own cell phone to take a photo of the numbers. He hadn't used his cell since he'd left Eden, but the sat phone didn't have a camera. He was about to slide his phone back into his pocket when he saw the missed calls.

Ten missed calls, all in the last two hours. *What the actual fuck?*

The only person alive who had this number was Pastor, and he had no way of accessing a signal. Not in the caves. If he'd climbed high enough on the mountain, he might have, but the old man wasn't as spry as he used to be.

Something had to be wrong. *Dammit.*

Heart hammering, he put his cell phone away. If Pastor had access to a signal, he might have access to the Internet. If that happened, and he saw a story about Mercy Callahan?

"Fucking hell," he hissed quietly.

Frowning, he stared at the tools he'd left at the kitchen door. He needed to fix the damn lock, but he also needed to find out what was wrong in Eden.

He took a breath, forcing himself to think logically. Kowalski didn't want any suspicion on this job, and he was the biggest threat.

Decision made. He quickly added wood putty to the door frame he'd splintered when he'd forced the lock. It needed to set for an hour before sanding, so he left the door slightly askew and slipped back into his own house.

His hands were trembling as he hit the notification for the first voice mail, then blinked in surprise when it wasn't Pastor's voice.

It was Sister Coleen, the healer. She was the only person outside of the Founding Elders who knew about their ability to stay connected with the outside world. She was the primary user of the desktop computer, researching ways to treat the people of Eden.

Of course, sometimes there was no treatment. Cancer, for example. The community prayed over the patient, but in all cases, they died. The Internet was useful for setting broken bones and treating mild coughs and colds. At least they hadn't had to deal with the flu. Being isolated from the outside world did have its benefits.

"DJ?" Coleen sounded breathless and scared. "Please call me. I've got Pastor's phone because he's hurt. I need you to call me right away and come back now."

Well, shit. What could have happened to him?

He didn't have to wait long to find out, because his phone buzzed in his hand before he could listen to the next voice mail. "Yeah," he answered tersely.

"Oh, thank God," Coleen said on a relieved exhale. "You finally picked up. I was afraid this thing didn't work."

"What's happened?"

"Pastor fell. He was above the cave entrance and it was raining. He must've slipped. He fell down some rocks. He's in a lot of pain."

"What's wrong with him? Exactly?"

"Broken ribs, a broken arm, a badly broken leg, and probably a torn-up knee. And a concussion. He hit his head when he fell. He's been in and out of consciousness all day. I found his phone in his pocket and hid it away so the others wouldn't see. One of the times he came to, he told me to climb the mountain until I got a signal, so I did. I've been here for two hours, waiting for you to answer."

The last sentence was said in a slightly accusatory way, but DJ let it go. Coleen was only in her fifties, but she had a bad knee and the climb couldn't have been easy for her.

"What do you want me to do about it?" he asked cautiously.

She hesitated. "He needs a hospital with real doctors."

"The community won't like that. They'll ask why he gets special treatment."

"He's Pastor," Coleen said, as if that explained everything. In a way it did. Pastor was like a god in the community's eyes. "I've had a few of the men privately ask me if we can take him to the city. They're worried that the government will find him and force him to reveal our location, but they realize he needs appropriate care."

"Who asked you this?" DJ pressed.

"Joshua and Isaac were the most insistent. They're worried that the community will implode without Pastor."

It was fair. Pastor held Eden together. "Is anyone saying he shouldn't go to a doctor?"

"Not out loud where anyone can hear. I noticed that a few members were scowling at the discussion of outside medical help for him. Mostly those whose family members have died. But they won't fight it publicly."

"Can't we just see if he improves on his own?"

She was quiet for a moment. "He has broken bones. And I think he's got internal bleeding. I don't have the equipment or training to know for sure, but . . . I don't think he's going to magically get better, DJ."

No, he wanted to scream. He didn't have time for this now. He needed to kill Mercy Callahan and Gideon Reynolds.

Although if Pastor died, it wouldn't matter. Especially if DJ managed to get him to cough up the bank account passwords first.

Suddenly the situation looked brighter. "What was he doing when he fell?"

"He'd gone to call his banker. He said that he needed to check the accounts."

It was how Pastor normally managed financial transactions. He would either e-mail or call his banker to check balances. He never logged on to the account himself. If he had, DJ could have tracked his keystrokes long ago. But the bastard was a wily old fucker.

The wily old fucker just might have met his end, though. "I'll be there as soon as I can. Get back to Pastor and make sure he's comfortable and not so out of it that he spills secrets."

"I will. Thank you."

He ended the call, realizing that her thanks were heartfelt. After having three husbands die over the last thirty years—two of natural causes, and McPhearson, who'd been murdered—she'd been married to Pastor for over a decade.

DJ wondered if she genuinely loved the man.

DJ did not. Pastor feigned amiability and exuded competence. Under all the charisma, though, lay a snake.

DJ knew that Pastor had instructed Ephraim to kill people who'd spoken out against Eden's leadership. It was always done in a way to make it look like an accident. Sometimes they'd "fallen" or, more frequently, they'd "wandered" too far from the compound and were "mauled by wolves or bears."

Ephraim had enjoyed his job as Eden's enforcer. A lot.

DJ preferred to do his killing with a gun and from far enough away to escape if need be, but a pillow over Pastor's face while they were en route to the hospital would also work.

He set his cell phone aside and called Kowalski on the sat phone.

"Yeah?" Kowalski barked over voices in the background. "This better be important."

"Daddy! Daddy!" A little boy's voice came through the phone.

"Just a minute," Kowalski said, his tone much gentler. "Daddy needs to take this call. Go wait with your mother. I'll be right there." A second later his demeanor was surly again. "What?"

"There's been an accident back home."

"What kind of accident?" Kowalski asked coolly.

"My father took a fall. He needs a doctor." DJ managed to call Pastor his father without a snarl. The man had taken him in when he was barely nine years old, even though Waylon had still been alive. Marcia, Pastor's wife, had died, along with their children, and he'd decided that DJ would be his next heir.

DJ always wondered why his biological father had gone along with it, but had figured that Pastor held something incriminating over Waylon's head. All of Eden's founders had nasty skeletons in their closets.

"Can't somebody else take him?" Kowalski demanded. "You have a crop to harvest."

The grow houses. *Shit.* Kowalski was right about that. Kowalski would send a few of his guys to help, but the responsibility was DJ's. His mind searched for a solution. "The doctor I need to use is in Santa Rosa. I can drive back and forth. It'll be no problem."

"What's the doctor's name?" Kowalski asked suspiciously, as if DJ had made it up.

Like I'd lie to Kowalski. Well, yeah, he would. He had. So he supposed Kowalski had a right to be suspicious.

"Burkett." The man had provided meds whenever Coleen had requested something specific.

Kowalski hummed, amused. "Jason Burkett?"

DJ's internal alarms began to scream. "Yes. Why?"

"Nothing. Just good luck with getting in touch with him. Not so sure that he's getting good cell reception where he's at right now."

DJ blinked. "You know Burkett?"

"Not personally. He was all over the news a month ago. He was murdered in his home. Neck snapped like a twig. What's *really* interesting, though, is that would have been less than twenty-four hours before you were shot."

"Do they know who killed him?" DJ asked tightly, because he was pretty sure he knew.

"Some guy named Harry Franklin, who also went by Ephraim Burton."

Fucking hell. DJ hadn't realized that Ephraim had killed the man. *Fucking Ephraim.*

"Okay, then. I'm going to need to find another doctor."

"There's the Yellow Pages," Kowalski offered with faux helpfulness.

"You know that's not an option," DJ growled. "We live off the grid for a reason."

"Which I'd love to hear more about," Kowalski practically purred.

"It's . . . it's not my story to tell."

"Bullshit," the man murmured. "Bull. Shit. But your story can wait. I'm willing to help you with another doctor."

DJ bit his tongue, because he wanted to tell Kowalski to go to hell. "I think we'll be okay."

Because he didn't actually *need* to take Pastor to a doctor. He just needed Eden to think that he was. Pastor needed to stay alive long enough to give him the account information. Once he got the passwords, he'd take Pastor's body back to Eden, lamenting that he hadn't made it.

"Fine," Kowalski agreed affably. "Let me know if you change your mind."

I won't. "Of course," he lied.

"Uh, before you hang up, did you take care of that small matter we discussed?"

Mrs. Ellis. "Yes."

"Then I guess I'll see you after you've gotten your father to a hospital."

The call ended abruptly and DJ let his head fall forward, suddenly weary. But he didn't have time to be weary. He had things to do before leaving for Eden.

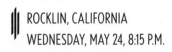

ROCKLIN, CALIFORNIA
WEDNESDAY, MAY 24, 8:15 P.M.

Rafe tapped his notepad with a pen. "I'm sure you know everything I'm about to tell you."

"Maybe, maybe not. What do you know?" Tom couldn't feed Rafe information, but he could confirm what the man had discovered.

"I started with Terminal Island, where Pastor and Waylon met and where Edward McPhearson came after he was arrested for his first bank heist. It was after the second bank robbery that he hid in Eden. When they met in prison, McPhearson was Aubrey Franklin and Pastor was Benton Travis."

"Right." Tom hoped Rafe's review would at least trigger a new approach. "Keep going."

"Waylon was Pastor's protector in prison, but McPhearson also saved Pastor's life once and this seems to have cemented their friendship. Marcia came along later. She was part of a prison reform movement and connected with Waylon there. The visitation records show that Marcia visited Waylon every two weeks without fail."

"She was a devoted girlfriend," Tom noted.

"Who became a devoted wife. They got married as soon as Waylon was released."

Tom had also found the marriage license—and the divorce decree. "And divorced him shortly thereafter. McPhearson didn't get out for a few more years."

"So we're really going to do this dance? Me telling you what you already know?"

"You might be able to fill in some blanks."

"I doubt it," Rafe muttered. "Pastor changed his name a few months after his release and married Marcia himself."

"As soon as the ink on her divorce was dry," Tom commented.

Rafe nodded. "I saw that. It looks like she divorced Waylon so that she could marry Pastor. Maybe for love? Or maybe to help perpetrate their church scam. Pastor was born Benton Travis, but changed it to Herbert Hampton and applied to be the pastor of a small church outside L.A. He fabricated the backstory that he was a preacher, complete with phony ordination certificate and seminary diplomas." He glanced up from his notepad. "All of this was in the newspaper because a decade later he was discovered to have lied about everything and embezzled tens of thousands from his parishioners."

"Helluva guy."

Rafe turned the page in his notepad. "Amos provided a list of the parishioners who sold everything and joined Pastor in Eden. I assume you have this as well."

"I do. He told me which ones had died over the last thirty years. It was most of the original members, because most of the people who followed Pastor from the L.A. church after the financial scandal were already retired thirty years ago. Pastor picked the right congregation to fleece."

All of the parishioners had had money, some more than others. When they'd sold their land and cars and belongings, then signed the proceeds over to Pastor, it had been the start of the Eden nest egg that had grown into fifty million dollars.

"I talked to a few of the L.A. church members who didn't follow Pastor," Rafe said. "They still hate him, thirty years later."

"It was a huge breach of trust," Tom agreed. "They were betrayed by their spiritual leader. But at least they weren't also fleeced out of their savings and land."

"True." Rafe flipped a few pages in the notebook. "People in the church remembered Waylon. He did handyman-type work for the church and for Pastor personally. Most of the congregation was afraid of him because of his tattoos and his appearance. But Pastor looked like a college professor and was very charming." He looked up from the notebook. "Almost every person used that word. 'Charming.'"

"Charisma is important for cult leaders," Tom said dryly. "After sociopathy and narcissism."

Rafe scowled. "And plain old evil."

"In Pastor's case? Yes, definitely."

Rafe flipped a few more pages in his notebook. "I've been looking for Pastor's wife, Marcia, and the kids—who were named Bernice and Boaz. I found their birth certificates."

This surprised Tom. "Why? Amos said they were dead. Gideon said they were dead. They both saw their bodies and . . ." *Oh.*

Waylon had brought back the bodies of Pastor's wife and twins after they'd fallen into a ravine, but the remains had been so decomposed that they were unrecognizable.

Waylon had also brought back a body—also unrecognizable— claiming it was Gideon's.

"You think that Pastor's wife and kids escaped like Gideon and Mercy did," Tom murmured.

Rafe lifted a brow. "He shoots, he scores!"

Tom was still reeling. Why hadn't he thought of this himself? "What have you found?"

"Nothing. It was easier to become someone else twenty-five years ago," Rafe commented.

"It was easier even twenty years ago," Tom said, nodding when Rafe's gaze immediately met his. "My father was an abusive sonofabitch who beat my mother and physically abused me as well. My mother tried to escape several times, but he kept finding her."

Rafe looked surprised. "I thought your father was an NBA star turned history professor."

Tom smiled. "Max Hunter is my stepfather, and yeah, that's him. But my biological father was . . . well, he was a murdering bastard. My mother finally escaped after he tossed her down the stairs and broke her back."

"Oh my God," Rafe whispered. "Is she all right now?"

"Yeah. Mom is amazing. She knew he'd kill her if she stayed and that I'd be left alone with him. She had to go to rehab for her back, and made friends with one of the nurses there. The woman slipped her the name of a shelter in Chicago that helped women start over, find new identities. So Mom did that. She became Caroline Stewart and I became Tom."

"What was your name before?"

Tom's smile faded. "Robbie Winters. Mom was Mary Grace and the sonofabitch we lived with was Rob Winters." Old hatred rose to burn in his gut, and he had to draw a deep breath before burying it back down where it never seemed to die. "My mother got her name off a gravestone in St. Louis. The shelter where we hid got us the necessary documents."

"So you used fake social security numbers?"

"We did—until Rob Winters went to prison. Then we legally changed our names and took our old socials back."

"Rob Winters," Rafe said hesitantly. "Is he still in prison?"

"No." And the single word gave him immense satisfaction. "He was killed soon after he was incarcerated. Got shanked in the shower. News got around that he'd been a very dirty cop."

"Good," Rafe said simply. "I'm glad."

"Me too."

"Does Liza know?"

Tom nodded. "My mom's best friend is a woman named Dana Buchanan. Dana ran the shelter where we hunkered down for quite a while. She got us IDs and helped us start a new life."

"You have good people in your life," Rafe said.

"Yeah. I think your mother would love my mom and Dana. Anyway, Liza . . . You know about her background, right? How her sister was murdered?"

Rafe nodded sheepishly. "My mom and I looked her up."

"Somehow, I'm not surprised. Well, after Liza's sister's killer was caught, she was all alone and still only seventeen. Dana and my mom took her in. Dana and her husband Ethan have been her primary family all these years. But then she joined the army to pay for school."

Which still annoyed the hell out of him.

"And you went on to the NBA."

"I did," Tom said.

"So . . . I've been wondering. How *did* you get from the NBA to the FBI?"

"I was recruited during college. Do you know what DEF CON is? The hacker conference?"

"I've heard of it. It's in Vegas, right? I read that they're super paranoid about attendance. No registration. You just show up with cash, so there are no records. The FBI recruited you there?"

"They did. The FBI would try to infiltrate the con so that they could either arrest the criminal hackers or recruit the 'good' ones. They wanted me to work for them then, but I was already on the watch list for the NBA draft. I told them to give me a few years. That I wanted to play for a while, but I'd join when I was ready." He'd done some contract work for the FBI in the off-season to keep his hand in, but that wasn't something he could talk about with Rafe.

"What prompted you to be ready?"

The sorrow returned, and with it all the guilt that still plagued him. "I was at the end of my contract with the league. Tory and I talked about me retiring at the end of the season."

"Then you could go public and she could keep her job."

"Exactly. We wanted to go public. I still wasn't sure if I was ready to make the leap, though. I had a few good years left in me. But then she was taken and . . ." He shrugged. "I couldn't focus."

"You'd been a secret, so you couldn't grieve openly."

Tom nodded, grateful that Rafe understood. "I got hurt again, this time worse. It was kind of like a sign, I guess. I called my Bureau recruiter, asked if there was room in the next training class at Quantico. He said if I got my knee in shape, then yes. So I opted out of my contract, took an early retirement, then did what I had to for my knee. I made it to Quantico for the August class and graduated in December, right before Christmas, then started here in January."

"Liza was discharged from the army about that same time, wasn't she?"

"She was. She got home on Christmas Day. It was like . . . I don't know . . . almost fate that we ended up in the same place after only seeing each other on Skype all those years."

Rafe looked away for a few seconds. When he looked back, his expression was tentative. "You and Liza . . . Were you ever—"

"No," Tom interrupted. "No. She was seventeen, for God's sake."

"Well, *then* she was," Rafe allowed. "She's certainly not seventeen now."

Tom found himself taking a mental step back. "I was with Tory."

"But Tory's gone," Rafe said gently. "Liza's right here."

He knew that. Goddammit, he *knew* that.

Tom slid from the stool and grabbed the plate of untouched cheese. He slammed a few drawers before finding the plastic wrap and covering the plate. After shoving it into the fridge, he felt calm enough to face Rafe. "It's only been a year," he said stiffly. *Actually, fourteen months, nineteen days, and two hours. Our baby would have been seven months old by now.* "So no. Whatever you're suggesting . . . no."

Rafe sighed. "I'm sorry. I should have kept my mouth shut."

"Yeah, you should have. I think Mercy might be wanting to get home."

Rafe closed his notebook. "I can take a hint, Tom. We can compare more notes later."

"*Eden* notes."

"That too," Rafe murmured. "I'll see you later." He started for the door, then turned. "Life is short, Tom. If you find someone who makes you happy, don't let society tell you how long is 'proper' to wait. That someone may move on, and then you'll be alone."

Tom didn't answer. He didn't think he could. He watched Rafe leave, then reached for the beer he'd set aside. It was warm now. He really wanted to throw the bottle against the wall, but curbed his temper.

His father would have thrown the bottle. Rob Winters. Not Max Hunter. Never Max.

Eyes burning, he reached into one of the cabinets for the bottle of Jack he kept for company. He'd never been much of a drinker, because Winters had been a vicious drunk. But tonight he needed a little something to settle his nerves.

He poured himself two fingers' worth and tossed it back, wincing at the burn. Then he picked up his phone and hit the first number on his speed dial. It was answered on the first ring.

"Tom? Hey, honey. How are you?"

Tom's throat burned, but not from the whiskey. He blinked back the tears and drew a huge breath. "Hey, Mom. I'm doing okay. I just called to see how everyone is back home."

His mother was quiet. "We're fine, sweetheart. The kids are in bed and I'm making coffee."

Tom winced at the time. "I'm sorry, Mom. I forgot about the time zones." It was two hours later in Chicago.

"Silly boy. I always have time to talk to you." He heard the clink of mugs and the hiss of the coffee maker and pictured her in her kitchen, all smiles and love and . . . home. "How is Liza?"

He hesitated for just a heartbeat. "She's okay."

His mother's hesitation was five heartbeats. "That's good. Give me a minute, I'm taking my coffee into the living room." He heard the quiet creak of the rocking chair where she loved to sit and read and wished he could go home. Just for a few hours. "Okay. Tell me everything."

Oh no. He wasn't telling her anything. "I've been busy at work, and you know I can't talk about that. Tell me how everyone is doing there. Is Gracie still mooning after that boy?" His younger sister was nine years old and currently in love with a boy in her class.

His mother's chuckle was soothing. "Oh, that's a story and a half. How long do you have?"

"As much time as you'll give me."

This time her hesitation was longer, her voice softer. Warmer. Like a blanket right out of the dryer. "Well, get comfortable, son, and I'll tell you a story."

Tom did as he was told, grabbing another beer before settling into the corner of the sofa. Without thinking, he pulled an afghan over himself, flinching when Liza's scent hit his nose. She'd crocheted the damn thing and liked to cuddle in it when she came over to watch TV. Rafe's words pinged around in his head and he tightened his jaw.

I'm not ready. Even if she were interested, I'm not ready. He contemplated switching out Liza's afghan for the throw on the back of the love seat. It was within his reach, the love seat and the sofa arranged in an L. He only had to stretch a little to the left to grab it. But he didn't.

Instead he pulled Liza's afghan closer, inhaling her scent. "Okay, Mom. I'm ready." Again he flinched, this time at the words that had fallen from his mouth. "What's up with Gracie?"

YUBA CITY, CALIFORNIA
WEDNESDAY, MAY 24, 8:40 P.M.

DJ did a final sweep of the house, looking for anything that might be incriminating in case the ME suspected foul play and the cops came sniffing around.

He'd already swept the basement twice. It smelled like weed, but there wasn't even a leaf on the floor and Kowalski had already cleared out all of the product that DJ had harvested before he'd been shot. He'd planned to take some of that back to Eden with him and store it in the caves. Their mushroom production had been disrupted with the last two moves in such quick succession, and they'd had no Eden-grown product to sell all winter. DJ had sold most of the pot he'd skimmed from what he owed Kowalski, just to keep revenue coming in.

That money was supposed to have been his. He wasn't supposed to have shared it with Eden. But Pastor had demanded an accounting of their income and DJ hadn't wanted him to see that he'd been siphoning money from the community for years. So he'd dipped into his own stash to keep Eden's coffers full so that Pastor wouldn't go looking.

This room had no product, just DJ's electronics. He packed up his laptop and the hard drives he'd collected over the years. He knew the Feds could find stuff, even on wiped hard drives. So he'd never thrown anything away.

He'd learned his way around computers on the old machines. His father had never been interested in the Internet. Had never understood what it could do.

DJ had immediately seen the benefits—some for Eden, but mostly for himself. Once Waylon was dead and DJ was in charge of supply runs, he'd met Kowalski, who'd taught him how to use software, how to manipulate photographs, how to use the surface web to sell Eden's quilts and sundries, and, importantly, how to use the dark web to sell the drugs they grew.

Once all of his old laptops were boxed up, he turned to the printers. There was no way he was leaving them. Cops could get copies of things a printer had produced by checking the device's memory. If DJ was suspected in Mrs. Ellis's death by virtue of being her "weird and antisocial" neighbor, the cops could come sniffing.

If the cops got evidence from his electronics, Kowalski would drop him like a hot potato. DJ didn't hold it against the man. He'd do the very same thing. Business was business, after all.

DJ loaded everything into his truck and took a last look at his house before driving away. He didn't think he'd be coming back. Even if Mrs. Ellis's death was assumed to be from natural causes, Kowalski had wired his house with cameras. He had no intention of allowing the dealer to monitor his every move.

He got enough of that from Pastor.

NINE

From her front window, Liza watched Rafe sheltering Mercy with his body until she was safely in his Subaru. Something needed to give before Mercy broke. Liza had seen soldiers break under the stress, and Mercy wasn't too far from that point.

They needed a distraction, something that would take Mercy's mind off the fact that DJ was out there without allowing her to lower her guard. Putting the leftovers that Irina had sent into the oven, Liza sat at the counter and dialed a known compatriot.

"Liza!" Daisy Dawson sounded chipper as always.

"Hi, Daisy. I hope I'm not calling too late. I know you get up early for work." Daisy was the cohost of a morning radio show, and her bedtime was surely approaching.

"It's fine." She laughed softly, a deep husky sound for which she was famous. "Even if you'd woken me up it would be fine. You saved Mercy's life today. Gideon and I are grateful."

Daisy was Gideon Reynolds's girlfriend and had inadvertently started the official investigation into Eden when she'd grabbed a locket from the neck of a killer who'd been trying to drag her away. Through the investigation, she and Gideon had connected.

"I did what any of you would have done."

"We're still grateful. What's up, Liza?"

That Daisy got to the point wasn't a surprise. Their friendship was a cordial one, but not on the same level as Liza and Mercy's. "It's Mercy."

"What's wrong? Has DJ tried again?"

"No, it's nothing physical," Liza assured her. "This whole situation is starting to get to her." She would not share Mercy's desire to make herself bait. That had been said in confidence. "I know Tom got a few leads today, but everything is still moving too slowly, and Mercy's going stir-crazy. I was hoping you'd have ideas about a distraction, something she can do that will make her feel like she's still got some control over this situation."

"Like what?" Daisy asked, curious. "A hobby?"

"I think Mercy's too intense for that right now. I was thinking more in line with something she can do to contribute to the search for Eden or to prepare for when the people there are finally rescued. Channeling her energy into a positive endeavor might help her right now."

Daisy hummed thoughtfully. "Like I'm doing with the escapees."

Liza's brows shot up in surprise. "What escapees?"

"Well, you know about the Eden tattoos, right?"

"Yes. Boys get them on their thirteenth birthdays. They're the official Eden symbol, the children kneeling beneath an olive tree, all beneath the wings of an angel with a flaming sword."

"Exactly. I started searching for other people with this tattoo on Instagram, looking for keywords like 'olive tree,' 'children praying,' and 'angel with flaming sword.'"

Liza was intrigued. "Oh, wow. Did you find anything?"

"I did. Initially I found two. One was a close replica. A college kid had copied it from his lover—an escapee who'd taken his own life.

That shook Mercy up. The second was exact—and belonged to an escapee both Mercy and Gideon had known. His Eden tattoo had been done in Eden on his thirteenth birthday, but he'd added a tat of a dragon breathing fire, like it was going to destroy it. His name was Judah."

Liza winced. "Was?"

Daisy sighed. "He was killed in a car accident last year. I haven't told Mercy yet. She's been so sad, I didn't want to add to it. Gideon took it hard enough."

Liza understood that. "You said you 'initially' found two tattoos. Did you find more?"

"One more, another exact copy, but this one was done by the artist who posted it. The client who got the tattoo isn't from Eden, as he'd have gotten it there, but he's got to know someone who escaped. I found the tattoo artist on Instagram and we exchanged a few e-mails, but then he ghosted me after the Feds visited him at the studio where he worked. He's taken down his Instagram page, so whatever happened, it rattled him. Artists use Instagram to advertise."

"Do you know where this guy is located? What's his name?"

"He was in San Jose. His name is Sergio Iglesias. He might have just changed studios."

"But he probably wouldn't have taken down his Instagram if he only moved. Does he have a police record?"

"No, but a lot of people get nervous when the Feds show up. They never actually got to talk to him. He skipped out the back door. He's gone under, according to Gideon. He got the information from Tom, who got it from someone else because he wasn't working that part of the case, but I'm not supposed to know any of that."

Liza's chest warmed. Tom was a Dudley Do-Right, a stickler for procedure, but he had a huge heart. He was capable of bending rules if necessary to help someone. "I won't tell anyone."

Daisy chuckled. "I would guess not, considering it would hurt your guy more than mine."

Not my guy. Roughly, she cleared her throat. "I don't want to get *anyone* in trouble." She thought she'd sounded pretty upbeat, but Daisy's extended silence said that she had not.

"I'm sorry, Liza. I just figured—"

"It's all right. Now," Liza said briskly, "back to the tattoo artist, Sergio Iglesias. The Feds haven't been able to get any whiff of where he went?"

"None. I think the FBI backburnered their search because they figured that an adult who'd gotten an Eden tattoo wasn't an actual escapee. And even if they know an escapee, that person won't be able to give them a current location, because Eden moves around too much."

Liza started up her laptop. "I keep thinking about the guy's Instagram account. If he continues tattooing, he'll need one. When did he take his Instagram down?"

"Three weeks ago. The day after he got a visit from the Feds."

"Did the Feds go looking for him? At his home, I mean."

"I don't know." She hesitated. "You'd have to ask Tom that question."

Which I'm not going to do. "Can you send me the screenshots you took of his old page?"

"Sure, but tell me what you're thinking, because I'm dying here."

"What if Iglesias started up a new Instagram account? If it were me, I'd post a few of my most popular photos under a different name."

"Oh." Daisy sounded impressed. "I'm kicking myself for not thinking of that."

"Fresh eyes help. What were you planning to ask this guy if he hadn't ghosted?"

"The name of the person who got the Eden tattoo. They have to have *known* an escapee, because the design is an exact replica. It's far too detailed to be a coincidence."

"And when you found the escapee?"

"I'd make sure they were all right, because Gideon and Mercy sure aren't. Maybe they can support each other, because none of us really knows what they went through. But I'd also ask how they got out and where their Eden was located. I'm frustrated that the FBI doesn't seem interested in doing any of this."

"I agree." That the FBI wasn't looking for the man was both frustrating and puzzling. "Look, it's late and you need to go to sleep. I'm going to do some searching online and I'll let you know what I find."

"You promise? You won't try to go alone if you do find him?"

"No, I won't go alone. I promise."

But she would go. Everyone else was either personally known to Eden—like Gideon, Mercy, Amos, and Abigail—or had been featured in the news stories about Ephraim's murder spree.

Liza had the only face that nobody would know. And she liked tattoos.

She looked down at the rose and musical note twined together and inked over her heart. The tattoo had given her ease. It had made remembrance of her family a physical part of her. A visible reminder that she'd been loved and had loved in return.

She had a second tattoo that no one had ever seen. It covered the scar on her hip, the remnants of that awful day when her unit had been broken apart. It hadn't been for comfort. She'd wanted to hide her scar, even from herself, out of guilt. But now she wanted comfort.

She closed Daisy's e-mail and stared at the desktop image on her screen. Arrayed in front of a Humvee, twelve people smiled at the camera. All were in uniform, all held their weapons.

They'd all been happy that day. *Even me.*

The next day, only five of the twelve still lived. *We weren't happy anymore.* But they had been once, which was why she'd kept this photo to remember her military family. Even in her nightmares about the day they'd died, she knew they'd protected one another with their lives.

Now she'd been invited into a new family. She'd protect them as well. Especially Mercy, who at times reminded her so much of her sister that it hurt Liza's heart.

She took one last look at the photo of the twelve smiling faces. They deserved permanent remembrance. She was going to find Sergio Iglesias. For Mercy. *And for myself.*

Because she was considering a new tattoo.

EDEN, CALIFORNIA
THURSDAY, MAY 25, 12:45 A.M.

DJ parked the truck close to the cave entrance. There was a rocky path that many of their members had found difficult to climb, but they were all inside the network of caves now with no need to leave.

Unless they got hurt. *Way to go, Pastor,* DJ thought with a sneer.

He found Coleen waiting at the entrance. "I'm so glad you're back," she said in relief.

"How is he?" DJ asked, because he didn't want the old man dead just yet.

"Conscious," Coleen replied. "He's talking, but he's in a lot of pain." She winced. "He's babbled a little, but nothing I couldn't explain away."

"Good. Is he ready to go?" It was then that DJ spied the small bag leaning against the cave wall. "Is that his bag?"

"No, it's mine." Coleen met his gaze directly. "I'm going with you."

DJ laughed and it wasn't a nice sound. "No, you're not."

"I am. Pastor wants me there. The community wants me to go with him."

DJ stopped laughing. "You're staying. I outrank you."

"Pastor outranks us all. The members will be displeased if he's not getting the best care."

Oh, you fucking little bitch. "Are you threatening me?" he asked softly. Menacingly.

She paled. "No. I'm letting you know that the community knows Pastor has asked me to come with him. He hasn't left the confines of the compound for nearly ten years, except when we move. This last move was especially hard on him."

Because the old man had needed to pull his own weight for a change. Ephraim was dead, and DJ had been unconscious when they'd arrived in the caves the month before.

"He's in pain and frightened, DJ. Let him have his way in this."

DJ seethed. When he killed Pastor, he'd have to kill her, too. He'd make sure it was a car accident, so that their deaths could be explained away.

The community might miss their healer, but Coleen was just a woman. Utterly replaceable. She was not meant to tell him what to do. None of the women were.

None of the men, either. Between Pastor and Kowalski, he'd about had it with people telling him what to do.

"Fine," he snapped. "Be ready to leave in five minutes." He stalked to Pastor's quarters, opening the makeshift door without knocking. Pastor got a piece of plywood to give him privacy. Most of the members had only a curtain. Some didn't have that much.

"Close the door," Pastor said weakly.

DJ obeyed, startled at the old man's appearance. He was . . . old. Frail, even. "How did you fall?" he asked, suddenly suspicious. "Did someone push you?"

"No. I was coming down the mountain. I had to climb to get a signal for my cell phone. I had to call my banker. You wouldn't set the dish up for me to e-mail him, so I had no choice."

DJ scowled. "So did you talk to your banker?"

Pastor nodded absently. "I'll call him again to make a financial transfer to whatever hospital you're taking me to."

And then DJ would learn the access code. He kept his voice calm, even though he wanted to shout with excitement. "All right."

"Where are you taking me?"

Straight to hell, motherfucker. "I'm not sure yet. I need to find a doctor who'll take cash."

"My banker has my personal papers."

DJ blinked. "What?"

Pastor struggled to open his eyes. "Specifically my will that states you are my heir."

Yes. He bowed his head so that Pastor couldn't see his glee. "I see."

Pastor huffed, a weary, sick little sound. "I'm sure you think you do, but you'd be mistaken. If I don't show up at a hospital by morning, my banker is instructed to mail all of the sealed envelopes in his possession. I send him a new one every year detailing everyone's personal sins. Including yours. He also knows to place my money in a series of trusts if I'm declared missing or dead. One trust is for the people of Eden. One is for you. You will get a stipend once a year."

Motherfucker. "I see," DJ said levelly. Because he did. The old man was ever cagey. "You said a series of trusts. Are there more?"

"Yes. One goes to my wives. One to my banker."

"Your banker gets a trust?"

"He's served me well." Pastor coughed, moaning at the resulting pain. "The point is, I better show up at a hospital. If I don't, you'd better hope it was an accident and we *all* died, otherwise your face will be on an FBI wanted poster."

Too late, asshole. The FBI already had his prints. If there was camera surveillance in the office building he'd used Wednesday morning, his face was now known to the Feds as well.

Then a detail popped up, distracting him. "Wait. How does your banker know all of this?"

"I told Coleen to call him. Gave her a onetime code."

"Where are the other codes?"

A crooked smile. "In my head. Better hope I wake up from surgery, or they die with me."

And then the money would be divided and put into trust. He had killed Ephraim in part to keep from having to share that money with anyone. Unless he could find another way, he'd still be sharing it. Despite being bruised and bloody and frail from his fall, Pastor looked smug.

It took every ounce of DJ's self-control not to ball his hands into fists and beat the fucker into a bloody pulp. Instead DJ breathed until he could be sure his voice was steady. "Is that why you want Coleen to come with us? To make sure I don't do anything—"

"Evil?" Pastor interrupted with a laugh that sounded more like a geriatric bark. "I don't need to give you any reason, but if you must have one, then yes, that is why. When do we leave?"

DJ gritted his teeth. "As soon as you're ready. I'll ask some of the men to carry you down to the truck. I need to make arrangements for a hospital."

Pastor closed his eyes. "Good boy."

Not a damn boy. Not anymore. He had been once, before Pastor had given him to Edward McPhearson. DJ had been his apprentice. Edward had been a brutal master. Once Edward was dead, McPhearson no longer owned him. But Pastor still did. Not sexually, but DJ was owned.

And he still owns me.

Because Pastor knew that the lure of fifty million dollars was too strong for anyone to ignore.

DJ turned to go. "I'll be waiting at the truck."

ROCKLIN, CALIFORNIA
THURSDAY, MAY 25, 1:15 A.M.

Finding Sergio Iglesias didn't take as long as Liza had thought it would, at least compared to the hours Daisy had spent identifying him to begin with. A week after the Feds visited his old studio, fifteen of Iglesias's photos had appeared on Instagram under the account of Sal Ibarra, the new name allowing Iglesias to continue using his initials as his signature.

According to his profile, Sal Iberra was an artist, located in Monterey. His last location had been San Jose, so he hadn't gone all that far. At least he hadn't skipped the state. Which made her wonder why.

She found her answer in one of the screenshots that Daisy had made of Iglesias's old Instagram account. The photo showed a woman in profile, hands cupping her pregnant stomach. The photo was captioned, *My beautiful wife, Felicidad.* It was originally uploaded six years ago.

"Yes," Liza whispered aloud. Sergio Iglesias had a good reason for staying close by.

Liza knew she had to tell someone what she'd found, but she didn't want the man to feel like he needed to run again. He had a family. Sending him running again seemed cruel.

She'd contact him first. If he had no relevant information, she'd let it go. If he could tell them who had gotten the Eden tattoo, she'd pass that information on to Tom.

On finding the tattoo parlor's website, she was pleased to see that they had an online appointment tool. "Sal Ibarra" had openings the next afternoon. According to Google, Monterey was about a three-hour drive from Sacramento. She requested a three o'clock session.

She could leave after giving Abigail the reading lesson she'd promised and be back before dinnertime. Hopefully with information.

And maybe a new tattoo. She had an idea now of what she'd like.

She cleaned up her dinner dishes, then took her laptop and a spiral notebook up to her bedroom. Pulling on her pj's, she stared at the place on the bed where Tom had so carefully perched that afternoon.

It hadn't been the first time he'd come to her room. He'd brought her chocolate once when she'd had cramps so bad that she couldn't get out of bed. Another time he'd brought her some of Irina's chicken soup when she'd had a cold. And more than once he'd come crashing through her door when he'd heard her scream while having a nightmare.

The nightmare. The one where all of her friends bled out while she fruitlessly tried to save them. She'd woken those nights to find herself in Tom's strong arms, his murmurs in her ear. He'd asked her to talk to him about the nightmares, but she hadn't wanted to and he hadn't pushed. At the time she'd been relieved.

Now she wished he'd pushed. She could have told him about Fritz. About how she'd married him. About how she hadn't loved him like she should have. How Fritz had been a substitute.

At the time she'd worried that it might make Tom think less of her, that maybe he wouldn't want her. Now she wanted him to know. It was wrong for her to keep Fritz a secret. He'd deserved so much more than that.

She crawled under the blankets, able to hear Tom working. His home office was adjacent to her bedroom. Muted strains of Pavarotti made her smile sadly. Pavarotti was his "thinking music." She'd mentioned once that she could hear it and he'd immediately offered to turn his music down. She'd told him that was ridiculous, that the music soothed her.

Not so much tonight.

She put in earbuds, turned up her Garth Brooks playlist, and opened the spiral notebook to a fresh page. She was no artist, but she had a few ideas about the tattoo she'd like. Sergio did good work, and having left the studio where he'd already built a clientele, he probably needed the money. If he turned her away after learning who she was and what she wanted to know about the Eden tattoo, she'd find another tattooist.

It was time to lay her friends to rest, once and for all.

MCARTHUR, CALIFORNIA
THURSDAY, MAY 25, 1:35 A.M.

DJ scowled at his sat phone, knowing he'd put off calling Kowalski as long as he could. The man would be meeting with customers and suppliers soon. Most of their work was done in the wee hours when most people were asleep.

He hated having to call Kowalski. Hated having to owe the man anything.

Hated having Kowalski know where Pastor was, because he would if they used the doctor he recommended. He did not want Kowalski meeting Pastor and asking him questions, especially now, when the old man wasn't firing on all cylinders.

Gritting his teeth, he dialed Kowalski's number, swallowing a snarl when the man answered, his tone smug. "Changed your mind about the doctor, huh?"

"Yes. My father was hurt worse than I'd been led to believe."

"That's too bad," Kowalski said, his words dripping with mock concern. "The doctor's name is Ralph Arnold. I'll text you his number. Wait a few minutes before calling. I'll have to let him know to expect you. He doesn't take calls from just anyone. He runs a very *private* hospital."

"Thank you." He swallowed the snarl that was crawling out of his throat. "I appreciate this."

"Oh, don't worry. You'll be able to return the favor at some point in the future."

That's what I'm afraid of. "Of course. But . . . what do you mean by 'private' hospital?"

"He's a legit doctor, if that's what you're asking. His patients have one thing in common—the need for privacy. Most of his patients are celebrities looking to avoid the media. Others are . . . like us. People who don't want their DNA falling into the wrong hands. He operated on my knee a few years ago and it's as good as new now."

DJ's phone buzzed with the incoming texted contact information. "I got the doctor's number, thank you. I'll wait to call him. I need to go. Road's dicey here."

Ending the call, he set the phone aside, gripping the wheel with both hands to navigate a hairpin turn. He hated driving this big truck on these curves. He didn't know how drivers of semitrucks did it without careening over the cliff to instant death, but they did, so he could, too.

The pickup in which Waylon had taught him to drive had been a standard Ford F-150. This box truck that he'd stolen from the itinerant farmhand was considerably bigger.

The road evened out after a few minutes, and DJ tapped the doctor's contact information to dial his number.

"Yes?" The voice was deep and musical.

"I'd like to speak to Dr. Ralph Arnold," DJ said.

"Speaking. Is this Mr. Belmont?"

"It is. Can you help my father?"

"I won't know until I see him. But I will see him, as Mr. Kowalski has vouched for you. Head toward the Sacramento airport. When I get your payment, I'll text you the address."

DJ rolled his eyes at the cloak-and-dagger approach. "What is the payment?"

"One hundred thousand."

What the fuck? A hundred thousand *dollars?* DJ opened his mouth, but no words came out.

"Mr. Belmont? Are you still there?"

"Yes." DJ cleared his throat because the word had come out hoarse. "I am."

"Can you afford my services?"

Uppity sonofabitch. "Yes. Of course." Pastor had fifty million bucks. A hundred thou was nothing. He hoped. "If you can text me the transfer instructions, I'll get that underway. It might be a little while. We're still in the mountains and unlikely to have a cell signal."

A short pause. "But you are talking to me."

"This sat phone is my business line. My father will be arranging the payment himself on his cell phone. He is . . . unaware of my business relationship with Mr. Kowalski."

"Oh. I see. Well, that's fine. We won't be revealing any information to him. We'll be focused on fixing what's broken."

"Thank you, Doctor. I'll be wiring the payment as soon as I can."

It was another hour before DJ could safely pull off the road into a gas station. He stuffed the sat phone into his pocket and zipped the pocket closed. He did not want Pastor or Coleen to see it. Looking both ways to ensure that they were alone, he opened one of the back doors.

The old man lay on the floor, eyes closed, his head in Coleen's lap. The healer looked up, her skin even paler than it had been in Eden. She looked a little green. "Are we there?"

"No," DJ replied. "But the curvy parts are over."

"Thank God," she breathed. "Pastor didn't do well. He's thrown up a few times, which is going to dehydrate him. When will we arrive?"

"Not for another three hours, if there's no traffic on the freeway."

She gasped. "Three *hours*? DJ, he's in pain *now*."

"And I'm sorry," DJ said. Even though he really wasn't. "But we can't just take him to a regular hospital. They'll ask for his insurance card and ID. Things are much different now than they were when you entered Eden. It's much harder to fake your identity. Especially when insurance is involved. We don't have insurance cards and they might not treat him without one."

That was probably not true, but DJ wasn't taking any chances. Pastor needed good care, because if he died, the codes died with him.

"I know," Coleen fretted. "I just hate seeing him in pain."

DJ didn't mind at all. "Is he conscious?"

"Yes," Pastor wheezed. "Why?"

"I need you to authorize a transfer from our bank account to the doctor."

Pastor's nod was barely perceptible. "How much?"

"A hundred grand."

Coleen gasped again and Pastor turned his head to glare at DJ. "Are you insane, boy?"

"I am not," DJ said levelly. *Insane or a boy.* "Hospitals are very expensive now."

"Coleen, please give the phone to me. DJ, have the information ready."

DJ took another look around. Luckily, it was early enough that no one was around.

"It's Ben," Pastor said a moment later, and DJ blinked. He'd never heard Pastor called anything but Pastor. Once or twice he'd heard Waylon call him Brother Herbert.

Pastor motioned for DJ to come up into the back of the truck. Drawing his weapon, DJ complied, closing the door. If anyone got nosy, he'd blow their head off and ask questions later.

"No, I'm not fine," Pastor snapped to his banker. "I'm on my way to a private hospital. I need you to wire a hundred grand to the following account ASAP." He listened for a moment, then turned his gaze up to DJ. "He says that a hundred Gs is pretty cheap for private treatment."

The grudging acknowledgment was as close to a "please," "thank you," and "I'm sorry" as Pastor would ever give.

Pastor put the phone on speaker. "DJ, give the man the information."

DJ read the account and routing number aloud. "The doctor's name is Ralph Arnold."

"Good," Pastor muttered. "An American name. Don't want a foreigner working on me."

"But you find a foreigner handling your money acceptable?" the banker asked congenially in lightly accented English. Not for the first time, DJ wondered who this man was and why Pastor trusted him with that much cash.

Pastor's expression chilled at the veiled criticism. "You know I'm not talking about you."

"Of course not," the banker said dryly. "I'll need your authorization code."

Pastor glanced up at DJ before saying, "B-e-B-o-11," into the speaker.

The code. That was *the* code. Short for Bernice-Boaz-11. The names of his dead twins and their age when they died. DJ tried not to let his excitement show, keeping his expression bland.

Inside he was jumping up and down and screaming in triumph. Until Pastor spoke again.

"Delete that code from our approved list. The new code will be the next in the cipher series."

Cipher series? What the hell? The bastard hadn't merely memorized some passwords, DJ realized. He and his banker had some kind of prearranged code. *Meaning I can't break it. Motherfucking sonofabitch.* DJ couldn't contain his glare. *Damn you to hell, old man.*

Pastor's lips twitched. He knew what DJ had assumed and had enjoyed cutting him back down to size.

Once I get that money, you are dead, old man. Dead. And it's going to fucking hurt.

"Understood," the banker replied. "I've sent the wire. It might be a few hours before it goes through."

"That's all right," Pastor said. "Apparently I'm a few hours from this Dr. Arnold. I'll check in again before I go into surgery to ensure the wire transfer was successful."

Pastor ended the call and gave his phone to Coleen, who still sat, looking shocked at the amount of money he'd so casually transferred. It appeared the healer didn't know about the fifty million that Pastor had been hoarding and building for thirty years.

DJ wasn't sure if that was a good thing or a bad thing, but it was certainly something he'd use for his own benefit if he could.

"Water, Coleen." The old man still managed to sound like a pompous king.

"Of course. I'm sorry, Pastor."

"As you should be," the old man muttered, closing his eyes. "Hurry up, boy. Get us there."

"Absolutely," DJ promised. And he'd make sure he hit every damn pothole along the way.

TEN

Hayley missed indoor plumbing. At least at the last Eden site they'd had outhouses. Here in the caves, the toilet was basically a bench with a hole cut into it. They literally peed in the pot that was stuck beneath the hole.

The smell . . . She had to fight not to gag, because if she gagged, she puked. Which just made it all worse. Plus, she didn't know if throwing up might start up her labor.

She didn't think so, but she didn't know. She didn't know because she didn't have access to a damn doctor. Even the healer was gone, having accompanied Pastor to the hospital in the city.

Because, of course, *Pastor* got to go to the hospital. She had to stay here, in a fucking cave.

She was having this baby in a fucking cave. Cameron wasn't coming. Nobody was coming. Nobody could help. She'd considered an escape attempt, but Graham had told her that there was a guard at the entrance—with a rifle. Graham might be able to slip out, but she wouldn't be able to, not as big as she'd become.

I'm going to have this baby and she's going to be taken away from me. To give to Sister Rebecca, the vile whore. *She thinks she's gonna steal* my *baby? No. Not gonna happen.*

Except that she might not have a choice. She needed to think. But all she seemed able to do was sleep, cry, and pee. She caressed her belly. "I'm so sorry, Jellybean," she whispered. "This isn't your fault."

It's not mine, either. She laid the blame of this nightmare directly on her mother's shoulders. If they ever got back to civilization, Hayley was going to have her charged. Because this was kidnapping. This was a crime.

Her ire fizzled, exhaustion retaking her. *This is my new life.* Sniffling back tears, she stepped away from the toilet, pulled the curtain closed, then lifted the lantern to find her way back.

A lantern, goddammit. A real one, not battery powered. It had actual fire inside it. At least most of the caves were wide and had decent airflow throughout. Otherwise, between the fumes from the toilet and the smoke from the lanterns, they'd all suffocate.

"Psst."

Hayley jumped, spinning around, barely holding on to the lantern. "Graham," she hissed. "You scared me to death. What are you doing here?"

He grinned, the flickering light giving him a devilish appearance. "Came to empty the pot. I'm on duty today."

Her stomach roiled. "You did it yesterday." She frowned. "And the day before. Why?" The disgusting jobs were rotated among the younger boys, unless someone was being punished.

"Gets me outside. I can breathe fresh air." Graham leaned closer and whispered, "And search for stuff. And hide other stuff."

Stuff. Like the computer. And the drugs he'd found the day before. Her heart clenched. "You're doing this for me?"

Graham shrugged. "More for Jellybean. Gonna be her favorite uncle."

Hayley's eyes stung. "I love you, Cookie."

His lips curved up. "I know." He hesitated. "You know."

She smiled at him. She did know that he loved her, too. "You need to go back to bed."

"After I dump the pot."

"Gra—," a shrill voice said before cutting away. "Achan," their mother whispered. "Why are you whispering to Magdalena?"

The thief and the whore, Hayley thought, having to close her eyes. She couldn't look at her mother anymore. The bubbling rage was just too much.

"She had to pee," Graham said, somehow hiding his contempt for the woman who'd brought them here. "Because she's pregnant. I'm dumping the pot, because it's my job." He darted into the toilet area, returning with the pot, full and foul. "Do you need to pee in it, Mother?"

Hayley gagged. "Graham. Oh my God, that reeks." Then her head snapped back as her mother slapped her. Hard.

"His *name* is Achan. Your name is Magdalena. You *will* be respectful, and you *will* follow the rules. Do you understand?"

Hayley worked her jaw, tasting blood. "Fuck you," she spat, suddenly not caring who heard.

Her mother gasped, and Graham winced. "She's hormonal," he said. "It's not her fault."

"It most certainly *is* her fault. She had relations with a man who is not her husband. Whatever happens to her is her fault."

Hayley clenched her fists. "Why, you smarmy little bi—"

"Mother," Graham interrupted, taking a step closer to their mother, holding the pot up so that the old bitch took a giant step back. "Let my sister go to bed. She's tired and scared. You had both of us in a hospital, didn't you? You had an epidural and a real doctor. She won't, and she's scared. You would have been, too, don't you think?"

"No. I was fine, and she will be, too. Unless God's will is otherwise."

Hayley took a step back of her own, partly to get away from the pot Graham held and partly so that she wouldn't drop her mother to the cave floor with an uppercut. Cameron had taught her how as part of her self-defense lessons. Fat lot of good those had done her, because she couldn't defend herself now. And if she couldn't defend herself, how could she defend their baby?

Longing for Cameron and a bone-deep sorrow hit her hard. She missed Cameron's mother. The woman had been a true mother to her. Not like the evil sack of shit that was trying to scare her by insinuating it might not be God's will for her or her baby to survive. "I'm going back to bed," she said, teeth clenched.

"I'll walk you there," her mother said silkily, taking her arm and digging her fingers into Hayley's flesh.

Hayley struggled, but her mother was strong. "Mom, you're hurting me. Don't—"

Hayley's protest was suddenly cut off by her mother's scream, the bitch's grip abruptly disappearing. Hayley caught Graham's small wink and bit back her grin. Graham had sloshed some of the contents of the pot onto his mother's feet, and it was soaking into her shoes.

"Oh, Mother. I am *so* sorry," Graham said.

"You did that on purpose!" she screeched.

Murmurs arose from the curtained-off rooms.

"Good job, Mom," Hayley snapped. "You've woken everyone. I'm going back to bed."

She turned on her heel and headed back for the cubicle she shared with Joshua's other wives. And ran right into Brother Joshua himself. He gripped her arms, steadying her before she could fall. His grip wasn't punishing, like her mother's had been, but she winced.

"What is the meaning of this?" he growled.

Sister Rebecca, the baby-stealer, sidled up beside him. "She's a troublemaker."

"Her mother slapped her," a calm voice said, and Hayley wanted to sag in relief. Sister Tamar had rescued her once again. "She slapped her, then grabbed her arm. She probably has bruises."

Joshua frowned. "Is this true?"

Hayley started to answer but caught Tamar's shake of the head. Looking over her shoulder, she saw that the question had been addressed to Graham. Who still held the damn pot of piss.

"Yes, sir," Graham said respectfully, and Hayley had the urge to giggle. His tone was so respectful. Only Hayley knew that he was laying it on with a trowel.

Joshua let Hayley go. "Go back to bed," he said with surprising gentleness. "I'll deal with your mother."

Hayley blinked in surprise, then bit back a flinch at the venomous look on Sister Rebecca's face. *If looks could kill, I'd be dead.*

"I'll help you," Tamar said, sliding her arm around Hayley's shoulders. She looked up at Joshua. "She's due any day. If she falls, she could harm the baby."

Joshua glanced at his first wife. "We don't want that."

Rebecca's expression had shifted from venomous to beatific. "No, we don't."

"Come," Tamar said, giving Hayley a tug.

Once they were back in Hayley's space, Tamar shook her head. "What were you thinking? You can't provoke your mother like that."

Now that it was over, Hayley realized that Tamar was right. She'd let her words fly without thinking. "I'm sorry. When she hit me, I . . ."

"I know. But you *must* control your temper."

"I know." Hayley sighed. "You're right."

"And you're tense." Tamar started a lower back massage that made Hayley groan. "Have you felt any contractions?"

"Not yet." Hayley hugged her belly. "I've been hoping she'll stay put a little longer."

"I understand that you're scared, but if the contractions start, do not fight them. Send Graham to find me immediately. I'm serious. You could be endangering your life and your baby's. Now, tell me why Graham was really out there. He's been dumping the pots for a few days now, without complaint. People are talking about it. Now they're singing his praises, but that could change on a dime."

Hayley looked at the curtain. It was pulled and there were no feet visible beneath it, so no one was eavesdropping. Unless they were waiting at the curtain's edge. "He's looking for something," Hayley said, trying to keep it generic.

"Something to help you escape?"

Hayley inhaled sharply. "I . . ."

"It's all right," Tamar said. "I don't think anyone else suspects. I won't ask more questions for now, because the other wives will be back soon. But I *will* help you. I want out, too."

She'd said it once before and Hayley needed to decide if she could trust her. Tamar could be working on the side of her mother, Rebecca, and Eden. Although Tamar had also lost her child, not to death, but to Rebecca.

"They have a computer," Hayley whispered.

Tamar's eyes widened, then filled with excitement. "For real?" Then she shut down like someone had flipped a switch. "There you go, Sister Magdalena," she said, her voice back to soothing and calm. A second later the curtain was whipped back and Joshua's other wives filed in. "Hopefully the massage helped."

One of the wives offered Hayley a cup of water. "Sister Tamar gives the best massages. She'll be an amazing midwife, even if Sister Coleen isn't back before your baby arrives."

Tamar patted her hand. "I've delivered five babies in the past year. Haven't lost a single one, nor their mothers, so don't worry. I'm going back to bed as well. Tomorrow, I'll ask Brother Joshua if I can move my pallet in here, so that I can be close by if you need me. Now, try to rest. You're going to be needing all the strength you can muster." She met Hayley's gaze with determination. "I *will* help you."

I will help you. Tamar hadn't just been talking about the baby. She'd been talking about their escape. She was moving her pallet tomorrow so that she could be nearby. To help with the baby *and* their escape.

Hayley thought about that and about Graham doing the most disgusting of all the compound's chores so that he could find the satellite dish that was their only hope of communication with the outside world. That was love.

She curled around her meager pillow, letting that love settle around her and within her. *I hope you know we love you, Jellybean. We're going to find a way to save you.*

ROCKLIN, CALIFORNIA
THURSDAY, MAY 25, 4:35 A.M.

Tom leaned forward, bracing his elbows on his desk and stretching his back. His muscles had grown stiff from sitting at his keyboard for far too long. He glanced at the wall of his office that faced Liza's bedroom, wishing things weren't so weird between them. He could have used one of her shoulder massages right about now. He loved the feel of her hands on his skin.

But she was probably asleep. Curled up in the nest of soft blankets she liked so much. Warm and pliant, smelling like apples and tasting like chocolate because she always had some for a bedtime snack.

He stiffened, in more ways than one. *Goddammit.*

He was hard. He'd felt desire since Tory died. Always when he'd been with Liza. Always he'd shoved it back, but tonight denial was much more difficult. He wanted Liza. *Dammit.*

Clenching his eyes shut, he swallowed a groan, wanting to call Rafe Sokolov and curse him to hell and back. Putting thoughts in his mind like that.

That Liza might be for me. That she might want me. That I could have her for my own.

Because it was not true. She was his friend, one of his oldest friends. They loved each other, true, but like friends. They took care of each other and that was all.

Tell that to your cock, buddy.

This was lust and it was wrong. *If I give in—which I won't—it will ruin our friendship.*

"Do we still have a friendship?" he asked, and Pebbles looked at him. The Great Dane lay pressed against the common wall, as if she knew that Liza was just beyond it. "Well? Do we?"

Pebbles snorted like the small horse she was and went back to sleep.

Tom sighed. He was getting nothing done. After his conversations with Rafe and then his mother, he'd returned to his office and picked up his attempt at tracing Cameron Cook's e-mail.

From Hayley, who was pregnant and scared and about to give birth in that horrible place. His arousal fled as he imagined Tory being scared the night she'd been killed, certain that she'd been more afraid for their baby than for herself. No one had saved Tory that night.

Everything in Tom yearned to get Hayley to safety. He'd tried everything he knew, both legal and illegal, but kept slamming up against nothing. It was like Eden's network had disappeared—maybe at the same time as their last move?

It was possible that they'd gone someplace where they couldn't get online. It was also possible that their equipment—the satellite dish that Amos had discovered at their most recent location—had been damaged.

They had taken it with them when they evacuated. Tom had checked himself, searching the perimeter of the compound Amos had described a month ago when he'd first escaped with Abigail. Tom had found evidence that a cable had been buried and then dug up. Maybe they'd damaged the cable when they'd ripped it from the earth.

Maybe, maybe, maybe. He blew out a breath and pushed away from his desk, needing . . . something. Exercise? Food? More booze?

No, definitely not more booze. He'd had more alcohol tonight than he usually consumed in a month.

His glance flitted to the wall again and he had to fight the urge to bang on it with his fists, to wake Liza up and demand that she tell him what was wrong.

You know what's wrong. Stop being an obtuse dick.

He hung his head, suddenly too weary to ignore it any longer. "I am a dick," he whispered.

Karl had tried to tell him, and he'd made a joke.

Rafe had tried to tell him, and he'd thrown him out.

His mother had tried to tell him multiple times as they'd talked on the phone, but each time Tom had changed the subject and his mother had allowed him to do so, albeit reluctantly.

Even Croft had tried to tell him that Liza's wants and needs might have changed during the seven years of their friendship, but he'd pretended to be clueless.

Dammit all to hell. "I don't want this," he growled to Pebbles. "I don't want to want her." But he did want her. He could lie to himself, but his body apparently knew the truth. He wanted her friendship, her laughter, all of her smiles. And he wanted to curl up with her under those soft blankets and see what would happen. "I *can't* want her."

Huffing a groan, Pebbles rolled over to press her face against the wall, shutting him out.

"*Et tu,* Pebbles?" he muttered. He closed all of the browser tabs he'd been using to trace that damn e-mail and stared at the image that remained on his screen.

Tory laughed at the camera, all bubbly happiness and dancing delight as she waggled her fingers to show off the diamond he'd just put on her finger. It was the night she'd agreed to be his wife. A month later, she was gone. The diamond on her finger was gone. The smile on her face, gone. The light in her eyes . . . all gone. All stolen by the brute who'd killed her.

He drew a breath and stared hard at her face. They'd fallen hard and fast, going from dating to storing toothbrushes in each other's bathrooms in a matter of weeks. And the only person he'd told was Liza.

He closed his eyes, remembering the night he'd told her about Tory on a Skype call. Liza had been laughing about something he'd said when he'd blurted it out. *I met someone. She's amazing.* Liza's smile had disappeared, and then hurt had flitted across her face.

I hurt her. I was clumsy and bumbling and I hurt her. He could see that now, in his memory. He'd either missed it or ignored it then. Either way, she'd schooled her features into a tight smile and had wished him all the happiness in the world. Had even asked all about Tory.

And he'd told her everything. Well, not about the sex. "Thank God for that," he muttered.

Because now . . . now he could see what everyone else had always seen. She'd cared for him then. At least a year and a half ago. Maybe before that.

Not as friends. Not just as friends, anyway.

Goddammit.

He had no idea what to do with this epiphany. He didn't *want* this epiphany.

He pushed back from his desk and paced the length of his little office. He was edgy, felt caged in. He needed to run. The ten-mile route he took around the neighborhood always cleared his head. But he wasn't leaving her alone. Not when she'd been in a killer's sights less than twenty-four hours before.

So, no, he wasn't leaving her here alone to go for a run. He had a treadmill downstairs.

He'd turned to go there when his phone shrilled an alarm. He sucked in a startled breath—that was the alarm for Eden's bank account. Dropping back into his chair, he quickly brought up the offshore account.

"Whoa," he whispered. One hundred grand was gone. Transferred.

He clicked on the transaction and stared at his screen. The money had been wired to a Dr. Ralph Arnold of Sacramento.

Fingers flying, Tom googled the man and found absolutely nothing of note in the standard search results. No address, not even a photograph. He then checked the California DMV database and found the man's photo.

Ralph Arnold was . . . ordinary. Medium height, medium build. Dishwater-blond hair that had grayed at the temples. He could be anyone.

But he was someone—someone who Eden trusted and needed enough to wire a hundred grand to. Right off, that made the man a definite person of interest.

Tom unlocked his safe and pulled out the laptop he used for the dark web. He was protected by multiple levels of proxy servers on his main computer, but he'd been taught to be careful by his first white-hat mentor, Ethan Buchanan.

Ethan had taken Tom under his wing when he'd been a junior in high school. Tom had managed to break into a protected government website and realized how vulnerable he was. He'd backed out quickly and had never been approached by men in black asking questions, but he'd realized that he could have been in real trouble. Life-destroying, going-to-prison trouble. So he'd taken his laptop to Ethan and asked for help.

Ethan's brows had nearly shot off his forehead when he'd seen what Tom had accomplished on his own, but then he'd rolled up his sleeves and taught Tom to be a white hat, too.

Tom owed the man a great deal and thought about him every time he delved into the dark web. *Be safe*, was Ethan's first rule. *Don't compromise your everyday workstation.*

Tom signed in on his throwaway laptop and opened the browser that provided entrée into the dark web. He wasn't going to dig that deep yet. He'd do a quick search, then report the Eden activity to Molina.

He sighed. No, he'd send it to Raeburn first and call Molina right after. He didn't want her kept in the dark, and it seemed that Raeburn was capable of doing just that.

Ralph Arnold MD, he typed into the search window. Then whistled softly when his screen filled with links, all referencing Arnold's very private practice. He operated a surgery out of his home, which was well guarded. He accepted U.S. dollars, euros, rubles, pesos, and yuan.

References abounded—many from satisfied former patients with code names like Coyote and Scarface and Moll. The man appeared to be a doctor to both Hollywood celebrities and the stars of organized crime.

Having sufficient information for the moment, Tom dialed Agent Raeburn.

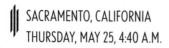

SACRAMENTO, CALIFORNIA
THURSDAY, MAY 25, 4:40 A.M.

DJ pulled the truck through the wrought iron gates that marked the entrance to Dr. Arnold's home. He'd received a call from Dr. Arnold's office manager confirming that payment had been received and that the address had been texted to his phone only minutes before.

Way to leave things till the last minute, he thought, feeling manipulated, distrusted, and surly. Most of which had been caused by Pastor, the bastard.

The house was located in an upscale neighborhood about fifteen minutes from the airport. DJ figured that made transport more convenient for the celebrities and crime bosses coming from out of town.

He half-expected to see Kowalski at the doctor's house, waiting for them, but the drug dealer was nowhere in sight.

DJ drove around to the back as he'd been instructed and stopped the truck in front of a large garage. The doors rolled up, revealing an ambulance, two nurses in white scrubs, and a muscled man about the size of a gorilla who held a rifle in his arms.

"Mr. Belmont?" one of the nurses asked. Her name tag read *Jones*.

"Yes. My father is in the back of the truck. His wife is with him."

"We'll get your father checked in and have your mother fill out his paperwork."

"She's not my mother." DJ had to bite back a wince, because he hadn't intended to say that aloud. The less information he provided, the safer he'd stay. "What paperwork? I was assured the doctor would require no paperwork."

The woman smiled. "Just his medical history. No identification required."

A hundred thousand bucks seemed to be enough identification for Dr. Arnold.

DJ opened the back of the truck. Coleen looked exhausted and Pastor was either asleep or unconscious.

"Asleep," Coleen said, reading the question in DJ's expression.

Nurse Jones climbed up into the back of the truck, the muscled man taking position at the open truck door. She knelt beside Pastor and took his wrist, frowning. "His pulse is very weak."

"I know," Coleen told her, her manner as professional as DJ had ever seen. "I've been monitoring it since we left home. The ride was difficult for him."

Coleen was not, to DJ's knowledge, a real nurse. Her first husband in Eden had been both a Founding Elder and the compound's actual doctor. He'd taught her to be his assistant. When he'd died they'd been unable to get a replacement and Coleen had become the healer.

Pastor was moved to a stretcher and the second nurse began setting up an IV. "We're going to run some scans before the doctor scrubs in," she said. "We need to know the extent of his injuries before he's put under anesthesia. Has he received anesthesia before?"

"Not that I know of," Coleen replied. She climbed down from the truck, her body swaying a little. Probably from exhaustion. "I've been our community's healer for thirty years."

Both nurses lifted their brows at the term "healer."

"We live in a remote town and we don't have a board-certified physician," DJ hastily explained, shooting Coleen a warning glare. "We've learned to be self-sufficient. This injury was outside our expertise."

Coleen dropped her gaze to her feet, folding her hands at her waist. The picture of female subservience. Just as Pastor demanded. "Can you help him?"

"We'll do our best," Nurse Jones promised, then turned to the man with the rifle. "Mr. Saltrick, please show our guests to the family lounge. Get them a meal and a place to rest."

"This way," the man commanded.

Coleen hesitated, casting a worried glance at Pastor. The nurses pushed the stretcher up a ramp and into the garage before disappearing through a door marked *Employees Only.*

"This way," Saltrick repeated.

DJ and Coleen followed. Once they were in a lounge with comfortable sofas and chairs that reclined into beds, Saltrick pointed to the refrigerator, a cabinet full of soup, and a microwave. "Help yourself," he grunted. "If you'll give me your keys, I'll park your vehicle."

DJ hesitated, then handed the man the keys to the truck. They could have had the cops waiting here for them had they been so inclined. That they hadn't suggested he and Coleen would be safe here.

Saltrick gave each of them a folder with no external labels or markings. "Inside you'll find an explanation of how things are done here. Once your father is finished with surgery, he'll be taken to a rehabilitation center for his recovery and for any other medical services he might require. Sunnyside Oaks's key mission is to provide quality care with the utmost privacy. We serve mostly celebrities—stars of film, TV, and sports. Some of our patients require privacy of a different sort, like your father."

In other words, DJ thought, protection from law enforcement.

"Due to privacy concerns," Saltrick continued, "we do not file claims with insurance companies. We require all patients to pay with cash. When your father is ready to be transferred, there will be an additional payment due for the rehab services. Dr. Arnold's office manager will provide the details. Please familiarize yourself with the rehab center. Do you have questions?"

Coleen timidly raised her hand. "The nurse said they'd do scans. What kind of scans?"

"CT scan," the man replied brusquely. "And an MRI, should he need one."

Coleen nodded like she understood the terms, which surprised DJ. "Do you have the equipment here?" she asked.

"We do," Saltrick said. "Now, if you'll excuse me."

He strode to the door, leaving DJ and Coleen alone. She was staring at the microwave with confusion and fear.

"What?" DJ barked.

She flinched. "I haven't used a microwave in thirty years. I'm not sure I remember how."

DJ was starving, so he got up to make them a meal. "I'll show you. It isn't difficult."

"Brother DJ? Will we have enough money to pay for the rehabilitation center?"

"Yes. We'll have enough." He opened the cupboard. "We have chicken soup, clam chowder, and beef stew. Which do you want?"

Coleen's eyes were wide before she dropped her gaze to her feet. "Choose for me, please."

It didn't surprise him. Women of Eden did not make their own choices. Ever.

"Come and watch me," he commanded. "You can make my food from then on."

"Yes, Brother DJ."

ROCKLIN, CALIFORNIA
THURSDAY, MAY 25, 4:45 A.M.

"Yes?" Raeburn snapped. "It's four forty-five, Agent Hunter. I assume this is important."

"Critical, sir. There's been a wire transfer from the offshore Eden account."

"Oh." The word was uttered on a huff of surprise. "When?"

"Four minutes ago. I got an activity alert. One hundred thousand dollars was wired to a Dr. Arnold in Sacramento."

"Give me a minute." A woman's murmur was followed by rustling sheets and creaking springs. A door closed and then Raeburn asked, "Sacramento? I would have thought they'd seek medical help in Redding or Eureka—cities closer to where you think they're hiding."

"I agree, but I'm frankly shocked that they're seeking medical help at all. Amos Terrill said that, in general, if members of Eden got sick, they either recovered on their own or they died. Outside help was never sought."

"Didn't Ephraim Burton get a glass eye?"

Huh. He does read the briefs I send him. "Yes. Ephraim Burton's eye surgery seems to have been an outlier, and one that was kept from. the community as a whole. Amos said he continued to wear his patch whenever he was in the compound. We think Burton got a doctor in Santa Rosa to perform the surgery during one of his quarterly hiatuses from Eden, but again, that's an outlier. For them to leave Eden and seek outside medical assistance—"

"It has to be a grave injury," Raeburn finished.

"Yes, sir. I think so. It would almost have to be one of the leaders."

"Belmont's hurt," Raeburn said.

"True. He was wearing a sling in the surveillance video we took from the office building he used to target Mercy Callahan." And Liza.

"Maybe he arranged for Dr. Arnold's services because he was back in Sacramento intending to finish off Mercy Callahan."

"That makes sense, sir."

"So who is this guy? Is he associated with a hospital?"

"I don't think so. Dr. Arnold's name doesn't get any hits on the surface web, but he's quite popular on the dark web."

"Not a shock," Raeburn muttered. "What did you find out about him?"

"He's recommended by movie stars, TV personalities, and mob bosses all over the world. He does surgery from his home, but his former patients say they convalesced and received rehab services at Sunnyside Oaks Convalescence and Rehabilitation Center. Again, patients include both A-list celebrities and criminals."

"Excellent work, Hunter. Can you find an address for Arnold's home surgery?"

"Not in these search results. It seems like his patients agreed to keep the location secret. A few say that they don't want to make the doctor angry in case they have family members who need help in the future."

"What about the rehab facility?"

Tom opened a new search window and typed in the name. He was a little surprised when an address surfaced. "That's available. The place is very private, but . . ." He turned to his primary computer and typed the name again. "It shows up on both the dark and surface webs. I'll send you the surface link with the address, but their website is very basic and says little of substance."

"It's something, though. This is our first real break. I assume you haven't traced the e-mail allegedly sent from Eden, since I haven't heard from you on that."

"Not yet. Still working on it."

"Keep me up to speed. I'll see you back in the office first thing."

It wasn't a request. Tom grimaced, wondering how he'd ensure Liza's safety tomorrow. He needed to hire someone to watch her, ASAP. "Yes, sir."

"And you will not be sharing this information with anyone, even Agent Reynolds, correct?"

Tom gritted his teeth, but forced his voice to remain level. "Of course not, sir."

"Good night, then." Raeburn ended the call before Tom could say another word.

Not that he'd wanted to say more, not after being chastised like a teenager skipping school. Telling Molina would help soothe the irritation. He started to dial from his work phone, but stopped himself. He didn't want either of them to get into trouble.

Using his burner phone, he dialed Molina's number. She answered on the first ring, wary but alert. "Yes?"

"Agent Molina, this is Tom Hunter."

"Agent Hunter. Why are you calling from this number?"

"Because I have information."

"Well, what are you waiting for? Tell me!"

He chuckled. "Yes, ma'am." He relayed the information that he'd shared with Raeburn.

"Good. Agent Hunter . . ." She sighed. "Tom. You know I've been recused."

"I know."

"Which is why you used the burner."

"Yes, ma'am. Would you prefer that I don't call you?"

She made a rude sound. "No. I want you to use another number." She rattled it off.

Tom grinned. "You have a burner? Agent Molina, I must admit that you've surprised me."

"Baby agents," she muttered. "You think you invented all the tricks. But thank you. I appreciate the heads-up. Good night."

Tom shut down his throwaway laptop and returned it to the safe. He'd been antsy and had needed to run, but now he was exhausted. Time for bed.

"Come on, Pebbles. You want to go out one more time?"

But Pebbles didn't follow him to the office door. She tensed, then growled low, head cocked toward the shared wall.

Concerned, Tom pressed his ear to the wall and a moment later heard what Pebbles had. Liza was screaming. His pulse rocketed up. *No.* He would not lose her, too. "Pebbles, come."

Grabbing his gun and the keys to Liza's side of the duplex, he ran down the stairs and through the kitchen into the backyard, calling up the cameras on his phone. No one was at the front and the alarm was still set. His hands were shaking as he shoved the key into the lock on her kitchen door.

He didn't disarm the alarm, leaving it to count down. In sixty seconds, it would go off. If there was an intruder, the blaring sound might startle them. *And if something happens to me, the police will still be called.*

Cell phone in one hand, his gun in the other, he took the stairs three at a time. Midway up, Pebbles raced past him and through Liza's open bedroom door.

"Pebbles? What the hell?" he heard her say, but her voice was hoarse and broken.

He stopped in her doorway to disable the alarm. But also to let his heart calm down. She was okay. She was unhurt, at least. But even though the screams had stopped, she was sobbing. Pebbles had climbed onto her bed and she had her arms around the dog, rocking her.

"Liza?" Tom asked, then entered when she didn't answer. He figured she would have told him to leave if that was what she'd wanted. She still might, and he'd cede to her wishes.

At least he knew she was all right. Physically. Psychologically, not so much. She visibly shook as she rocked Pebbles, her fingers clenched in the dog's short hair.

He couldn't let her cry. Nudging Pebbles off the bed, Tom took her place and pulled Liza onto his lap, blankets and all. She didn't fight him when he wrapped his arms around her and held her tight. She grabbed handfuls of his shirt and held on, burying her face against his chest.

"Shhh," he soothed, her sobs breaking his heart. "It was a nightmare. It's not real."

She shook her head but said nothing. Just clung harder.

It was then that he realized she'd fallen asleep with the light on and earbuds in her ears. They'd fallen out at some point, the cords visible against the white of her pillow. He lifted one of the buds to his own ear and heard Garth Brooks singing. Her laptop was overturned on its side, still open, and next to it was a spiral notebook.

Keeping one arm tightly around her, he righted her laptop. The screen woke up, displaying the photo she kept as her wallpaper. He'd have to lecture her again about computer security. She didn't use a password even though he'd set one up for her.

He'd seen the wallpaper photo before. It was Liza and eleven other soldiers, all holding their weapons and smiling. All he knew was that it had been taken while she'd been deployed in Kabul.

The notebook was opened to a page bearing a sketch that he'd never seen before. He tugged the notebook closer so that he could see the sketch more clearly. It wasn't particularly artistic, but it didn't have to be for him to get the gist of its purpose.

An angel held the caduceus staff in both hands, the smaller wings of the caduceus the same shape as the larger outspread wings of the angel. Instead of snakes, a stethoscope wound around the staff. Which, on closer inspection, wasn't a staff at all. It was a semiautomatic rifle. But the detail that grabbed his attention was the names written on the feathers of the angel's wings, three on the left, four on the right.

Seven names, each with a different symbol sketched below. Ted had a football. Lenny, a violin. Judy, a baby bottle. Odell, a smiling sun. Neil's name was surrounded by the ABCs. Christie had a medal on a ribbon. And Fritz had two connected rings against a broken heart.

His gaze lingered on the broken heart, wondering what it meant. Wondering what the rings meant. Wondering who Fritz had been. Wondering who all of the people had been.

Had been being the operative phrase. This was clearly a memorial. A helmet hung from the top of the rifle. A pair of empty boots was positioned at its base.

These people had meant something to Liza. And they'd died.

Eyes stinging, he hugged Liza harder, and the question just slipped out. "Who was Fritz?"

ELEVEN

Who was Fritz?"

Liza went still, Tom's softly spoken words glaringly loud in the quiet of the night. *You wanted him to know. You wanted to talk about Fritz. To acknowledge him as being important.*

"My husband."

Tom's shocked gasp seemed to echo off the walls. "Your . . . *what?*" He reared back, their gazes colliding. "You were *married?*"

Liza used her sleeve to wipe her face. Dammit, her eyes hurt. Resting her head against his broad chest had felt so good while it had lasted. That comfort was gone, and although he still held her, there was confused accusation in his eyes.

"For a little while, yes," she murmured.

"How long?"

"A month."

"And then?"

She inhaled deeply, then let it out. Stalling, because saying the words aloud hurt. Knowing that she should move off his lap, but unable to make her body obey the command. "He died."

"Oh." The word was uttered on a huff of breath, then she felt him straightening his back and bracing his shoulders. But he still held her. Not tightly, but he hadn't let her go. "In combat?"

"Yes."

"Is that . . ." He hesitated. "Is that what you were dreaming about? You screamed."

"Yes." She closed her eyes. "I see it when I'm asleep. See them all."

"I'm sorry." He stroked her hair, pushing it off her face. "So sorry."

She nodded, new tears welling against her closed eyelids. "I miss him. Fritz." It was true. She hadn't loved him like he'd loved her, but she *had* loved him. For a long time, Fritz had been a dear friend. *Kind of like Tom sees me now.* Maybe this was karma, coming to exact its due.

I deserve it. I'm sorry, Fritz. More tears welled in her throat and she harshly cleared it, carefully disengaging herself from the only place she'd ever wanted to be. Tom Hunter's arms.

She slid from the bed, going to stand at the window. She'd barely peeked through the blinds at the darkened street below when Tom pulled her back, his hands gentle but insistent.

"Not in front of the window," he murmured. "It's too dangerous."

She stared at him, not understanding. Until her mind clicked. The rooftop gunman who'd been aiming for Mercy the morning before. "Right. Sorry."

He led her back to the bed and urged her to sit, then retrieved the small stool from under her makeup vanity. Completely dwarfing it, he sat next to the bed.

But then he took both of her hands in his and all she could focus on were his eyes, blue as a summer sky. "Tell me about the dream," he murmured.

"I . . ." She had to look away, because he was being her friend. Just her friend. *I'm the one wishing this were more than it really is.* "I don't talk about it."

"Don't?" His tone was careful and he didn't release her hands. "Or don't want to?"

She laughed and it sounded bitter. "Both."

"You haven't talked to anyone about these nightmares? This isn't the first one you've had."

She knew this. She didn't scream every time. Usually she woke in a cold sweat, sobbing. But tonight's nightmare had been especially vivid. Probably because she'd been remembering each of the souls they'd lost that day. "It isn't something I discuss with just anyone."

He lightly gripped her chin. "I'm not just anyone. I'm your friend."

The word was like an ax to the chest. "I know," she managed. "And I appreciate it."

His sigh was barely audible. "Please talk to me, Liza. Tell me about them. There are seven names on those angel wings. Tell me about them. Please. It might help." His smile was a little lopsided and a lot sad. "Can it hurt?"

God, yes. It could hurt. It *did* hurt.

But she owed it to Fritz. The others deserved to be remembered as well. Behind her, the bed dipped and a moment later, a big doggy head rested on her shoulder as Pebbles pressed her muzzle to Liza's cheek.

Tugging one of her hands free from Tom's grip, she wrapped her arm around the big dog's neck. This kind of unadulterated love was addictive.

"They were a unit, and Ted and I were their field medics. Ted had played college football and had a girl back home in Texas. Lenny was a violinist from upstate New York. He'd play for us between missions. Judy had a two-year-old back home in Indiana. She loved that boy more than the world. Odell was a career soldier with a smile that lit up any room. Neil was going to be an elementary school teacher. He cheated at Scrabble, but I still played with him because he was so damn funny. Christie ran track in high school. She wanted to go to the Olympics."

"She never made it," Tom murmured.

"No."

"And Fritz?"

"He was the heart of us. Never forgot a birthday, always had a smile or a joke to lift our spirits when we were homesick. He was a good man. Such a good man."

Tom's jaw clenched, ever so slightly. "I wouldn't have thought you'd choose a bad man." He pointed to the sketch she'd made of the tattoo she planned to get. "What happened to them?"

Liza tilted her head, gesturing to the laptop screen, gone dark again. "That was taken the morning before the attack. We'd gone to a village to distribute supplies and meds. One of the villagers saw the cross on my uniform and begged me to help his wife. She was in labor and there was no doctor available." She leaned into Pebbles, remembering the village, devastated and battle-torn. "They'd been bombed and there was very little left. Which was why we were there with supplies."

He squeezed the hand he still held. "Did you deliver the baby?"

"Yes. It was a little boy. A healthy little boy with such a pair of lungs." She sighed. "We were leaving the house and our spirits were a little high. Even the gruffest of the guys melted at the cry of a newborn baby. Plus, the villagers were so grateful. They'd congregated in the street to take the supplies we were giving out. Some sang and celebrated the new baby. They'd lost so many people and they had a tiny spark of something good. That kind of happiness is kind of contagious and we were distracted. Just a little, but it was enough. I looked up and saw a flash of light on the rooftop across the street."

"A sniper," he murmured. "Like yesterday morning."

"Yes, but this wasn't just one. There were three men on the roof, and they fired. A lot."

"But you weren't hit," he said, a hint of desperation in his voice.

"Yes, I was, but it was only a graze. A few of us had seen them at the same time and screamed 'gun,' and then everything went sideways. There was chaos and so much gunfire." She had to stop for a moment, her anxiety starting to spike. "And screaming." *So much screaming.* "The village residents were running for cover, falling in the streets. Not getting up."

"But your unit fired back?"

"Those of us who were still alive." She looked down, concentrated on the big hand still holding hers. "Fritz wasn't one of them. He'd thrown himself over me. To protect me. By the time I pushed him off me, he was already dead."

Tom hesitated. "I thought married couples weren't allowed to serve together?"

"They're not. We'd gotten married a few weeks before that—we'd gotten two weeks of R&R stateside, and Fritz proposed. Took me home to meet his family. They wanted to be a part of the ceremony, so . . . I said yes."

"They were good people? Fritz's family?"

"Yes. Very good people." Too good for a woman who'd only married their son because she couldn't have the man she wanted. "I liked them very much."

"Have you seen them? Since Fritz was killed, I mean."

"Yes, as soon as I landed in the U.S. after my discharge. They live in Jersey City and I flew into Newark, so it was close by." They'd held on to her as they'd all cried, and she'd cried with them. "And then I got on a plane to Chicago to see you all."

"Last Christmas," he murmured.

"Yes." She'd arrived as the Hunters and the Buchanans—the family who'd taken her in after her sister's murder—were sitting down to Christmas dinner. It was then that she'd learned Tom's Tory was dead.

"You didn't say anything," he said. "Why didn't you tell us about Fritz then?"

She turned her face into Pebbles's soft muzzle, shaking her head.

"What?" he demanded, his tone going sharp. "Why didn't you?"

The thinly veiled anger in his tone snapped the lid off her own temper. "Because someone would have asked to see his picture," she spat. "And then they would have known the truth."

"What truth?"

Yanking her hand free of his, she unlocked her cell phone and found Fritz's official army photo. Dressed in a pressed uniform, his body ramrod straight, he'd been so handsome. So stern. But that hadn't been him. Fritz had laughed and loved and was generous to a fault.

She shoved her phone at Tom, who sucked in a harsh breath. "Oh."

She laughed bitterly. "Yeah. Oh."

Because Fritz Pohlmann and Tom Hunter could have been brothers. Same body type, same size, same chiseled jaw, same blond hair. Fritz's eyes had been brown, though. At least when she'd looked into his eyes, she'd seen Fritz. Not Tom.

"He looks like . . ." He trailed off, staring at the screen.

She took her phone from his hand and turned it off. "You. He looks like you."

Tom lifted his gaze to hers, searching for what, she wasn't sure. "Why did you marry him?"

She swallowed hard, shame forming like a boulder in her chest. "I shouldn't have. But . . ." She sighed. "You'd met Tory. You'd popped the question and she'd said yes."

He flinched. "When did you get married?"

"February first would have been our first anniversary. He was dead by March first." She'd gone to New Jersey on the anniversary of his death, to grieve with his family. It had nearly torn her apart. Meeting Mercy and the Sokolovs a month later had pulled her out of a dark place.

"Tory died on March fifth," he whispered. "I told you that she was pregnant around the end of January. Is that why you married him?"

"No." And that was true. "I'd already let you go by then. It was a wake-up call, though. You were living your life. I wanted to live mine. Fritz wanted me." Which couldn't have sounded more pathetic if she'd tried.

His expression went carefully blank. "I'm sorry, Liza. I didn't know how you felt."

He was sorry. That hurt more than anything. "Didn't matter. You didn't feel the same way."

"No," he said simply. "I didn't."

She recoiled, his words a physical blow. She'd thought it couldn't hurt worse, but she'd been very wrong. "I know."

His very audible swallow was followed by a less than graceful escape. He lurched to his feet, backing from her room. When he cleared the door, he bolted and ran down the stairs.

She heard the kitchen door close and the house was silent once more.

She stared at the place where he had been for a minute, shocked by his sudden departure, shocked by the bluntness of his words.

He'd run. *From me.* He'd been disgusted and he'd run. Her vision blurred, and she wasn't sure she'd ever been so weary. *I can't keep doing this.* Something had to change.

She cleared the laptop and notebook from her bed and straightened the blankets as best she could with a one-hundred-twenty-pound Great Dane sprawled over them. "I can't stay here," she told Pebbles, who got up, turned in a circle, and flopped down beside her, big doggy head on the other pillow. "I'll find a new place to live and come back to see you when I can."

But she knew deep down that wasn't going to happen. She needed to cut Tom Hunter out of her life completely and move on. Again.

ROCKLIN, CALIFORNIA
THURSDAY, MAY 25, 5:30 A.M.

Tom stared at the image that filled his computer screen. Friedrich Pohlmann, known as Fritz to his family and friends. It was his official army photo.

It was also his obituary.

Fritz Pohlmann was the beloved son of Marian and Kristofer Pohlmann and was survived by two brothers and two sisters. And by his wife, Liza.

Liza had been married. *To a man who looked like me.*

Tom didn't know what to think. How to feel. It was . . . shocking. Numbing. But below that was a current of hurt. Maybe even betrayal.

She hadn't told him about Fritz.

He wondered if she'd told Fritz about him.

He studied Fritz's face, stoic and unsmiling in his uniform. It wasn't like they could have been twins. But the resemblance was obvious at a glance. Same jaw, same hair. Same build.

Different eyes. Fritz's were brown and, in the more personal family photos attached to the online obit, appeared joyful. His smile was broad.

Especially in the photo taken the day he and Liza had married. The man looked too damn happy as he stared adoringly at his wife.

Wife.

It was too much, and Tom had to click away from their wedding photo. He wasn't even sure why. Because she'd been married at all? Because she'd married someone else?

No, that wasn't it. Tom was sure of that. Mostly sure.

It was, he decided, because she'd never told anyone. Or had she? Had she told Dana and Ethan Buchanan? She hadn't at Christmas. She'd said so. But later?

Tom had a hard time believing that she had, because he hadn't heard it through the family grapevine. Dana Buchanan was his mother's best friend. If Dana knew, his mother knew.

If his mother knew, she would have sounded different when they'd spoken on the phone the evening before. At one time, back when they were hiding from his biological father, his mother had been the master of controlling her emotions. All these years later, not so much. Thirteen years of living with Max Hunter had given her the freedom to be herself without fear.

But Dana was cagey. She'd run a women's shelter for years, protecting her clients' secrets. Now she operated a halfway house for victims of sexual assault. She kept their secrets.

Maybe she'd kept Liza's, too. Suddenly knowing if Liza had told her Chicago family was more important than anything else.

He glanced at the clock. It was seven thirty in Chicago. Dana would be awake. His fingers were typing out a text before he realized his own intention, but this wasn't anyone else's business. Only Liza's. *Not even mine. I don't have the right.*

Because he'd hurt her.

You didn't feel the same way.

No. I didn't.

I know.

He hadn't been able to stop the words at that moment. Because he hadn't felt that way, and letting her believe otherwise was cruel.

Except . . . that wasn't entirely true. He *had* felt that way once. He'd almost told her on her eighteenth birthday, but she'd shocked him with the news that she was joining the army. He'd stopped himself that night, too stunned, too *hurt* to bare his soul.

Tom stared at his screen, at the photo of the man who'd been there when she'd needed someone. "I'm sorry you died," he whispered to Fritz. "But I'm not sorry you saved her life. Thank you for that."

Then he closed both the browser tab and the compartment in his heart. He had work to do.

He'd gotten into Sunnyside Oaks's network and it was so easy, it was scary. He bet their system administrator believed he'd constructed a hackproof network. That admin would be wrong. A nurse working the night shift had clicked on a link he'd embedded in an e-mail to the staff in general with a bogus offer of free samples from a nonexistent pharmaceutical company.

He'd sent his message to two dozen different accounts, all with names he'd simply guessed at based on work he'd done with other medical facilities. One had worked.

Tom was violating the most basic of privacy laws at the moment, sifting through the facility's patient database, looking for anyone who might be tied to Eden. So far, he'd found evidence of medical procedures done on movie stars and mob bosses, but nothing that resembled any of the Eden bigwigs. The facility hadn't had a new arrival in more than five days.

Tom put an alert on the database so that he'd know when they added any new patients and closed that tab as well. He needed to get a few hours' sleep or he'd be of no use to Croft in the morning. He stood, starting to call for Pebbles, but remembered he'd left her next door.

She'd be fine with Liza for a few more hours. He wasn't going to bother Liza again tonight.

Because you are the biggest coward ever.

It was true. He didn't want to face her again. His emotions were too raw and too unclear.

What was clear, though, was his need to see her safe. He'd go over in the morning before he went to work. He'd make her promise to stay home. To stay safe.

SACRAMENTO, CALIFORNIA
THURSDAY, MAY 25, 7:00 A.M.

"He's awake. DJ, he's awake. Come—"

DJ jolted to consciousness, his hands halfway to Coleen's throat before he realized where he was. "God." He shook himself, trying to dispel the sudden surge of adrenaline that was too much to handle on so little sleep. He felt like he had nodded off just minutes ago.

Fuck. He searched frantically for his phone, finding it on the chair beside him. It must have slipped from his hand. The screen was dark, so no one had seen what he'd been looking at.

After Kowalski's revelation that Ephraim had murdered his old doctor, DJ had spent most of the hours of Pastor's surgery reading articles about Ephraim Burton's recent tangle with the law. He'd learned that Ephraim had killed a buttload of people, dropping clues along with every corpse. He'd also noticed that Eden hadn't been mentioned once in any of the articles.

That was good. But also bad. It was good that Eden wasn't on anyone's radar, so if Pastor muttered it in his sleep, the rehab staff wouldn't know what it meant. However, the Feds knew about Eden. Gideon, Mercy, and Amos had to have told them. That they were holding the knowledge from the press didn't bode well at all. The only reference to Eden that he'd seen had been a picture of one of the lockets. The locket had come up in another case, having belonged to a victim of a serial killer who'd killed one of Ephraim's former wives.

The wife that Ephraim had claimed died while trying to escape. The wife whose "body" he'd brought back, too decomposed to identify. In other words, he'd lied. Like they all did.

DJ would have loved for Pastor to hear about Ephraim's lies, to keep him angry about Ephraim and *not* angry at DJ, but that same news story had featured photos of Mercy Callahan. It would be like shooting himself in the face.

He looked up to see that Coleen had jumped back at least three feet, her palm pressed to her chest, which rose and fell rapidly. "You scared me to death."

"Don't sneak up on me," he warned.

"I was trying to wake you up."

"Do not sneak up on me," he repeated slowly. "For any reason." He'd learned to defend himself the hard way. "The last guy who did that didn't survive." He'd been a drug dealer who'd snuck up on DJ, trying to attack while he'd been asleep.

Coleen looked shaken. "He's awake and asking for you."

DJ slowly got to his feet, rolling his head until his neck cracked. "On my way." *To His Majesty*, he added silently, still furious over

Pastor's little code word stunt the night before. *Get my hopes up and then laugh at me? Fucker's going down.*

He'd known for years that Pastor had memorized the access codes. It was the old man's way of ensuring he never typed a password into the computer. Normally, he went off by himself to call his banker, only using the computer to research stock trades. His banker handled that, too.

There had to be a way to get access to that account.

DJ entered the recovery room, where Pastor was lying on a bed, hooked up to several machines. A cannula provided oxygen into his nose. He was breathing on his own, though. His skin was pale, but not nearly as bad as it had been.

"You look better."

"I feel like shit," Pastor muttered. "Did you talk to the doctor?"

"No. He might have spoken to Coleen. Why?" Was there more wrong? Was Pastor dying of something else? *One can only hope*, he thought dryly.

"I'm not dying," Pastor snapped.

DJ wondered if his expression was that transparent. "I'm glad."

"I wonder if you are." Pastor gestured at him. "Come closer. I don't want to yell."

As if you could. The old man's breaths were too labored to do much more than whisper.

"I'm going to be in the rehab facility for six weeks."

DJ blinked, shocked. "What?"

No. No fucking way. A week he could have handled. He could have kept Pastor off the TV and online news for a week. Six weeks? *Hell no.*

"That's what the doctor said. Six weeks. I have a broken arm and a few broken ribs. My knee is toast and I have a concussion. My femur is broken in two places. I'm going to have to learn to walk again. So six weeks."

DJ opened his mouth, then closed it again. "Wow" was all he could muster.

"I want you back in Eden. Get the people to a better location. The caves are killing them."

"What about Coleen?"

"She's going to stay with me, at least until I'm comfortable with this rehabilitation center the doctor was going on about. I want you to make sure the members stay calm. You stay put once you've moved them."

"All right," DJ said quietly. He had no intention of going back to Eden until he'd eliminated Mercy Callahan. He also had no intention of telling this to Pastor.

"I want you to bring Joshua in," Pastor added, then coughed.

DJ held a cup of water so that the old man could sip from a straw. "In where?" he asked, being deliberately obtuse.

Pastor glared at him out of watery eyes. "Idiot," he wheezed. "You know what I mean."

"And if he objects on moral grounds?" It was unlikely, but one never knew. Joshua was a pompous prick who'd taken well to keeping multiple wives who satisfied his every whim. He'd probably have no issue with any of the truth.

"Tell him there's money in it for him. That'll level his moral ground. I want you to make a video of him swearing his loyalty and his silence with that phone of yours. Then bring it to me and prove that you've done as I ask."

Motherfucker. DJ made himself smile. "That's fine. What about the additional payment? That security guy last night said you'd have to make another payment for the rehab center once the surgery was completed."

Pastor's eyes fluttered shut. His breathing was deeper now. More regular. They must have given him a painkiller. "Already . . . took care of it."

"*What?*" DJ clamped his lips together after nearly shouting the word. He hadn't meant for it to come out so loud. "When?"

Pastor smiled with the same smugness that he'd exhibited last night. "Coleen dialed my banker and gave me the phone. All done," he said in a drunken singsong.

DJ gritted his teeth. "How much?"

"Quarter mil."

DJ tried for control when he realized his fists were clenched and fantasies of beating Pastor to a pulp were going through his mind. "That's a lot of money."

"Not your money," Pastor murmured. "Not your concern."

Not my money? "It *is* mine. Half of it, at least."

"Not until I'm dead. Which is why I'm not giving you the access code."

DJ scowled. "You don't trust me?"

"I don't trust anyone. Don't forget that I raised you, boy. I know what you'd do if you had those codes. I wouldn't be . . ." He began slurring the words toward the end and trailed off.

"He'll sleep for a while," a voice said from behind him.

DJ whirled around to see a nurse watching him. "You shouldn't have eavesdropped."

She shrugged. "I hear a lot. I say nothing. I stay employed and alive. As I said, your father will sleep for a while now. We'll move him to the rehabilitation center in an hour or so. He'll sleep through the transport. That way we can keep him comfortable."

Like DJ cared about Pastor's comfort. Fucking bastard. "I see. What are visiting hours at the rehab center?"

"That depends on the patient. Some patients' families are more comfortable visiting under the cover of darkness. Others don't care. You can speak with the charge nurse once he's settled in." She stepped aside, gesturing for him to leave. "You can pick up the keys to your vehicle at the back door. Your mother is waiting for you there."

"She's not my mother," DJ bit out.

The nurse shrugged again. "Either way, she's waiting for you. I'd advise getting something to eat. By the time you're finished, your father will be transported."

There didn't seem to be much more to say. Pastor was sleeping. DJ wasn't certain that the old man had intended to disclose his reasons for not sharing the access codes. It didn't really matter now. The cat was out of the bag. So DJ went to the back door, where Coleen waited.

The muscle man from the night before had been replaced by a different muscle man, clad in a similar suit, carrying a similar rifle. And holding his keys.

Without a word, DJ took the keys and stalked out, Coleen following behind him. Once he'd made sure that the rifle he'd left in the back of the truck had not been stolen or tampered with, he got behind the wheel and glared at her. "What was the access code?"

She stared at him. "What?"

"The access code," he said from behind clenched teeth. "The words that Pastor told his banker. Who you called for him."

"I don't know. He told me to leave the room."

For the love of . . . "And you obeyed?"

Her eyes widened. "Yes."

Right. Because they'd trained the women to do so. "Fine. I'm going to a drive-through for breakfast and then I'll drop you off at the rehab facility. He's ordered me back to Eden."

"I know."

"So he told you that, but not the codes?"

"Yes."

DJ rolled his eyes and stared the engine.

"Brother Joshua knows something isn't right," Coleen offered. "I caught him trying to get into the clinic a month ago, on the night you came back wounded."

So that was interesting. "What was he trying to find in the clinic? Drugs?"

"Maybe. Maybe he knows about the computer." She hesitated. "I think Amos knew. I think he saw it. It was a few days before he took Abigail and ran."

DJ whipped his head around to stare at her. "Why didn't you mention it?"

"I . . ." She exhaled. "I don't know. I don't think I really suspected it until he was gone. And then everything went crazy. You got shot, we moved to the caves . . . And by then it didn't matter anymore. Amos was gone."

"Who else knows about the computer?"

"Nobody. At least nobody I know of. I figured if you were going back to Eden, you needed to know that Joshua might not be as surprised as you expect."

"Thank you, Sister Coleen," DJ said, and meant it. He didn't sincerely thank people often, but Coleen was watching his back.

She folded her hands in her lap. "Can we go to Carl's Jr.? I've missed their food."

DJ chuckled. "*That's* what you've missed?"

"Mmm. Yes."

She'd scratched his back, he could return the favor. "Sure. I'll find one and take you there."

And then he'd find Mercy Callahan.

ROCKLIN, CALIFORNIA
THURSDAY, MAY 25, 8:30 A.M.

Tom blinked, trying to figure out where the pinging was coming from. When it registered, he sat bolt upright in bed, grabbing his phone. Something was happening with the Eden account. Racing from his bedroom to his office, he checked the account and gasped.

Two hundred fifty thousand dollars this time. Payable to Sunnyside Oaks Convalescence and Rehabilitation Center.

Bingo. He dialed Raeburn, wincing at the time. He was officially late to work already.

"Hunter," Raeburn answered, forgoing any greeting. "Why are you late?"

Because I was up all night worrying about my best friend who appears to be in love with me, you asshole. "I was able to get into the rehab center and was running scans on their patient database most of the night." Also true. "I'll be in ASAP. In the meantime, you should know that there was another wire transfer from the Eden account. This time to the rehab center itself."

"How much?" Raeburn sounded less annoyed, at least.

"Two fifty."

Raeburn whistled quietly. "A hefty chunk of change. You get ID on the Eden leader who'll be there?"

"No, not yet." He opened a window into the database and saw nothing new. "They haven't checked him in yet, whoever it is. I've added an alert, so I'll know when they update."

"Sounds good. You'll be here soon, yes?"

Tom swallowed his sigh. "Of course."

He ended the call and leaned back in his chair, trying to organize the things he needed to do that day. *Get dressed. Make sure Liza stays the fuck at home. Go to work. Warn Rafe to keep Mercy close.* Not that the final item was really necessary, because Rafe wasn't about to let Mercy out of his sight after yesterday.

Oh, and he needed to tell Molina the latest as well. Somewhere in there he needed to get some food, because his stomach was growling loudly.

Showered and shaved, he felt more human. And then he tripped over Pebbles, who lay across the bathroom doorway, waiting for him to emerge.

"What are you doing here?" he asked her, scratching her ears. She leaned into him and he sighed because he'd have short dog hairs all over his clean suit. At least he had a sticky roller in his desk drawer at work. Courtesy of Liza.

The thought made him frown. If Pebbles was here, Liza had to have brought her over. He hoped she hadn't gone on her morning run. Surely she wouldn't be so foolish.

He ran down the stairs and almost went out his kitchen door. Then realized that maybe Liza wouldn't want him just walking in anymore. Not after last night.

Feeling more awkward than he had in forever, he went out his front door, crossed the small yard they shared, and knocked on hers. And knocked again. Alarm had his heart racing and he pounded on her door with one hand while he dug in his trouser pocket for his keys with the other.

"She's gone already."

Tom looked to his left where their neighbor, a retired teacher, stood on his stoop, puffing on his pipe while his Yorkie busily sniffed the grass. "Good morning, Mr. Tolliver. What do you mean she's gone already?"

Mr. Tolliver shrugged. "She left. I was letting Sweetie-Pie out for her morning pee and saw Liza driving out of the garage. Her car was filled with boxes."

Tom's mouth opened. "Boxes?"

"Yes, young man. Boxes. Like, you know," he added sarcastically, "cardboard things that you put stuff in? Boxes."

Tom couldn't find a suitable reply so he merely said, "Thank you, sir." His hands were shaking when he found his keys and he had to try twice before getting the key into the lock.

"She was crying."

Tom froze at the old man's words. *Fuck.* He forced himself to look left again, finding Tolliver's face creased in concern. "Excuse me?"

"I said that she was crying. And I think she had been for a while. Her face was swollen and red. She just carried boxes to her car and cried, not even stopping to wipe her eyes."

Oh my God. Fear gripped his heart. "Thank you, sir. I'll make sure she's okay."

"See that you do," he said gruffly. "She's a nice girl, that one. Brings me fresh-baked brownies once a week without fail. And she likes Sweetie-Pie."

Which alone made Liza a saint. The man's dog was an evil ankle biter. "Thank you," he said once more and entered Liza's house.

At first glance, it looked normal. Alarm system armed, all the furniture in the same place. But then he noticed all the things missing. The afghan that her mother had made was gone. The photos of her mother and sister that had lined the mantel. All gone.

Numbly he walked into the kitchen and opened a cupboard. Her dishes were still there, but all the cookware that had been her mother's was gone.

Slowly he climbed the stairs, knowing what he'd find. It still hurt to see.

Her bed was made with military precision, and not a single speck of dust was on the furniture she'd bought when they'd moved in. But the closet and drawers were empty, all the clothing gone. Her suitcases were gone. As was her gun safe.

Her bathroom was so clean that it sparkled, but every shelf was empty of toiletries. No shampoo that smelled like crisp apples. No makeup.

She *had* left a roll of toilet paper in the cabinet and a hand towel on the rack.

He swallowed hard.

She's gone. She left me.

No, she left, period. Not you. There was no you to leave.

"Bullshit," he hissed aloud. They were still friends. He still deserved a damn goodbye. But then he heard her voice, tentative and small.

You didn't feel the same way.

No. I didn't.

"Goddammit." He pulled out his personal phone and dialed her number. It rang several times before going to voice mail. Swearing viciously, he called again. This time she answered.

"Hello, Tom." The words were heavy and sad and he swallowed again.

I'm sorry. Come back. I'll try.

But none of those words would come out. Instead he snarled. "Where the *fuck* are you?"

He could hear her indrawn breath. "At Irina's."

I'm sorry. Come back. Please come back.

But once again, his mouth betrayed him. "You were supposed to stay home," he snapped. "What part of being in a sniper's sights did you not understand?"

This time the breath she drew was even and measured. "I'm fine. I am not your worry."

Anymore hung between them.

"I left a note on the fridge along with a check for next month's rent," she went on. "I'll set up autopay through my bank for the future."

"I don't care about the fucking rent!" he shouted.

"I do."

He opened his mouth to say . . . what, he had no idea, but just then his work phone pinged with an alert.

Dammit. Sunnyside Oaks's patient database had just been updated. "I need to call you back."

"No, you really don't. It's okay. Just find Eden so that Mercy will be safe."

And then she hung up, leaving him staring at his personal phone while his work phone continued to ping.

Fucking hell. Backing out of her bedroom, he slowly trudged down the stairs, wondering what to do. Wishing . . . but for what he didn't know.

He locked her door and, after checking to be sure his neighbor was gone, marched into his own house and up the stairs and sat down at his computer. Pulling up the window into Sunnyside's database, he saw that a new patient had been registered: Timothy Alcalde, age seventy-two, Caucasian male.

Not DJ Belmont, then. It had to be Pastor.

On autopilot, Tom took a screenshot of the file and carefully backed out, making sure he left no trace that he'd broken in. Then he sent the file to his own secure e-mail. He could upload it to the Bureau's servers when he got into the office.

He considered calling Raeburn, but had no energy for the conversation. So he texted instead. *New patient, 72yo man, Timothy Alcalde. Right age for Pastor.* He'd been forty-two when he'd fled to Eden thirty years ago.

And "Alcalde" meant "mayor" in Spanish. On another day, Tom might have appreciated the joke. The Eden assholes had already demonstrated that they put thought into names. He supposed "Timothy Pastora" would have been too obvious, even for them.

Excellent, was Raeburn's reply. *We'll apprehend ASAP.*

Um, no. That would be the wrong move. Fearing that Raeburn would go off half-cocked, Tom called his boss. "We can't just bust in and arrest him," Tom said when Raeburn answered.

"Why not?" Raeburn snapped. "I can have a warrant in ten minutes."

"Because we still don't know where Eden is. Do you want to bet those people's safety on Pastor rolling over and telling us? They've already demonstrated how ruthless they can be and we don't have any physical evidence on Pastor himself, only DJ. Without leverage, he's not going to simply give in."

Raeburn huffed, a frustrated sound. "No. I don't suppose he would."

Encouraged, Tom went on. "And we have to make sure we get Belmont at the same time, or he'll go under so far that we'll never find him. He'll keep coming after Mercy and Gideon."

"True," Raeburn admitted, disgruntled. "I doubt they'll discuss the compound's location specifically, but even a mention of Eden might be the leverage we need. I want eyes and ears inside that facility. Come in and we'll discuss our options."

Tom slipped his phone into his pocket. He should be energized and thrilled that they knew exactly where Pastor was, but he wasn't. He was too numb. *At least Liza is okay. Safe, anyway.*

He didn't think either of them was okay. He wasn't sure he'd ever be okay again.

TWELVE

Liza put her phone on Irina's kitchen table and picked up her fork, avoiding the older woman's eyes as she focused on the plate of eggs and bacon in front of her. Irina had seen the look on her face when she'd knocked on the front door that morning and insisted that she eat.

"Well," Irina said, "that explains the boxes in your car. You're moving out of Tom's place?"

"I'm moving out of the side of the duplex that I've been renting from Tom," she corrected, grateful that it was only the two of them in the homey quiet of Irina's kitchen. She couldn't have handled all of the Sokolovs that morning.

"Want to talk about it?"

"Not really. Unless you know someone who's looking to rent in a family-oriented neighborhood. Plenty of room for kids to run in the backyard."

Not that she'd dreamed about kids of her own.

Of course she had. *God, I was so stupid.* Tom had lost his child with Tory, and Liza had dreamed of giving him the family he'd always wanted. But he didn't think of her like that.

You didn't feel the same way.

No. I didn't.

"No, but you can post it on a realty site and we can put out some feelers."

"I appreciate it. I'm also looking for a job. Just until school starts in July."

Irina's brows lifted. "I thought you were going to take a holiday."

"Not now," Liza murmured. "My job at the veterans' home was only as a fill-in for a woman on maternity leave, so going back there isn't an option. I checked the want ads last night but didn't find anything."

She'd done a lot of things last night, because sleep had eluded her. She'd scoured the want ads, updated her résumé, gathered her letters of recommendation, and packed up her belongings.

"I know some people I can ask," Irina said. "There's always a demand for nursing assistants. Can you send me your résumé?"

"I have it with me." Liza retrieved her résumé and letters of recommendation from her handbag and slid them across the table so that Irina could examine them.

"Impressive. Coupled with your military service, you'll have no trouble getting work."

"That's what my nursing school advisor said. She was also army, back in the day, and helped me with financial aid for school and helped me find a job in the interim. She also helped me get my CNA license, all before my discharge was effective."

"Have you called her yet?"

"I plan to, later today." She'd be able to call on the drive to her tattoo appointment. The sketch was also in her handbag, carefully folded, just in case Sergio Iglesias was a nice guy and didn't throw her out after she asked him about the Eden tattoo.

She'd already texted Daisy to ask the woman to accompany her and gotten a "Hell, yeah" reply. Which presented another problem.

"Can I store my boxes in your garage? Just for today. I need to go somewhere with Daisy and she won't fit in my car right now."

Irina nodded. "Where will you go?"

"With Daisy?"

"No. Well, yes, but I meant where will you live now that you've moved out?"

"I don't know. I'll find a hotel for a few days while I look for a place. Just temporarily," she added hastily when Irina opened her mouth to speak. "I may be able to get a place in the dorm for the up-coming semester."

"You will stay here," Irina declared, her mouth set stubbornly.

"I will *not* stay here," Liza replied, calmly sipping her tea.

"With Sasha, then." Sasha was Irina's second-youngest daughter and lived in the house that Rafe had converted into apartments. Amos and Abigail lived on the top floor, Sasha on the middle, and Rafe and Mercy on the ground floor.

"Nope," Liza said with a smile to soften the refusal. "She and Erin are in the gooey and sweet phase at the moment and I won't impose. Right now, I need my own space."

Irina nodded, resigned. "I understand. If you won't live here or with Sasha, will you let me find you a place in a safe neighborhood until your school begins?"

Liza's smile felt wobbly. "Yes. Thank you. I can't be picky right now, but if the rent is affordable, I'd be grateful. That would be one thing I wouldn't have to worry about."

Irina released her hand but didn't move away, instead resting her chin on her fist, creating an air of companionable commiseration. "What else do you worry about?"

Liza was literally saved by the bell when the front door opened, making an alarm beep. That was new. "You have a new alarm?"

"No. I just set it to beep when anyone enters or leaves the house. I didn't ground Zoya for driving to San Francisco with Jeff yesterday morning, because her heart was in the right place and she is a safe driver. But I don't like the idea of her being able to sneak out, either."

"My mom would have loved you," Liza said with a genuine smile, and then she turned to embrace the child flying into her arms. "Miss Abigail! Good morning!"

"Morning, Liza! Morning, Miss Irina," Abigail added, her smile sunny. "Is there breakfast?"

"Abigail," Amos chided. He'd followed Abigail at a more sedate pace. "Don't be rude."

Abigail sighed. "Sorry, Papa."

"It is okay, *lubimaya*," Irina said. "You want some eggs? Or pancakes?"

Abigail looked undecided. "Both?"

Irina chuckled. "Wash your hands and set the table for you and your papa."

"Karl and Zoya, too?" Abigail asked.

"No, they're already gone." Irina turned to Amos. "Is Mercy coming?"

He shook his head. "No. She's staying with Rafe today. She said she'd do Abigail's science lesson with her this afternoon back at our house."

Abigail sobered. "It's because of Brother DJ. Rafe is afraid she'll be hurt. Mercy said that she'd stay to keep Rafe happy. And to bake me some cookies." She sidled up to Liza. "I brought my book. See?" She produced a copy of *Who Was Sally Ride?* from her book bag.

"And we will read it after breakfast," Liza promised, hugging her. "You have your orders, Private," she barked, pretending to be a commanding officer. "Wash hands. Set table. Go."

Abigail saluted, giggling when she accidentally poked her eye. "Yes, sir!"

GRANITE BAY, CALIFORNIA
THURSDAY, MAY 25, 9:45 A.M.

DJ slowly drove up and down the streets of the Sokolovs' neighborhood, searching for the best surveillance angle. He wasn't going to park here like he'd done the morning before.

This seemed like exactly the kind of place that would have an intrusive neighborhood watch program that might notice his truck parked for hours a second time. He'd already killed Mrs. Ellis for spying on him. He didn't want to kill anyone else.

Not that he minded killing people. He'd gotten very good at it. But a trail of dead bodies would be like a neon sign indicating his movements. Cops had forensics, and *those* were the guys who made him nervous. They already had his prints and his face. He wasn't going to telegraph his plans by leaving a bunch of dead bodies.

After breakfast with Coleen, DJ had taken her to the rehab center, where they'd gotten the welcome spiel, including the level of care Pastor would be receiving and all the security features the place provided. The facility and its grounds were surrounded by a wrought iron fence. The gate was activated by key card and every staff member was vetted. Families were offered wigs and other disguises so that they could visit undetected. Security cameras were placed everywhere. Halls and common areas were monitored twenty-four-seven. Cameras in the patients' rooms were only monitored by request or if there was a disturbance.

Which had made DJ think of Kowalski and all the cameras the bastard had installed in both his house and Mrs. Ellis's. And had prompted his early-morning visit to Walmart.

He'd taken a calculated risk going into the big store. He figured that the cops might have his face from a surveillance tape of his botched roof job the morning before, but nothing had shown up online. So maybe the office building hadn't had a security camera and he'd worried for nothing. Even if they had one, they hadn't posted footage in the media, so it was unlikely that anyone inside would recognize him.

If they had, his handgun was holstered under his jacket. Luckily no one had and he'd been left alone to shop. There were more eyes watching the electronics aisle, so he'd chosen the baby supply aisle instead. Baby monitors came with cameras, and cameras were what he needed. He'd bought one that had a video recording feature, paid cash, and walked out without a single raised eyebrow.

Now he needed to find the proper place to set up the camera. There was no rain in the forecast, so even though the unit wasn't waterproof, it would be okay for a few days.

He stopped the truck in front of the house he'd deemed to have the best view. It wasn't across the street from the Sokolovs, unfortunately. Ephraim had tried that, a fact included in the media coverage DJ had read while waiting for Pastor's surgery to be over. He'd also read that the homeowner had been saved by his daughter, who'd declared that she'd had extra security installed, so sitting too close to the Sokolovs' house was not an option.

Some assholes spoil it for the rest of us.

The house DJ had chosen was behind and to the right of the Sokolovs'. There was a gap in the trees, through which the street just beyond the Sokolovs' house was visible. A camera wouldn't capture the activities of individuals, but it would capture vehicles and license plates.

Getting out of his truck, he double-checked the magnetic sign he'd applied to the driver's door. Today he was posing as a contractor for PG&E.

Nobody questioned the presence of the utility company.

He crossed the homeowner's back lawn, along the man's eight-foot privacy fence, looking for the best spot for the baby monitor camera. It was light pink and would show up if he mounted it to the fence itself. But if he mounted it to one of the trees, he might be able to camouflage it with leaves.

He chose the tree and went down on one knee, laying out his tools, cursing his left arm, which still hung in the sling. Even though he'd developed the dexterity of his right hand, it was still his less dominant and clumsier. This injury made everything take longer.

"Hey! You there!"

DJ stilled. *Fucking hell.* Slowly he rose, tugging on the brim of his ball cap to hide his face. A man in his sixties stood near the fence, scowling. He'd either come from the house or just been walking down the street, paying attention to things not his business.

Damn neighborhood watchers.

"Good morning, sir," DJ said pleasantly.

The man's scowl slipped a little. "What are you doing?"

"I work for PG&E. We're monitoring the moisture level of the soil. Dry spots are tinder for wildfires." Kowalski had taught him that spiel as well.

"Okay." The man took a step forward, then stopped. "But that looks like a camera to me."

"It monitors temperature and moisture content," DJ explained, calm on the outside, but inside he was starting to worry.

"So you say. Looks like a camera to me. Maybe I should call your manager." The man's chin lifted slightly. "Or even the police."

For fuck's sake. Really? It appeared he might have to kill the man after all.

"Whoa, whoa." DJ took a step closer. "No need for that. I'll give you my number and you can call my boss." Of course the number was a fake and the man would probably end up talking to a contractor in L.A. who'd tell him he had the wrong number. But by then, DJ would be gone.

"No. I'm going to call the police." The man took out his cell phone and stared into the screen, unlocking it.

Sighing, DJ took out his gun. Of course it wouldn't be simple.

The man took a step back, wide-eyed. "What the hell?"

DJ approached the man slowly. "Drop the phone."

"I knew it," he hissed. "I called the cops already. They're on their way."

But he was clearly lying. The color had drained from his face and he was twitchy.

"Drop the phone," DJ repeated.

The man dropped the phone. Slipping his left arm from the sling, DJ managed to grab the phone while holding his gun on the trembling man. The phone was still unlocked and he confirmed that no outgoing calls had been made.

"I wish you'd just accepted that I was from PG&E. Give me your wallet."

Shaking, the man tossed his wallet to the ground. DJ fumbled with it, dropping his gaze only long enough to see the man's name and address. Sure enough, the man lived in the house behind the fence.

"Let's go home, Mr. Smythe," he said, gesturing with his gun. "Don't make a scene and you'll live to see another day. This gun has a silencer and I will drop you where you stand."

Nelson Smythe obeyed. "What are you going to do to me?"

"I'll tie you up until I can get away—if you cooperate. Make a fuss and you're dead. Got it?" They entered Smythe's backyard through a door in the fence. "Are you home alone?"

Smythe nodded again. "My wife is out of town until next week," he stammered. "I won't report you, I swear. Take my phone, my car, my money. Just don't tie me up. Nobody will find me. I'll die."

"Fine. Show me your car."

Body sagging in relief, Smythe led him into the garage, where a Lexus was parked. More importantly, there was a chest freezer up against the far wall.

"Stand next to the freezer," DJ commanded, and Smythe obeyed. "Now open it. I want to see what you have stored inside."

Frown deepening, Smythe lifted the freezer lid. "It's just frozen meat and—"

DJ fired, hitting Smythe right between the eyes. He used the backward momentum to push with his right shoulder, toppling the man into the freezer, where there was just enough room for him. DJ fired again, just to make sure.

Kowalski had taught him that, too. He'd learned more from Kowalski than he'd thought.

Holstering his gun, DJ checked Smythe's pockets, finding an engraved lighter, a half-smoked pack of Lucky Strikes, and the keys to the Lexus.

Excellent in more ways than one. DJ hadn't had a smoke in over a month and he'd missed it. He lit up a cigarette and inhaled, feeling his body relax. Now that Smythe was taken care of, he'd finish mounting the camera on the tree outside and get out of here.

Or . . . if the house was truly empty until Mrs. Smythe returned, he could hole up here.

Like Ephraim did in the house across from the Sokolovs?

Well, shit. Except DJ knew there was a wife who'd be arriving home at some point. If he could keep track of the wife's movements, it could work. For a day or two, at least.

He looked at Smythe's phone and cursed. It was locked again. *But . . .* Examining the phone's make and model, he was encouraged. Some of those phones had a major glitch—the facial recognition software worked even when the phone owner was asleep, unconscious, or even dead.

This, he'd determined on his own and had shared with Kowalski. Kowalski had been very pleased to learn this tidbit.

DJ held the phone screen over Nelson Smythe's face and, bingo, the phone unlocked. It wasn't a permanent solution, but he could at least find the wife's texts and Facebook and figure out where she was. As long as she wasn't headed to this house anytime soon, it could work.

He scrolled through the man's phone. She'd gone to her daughter's house. She'd been gone for a week and would stay through Memorial Day, returning home on Tuesday.

DJ was always mildly surprised when holidays like Memorial Day happened. Only Christmas and Easter were celebrated in Eden. All of the other holidays were either ignored or reviled. Valentine's Day was ignored. Halloween, the devil's day, was reviled. Fourth of July was also reviled, as it celebrated the government. Which Pastor said was evil.

It was the best way to frighten and manipulate his congregation.

Why are we moving? The government is coming. They destroyed the Branch Davidians. They will destroy us, too.

He'd believed Pastor's words until he was seventeen. Until DJ had killed his father and taken over as Eden's shopper. One glimpse at the real world and DJ had known Pastor's lies for what they were.

But he still didn't buy into the holidays. They were only good because sales of narcotics skyrocketed over long holiday weekends.

He'd take Memorial Day, though, if it meant he had the house through Monday. It wasn't like he planned to stay forever anyway. Just until he could figure out where Mercy was living.

The Smythes appeared to communicate through texts. There had been no calls between them, either incoming or outgoing, which was encouraging. It was less likely that the wife would be worried if her calls went unanswered, and as long as the dead man's face continued to unlock his phone screen, DJ could text back, keeping her from becoming suspicious.

Closing the freezer lid, he scouted every room in the house and found it unoccupied. The spare room was filled with sewing equipment, but it had a twin bed—and a view of the street he'd wanted to monitor in the first place. He could put the camera in the window and not worry about anyone else finding it.

Exhausted from all the driving the night before, DJ was tempted to take a nap, but he needed to get the camera from outside. Once it was in place, he could finally sleep.

SACRAMENTO, CALIFORNIA
THURSDAY, MAY 25, 10:30 A.M.

"This is fantastic work, Hunter," Croft said as Tom drove them across town. She was studying Pastor's medical file on her phone. "Looks like he took either a beating or a fall."

Tom wished he had an ounce of her enthusiasm, but all he could think about was Liza's empty closets. And how he'd yelled at her when that was the last thing he'd wanted to do.

Rob Winters had been a yeller. *God, don't let me be like him. Please.*

Tom thought he'd rather be dead than have an iota of his father's personality. But genetics were a bitch sometimes.

I'll go to Irina's as soon as I have a break. I'll take Liza flowers. She liked bright, happy flowers. He had to make this right.

"Hunter." Croft sounded annoyed. "Are you even listening to me?"

Tom realized that he'd completely missed what she'd said. "I'm sorry. My mind wandered."

"To the moon," Croft confirmed. "Are you okay?"

Nope. "Of course. I was thinking about the employee file." Raeburn had announced in the morning meeting that they wouldn't be storming the Sunnyside rehab center, but that they'd be focusing on recording conversations between Pastor and DJ while Pastor was recuperating. The mission was first to find Eden, then to punish those who'd committed crimes against its people. Raeburn had made it sound like it was all his own idea, but Tom wasn't going to call him on it. As long as they got eyes and ears inside, Tom was on board.

"Did you find anyone who might turn informant?"

"Maybe. I gave the list to Raeburn with a few recommendations." Raeburn was hoping to find someone who could be pressured to plant a few bugs in Pastor's hospital room and to keep tabs on DJ.

"Don't worry," Croft said quietly. "Raeburn may be a jackass on a personal level, but he's a good agent. If he said he won't raid the rehab center, then he won't."

Tom managed a smile, both grateful and a little irritated that Croft read him so well. "What's this tattoo artist's name again?" he asked, changing the subject. "Your top pick, I mean."

They were headed to a tattoo parlor in Natomas. Croft's source had never seen DJ Belmont or anyone with the Chicos gang tat but had recognized the style. They now had the names of a few possible tattoo artists and were following up on the most likely offender.

"Dixie Serratt. She's on parole, by the way, so if she did the Chicos tats or knows who did, she might be persuaded to tell us."

"Excellent."

They were silent for a time, and then Croft sighed. "If you're in a bad headspace right now, I need to know. We don't know what we're walking into. If you're not sharp, you need to say so."

Tom wanted to punch himself in the face. Liza deserved better than his anger, and Croft deserved a partner who had her back. "I'm good. Read me Dixie Serratt's rap sheet."

Croft complied, and hearing the severity and breadth of Dixie's crimes helped Tom's focus more than anything else. The fifty-five-year-old woman had committed everything from manslaughter and kidnapping to petty theft. There was a vehicular homicide in there, too.

"She's a bad motherfucker," Tom commented as they stopped outside Dixie's studio.

"She really is. I'm glad you're not a person who thinks that women can't be evil."

"Oh, I know they can. My aunt Dana had a female serial killer terrorize her women's shelter, back when I was a teenager. That woman had no soul. She burned our house down and even hit my mother with a car, trying to kill her."

"Oh my God! Was your mother okay?"

"Yes, thankfully. My mom is pretty resilient. You ready to talk to Dixie?"

"I'm ready to try. She may not talk to us if she's been doing tats for the Chicos, as it would be a violation of her parole, but hopefully she'll let something useful slip."

The inside of the studio was what Tom expected. He'd never gotten a tattoo himself but had accompanied Liza when she'd gotten hers. This place was clean and the buzzing sound of the needles was almost soothing.

Behind the counter stood a man wearing a short-sleeved button-down shirt and a paisley tie. Both forearms bore colorful sleeves. "Can I help you?" he asked, giving them a suspicious look.

"We're here to see Dixie Serratt," Croft said, without showing her badge.

The man sighed. "Dixie!" he called. "You got POs here again." He looked back at them with a mild sneer. "You people just won't leave her alone, will you?"

A tiny woman with tats covering nearly every inch of skin appeared from the back of the shop. "What?" she asked rudely. "Who are you? What happened to O'Leary?"

"We're not parole officers," Croft said. "I'm Special Agent Croft and this is Special Agent Hunter. We'd like to ask you some questions."

Tom was watching Dixie carefully. She'd stiffened, her expression briefly telegraphing that she was considering running.

Croft tilted her head toward Tom. "He'll just chase you, Miss Serratt. And he's young enough and his legs are long enough to catch you."

Dixie drew a breath and let it out. "Fine. We're just talking, right?"

"Yes, ma'am," Tom said. *Unless you've done something illegal.*

"Then come with me." They followed her to one of the unoccupied rooms, where she gestured at the two chairs.

Croft sat, the picture of calm. Tom sat, kind of wishing that Dixie had run. He had a lot of pent-up energy he would have liked to expel.

"Chinese Cobras, also known as Chicos," Croft said, and Dixie flinched.

"You don't start out throwin' softballs, do you, lady? I don't have nothin' to do with them."

"But you have," Tom said. "In the past?"

"In the far past," Dixie claimed. "Way far. I got nothin' for you guys." She was halfway to the curtain separating the room from the hallway when Croft stopped her in her tracks.

"You are required to cooperate with law enforcement, Miss Serratt. Otherwise you're violating your parole. We'd appreciate your help."

Dixie turned to confront them, face hard and fists clenched harder. "Right. Like I have a fuckin' choice." She rolled her eyes but plopped down on a stool.

Croft pulled a photo of DJ Belmont from her pocket. It was the still Tom had printed from the office building surveillance video. "This guy. You seen him?"

Dixie snatched the photo and peered down at it. Tom could see the moment that she recognized DJ's face. And that she briefly considered denying that recognition. "Yeah." She returned the photo to Croft and settled herself in her chair, crossing her arms over her chest.

Croft just smiled, unperturbed. "When did you first see him?"

"The night I did his tat."

Tom noted it on his tablet. "When was that, ma'am?"

"You can cut the 'ma'am' bullshit, buddy. You think you can butter me up?"

Tom didn't rise to the bait. "When was that, ma'am?" he repeated.

Dixie's shoulders slumped. "Has to have been at least five years. I don't know his name, so don't ask. They paid cash, so don't ask about receipts, either."

"Five years is a long time ago," Croft remarked. "Was there something about him that made you recall his face after so much time?"

Dixie looked away, but not before a spark of fear flickered in her eyes.

"Did he hurt you, ma'am?" Tom asked kindly. "Or threaten you?"

"No," Dixie said, but too quickly. "I didn't want to do the tat. I was done with that life. But he'd been sent by his boss and he wasn't leaving until he got one. It was some kind of initiation thing, I think." She swallowed. "I didn't want to do it."

"But he forced you to," Croft said sympathetically.

Dixie simply shook her head, making it clear she'd said all she would on the topic.

"You mentioned this man's boss," Tom said. "Who was he?"

Dixie paled, shaking her head harder. "Haul me in for breaking parole if you want to. I'll be safer back in prison."

Croft frowned, holding up DJ's photo. "Are you afraid of this man or his boss?"

"Both." The word was barely audible. Her skin had grown sweaty, her fear palpable. "Mostly his boss."

"What did he do?" Tom asked.

She held out her arms wordlessly. Tattooed vines covered her skin, but there were areas where the ink hadn't taken as well. Scars. Round, about a centimeter in diameter.

Tom's stomach roiled, because he recognized those scars. He had several. His biological father had given them to him, trying to make Tom into a man. He'd been six years old. He could still smell the tobacco. And the burning skin.

Someone had held Dixie Serratt down and burned her skin with cigarettes. He found himself unable to speak and was grateful when Croft stepped in.

"This boss person did this to you?" she asked. "With cigarettes?"

"Yeah, because I didn't want to do any more tats for his boys. The next time one of his boys came in, I said yes."

Tom blew out a breath, trying to get hold of himself. "Can you tell us anything about him?"

Dixie's eyes narrowed, like she saw his reaction and understood. "No. He's a big deal in these parts. Dig into the Chicos and his name will come up. Talk to the high school kids. They know the dealers. The dealers know *him*."

"Thank you," Tom said, somehow keeping his voice level.

"When was the last tat you did for them?" Croft asked.

"Three years ago. Right before I went in again." She grimaced. "I drove when I was high. My fault." She dug in her pocket and pulled out an NA chip. "Two years sober. I'm trying to get my life right, but I draw the line at having my throat slit or getting a needle full of heart medicine."

Tom's eyes widened and Dixie's slammed shut.

"Shit," she muttered, covering her face with her hands. "I'm done talking to you. Please go."

Croft glanced over at him, then gestured at the curtain with a tilt of her head. "Thank you, Miss Serratt. We'll leave our cards here on the table. If you think of anything else or receive any threats from the Chicos or their associates, please call. We'll see ourselves out."

Tom waited until they were both in the SUV to lean his head back and close his eyes. "Fucking hell," he whispered.

"You gonna tell me what got you going in there?" Croft asked.

"My biological father was abusive. I know what it feels like to get those scars."

"Ah, shit, Hunter," Croft murmured. "Good to know. For what it's worth, you rallied well. So. You believed her?"

"I did. She's no angel, but I don't think she was lying today. I didn't want to force her to talk. Felt like we wouldn't have anywhere to go in the future if we shoved her over the edge."

"Good instincts. I was in the same place. At least now we can confirm that DJ has a Chicos tat, like the little girl described. If we can track down other gang members, we might be able to find out where he's hiding."

The mention of Abigail made Tom think of Liza. *Not now.* "Where to?"

"The local precinct. They might know where the Chicos hang out. I agree with waiting to grab both DJ and Pastor until we know where Eden is, but we need to keep tabs on DJ until then. Mercy's life depends on it."

"We're one hundred percent on the same page." Tom had put the SUV into gear when his work phone buzzed. "Special Agent Hunter."

"Special Agent Hunter, this is Sergeant Farley with the Yuba City PD. I got your name from Sergeant Howell of SacPD. We have a crime scene you should see."

Howell was the guy they'd met on the rooftop the morning before.

This has to be about Belmont. "Can I put you on speaker? I'm with my partner, Special Agent Croft." The man agreed and Tom put his phone on the center console. "Agent Croft, we've got Sergeant Farley, Yuba City PD, on the line. What do you have?"

"A homicide. Victim is Minnie Ellis, seventy-five, Caucasian. Found by her friend this morning, dead in her bed. There are signs of forced entry. The night before last, Mrs. Ellis told her friend that she suspected her neighbor of fishy business. Nobody is answering at the house next door. It appears to be empty, but we found trash in the can on the curb. Dusted a beer can for prints and came up with a match. Seems Mrs. Ellis's neighbor's prints were also found on a railing of a rooftop yesterday morning at Sergeant Howell's crime scene. DJ Belmont. Ring a bell?"

"Can you text me the address?" Tom asked, his pulse ticking up. "We're on our way."

THIRTEEN

W e're looking for Sergeant Farley," Croft said when they got to Minnie Ellis's home in Yuba City. She held out her badge, as did Tom. "Special Agents Croft and Hunter."

The uniformed officer standing guard at the front door frowned. "Hunter? Tom Hunter?"

Tom knew that the cop had recognized him from his pro days, but Croft seemed oblivious. "Farley is expecting us," she said tartly.

The cop blushed. "It's just that I—Never mind. Here are your booties. Follow me."

Slipping the booties over his shoes, Tom gave the man a smile. "She's not a basketball fan."

The cop laughed. "Well, I am. Miss seeing you on the court. Didn't know you were . . ." He gestured at Tom's badge. "You know."

Tom lips twitched. "I know."

Croft finished putting on her booties with a frown. "Really? You have fans?"

"Only a few," Tom said.

"A few," the officer agreed with sham gravity.

She sighed. "Officer, can you just take us to Sergeant Farley?"

"Of course." He led them to a bedroom, where Farley stood next to a CSU tech standing on a stepladder, pulling something from the ceiling. "Sergeant Farley? The FBI is here, sir."

Farley turned, his expression sour. "Hunter and Croft, right? Okay, this went from bad to worse. The victim, Minnie Ellis, was found in her bed by her friend, like I told you. I'll show you the rush job the killer did to repair the broken door frame. Might have passed muster if the friend hadn't made a fuss. ME found a needle prick in the victim's arm." He touched the inside of his elbow. "They'll test for the usual heart-stoppers. Again, it might have passed muster as natural causes without the friend's testimony. And now this." He pointed to the CSU tech.

Tom walked as close as he could without knocking the tech off the ladder. The tech held a small wireless camera. "Was it active?"

"Still is. We might be able to trace the signal. Or not," he added when the red light on the device suddenly died. "Looks like we were made. Dammit."

"Dammit indeed," Tom agreed with a scowl. "Maybe we can get prints off it."

"Maybe," the tech said, huffing in frustration. "There are cameras in every room. Including the bathroom."

"Who spies on a seventy-five-year-old woman?" Croft asked. "In her bathroom?"

"Good question," Farley said. "Somebody's been watching her. From the dust on the camera lens, it's likely been for a while. We don't know who planted them, but the neighbor is a suspect in her death based on her friend's statement, like I told you on the phone. We went to question him, which was when we found his trash."

"This guy had a sniper rifle on that rooftop yesterday," Tom said. "He could have shot Mrs. Ellis, but he must not have wanted the attention, so he tried to make it look like a natural death."

"That's what I think." Farley checked his phone. "Excellent. We got a warrant for the house next door. I assume you want to join me?"

"You assume correctly," Croft said. "Lead the way."

The four of them moved through the house toward the kitchen. All of the walls were covered in photographs. Mrs. Ellis had a lot of grand-children who seemed to love her. Plastic containers of cookies sat piled on the kitchen table along with several pies, all with little name tags.

"She loved with food," Tom said. "Has her family been notified?"

"Her son," Farley replied. "He was supposed to get one of the pies. The other says 'Johnny.' Her friend says that's the neighbor's name."

"She made him a *pie* and he *killed* her?" Croft demanded incredu-lously. "What an asshole."

Tom barked out a surprised laugh. "Well, yeah. But we already knew that," he said, joining Farley at the kitchen door. The door frame had been spackled and sanded. It wasn't an awful job. "I might not have noticed that if I wasn't looking."

"Which was his intent." Farley shot an amused glance at Croft. "Him being an asshole."

Croft wasn't offended. "My opinion stands. Let's check the house next door. Who owns it?"

Farley checked his notes. "Mr. Johnny Derby. My men are waiting on me to open Mr. Derby's door. Garvin, you're to continue securing the crime scene."

The officer who'd recognized Tom seemed disappointed, but didn't argue. "Yes, sir."

DJ Belmont's house was similar to the one they'd just left, except for the broken front door. The two officers who'd busted it were rub-bing their shoulders. "Ready for you, sir."

"He owns a house," Croft muttered under her breath as they walked through the kitchen.

"He was the only one to leave—" Tom stopped himself from say-ing *Eden*. "Looks like he kept a separate life." But sterile. There were no photographs or any personal belongings.

"But why?" Croft pressed. "Did he just flop here on the weekends?"

"Maybe." On a hunch, he checked the corners of the ceiling. *Yep.*

That was what he'd thought. "But look at that." He pointed to a camera, similar to the one they'd found in Mrs. Ellis's house.

"Why?" Farley asked. "Was someone spying on him while he was spying on the old lady?"

Tom remembered what Dixie Serratt had said about DJ's boss. "Or his boss distrusts him."

Farley gave him a sharp look. "Care to explain that?"

Croft had made the connection. "We have information that the suspect has a Chicos tattoo."

Farley blinked. "Oh shit. That drug gang is here? In my town?"

"So it would seem," Croft said. "And his boss is not a kind individual. I'd have your Latent team dust every damn inch of this place. You might get a lucky hit."

"I will," Farley said grimly. "Thank you. Let's check out his bedroom."

The first bedroom had a queen-sized bed that appeared to have been slept in recently, but the closets were empty.

Like Liza's closets. Tom's chest squeezed hard. *Dammit. Not now.* He forced thoughts of Liza from his mind. *Focus on your damn job, Hunter.*

Tom took the second bedroom, which appeared to have been used as an office. There were three dust-free areas on the desk. Two were about the size of a printer, and the third might have been a laptop. "He took his electronics with him." He sniffed the air. "Do you smell that?"

Croft inhaled through her nose, then frowned. "Waffles?"

"It's the 3D filament," Tom told her. "It's derived from corn. Smells like waffles."

"So your theory about the license plate holds water." She smiled at him. "Nice job, rookie."

"It also means that he was running the 3D printer recently. Maybe last night. He's probably made new license plates."

"I figured he would," Croft said grimly. "The BOLO on the box truck is worthless now."

"Sergeant Farley." One of the uniformed officers was standing in the doorway. "There's something in the basement you want to see. Or not see. Maybe just smell."

Tom had followed Farley one step down the basement stairs when he smelled it. "Whoa." The skunky odor of weed became stronger as he descended the stairs. But the basement was empty. "They moved it out."

"It was on pallets," the officer said, shining his flashlight at the disturbances in the dust. "Looks like they had a significant stash, even if the pallets were only stacked one high. But there are scrapes along the walls where a second level of pallets might have sat."

"Good work," Farley said. His phone buzzed. "Excuse me. I need to take this. It's my clerk." He walked toward a door to the side yard, checking his signal. "Yes?" he answered, then listened. "You got a warrant started?" Then he smiled. "Good job. Yes, I'll bring you a milkshake. Yes, it'll be chocolate." He ended the call and returned to Tom and Croft. "The house next door is owned by an Oakland couple. Their tenant's name also is Mr. Derby, and I have a very smart clerk. When she saw the name, she immediately started another warrant."

"Then she deserves a chocolate milkshake," Tom said.

"There's a path between the house next door and this one," Farley explained as they ascended the stairs. "Not a paved path, but one beaten into the dirt. Lots of foot traffic between this place and the one next door. Like boxes being carried, maybe?"

"You're thinking a grow house?" Croft asked.

Farley nodded. "I was afraid this would sprout back up. You Feds took out so many of those grow houses a few years back. The part of me that still believes in the Easter Bunny hoped that would be the end of it."

His officers broke through this door as they had the last one, and Tom whistled from the threshold, because there was no real floor to walk on. "That is a lot of weed."

The floors were covered in dirt, and marijuana plants grew in neat rows. A watering system hung from the ceiling and grow lights were positioned at regular intervals, bolted to the walls. Extension cords ran every which direction.

Crouching down, Farley pulled a leaf from the plant closest to the door. "Ready to harvest." He stood up, dusting the dirt from his hands. "Not a bad haul."

Croft stuck her head in the open door. "That's a lot of pot to remove. This house is trashed. Let's check it out. He might have left something behind."

But he hadn't. There were no beds or clothing in the bedrooms, no food in the kitchen, no appliances of any kind. There wasn't even a refrigerator, all the power going instead to the grow lamps.

"We're heading back to the field office," Croft said once they'd searched the small house. "Thank you for getting in touch with us, Sergeant Farley. If your team turns anything up, please let us know."

"Of course." Farley looked across the lawn at Officer Garvin, the uniform left behind to protect the crime scene. "I think my officer really wants to talk to you, Agent Hunter. He'll probably ask for an autograph, just to prepare you."

Croft frowned. "Wait. You knew who Agent Hunter was, too?"

"Before you got here," Farley said. "I looked you two up. Not much on you, Agent Croft—no offense—but this guy? His name gets a shit ton of hits."

"Wonderful," Croft grumbled. "Although I have to say, he's pretty humble to be so famous."

"Thank you," Tom said graciously. "I'll meet you at the car." He ambled over to where Officer Garvin stood nervously. "What can I do for you, Officer?"

Garvin exhaled nervously. "My kid's birthday's next week. He's a huge fan. Can't rip him away from the TV when a game is on. Knows all the stats. He'd love an autograph from you."

Tom gave the man his card. "E-mail me your address. I've got gear just cluttering a closet. I may have a few basketballs. Won't be a game ball, but hopefully he'll still like it."

"Thank you," Garvin said. "He will be over the moon."

Tom shook the very happy father's hand. "Nice to meet you. Have a great day."

When he got back to the SUV, Croft was rolling her eyes. "Does this happen often?"

"Not really. As time passes it'll be even less frequent." He settled into his seat and started the engine but didn't drive away.

"What are you thinking about?" she asked.

"DJ Belmont's houses," Tom said. "If this was where he slept when he came down from Eden, where will he sleep now? He has to know that he can't come back here."

"He did clean his place out," Croft agreed. "We can send his photo to hotels and B and Bs around Sacramento. He might also be staying at the rehab center with Pastor."

"Which is why I want eyes and ears inside the place. If he's there with Pastor and they talk, we need to know what they're saying."

"I agree and so does Raeburn. He's working on that. So why are you still frowning?"

"He *has* to know that we're looking for him. He might not know that we got his photo from the security cameras from yesterday's office building, but he has to know that we have his description from Mercy, Gideon, and Amos. If I were him, I wouldn't stay at a hotel."

Her smile was encouraging. "Where would you stay, Tom?"

"Somewhere I trusted. Where I'd be safe."

"Friends, maybe? I'd say family, but he doesn't have any. His father's dead."

That was what had been bothering him. "But his father's family isn't." Tom searched the files on his phone for the folder on Eden. "We checked out Waylon Belmont's family weeks ago. He was from Benicia and his mother and his brother still live there. The brother, Merle, was the one who filed the missing-person report on DJ Belmont when he disappeared when he was a little boy."

"When he was taken to Eden."

Tom nodded. "I believe so. The timeline matches up, anyway. He disappeared with his mother when he was four years old, a few months after Eden was started. I called Waylon's brother, but he hadn't heard from DJ and had no idea where he'd be. He and his wife thought DJ had to be dead after so much time. At the time I hoped he *was* dead."

"Maybe we should pay them a visit now that we know he's not dead, if for no other reason than to warn them."

"I think so too, but first . . ." He found the paragraph in his Eden file and passed his phone to Croft. "The Belmonts own a house that they rent out, also in Benicia. It's a long shot, but . . ." He shrugged. "It's only an hour away, so not too much time lost if it's a bust."

Croft tapped her finger against her chin as she considered it. "It *is* a long shot. I think it's more likely that he'd stay with a gang member around here. Let's check with the local PD and see if they can tell us where Chicos members hang out. If we come up dry, we'll drive out to Benicia. And if we come up dry there, we can cross it off as where he isn't. Sound good?"

Tom put the SUV into gear. "Sounds good to me."

GRANITE BAY, CALIFORNIA
THURSDAY, MAY 25, 2:00 P.M.

DJ woke abruptly, panicking for the second it took him to remember where he was.

Nelson Smythe. The man was dead in his own freezer and this was his spare room.

DJ lay there for another minute while his racing pulse slowed. Then for another few minutes while he appreciated the softness of the bed. He'd thought that the bed in his Yuba City house was comfortable, especially compared to the hard pallet on the harder cave floor.

This bed, though . . . It was like a goddamn cloud. Nothing hurt, he realized. His back wasn't sore and his arm wasn't throbbing. He tested his shoulder joint gingerly. It was still stiff. Still sore. But the overwhelming pain was gone.

He didn't care what Pastor said. He was getting himself a mattress like this when he returned to Eden. He didn't care if it was vanity or any of the shit Pastor spewed.

DJ found his phone and tapped the screen, only to have his pulse start racing again. "No way." There was no way that it was two o'clock in the fucking afternoon. He'd only meant to rest for an hour. He'd set an alarm on his phone, for God's sake. Hadn't he?

He opened the clock app and blew out a frustrated breath. He'd set the alarm for eleven p.m., not a.m. *Goddammit.* Then he spied the light pink camera on the window and remembered why he'd come here to begin with.

"Shit." He lurched from the bed, making his arm throb again. "Fuck." He'd set his alarm for one hour. One hour. He'd wanted to check the camera feed, to make sure it was recording properly. If it wasn't, he'd only have lost an hour.

Now he'd lost four.

Snarling under his breath, he connected the camera to his laptop. It downloaded, thankfully, so it had recorded something. He reset the camera on the windowsill and returned to the soft bed to review the footage.

Nothing happened for the longest time, and then a UPS truck passed by. A few minutes later the same UPS truck came from the opposite direction. DJ paused the video and zoomed in on the driver. Nobody he knew. Certainly not Mercy.

Unless she was hiding in the back of the truck. *It's what I would do.*

He noted the license plate and restarted the video. After ten minutes he grew impatient and began fast-forwarding. At about sixty minutes, a pickup truck passed by the camera's lens.

DJ paused the video. The truck looked familiar. It was a black Ford F-150 and he'd owned one similar to it—just a lot older. His had belonged to his father and was a few years old when he'd inherited it, seventeen years ago. Waylon had bought a similar one new in '89, days before he and Pastor had headed up to the first Eden site. DJ had helped his father work on it.

When the truck had worn out, Waylon had wanted a new one, but Pastor had insisted he buy the same make and model—and not new. He'd been insistent that as much around the compound stay the same as was possible.

It was Pastor's way of trapping time in a bubble. If the congregation got dulled to the passage of time, they would grow more compliant.

The concept had made sense to DJ. He'd planned to replace his truck and was going to get another used black Ford F-150.

Except his truck had been stolen by that bastard Amos Terrill. The man had stowed away in the back and, when DJ was occupied, had driven away in it.

DJ's temper boiled. He hadn't been aiming at Amos that day a month ago. He'd meant to shoot Mercy Callahan, but Amos had come running from the woods to throw himself on top of her. The bullet had gotten Amos in the neck and DJ had spent the last month satisfied that the man had bled out.

DJ paused the video. This F-150 was brand spanking new. The chrome still shone and there wasn't a trace of rust. Slightly envious, he noted its license plate, then zoomed in. And—

"Motherfucker," he hissed. "What the fuck? What is he doing here?"

It was *Amos*. Amos Terrill. It was just a glimpse, less than a half second of video, but DJ would know that bearded aw-shucks face anywhere.

The fucker was alive. And he'd had the nerve to get a truck just like the one he'd stolen.

DJ's fists clenched and he had to draw a breath to calm himself, because he was angry. Furious. And tempted to throw his laptop into the wall.

But you can't kill him if you can't track him. And you can't track him without your laptop.

When he'd sufficiently calmed, he examined the truck's interior.

There was someone in the back seat, but the windows were covered by shades, too dark for him to see any details other than the fact that they were small.

That could be Abigail, he thought, encouraged. When he found out where Amos was living, he could kill him, grab the kid, and deliver her to Eden. That would make Pastor happy, at least.

Hitting play, he shrank the video screen so that it was side by side with the browser tab he opened next. He could keep an eye on the video as he ran a search on Amos's license plates.

He stole a lot of the information he came across, but he paid for the search tools that he used. They were more reliable and, as he'd found out the hard way, could make a critical difference when approaching a new customer or supplier.

"Well, fuck," he muttered when the results flashed on his screen. The truck had been bought by a corporation. That was going to take a little more time.

He'd maximized the video screen, focusing again on the traffic up and down the street, when his sat phone buzzed. Startled, he jumped a little, then groaned. It was Kowalski.

"Where the fuck are you?" Kowalski shouted when DJ hit accept.

DJ bit back a shout of his own. "Why?" he asked calmly. "Why are you shouting?"

"You are on the fucking news! Your stupid face is on the fucking news! I told you to make it look like natural causes!"

Shit. Mrs. Ellis. DJ hadn't believed the cops would buy it.

"I did everything you said," he replied, keeping the defensive challenge from his tone.

"No," Kowalski said coldly, and his stone-cold quiet was far scarier than his screaming had been. "You did only a *third* of what I told you to do, and now her house is crawling with cops."

"I killed her. I didn't leave a trace. I even fixed her fucking door after I broke in. What didn't I do?" DJ demanded, exasperated.

"The friend. Remember her? The one the old lady called?"

DJ's blood chilled and his gut clenched. *Fuck.* "I got her number from the caller ID on old lady Ellis's phone."

"But you did not kill her."

No, I didn't. How had he forgotten? Pastor. That was how he'd forgotten. He'd gotten the call from Coleen and he'd immediately packed up and headed to Eden. "Shit," he whispered.

"Yeah. Shit. You are an idiot. She discovered the old woman's body. I thought for a while that the police would search her place and let it go, but no. She told them you were antisocial and that the old lady feared you, so they brought in a forensics team, who found the cameras that you *didn't cover up.* Now they know someone was watching her."

DJ swallowed hard. *Dammit.* "I—" His heart was pounding hard. *Damn you, Pastor. And damn me for being at your beck and call.* "I'm . . . I'm sorry. I fucked up."

"You think?" Kowalski asked coldly. "The cops believed the old bitch's friend and now your fucking face is on every TV and computer screen. Way to go, kid."

DJ bristled. He was so damn tired of being browbeaten. He was also annoyed, because he'd hoped yesterday's office building hadn't had cameras. He couldn't fix that now.

But Kowalski was right about the Ellis situation. He needed to fix that. "What can I do?"

Kowalski sighed. "I already took care of it. Where are you right now?"

"At a hotel," he lied. "My father is in the rehab center and I wanted to stay close for the first day or two."

"Okay." Kowalski sounded weary now. "You owe me, though. I had to pull strings to get your name cleared."

"It's cleared?" DJ asked, stunned.

"It will be. I can't have one of my top men hiding from the cops. If you're going to be in the top tier of my organization, you have to be able to rub elbows with the politicians."

DJ frowned. "What does that mean?"

"It means I'd planned to promote you, asshole," Kowalski snapped. "Jesus, maybe I should reconsider. You're sounding stupid today."

"Just tired," DJ said. "Sorry."

"Yeah, well. I need you to run an errand for me."

"What kind of errand?" DJ asked warily.

"The kind I need run," Kowalski snapped again. "Pick up a package for me. I'll text you the address. When you've picked it up, let me know and I'll send you my address. Come to the house. We'll talk about your promotion."

DJ blinked. He'd never been invited to Kowalski's home before. He didn't even know where the man lived. "Of course. Send me the package pickup address."

"Don't disappoint me again, boy. I'm giving you another chance. Do not fuck it up."

I'm not your damn boy. "I won't," DJ promised, swallowing back his irritation.

A minute later, an address in Stockton popped up in a text. Along with: ***Don't fuck it up.***

"Asshole," DJ muttered. But he couldn't really blame Kowalski for being angry. He had dropped the ball with Mrs. Ellis. *Good thing I cleaned out the house.*

The cops could search all they wanted. They weren't going to find anything of his.

MONTEREY, CALIFORNIA
THURSDAY, MAY 25, 2:50 P.M.

"This is the place," Daisy said from the back seat. "Sal Ibarra a.k.a. Sergio Iglesias's tattoo parlor. Made it with ten minutes to spare."

Gideon was searching the street, gun in hand, as it had been for the entire trip. "What's your plan again?"

Liza hadn't been pleased when Daisy's VW Beetle had pulled into Irina's garage with Gideon's Chevy Suburban following behind her, but he'd promised he would only be involved in a civilian role and that he wouldn't frighten the tattoo artist by questioning him. He was there as protection, firmly stating that while he couldn't stop Liza from driving to Monterey on her own, Daisy would not be joining her without him.

The more Liza had considered it, though, the more relieved she'd been. She hadn't been afraid for herself, but she'd never be able to live with herself if Daisy somehow got hurt. So Liza had driven Gideon's Suburban while Gideon had ridden shotgun, making sure that no one had followed them. Daisy sat in the back with her rifle ready.

They had Liza's back and she was grateful. "I was going to ask him about the person he tattooed with the Eden design and hope he doesn't run from me, too."

"And then you're going to ask him to tattoo you," Gideon said flatly. "I still think this is a bad plan."

"Which part?" Liza asked. "The part where I ask him about the Eden tattoo, or getting a tattoo?" She'd told them about wanting the tattoo before they'd left Irina's house, because that would add a few hours to their trip.

"Both parts." Gideon shook his head. "Why are you getting a tattoo today? From this guy?"

"Because Liza is a nice person," Daisy answered for her. "She thinks he needs the money because he left his old tattoo business behind when the Feds scared him to death. And he's got a little kid, so they probably need the cash."

"I guess so," Gideon said begrudgingly. "But why do you want a tattoo today?"

Liza pulled her sketch from her handbag and handed it to him. "This is what I want done."

"It's a memorial tattoo," he said quietly, all irritation gone from his voice.

Liza thought of Fritz, of how he'd given his life for her. "For the friends I lost. And . . ." She drew a deep breath and let it out slowly. "And for my husband, who died saving my life."

The car went utterly silent.

Then Daisy whistled. "You are a vault, Liza Barkley. I never would have guessed that you kept a secret like that. Now I know who to tell if I ever have a burning secret I can't tell Gideon."

"Hey," Gideon protested.

"Like a birthday present," Daisy told him, then turned to Liza, her eyes gone soft. "If you ever want to talk about him, I'm always ready to listen. If you don't, that's okay, too."

"Thank you. I might take you up on it." Liza was surprised to realize that she just might. Telling them hadn't been as hard as she'd anticipated. "I have nightmares about them. Last night's was really bad. I'm hoping that carrying them on my back will help me lay them to rest."

Gideon returned the sketch to Liza with a gentle smile. "I understand now. Do you want me to come in with you or wait out here?"

Liza folded the sketch and put it back in her bag. "I think I should talk to him first and feel him out. You might need to stay out here the whole time."

"That's okay," he said. "I can watch for trouble better from out here. What about Daisy?"

Liza turned to the back seat. "What do you think, Daisy?"

Daisy grimaced. "Maybe I should wait here with Gideon until you calm him down. Text me when I should come in. I've got e-mail to catch up on, so it's fine."

"Good luck," Gideon said sincerely. "Wave if you need us."

Liza hoped that she wouldn't. *Please let Sergio know something. Please let him tell me.*

Sergio stood behind the counter, welcoming her with a wide smile. He appeared to be in his midthirties. "I'm Sal Ibarra." His new name. "You must be Liza?"

"I am," Liza said.

"Please come in." He motioned her to a sitting area.

"Can we talk a little first?" Liza asked when they were seated.

"Of course. You've booked out my afternoon, so you must know what you want."

"I do." She patted her handbag. "I made a sketch." She drew a breath. *Forward, soldier. Just do it.* "I'm hoping you'll still be willing to tattoo me after we've talked."

Fear flickered in his eyes. "What is this?"

"Nothing bad," Liza assured him. "I'm not law enforcement. I'm a normal person."

Sergio edged forward, looking like he was preparing to bolt. "A normal person," he repeated.

"Well, I served in the army," Liza amended. "But I'm not a cop and I'm not FBI or ICE. I wanted to talk to you about a tattoo you did." From her handbag, she pulled a copy of the Eden tattoo that he'd posted on his old Instagram account. "This one."

Sergio lurched to his feet. "No. Please go. The last time someone talked to me about this, the FBI came. I am not a criminal."

Liza slowly rose, her hands out in an attempt to calm him. "Mr. Iglesias, please, just hear me out. I don't believe you are a criminal. I think you're a father trying to support his family. But my family is in danger right now and I really hope you can help us."

Sergio still looked ready to run. "Why? Why are you interested in this tattoo? It's old."

"Because it's a symbol of slavery. My friend was forced to wear a locket with this design on a chain around her neck. *A dog chain.* Nothing pretty. Her brother was forced to get the tattoo. Both were assaulted. Both nearly died, but they were able to escape. Now they're in danger because the people who hurt them don't want them to talk."

"I'm so sorry." Sergio sank back down to the sofa and seemed to deflate. "But I don't want any trouble."

"You won't get any trouble from us," Liza promised.

Sergio tensed again. "Us?" He looked through the window to Gideon's Suburban parked on the curb. "Who is 'us'?"

"The people who don't want my friends to talk tried to shoot me a few days ago, so I brought protection. We don't care if you're undocumented or not. I swear."

Sergio's jaw tightened. "But I'm not undocumented. I've had a green card since I was a boy, just arriving from El Salvador with my parents. But a customer of mine didn't like the tattoo I gave her, even though she signed off on the design before I started. She threatened to have me deported. I told her I had a green card, but she said that her father was with ICE and that it wouldn't matter. Men claiming to be ICE agents came to my old studio and threatened me. I don't know if they were ICE or not, but they scared me. And they scared my wife."

Liza ignored the temper that fizzled under her skin on his behalf. "The FBI showing up at your old studio must have been terrifying."

"It was. My wife, my child . . . they were very afraid. Not for themselves. My wife is a citizen. She was born in Florida. But she was afraid for me, afraid I'd be deported."

"I'm so sorry." Liza considered hiding Gideon's profession, but she was asking this man to trust her. She couldn't lie to him. "Full disclosure: Daisy Dawson came with me. She's the one who contacted you before. She's waiting in the truck with her boyfriend, Gideon. He's the friend who was forced to get the tattoo as a young man. He's also with the FBI, but he's here as a civilian," she rushed to add, because Sergio looked like he'd run again. "He's not on duty or here in any official capacity. He will not report you, but he wouldn't let Daisy come without him. You know, because the people who hurt them are dangerous."

"Is Daisy FBI?" Sergio asked suspiciously.

Liza had to chuckle. "No. I don't think that the FBI would survive Daisy. Can she come in?"

"What about the FBI agent?" Sergio asked nervously.

"The *off-duty* FBI agent is going to stay outside," Liza replied. "Partly out of respect for you and partly to make sure that the people who want to hurt our family don't catch us unaware. They didn't follow us here, so you're safe. But Gideon is super careful about our safety."

Sergio drew a breath. "Yes, Miss Dawson may come in."

"I'll let her know." Liza sent a text, then withdrew her sketch from her handbag. "So you don't worry about me blocking out your afternoon, I really do want a tattoo. I wasn't being deceitful. I loved the detail you achieved on the angel feathers on the tattoo we're asking about."

Sergio studied her sketch. "A memorial tattoo?"

"Yes," she murmured. "For people who were my family over there."

"I can do this," he said. "When we are finished talking, I will work up a design. When you are satisfied, we can begin. You will probably need a second session. Maybe a third."

"I figured as much. I thought maybe you could just outline it today."

His lips curved. "Not your first tattoo, I take it?"

"No. Not even my first memorial tattoo."

He sobered. "Then you have known much loss."

She was saved a reply by Daisy's entrance. Daisy was her typical self, striding forward, hand outstretched. "Sergio. So nice to meet you in person. I'm Daisy."

"Please, sit. The studio is empty, so no one will hear us talking here. Shall we begin?"

FOURTEEN

Sergio Iglesias studied the photo of the Eden tattoo for a long moment. "My wife set up my Instagram account a few years ago. She went through all the photos I'd kept since I started tattooing and picked the ones she liked. This was one she liked."

"It's beautiful work," Liza murmured.

He dipped his head once. "Thank you."

"Do you remember the subject?" Daisy asked.

"I didn't when you first contacted me, Daisy. I had to go back into my files to jog my memory. Once I saw the file, though, I remembered him well."

The photo was of the tattoo itself, so only the person's left pectoral was visible. It had the grainy quality of a photo taken with a cheap camera, then scanned.

"When did you ink this tattoo?" Daisy asked.

"Eighteen years ago."

Liza was surprised. "You keep your files that long?"

"I do. I've kept them all, a file for every tattoo I've ever done, including signed documents stating that they are not intoxicated, and that they approve my design. It was the way I was taught by my mentor, almost twenty years ago."

"Why do you remember him specifically?" Daisy asked.

"Partly because it was one of my first, and I was really proud of how it turned out. But mostly because I almost didn't do this tattoo. He seemed really young and immature, which was funny, because we were about the same age. The day he came in was his eighteenth birthday and I'd had mine only a few weeks before. But he had ID and there wasn't anything offensive about the design, so I did it." He hesitated. "Why do you want to find him?"

"The short answer is, we don't know," Daisy admitted. "We're looking at every connection to the community from which our friends escaped. This person"—Daisy pointed at the photo—"wouldn't have been from their community, because he would have already had a tattoo by his thirteenth birthday. But he has to have known someone who had one. The tattoo you inked is identical to the one my boyfriend had inked over when he was eighteen."

"We ultimately want to talk to whoever told this guy about the tattoo," Liza said. "That person may give us information about the community and the people who are trying to hurt us."

Sergio inhaled sharply. "It was like a cult?"

"Yes," Daisy said. "My boyfriend still wakes with nightmares from that place, and he's been gone for seventeen years."

"The young man who got this tattoo was very happy to be eighteen, to 'finally be free.'"

"Free from what?" Liza asked.

"I asked him that. He said it was from his mother's control. She was apparently quite overbearing and he was very unhappy at home. He said that the tattoo would 'show her.' I got a bad feeling while I was working on him. I might have stopped, but he was eighteen. I made a copy of his driver's license. Just to cover myself, you know. He's one of the reasons I keep all my files with signed releases. Just in case someone comes forward years later and complains."

"Oh wow!" Daisy exclaimed, excited. "Please say you still have it!"

Sergio's smile was faint, but genuine. "Yes, I have it. I scanned the files to my phone when you first contacted me." He tapped his phone and turned it so that they could see the screen.

"May I?" Liza asked, reaching for the phone.

"Yes," Sergio said warily, handing it over.

The driver's license photo showed a young man with a baby face, but his lips curled down, giving him a sullen appearance. His hair was blond, cut military short. Nearly black eyes stared defiantly through round-rimmed eyeglasses.

"William Holly," Daisy murmured, looking over Liza's shoulder. "The name doesn't mean anything to me, but it might to Gideon. Can you send us this file?"

Sergio nodded. "Of course."

Liza tried to enlarge the photo, but it swiped left, revealing the original tattoo design with a scrawled signature beneath. "Oh, I'm sorry. I didn't mean to—"

"It's fine," Sergio said. "That's the design he approved."

"What's this?" Daisy pointed to a second signature in the margin.

Liza enlarged the sketch. The children kneeling in prayer had something written beneath them. "Are these names?" She peered harder. "Bo and Bernie."

"Yes," Sergio confirmed. "For him and his sister, but when I got to that part, he decided he didn't want the names after all, so I updated the release and had him sign off on the changes."

Liza frowned to herself. She'd heard those names before, and in conjunction with Eden.

Sergio was also frowning, but at Daisy. "You know who they are."

Liza turned her attention to the other woman and knew that Sergio was right. Daisy appeared stunned, but her eyes were coming back into sharp focus.

"Where were you when you did his tattoo?" Daisy asked. "Which city?"

"Benicia, same city as is on his ID. It's outside of Oakland."

"I know it," Daisy said quietly. "I lived in Oakland when I was a little girl."

Liza wanted to ask questions but held them. She could ask once they were in the SUV.

"Can you send this to my phone?" Daisy asked. "It's the number I called you from a few weeks ago."

Liza returned his phone and Sergio sent the files via text, paling at the concern etched into Daisy's brow. "Is this man a danger to me and my family?"

"I don't know," Daisy said honestly. "It's unlikely, but . . ."

Sergio's expression became grim. "But I should be very aware."

Daisy nodded. "I would be."

Sergio ran his hands through his hair before turning to Liza with a strained smile. "Do you still want the memorial tattoo? No worries if you don't."

"I really do. But can you give us a minute to talk privately?"

"Of course. I'll go in the back and prepare your design. It will take me fifteen minutes."

"Who is he?" Liza asked as soon as they'd shut all the doors to Gideon's Suburban.

Daisy quickly brought Gideon up to date, his eyes widening at the mention of Bo and Bernie.

Gideon's mouth fell open. "Are you fucking kidding me? The guy who got the tattoo was Bo? Pastor's dead son, Bo?"

Daisy nodded. "He initially wanted his and his sister's names included on the tattoo."

Gideon stared at the driver's license photo in disbelief. "I don't recognize him, but I was very young when he and his mother and sister were declared dead, and he was a lot younger than he is in this photo. Plus it's been twenty-five years. We need to show this photo to Amos. He might be a better judge."

"Oh," Liza breathed. "Bo and Bernie. Boaz and Bernice." That was where she'd heard the names. They were Pastor's children.

Gideon was shaking his head, stunned. "This . . . this is not what I expected. We were told that they were lost in the wilderness."

"Which is what they said about you," Daisy said softly.

Gideon's laugh was bitter. "True. Marcia—she was Pastor's wife—had taken the kids on a hike to gather herbs and they never came back. Pastor looked and Waylon looked. All the men searched, but never found them. Eventually Waylon found their remains at the bottom of a ravine. They were not recognizable. Or so goes the story we were told as kids. It was something the leaders told us to keep us from venturing far from the compound."

"Those remains belonged to someone else," Liza said, feeling foolish for stating the obvious. "Hopefully victims of an unrelated accident."

"But possibly murder victims," Daisy said soberly. "Waylon brought back a body after Gideon escaped. Told everyone it was him, but he was also unrecognizable."

"So Pastor's wife and kids survived," Liza murmured. "I wonder why she ran? How old were they when they disappeared?"

"Eleven," Gideon said, still staring at the photo. Then he looked up, understanding in his eyes. "Almost twelve. Bernice would have been married off very soon."

"And her mother didn't want her daughter raped in the name of marriage at twelve years old," Daisy finished. "What a hypocrite."

"Yes, but also a mother who saved her kids," Liza said. "Although it sounds like Bo didn't like being saved all that well if he *wanted* an Eden tattoo." She sighed. "So which of us is going to tell Tom?"

Daisy and Gideon shared an uncomfortable glance. "I'm not supposed to be here right now," Gideon said. "I'm recused."

"I'll tell him," Liza said. Having an appointment for a tattoo would make a good reason to cut her conversation short. "Are you going to stay here? Or go get some food or something?"

"We're staying," Gideon said firmly. "No way are we leaving you alone. Go ahead and call Tom. We'll have your back if he gets angry with you like Irina said he did this morning on the telephone."

"Let him even try," Daisy added. "He'll be sorry he decided to tangle with me."

The thought of five-foot-nothing Daisy facing off against six-foot-six Tom was enough to make her grin. "That is exactly the image I needed today, Daisy. You, fists on your hips, glaring up at Tom. I think he'd be quaking in his boots, quite honestly."

Daisy grinned back. "As he should. But I hadn't planned to personally confront him. I just took a page from his book and got one of these." From a pocket in her jacket she produced a flip phone. "It's a burner. Got it at Walmart. The FBI won't be able to track us back to Sergio."

"Seriously, Daisy?" Gideon asked. "What have you used it for?"

"Nothing. This is its inaugural call. I like carrying it. Makes me feel all clandestine."

Gideon's smile was fond. "You're impossible."

Liza took the phone, completely impressed. "I'm just glad you're on my side."

"Many people say this," Daisy said loftily.

Liza laughed softly. "Thanks, guys. I appreciate it."

Daisy winked at her. "That's what family's for. Make your call."

BENICIA, CALIFORNIA
THURSDAY, MAY 25, 4:00 P.M.

"It's empty," Croft said, peering into a window of the Belmonts' rental home.

Tom joined her after taking a walk around the perimeter of the house. "Basement too."

They'd come up empty on their search for members of the Chicos gang. The local PDs knew of them, but no one knew any names or locations where they might hide out. The gang, which seemed to have ceased recruiting new members, stayed under the radar through both skill and intimidation. Every cop they'd asked requested they share any information they dug up.

A call to Raeburn yielded his agreement that they should at least check DJ's surviving family off their list of suspects, so they'd made the hour drive to Benicia, a quiet community northeast of Oakland. But if DJ was here, he was hiding his presence well.

Tom wanted to sigh. It was more likely that DJ hadn't been hiding here and didn't intend to.

Croft patted his shoulder as they returned to the SUV. "Don't look so glum."

"I wasted our time," Tom said when they'd closed the SUV's doors. "You were right."

"Nah." Croft clicked her seat belt into place. "It wasn't a bad guess and we needed to check it out, especially since this was the address listed on his missing-person report." Tom had sent his Eden file to her phone and she'd refreshed her memory by reading it aloud as they'd made the drive. "This was the last place he lived before Eden. He might have remembered it. Look, kid, most of the job is paperwork, checking off things that aren't relevant, chasing dead ends, and waiting for new leads. Didn't they teach you that at the Academy?"

"I thought they were exaggerating," he muttered.

Croft chuckled. "Nope. Let's check off another box by talking to DJ's aunt and uncle."

"Waylon's brother and sister-in-law," Tom agreed. "They seemed to be telling the truth when I met them a month ago, but I'm interested in your take."

"Merle Belmont is Waylon's younger brother," Croft said, referring to the Eden file on her phone. "Unlike Waylon, who spent time in the federal pen, Merle's kept his nose clean. He's had a few traffic tickets, but nothing more than that. He might think he's doing a good deed, giving his nephew a place to hide. The missing-person report says that DJ's mother disappeared at the same time as DJ. Only a few months after Waylon went to Eden. Did Amos tell you anything about how DJ got to Eden?"

"Only that he showed up with Waylon one day, but Ephraim talked about it." He leaned over the center console to swipe her phone screen until he came to a part of the Eden file she hadn't read aloud. "Did you see these? The photocopies of the notebooks that Ephraim Burton left behind in his safe-deposit box?"

"I read the parts that Raeburn highlighted—mostly about the fifty million in the offshore accounts. Which part specifically?"

Tom was annoyed. Raeburn had dismissed much of Ephraim's record as interesting reading but not integral to finding Eden. "Read the page I turned to. W is Waylon and P is Pastor."

"'I got goods on W. I'm saving it for now, but I'll tell P if W gets in my way. W killed a chick who showed up at Eden's gate in a very hot car with a kid—his kid, she said. W called the chick Charlie. She said she was tired of babysitting his kid, that she wanted to have fun, so it was his turn. He twisted her neck. Snapped it like a twig, then saw me standing there. He was not happy to see me, but I told him that if he taught me to snap necks and gave me the car, I wouldn't tell P that he let a woman follow him to the compound. He agreed to both and now I have a very hot car and I can kill with my bare hands.'"

Croft looked up, her expression grim. "I wonder if Waylon's brother suspected that Waylon was involved in DJ and his mother's disappearance."

"Waylon was a suspect at the time, mostly because of his prior record and the years he spent in the pen, but they never found him, of course. It's all in the file."

"Dammit. I need to read all of this, don't I?"

Tom wanted to roll his eyes, but he didn't. "I'd recommend it."

"I deserve that." Croft frowned. "But didn't I read that Pastor adopted DJ?"

"You did. It was a casual arrangement, according to Amos. Pastor's own children had died and he wanted to raise DJ. But this was years *before* Waylon died."

"Why would Waylon allow that?" Croft wondered. "Unless DJ was a hell-child even then."

"Possibly. But Gideon remembers that DJ was nice to him when they were little. DJ was four years older and played with Gideon sometimes. But DJ changed when he was thirteen and became Edward McPhearson's apprentice."

"The pedophile blacksmith," Croft said. "Who targeted adolescent boys."

"Exactly. As opposed to his brother Ephraim, the pedophile who targeted adolescent girls."

Croft rolled her eyes. "Their mother must be *so* proud."

Tom grimaced. "She is. I listened when Mercy visited her in her nursing home last month. The woman was convinced her sons were angels. I don't think that was her dementia talking."

Croft tilted her head. "Liza Barkley was with Mercy that day," she noted.

"Yes." Which had been both a good and colossally bad idea on his part. "Liza worked with Alzheimer's patients at the VA home and she's levelheaded in a crisis, so I thought she'd be a good companion for Mercy." It had also bonded the two women, creating an instantly deep friendship and further drawing Liza into Mercy's troubles.

Which was why she'd been in a killer's crosshairs the day before. *I set Liza up for that.*

"I read the transcript of the nursing home visit," Croft said, interrupting his guilt fest. "Miss Barkley was really good at distracting and redirecting Ephraim's mother."

"She was." Of course she was. Liza was good at everything she did.

Except picking men, apparently. *Present company definitely included.*

"But back to DJ," Croft said, her gaze far too knowing for Tom's comfort. "If he was apprenticed to McPhearson and his behavior changed, it's not a huge leap that he was molested as well."

"I agree. Doesn't excuse him being a monster."

"I couldn't agree more. Let's go talk to the aunt and uncle. And I'm going to go over Ephraim's notes with a fine-tooth comb. I should have anyway. Glad you did."

Tom nodded once, because she was right. She should have. He'd started to put the SUV in gear when his work phone buzzed in his hand. "I don't recognize the number." He answered, putting it on speaker. "Special Agent Hunter."

"Tom, it's Liza."

He immediately sat up straighter, his heart taking off. "Liza? Why are you calling from this number? Are you all right?"

"I'm fine. I'm with some friends. I just wanted to pass on a tip. Do you remember the Eden tattoo that Daisy was trying to track down? The one she saw on Instagram?"

"Yes. We got a name and address for the artist, but when agents went to question him, he ran. He went underground. Why?"

"The person who got the tattoo is named William Holly, who got it on his eighteenth birthday, eighteen years ago. He originally asked that the children kneeling be labeled as 'Bo and Bernie.' For him and his sister."

"*Holy shit.*" Bo and Bernie were Pastor's twins, whose bodies had been found at the bottom of a ravine—unrecognizable. "How do you know this? Did you find the tattoo artist?"

"William Holly's address eighteen years ago was 966 Elvis Lane in Benicia," Liza replied.

Tom stared at the Belmonts' empty rental property—*966 Elvis Lane, Benicia.* Rafe was right. Pastor's wife and kids hadn't died in that ravine. He set the revelation aside for a moment, refocusing on Liza. "You didn't answer my question. Did you find the tattoo artist? Whose phone is this? Where the hell are you?"

"I'm texting you the photo ID William Holly used when he got the tattoo," Liza said very calmly. "I thought this information might be useful to you right away."

"Goddammit, Liza," he snarled. "I need to know where you are and if you're safe."

"I'm safe. I promise. I'll call you later, but I need to go now." And the call ended.

"Fucking hell." He tried redialing the unfamiliar number, but it just rang. He tried Liza's cell number and it went to voice mail without ringing once. She was either quick to hit decline, she was talking to someone else, or she'd blocked him. The latter stung.

"Which friends do you think she's with?" Croft asked.

Tom made himself breathe, not allowing his frantic anger to consume his logic. "Daisy's gotta be one of them. She's been pushing to find the owners of the Eden tattoos she discovered online." He dialed Daisy's cell, but it went to voice mail. "Fucking hell," he muttered, then dialed Irina's number.

"Yes, Tom?" she answered.

"May I speak with Liza, please? I think she had a lesson with Abigail today."

"Oh, that's long over. Liza's no longer here."

"Is Mercy there?"

"No. Mercy is with Raphael today. He didn't want her to leave the safety of their home."

She said she's with friends. Who else did she consider her friend? Immediately the image of Mike the Groper popped into his mind, but he shoved it aside. She wouldn't involve a stranger in an active investigation. "Did she mention where she'd be going this afternoon?"

"Why don't you ask *her*, Tom?" Irina asked, her tone heavy with maternal disappointment.

"She's not answering my calls."

"That is not good to hear. I recommend you try harder."

The call ended. Tom gaped. "She hung up on me."

"She totally did," Croft said. "Okay then, your personal drama aside, why has Daisy been searching for the owners of Eden tattoos? Why has she been searching for Eden tattoos at all?"

Tom pinched the bridge of his nose. He felt a headache coming on. "She's looking for other escapees because she thinks that they might be able to lead them to old Eden locations."

"But we know all of the old Eden locations." Then she nodded, understanding filling her eyes. "But Daisy doesn't know that because you're not allowed to tell her."

Tom nodded. "Exactly. Up until today she'd only located two people with Eden or Eden-like tattoos. Both are dead—one suicide and one car accident. I should have known she wouldn't give up—and that Liza would get sucked into it."

"All right." Croft was calm. "Then we need to figure out what to do with this information—if anything."

Tom closed his eyes, forcing himself to focus. "Probably nothing? This would be more important if we didn't already know where Pastor is. We just don't know where Eden is, which is why we haven't rushed in to arrest him. That's the big prize. Finding Eden."

"But Daisy and the others don't know that, either—that we know where Pastor is, I mean."

"Right." He sighed. "I mean, I'd love to find Pastor's wife, because she could fill in our knowledge gaps—how Eden came to be and all that. But to be brutally logical, she's been gone for nearly twenty-five years. I don't think she can help us find Eden now."

"But," Croft mused, "this does tell us that Pastor's wife and children probably didn't die and probably lived in Waylon Belmont's brother's rental house. Waylon was the one who supposedly found their bodies, so it's fair to assume he's the one who helped them escape."

"Like he helped Gideon. It makes sense, actually. Waylon was married to Pastor's wife for a little while. She left Waylon to marry Pastor right about the time he assumed a new identity and claimed to be a minister."

"Which was when the embezzlement began."

"Exactly," Tom said. "And, if Waylon helped her escape and at some point she lived in his brother's house, it might also mean that Waylon continued to have contact with his family long after he went into Eden. Unless his brother had no idea who he was renting to."

Croft held up one finger. "But if the brother did know back then, it means he was in touch with Waylon and possibly with DJ."

"That's a lot of 'mights' and 'maybes,'" Tom said doubtfully.

Croft shrugged. "I know. We could be veering down a garden path, but if Waylon's brother knows where DJ is, we need to find that out, because while we know where Pastor is, DJ is still out there with a rifle. Drive, please."

Tom started the SUV. "So what's the plan?"

"For now? Let's let them talk and see where it goes. I'll ask more targeted questions if we're not getting the answers we need."

FIFTEEN

BENICIA, CALIFORNIA
THURSDAY, MAY 25, 4:30 P.M.

Can I help—" Merle Belmont's expression fell when he realized who stood on his doorstep. "Oh. Special Agent Hunter." He sighed. "I suppose you want to come in."

Okay . . . "Yes, please. This is my partner, Special Agent Croft."

Merle sighed again. "I guess I knew this was coming. Doesn't make it easier. Follow me."

"Thank you," Tom murmured as he and Croft followed Merle into the foyer, where they were met by Merle's wife Joni, who patted her husband's arm sympathetically.

"I'm glad you called him, honey," she said. "It was the right thing to do. And you'll get it back, eventually."

Merle's eyes dropped to his feet. "I . . . well, I didn't exactly . . ."

"Merle Belmont," Joni scolded. "You didn't call him? You *promised* me. Now this will be a mess." She looked at Tom and Croft apologetically. "Please come in. Can I get you something to drink? Tea? Lemonade?"

"We're fine, but thank you for offering," Croft said. "I'm Special Agent Croft, ma'am."

"My wife, Joni," Merle mumbled, then followed his wife, his shoulders slumping.

When the couple's backs were turned, Croft gave Tom a what-the-hell look. Tom shrugged.

"Well," Joni said brightly when they were all sitting in the living room. "I suppose you'll be wanting the keys."

"I want a receipt," Merle said, his chin coming up. "And if there's one scratch on that car when I get it back . . ."

"Merle," Joni hissed, then sighed. "Please excuse my husband. He's just disappointed."

"I don't understand," Croft said. "Agent Hunter?"

"I don't understand, either," Tom admitted. "What is this about a car?"

Merle visibly brightened. "You're not here for the car?"

"What car?" Tom asked slowly.

Merle and Joni exchanged a long glance. "Well," Joni said again. "We assumed you were here to take custody of the Camaro. You know, Waylon's Camaro. We just got it back from the nice policemen in San Francisco. Merle hasn't even driven it yet."

Tom frowned, then remembered the set of GM keys they'd found in Ephraim Burton's pocket and the *very hot* car he'd extorted from Waylon Belmont. They must have been one and the same. "I see. Where was the car found?"

"At the airport," Merle said. "It had been parked there for several weeks before one of the security guards ran a check on the VIN and saw that my father had reported it stolen."

Makes sense. Tom kicked himself for not thinking to check the San Francisco airport himself. Using his tablet, he pretended to be taking notes as he typed out a message to Croft.

Ephraim Burton had a set of GM keys in his pocket when he died. He left out of SFO when he flew to New Orleans to stalk Mercy last month. This has to be the car he took from Waylon.

He angled the tablet so that Croft could see, and her small nod indicated that she'd read and understood. "When was the car reported stolen, sir?" she asked.

"Almost thirty years ago." Merle exhaled, his expression becoming pained. "My father had loaned it to DJ's mother because she wanted a night on the town with her friends. She had DJ with her. Said she was taking him to a babysitter."

"It was the last time we saw them," Joni added soberly. "We figured whoever had taken them had stolen the car, too. That maybe they were carjacked. It was a valuable car even then."

"It's a '69 Camaro," Merle explained. "Mint condition."

"A *very hot* car," Tom said quietly. "Did you wonder where it had been?"

"Of course," Merle said. "But whoever stole it took really good care of it. I'm grateful for that, at least." He frowned, then sucked in a breath. "Wait. You asked about DJ the last time you were here. Are you saying that he had it?"

"No," Tom said easily. "I'm not saying that at all."

"Have you found DJ?" Joni asked. "Is that why you're here?"

"No, ma'am," Croft replied. "We haven't found him. But he is why we're here. We were wondering if you knew anywhere he might go."

Both Joni and Merle shook their heads. "No," Merle said warily. "We told you—we haven't seen him since he was four years old. Why are you asking us this again?"

The couple joined hands, appearing anxious now.

Croft met their eyes squarely. "Would he stay at your other house?"

The couple glanced at each other in confusion. "You mean our house on Elvis Lane?" Joni asked. "Why would he? You're scaring me, Agent Croft. What's going on here?"

"He lived there once," Croft pressed.

"When he was four years old!" Merle exclaimed. "The house stood empty for years after he and Charlene disappeared. My father went over there every day, sometimes multiple times a day, hoping that they'd magically come home, but they never did. He refused to rent the place to anyone else. For *years*."

This was the opening Tom had been hoping for. "How many years, sir?"

Again Joni and Merle shared an anxious glance. "Maybe five years?" Joni said slowly.

"That's about right," Merle agreed. "Dad heard about this single mom and her two kids who needed a place to live. Margo had run from her husband, who was abusing her, and she needed a place to hide. Mom and Dad took her under their wing, you know? Her kids—twins—were only a few years older than DJ would have been. I think Mom and Dad kind of connected with the kids, so they let them stay."

Bingo. The timelines matched. Pastor's wife and kids had disappeared five years after DJ had arrived in Eden, according to Amos. Tom smiled at the couple, hoping to put them at ease, because Croft had them on high alert. "What were their names?"

Joni smiled back tentatively. "Will and Tracy Holly."

"Nice kids," Merle added, "but too quiet. Always scared, always looking over their shoulders. Margo wouldn't leave the house for years. I remember Mom going to meetings with the kids' teachers at the school. Mom and Dad were like the kids' grandparents. Joni and I weren't blessed, so . . ." He shrugged self-consciously.

"His folks adopted the kids," Joni finished. "Not officially, of course."

"And, as time passed, Mom and Dad lost hope that DJ would come home," Merle said sadly.

"I'm sure the twins were a comfort to them," Tom said. "How long did they live there?"

"Until Tracy graduated from college," Joni answered. "Will left home when he was eighteen. Mom and Dad got postcards from him for a few years."

Merle sighed. "Until he killed himself."

Oh. Shit. "How terrible," Tom murmured. "Your parents must have been devastated."

Joni nodded unhappily. "They were. We all were. Margo . . . she was . . . well, I'm glad she still had Tracy. That girl held her together until Margo met her new husband."

"She married again?" Tom asked, hoping he sounded casual.

Merle nodded. "She did. A good guy this time. An architect. Dad met him and approved."

"Do you still see them?" Croft asked, also casually.

Joni shook her head. "No. Margo left her life here behind, and I can't blame her. So many sad memories in that house, what with Will's suicide and all. Last I heard, she lived in Modesto. We lost touch with Tracy, too, but Merle's mom gets a postcard from her occasionally. Never from the same place, though, so I don't know where she ended up."

"And your father?" Croft asked.

"He died ten years ago," Merle said gruffly. "He was never the same after Will's suicide." He cleared his throat. "But enough talk of sad times. What else can we help you with?"

"Did your parents continue to rent the house after Margo moved away?" Croft asked.

"They did," Merle confirmed. "It was nearly always occupied, although it's been sitting empty for the past few months. We're probably going to sell it. Mom's nursing home is pretty expensive." He made a face. "I should probably sell the car, too."

"No," Joni said quickly. "You need to keep that car for yourself. As a memory of your dad."

"I guess we'll have to see," Merle said. "Will you need the car, Agent Hunter?"

Tom turned to Croft. "I don't know. Will we?"

"For a little while, yes," Croft replied. "It might have been used in the commission of a crime, so we'll want our forensics team to examine it."

Merle's mouth dropped open. "A crime? What kind of crime? Does this involve DJ? Is that why you're here?"

Croft threw a quick glance at Tom before turning back to the couple. "We don't know if DJ is connected to the car, but we do have evidence that he's involved in our investigation."

Joni gasped softly. "So he is alive?"

"We believe so," Croft said. "If he should come to see you, please contact us. Don't invite him into your home."

"He's turned out like his father, then," Merle said heavily. "Has he been in prison, too?"

"We don't know," Croft said kindly. "But he is dangerous. He might not bother you, but if he does, please let us know."

"We will," Merle said, his voice faltering. "This . . . is not what I expected."

Tom believed him and it seemed that Croft did, too. "Can we see the car?" he asked.

Merle rose unsteadily, Joni at his side. "Of course. It's this way."

Tom and Croft followed the couple to the back of the house, passing along a wall covered in framed photos. Tom paused at one that caught his eye—two photos side by side, both of small boys about four years old, both blond, nearly identical in appearance. But one was in color while the other was black-and-white and appeared much older.

"That's Waylon as a baby," Joni said when she realized what he was staring at. "Waylon and DJ at the same age. There's a strong resemblance, isn't there?"

"There really is." Tom met Joni's gaze. "May I snap a photo of these pictures?"

"I don't see why not." Joni stepped back, allowing Tom to take the photo.

"Thank you." Tom scanned the wall. There were several photos featuring an older couple—Merle's parents, he figured. In one of the photos, Merle and his father stood in front of the classic Camaro, wearing matching grins. There was another photo with the older couple and DJ, dressed for church. But there was no sign of Pastor's wife and children. "No photos of Margo and the twins?"

"Mom has a few at the nursing home," Merle said. "The rest are in storage. Why?"

Tom smiled at him. "Just curious. I apologize if I overstepped."

"No worries." Merle jerked his head in the direction they'd been walking. "Car's this way."

Tom whistled softly when Merle opened the door to the garage. "Sweet." It really was. Even from several feet away, it was obvious that the car had been well taken care of.

Tom wondered where Ephraim had kept the car all this time. They might never know now.

"Your forensics guys won't hurt her?" Merle asked.

"They'll take good care of her," Croft assured him. "We'll just wait out in our vehicle for the flatbed truck to arrive. Can I have the keys?"

Merle handed them over reluctantly and Tom and Croft returned to the SUV, where Croft called for a truck while Tom called San Francisco PD about the Camaro.

A half hour later, a truck was on its way and Tom had confirmed that the Camaro had only been cursorily searched by SFPD. "Not sure if the car will yield anything new, but it can't hurt to check," he told Croft.

"I agree." She glanced up at the Belmonts' house. "I believed them."

"I did, too."

"Why did you ask for the photo?"

Tom shrugged uncomfortably. "I'm not sure. Maybe just to fill in some gaps on my case wall." He'd been collecting documents and photos for the past month, keeping them organized both on the wall of his office at work and at his home office. "Maybe I'm just curious."

"Curiosity isn't a bad thing," Croft said. "So we know Pastor's wife is still alive. Not sure what that gets us, if anything. We also can be fairly certain that DJ hasn't contacted his aunt and uncle. So we can cross them off our list and refocus on trying to track him through his connection with the Chicos and with the rehab center where Pastor is. Sound like a plan?"

Tom nodded, aware that she was kindly telling him to stop chasing after Eden's past. "Sure."

She gave him an understanding smile. "It's okay, Tom. We'll likely chase down a ton of leads before we find the right one. It's the nature of the business."

Tom managed to smile back. "Thanks. I'll dig into the dark web when we get back. If DJ is selling drugs for the Chicos, there should be some record somewhere."

"That's good thinking. And I'm going to reread your Eden file while we wait for the truck."

Leaving Tom to check his phone for any messages from Liza. There were none. He sent her a text, asking if she was okay, but got no answer.

I need to fix this. But if she shut him out, he wasn't sure how.

SACRAMENTO, CALIFORNIA
THURSDAY, MAY 25, 5:15 P.M.

DJ's eye twitched as he was beeped into the rehab center through the back door. He was still shaking an hour later.

Kowalski had lured him into a trap. The package that DJ was supposed to pick up had been a trap. His last-minute decision to take Smythe's Lexus might have saved his life. His gut hadn't liked the setup—the warehouse in Stockton had been too quiet. He'd been right.

He'd pulled into the loading area of the next warehouse and looked through his scope. And there had been Kowalski, waiting with two of his biggest thugs. His finger had itched on the trigger, but he hadn't fired a shot. If DJ had fired, he would have been made, and likely wouldn't have been able to escape.

So now he was sneaking into Sunnyside Oaks through the employees' entrance, wearing a cheap goddamn wig that he'd been forced to buy at a party store, because his drug-dealing boss wanted to kill him because his fucking face was all over the fucking Internet.

A nurse met him at the door, a surgical mask in her hand. "You're wanted by cops in several jurisdictions and by the FBI. I think covering your face may be in your best interest, since that wig won't fool anyone, and not everyone here is paid to look the other way."

DJ rolled his eyes, but he took off the wig and put on the mask. *Dammit.* "How is my father doing?" he asked as she led him down a hallway where the stainless-steel wall tiles gleamed so brightly he was tempted to put on his sunglasses.

"He's awake and talking."

Alarm skittered down DJ's spine as he imagined all the things Pastor might say if he was high on painkillers. All the truths he might speak that both DJ and Pastor would prefer he keep quiet.

"What's he saying?" he asked casually, but the nurse wasn't fooled.

"Nothing like that, sir. You're not alone in your worry, though. We keep all recovering patients who are still on painkillers in their own rooms with specialized personnel who are trained and vetted. They won't share anything they hear."

"Or what?"

"Or they're terminated," she replied without a heartbeat of hesitation.

DJ wasn't sure if that meant fired or killed, but he didn't really care if it was the latter. "I see. Thank you for letting me know. What's he talking about?"

"His children mostly." A sad note entered her tone. "The ones who died. That's not uncommon, though. Painkillers can fog the patient's brain and make old memories resurface."

DJ remembered Pastor's twins. They'd been a few years older than him and real assholes. They'd been the prince and princess of the community and had never let anyone forget it. They'd also believed they were invincible and ignored the warnings to stay out of the forest. Their mother had gone hiking with them and nobody had seen any of them alive again.

It might have been the only case where Edenites truly *had* been killed by wolves.

Pastor had disappeared for two weeks, searching and then mourning. When Pastor had returned, he'd immediately adopted DJ and declared him his new heir.

Fat lot of good it's done me.

"He's a real sweetheart," the nurse continued. "All of his nurses love him already."

A sweetheart? Pastor? "I'm glad," DJ managed, and she smiled.

"They're often nicer here than they are at home. Don't take it personally."

They walked the rest of the way in silence, for which DJ was grateful. He was still trying to wrap his mind around Pastor being a "sweetheart." He was loved by his congregation, but that was more of an awed worship. Not affection.

DJ felt no affection for the old bastard. Especially after the stunt he'd pulled that morning with the access code. He wondered if Coleen loved Pastor. She might. She'd been sufficiently brainwashed over thirty years, despite knowing the deep, dark truth.

He was momentarily stunned when the nurse showed him into Pastor's room, which wasn't a room at all. It was a suite with several rooms—a master bedroom with an en suite bath, a second bedroom also with an en suite, a third bathroom, a living room, a kitchen, and a dining room.

Holy fucking shit. "How much does this run us a day?"

"It's all part of the prepaid package," the nurse said, not answering his question. "Your father is in the master bedroom, through there. If he's asleep, let him sleep. Your mother is sleeping in the other bedroom."

She is not my mother. But DJ smiled tightly. "That's good. She must have been tired."

"She was, poor thing. The bedrooms are soundproofed, so if you want to watch TV out here, you won't disturb them. His private nurse will stay in there with him. Her name is Nurse Gaynor and she's one of our best. She's been with us for almost ten years. I'm Nurse Innes, the charge nurse, by the way. Contact me with any concerns. Speed dial one on the house phone goes right to my cell." She held up a smartphone. "Cell coverage is very good here and there is Wi-Fi. Password is changed daily. Your father's nurse will have it for you. Nurse Gaynor just came on shift, so she's probably checking his vitals. I'll leave you to your visit. Call me when you're ready to leave and I'll escort you out."

As soon as she was gone, he took off the wig and the mask, wondering if last night's surgeon did plastic surgery. He might need it when this was over and he skipped the country with his fifty million.

He turned off all the lights in the living room and opened Coleen's bedroom door to ensure that she was really asleep and not going to spy on him. She was under the covers, visible by the light from the bathroom that she'd left burning. Her chest rose and fell rhythmically. If she was awake, she was good at faking it.

She wore a simple nightgown, the sleeping uniform of all Eden women. The neckline wasn't high like a turtleneck, but it exposed nothing below the hollow of the throat. Where her locket lay, glinting in the dim light. Even Coleen had to wear a locket. No discussions. No exceptions.

Satisfied that she slept, he closed her door and approached the master bedroom, remaining quiet. He really didn't care if he woke Pastor, because the old man was a douchey motherfucker. He was more concerned with hearing what Pastor was saying in his nurse's presence, and whether he was aware.

Nurse Innes might be convinced that their staff was trustworthy, but DJ was not. The only person he could trust was himself. Everyone else had an agenda that conflicted with his—getting the money and living in luxury on a tropical island. Even Coleen had an agenda, but DJ hadn't figured that out yet. Maybe it was just to remain in power at Pastor's side. If he died, she'd become the bottom-rung wife of another man in Eden and it would suck to be her.

He opened Pastor's door a mere crack, not wanting to alert the old man.

What the hell? He froze, staring as the nurse in Pastor's room rocked back on her heels, having been standing on her toes to reach a lampshade.

She then pulled something from her pocket and slipped it under the nightstand lamp. The light was dim, and DJ couldn't see exactly what she'd deposited there, but he had a fair idea.

She was bugging the room. *What the actual fuck?*

His mind raced, analyzing all the possible responses. He decided on pretending he hadn't seen it. He wanted to find out if this was a plot by the facility's owners to gather incriminating information that they could use for future blackmail.

Or . . . it could be that someone else was pulling the nurse's strings. Kowalski was the top contender, considering the man wanted him dead. And since he'd recommended the doctor. He was the only one who knew for sure where they were.

The other option was the Feds. That was least likely, though, because it made no sense that either Kowalski or the facility's owners would be giving the Feds information.

So . . . probably Kowalski. *Fucking Kowalski.*

DJ closed the door and took a step back, giving the nurse a minute to resettle herself wherever she'd been sitting or to do whatever she'd be pretending to do when he knocked.

He turned on the lights, then knocked lightly on the bedroom door, opening the door a fraction. "Is he asleep?" he whispered.

The nurse startled, whipping around to face him, and even in the dim light he could see her face flush with color. "Yes," she whispered back. "But you're welcome to sit with him."

DJ entered, shutting the door behind him. The master bedroom was elegant. Pastor probably hadn't slept anywhere so nice since the last time he'd left Eden and stayed in a hotel. That had been a decade at least.

He took the chair next to the one in which she'd been sitting and waited for her to follow. "Has he been eating?"

"He had some chicken broth and applesauce. Tomorrow we'll give him food that's more solid, and we'll work him up to his favorites. Do you know what food he likes?"

"He eats a lot of lamb." Pastor hated lamb. "Also he loves tomatoes." Pastor got hives when he ate tomatoes. "And chocolate, of course. Everyone loves chocolate." Chocolate gave Pastor heartburn. Of course, the old man would never admit to having a physical weakness. He felt that admitting a weakness lessened his status as a pseudo-deity.

DJ had brought him chocolate at least once a month during the seventeen years since he'd taken over as the community's buyer, feigning ignorance of Pastor's plight. The second to the last time they'd moved, DJ had found a pile of chocolate in one of Pastor's desk drawers, much of it white with age.

"Chocolate gives me gas," Pastor whispered. The raspy admission made DJ want to smile, but he bit it back.

"Why didn't you say so?" DJ asked, dragging his chair to sit closer to Pastor's bedside.

"You're a vicious little cunt," Pastor wheezed. "You knew. You gave it to me on purpose."

Damn straight.

"That's why you're not getting the access codes," Pastor added.

Motherfucker.

"Aw, Dad," DJ said with mock affection. He wasn't sure if he was hamming it up for the nurse or for the bug. "You know that's not true. I'm sorry. You know I would never have caused you pain on purpose."

Pastor's eyes narrowed. "Asshole."

It was fair. "How are you feeling, Pops?"

Pastor's eyes narrowed further, to tiny slits. "Watch it."

The old man was right. DJ was pushing him, which could result in him changing his will entirely. The pleasure he got from the verbal jabs wasn't worth it in the long run.

DJ nodded once, which seemed to pacify the old man. Either that, or the act of narrowing his eyes had tired him out.

"Did you talk to Brother Joshua?"

"I did," DJ lied smoothly. He had no intention of ever bringing Joshua into the fold. That would be one more person who knew about the money, and that didn't fit with DJ's plan. "He's completely on board."

Pastor smiled wearily. "Knew he would be. He's going to make a good right hand."

DJ maintained his pleasant expression, even though inside he was fuming. *I'm your right hand.* He suspected Pastor didn't realize he'd admitted that, but it was good to know his true intentions. Not that it was that much of a shock.

Pastor said no more, dropping back into a deep sleep.

"He'll do that for a few more days," the nurse murmured from her chair. "The painkillers are strong because his body needs rest to heal. All perfectly normal."

DJ pulled his chair until he and the nurse were side by side again. "Is there a pad of paper in this room?"

"Desk drawer."

"Thanks." He got the paper and a pen and sat down to write. *I know what you did. If you don't want your management to know, walk with me to the parking lot, where you can explain.*

He placed the notepad atop her electronic tablet. He knew when she'd read it, because her body stiffened. She glanced up, eyes full of fear. *Excellent.* DJ pulled his jacket back enough for her to see the gun in his shoulder holster. She inhaled sharply, her nostrils flaring.

He tilted his head toward the door, secretly relieved when she stood up.

Kowalski, then. If it had been the facility owners, she wouldn't have been afraid for them to know.

He left the bugs in place. He'd deal with them once he learned the extent of this treachery.

When they got to the living room, DJ leaned down to whisper in her ear. "You're giving me a tour if anyone asks. Got it?"

She nodded, her body trembling.

"And if you fuck it up," he added silkily, "I will kill you and anyone who has the misfortune to stop us. Nod if you understand."

She swallowed hard and nodded.

He put the damn mask back on. "Hands where I can see them," he murmured as they left Pastor's suite and began the walk to the back door. No one stopped them. No one even passed them. The halls were so quiet, it was creepy. DJ didn't breathe until they were outside.

He pointed at the lot. "Which car is yours?"

"The Audi."

"Fancy. Let's get in it so that we can talk."

The woman was shaking so hard she could barely walk, but she made it to the car. DJ stopped her, making it look like he was opening the passenger door for her. Instead he patted her down, hissing when he found a wire.

A fucking wire. Bugs weren't enough? Kowalski had to wire her as well?

He yanked it off her and tossed it on the asphalt, where he crushed it with his shoe. He then opened the door and showed her his gun again.

She got in and immediately began to cry. It was good that women's tears had no effect on him. He took her keys and got behind the wheel.

"Don't kill me," she begged. "This is the first time I've done anything like this. I swear."

I don't care. He pulled the mask down, giving her his kindest smile. "I won't kill you if you cooperate." He totally would, regardless. "How much is Kowalski paying you?"

She frowned in confusion. "I didn't talk to him."

He believed this as well. Kowalski could, however, have sent one of his underlings. He likely had, in fact. "Who put you up to this?"

"Mr. Raeburn."

DJ didn't recognize the name, but he didn't know most of Kowalski's men. "What did he offer you?"

Tears were flowing down her face. "Help for my son. He's in prison, waiting for his trial. Mr. Raeburn promised to get him out."

Now *that* sounded like Kowalski. Of course, the man had no ability to spring people from prison. He'd lied to the nurse just as DJ had.

"Do your employers know your son is in prison?"

She shook her head. "He was recently charged. I was trying to find him an attorney."

"Charged with what?"

"Murder. But he didn't do it!"

"Of course he didn't," DJ said dryly. He started the car and headed toward the security gate.

She paled. "You said you wouldn't kill me."

"And I won't," DJ said. *Here in this parking lot, anyway.* He needed to get her off the property so that the rehab center wouldn't have him charged with her murder. He noted the card reader and grabbed the badge clipped to her scrubs. He pulled the mask up to cover his face in case there were cameras at the gate. At least he learned from his stupid mistakes.

He exited the lot after swiping her card through the reader. He'd made it to the end of the street when a plain white panel van pulled out of a side street behind him.

Oh goody. Kowalski sent a tail.

"How many bugs?" he asked.

To her credit, she didn't play dumb. "Three."

"I know about the lampshade and under the nightstand lamp. Where is the third?"

She closed her eyes and said nothing.

"Nurse Gaynor? I asked you a question."

"You're going to kill me either way," she said hoarsely.

"No. I won't kill you if you cooperate." He might have even believed himself, he sounded so fucking sincere. "I will definitely kill you if you don't."

"In his Bible. I figured with him being a pastor, he'd keep it close."

DJ snorted. "Thank you."

"You won't kill me, then?"

"Of course not." He'd wait until he got free of Kowalski's tail.

They were only after him, at least. Kowalski didn't care about Pastor, so the old man was safe for now. Not that DJ cared about Pastor. He just didn't want Kowalski getting those access codes before he could.

The van behind him kept a steady pace, leaving three cars between them. *Like that's supposed to fool me.* He bided his time until he came to an intersection at which the light was yellow, about to turn red. Gunning it, he flew through the intersection a second after the light turned red, earning him a cacophony of blown horns.

Ignoring them, he turned at the next corner, following the road to the rear lot of a grocery store, where he parked and made sure his mask was still in place.

"Where are we going?" the nurse asked fearfully.

"Well, you're going to hell," he said pleasantly. Not prolonging things, he dragged her across the console and out of the car and tossed her to the pavement. She immediately tried to run, but he drew his gun, tightened the silencer, and shot her in the head.

She dropped and he shot her in the head a second time, just to be certain. Then he slid behind the wheel of her car and drove away—just in the nick of time. In his rearview mirror he saw the white panel van pulling into the grocery store lot as he turned the corner. He didn't see anyone following him the rest of the way back to Sunnyside Oaks.

He was met by the same charge nurse, who wore a forbidding frown. Standing behind her was the big-ass security guy from that morning. He did not look pleased.

"Where did you go? Where is Nurse Gaynor?" she demanded.

"She's permanently resigned," DJ snapped. "She agreed that she wasn't competent enough to care for my father. I dropped her off at a grocery store nearby. Come with me."

The two followed him into Pastor's bedroom. Putting a finger to his lips, DJ lifted the lamp on the nightstand, holding it so that the underside of its base was visible. He could see when the security guy saw the bug. The man's jaw tightened, making a cheek muscle twitch.

DJ laid the lamp on its side, then pointed at the lampshade, showing them the second bug. He opened the nightstand drawer and withdrew the Bible, exposing the third bug.

It wasn't Pastor's Bible. Pastor only waved one when he was preaching. Wasn't like he read it every day. Or any day, for that matter.

Nurse Innes's lips had thinned. She motioned to DJ and the security guy, leading them into the hallway.

"Who?" she asked sharply.

"A guy who wants to kill me," DJ told her. "He already tried once today."

"How did he turn her?" the security guy wanted to know.

"Her son is in prison, waiting for trial."

Innes shook her head. "We would have known."

"It's new, apparently. You can check it out."

The security guy made a call, then scowled at whatever he heard. He ended the call and gave Innes a nod before turning to DJ. "Was she ambulatory when you dropped her off?"

"Not really," DJ said.

The man sighed. "Can't say I blame you. Which store? I'm going to need to grab her before the cops find her. Did you use a silencer, at least?" DJ gave him a look and the man sighed again. "Of course you did. What a mess."

Innes suddenly looked exhausted. "I told you to come to me with concerns, Mr. Belmont."

DJ blinked at her. "I thought you meant if my father needed extra pillows."

Innes rolled her eyes. "Get her body," she said to the security guy. "You may return to your father's room," she said to DJ. "I'll send our tech guy to retrieve the bugs. We'll destroy them."

DJ shrugged, unconcerned. "I'll sit with my father until you assign him another nurse." He turned away, but not before he saw Innes shaking her head. It was her mess now.

SIXTEEN

Raeburn was staring down at the body when Tom and Croft arrived at the crime scene, located behind a grocery store. The victim lay on her back about a foot from the dumpster, two gunshot wounds in her head.

One of the head shots had taken a chunk of her skull with it.

"Which one is she?" Tom asked quietly. All they'd been told was that their mole was dead.

Raeburn was visibly disturbed. Likely not at the gruesome scene but at the reason this woman had been targeted. "Penny Gaynor."

Tom closed his eyes, visualizing the pages of the employee database scrolling in his mind. Penny Gaynor, age fifty-three. Mother of four. She'd been a nurse at the rehab facility for nearly ten years and was one of their most trusted employees.

"The one whose son is sitting in prison awaiting trial?"

"Yes," Raeburn said. "She was only supposed to plant a few bugs and wear a wire."

She wasn't supposed to die hung in the air like a dark cloud.

That DJ was involved in the killing was to be assumed. Which meant he knew that the FBI knew where he was. *Shit*. Tom hoped this wouldn't lead to Raeburn sending in a team to arrest Pastor and DJ, if he was hiding in Sunnyside. They still had no idea where to find Eden.

"She catered to killers and mob bosses," Croft said rationally. "She looked the other way when killers crossed her path. She's not completely innocent, boss."

Raeburn drew in a breath and let it out. "I know, Agent Croft." His words were crisp, intended to intimidate, but the slight tremble in his voice ruined the effect.

Tom's respect for the man ratcheted way up. "Who found her?"

Raeburn pointed to a white panel van parked a short distance away. "The agents who were in the surveillance van radioed as soon as they knew she was in trouble. They followed her car when it exited the parking lot, but lost her when her car ran a red light. They found her not even two minutes later, but she was already dead."

"Does the store have security cameras?" Tom asked.

Raeburn nodded. "It was Belmont. He was wearing a surgical mask, but based on hair, eyes, and build? It was him. He found the wire and yanked it out. Destroyed and dropped it on Sunnyside's parking lot."

Croft frowned. "So he's onto us?"

"No." Raeburn pointed to the pendant that hung around the nurse's throat, covered in blood and brain matter.

Tom's momentary elation at their not having been made withered as his gut roiled. He recognized the pendant as one of the Bureau's comm devices. It was similar to the one he'd given Liza to wear the day she'd accompanied Mercy to the nursing home where Ephraim Burton's mother lived. He had to force himself to see the nurse's features and not transpose Liza's over them.

"DJ didn't know it was a transmitter," Tom said, grateful that his voice was even.

"No. We heard them talking in the car. He asked her how much

'Kowalski' was paying her. Luckily when she denied knowing him, she called me 'Mr. Raeburn,' not 'Agent.' He doesn't appear to know that we're the ones behind the bugs. That'll hopefully give us a little more time to line something else up."

Some*thing* else, Tom noted. Not some*one* else.

"We know Pastor's still in there," Croft said. "Maybe we just wait for him to be brought out and follow them back to Eden."

Tom didn't like that. "Leaving Belmont free to stalk Mercy while Pastor recuperates? That could be weeks. Where is DJ now?"

"We don't know," Raeburn admitted. "The van lost him a few minutes after he took the nurse from the rehab center. He might have gone back inside or he might have run."

Croft sighed. "Dammit. Who is Kowalski?"

Raeburn brightened a fraction. "That's the good news. He's a local gang leader."

Croft's eyes lit up. "Of the Chicos?"

"We hope so. The Chicos have become insular and a lot harder to pin down since the men at the top were taken down a few years ago. No one seems to know much about their new power structure. Local PDs had heard his name but knew nothing more. No photos or even a description. I've got a team searching for him now."

"What do you need from us?" Tom asked. He thought of Dixie Serratt and wondered if they should have pushed harder. She knew what Kowalski looked like. Tom was sure of it.

"I need you to find a way to get audio and video from Pastor's room. Find out if they've got a leaky faucet or a broken window. Anything that would require the services of an outside contractor. We'll get one of ours in that way. That Belmont doesn't know that we were behind the bugs buys us some time, but I think the Sunnyside employees will be hyperaware of anyone approaching them the way Gaynor was approached. We can't try turning one of theirs again."

Tom was already considering the possibilities. "I could manufacture an IT crisis."

"Do it fast," Raeburn warned. "And thank you, Hunter. That would be most helpful."

"And me?" Croft asked.

"You're with me. I want a description of Kowalski. I'm betting on him being with the Chicos, so I'm bringing the Serratt woman in for an interview. I want you to lead it. She doesn't leave until she tells us what the man looks like."

"We're more likely to get information out of her if we can offer protection," Croft murmured. "She seemed genuinely terrified for her life."

"I've already started the paperwork for protection," Raeburn said. "And I'll have the state's attorney involved. We may be able to offer her a reduced parole period. You've got your assignments."

Tom knew that Raeburn was right. But he also had a gut feeling about Pastor's wife. At a minimum, the woman could fill in a number of unknowns. He gave his boss and his partner a nod and started back for the field office so that he could return the Bureau's SUV and get his own back. He already had ideas on how to manufacture a network failure that would force Sunnyside to call for IT help.

Once he was on the road, he dialed Liza's number again. This time it rang a few times before going to voice mail. Which meant she'd directed it there. Which still stung, but at least she was actively involved in avoiding him, so that meant she was okay.

He hoped. He needed to know. Using the SUV's handsfree, he dialed Irina's number, hoping she'd be more helpful than she'd been earlier in the day.

"Yes, Tom?" she answered, sounding like his mother before she'd grounded him as a kid.

"Just tell me if she's all right." There were voices in the background. It seemed they were having fun. He listened hard for Liza's voice, but then Irina spoke again.

"Hold on." A minute later the background noise became hushed. "She is fine."

Tom sighed in relief, then tensed. "Who is she with?"

"I am not TMZ, Agent Hunter. I do not give out titillating sound bites and call them facts."

"Titillating?" He frowned. "What's titillating? Who's with her?" *Don't be Mike the Groper. Please don't be Mike the Groper.* "Is it that Mike the Groper?" *Dammit.*

Irina coughed, but had clearly covered a laugh. "Mike the Groper?"

Tom's cheeks flamed. "Well, is he with her?"

Irina sighed. "I think you should talk to Liza."

"She keeps sending my calls to voice mail. Where is she?"

"That, I will not tell you. If she doesn't wish to see you, I will respect that. I'd do the same for you."

"I know," Tom grumbled. "Will you at least tell her that I'm sorry that I shouted at her? I was worried and . . . well, I shouldn't have done that."

"No, you really shouldn't have. I'll tell her. I have to go now. Good night, Tom."

Tom ended the call, frustrated. He didn't know where Liza was and who she was with, which sucked. At least he knew that she was all right. Wherever she was.

She'll calm down in time, he told himself. She'd come back.

But as what? *As a friend*, he told himself firmly, although the words no longer felt right.

And if she never did? The prospect of a life without Liza wasn't something he could even think about. Every aspect of the life he'd built since coming to Sacramento was tied to Liza.

Everything but his job. Which he'd now go home to do.

GRANITE BAY, CALIFORNIA
THURSDAY, MAY 25, 10:15 P.M.

"Thank you," Liza said, hugging Karl Sokolov first, then Irina as she walked them to her new front door. "You guys are insane, letting me have this place until July." The posh apartment was one that Karl made available to clients visiting his marketing firm. "This is the nicest place I've ever lived."

The poshest, at any rate. The nicest place she'd ever lived was the place she'd left that morning, and she was already homesick.

"This place sits empty most of the time," Karl said. "I'm glad someone is using it."

Liza shook her head helplessly. "I think you're lying about that, but again, I thank you."

"Did you show her the alarm panel, Karl?" Irina asked.

"I did, my love."

"Did you introduce her to the guard in the lobby?"

Karl kissed Irina soundly. "I most certainly did."

"Good. Liza, there are clean sheets on the bed and food in the pantry and the fridge. There is also a list of restaurants that deliver in the drawer next to the stove. Karl's company has an account with all of them, so you will not need to pay."

Liza's brows shot up. "I most certainly will pay. I have funds. I was Fritz's beneficiary. I got his death benefits." She'd told them about Fritz when she'd returned from Monterey, and it seemed that telling people about Fritz got easier every time. She needed to tell her Chicago family soon. She didn't want them hearing it from Tom. *They need to hear it from me.* "I put half of the money in a trust for his parents to use for their retirement, and I'll use the rest for living expenses and tuition not covered by my GI benefits and financial aid. I'll be fine."

Karl's smile was both proud and sad. "Do his parents know about the trust?"

"No. I thought I'd tell them . . . later. Their grief is still too fresh."

"You are a good girl, Liza." Irina took Liza's cheeks in her palms and brought their foreheads together. "Your mother would be so proud of the woman you've become."

Liza had to clear her throat. "Stop making me cry, Irina."

Karl tugged at Irina's sleeve. "Come on, my love. Let her get some rest."

Irina had called her as she, Gideon, and Daisy were driving back from Monterey to tell her that they'd found her a place and had moved her boxes and her car. Gideon had stopped first at the Sokolovs' house so that Daisy could get her car, then the two of them had escorted her up to the apartment, where they'd helped unpack Liza's things. With so many hands working, her boxes had been unpacked before she could blink.

"I'll be by tomorrow to read with Abigail," Liza assured Irina. "Thank you again."

Everyone hugged her a final time, then left.

And the silence was . . . awful.

Liza hadn't realized how much noise there'd been at her old place. Tom always had either a TV on or his opera music blaring. Pebbles was always barking at something.

But this place was quiet. Too quiet.

"Buck up, soldier," she murmured. "You're blessed. Be grateful."

And she was. She really was. She had everything she'd ever wanted.

Except for the one thing she couldn't have. Exhausted, but too wired to sleep, she sat down at the mahogany desk and opened her laptop.

Step one: Post an ad for someone to sublet my side of the duplex. She wasn't poor, but she wasn't going to waste Fritz's money on rent for a place she wasn't using. She e-mailed Tom to let him know she'd placed the ad, because he'd ultimately have to approve the new renter.

Step two: Sift through the want ads and apply for a temporary job. Irina had pointed her toward a temp service that hired out nursing assistants, so she'd go there.

Step three: Run on the treadmill in the gym in the apartment building's basement until I'm too tired not to sleep.

Step four: Do not dream.

That last one would be far easier said than done, but if she did dream of the sniper attack, at least she wouldn't be hit with the guilt of keeping Fritz a secret. She leaned back in the desk chair and winced. Her tattoo was gorgeous and she loved it, but it was sore. Sergio had outdone himself, thanking her for allowing him to create such a moving memorial. Liza would need to go back in a few weeks to get the shading done, but even without that, the memorial was all she'd envisioned.

She'd completed steps one and two and was trying to remember where she'd put her running shoes when her phone rang. She almost let it go to voice mail but then saw the caller.

It was Mr. Tolliver, her old next-door neighbor. Something had to be wrong. Mr. Tolliver never called this late.

"Hi, Mr. T, what's wrong?"

"I'm glad *you* answered. Your dog has escaped."

"Pebbles? Oh my God. How do you know? Did you see her running by?"

"No, I see her on my front stoop, playing with Sweetie-Pie."

Liza exhaled, relieved. "Oh good. At least she's all right."

"Can you come and get her? It's after my bedtime. I'm an old man, y'know."

"Of course I'd come over to get her, but . . . I don't live there anymore."

"I figured that. I saw you moving this morning. Did that man throw you out?"

"No. Of course not. I left because . . . I just needed to leave."

"What are we going to do about your dog, then?"

"Did you call Tom?"

"Don't have his number," Mr. Tolliver said tartly. "Just yours."

Liza wasn't giving out Tom's number without his permission. Nor was she calling him herself. He'd ask her to come back and she wasn't sure she was strong enough to say no. "Can you knock on the front door?"

"As if I haven't done that already! If he's there, he's not answering, because he's killing his hearing by playing that music so loud. It's not rock, either. That I could take. It's . . . opera."

Liza had to chuckle because he'd said *opera* like it was dog doo. "Fine. I'll be over to get Pebbles. I still have a key. I can put her in Tom's house. Do you know how she got out?"

"She tunneled under the fence. He must have let her out and she got bored. Or lonesome. She went right up to your front door and lay on the welcome mat for the longest time."

"Oh." Liza's heart cracked. She loved that dog so much. "I'll be there in about fifteen or twenty minutes. See you soon."

Liza waved to the man at the security desk on her way to the parking garage elevator. Irina had cited two separate elevators as additional security, and it made Liza feel safer to know that someone couldn't come all the way up to her floor from the parking garage.

ROCKLIN, CALIFORNIA
THURSDAY, MAY 25, 11:00 P.M.

Pebbles perked up when Liza got out of her car, running up to meet her. Liza was glad she'd been leaning against the car when Pebbles had leaped to lick her face, otherwise she'd be on her ass.

Liza gently pushed Pebbles back to all fours and wiped her face with her sleeve. "Tom doesn't like it when you lick faces," she told Pebbles sternly.

"Tom isn't *here*," Mr. Tolliver said with attitude. "He can train her when he's *around*."

Liza looked up at his side of the duplex. All the upstairs lights were on and she could hear the faint strains of Pavarotti's "Nessun dorma" all the way from where she stood.

"He's working. That's his working music."

"Hmph." Mr. Tolliver lifted his chin. "It's loud."

"What's your favorite band, Mr. T? You said you'd have preferred rock."

Mr. Tolliver grinned. "I saw Black Sabbath in concert six times one summer. That's where I met Mrs. Tolliver, God rest her soul."

Liza grinned back. "You are awesome, Mr. T. I'd love to chat, but I'm going to take Pebbles back inside now. I've had a really long day."

Mr. Tolliver took a step forward, his expression now wistful. "Come back every now and then, okay? Pebbles will miss you. And so will I."

Another piece of Liza's heart cracked. "You bet. I promise."

"You'd better. I just got used to you, girl."

"And my Dream Bars." Mr. Tolliver loved her Caramel-Pecan Dream Bars.

He grinned. "Those too."

Liza slapped her thigh. "Pebbles, come. You're going home." Pebbles followed her across the lawn but stopped at Liza's front door. "No, girl. That's not your home. Not anymore." She could have sworn that Pebbles pouted. "Come. I'm too tired to drag you."

Pebbles snorted, shaking herself before following Liza to Tom's front door.

Liza unlocked the door, disabling the alarm. "Go on." But Pebbles didn't move. Exasperated, Liza pulled on the dog's collar, dragging her inside. Tom might not even have known that Pebbles had gone out to the backyard, so she checked the massive doggy door they'd put in after Tom had first brought Pebbles home. Sure enough, the doggy door was unlocked.

Liza locked it, all under the cover of Pavarotti singing at the top of his lungs.

Then froze when she heard Tom's shout.

"Goddammit, Liza!"

She stood in place, hardly daring to breathe, hoping he didn't come down the stairs.

But also hoping that he did. When he didn't, she edged toward the front door and the music abruptly stopped. Again she froze, staring up at the stairs. Hoping she wouldn't see him.

Praying that she would. *Just a glimpse.*

Stop it. This is over. Get out of here.

But Tom still didn't come down the stairs. Instead she heard him pacing in his office. "I might have a way in," she heard him say.

Against her better judgment, she climbed the first few stairs.

"Good," another voice said, sounding tinny. Tom was on the phone. "What can you do?"

"I tried shutting down their security network from my end, but whoever developed it put in too many fail-safes, so I constructed an e-mail that looks like a bill with late charges. If their bookkeeper clicks the link to pay, it'll allow me to shut down all nonessential network function. I'm not going to touch anything that has to do with patient treatment or medication, though."

"But it will shut down enough of it, yes?"

"Yes. Sunnyside Oaks won't be able to operate any of their personnel, accounting, or admin functions. Hopefully they'll call tech support so we can get an agent physically in there."

"I'll get the warrant expanded to cover wiretaps so we can intercept their calls."

"Just to let you know," Tom said cautiously, "in case this doesn't work, Sunnyside Oaks posted a job opening for a nursing assistant. I found it when I did a wider search on the place."

"Not a nurse?"

"No, this was posted earlier in the day, before Nurse Gaynor was discovered. If you want to try to get someone in there . . ."

"We'll do that. Do you know on which job websites they've posted the opening?"

Liza frowned as Tom rattled off two websites she hadn't found in her earlier searches. What was Sunnyside Oaks? And why was Tom interested in it? Who was he talking to? Sounded like his boss. Why were they interested in a nursing assistant position?

"Just because the nursing assistant position is open, that doesn't mean that the individual will have access to Pastor or DJ," Tom cautioned.

Liza's mouth fell open. *DJ? And Pastor?* They knew where *Pastor* was?

Apparently so. He was at some place called Sunnyside Oaks, which needed a nursing assistant.

No one had informed Mercy or Rafe or Gideon. They would have been unable to stay silent about something this huge. Which pissed her off, because they had a right to know.

"I know that," the other man said. "But an in is an in."

Yeah. It is. And Liza was going to apply to be that in. This was finally *something* she could do. Yes, they'd tracked down the Eden tattoo and might be able to find Pastor's wife and kids. But this was Pastor *himself.* He could lead them to Eden.

And Liza was uniquely qualified to help. *So I will.*

Tom said good night to his boss and for a brief moment she considered sneaking out without letting him know she'd been there. But that was childish. And dishonest. And cowardly.

She glanced down at Pebbles, who leaned into her hip, staring up adoringly as her tongue lolled to the side. "Wish me luck," she whispered, giving the dog's muzzle a soft stroke.

Drawing a breath, she went to the bottom of the stairs and called out, "Tom?" Straightening her spine, she braced herself for the sight of him, like she always did.

Because he took her breath away. He always had.

And then he was standing at the head of the stairs, gaping. "You're here."

"I am."

He came down two of the steps, then paused uncertainly. "Are you back?"

"No." She backed up a few feet, giving him room as he descended the rest of the way. "I got a call from Mr. Tolliver. Pebbles got loose, so I came back to bring her in."

Startled concern flickered across his features. He dropped to his knees in front of the dog, checking her for injuries. "Is she okay?"

"Yes. She dug a hole under the fence. You should probably get it filled in. Apparently she only went as far as next door to play with Sweetie-Pie."

He looked up, blue eyes uncertain as he seemed to drink her in. "Is the Yorkie okay?"

Liza forced her lips to curve. "Of course. They're BFFs. Anyway, I brought her inside, fed her, and locked the doggy door so she can't get out again."

He swallowed hard, and then, not breaking eye contact, rose to his full height.

Liza looked up. She'd always loved that she had to look up at him. But not tonight. He looked pained. And awkward.

"Thank you," he murmured. "You want to . . . sit? Talk?"

She shook her head. "Today was a busy day. I need to get back to my new place and sleep."

"Where is your new place?" He held up his hands, surrender style. "Wait. First, I need to tell you I'm sorry. For yelling at you this morning."

"I know. Irina gave me the message. It's okay. I'm okay. I need to tell—"

"No!" he shouted, then groaned. "I did it again. Just . . . don't leave. Please. I'm sorry."

"And I *said* it's *okay*. Listen, I—"

He cut her off before she could tell him about the conversation she'd overheard. "But I'm *not* okay," he said hoarsely. "Please. Let me say some things. I need to say this."

The agony in his voice stunned her into silence.

"I was scared," he said in a rush of words. "Really scared."

Her heart softened, and she hated that it did. Hated that she wanted to soothe him. To tell him that everything would be all right. That she'd come back. That they could go back to the way things had been before she'd shown him Fritz's picture.

But they couldn't go back. Eventually it would eat her up inside. So she forced lightness into her tone that she did not feel. "That I'd been kidnapped by aliens or something?"

His eyes narrowed. "No. By a killer who had you in his crosshairs yesterday morning."

"Oh." She winced guiltily. "I didn't mean to scare you like that. I left a note on the fridge."

"Yeah," he said bitterly. "I read it. 'Tom, I'm moving. Don't worry, I'll keep paying the rent.' Which was the last thing I was thinking about." He exhaled, visibly trying to calm his temper. "Will you at least tell me where you're living?"

She hesitated, tempted not to tell him. But that would also be childish. "Karl's company keeps an apartment in Granite Bay for VIP clients. Top-of-the-line security, a guard in the lobby. A gated, guarded parking garage. Cameras everywhere. It's very safe." And because she needed to reclaim a little of her pride, she lifted her chin. "You don't need to worry about me anymore. I can take care of myself."

"But I *liked* taking care of you. You're important. You're my—" He went abruptly silent, as if realizing he was about to say the very wrong thing.

Too late. "Your friend," she said, trying so hard not to sound bitter.

He took a step closer. "Because we are. Aren't we?"

Liza took a step back, her eyes filling with tears. "I need more than that."

He flinched, then shook his head helplessly.

Get this back on track. Back to business. "Did you get the copy of the photo ID that I sent you? The one that William Holly used eighteen years ago to get that Eden tattoo?"

"I did. I've already got it printed out and tacked to my bulletin board. Thank you."

"You're welcome, but I didn't do it for you. I did it for Mercy, Gideon, Amos, and Abigail."

"I know." He looked at his feet for a moment before lifting his gaze, filled with hurt. "Will you tell me where you went today?"

"I promised the artist that I wouldn't. The FBI scared him into moving away the last time you visited."

"I didn't visit him," Tom said defensively. "It wasn't me who scared him."

"I know. I meant 'you' in the sense of 'you FBI guys.' I won't expose him. I promised."

"You also promised you'd live here with me," he blurted out. "But you e-mailed me that you placed an ad for someone to sublet your side."

"Oh, that's why you swore at me," she murmured. "You saw my e-mail."

"I have to approve whoever you choose." Now he sounded arrogant, but she could still hear the hurt underneath. "It's in your lease."

She knew that, and it was a fair requirement. "If you don't approve them, I'll continue to pay the rent myself."

"And not live here?" he asked, stunned. "How can you afford to pay rent on two places?"

"It'll cut into my savings, but it'll only be for a little while. I've applied for dorm housing starting in July and there may be financial aid for that."

"Liza." Then he frowned. "Wait. What do you mean, 'that's why you swore at me'?" His face paled. "How long were you standing there? What did you hear?"

"Long enough. And everything you and your boss discussed."

Twin red stripes rose on his cheekbones. His breathing ticked up. He was angry. But she wasn't afraid. She'd never been afraid of Tom

Hunter. She was only afraid of how he made her feel. And what she was willing to do to make him happy.

"You had no right," he hissed.

"You're right. I didn't. I didn't plan to overhear you, but I did. And now I know that they are hiring a nursing assistant at Sunnyside Oaks."

Tom staggered back a step, anger now mixed with fear. "You wouldn't. You *can't*."

"I will and I *can*. I'm qualified for the position."

"Liza, no." His jaw went tight. "I forbid it."

She gaped at him. "You *what*?"

"I. Forbid. It."

A tendril of temper unfurled in her chest and she welcomed it. Anger was a million times better than despair. "You can't stop me."

He was in her space before she was aware that he'd started to move, his big hands gripping her upper arms. His grip was firm, but not punishing. She still wasn't afraid.

She was pissed off, but she didn't shrug him off, because he was touching her and she was pathetically needy. She swallowed a whimper. Barely.

"Watch me," he said in a low growl.

His face was close, his nose millimeters from hers. His mouth was unsmiling. Still, she wanted it more than she wanted to breathe. She swallowed hard, her gaze dropping to his lips. Would they be soft? Or hard? How would he taste?

No, no, no, no. Stop it. Stop it now.

She yanked her gaze up. And froze.

Because he was looking at her mouth, too. For a moment she thought . . .

She hoped . . .

But when he yanked his gaze up, all she saw was shock. He was . . . *appalled*, and her pounding heart seemed to freeze in her chest.

His hands fell from her arms as if she'd burned him, and he took a huge step back, so huge that he nearly tripped up the stairs. He shook his head hard, saying nothing. But his rejection couldn't be clearer.

"Well," she said, wondering if he could hear her frozen heart shattering into tiny pieces. "I'm glad we had this chat. I'll be going now." She had her hand on the doorknob when he finally spoke.

"Liza, wait."

She paused but didn't look back. She could hear that he still stood by the stairs. He hadn't moved an inch after that colossal retreat. "*What*, Tom?" she snapped.

"You can't apply for that job."

Not wanting to argue, she simply shook her head and opened the door, but the knob was ripped from her hand, the door slamming shut. Tom's hand lay flat against the door, his big body close enough that she could feel his heat.

"Pastor is there," he hissed, his breath hot on her neck. "DJ will be there. If he sees you, he will kill you."

"It is a risk," she allowed, because to deny it would be foolhardy. To deny that her heart beat faster at the thought would be a lie. But she wasn't afraid, not enough to quit before she tried.

If she could meet Pastor, talk to him . . . maybe she could get him to talk about Eden. Maybe even tell her where it was. Especially if he was hurt or in detox, which she assumed he was, because he was in a rehab center. People said things when they were in pain, things they might not otherwise say. And if he didn't tell her directly, maybe she could overhear something useful.

She only knew that she needed to try. "But a risk I'm willing to take," she added.

"It is a *certainty*." He didn't shout, not really. But his voice was so loud that she recoiled involuntarily. "I'm sorry," he said quickly, far more quietly. "I didn't mean to yell again, but, Liza, this is madness. We had someone on the inside—one of Sunnyside's nurses who'd agreed to work with us. She planted bugs in Pastor's room. But DJ caught her."

Liza's heart raced faster. "What happened to her?"

"He dragged her out of the facility, drove her a few miles, lost our surveillance van." There was a sudden pressure at the base of her neck, a few inches above her new tattoo. Tom's forehead. He was leaning on her. "Then he pulled her out of her own car," he whispered, "onto the back lot of a grocery store and shot her in the head. Twice. My boss wanted to storm the place and arrest the bastard, but I convinced him to wait. To use this time to get intel. To find Eden. So we recruited the nurse and she's dead. I have to live with that, but I couldn't live if you got hurt. So I *forbid* this."

Liza swallowed, wanting to assure him that she'd forget about Sunnyside, that she'd stay safe for him. But this was bigger than either of them. So many innocent lives lay in the balance. And she'd risked her life before, every time she'd entered a battle zone. She could and would do it again for Mercy and Abigail. They deserved to live without fear.

"I'm sorry for the nurse who was killed. I really am. But I'm qualified and I'm careful. I won't take stupid risks. *If* I even get the job."

The pressure on her back disappeared as his hands gripped her upper arms again, spinning her to face him. "Goddammit, Liza," he cursed from behind clenched teeth. His eyes were wild. Afraid. And still angry.

At least he no longer seemed appalled at the thought of kissing her. A small balm.

She looked up into his face, the need to soothe outweighing the urge to run. She loved him. She always had. And even though he didn't feel the same way, simply seeing him like this, so helpless and afraid, was devastating. She needed to fix him. Heal him.

So she cupped his face in her hands, her chest hurting when he shuddered into her touch. "I survived three deployments. I was a combat medic. I've been shot at. I shot back, and I'm still here. I can take care of myself."

He closed his eyes wearily. "Why? Why would you do this?"

She didn't hesitate. "For Mercy and Gideon. Amos and Abigail.

And for that young girl who's pregnant, who must be so scared. This has to stop, Tom. I can help. I *need* to help."

He opened his eyes and now she only saw despair. "But why you?"

"Why not me? I'm qualified for the job. I know about Eden. I'm not foolish. You can even wire me if you want."

His expression flickered, despair becoming fear. Fear for her.

He stepped back, and her hands fell from his face to dangle uselessly at her sides. "We wired the nurse who agreed to work with us. She's still dead."

Liza was too tired to debate with him any further. He wasn't going to change his mind any more than she was going to change hers. "I'll see you around."

And this time when she opened the front door, he let her go.

SEVENTEEN

Tom stood staring at the door after Liza left. This had to be coming from her PTSD. Survivor guilt. She'd experienced enough loss. Her mother, her sister. *Her husband.*

Tom hadn't seen this coming. *Because you didn't ask the right questions.* He'd known something was wrong, that she was experiencing PTSD, but he'd let it go on way too long.

Well, that was history. From here on out, he was asking *all* the questions. *Because I'm not going to let her undertake a damn suicide mission.*

You can't stop me.

Watch me. He *could* stop her. True, he couldn't keep her from applying, short of putting her into protective custody. Briefly he considered it. Because the alternative was ruining her résumé, altering her references so that they gave her a bad review. He could do it.

But he didn't want to. He didn't want to hurt her. He wanted to save her from herself.

He locked the front door, resetting the alarm, then climbed the stairs to his office, his thoughts a whirlwind. Pebbles ambled after him, settling down in her preferred place against the wall.

The sight of the dog curled up against what had been Liza's bedroom wall had Tom's eyes burning. "She's not there," he said, his voice breaking. Because she wasn't coming back.

Heavily he sat in his chair, all thoughts of her résumé fading as the words she'd whispered in pain echoed in his mind. *I need more than that.*

Pebbles's growl cut into his mental fog, the sound low and ominous. Her head was tilted, her uncropped ears pricking up. Then Tom heard it too, the quiet buzzing of an incoming call.

It was Molina. Grateful for the respite of work, he answered. "Hunter."

"Agent Hunter, I've got Agent Raeburn patched in. We'd like to talk to you."

Tom frowned, not liking the sound of that at all. "Of course. Is something wrong?"

"No," Raeburn said. "In fact, I think something could be very right."

"I'll cut to the chase," Molina said. "Liza Barkley just called me."

Tom's breath got stuck in his chest. "Wh-what?"

"Liza called. She informed me that, through no fault of your own, she overheard a conversation she wasn't meant to hear."

"Not her fault, either. She was bringing the dog in. I thought I was alone in my house."

"Tom," Molina said overly patiently. "We're not calling to hand out demerits."

Tom's blood turned to ice as the implications sank in. *She wouldn't. She couldn't.*

"She intends to apply for the nursing assistant job at Sunnyside Oaks," Molina went on.

Oh my God. She did. His fury with her reignited and he had to draw a calming breath before he spoke. "You set her straight, I assume," he said, grateful that his voice didn't shake.

"By setting her straight," Raeburn said, not one iota of levity in his tone, "you mean we said, 'Yes, please, and let us help you get that job.' Correct?"

Tom was speechless. "But . . ."

"She said you turned her down," Molina said. "She said that you forbade it. Which, just for your own edification, was a really stupid thing to say, Tom."

"Extremely stupid," Raeburn added.

Tom's temper was about to explode and he had to remind himself that the two people on the phone were his bosses. That he had to remain respectful. "She is a civilian. It's too dangerous."

"According to her résumé, which she's already sent to me, she is a trained, decorated soldier who is also a trained, highly skilled combat medic," Molina corrected tartly, then seemed to soften. "And she's not our first choice, if that makes you feel better. We've identified two undercover agents who will also apply. You can cross your fingers and toes for them if you like. In the meantime, we want a virus that can be embedded in their résumés. When they're reviewed by Sunnyside's HR person, I want that virus to take over that person's computer. Even if we can't see the entire network, we can see employee records and we can follow the hiring process."

Goddammit, Liza. He couldn't believe she'd gone over his head like that. He took a second to ensure he'd be appropriately respectful when he spoke. "When do you need the virus?"

"One hour."

"What the f—?" He drew another breath. Started to say it was impossible. Then realized it was perfectly possible. And a good idea. For the *other* two applicants. Not for Liza.

But it appeared that he'd been both outmaneuvered and overruled. "I'll provide you with the embedded code in one hour with instructions on how to add it into the résumé documents."

"Thank you, Agent Hunter," Raeburn said formally. "We'll have all three résumés ready to be uploaded into Sunnyside's application form on receipt of your e-mail."

"Yes, sir. I assume shutting down Sunnyside's network, thus requiring them to call in IT support, is also still a goal."

"You assume correctly," Raeburn replied. "I want the résumé viruses first. We've already developed identities and backgrounds for the two undercover nursing assistant applicants. We'll have the same for an 'IT support team' sometime tomorrow. It's possible that Sunnyside won't hire any of our applicants. It's possible that none of them will even be called in for an interview. However, if one of ours is hired, we still want support for them inside the facility."

"Any decent IT team will be able to fix the problem in an afternoon," Tom said. "If one of ours does get the nursing assistant job, he or she won't have support for very long."

"Then they'll find a way to further sabotage Sunnyside's network, requiring a longer presence," Raeburn replied coolly.

Tom swallowed a sigh of resignation. "Then I'll get right to it."

"Thank you, Agent Hunter," Molina said quietly. "Agent Raeburn, you're free to hang up. I'd like to speak with Agent Hunter alone, if you don't mind."

"Of course not," Raeburn said. "Call me if you learn anything new, Hunter."

Molina waited until Raeburn had ended his connection. "You know," she said, "I talked to Liza's former commanding officer."

"You mean, in the army?" Tom asked, startled at the topic change. "When?"

"The first time was before she and Mercy visited Ephraim Burton's mother in that nursing home. I wanted to be sure that she wasn't a security risk and that she had the skills we required."

Tom knew he shouldn't have been surprised. Molina had accepted Liza's involvement, had allowed her to know about Eden, had permitted her proximity to Mercy. He'd thought at the time that Molina simply valued his opinion and approved Liza's involvement on his say-so. *How naive was I? How arrogant?*

"What did he say?" he asked, a little subdued. "Her former CO, I mean?"

"He said that we couldn't have picked anyone better suited to shoulder the responsibility. That she was levelheaded in a crisis, that she employed diplomacy when dealing with delicate situations, and that she could shoot her way out when diplomacy was no longer an option. He said she was one of the finest soldiers that he'd ever had the privilege to command. And that her nursing skills were exemplary. Combat surgeons credited her with saving lives because she stabilized field wounds so well. Patients who might have otherwise died didn't."

Pride swelled in his chest. He hadn't known any of that. She hadn't told him.

You didn't ask.

God, I'm an asshole.

"You said the first time. Did you call him again?"

"Yes, after she started visiting me at home when I was recuperating."

"When she did your laundry and cooked for you?"

"Yes. And sat with me, just chatting."

"Why did you call him a second time? And what did he say?"

"I called him because I had concerns regarding her intentions. She was in my home, after all. He told me that Liza has a nearly limitless need to help and that it's genuine. You know about the attack on her mission, right? The one where members of her unit were killed?"

"She told me about it."

"Did she tell you that she saved the lives of four soldiers and five villagers that day, after they'd been shot? That doesn't include the lives that might have been lost had she not grabbed her rifle and started shooting the rooftop snipers who'd attacked U.S. soldiers on a humanitarian mission and the villagers they'd gone to serve."

"No. I didn't know that part. She told me that her . . ." He swallowed. "That her husband had thrown himself over her to shield her, and that he'd died."

"That's true, he did save her life. But once she realized he was dead, she went into crisis management mode. Took out one of the snipers while a few other soldiers took out the others. Then she was like . . .

how did her CO say it? Oh, yes. Like Florence Nightingale on speed, running from person to person, triaging, doing first aid. She took a bullet in the hip, kept on going."

"I knew about the graze, but not that she'd kept going," Tom said quietly. *And I should have.*

"It was enough of an injury that she was awarded a Purple Heart." Molina made a sound halfway between a fond huff and a dry chuckle. "I tried to recruit her. She said no, that there was already one FBI agent in the family. She just wanted to be a nurse. If I could have her as one of my agents, I'd jump at the chance. Since she already told me no, I'll take her involvement with Sunnyside Oaks. I only tell you all this because I know you'll continue to worry."

"Of course I'm going to worry," Tom snapped. "She's already been in his crosshairs once."

"I know. But when that picture fills your mind, replace it with one of her grabbing her rifle and shooting rooftop snipers to save her fellow soldiers and innocent villagers."

He hesitated. "That sounds like personal experience talking."

"It is. My daughter is a cop. Says she's following in my footsteps. Sometimes I wish she'd followed her father's footsteps into culinary school. I remind myself daily that she is smart, highly skilled, and makes a difference."

Tom knew it was time to surrender. "I still don't want Liza there, for the record. But I understand and I'll do everything I can to make sure she and the others are as safe as possible."

"I knew you would. Now, get to work."

GRANITE BAY, CALIFORNIA
THURSDAY, MAY 25, 11:50 P.M.

DJ blinked hard and rewound the camera's video back to the point where he'd dozed off. Again. He was tired. And he hurt again. He'd pulled something dragging Nurse Gaynor from the car, and the ibuprofen he'd bought at a convenience store hadn't touched the pain.

He wished he had some of the pot that had once filled the basement of his home in Yuba City. Or the house he'd rented next door. The one the cops had seized. *Fucking sonsofbitches.*

Kowalski had probably been pissed off by that more than the Ellis woman being tagged as a homicide. The marijuana in the grow house had been ready to harvest. He didn't want to think of how much of his income the cops now held.

Better than holding you *in a prison cell, though.* Which was true enough.

After ensuring that Pastor's new nurse wouldn't even consider selling out to Kowalski, he'd borrowed a wig from Nurse Innes in case Kowalski's men had returned to watching the gate. Then he'd driven Smythe's Lexus back to the house and downloaded the video from the pink camera in the window. It was *so* boring. And this bed was *so* comfortable.

He sighed and pulled himself up to sit straight against the pillows. He hit play, fast-forwarding until he came to the next vehicle that drove down the Sokolovs' street.

It was an older-model Mazda and was filled with so many boxes that they obscured the view of the driver. He noted the license number, just in case, but a beat-up old Mazda didn't seem like it would fit into the Sokolovs' neighborhood. The residents here tended to favor BMWs and Teslas. Like the one that had just driven by.

He noted plate numbers for both the Mazda and the Tesla, then continued to fast-forward. And scowled. A gray Suburban approached the Sokolovs' house but the windows were too darkly tinted for him to see inside. A few minutes later the Suburban reappeared, followed by an orange VW Beetle, and *that* driver's face he could see. It was a face he knew.

He hissed a curse. *"Her."* The woman who'd shot him after Amos had taken the shot he'd aimed at Mercy. *Daisy Dawson*. Gideon Reynolds's girlfriend.

She was already on his list but seeing her face redoubled his determination to see her dead. He noted the license plate, paused the video, then opened a browser to check all three plates.

The Tesla was registered to the same corporation as the black F-150 he'd seen that morning. That was interesting.

DJ had googled the corporation's name and had come up with a lot of nothing. But he had a hunch now and googled *Karl Sokolov* and *Tesla*. And, sure enough, a picture surfaced of Karl and his wife standing next to the fancy car, apparently on their way to a charity gala. The photo had been posted to the Facebook account belonging to Karl Sokolov's marketing firm. The corporation didn't bear the man's business's name, but it really didn't need to. The connection was obvious.

Sokolov had loaned his truck to Amos. They'd regret helping him, just like they'd regret helping Mercy and Gideon.

He added the two Sokolovs to his list. If he could get Mercy and Gideon, all the others would show up to the funeral. It would be like shooting fish in a barrel.

He ran the plates on the Beetle and the gray Suburban, expecting to see actual owners' names, but instead he got another corporation, this one based in Maryland.

The final plate belonged to the red Mazda that had been full of boxes.

"Oh my fucking God," he snarled after its search results came up. "You've got to be kidding me." *Another* corporation. Which, of course, wasn't tied to any one individual.

Weren't any of these people *normal*, for fuck's sake? *Normal* people registered cars in their own fucking names with their own fucking addresses.

The lawyers must be making a mint off these assholes. He fast-forwarded the video, noting the time and the other vehicles that passed by, all belonging to neighbors. *Those* had normal registrations. *They* were normal people.

Too bad they weren't the people he wanted to kill.

He made sure that the camera was reset and unpacked the bag of items he'd gotten at the convenience store on the way back from Sunnyside. He shook a few more ibuprofen from the bottle and swallowed them with water he'd found in Smythe's fridge.

The cigarettes went on the nightstand along with Smythe's lighter. He'd smoked all that he'd found in Smythe's pockets and had treated himself to more. He'd always smoked sparingly so that Pastor didn't smell it on him when he returned to Eden. But tonight he'd smoked a whole pack and a half.

The box of hair color he put in the bathroom along with the reading glasses he'd bought to wear on the end of his nose. Tomorrow morning, his blond hair would become . . . He squinted at the box.

"Deep Dark Brown," he muttered.

He rubbed his palm along his jaw. He couldn't grow a decent beard no matter how hard he tried, but he could trim and dye the scruff. It didn't have to be pretty. He just had to make himself look like someone else.

ROCKLIN, CALIFORNIA
FRIDAY, MAY 26, 12:45 A.M.

Tom gave his e-mail to Raeburn one last look, triple-checking the virus-embedded text he'd prepared for the résumés the Bureau would be submitting to Sunnyside Oaks. Including Liza's, which made him want to scream. But the file was complete, so he hit SEND.

Then sagged into his chair as the full import of what she'd done hit him once again. She hadn't argued with him. Hadn't screamed or yelled back at him. She'd stayed calm.

And had promptly gone over his head, scaring him shitless. *She is competent*, he kept telling himself. *More than competent. She's amazing.*

She really was. Even though he'd hurt her, even though he'd yelled, she'd been gentle. She'd faced him squarely.

She'd even held his face tenderly. Her hands were always a little rough because she washed them so often. He wished he could free her from that, from having to work at all. Except that Molina was right. Liza did have a nearly limitless need to help others. She would never be happy unless she had something useful to do.

But this . . . He thought of Penny Gaynor's body, the way the bullet had torn her skull apart. He thought of the pendant around her neck, covered in blood and brain matter.

Too close to the pendant he'd given to Liza when she'd accompanied Mercy into that nursing home. He swallowed hard, his gorge rising at the thought of DJ Belmont laying a hand on her. Hurting her. Then he did as Molina had advised, picturing her in combat fatigues, taking up a rifle and protecting her unit.

And then becoming like Florence Nightingale on speed. *That* he could easily visualize.

She'd survived a war zone. He had to believe she could survive this, because he couldn't fathom his life without her in it. Except now she wasn't in it. Not anymore.

I need more than that.

He closed his eyes, thinking of that one moment earlier, that one moment he'd forgotten himself. It had been an electric moment as she'd stared at his mouth, desire plain on her face.

She'd wanted him to kiss her.

And for that one electric moment, he'd wanted that, too. More than anything.

Which would have been very bad for both of them.

Why? a small voice whispered in his mind. *Why would that be so very bad?*

He recognized the voice. He'd heard it before, every time he'd fleetingly considered kissing her. Used to be a lot more frequent. His answer back then had been a simple one.

She's too young. So he'd shoved his feelings into the box inside his heart, the one where he kept all of the other emotions he couldn't allow himself to feel—the rage with his father, the terror that one day his own temper would defy his control, and the unmitigated want he'd felt for Liza Barkley. They were taboo. They were untenable. They needed to stay locked in the damn box. But keeping Liza at arm's length had always been a challenge at which he'd failed.

She'd been his biggest temptation. She still was.

But she wasn't seventeen anymore. She wasn't a traumatized teenage girl who'd just lost her sister to a killer. She was all grown up now and that small voice had become much less frequent as time had passed. He'd heard it mainly when she'd been home on leave. When he'd sat in the same room with her, able to smell her hair or feel the weight of her head on his shoulder when she'd fallen asleep watching TV.

Those were the times he'd wanted to touch her, but he'd shut those wants down every single time, despite the small *why* that tormented him.

They were friends. If they tried for more and it didn't work out, they wouldn't be anymore.

Are you friends now?

He was saved from answering himself by the light buzzing of his personal cell phone. Surprised that anyone would call him so late, he checked the caller ID.

Rafe Sokolov. *Oh joy.* Just one more person who'd tell him that he was fucking Liza up.

"Yeah?" Tom asked wearily.

"Did I wake you up?" Rafe asked, sounding concerned. "Gideon just drove by your place on his way home and said your office light was on."

"It's fine. I'm . . . working." Actually, no. He wasn't. He wasn't working. He was brooding, which wasn't going to help anyone. "Why was Gideon driving by my house?"

"He went to Walmart to get a nine-volt battery because his smoke detector was beeping every few minutes and making him crazy. I asked him to see if your lights were on since he lives so close. I won't keep you, but I wanted to let you know that Liza is safe."

Tom frowned. "What does that mean?"

"She's moved into a very safe place. Good security. I thought it might ease your mind since my mother won't tell you where she is, but she is safe. Gideon made sure to check every point of entry when he helped her move in."

"He apparently didn't lock her in," Tom said sarcastically. "Because she was here."

There was a beat of silence. "She was where?"

"Here, in my house."

"Oh. Well, she's back in her place now. She and Mercy are on the phone. Mercy's eating ice cream because Liza is, and apparently there's some girl-commiseration pact or something."

"Rocky road," Tom murmured. It was Liza's go-to flavor when she was sad. He wondered how many times his actions had driven her to drown her sorrows in rocky road. "Thanks for letting me know. It was good of you."

"Anytime," Rafe said kindly. "You sound rough, Tom. Call one of us if you need anything, okay? Even my mom. She's annoyed with you, but she'll still listen and give you good advice. Maybe not the advice you want to hear, but . . . Anyway, have a good night."

"Wait," Tom said. "I need to tell you something." Because Rafe had done him a solid when he hadn't needed to. "Belmont is still lurking around Sacramento."

A long moment of silence. "Give me another minute." This time, the sounds were of a door closing and Rafe's quiet groan. "I need to get a chair out here in the foyer. These steps are hard on my ass. But now I'm all comfortable and you're going to tell me what you meant by that."

"Just that. He's here in the city, but we have a lead." Actually, they knew exactly where he'd be . . . eventually. The surveillance vehicle they'd placed near Sunnyside's entrance hadn't seen him return after killing Penny Gaynor, but he would. Unless Pastor died inside.

That wouldn't be such a bad thing. Kind of like Rob Winters being shanked in prison. Tom would not mourn Pastor's death any more than he'd mourned his father's.

"You should keep Mercy at home this weekend," he told Rafe. "Keep her safe."

Rafe blew out a breath. "I can't. Can't keep her home, anyway. We're having a surprise party for her on Sunday."

Tom knew about the party, had even requested the following day off from work so that he could help with cleanup. He didn't hesitate with his reply. "Cancel it." That was simple enough. Mercy couldn't celebrate her birthday if she was dead.

"I can't. We've got people coming in from New Orleans. A lot of people." There was a pause during which Tom could hear Rafe's muttered counting. "Ten, at least."

"Tell them not to come," Tom said, speaking slowly and enunciating.

"No," Rafe insisted. "I'm not going to deprive her of this. She's lost enough in her life."

"She could lose her life," Tom snapped.

"Don't you think I've thought of that?" Rafe hissed. "We've been living with the threat of DJ Belmont for a month, Tom. A fucking month. I'd already hired security for the weekend. I just bumped it up."

Tom heard the desperation in Rafe's voice. He also heard determination. "How much security and what organization are they out of?"

"I had six guys. After the attempt at the eyeglass store, I bumped it up to ten. All active or recently retired cops, friends of mine from SacPD."

"Where are your guests staying?"

"With Mom and Dad. A few of Mercy's siblings are only flying in on Sunday and taking the red-eye back that night."

Tom knew that Mercy had relied heavily on her half brothers and half sisters when she'd lived in New Orleans. They, along with her best friend Farrah's family, had been her support system as she emotionally recovered from the abuse she'd suffered at the hands of Ephraim Burton, DJ Belmont, and all of Eden.

Rafe was right. Mercy had lost enough in her life.

"How were you planning to transport the guests to and from the airport?"

Rafe hesitated. "In our vehicles?"

"And if DJ Belmont is watching? He has to have followed the SUV Agent Rodriguez was driving the day they went to the eye doctor. I don't know exactly where DJ is right now, but we must assume that he's still watching."

"Right." Rafe's swallow was audible. "I'll rent cars, then."

"That's an option. You could also let me help. Will you let me provide the vehicles? I'll get SUVs. Armored with bullet-resistant glass."

"You or the Feds?"

"Does it make a difference?"

"Of course it does. Who's paying the bill?"

"Me."

"Why?"

Tom frowned. "Because your mother gave me cake and has fed me nearly every Sunday for a month. Because your family has taken Liza and me in. Because Irina loves Liza like a daughter and Liza loves Mercy like a sister. Because I *can*. Jesus, Rafe. Why do you think?"

Rafe shuddered out a breath. "Sorry. I know you care, and I appreciate it. It's just my pride balking. Okay, please provide the vehicles. Thanks."

"All right, then. There's a firm that the pro athletes use when they want to avoid the press. They also serve politicians and celebrities. I'll make the arrangements as soon as we hang up."

"Don't hang up yet. I need to know more about the lead on Belmont. Don't think that I forgot you said that."

"I can't tell you more. I'm not supposed to be telling you this much."

"He killed a woman," Rafe said abruptly. "Last night. An elderly woman in Yuba City. His face is all over the news."

Tom had seen the reports. "He's a suspect, yes."

"Oh, for fuck's sake," Rafe hissed. "Do *not* fuck around with me, Hunter. I'm not in the goddamn mood. He killed the old lady. Why?"

"It's possible that she suspected him." He'd heard back from Yuba City PD. They'd found another set of prints on another beer can in the trash, and that person could also have killed her.

Could have been Kowalski, even. The man didn't trust DJ, evidenced by the cameras he'd planted. "There is another possibility on the Ellis murder, still linked to Belmont. Have you ever heard of a guy called Kowalski? You said you knew some of the members of the Chicos, and he's supposed to be one of their higher-ups."

"Kowalski," Rafe growled. "Yeah. I know him. Low-to-mid-level thug. Did a few deals with him when I was undercover. If he's a possibility for the Ellis woman's murder, that means he was also there. With Belmont."

Tom had hoped Rafe would make that connection. "Can you describe him?"

"I can do better than that. I can give you a photo. It's five years old, but his face is clear. It was one of my surveillance photos and . . . well, I'm not supposed to still have it."

That was a helluva lot more than they'd gotten from any of the local PDs, and Tom wondered why. That Kowalski had cops in his pocket was a possibility. "I won't say it was from you."

"At this point, I don't care. It's unlikely that I'll return to SacPD, at least in my old role."

A month ago, Rafe had been bitter about an injury keeping him from being a detective again. He was sounding resigned now. No, not resigned. Accepting. There was a difference.

"I still won't tell," Tom said, "unless it's unavoidable, and I'll give you a heads-up first."

"Thanks. I assume you'll want this photo sent to your burner? I still have the number."

"No, you don't. I tossed that burner two weeks ago. Never keep them for long." He gave Rafe the new number, then had a thought. "Does Gideon have a burner?" Because Liza had called him about William Holly's—a.k.a. Pastor's son Bo's—tattoo on a burner phone.

"You don't quit, do you?" Rafe asked, amused. "Talk to Gideon. I'm not involved."

"I will." His burner chimed and Tom immediately opened the text from Rafe. "You have a burner, too, I see. This isn't your normal number."

"We see, we learn," Rafe said lightly. "I always carried one when I was undercover, but I'm finding it has its uses even now."

Tom looked at the photo of Kowalski. "He looks ordinary."

"Best way to blend," Rafe said.

Tom glanced at the signed basketball on the edge of his desk—the child's birthday gift he'd promised the officer in Yuba City—with a sigh. He might always be recognized. He'd likely never be able to blend. "True enough. What do you remember about him?"

"He seemed educated and too polite. The kind of polite that makes you check for your wallet and to be sure there's no knife in your back. He once took a personal call when we were doing a deal. Left in a flash. His partner said his wife had just gone into labor. That was six years ago."

"So we're looking for a family man with a six-year-old kid."

"Six-year-old boy. His partner yelled after him to remember that he'd promised to name the baby after him. So maybe they were brothers."

"What was the partner's name?"

"Jed, but none of them used their real names. I got something else that will help."

"What is it?"

"Kowalski always dressed very well. His shirts were always starched and pressed. Even his jeans were pressed. Hell, he even wore Gucci loafers once. He was a show-off."

Tom winced, because he had a pair of Gucci loafers, too. "So he liked to look good?"

"No, he liked to look good, *and* he carried a hankie in his pocket. Pulled it out once to wipe the sweat from his forehead on a hundred-and-six-degree day. The hankie was monogrammed. 'A.W.'"

"A.W.," Tom repeated, his pulse starting to thrum. "Initials and facial recognition software might be enough to find this guy. Did SacPD try to find him?"

"If they did, they didn't try very hard, because they never managed a true ID. But Kowalski was a minor player at the time. Definitely still clawing his way up the ladder. The brass had arrested all the top guys in the organized crime syndicate. After that, the momentum fizzled."

"And you never tried?"

"No," Rafe said. "After I closed that case, I took some time off to grieve Bella."

The woman he'd lost at the crime boss's hands. "Got it."

"Did you grieve your Tory, Tom?" Rafe asked gently.

"I saw her murderer get justice," Tom said grimly.

"Not the same. Not even close. If you haven't grieved, you can't move on."

Tom closed his eyes, not wanting to have this conversation. "I grieved, okay?" he snapped, mostly to make Rafe shut up. Then realized that he really had grieved. "Liza let me talk about her," he added quietly.

"Oh," Rafe breathed.

Tom cleared his throat, remembering the gentle but pained expression on Liza's face as he'd talked about Tory for hours as they'd made the drive from Chicago to Sacramento after the holidays. "Yeah. I thought she was grieving with me."

"Maybe she was, and maybe she was grieving more than Tory. She, um, well, Gideon said that she talked about Fritz when they were helping her move in. Said you know about him."

"Yes, I know."

"She said it was easier to tell us because she'd already told you and—" Rafe cut himself off. "Others," he finished lamely.

"'Others.' Like Daisy and whoever else she went with this afternoon."

"Gotta go, Hunter. Call if you need anything else on Kowalski. I'll do a lineup if you need me to. Night." The line went dead.

Tom barked out a frustrated laugh. At least Liza had people who cared about her. Rafe wasn't going to betray her confidence any more than Irina had.

He stared at his phone again, seeing the day's ignored calls to Liza in his call log. She'd avoided him all day long. *Get used to it.* Because he didn't think she was coming back.

I need more than that, she'd said, her voice breaking.

Absently, Tom pressed the heel of his hand to his heart. Did he need more?

He had no fucking idea. He only knew that he couldn't let her go.

He picked up the phone and started a text to her. But what to say? He'd already said he was sorry. He'd told her that he wasn't okay.

If he were a better man, he'd say goodbye. He'd let her go.

He needed to end this. He needed to let her go before he hurt her any more. He started to type. *Good—*

He couldn't do it. He could not force himself to type "goodbye." "I guess I'm not a very good man," he whispered, his feelings too raw and torn to analyze.

His finger pecked out the rest of the phrase. —*night*.

Saying good night was the best he could do. He hit SEND, set that phone aside, then picked up his work phone and dialed Raeburn. It rang so many times that Tom didn't think his boss would answer, but then he did.

"What have you found?" Raeburn demanded, abandoning any pretense of politeness.

"I've got a photo of Kowalski. I'm sending it to you right now." He transferred the photo from his burner to his work phone and forwarded it to Raeburn. "His initials are A.W. and he has a six-year-old son."

Raeburn whistled. "Where did you get this?"

"From one of my sources. You want me to start running facial recognition?"

"Hell, yeah." Raeburn sounded exhausted. "This is the best news I've had all day. I'd just sent Croft home when Molina called about Miss Barkley. Croft was unable to get anything out of Dixie Serratt. Finally I had SacPD take her to booking for parole violation."

Tom hadn't thought the woman would talk. "Hopefully finding Kowalski will lead us to Belmont." And Eden.

"Get on it. Call me with updates. I don't care what time it is."

"I will, sir." The call ended and Tom got to work loading his facial recognition software. It was going to be a long night.

EIGHTEEN

He did a good job," Irina said as she applied moisturizer to the tattoo nestled between Liza's shoulder blades, exposed by the tank top that dipped just enough in the back. "The artist in Monterey."

"He really did. Thank you for doing this for me. I couldn't reach it myself."

A month ago, she would have asked Tom to help her. Except she knew that she wouldn't have a month ago, because she hadn't been ready for this tattoo then.

"I like it," Karl said, glancing at her back as he walked to the coffeepot.

"Ooh," Zoya said, coming over to stare. "Me too. Can I have one, Mom?"

"When you're eighteen. Then I cannot stop you."

"What'll you get?" Karl asked, tugging on Zoya's ponytail.

"I'll think about it," the teenager replied. "I'm not getting a tramp stamp for the hell of it."

"Language," Irina scolded.

"Bullshit," Zoya coughed.

"Zoya, do not sass your mother," Karl snapped.

Liza fought a smile. "My mom would have gotten out a sewing needle and offered to do the tattoo for me. Just like she did when I wanted to have my lip pierced."

"But your lip isn't pierced," Zoya said.

"Exactly," Liza said, and Irina chuckled.

"Your mother and I would have had a lot of long talks," Irina said fondly.

"She would have loved you. You have so much in common, but mostly because you've been so good to me."

"You are deserving of people being good to you." Irina hesitated. "Tom's called me a few times and I'm not sure what to say to him. Did you tell him that you were moving out?"

Liza sighed. "Yes. I told him I'd keep paying rent when he hinted that he wouldn't approve whoever I got to sublet my side of the duplex."

Irina went to the sink to wash her hands, her face set in a scowl. "He *threatened* you?"

"What a dick!" Zoya said.

"Language," Irina scolded.

"But Zoya's not wrong," Karl said, frowning.

"Yes, she is." Liza couldn't let them believe that about Tom. "He was hurt that I was moving. And it *is* in our contract. He didn't want just anyone renting from him, because sports fans can be intense. Everything he owns is bought in the name of a corporation so that people can't stalk him. And that was *before* he joined the FBI and made criminals hate him."

"I can understand that," Irina allowed, pouring from the ever-present teapot.

"So no calling him a dick, Zoya," Liza said. "He even registered my car under his corporation, so that anyone looking for him wouldn't come at me." She was going to have to register it in her own name when it expired. But that wouldn't be until mid-January of the following year, so she had time to figure it out.

"Oh, all right," Zoya muttered. "I just don't like people hurting you."

Liza smiled at the teenager. "And I appreciate that. Thank you," she added when Irina filled her cup. She'd taken her first sip of the tea—not "special tea," Irina assured her—when her cell phone began to ring. On the off chance that it wasn't Tom, she checked the caller ID.

It was a number she didn't recognize. *I swear to God, Tom, if this is one of your burners . . .* She hit ACCEPT and went nearly limp with relief when a woman asked to speak to Miss Barkley. *God. I don't even care if she's a telemarketer.* "This is she."

"Hello. My name is Portia Sinclair. I'm the head of HR at Sunnyside Oaks Convalescence and Rehabilitation Center."

"Oh." Liza blinked. "That was fast. I just sent in my application last night."

"Well, your résumé is very impressive, Miss Barkley. Would you be available to come in for an interview today? Say, noon? We have a pressing need to fill this position."

Liza's heart was racing. *Yes.* This was what she was meant to do, how she was meant to protect this family who'd taken her in. "Yes, that sounds wonderful."

"Then I'll text you the address. When you arrive, have the front desk call me."

"I will. Thank you." Liza ended the call and met three curious gazes. "Job interview."

"We figured that out," Irina said with a smile. "What facility?"

"It's a convalescence and rehabilitation center," Liza said, hedging on the name.

"Which one?" Karl asked, buttering his toast.

To hedge further would be more suspicious at this point. "Sunnyside Oaks."

Irina frowned. So did Karl. "I . . . have heard of this place," Irina said slowly.

"So have I," Karl said, "but I can't remember where."

"Me too." Zoya was busily typing into her phone. She grimaced. "One of their nurses was murdered last night. Penny Gaynor."

Karl snapped his fingers. "That's where I heard it, too. It sounds dangerous."

Irina was still frowning. "I don't know if it's dangerous or not, but I knew a few nurses who took jobs there. None of them were women I'd call friends."

Well, they are *caring for Pastor,* Liza thought. "Were they bad people, the nurses?"

"No, but they weren't nice, either. The only one I remember being suspicious was a woman named Innes." She tapped the rim of her cup, thinking. "She was accused of stealing narcotics by a patient's family. There was never any proof, but no one had any trouble believing it was true. The woman had a hardened quality that made her difficult to warm up to."

Good to know. Avoid Nurse Innes. "I see."

Irina's eyes narrowed. "Zoya, you're going to be late for school."

Zoya crossed her arms with a scowl. "I'm staying home. Dad told me to, remember? It's why Abigail isn't here. Amos kept her home, too. Does DJ Belmont ring a bell?"

"Zoya," Irina warned. "Watch your tone."

Zoya slumped in her chair. "Mom, if you want me to leave, just tell me to leave."

"Leave," Irina ordered.

Karl coughed to cover a laugh. "Come on, Zoya. We'll find something to do."

Keeping her gaze on Liza's face, Irina grabbed a handful of Karl's jacket. "Stay, please."

"Oh, for the love of—," Zoya grumbled. "I never get to hear the good stuff." She stomped from the room, muttering under her breath.

"You know she's waiting in the hall, eavesdropping," Karl said.

"I know. Zoya!" Irina said no more until she heard Zoya's footsteps above them. "We have a minute before she sneaks back down. You're hiding something from us, Liza. Spill it."

Liza blinked. Innocently, she thought.

Karl just chuckled. "We've raised eight children, Liza. Just tell her. She won't give it up."

Liza sighed, wishing she'd retreated with Zoya. She was torn. On one hand, she wasn't supposed to speak of it per Molina and Raeburn, but on the other hand she trusted Irina and Karl. And having Irina's take on the nurses she'd known who now worked for Sunnyside could be valuable. "I can't tell you a lot, except that this place is important."

Irina's eyes narrowed. "To whom?"

Liza hesitated, then came as clean as she could. "To Mercy."

Karl sucked in a shocked breath. "Then this place *is* dangerous."

"Did Tom put you up to this?" Irina demanded.

"*No.* This was my decision. He knows, as do his superiors. He was not pleased."

"This is wrong," Irina said, shaking her head. "You cannot do this, *lubimaya.* I forbid it."

Liza's hackles shot up just as they had when Tom had forbidden her the night before. But she remained calm, because, like Tom, Irina's expression was full of fear. "Irina," she said gently. "Mercy should live without fear. Gideon, Amos, and Abigail, too. That's worth a risk."

"No," Irina insisted. "I cannot sit idly while one of my girls sacrifices for another. It's like asking me to choose one child over the other."

"Thank you." Affection roughened her voice. "Truly. But I went into combat zones. I'm trained to defend myself. And I'm qualified for this role. I'm a good choice."

"I can't . . ." Irina looked at Karl beseechingly. "How can we change her mind?"

"I don't think we can. Or that we should. Liza has proven herself capable of making wise decisions." He wagged his finger at Liza. "But you won't take any undue risks."

"None." She crossed her heart. "Of course, you're assuming I'll even *get* the job."

"You will," Irina said sadly. "Because Portia Sinclair finds your résumé very impressive."

Liza blinked. "You heard her say that? The HR lady on the phone?"

"I have good ears. I hear much." She raised her voice. "Like footsteps in the hallway!"

"Dammit!" Zoya snapped. Her stomping footsteps could be heard going back up the stairs.

Karl shook his head. "She's yours."

"Remember that when she is valedictorian of her graduating class," Irina said.

He leaned over to kiss Irina's temple. "Then she's mine." He turned to Liza. "Okay, here's how this is going to go. Because you are important to us. You get that, right?"

She smiled. "I do. Thank you. Now I need to get home and get ready for the interview."

"Not so fast," Karl said. "I know you're a soldier and I know you can take care of yourself, but there's also DJ Belmont to consider. If he knows that you were the one who spoiled his shot on Wednesday, he might be looking for you. I don't want you driving around in a car he can follow. I've already given instructions to the guards in the lobby of your apartment to watch for Belmont and call 911 if they see him anywhere on or around the premises. Now I'm going to worry about people from Sunnyside Oaks lurking outside and following you. Especially if they find out where you used to live."

"How could they?" Liza asked. "How could DJ? Nothing I own is in my name."

"If someone wants to badly enough, they can," Karl said darkly. "Do this for me, okay? Drive your car back to the apartment, and when you leave for the interview, take mine."

Liza choked. "Your Tesla? Hell, no. I'd wreck it."

"Not the Tesla." Karl took a pen from his pocket and wrote something on the back of a napkin. "I keep an SUV there for VIP clients. It's a Ford Expedition and has tinted windows. It's made for privacy. The keys are hanging on a hook in the laundry room." He gave her the napkin. "This is the slot where it's parked. Please drive it when you go on your interview."

"And any other time you drive yourself somewhere," Irina added.

Liza folded the napkin and slipped it into her handbag, touched beyond words. "Thank you."

Karl nodded once. "I don't like this, nor do I understand what you're doing, but I understand why you're doing it. If I could do whatever this is in your place, I would, just to ensure that Mercy and the others have a normal life. But if there is any whiff of danger, we want you out of there."

Liza nodded, knowing that by keeping Pastor's presence a secret she was deceiving them, and she hated that. At the same time, having a car that could possibly be traced to an FBI agent was probably not the best idea. Having a car that could be traced to Karl wasn't, either.

"The Expedition can't be traced to you?"

"No. I've got a tangle of corporations that would keep even the most talented hackers scratching their heads for a while. I should know," Karl added dryly. "I paid enough for hackers to try to bust in."

"You're that scared of stalkers?" Liza asked, now worried for Karl and Irina.

"No, *dorogaya maya*," Irina said. "Karl, you have made her afraid for us. Liza, Karl's marketing business works with celebrities who film endorsements and commercials. There is a lot of information in the company's computer that could damage some very influential people. Their addresses, phone numbers, children's names, products or brands that they haven't yet launched, for example. Good security is necessary."

"That makes me feel better." Liza stood, kissing both of them on the cheek. "Thank you. I'll be careful with your SUV."

"Be careful with *yourself*," Karl said gruffly.

"I will."

SACRAMENTO, CALIFORNIA
FRIDAY, MAY 26, 8:30 A.M.

"You got all this in eight hours?" Croft asked, looking at the photographs Tom had spread over the conference table in Raeburn's office, products of his overnight facial recognition searches. "Wow. Did you sleep at all?"

"A little," Tom lied. He hadn't closed his eyes all night, Liza's words banging in his head like sledgehammers. *I need more than that.*

He'd worked at his keyboard for hours, then had run on the treadmill. He'd even bathed Pebbles and baked a cake, but nothing had helped.

I need more than that. At some point he'd stopped hearing her voice say the words, instead hearing his own. *I need more than that.*

But did he? He didn't have any idea.

"I mostly let the facial recognition software run," he went on. "Knowing his initials and that he had a six-year-old son helped narrow things down."

"So this is Kowalski," Raeburn mused, examining each photo.

"Roland Kowalski," Tom said, "when he's working his drug business."

Croft was looking at a photo of the man in a fancy three-piece suit. "And Anthony Ward when he's developing real estate."

"His office is in Granite Bay," Tom said. *Too close to the Sokolovs' house.*

"Lots of pricey real estate out there," Raeburn said, turning to the second stack of photos. "His wife and kids, too? How did you find these?"

"His wife's Facebook page," Tom said. "Her name is Angelina. Their six-year-old son is Anthony Junior. They call him Tony. They have another son who's about two."

Raeburn's brows went up. "The wife didn't have her Facebook account locked?"

Tom shrugged.

Raeburn chuckled. "Right. No locks can keep you out."

"I never said that." But her password had been criminally easy to break. Her son's birthday, easy to find from his birth certificate once he had the father's name. *Amateurs.*

Raeburn waved a hand as if his denial was of no consequence. "Never mind. Bring the bastard in."

"We'll start at his business," Croft said. "We're more likely to be allowed in."

Raeburn nodded. "Take Hall and Summerfield with you. I doubt he'll come in easily."

Tom felt a rush of adrenaline at that. He hadn't been in a takedown situation since Ephraim's last stand at Dunsmuir. He really wanted to take someone down today.

"Will do," Croft said. "Anything else?"

Raeburn nodded. "I had your tattoo artist, Dixie Serratt, put in protective custody. She can't ID Kowalski if she's been harmed in the general population. When you bring Kowalski in, we'll put him in a lineup. Any chance that your source would agree to do a visual?"

"Yes. He's already agreed to that."

"Good." Raeburn pushed away from the conference table and returned to the chair behind his desk. "You have your orders. Keep me informed."

When they were in the hall, Croft lifted a brow. "Who's your source, Hunter? That sixteen-year-old who brought us Cameron Cook?"

"No." Tom was saved further reply by the buzzing of his work phone. It was a San Francisco area code. "This is Agent Hunter."

"This is Cameron Cook."

Speaking of. Tom stopped midstep and leaned his back against the hallway wall, letting others pass. Croft stood beside him, looking concerned. "Cameron," Tom said, and Croft tilted her head, hopeful excitement in her eyes. "How are you?"

"Not good," Cameron confessed. "Have you heard anything? I'm so worried. Hayley's due any day now. She must be so scared. And I can't even think of my Jellybean in that place."

Tom's shoulders sagged. He fully understood Cameron's fear. "I have some leads, but nothing that tells me where she is. I was hoping you'd gotten another e-mail."

"No. Sometimes I stare at my screen for hours at a time, hitting refresh over and over."

"I get that," Tom said. And he did. It had been like that for him when Tory was murdered. He'd stalked her killer through Internet forums that no decent person should ever see, clicking refresh in the hope that the vile monster would show his virtual face. "I don't have anything I can tell you, though. I'm sorry, Cameron."

A choked sob met his ears. "Thank you anyway. I'm . . . I'm sorry I bothered you."

"You didn't," Tom said firmly. "I promise you didn't. But keep watching your e-mail. Maybe Hayley and her brother will be able to send you another message." Especially if Pastor and DJ were both in Sacramento. Tom wondered who was minding Eden in their absence.

"I hope so." Cameron shuddered out a sigh. "I'll call you as soon as I see something."

"Thank you. Listen, Cameron, do you have someone with you?"

"My mom and dad. They let me take a few mental health days but they say I have to go back to school on Tuesday. So after that I can't watch my e-mail."

"If I have your permission, I can put an alert on your e-mail that will let me know if you get a message. I might see other personal messages, though."

"Do it," Cameron said quickly. "I got nothing to hide, Agent Hunter. I need to get Hayley back. I need her. And my daughter, too."

"All right, then. I'll send you a form you can sign, and then I can do it legally. I have to go now, but you have my number." He ended the call and looked at Croft helplessly. "I hate having to tell him that I've got nothing."

"But you don't," Croft encouraged. "You got a lot of somethings. We just don't know how they fit together yet. But we will. Come on. We need to round up Hall and Summerfield. If Raeburn offers backup, I am for sure taking it."

GRANITE BAY, CALIFORNIA
FRIDAY, MAY 26, 8:45 A.M.

"Oh my God." DJ grimaced at his reflection in Smythe's bathroom mirror. "This is awful."

It wasn't the dye's fault. It had done exactly what was advertised. His hair and scruff were now Deep Dark Brown. Just like the guy on the box. *So why do I look so bad?*

He didn't consider himself a vain man, but this was truly awful. "I look dead."

Which was true. His skin was pale, his face gaunt. It hadn't shown so much when his hair was blond, but it sure did now. His cheekbones jutted out in sharp relief, his dark eyes looking . . . *Dark. Like black-hole dark.*

Some people were not meant to go dark. He snorted. *With their hair, anyway.*

But, he thought objectively, he didn't look like himself anymore, which was the effect he'd been going for. He trimmed his scruff and slid on the glasses that he'd bought on a whim.

"Not bad." He stroked the edges of the goatee that was the only thing that looked better dark. The dye had made his blond scruff a little denser, and he'd been able to remove the stains left on his skin with some rubbing alcohol he'd found in the Smythes' medicine cabinet. The glasses were an excellent touch, drawing attention to the end of his nose where he settled them.

Grooming completed, he cleaned up his mess and bagged it. He'd noticed the neighbors putting all their trash cans out the night before and he hadn't heard the rumble of the garbage truck. He'd toss the bag into one of their cans on his way out. No way was he leaving any of his personal trash around any more bodies.

Nor would he leave any more extraneous bodies. That was what had led to Ephraim's capture. *I have to stop killing people and leaving them to be found.*

He wasn't sure what he himself could have done differently, though. Nurse Gaynor had deserved to die. She'd broken the trust of her patients and her employers. She'd been extortable.

Mrs. Ellis had also deserved it. She'd been a nosy busybody who'd probably never been told no in her life. This was what happened when women weren't kept on a leash and busy doing chores. They got gossipy and peeked in your windows and played armchair detective.

Mr. Smythe, now . . . DJ did regret having to kill him. But if the man had only minded his own business, he would still be alive. Storing his body in the freezer had been necessary, because he could no longer count on Kowalski for body disposal.

Kowalski had to have some kind of chipper shredder, because the bodies simply disappeared. Even when there had been half a dozen rival gang members dead on the ground. He'd always wondered where Kowalski put them.

He wondered how long it would take for Mrs. Smythe to think of looking in the freezer for her husband once she got home. Maybe he should move some of that frozen meat out of the chest into the kitchen freezer. That way she wouldn't need to open the chest for a while.

It would give him time, especially if he hadn't finished this by Tuesday when Mrs. Smythe came home. Luckily, she hadn't called yet, opting instead to send a few texts every day. He'd noticed a few new texts pop up on Nelson's locked phone screen that morning and needed to try to answer them, or the lady of the house might ditch her trip and come home early.

DJ hoped Smythe's face hadn't gotten freezer burn. He wasn't sure if it would still unlock his phone if there were ice crystals forming.

Hopefully it wouldn't matter, because hopefully he was getting out of here sooner rather than later.

He'd wasted too much time watching video that was after the fact. He had added the camera to Smythe's Wi-Fi, which enabled him to watch the feed in real time when he wasn't physically in the bedroom, but that was still playing defense. It was time to get ahead of the power curve.

After a good night's sleep, he'd realized that he had a valuable piece of information: Daisy Dawson's place of employment. Everyone else had either hidden their addresses behind fucking corporations or, like the Sokolovs, had round-the-clock security.

Daisy worked at a radio station in Midtown Sacramento. She was on the air right now, so she was there. Her show was over at ten, so he needed to get his ass in gear.

He was going to shoot her as she left work. With any luck, he'd kill her, and then all he'd need to do was pick off Gideon, Mercy, and Amos at the funeral. And if she survived, Gideon would rush to the hospital. *I can follow him home from there.*

Then, eventually, the prick would visit his sister. *And then I'll have them both.*

GRANITE BAY, CALIFORNIA
FRIDAY, MAY 26, 12:00 P.M.

"Wow." From behind the wheel of the Bureau-issued SUV, Croft stared up at the mansion that Anthony Ward—a.k.a. Roland Kowalski—and his wife Angelina called home.

Ward's business location had been a bust. Mr. Ward had not been in, according to his receptionist. She'd told them that Mr. Ward would call them if he wanted to and, unless they had a warrant, to remove themselves from the premises or she was calling security.

Tom had low expectations for this home visit. Anthony Ward

would already be in hiding. Or manufacturing an alibi. But maybe they could get through to Mrs. Ward.

Croft glanced at Tom from the corner of her eye as she turned into the grand driveway. "I guess this kind of place is old hat to you, though."

The Wards' house resembled an old manor home. "I've seen a few like this. A lot of my former teammates had estates like this, with electric fences and security guards."

"Why don't you?" Croft asked. "I've wondered why you bought a duplex in Rocklin when you could have had something like this."

"I didn't want something like this."

Her glance had become disbelieving. "What did you want, then?"

"I lived in the house that my stepfather grew up in. When it got burned down, we rebuilt on the same foundation. It's a home. Not a mansion. I wanted something like that."

"But a duplex?"

"I liked the neighborhood," he said defensively. "There are real families there that you can smile at, and you can buy their kids' lemonade."

She smiled. "Even though it was awful."

He smiled back, not surprised that she remembered the detail from their conversation on Wednesday. "Even though."

"But you could have afforded more."

"Liza couldn't." The words were out of his mouth before he could call them back.

Croft's brows went up. "Liza couldn't? Did she buy the house with you?"

"No. But we'd agreed that she'd rent from me, and she stipulated that it be a place she could afford. She spent hours while we were driving down from Chicago researching neighborhoods and rent values. She found the duplex online."

And he hadn't argued. He'd been so damn grateful to know that she was on the other side of the wall that he'd made an offer on the duplex the day after they'd arrived in Sacramento.

"But don't you want security?"

He shrugged. Hiding his address behind layers of corporations was good security, in his book. "I'm not that recognizable. That guy yesterday in Yuba City wasn't rare, per se, but it doesn't happen that often. And fans aren't exactly a threat, except to my privacy."

Croft shook her head fondly. "You already signed something for that cop's kid, didn't you?"

"Yes. Liza had—" His words stumbled to a halt and he felt his cheeks heat at Croft's too-insightful gaze.

"Liza had?" Croft prompted.

"She bought some basketballs when we first moved in. For some of the kids I met at a charity event. They were raising money to help kids who'd come from abusive homes. Liza asked if I'd offer up some signed gear and told me that she'd found a sale on basketballs at the local sporting goods store. She bought four dozen."

"Four dozen basketballs?" Croft laughed. "Where did she put them?"

"In my spare bedroom closet," he said wryly. "Half of them are still there, and I'm terrified to open the door. It's like snakes in a can." He spread his hands like an explosion. "*Boing.* They rain down on my head and she laughs."

Laughed. She *laughed.* Because she'd left and wasn't laughing anymore.

Croft, having pulled to a stop in the circular driveway near the front door, turned in her seat to give him her full attention, so he forged on.

"Anyway, she donated the basketballs and the organization auctioned some of them off. The others they gave to kids as prizes for selling the most raffle tickets, that kind of thing."

Croft tilted her head, studying him. "Did she buy the basketballs herself?"

He nodded, remembering that argument all too well. "I told her to use my credit card, but she's stubborn. Said she had money saved and wanted to do some good." His throat closed. "She said that she wished there'd been an organization like that to help me when I was a kid."

"She knows about your bio-father, then?"

"Yes. She knows my whole family."

She is *my family.*

I need more than that.

He cleared his throat again. "Let's talk about Angelina Ward. You want to take the lead?"

"Nah. She might like the looks of you better. I'll be bad cop this morning."

"Only this morning?" Tom teased.

"Shut your pie hole," she said, but with obvious affection. "You're growing on me, kid."

"Let's do this. I assume she won't want to let us in, but I'll bat my eyelashes or something."

"She's not going to tell us anything, and if she lets us in, I'll be shocked. But if she does let us in, be on the lookout for anything we can use to track her husband. Sometimes it's as simple as a hotel brochure they've set aside or a Post-it Note on a fridge."

A maid answered their knock. "We don't accept solicitors." She started to close the door.

Producing her badge, Croft rested her hand on the door, halting its progress. "Special Agents Croft and Hunter, here to see Mr. Ward."

The maid's eyes widened. "He's—"

"That will be all, Carmela." The words were delivered in a clipped staccato by a woman with waist-length black hair who wore a spotless white pantsuit. "Please return to your duties." When the maid was gone, Angelina Ward glared at them with unveiled malice. "Get off my property."

Tom smiled. "Ma'am, we'd just like to talk to your husband. That's all."

Angelina's chin lifted. "He's at work."

"No, he's actually not," Tom said. "We've just come from there."

"Well, he isn't here. Leave, or I'll report you for trespassing and harassment."

Tom wanted to roll his eyes, but he held his smile. "We're merely trying to get information on one of his business associates. Maybe you know him? Roland Kowalski?"

The woman's nostrils flared and her jaw tightened. "Leave. Immediately."

"Mommy?" a little boy's voice asked uncertainly.

Angelina instantly changed from vicious to warmly maternal as she turned to the child who was hidden behind the door. "It's all fine. These people are salesmen and are leaving."

"I'll make them leave," the boy said, and Tom could picture the child's chin lifting just as his mother's had.

"No, sweetheart. Let Mommy handle this."

"Call the police, Mommy. My teacher said so. I'll call them. I know the number—911."

"Smart kid," Croft said, and Angelina glared at her.

"Go find Carmela, baby."

A small foot stomped. "I am not a baby."

"She's got cookies," Angelina said, ignoring the tiny tantrum. "Chocolate chip."

"Okay!" The child ran, his footsteps growing softer as he raced toward cookie goodness.

Angelina turned back to face them, teeth bared. "Leave."

Tom took a measured step back. "You should be protecting your son. With all due respect."

"I am," she snarled. "From the likes of you."

"You know what your husband is," Tom said softly. "You know the kind of enemies he makes. We're trying to warn you about one of his enemies." He didn't know if that was true yet, but he had no doubt that DJ would turn on Kowalski's family if he were cornered. "His name is DJ Belmont. You might know him as John Derby. He's killed before and he'll kill again. Don't make the mistake of believing that he'd spare your child."

The woman was breathing shallowly, her eyes flickering in fear for a moment before she shuttered her expression. "I've asked you nicely. Now I'm calling the police."

Tom followed her quick glance skyward and noticed the security camera mounted above the door. *She knows her husband is listening.* "Well, if you think of anything or have any concern that this man will hurt you or your little boys, please call us." He gave her his card and watched her rip it into pieces.

But she kept the pieces clenched in one closed fist. He hoped she would be able to reconstruct his number later. That would have to be enough for now.

"Thank you for your time," he said. "We're sorry to have troubled you, but this man is very dangerous." He ventured another smile. "And your sons are very small."

The door slammed and Croft shrugged. "Let's go." Back in the SUV, she belted up and turned to him. "Well?"

"She was being watched. There was a camera above her head."

Croft nodded. "I caught that, too. Think she's taping those pieces of your card together?"

"I hope so. Although she might be flushing them." He checked his watch and made a decision. "Can we stop by the Sokolovs' place on our way back?"

Croft started the engine. "Sure, but why?"

He sighed. "Liza has a lesson with Abigail today."

"She's still not answering your calls?"

I need more than that. He cleared his throat. "Something like that."

The Sokolov house was unusually quiet. The only evidence of life was the security guard that Karl had hired to protect them when Mercy and her FBI protection detail were elsewhere.

Irina answered the door. "She's not here. You can come in and check if you want."

"No." Tom sighed. "I believe you."

Irina's expression softened. "Good. You look tired, Tom. Come inside and have some tea."

"I can't now. Croft is waiting for me in the SUV. But thank you."

"It is I who should be thanking you. Raphael told me that you are providing secure vehicles for Mercy's birthday guests. We appreciate that, more than you know. Raphael is kicking himself for not thinking of it himself."

Tom managed a smile. "He's had a little bit on his mind." He needed to try one more time. "Is Liza coming back today? Doesn't she help with Abigail's lessons?"

"Amos kept Abigail home today. Rafe told him to."

Tom frowned. There was something Irina wasn't telling him. "Where is Liza?" When she just shook her head, he glanced up, hearing a window open. Zoya looked down at him. "Care to share?" he called up.

"Nope," she called back. "You're walking the stalking line, Agent Hunter."

Tom bit back a retort. Because the girl wasn't wrong. "But she's all right?" he asked Irina.

Irina's smile was sad. "She'll be fine, in time. But I do feel the need to ask why you keep bothering her. I haven't known you long, but you don't seem like the kind of man to push yourself on a woman who's asked you to back off."

Tom flinched. He opened his mouth, then closed it again, having no idea how to answer.

She patted his arm. "Think on that. Then we will talk further. Be safe."

And then she shut the door in his face. Numbly, he walked back to the SUV, feeling Croft's gaze with every step. He got in and closed the door.

"Don't ask. Please," he said, pulling his seat belt on. "Let's go back to the office, okay? We can figure out our next steps on Kowalski."

"Okey-dokey." She had started to back out of the driveway when Tom's work cell began to buzz. "You are the most popular partner I've ever had," she drawled.

Tom frowned. "It's Gideon."

Croft stopped the SUV and put it into PARK. "Answer it. On speaker, please."

Tom wasn't sure if she thought he'd given Gideon more Eden information or not, but he didn't argue. "I'm with Croft," he said by way of greeting. "You're on speaker."

"Someone tried to lure Daisy out of the radio station," Gideon said, a tremble in his voice.

Croft's mouth tightened. "What happened, Gideon?"

"I drove her in to work this morning. All this DJ Belmont stuff has had me rattled. About an hour ago, a man called asking if Poppy was still in the station."

"Poppy is Daisy's radio name," Tom explained to Croft.

Croft rolled her eyes. "I know. I'm a listener. Go on, Gideon."

"I'd already told the receptionist to let me know if Daisy got any calls. Daisy shot Belmont a month ago. If he knows that, he'll be gunning for her, too."

"Or he might use her to get to you," Croft murmured. "And to Mercy through you."

"Yeah," Gideon bit out. "I figured that out myself. Another reason why I'm Daisy's Velcro for the foreseeable future. The guy didn't get anywhere with the receptionist, who taped the call. I checked it out and it came from a burner. An hour later, a bouquet of flowers arrived. The card said they were from one of the charities that she featured on the show last week."

"But they weren't?" Tom asked.

"No. I called, because my gut was in knots, and the flowers seemed too timely. The charity said that while they did appreciate Daisy's shout-out, the flowers were not from them."

"And then?" Tom didn't think he was going to like the answer.

"And then I got mad. I took the flowers out to the dumpster and chucked them in."

Croft winced. "And then?"

Gideon's laugh was bitter. "And then the bastard shot me from a goddamn Lexus."

Tom shared a tense glance with Croft. "Belmont? Did he hit you?" he asked, because Gideon was still talking. Therefore he hadn't been hurt that badly, if at all.

"Vest."

Croft's cheeks flushed in anger. "Motherfucker. He shot you in the chest?"

"Yep. It'll bruise, but I'll live. I pulled my gun, but he drove away and there was too much foot traffic to risk shooting back. I called it in, but the license plates were another fake. Marin County issued the original plates to a Lexus in the same color six months ago."

"He has access to private citizen information, then," Croft said. "Not a surprise."

"No, but also, he's changed his appearance. It all happened so fast that I didn't realize it until I watched the station's security tapes. He's dyed his hair dark. Has a goatee, too. His left arm was in a sling, so he's still injured. Molina said she was updating the BOLO to reflect."

"We need to roll, Gideon," Croft said. "Do you need a ride out of there?"

"No. We're sitting tight here for a while. Molina arranged for a Bureau transport van to pick us up. It'll be disguised as a delivery van and will back up to the door so that we can crawl in and hide. I fucking hate this guy," he finished.

"You're not the only one." Croft ended the call. "Let's head back. We've got work to do."

NINETEEN

DJ exited the interstate and wound his way toward the zoo. He could lose himself in traffic there. Once he felt sure that no one was following him, he pulled into an alley, released his iron grip on the steering wheel, and sagged against the seat.

Oh my God, how could I have been so stupid? He wanted to scream. But he didn't, drawing deep, even breaths instead, trying to calm himself.

He'd been frustrated when he'd noted that Daisy's orange Beetle wasn't in the parking lot, but she'd been live on the air, so he knew she was inside. He'd been annoyed when she hadn't emerged from the building, but he'd still been okay. He'd been logical. Thought driven. His emotions had been in check.

When the damn receptionist had told him to leave a message for "Poppy," and that she'd call him back at her earliest convenience, he'd only been mildly irritated.

He'd still been clearheaded when he'd come up with the idea to send her flowers, hoping she'd come to the door to receive them, but another woman did. Probably the bitch receptionist who'd told him to leave a message.

Still, the flowers would have been useful. He could have spotted her leaving the station from across the street. Also, the flower arrangement was so large that her vision would be impaired. She wouldn't see him when he shot her.

What he hadn't expected was to see Gideon Reynolds carrying the flowers from the station, as cocky and arrogant as he'd always been, even when he was a kid. And then Gideon Reynolds had thrown the flowers into the dumpster, vase and all.

He hadn't expected his mind to flash back to the image of thirteen-year-old Gideon, covered in blood after shoving Edward McPhearson so hard that his head hit his own anvil. So hard that McPhearson had died.

And he hadn't expected that image of Gideon's face to morph into Waylon's at the moment that DJ had smothered him to death with a pillow.

He definitely hadn't expected the swell of rage that exploded inside him or the suppressed *pop* of the gunshot that followed. It was as if he'd been taken over, his actions not his own.

Gideon had staggered back against the dumpster, clutching at his chest, and DJ had felt that rage become a visceral jubilation.

He'd done it. He'd killed Gideon Reynolds. The fucker had finally paid.

But then the man had stood, chest heaving. Because he was still breathing.

Breathing. Gideon didn't deserve to breathe. He needed to die. He'd needed to die seventeen years ago when he'd killed Edward Mc-Phearson.

Just like DJ's father had died for helping Gideon escape.

DJ remembered the look in Waylon's eyes as he'd breathed his last. The fear.

The guilt.

The acceptance.

Because Waylon had known that he deserved to die.

A sound cut through the storm in his mind, a wail, an animal howl. For a moment DJ wondered what it was that could make that sound. Until he realized.

It's me. Shocked, DJ covered his mouth, his whole body shaking. His face was wet.

Shit. He was crying. Sobbing.

He hadn't cried since the day he'd turned thirteen years old. Not since Edward McPhearson had welcomed him into the smithy as his newest apprentice. He'd been so proud of himself. Until Edward had . . .

DJ closed his eyes, hand still pressed tight to his mouth, muffling the cries that continued to spill from his throat.

It had hurt. God, how it had hurt.

And when he'd told Pastor, the bastard had smiled.

He'd *smiled*. And told DJ that he'd been honored by the love of a Founding Elder.

Love. There was no such thing as love.

DJ knew this, because he'd gone to his father, still bleeding. Still in shock, but believing that his father could fix this. That he'd help. That he'd make this right.

Waylon's fists had clenched as DJ had haltingly told his father what Edward had done, every one of his father's considerable muscles hardening as his body seemed prepared to rip someone up. But then Waylon had exhaled.

And told DJ that it was something to be accepted. That there wasn't anything he could do. That Edward would tire of him and there would soon be another.

DJ had left his father's house that night, never to return until four years later when he'd killed him. He'd gone back to Pastor's house, because he'd had no other place to go.

And the next day he'd gone back to Edward. To work. Because he was Edward's apprentice, and that was what apprentices did. They worked.

But work wasn't all they did.

Waylon had been wrong. Edward hadn't tired of him. Not until Gideon had turned thirteen, four long years later.

It was finally going to be over. There would be a new apprentice. DJ would be a blacksmith.

Edward would take Gideon to his bed. He'd said so. He'd said DJ was now "too old." He'd even said that DJ could participate, if he wished.

DJ hadn't wished that. But he had been happy that someone else was going to have to take it from Edward.

But that didn't happen. *Gideon* had happened. *Gideon* hadn't been raped, because he'd fought back.

Gideon had killed Edward. And he'd gotten away with it.

Because of DJ's own piece-of-trash father. The howl clawing from his throat had subsided, leaving whimpers in its place.

He hadn't understood when he'd witnessed Waylon in the bed of his truck, a steel claw gripped in his fist, hastily ripping at the face of a dark-haired kid. Only slivers of tattooed skin on his chest remained, tendons and bone mostly visible. The kid's eyes were gone.

Now, seventeen years later, DJ understood why his father had been doing that—because Gideon's were green and Waylon hadn't found a boy with eyes to match. Now, seventeen years later, DJ realized that his father must have tattooed the nameless boy's chest to make it look like Gideon. His father had been the first tattoo artist in Eden. He'd done DJ's tattoo, after all.

Now, seventeen years later, he knew it had all been a farce, because Gideon was not dead. He'd escaped.

But then, DJ had been so shocked that all reason had fled from his mind. It had been the first time he'd seen the claw, which he'd later learned was responsible for all the mutilations of Edenites who'd been "devoured by wolves" because they'd "strayed too far from the compound." In reality they'd questioned, dissented, or tried to escape.

He'd been out searching for Gideon, who'd gone missing after running from his punishment for murdering Edward McPhearson. Everyone had been searching—everyone except his father, who'd disappeared some time during the night with his truck. Pastor had told them that Waylon was searching the forest road.

DJ had believed him—until he'd come upon his father's truck in the forest near the river. Gideon's mother had been curled up in a corner of the truck's bed, sobbing. His father had looked up, wild-eyed and equally shocked to see DJ as DJ had been to see him.

And in that moment of unguarded shock, guilt had flashed across Waylon's face, crystal clear in the dim glow of dawn.

What are you doing? Where have you been?

Driving around the forest. Go home, DJ. Go back to Pastor.

But DJ had been suspicious, so he'd checked the odometer. Waylon had gone more than two hundred miles since his last trip from Eden. DJ knew because he'd been tasked with keeping Waylon's truck running. He knew every nut and bolt of the old vehicle.

No way you drove two hundred miles around the forest. You went into the city. Why?

Waylon had swallowed then, a grotesque sight all covered in blood and gore. *Go home.*

No. Tell me. And then a terrible thought had occurred to him. *You were helping him?*

His father's guilty expression was the only answer DJ had needed. *Why?* he'd demanded. *Why did you help him?*

Waylon had stared at him miserably. *Because I couldn't help you,* he'd said.

With McPhearson. DJ had known exactly why Gideon had been fighting the blacksmith.

Why wouldn't you help me? It had been an agonized cry. Much like he was doing right now.

They know things. I've done things. Waylon had been babbling. All but confessing.

And then it had all clicked. His big, bad enforcer father had been afraid of what Edward McPhearson would say about him. He was afraid of what the bastard would reveal. Waylon's fear of Edward had been stronger than any love he'd ever felt for his son.

You gave *me to him,* DJ remembered saying the words, dry-eyed and steel-spined.

I had no choice.

You had a fucking choice. You always *had a choice. You just didn't choose me.*

Listen to me. I wanted to help you, but I couldn't.

So you helped him? DJ had spat the words, pointing to the body that he now knew had not been Gideon's after all. *Why did you take him to the city?*

Waylon's gaze had flicked to the body. *He died by the time we got there. They beat him bad.*

Like that made the betrayal better, somehow. Easier to accept.

DJ had stepped forward, fists clenched. *And if he hadn't died? What would you have done?*

His father's silence was his answer, once again.

You would have let him go. You would have set him free.

That had been the brutal truth. His father had risked Pastor's wrath for Gideon Reynolds. Because of some misplaced sense of guilt, of responsibility that he hadn't felt for his own flesh and blood.

"But not for me," DJ whispered into the quiet of the car. Waylon hadn't acknowledged his accusation. He'd merely jumped from the truck bed, leaving the body destroyed and unrecognizable to wade into the river and wash away the blood and gore.

That had been the moment that DJ had known that Waylon had to die. Now, all these years later, he replayed Waylon's final moments in his mind, so glad that he'd killed the bastard.

Seventeen years had passed since Gideon's escape, and DJ was just as angry now as he'd been then. Seeing Gideon's face . . . He'd snapped. Before he'd even been aware of it, he'd pointed his gun straight at Gideon's chest. And fired.

But the bastard had not died.

Not today, he told himself. He hadn't died today. *But he will.*

DJ's pulse was slowing, his mind gradually clearing again.

He will die, but Mercy needs to be first. Mercy was the greater threat. Gideon was Waylon's shame and Waylon had paid. Mercy was DJ's shame.

He'd claimed to have killed her and buried her body. He'd thought he *had* killed her. He'd lied to Pastor just as Waylon had lied. But DJ had had a better reason. He'd been chased away by a fucking bystander before he could finish the job.

Waylon had known that Gideon still breathed when he'd dumped him. Waylon had *wanted* Gideon to escape.

I am not like my father. Not in any way. Except for the fact that he had lied and now couldn't let Pastor find out that Mercy was alive. Pastor would brand him a liar and would never tell him the access codes that the old fucker had memorized.

So he was back to the same plan he'd had before. Mercy needed to die.

Except now Gideon and Daisy Dawson would be on alert, because his brain was stupid and had reacted to seeing Gideon's face. He hadn't seen him clearly a month ago, that day in Dunsmuir. He'd been focused on killing Ephraim and Mercy. And then Daisy had shot him.

"Except you just made your job a thousand times harder," he muttered to himself. "Fuck."

Now the cops would be looking for a Lexus. He needed another car, but for now he'd change the license plates and keep his gun close. He wouldn't risk stealing another car right now. Nobody would report the Lexus missing until Mrs. Smythe returned home. He didn't know the same about any vehicle he could steal today.

He got out of the Lexus on legs that felt like Jell-O. Holding on to the car for support, he opened the trunk, found two matching license plates, and switched them with the set of fakes he'd made that morning.

Then he headed back for the Smythe house, exhausted and in pain. His head hurt, his arm hurt. His body ached.

He needed a safe place to hide, a place where neither the cops nor Kowalski could find him.

Kowalski. He wanted to groan. Now he was fighting a war on two fronts. He didn't expect to turn the cops to his way of thinking. But Kowalski he might be able to manage.

He considered his father again. Waylon had been afraid of what would happen if Pastor and McPhearson spilled all they knew.

Kowalski had a family. He could be vulnerable if DJ spilled all that *he* knew. If he couldn't be persuaded to help DJ, he might be convinced to call off his thugs.

It would be good not to have to look over his shoulder. So that was the plan. Get Kowalski to back off while he looked for another place to live.

He thought about staying with Pastor and Coleen in the rehab center. But Pastor kept whining for him to leave Sacramento and return to Eden, so the rehab center wasn't a good idea.

He'd have to keep looking for a place, because Mrs. Smythe would be home soon. He'd kill her if he had to—the chest freezer could hold one more—but he ran the risk that her daughter would call to confirm that she'd made it home all right.

So his priorities were building a file on Kowalski, locating a new house, and finding Mercy. He still felt shitty and stupid, but a little more in control now that he had a plan. That would have to be enough.

SACRAMENTO, CALIFORNIA
FRIDAY, MAY 26, 12:30 P.M.

Portia Sinclair folded her hands atop Liza's résumé. "So do you have any questions for me?"

The interview at Sunnyside Oaks had gone well and Liza was cautiously optimistic.

"Yes, ma'am." She hadn't mentioned that she was only applying for a short-term gig. She hoped that she'd be able to get whatever Tom needed long before she started school. "What will my responsibilities be and for how many patients will I be providing care? On average, of course. I'm aware that your needs will vary from day to day."

"You'll be assigned one or two patients during the day, five at night. Sometimes you'll go as high as three during the day and seven at night, but that is our ratio cap. Will that be a problem?"

Liza blinked. "No, ma'am. My ratios were one to five during the day and one to ten at night. So, no, this won't be a problem at all."

"Well, you were working in the veterans' home," Sinclair said, not bothering to mask her disdain. "This is a private facility and we have higher standards."

Well, bully for you, Liza thought, but kept her smile firmly in place. "That's wonderful. What is the range of patient conditions?"

"Anything from a short-term surgical recovery to long-term rehabilitation after a stroke. Patients vary in age from pediatric to geriatric. We really cover the spectrum."

Including killers. Because Pastor was here somewhere. "I can handle that."

"I'm sure that you can. You'll have to sign an NDA. Many of our patients are public figures and won't look as polished as they do in their outside life. You will not take photographs. You will not carry your phone with you while you are on shift. We provide a locker for your things."

Which would probably be searched. "Those are standard policies. Not a problem."

"Good." She tilted her head. "How did you learn about us?"

"I found you online. I was looking for a position as a nursing assistant and applied for about a dozen positions. You're the first to call me in for an interview. As I said on the phone this morning, I was surprised you called me so quickly."

"You don't know any former patients or other employees of our facility?"

"No, ma'am. I'm relatively new to Sacramento. I don't know many people yet. It's been a little difficult to reintegrate with civilians after my discharge."

"I can imagine. You have no family here in Sacramento?"

"No, ma'am. My family is gone."

Sinclair's expression softened in sympathy. "What happened?"

Like you haven't looked me up six ways to Tuesday. "My mother died of cancer. My sister was murdered."

"How horrible."

"It was. I was only a few months from high school graduation. I somehow made it through, and then, after that, I joined up."

"You have a stellar military record. How did you get the job at the veterans' home? It appears you started just a few weeks after your discharge?"

Liza told her what she'd told Irina—the truth. "My nursing school advisor helped me. She'd been in the army and took me under her wing."

"So you'll be starting school soon?"

"July, ma'am."

"Would you be staying on here as well?"

"Yes, ma'am," she lied. "I'm not wealthy. I need to eat."

"But surely you have funds. Your husband's death benefits. Didn't you receive those?"

Liza flinched, not expecting that question. It was also none of this woman's business. But she answered, because on this point she could be honest. "I did. I put enough away for tuition and lab fees, textbooks, that kind of thing. I put most of Fritz's money in a trust for his family. He'd have wanted his parents to have a retirement cushion."

"How kind of you," Sinclair said, and she sounded so sincere that Liza wondered if the woman knew that they harbored a criminal like Pastor. But of course she knew. Molina and Raeburn had prepped Liza on the nature of the facility's clientele. Mostly celebrities, but a fair share of drug kingpins and mafia bosses.

Liza shrugged uncomfortably. "It seemed like the right thing to do."

"I'm sorry to have to ask you about your husband. I hope I didn't offend."

"Of course not."

"I assumed that it had been a long time since his death. I was surprised to see it upset you."

Aren't you the bitch? "How long is long enough?" Liza asked, thinking about Tom and Tory and their unborn child. "I saw Fritz die, so perhaps my feelings are a bit more raw."

Sinclair nodded. "I suppose they would be. How do you feel about children?"

Liza frowned. "I don't think you're allowed to ask if I have children or plans to have any."

Sinclair chuckled. "No, I meant in a general sense. Can you deal with a pediatric patient?"

"Oh. Then, yes, I can deal quite easily."

"Even if the child is terminal?"

Liza froze for a few seconds, then exhaled as it hit her that her patient would be a real person—a real *sick* person—and not an FBI plant. "It wouldn't be easy, but I could still deal."

"Good. If we decide to hire you, when can you start?"

"As soon as you need me to."

Sinclair stood, extending her hand. "Thank you for coming in. We plan to hire someone quickly, so I'll be able to let you know fairly soon one way or the other."

Liza shook her hand. "I'll be looking forward to your call."

Sinclair took her to the lobby, passing through a different series of hallways on the way out than they'd used on the way in.

Liza tried not to be obvious about looking into the patient rooms, but Sinclair noticed. "Apologies," Liza said. "I'm not trying to be nosy. I'd like a feel for the layout and the kind of equipment you're using here."

"We have all the equipment you'll find in any other facility," Sinclair said proudly. "And if a patient needs what we don't have, we get it."

"Wow," Liza murmured.

"Indeed. Well, here is the lobby, Miss Barkley. I hope you have a delightful afternoon."

"Thank you."

Liza walked to the visitors' lot, where she'd parked Karl's SUV, noting the cameras pointed in her direction. There were a number of them. There was also a tall iron fence with a gate behind it, which, according to Sinclair, was parking for employees and the families of their patients.

The atmosphere was every bit as oppressive and severe as the army base outside Kabul.

She pulled out of the parking lot, noticing a dark sedan pull into traffic behind her. It followed her all the way back to her apartment, not seeming to care that she noticed it.

It could be DJ, she thought. *That would be bad.*

Or it could be Sunnyside Oaks's security staff, checking to see that she lived where she said she did.

Or it could even be the FBI. She hadn't seen Tom in the sedan, but she wouldn't put it past him to have followed her.

Regardless, she was glad for the relative anonymity of the apartment and Karl's SUV. As soon as she was back in her apartment, she flopped onto the sofa and heaved out a relieved breath.

"So far, so good," she muttered.

She checked her texts, expecting one from Tom, but seeing one from Mercy. Or, rather, from Abigail, who had used Mercy's phone. It was an invitation to a sleepover tonight at Mercy's. There would be nail painting, hair braiding, and makeovers. And ice cream.

The sleepover had been Mercy's idea. Her friend had called her the night before when she'd been crying and eating rocky road. Mercy had floated the idea then.

Except that last night, she hadn't been a part of a potential undercover operation. But if she backed out of this party, not only would she disappoint Mercy and Abigail but she'd raise a lot of questions that she didn't want to answer. This had just gotten complicated.

Except . . . this apartment was for Karl's clients. Many who wanted anonymity. It was why the ownership of the unit and the registration on the SUV were—hopefully—untraceable.

She opened a text window to Karl. *All is well. Am at apt. Do you have disguises here?*

Okaaaay. Why? was Karl's immediate reply.

Going to Mercy's tonight. Don't want to lead anyone there if someone is watching. Paranoid maybe but want to be safe.

Are you claustrophobic?

Liza frowned at the question. *No. Why?*

Her phone rang a moment later with a call from Karl. "I hate texting," he said. "We sometimes have to transport celebrities who do our commercials. There's a large box in one of the bedrooms. Big enough to sit in. It's a nice box, and has its own chair. You get in, the driver takes you out on a dolly, and once you're loaded in his delivery truck and he's on the road, you can get out. Sound like something you can do?"

"Yes, I can handle a box. I should leave by five p.m. if that works. Thank you."

"Five p.m. will work, and you're welcome. Be careful," he said and ended the call.

With a satisfied smile, Liza switched back to her conversation with Abigail. *I'll bring nail polish and scrunchies. See you soon, Shrimpkin.*

She had a life. She had friends. She had a family in Chicago who cared about her. She had a new family in Sacramento who cared about her, too.

And if she didn't have Tom Hunter? She'd cope. She always did.

EDEN, CALIFORNIA
FRIDAY, MAY 26, 2:00 P.M.

Graham crouched next to Hayley's pallet, a plate in his hands. "How're you?"

"Ready to pop," Hayley grumbled, curled up on her side, grateful that at this time of day the other wives were elsewhere doing chores. She needed to talk to Graham about their mother. She'd been worried sick about him since he'd splashed their mother's shoes with piss. "Like a huge pus-filled zit."

Graham snorted. "I'm gonna rename Jellybean. From here on out, she's Zit."

Hayley shoved herself to a sitting position, patting her stomach. "I won't let him call you Zit." She eyed the plate, then sighed. "Jerky again, huh?"

"Sorry." He dipped his head closer. "There's a little bit of chicken hidden underneath."

She frowned. "Hidden?"

"Nobody knows what's going on right now," he whispered. "Pastor's gone to the hospital and DJ and the healer went with him. Nobody knows when they're coming back. Or even *if* they're coming back. DJ never did bring back the supplies he went for, and he took the only set of wheels. Nobody's sure how to get more food. And even the jerky won't last forever. That chicken was the last of the animals they were able to bring from the old site."

Most of the animals—cows, goats, sheep, and pigs as well as chickens—had been slaughtered prior to their move to the caves. The meat had been cured and stored, but without DJ getting supplies from the nearest town, the food had been quickly consumed.

"So we might starve," Hayley said, trying not to panic.

"People are scared. Which isn't completely bad. Scared people rise up. You know, down with tyranny and the man and all that. If they get scared enough, they might all try to get out of this place. Eat the chicken first. I wasn't supposed to have it and don't want to get caught."

She popped it in her mouth obediently. When she'd swallowed she asked, "Did you steal it?"

"Duh. From Joshua. *He's* eating chicken. Because *he's* in charge."

"Doesn't surprise me," Hayley muttered. "One of the other wives said he'd be the next leader, now that Ephraim is dead. Did Mom hurt you after you ruined her shoes?"

That their mother had gotten human waste on her shoes had been whispered all over the compound. It seemed to entertain Eden's women. *This is what happens without TV.*

"No. Joshua told me to dump the piss pot, so I didn't hear what came after that. But Mom has been super quiet ever since. Isaac hasn't been speaking to her, so I think she's in trouble."

Isaac was the man to whom their mother had been married on day one of this hell. He didn't seem to be a violent man, but he was an Eden fanatic. One of the earliest members to join way back in the early nineties, he was the community tattooist and enjoyed a captive audience. Every male over thirteen in the compound wore his ink on their skin. All the younger ones, anyway. Apparently there used to be another tattooist, who'd died in his sleep. He'd tattooed all the older men.

Graham will be tattooed—or worse—if I can't get us out of here.
"I'm glad she didn't hurt you."

Graham touched Hayley's cheek gently. "She hurt you. There's a bruise here." His young face hardened, suddenly looking too adult. "I think that's why she's in trouble. But not because she hit you." His gaze dropped to her stomach, and Hayley understood.

"Because of Jellybean."

He nodded. "Sister Rebecca wants the baby alive and unharmed."

Hayley closed her eyes, once again feeling the panic swell in her throat. "How do I stop her?"

"By getting out of here with me."

Her eyes flew open, something in his tone grabbing her attention. "What did you find?"

"The computer *and* the satellite dish." He grinned. "They were in the clinic, in a box labeled *Birthing Supplies*. Tamar asked Joshua if I could fetch the box so that she could get ready to deliver your baby."

Hayley's eyes widened. "Did Tamar know it was in there?"

"Nah. She was as surprised as I was."

"Can you set them up? Especially the satellite dish? That doesn't sound simple."

"I'm going to try. I need a power source. I know they had one and it has to have been quiet. Some generators are silent. Or they had solar panels. I'm still searching for that. Tamar has been a huge help. She's provided distractions all day so that I could hide the stuff I found."

"Where did you put it?"

"Near where I dump the pee." He smirked. "One good thing came from the shoe incident. Everyone's giving me a super wide berth because I'm 'clumsy.' Nobody gets close enough to see what I'm carrying. But back to Tamar. Do you think we can trust her?"

"I hope so. She's going to deliver this baby unless Sister Coleen gets back really soon."

Graham's nod was grim. "When Coleen comes back, she'll take over. I know you're scared, but I think you have more of a shot keeping the baby with Tamar on the job than Coleen."

"I don't think so, Cookie," she said sadly. "Tamar couldn't keep Rebecca from taking *her* baby. She's not going to be able to keep her from taking mine."

Graham's mouth fell open in shock. "What?" he squeaked, rather loudly.

"Shhh." Worried, Hayley glanced around him, looking to see if someone was coming. "I thought you knew," she breathed softly. "I guess I forgot to tell you."

Graham looked down numbly before looking back up at Hayley. "Did she tell you this?"

"No. I figured it out. Her eyes are the same exact color as Rebecca's third child. The other wives told me that Rebecca's other children were born to mothers who didn't survive the births. Nobody said what happened to the mother of the third child. I wondered why. Now I know."

"So Tamar has a really good reason to help us."

"Yeah."

Graham's brow furrowed. She could almost see the gears turning. "That means," he said, "that when we go we'll be transporting two kids. Not only one. And that's assuming that Tamar's baby doesn't throw a tantrum because we're taking him away from Rebecca. We'll have to keep him quiet somehow. I'm considering the logistics of getting out of here. There's nothing but rocks and mountains and trees as far as I can see, and I've explored *way* up the mountain. If we're going to make it to civilization with two kids and you—who'll just have had a baby—we need to have the right gear. You ever rock climb?"

"No. I'm sorry," she added weakly.

"Don't be sorry. I'm just thinking. You know how I do that." Graham patted her stomach. "No worries, little Zit. Your uncle Graham is on the job." He rose fluidly. "Gotta go. More pots to empty." With a final wink, he was gone.

Hayley let the smile drop from her face, closing her eyes as the fear swamped her. "It'll be okay, Jellybean, like Uncle Graham said." But she wondered who she was trying to convince.

TWENTY

DJ refilled his glass with the whiskey he'd found in Nelson Smythe's very well-stocked bar. He normally wasn't a big drinker, but this afternoon had left him shaken.

He'd blown it. Nearly gotten himself caught.

He'd shot Gideon Reynolds, which should have had him celebrating— *if* the bastard had actually died. But the bastard *hadn't* died and now DJ's face was all over the Internet, the photo updated to the one that cops had pulled from the surveillance cameras at the radio station, reflecting his darker hair and his goatee.

He ran a hand over his newly bald scalp and freshly shaven face. He still had the wig he'd borrowed from Nurse Innes at Sunnyside, but that wouldn't be enough. Not if he ever intended to walk on a public street ever again.

Motherfucking Gideon. DJ drained the tumbler in his hand and hurled it, the glass hitting the dresser mirror. The mirror shattered along with the glass.

Just as well. He'd never been much for mirrors, but today, after the memories had obliterated the wall he'd built around them in his mind . . . he couldn't stand the sight of his own face.

He could have run from Pastor and Eden at any time after he'd turned seventeen. But he hadn't because he'd had something to prove.

To whom? He didn't have a clue. Hours later and he still didn't have a clue.

He could have held a knife to Pastor's throat at any time and demanded the old man give him the access codes to that damn bank account, but he hadn't. He should have, but he hadn't.

And objectively, he knew why. He'd been brainwashed. Groomed. He knew about victims of childhood abuse. Objectively, he knew he was one.

Never felt like it, though. He'd always felt powerful, like he was putting something over on Pastor and Eden. But he hadn't been. Not really.

In the end he was still tied to Pastor, even though he hated every cell in the old man's body.

In the end he was still tied to Eden, which was nothing but a prison. None of the fools who worshipped Pastor knew it, and if they did know they didn't admit it, and if they admitted it and fought to get free, they mostly hadn't survived it. But DJ had known the truth and had believed he'd made the *choice* to stay. For the money.

Which he'd never demanded. He gave the now half-full whiskey bottle a bleary glance. It had been unopened when he'd started.

He grabbed the bottle and took a healthy swig. Because who was really the fool?

Once he'd taken over his father's job delivering the drugs Eden produced, DJ had met Kowalski. He'd felt powerful dealing with Kowalski. Valued, even. The man had seen his potential and had taught him all of his tricks.

Bullshit. He'd used DJ just like he'd used everyone else. He'd told DJ that he'd have a house of his own. Now he realized that Kowalski had just wanted someone else's name on the deeds. On the leases. The bastard didn't want anything to be traced back to him.

We're just his stooges. He'd fallen into Kowalski's hands just like he'd fallen into Pastor's.

Because I'm the fool.

"Not anymore," he muttered, and if it sounded a little slurred, that was okay. Life owed him a little numbness, because everything had gone to shit.

He'd missed killing Mercy. He'd missed killing Gideon. He still didn't have Pastor's money. Kowalski had tried to eliminate him. And he was front and center on the FBI's radar.

He sat in a stolen house, drinking stolen whiskey. He didn't mind the stealing. But he'd had his own house. He'd had his own whiskey.

"Not anymore," he muttered again. The Feds had taken everything.

The worst part of it was, DJ was on his own. He hadn't realized how much he'd depended on Kowalski's organization until he'd been cut off.

Weapons, customers, safe houses. Hired muscle. Fellow operatives. *Gone.* He was alone.

"So get them back." He set the bottle aside and focused on his laptop. The document he'd been working on was nearly full. He'd noted the jobs that he'd pulled for Kowalski, the jobs that others had pulled, and the customers and suppliers he could recall.

The jobs, the names of customers and suppliers, those filled the page. But DJ realized he didn't know a single other member of the Chicos who had any power whatsoever.

Only Kowalski.

He laughed bitterly at his lists. Isolating a person from others? Making them dependent on a single source of financial and personal support?

Classic tactics of abusers.

He'd jumped from Pastor's frying pan into Kowalski's fire.

"Not anymore," he said again, so forcefully that he finally believed it himself.

He'd find a way to make Kowalski do what he wanted for a change. He'd get the weapons. He'd get those damn bank codes.

Then he'd blow everything up and shoot everyone down. It was time to take charge of his own damn life.

SACRAMENTO, CALIFORNIA
FRIDAY, MAY 26, 6:00 P.M.

"I'm glad you're all here." Raeburn sat at the conference room table, which was more crowded than it had been Wednesday morning.

Since DJ Belmont's attempt on Gideon's life that afternoon, the "Eden Team" had become significantly bigger. Molina sat at the table, although she'd told them that she was there to provide insight on Belmont's sniper skills, rather than taking a leadership role. Tom wasn't the only disappointed person at the table. It seemed that Molina, while not universally liked, was universally respected.

Raeburn was improving, though.

There were logistics experts and a few experts in the local gangs, including Agent Rodriguez, who'd been providing protection for Mercy until now. Mercy, therefore, had new protection, as did Gideon.

Liza finally had protection as well, which was the one good thing to come of her involvement with Sunnyside Oaks. But her detail would be staying outside Sunnyside's gates. Tom had been racking his brain trying to figure out a way to get someone inside with her. He'd considered hiring a bodyguard on his own.

Liza might not like the idea, but he couldn't concentrate if he was worrying about her safety. It was hard enough to concentrate with her voice in his damn head.

I need more than that.

"Agent Croft?" Raeburn asked, yanking Tom's attention back to the briefing. "Update?"

"SacPD ballistics analyzed the bullet that was lodged in Agent Reynolds's vest," Croft said, having been put in charge of communications between the FBI and SacPD.

Tom had spent most of the afternoon searching for any sign of Kowalski or Belmont, running facial recognition checks at airports and toll stations. So far, there'd been no sign of them.

"The bullet matches the two taken from Penny Gaynor's body," Croft went on. "It also matches a bullet taken from a drive-by shooting a year ago. The victim was a drug dealer who, according to witnesses at the time, was infringing on the Chicos' territory."

"That's a connection," Raeburn said. "Has Belmont been back to Sunnyside Oaks?"

"Not today," one of the agents answered. "We've had eyes on the place from outside the gates since last night. A Lexus like the one Belmont was driving when he shot Agent Reynolds was seen leaving the facility late last night, though. The driver had long dark hair and was not identified as Belmont. Unfortunately, we didn't know about the Lexus then."

"So he wore a wig last night," Raeburn said. "And had colored his hair by this morning. Agent Hunter, have you found any leads?"

"No sir, but it doesn't appear that Belmont's left the area. Kowalski either."

"Good." Raeburn's face had lines that hadn't been there that morning. "I talked to Agent Reynolds personally this afternoon. He was all right, but still in a bit of shock."

"Getting shot does that to a person," one of the other agents muttered. He was one of the SWAT members who'd survived Belmont's assault on the team the month before in Dunsmuir.

Raeburn gave the man a rueful glance. "True. Agent Reynolds seemed surprised that he'd been shot, though. He'd assumed that Belmont was trying to get to Mercy."

"I was surprised, too," Tom offered. "I figured he'd use Gideon to get to Mercy and kill them both at the same time."

"Reynolds said the same," Raeburn confirmed. "He also said that in the second he glimpsed Belmont's face, he thought Belmont was also shocked."

"Like Belmont hadn't planned to shoot him?" Molina asked.

Raeburn nodded. "And I'm not sure what to make of it. I'm happy to entertain suggestions."

Tom thought he might have an idea. He shared a long glance with Molina, who gave him a slight nod, seemingly thinking along the same lines.

Raeburn caught the look they'd shared. "Speak," he suggested with a slight edge to his tone.

Tom sighed. "It's not anything definite. But when Agent Reynolds was remembering Belmont from his own childhood, he said they were friends—until Belmont turned thirteen and was apprenticed to Edward McPhearson."

"The pedophile who tried to rape Gideon, but failed," Croft explained. "Gideon got away."

"Right," Tom said, noting a few shocked stares. Apparently, some of the team hadn't read the full brief he'd prepared weeks ago. "When Agent Reynolds fought back, McPhearson fell and hit his head on an anvil and died. The ensuing beating that Reynolds received was what prompted his mother to smuggle him out of Eden seventeen years ago."

"Gideon escaped," Raeburn said quietly. "He escaped, but Belmont did not. That might have made Belmont very angry indeed."

"But why didn't Belmont shoot Reynolds when he saw him in Dunsmuir a month ago?" one of the other agents asked.

Tom wanted to snarl, *Read the damn brief!* "Belmont was in the process of shooting Mercy Callahan when Amos Terrill threw himself over Mercy to protect her. Belmont's bullet hit Amos instead. Then Agent Reynolds's girlfriend shot Belmont. He was on the run after that. Who knows who else he would have shot that day had he not been stopped?"

"Everyone, I would assume," Molina said dryly.

Agent Collins, the SWAT survivor, grimaced. "Daisy Dawson took him out," he said with no small amount of self-disgust. "He almost took out a whole team and a civilian shot him."

"A civilian who is every bit as good a sharpshooter as I've ever met," Molina said. "But Belmont is as good as she is. Which is how he got the drop on us."

"It was fast," Collins remembered. "We were searching for Ephraim Burton and then all of a sudden, we were dropping like flies. He didn't need time to set up his next shot."

"Agent Reynolds said Belmont's left arm was in a sling," Raeburn noted. "He might not be as fast now."

Molina looked concerned. "But he's still accurate, because Agent Reynolds was standing across the street from him when he fired."

"A hundred feet away," Raeburn confirmed. "At least."

"We have to assume he's still as good a shot as he was before," Molina said. "He hit Agent Reynolds in his heart. If Gideon hadn't been wearing the vest, he wouldn't be here anymore."

Tom felt a shiver prickle his skin. "But Belmont's not as fast as he was before. Especially with a rifle. He used a tripod on the roof of that office building on Wednesday morning. If he uses the rifle, he's going to need that tripod as a crutch. That limits his range, his speed, and his choice of places from where he can shoot. Not a huge amount, but some."

"Some might be enough when it comes down to it," Raeburn said. "Belmont will return to Sunnyside Oaks sooner or later, because Pastor is still there. Correct?"

"I assume he'll return to Sunnyside Oaks, sir," Tom answered. "But Belmont has been hard to predict. Pastor is still there, though. There have been no changes to the patient roster."

"So worst case," Raeburn went on, "we wait him out while providing protection to Agent Reynolds and Mercy Callahan. How close are you to getting a virus into Sunnyside's network?"

"I have access to the HR manager's computer." Tom had had that as soon as Portia Sinclair had clicked on the résumés they'd uploaded. "We have ears on their phone calls now that we have the wiretap warrant. I got e-mail addresses for the network administrator and the accountant from HR's computer and sent them messages with embedded viruses. I'm hesitant to send any additional e-mails. They could compare notes and realize that someone's trying to break in. Now I have to wait until one of them clicks on the link. It's called a man-in-the-middle attack. I'll gain access to their server, but they'll believe that their network has shut itself off, so they'll call a network specialist to get them back up and running."

"Traceable to us?" one of the other agents asked.

Tom wanted to scoff. "No," was all he said.

"Good," Raeburn said. "We know that Sunnyside Oaks is hiring a nursing assistant. We've had several of our candidates apply. If one is hired, we'll use the IT network specialist role to provide backup inside. If none of our applicants are hired, the IT person will be our insider."

"What will the IT person do, exactly?" one of the agents asked.

"Damage the network physically, for one," Raeburn said. "And they can provide cover to our nursing assistant, helping to get her out if they're discovered."

"The IT person can also install cameras on the inside," Tom added. "I might be able to get control of some of the cameras connected through the facility's Wi-Fi, but hardwired cameras that we control would give us even broader visual access."

"We're covered either way," Croft said.

"That's the plan. You have your orders," Raeburn said, rising. "You're all on call."

They disbanded with Croft telling Tom to go home and take a break. Tom agreed, even though he had no intention of doing so.

Molina, however, had other ideas. "Walk with me, Tom," she said.

She made her way from the room, not even checking to be sure he was following.

"Can I do something for you, ma'am?"

She stopped and stared up at him, her shorter stature having no impact on her considerable ability to intimidate. "I'd tell you that I'll only say this once, but that's not true. I will say it over and over again as long as you are under my command."

Tom frowned, trying to figure out what he'd done now. "Ma'am?"

"Listen to me and listen well. If you're serious about a career in law enforcement, you need to understand that it is a marathon, not a sprint. You burn yourself out and . . . then you're done. Washed up. So go home. Eat food. Watch some sports thing on TV."

His lips twitched. "Some sports thing?"

One dark brow lifted. "'Thing.' It's a word, Hunter. A useful word. Look it up." Then she smiled at him. "You have the potential to be an amazing asset to the Bureau. It's my job to teach you how to do that. And I'm ordering you to go home."

"And if I work from home?"

"Then you do. I figure you will. But you'll be able to take breaks there. I understand you have a dog. Miss Barkley showed me photos. Pebbles, yes? Doesn't she need to be walked?"

"Liza always—" He cut himself off with a groan. *Pebbles*. Liza always walked her when he needed to work late. He'd probably be coming home to a mountain of Great Dane excrement.

Molina frowned. "Is Miss Barkley all right?"

"Yes." *I hope*. "She just . . . doesn't rent from me any longer."

Molina seemed to digest this, then shook her head. "Not my circus," she murmured.

Not my monkeys went unsaid.

"You might as well say what's on your mind," Tom said bitterly. "Everyone else has."

"Then I don't need to. Home, Hunter. Rest. Then be ready when we need you."

So Tom gathered his things and started for home. Luckily, the field office wasn't far from the duplex. It was one of the reasons Liza had chosen it. It was far from the veterans' home, though, and even farther from the nursing school. She'd said she hadn't minded.

She'd set up his life for his convenience and comfort at the expense of her own. He could see that now. He needed to talk to her. He *needed* to. He needed to make this right. But . . .

I need more than that.

She needed him to back away. But . . .

He'd been about to speed-dial her when his personal cell began to ring through his SUV's speakers. It was Rafe Sokolov. "Rafe, is there anything wrong?"

"No, nothing's wrong. Nothing new, anyway. I was hoping you could come to my house. I borrowed some tables for Mercy's party and I've been hiding them in the garage. Amos and I could use some help loading them into his truck. Neither of us is operating at full capacity."

"Of course. I need to stop by my house and walk Pebbles first, though."

"Bring her with you," Rafe said warmly. "Abigail will be so happy to see her. Then, after we move the tables, you can have dinner with us. We're ordering pizzas."

That sounded more than nice. Not spending the evening alone sounded like heaven.

"I'll be over as soon as I can."

SACRAMENTO, CALIFORNIA
FRIDAY, MAY 26, 7:05 P.M.

"I ordered the pizzas," Rafe announced as he came through the door to the studio apartment he and Mercy shared. "Double anchovies for everybody, right?"

Liza looked up from where she sat on the floor painting Abigail's nails to catch him wink.

"What's anchovies?" Abigail asked.

"Salty little fish," Liza said.

"Ew!" Abigail cried, scrunching up her face. "That's gross, Rafe."

"He's teasing," Mercy told her softly. Then she looked uncertain. "Aren't you, Rafe?"

"He totally is," Sasha Sokolov said, her hands soaking in a bowl of warm, sudsy water. Rafe's sister lived upstairs but was hanging with them on the lower floor for girls' night.

"I totally am," Rafe assured Abigail, tugging on her braid. "I got liver flavor instead."

Abigail rolled her eyes. "You're teasing again."

"He is," Daisy said firmly. She was painting Mercy's nails, taking special care because Mercy was going to be guest of honor at her birthday party. Everyone thought it was still a surprise, not knowing that Mercy had figured it out. "We're eating pepperoni and sausage and *all* the good things. And you don't even have to finish your supper to have ice cream."

Liza perked up. "What kind of ice cream?"

"*All* the flavors," Erin Rhee said from the sofa where she sat next to Gideon, who was watching them with silent, semihorrified fascination, as though if he asked them what they were doing, they'd somehow drag him into their little salon.

Gideon hadn't originally been invited, but his brush with one of DJ's bullets that afternoon had left him shaken and wanting company. Daisy was equally shaken, although she was wearing a brave face. Gideon's presence crowded them a bit in the small studio, but no one faulted the two for not wanting the other out of their sight, and Rafe couldn't manage the stairs. So they crowded in close on the ground floor, Liza finding comfort in their company.

"All the important flavors, anyway," Erin amended. Sasha's girlfriend had been shot by Ephraim a month ago along with so many others, and although she'd returned to desk duty in SacPD's homicide department, she was still in pain from her injuries. She couldn't sit on the floor with the rest of them but didn't want to miss the party. "Look in the freezer, if you want."

With a squeal of delight, Abigail ran to the freezer. "It's like an ice cream store!"

"There's even rocky road," Erin said. "For Liza."

"Because we are *here* for you, girl," Sasha said, because apparently *everyone* knew that Liza and Tom had argued. "No boys allowed in our clubhouse. Except for Rafe. He can stay."

Rafe mock-sneered at his sister. "Gee, thanks, considering it's my apartment."

"What about me?" Gideon asked.

"You can stay, too," Daisy said. "You can even be the next client in Daisy's nail salon."

"That's not necessary," Gideon assured her. "I'm just here for the pizza."

And the support from this tight-knit group of friends. No one had mentioned the shooting, but it was on everyone's mind.

Liza had heard about it from Karl's driver after she'd climbed from the box he'd used to smuggle her into his truck. The family was shaken, he'd shared. So was Liza, but it seemed they were getting very skilled at pretending that everything was all right.

Liza looked up from shaking the bottle of topcoat for Abigail's nails when she noticed that the room had grown quiet. And that Rafe was looking uncomfortable. "You okay, Rafe?"

Rafe made an awkward face as he scratched the back of his neck. "Liza, can I talk to you for a moment?" He pointed at the front door. "Out in the hall?"

Liza gave him a wary look. "Now?"

"Yeah."

Mercy's brows crunched together. "Rafe? What have you done?"

"Nothing." He winced. "Well, nothing bad. Too bad anyway. Nothing I can't fix."

Liza stood, dread settling on her shoulders. This would be about Tom, then. "Let's get it over with." She followed Rafe out and waited until he'd settled himself against the foyer wall, leaning on his cane. "Go ahead."

"I need some help with some heavy lifting for Mercy's party on Sunday. You know about the party, right?"

"Yes," Liza said, relieved. This wasn't about Tom, then. "What do you need lifted?"

Rafe opened his mouth, then closed it. Then sighed. "I don't need you to lift anything. I called Tom. He's coming over to help me load some tables into Amos's truck."

Liza closed her eyes. "Of course he is."

"Your car's not outside, so Tom won't know you're here. I didn't want you blindsided."

"Thank you. I can duck upstairs while he's here." But then Rafe winced again. "What?"

"I might have invited him to eat pizza with us."

Liza's temper popped. "Dammit, Rafe."

"I'm sorry! It sounded like a good idea at the time. He doesn't know you're here. I promise."

"When will he get here?" A knock at the front door was her answer. "Fucking hell, Rafe."

Rafe sighed. "I am sorry. I shouldn't have done it. But I do need help with the tables. I didn't make that up. You can go upstairs if you need to and I'll take him out for pizza."

A dog barked and Liza's resolve crumbled. "He brought Pebbles. Just . . . open the door."

Rafe did and Tom stepped in, his expression going slack in surprise. So at least Rafe hadn't lied about not telling him that she was here. Pebbles took advantage of Tom's distraction to tug her leash from Tom's hand and lunge at Liza.

"Whoa," Liza soothed, gently shoving Pebbles's massive paws from her chest. She crouched when the dog dropped to all fours, wrapping her arms around Pebbles's neck and burying her face in the dog's fur. "Missed you," she whispered, laughing when Pebbles licked her face.

"I'll . . ." Rafe hesitated. "Those tables are in the garage, Tom."

But Tom wasn't listening, his gaze frozen on Liza's face. "Can I talk to you?"

"Me?" Rafe asked.

Liza sighed. "No, he's not talking to you. He's talking to me. Like you didn't know."

Rafe looked uncomfortable. "You should go back with the girls, Liza. Tom, let's get busy."

Tom took a step forward, his gaze still locked with Liza's. "Please."

Liza opened the garage door. "Come on. Let's get this over with."

Tom crossed the space in two long strides. He closed the door in Rafe's face before descending the single step into the garage, where Liza had retreated to the far wall, leaning against the hood of Sasha's hot pink car.

"I didn't see your car outside," Tom said.

"I got a ride."

"Oh." Tom's throat worked as he swallowed. He approached warily, his eyes on hers.

She took a few steps back, stopping when she hit the wall. "Is there an issue with Sunny—" She cut herself off, not knowing who could overhear. "With my job application? I already told Raeburn about my interview. Have you heard anything?"

"No, this isn't about that place. Liza, are you afraid of me?"

Liza frowned. "No. Why would you ask me that?"

"Because you're standing as far away from me as you can. I can't . . . I couldn't handle it if you were afraid of me."

Liza hated seeing the apprehension on his handsome face. "I'm not afraid of you, Tom. It's just best if I keep my distance."

"Why?" he asked, the single syllable sounding tortured.

"Because I . . ." She stared at her feet, then looked up to see he'd come closer. Close enough to touch her now. Close enough for her to catch the scent of his aftershave. "Because it hurts, okay? Being close to you, smelling you, feeling how warm you are? It hurts, because I want more. I know that makes me stupid, but—"

He pressed his fingers to her lips. "Stop it. You are never stupid." He dropped his arm to his side and she missed his touch immediately. "I'm stupid, but not you."

"Why did you think I could be afraid of you?"

"Because I yelled." His blue eyes were filled with turmoil. "I lost my temper and I yelled."

"You've done that before. You'll—" She stopped herself before she could say that he'd do it again. Because she wouldn't be giving him that opportunity. Because she'd walked away.

"I'm sorry," he whispered. "I should never yell at you. My father yelled. I don't mean to."

"Oh." Liza's eyes stung. She knew all about Tom's father. Knew how the man had beaten Tom's mother until she'd nearly died. Knew that he'd tortured Tom as a child, burning his skin with cigarettes because Tom had tried to protect his mother when his father had been kicking her.

She knew how conflicted Tom was because he'd been happy when his father was killed in prison. She knew it made him worry that there was a monster inside him, too.

She knew all of this because he'd told her. He'd trusted her with his deepest secrets.

I should have thought of this. "Oh, Tom. You are not your father. You could never be like him. Erase that from your mind, because it never entered mine. I am afraid, but never of you."

"Then of who?" he asked, his whisper rough and hoarse.

"I'm afraid of myself. Of who I am when I'm near you." She squared her shoulders. "I'm afraid because you could convince me to come back, to live on the other side of your duplex, where we'd just be friends forever. And that would hurt too much. I'd rather you yelled at me."

He flinched. "Are we ever going to be friends again?"

God. He was breaking her heart. Because this wasn't an act. This wasn't manipulation. This was Liza, taking something away from him that he'd treasured.

He had treasured their friendship. Of that, she'd never had a single doubt.

"Yes, but not right now. I don't know how to be your friend right now," she confessed. "But I'm sure I'll figure it out."

He took another step forward, then another, until the tips of their shoes were millimeters apart. He searched her face before cupping her cheek in his palm.

Warm and strong. Just like he'd always been.

"How long?" he asked.

Knowing she was cracking, she pressed her cheek into his hand. "How long will it take me to figure it out?"

"No. How long have you felt this way?"

She wanted to scream *No!* She wanted to tell him that he couldn't have that piece of her. But then his thumb swept across her cheek. It was a tender touch. The touch of a lover.

But he wasn't and he never would be.

Still, the words came tumbling out. "Since I was seventeen years old."

He gasped. "You were too young. I was too old."

"You were twenty, Tom. Not too old. Not that it matters. I'm not seventeen anymore and you're not twenty, but you still don't have the same feelings that I do. That's why I moved out. You'll never feel the way I do and I can't live my life wishing that you did. Eventually you'll meet someone new and you'll bring her home and . . ." A sob choked her, but Liza forced it back down. "You'll have a good life," she finished in a whisper. "Which I really want for you."

She hadn't moved her face and he hadn't moved his hand.

He was staring down at her, his emotions too turbulent for her to read. But then, one emotion rose above the others and the sight stopped her heart. Longing.

She leaned closer and for a brief, shining moment, hope surged. Again.

And then he took a step back. Again. "All right," he said quietly. "I won't bother you anymore. Just let me know when you've figured out how we can be friends, okay?"

He left the garage, and a few seconds later, she heard Pebbles's yip and whine, Tom's deep rumble of chastisement, and then, *finally*, she heard Rafe's front door open and close.

She let out the breath she'd been holding and sagged against Sasha's car. For a few minutes she stood there, breathing. Collecting the pieces of her heart that had shattered. One by one, she rebuilt herself until she could stand firmly on her own two feet.

She had practice doing this. She'd done it before. When her mother had died. When her sister was killed. When she'd held Fritz's body, his life already having seeped away.

She'd rebuilt her life before. She'd do it again. And because she had a little girl waiting for her in Mercy's apartment, she forced her feet to move.

She opened the door to find Rafe waiting in the foyer, looking devastated.

He started to speak. "I'm—"

She held up her hand, stopping him with a smile. "It's all right, Rafe. Tom and I are friends." It was a lie, but Rafe seemed to believe it. "It's not the drama you think it is. He yelled at me the other night because he was upset that I hadn't told him about Fritz until now. He needed to be sure that he hadn't hurt my feelings."

"And did he?"

"Nope," she said with forced cheer. "I'm good."

"He'll come back tomorrow to help me with the tables. You can hide anywhere you like."

"If I'm still here," she said lightly. "I have to go home sometime. Although I do recall you promising pancakes for breakfast when I first got here, so I'll stay for those."

Rafe's smile was one of relief. "Okay. But maybe tell that to Mercy? Otherwise I'll be sleeping with Abigail's puppy in the doghouse tonight."

"It'll be quieter there," she told him. "Abigail wants to stay up all night telling stories. I give her till midnight before she conks out."

She opened the door to rejoin the party, only to stop short at the sight of Mercy holding one of the cartons of rocky road and a spoon.

Liza appreciated the gesture more than she could say, and she really, really wanted that ice cream, but she shook her head with a smile. "I'm good. Let's save the dessert until after the pizza. Abigail, we need to finish polishing your fingernails."

"Mercy did it for me."

Well, shit. Liza amped up her smile. "What about your toenails? You can't leave them naked. That would be too scandalous."

"Can I have stickers on them?"

"You sure can." Liza sat on the floor and patted her lap. "Come sit with me and we can choose your design." And if she squeezed Abigail a little harder than necessary, the little girl didn't complain.

TWENTY-ONE

Liza found everyone eating pancakes in Rafe's small studio apartment the next morning. They'd scattered among the three floors when it had been time for bed the night before. Liza had been worried that Abigail would want to camp on the floor with sleeping bags, but the girl had informed them that she'd slept on the floor "back there" and liked a soft bed better.

Liza had been the odd woman out, all the other adults—except for Amos—having partners. So she'd shared Abigail's bed with the little girl, telling herself to stop feeling sorry for herself.

Amos had prepared her for Abigail's nightmares. Liza was ready to hold Abigail and tell her that it would be all right. What she hadn't expected was that she'd wake up gasping herself. She'd dreamed about Fritz again, except that at the last minute, Fritz's face had become Tom's.

Equally unexpected was that Abigail had comforted her. The child had wrapped her arms around Liza's neck in a fierce hug, telling her sleepily that it was just a dream and that everything would be all right.

The aroma of bacon hit her nose as soon as she walked into Rafe's apartment. Gideon offered his chair, but Liza waved him away, sitting on the floor instead.

"I have eaten in far worse conditions," she assured him. She felt her phone buzz and tensed, instantly thinking it was Tom.

But it wasn't and she had to scold herself for being disappointed.

"Who is it?" Abigail asked, peeking at her screen.

"It's a text from the eye doctor," Liza said with a smile. "Our glasses are ready."

"No," Gideon and Rafe said together.

"Mercy isn't going anywhere near that place again," Rafe added.

Amos had grown pale. "Neither is Abigail. Neither will you."

Liza sighed. "I didn't say I was going to pick them up. Can one of the agents go?"

"I'll go," Sasha said. "Erin and I need to pick up some groceries and we aren't on anyone's hit list. But won't the glasses need to be fitted?"

"They took our measurements when we picked out the frames," Mercy said. "And we called them with our credit card information that afternoon, when everything calmed down. I really want to get glasses on Abigail. She's been getting headaches. Besides," she added fondly, "we're going to do a movie marathon later and it will be more fun for Abigail if she can see the TV screen."

"We'll leave after breakfast," Sasha promised while Rafe served the pancakes. "And, once you can see better, we'll catch a movie on a big screen, like in a real movie theater."

"When it's safe," Abigail said matter-of-factly, and Amos looked stricken.

So did the other adults in the room. *No child should ever treat danger like it's normal*, Liza thought, more determined than ever to help put DJ Belmont away forever.

"Yes," Amos managed. "The minute that it's safe."

"What was the last movie you saw in the theater?" Daisy asked Amos, to change the subject.

"*Batman*," he answered after a moment's thought.

"Which one?" Daisy countered.

Amos frowned. "What do you mean, which one?"

"Oh wow," Daisy breathed when she realized he was serious. "We need to Netflix you up."

They spent the rest of breakfast telling Amos about all the *Batman* movies he'd missed during his thirty years in Eden while Abigail listened, eyes wide.

"I think the *Batman* movies are too scary for me," Liza said, picking up on the child's apprehension. "Maybe we'll look for a new Disney flick."

"I like Disney," Abigail whispered, relieved.

"So do I," Liza whispered back.

Amos mouthed a *Thank you* and Liza gave him a wink.

Breakfast was finished and they were drawing lots for who would do the dishes when Liza's phone rang. Her pulse picked up because she knew this number. She'd hoped for a return call and dreaded it all at once.

"Sorry, I have to take this," she said, leaving Rafe's tiny studio apartment to sit on the steps in the foyer. "This is Liza," she answered once she was alone.

"Miss Barkley, this is Portia Sinclair from Sunnyside Oaks. I hope I haven't called too early on a Saturday."

"Oh no, ma'am. What can I do for you?" she asked, trying to sound calm and collected.

"We've completed our interviews and would like to offer you the nursing assistant's position."

Liza didn't have to fake her enthusiasm. "Thank you! That's wonderful! When do I start?"

Miss Sinclair chuckled again. "Don't you want to hear the salary?"

"Oh." Liza hoped she hadn't blown the opportunity. "Yes, please." Sinclair said a number and Liza's eyes widened. "That's . . . more than I was anticipating." It was double what she'd made at the veterans' home.

"We get that a lot," Sinclair said smugly. "Can you start on Tuesday? Your shift starts at seven thirty a.m., but we'd like you to arrive an hour early for orientation with your supervisor."

"I'll be there. Who should I ask for?"

"Nurse Innes. She's one of our charge nurses. She'll be training you."

Innes. The one person Liza had planned to avoid. "Should I bring my own scrubs?"

"No, dear. We have uniforms for you here. Wear comfortable shoes, of course."

"Of course. I'll see you on Tuesday."

Liza ended the call, her hands now trembling. She'd done it. She was in.

With any luck, she'd meet Pastor and be able to talk to him. With any luck, he'd be in pain, on meds with his guard down, and he'd tell her where Eden was. Or at a minimum she could plant a few bugs so that the FBI could listen to anything Pastor and DJ discussed when the younger man came to visit. And, with any luck, both Pastor and DJ Belmont would go to prison for a very long time and would never be able to hurt Mercy or the others again.

Clenching her teeth, she steadied her hands enough to type out a text to Special Agent Raeburn. *I was offered the job. Accepted. Starting Tuesday. Please advise.*

She looked up from her phone when the door to Rafe's apartment opened. Mercy stood in the doorway, looking anxious. "Is everything all right?"

Liza mustered up a smile. "Everything's good. I just got a new job."

Mercy frowned. "Then why do you look like you lost your best friend?"

Because I did.

Seeing Liza's expression, Mercy winced. "That wasn't what I meant to say."

"It's fine. Did I get the short straw on the breakfast dishes?"

"No. Sasha did. She's appealing the decision, saying that the straws were rigged, but Erin's already got most of the dishes in the dishwasher. Abigail is asking if you're coming back. We're getting ready to watch *The Little Mermaid*."

"Better than *Batman* for a seven-year-old," Liza agreed. She stood up. "I can watch one movie, and then I need to go home. I've got laundry to do."

"Would you consider staying here for one more night? We're worried about DJ. Especially after what he did yesterday." The evenness Mercy had displayed since she'd heard the news began to fracture as Liza watched. "If Gideon hadn't been wearing that vest . . ."

Liza shuddered. "Yeah. I get that. I'll be fine, though. He doesn't want me."

"You don't know that. You were there on Wednesday, too. Will you humor me?"

"Sure." She slid her arm around Mercy's shoulders and gave her a hug. "It'll be all right."

Mercy's smile was sad. "You don't know that," she repeated.

She was tempted to tell Mercy the truth—that Pastor was in a rehab facility and she'd just gotten a job there so that she could help Tom put him away forever. But there was no way she was saying any of that, so she went with what was in her heart.

"But I *do* know it'll be all right, because a seven-year-old told me so when I had a nightmare last night. Have faith, Mercy. I have a feeling things are going to get better very soon."

GRANITE BAY, CALIFORNIA
SATURDAY, MAY 27, 11:00 A.M.

The man was a motherfucking ghost. DJ had spent most of the morning trying to locate Roland Kowalski, which, of course, was not his real name.

It would be easier to search if he could think. Which would be easier if he didn't have the fucking hangover from hell.

This was why he didn't drink often. He'd woken to find he'd thrown up on Smythe's floor, the empty whiskey bottle next to him in bed. Not a drop remained.

He didn't remember finishing the bottle, which was alarming. He'd quickly checked all of his devices to be sure he hadn't e-mailed or texted or posted anything damning, nearly wilting with relief when he saw that he had not.

He was never going to drink again. Which wasn't going to be a problem if he didn't figure out a way out of this mess. Right now, he was one guy with a bum arm, a rifle, and a handgun. And a laptop, which wasn't worth jack shit, because Kowalski didn't show up in any police reports, and according to the Internet, he owned no land or vehicles. He did, of course. He owned several vehicles, but DJ had never seen a legit license plate on any of them.

Not a surprise. Kowalski had been the one to teach him to use a 3D printer to make fake license plates. None of the addresses DJ had visited with Kowalski were registered to any real people. Like DJ's house in Yuba City was owned by "John Derby."

He hit dead end after dead end. None of Kowalski's associates were traceable, because none of them used real names, either.

The cell phone charging on the nightstand pinged with an incoming text. DJ grabbed it to silence it but stopped when he saw the screen.

This was Nelson Smythe's cell phone and the man had missed at least five calls and twenty text messages from his wife while DJ slept. This latest one read: *Answer me or I'm calling 911. Did you have a stroke? Are you there? ANSWER ME!!!!*

"Shit," DJ muttered. He'd been good about keeping up with the woman's texts, providing one- or two-word replies, such as *Yes*, *No*, *Maybe*, *I'll check*, and *Love you*. Those were pretty typical of Smythe's replies over the past six months, so DJ felt pretty confident that the woman hadn't been suspicious.

Except then he'd drunk an entire bottle of whiskey and missed a whole assload of texts.

Groaning, he descended the stairs to the garage, where he grabbed a hair dryer and lifted the chest freezer's lid. Ice crystals had formed on Smythe's face, just like they had every day after he melted them off the day before.

Turning the hair dryer on, he blew warm air over Smythe's frozen face until it was ice-free, then held the phone over his face until the screen unlocked. He hadn't been that concerned about the texts until now, but if she called 911, it would suck. He needed a little time to pack his printers and the few belongings he'd taken from the Yuba City house.

I'm fine, he texted back. *Not dead. 24-hr bug. Feeling better. Love you.*

Glad u r not dead! The message was punctuated by heart emojis. *Will call tonight. Miss u.*

"Fuck," he muttered. If she called and he didn't answer, she might call 911. That was what he needed to avoid. *Miss u*, he replied.

He'd get the truck loaded up with his stuff, just in case. But he'd use some of the time to print more license plates. What he hoped for was to get Kowalski to back off and stop trying to kill him, but he didn't think that was likely. So now he was focused on finding Kowalski's hangouts. What he really wanted was Kowalski's weapons stash, but if he stumbled on a vehicle along the way, he'd take it, because the Lexus was too dangerous to drive now. The BOLO on him listed the car's make, model, and color along with the note that it would have fake plates.

Assholes. He was putting the blow dryer away when another text arrived on Smythe's phone. It was a photo of some really cute kids all lined up, mouths open like birds. They were singing.

The next text read: *Liam was the very best!*

Liam, DJ had deduced, was the couple's grandson, the event a concert at the kid's school.

Send video, DJ typed back, because that was what Smythe usually said. DJ had wondered why the man hadn't gone with his wife, but had realized through reading their texts that Smythe and his son-in-law did not get along.

He was lowering the freezer lid when a memory tickled his brain. *Concerts. Children.*

"Oh," he breathed.

Kowalski had a kid. A little boy, around six years old. On Wednesday, the kid had done a recital at his school. It was a private school, because DJ remembered Kowalski complaining about the cost of tuition when they'd been negotiating with a customer who'd wanted a break on the price of the kilo of coke they were selling.

This could work. He knew what the kid looked like, kind of, having once seen a photo of the boy while peeking at Kowalski's phone. He'd taken every opportunity to spy on Kowalski because, while he'd trusted him to a point, Kowalski was all about himself. *As are we all.*

He'd wanted to learn, wanted to know the important details, so he'd risked looking over Kowalski's shoulder. Therefore, DJ had a decent recollection of the boy's face.

Schools had Facebook pages and websites. It wouldn't hurt to try.

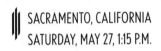

SACRAMENTO, CALIFORNIA
SATURDAY, MAY 27, 1:15 P.M.

King Triton embraced the newly wedded Ariel, drawing a happy sigh from Abigail, who cuddled between Mercy and Liza on the floor of Rafe's apartment. The place was small and its TV tiny, but they'd all congregated there because, even though last night had been a "girls' night," no one wanted to exclude Gideon and Rafe, who couldn't climb the stairs.

"Ariel's gonna be okay now, right?" Abigail asked.

Mercy kissed the top of the child's head. "She is. And she and Prince Eric are going to live happily ever after."

"Even though she's only sixteen and kind of a brat," Gideon commented dryly from the sofa.

Liza thought that Abigail would object to this, but the girl surprised her yet again.

"She really is," Abigail said. "She should have obeyed her papa."

Liza glanced at Amos, smiling at the contented look on his face.

But anything she was about to say fled from her mind when someone started knocking impatiently on the outer door.

A moment later, everyone relaxed. It was Sasha and Erin returning from doing their errands.

Rafe's cane thumped as he walked to his apartment door in irritation. "Why didn't you just use your key?" he demanded. "Instead of knocking loud enough for the neighbors to hear?"

"Hey, don't blame me," Sasha said. "I wasn't the one who made all that racket. I have a key." She leaned around Rafe, a plastic bag with the optometrist's logo dangling from her fingers. "Glasses, anyone?"

Liza pushed to her feet, crossing the room to retrieve the glasses. "Thanks, but who—"

She sighed. *Dammit.* Tom stood on the front stoop, his blue eyes flashing. Liza had no idea what he was angry about now.

"You knocked?" Liza asked him. "Loudly?"

"I didn't realize I was being loud," Tom said, penitent. In fact, someone who didn't know him well wouldn't be able to tell that he was angry at all. "May I speak to you, Liza?"

She smiled to put everyone at ease even though her heart was pounding. "Of course."

She crossed the foyer into the garage, once again not waiting to see if Tom followed.

He did, of course, closing the door behind him and walking right up to her, getting in her space. His body filled out the tight T-shirt he wore and his jeans were dirty, like he'd been working outside. She didn't care that he was filthy and sweaty. Hungry for the sight of him, she drank him in.

Until he spoke. "You didn't think to call me?"

"About?"

His expression was forbidding. "Sunnyside Oaks? Were you going to tell me that you got the job? Were you going to tell Raeburn?"

"I already did. I texted him as soon as I got off the phone with Sunnyside Oaks."

A muscle in his cheek twitched as he ground his teeth. "But you didn't text me?"

Okay. "I . . . didn't know I was supposed to."

Hurt flashed in his eyes. "*Supposed* to?"

She hesitated. "I was under the impression that Raeburn and Molina were my contacts."

He shoved a hand through his hair. "They are. Because you went over my head."

She squared her shoulders. "Yes, I did."

"Why?"

She wasn't sure what he expected her to say. "Because you weren't willing to support me."

His fingers tightened in his hair, yanking on it hard. He was hurting himself and she needed him to stop. But she said nothing, waiting for the flood of words that she could sense coming.

But when he finally spoke, it wasn't in a shout, but in a hoarse whisper. "Why are you doing this? Why is this so important?"

She told him the same thing she'd told him Thursday night. The same thing she'd told Molina and Raeburn. "If I can make contact with Pastor, I might be able to get him to tell me where Eden is. Then, once everyone in the compound is safe, you can use Pastor to lure DJ to the rehab center and arrest them both. Then this will be over. I can help Mercy this way. I can keep Abigail safe."

He dropped his hands to his sides, looking defeated. "Because you couldn't save your sister?" he asked quietly.

Her mouth fell open in stunned surprise. "What? No."

"*Yes,*" he said, shocking her further when he gripped her upper arms, his hold firm yet gentle. "You couldn't save Lindsay. You couldn't save your mother. You couldn't save Fritz. So you're saving Mercy and Abigail. Don't *tell* me that I'm wrong."

She started to tell him exactly that, but the words wouldn't come. *Was he wrong? Was she trying to play savior because she'd failed so many others?*

"Do you know when I saw Mercy for the first time?" she asked instead.

He frowned. "That day we saw Burton's mother at the nursing home."

"That was the first time I *met* her. I saw her for the first time a few days before that, on the news. She'd nearly been abducted by Burton at the airport when she returned to Sacramento."

He nodded, not sure where she was going. "She was in shock."

"She was terrified." Liza swallowed hard. "I saw the look in her eyes, the knowledge that someone she feared had just tried to hurt her again, and I thought of Lindsay. Of how terrified she must have been." Her voice broke. "Of how she died alone, because nobody was there to help her. So, yes. I'm doing this because I couldn't save my sister. But that doesn't change the fact that I'm doing what I believe is right."

He tilted his head to stare at the ceiling, his fingers kneading her arms, his touch still gentle. Finally, his gaze met hers again. "I don't want you to get hurt."

"I don't want you to get hurt, either."

He frowned. "I won't be."

"You don't know that. DJ tried to kill Gideon yesterday. When he finds out you're on the case, he might go after you. Don't *tell* me that I'm wrong." She echoed his words deliberately and his small flinch told her that she'd hit her mark. "Tell me this, and be honest. If you had the skills, would you have volunteered for the position?"

"Yes," he said without hesitation. "But I can't. Too many people know my face."

It's such a nice face. "But you would if you could."

"Yes."

"Then tell me this. What training have you had that makes you so sure you wouldn't be hurt if you were able to go undercover?"

"I went to the Academy. We were trained in—" He stopped abruptly, his eyes narrowing as he realized she'd set him up.

She smiled up at him sadly. "I went to boot camp. I've been trained as well. In addition to that, I've been in active war zones. That's more experience than you have."

He stared at her helplessly. "I want to shake some sense into your thick skull."

"But you won't," she murmured.

He frowned. "What?"

"You won't shake me. You won't hurt me. Ever."

His hands dropped immediately to his sides. "But I did hurt you."

She missed his touch, just as immediately. "Not physically. And not on purpose. Because you are not your father, Tom Hunter, and you never will be."

He opened his mouth, then closed it again. It appeared he had no argument left. "Thank you."

"You're welcome, but I only speak the truth." She paused a beat, then asked, "How did you know I'd gotten the job? If you thought I hadn't told Raeburn, he didn't tell you."

"I have access to Sunnyside's employee database. It's how I knew there was an opening."

"And how you identified Penny Gaynor as approachable."

He nodded once. "I was filling in that hole that Pebbles dug under the fence when I got an alert on my phone that the database had been updated."

That explained his dirty clothes. "And I've been added."

"Yes. They've done extensive background checks on you. They're still searching."

She lifted a brow. "Did they find anything that connects to you?"

"No. I did a deep check of my own, just to be sure that I knew about anything that was out there that could compromise you. You have no social media presence and no property registered to you, so that helps a lot. You're in the white pages, but there is no phone number or other mineable information. They have a copy of your military record. It's a damn good record, Liza."

"Thank you," she whispered. "That means a lot."

"I'm proud of you. I just wanted you to know." He cleared his throat. "When do you start?"

"Tuesday morning." She hesitated, then asked, "Were you following me yesterday?"

He paled. "No. Did someone follow you?"

"Yes. I was driving Karl's SUV. He keeps one at the apartment where I'm staying. I wasn't driving my Mazda, so they can't trace me to you."

"You think that's what I care about? Them tracing you to me? Really?"

She shifted uncomfortably. "No. But I thought you should know."

His chuckle was bitter. "Oh, so *now* you're telling me things I should know? Thank you so much." He shook his head and squared his shoulders. "Text me your new address. I'm not planning to drop by. I promise. I'm going call my boss to get you protection there in addition to the protection we're providing outside the Sunnyside gate."

She wanted to tell him that it wasn't necessary, but that would be wrong. It was necessary, if only to protect those she cared about. "All right."

He hesitated a moment more. "Did I . . . did I push you into doing this?"

"No, Tom. You did not break my heart so thoroughly that I did the first cockamamie, self-harming thing that I thought of. I accepted this job because I thought I could help. Because I needed to help my friends. Not because you don't love me."

He flinched at her blunt words but then nodded. And then he was gone.

When Liza left the garage, Mercy was leaning against Rafe's closed door, waiting for her. "You okay?" she asked quietly.

Liza managed to nod. "He was annoyed because Pebbles dug a hole under the fence and I forgot to tell him about it. He was worried that she'd gotten out."

Mercy wasn't buying it but had the grace to pretend that she was.

Saying nothing, she held open her arms, and Liza took the hug. Took the comfort.

"It'll be okay," Mercy murmured into her hair. "Somebody told me so this morning, so I'm having faith that it's true. You should, too."

GRANITE BAY, CALIFORNIA
SATURDAY, MAY 27, 8:00 P.M.

Something was going on at the Sokolovs' house. DJ was certain of it. He'd taken a break from his search for Kowalski when he'd noticed the SUVs driving back and forth. There were three different vehicles, none of which he'd been able to trace back to their owners. Each SUV had made at least two round trips, all spaced a few hours apart. The windows were so heavily tinted that DJ hadn't been able to get a look at the driver or the passengers.

Seemed like Mercy's team had upped their game. They were being a lot more careful. They had to know he was watching. Not from *where* he was watching, otherwise he'd have been surrounded by Feds already. But they knew he was watching.

Mercy could have been in one of the SUVs. She could be nearby, in the Sokolovs' house, even now. So could Gideon. And Amos.

A well-placed explosive could take care of the entire house, but he wasn't sure he could get close enough to plant a device, even if he could get his hands on one. Kowalski could, if he weren't actively trying to kill him.

But DJ was getting closer to finding Kowalski's family. Once he did, he'd put that on his list of conditions. He wanted Kowalski to back off from trying to kill him, first and foremost. But some weapons would also be good.

He frowned when one of the black SUVs passed by again, on its way to the Sokolovs' house. Suddenly restless, he grabbed the keys to his truck, his rifle and his handgun, a new magnetic sign, and a new set of license plates. Tonight he'd be a septic service technician.

He'd left his truck parked up against Smythe's privacy fence with signs for a landscaping company prominently displayed, but he wasn't really worried about his truck being reported. In the three days that he'd been there, none of Smythe's neighbors had come outside. The closest house had the lights come on at the same time every night, clearly on a timer.

It was hotter than hell and it was Memorial Day weekend. Maybe the rich folks went to the mountains where it was cooler. It was what DJ would do when he became rich.

Eyes on the prize, he thought as he lined up the edges of the new magnetic signs on each of the truck's doors. The license plates were next, and within minutes he was pulling onto the deserted street. He'd drive to the entrance to the neighborhood and wait there.

If the SUVs stuck to their pattern, the one that had been on its way to the Sokolovs' house would soon be heading out again. Sure enough, within five minutes, the SUV passed by on its way out of the neighborhood.

DJ waited until the SUV had turned toward the interstate before following, keeping a safe distance. From the height of the truck's cab, he could see over ninety-five percent of the vehicles on the road. He put five cars between himself and the SUV, then settled into a steady pace in the right lane. DJ made no move to get closer. It would only draw attention to him.

He followed for miles, hoping the SUV wasn't going to take the exits into the city. It would be harder to follow them there. His wish was granted when the black vehicle exited onto I-5, toward the airport. DJ continued to follow, now directly behind the SUV, assuming the airport would be their final destination when the vehicle exited onto Airport Boulevard.

And then everything went to hell.

"Fuck," he growled, his pulse shooting to the moon when a police cruiser came up on his left, lights flashing. He'd been made.

"Pull over," came the command from the cruiser's speaker.

"I don't think so," he muttered, glad that he had the truck. He swerved, forcing the cruiser off the road into the median. He then rammed into the back of the SUV in front of him, causing it to veer off the shoulder. He stomped the gas pedal to the floor, the truck accelerating so fast that it fishtailed, but he got it under control and thundered down the highway.

He made the most of his lead, knowing the cops wouldn't give up. After a minute of the fastest driving he'd ever done, he slammed on the brakes and turned onto one of the roads that led to the river. There was no place to hide the truck, so he'd use it to buy more time. He parked the truck sideways so that it blocked the road, then grabbed his rifle out of its case and ran into the trees that lined the river.

Slipping the rifle's strap over his shoulder, he let it rest on his back as he slowed his pace, trying to find a tree that he could easily climb. His arm was so much better since he'd been resting in Smythe's soft bed, but it still didn't have a lot of strength.

He found a tree with low-hanging limbs that appeared strong enough to support his weight and, one-armed, hefted himself to the first limb. He didn't need to climb high, just enough to be out of the cops' sight when they came looking for him.

It didn't take long. Within minutes, a pair of SacPD uniforms appeared, searching among the trees, shining their flashlights along the ground.

Surprise, he thought. Bracing his rifle on a tree limb, he got a line on the first cop's head, then the second's. Both were wearing vests over their uniforms, but neither wore a helmet. He pulled the trigger on the first, then the second.

They both dropped like bricks. Not wasting a minute, DJ swung down from the tree and raced to the first cop. He was bigger than DJ, but he'd do.

Removing the cop's vest, DJ tugged his shirt off, buttons going everywhere. DJ slipped it over his own shirt, setting his rifle on the ground only long enough to pull the shirt into place and the vest over it. The pants he left on the body. He didn't need them for what he had in mind.

The cop's gun belt was next. It hung low on DJ's leaner hips, but again, it would do for what he had in mind. The cop had dropped his handgun when he'd been hit. DJ scooped it up, grabbed his own rifle, and ran for the truck.

Sure enough, the cop car was parked behind it, lights still flashing. Engine still running.

Not stopping to think or second-guess himself, DJ got in the police cruiser and started toward the interstate. He saw his mark—a late-model Honda Civic—and fell into place behind the car.

The car pulled over to the shoulder like a good citizen. DJ approached the driver's window, his own silenced gun drawn. He didn't want to draw attention with more gunfire.

"Hands on the steering wheel!" he barked. But the young woman behind the wheel wasn't obeying. She was holding her damn phone. *Recording* him.

For fuck's sake.

"I haven't done anything wrong," she started. "I'm recording you for my own protection and I will be talking to your supervi—"

Reaching into the car, DJ grabbed her phone, dropped it to the asphalt, and shot it. The screen splintered. He kicked it under the tire.

"*Ohmygod!*" the woman screeched. "You can't—"

DJ opened her door, pulled her out, and dragged her to the cruiser. He tossed her in the back seat and shot her in the head, then shot her a second time. *Just to be sure.* He took off the cop's shirt and threw it over her face. The cop's vest and gun belt he kept.

Then he got into her car and drove away. Drawing a breath, he exhaled, his pulse slowly returning to normal. "Not exactly what I'd planned," he said aloud, "but it turned out okay."

He'd acquired a new vehicle and he knew that the SUVs had been making runs to the airport. The Sokolovs were entertaining company—quite a lot of company, based on the number of times the SUVs had passed by his camera's checkpoint.

One less SUV now, he thought, a laugh bubbling from his throat as he passed the SUV he'd been following, still on the shoulder on the other side of the road. A man stood at the back bumper, talking on his cell phone while examining the extensive damage done by DJ's truck.

DJ had been just quick enough. No fewer than ten cruisers came tearing up the opposite side of the road, sirens blaring, headed for the crime scene.

As soon as he was clear of the hubbub, he'd find a place to pull over and disengage the Honda's GPS and change the license plate. Then he'd return to his comfy bed and keep searching for Kowalski's kid.

He needed access to Kowalski's weapon reserves now more than ever. Something was going on at the Sokolovs' house and he needed to take advantage of whatever that was.

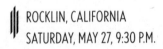

ROCKLIN, CALIFORNIA
SATURDAY, MAY 27, 9:30 P.M.

Tom scowled at the bulletin board on the wall of his home office. The board was half filled with photos, maps, and documents he'd gathered in the month he'd been searching for Eden. He had aerial maps of the sites listed in the notebook they'd found in Ephraim Burton's safe-deposit box. He had photos of Kowalski and his family, photos of DJ and Waylon that he'd taken at Joni Belmont's house, and photos of DJ Belmont's two victims.

The two who they knew of, anyway—Minnie Ellis and Penny Gaynor. Belmont had no compunction about murdering in cold blood. It was more than likely that he'd killed others and their bodies hadn't been found yet. Or ever would be.

But the photos, maps, and documents didn't represent progress and

Tom was frustrated. He had nothing new after hours spent searching for DJ Belmont. Searching for Kowalski.

Irritated and tired, he took a break from searching for the two men to try searching for Pastor's wife, who supposedly lived in Modesto with her architect husband.

He knew that the woman wouldn't likely be able to tell them where to find Eden. She'd run from the cult twenty-five years before. But Tom was curious. He wanted to know how Eden had begun and how they'd managed to hold on to power for so long. He was curious about what kind of woman would marry Waylon Belmont only to divorce him for Pastor.

Was she a criminal, too? Or had she been manipulated like everyone else?

Unfortunately, he hadn't found any architects in Modesto with a wife named Margo.

He'd had only one true success in all the hours he'd spent searching. He tacked the photo of eighteen-year-old William Holly—a.k.a. Boaz Travis—next to a photo he'd found in the archives of an L.A. newspaper. The photo featured Pastor, his wife, and their twins, five years old at the time, and had been taken for a Christmas newsletter the year before he'd been accused of embezzling tens of thousands of dollars from his church.

The quality of the photo wasn't good. The original had been photocopied for the newsletter before being included in the newspaper article, and the result was dark and grainy. It had been one of the few articles that Tom had been able to find on the investigation into Pastor's embezzlement and identity fraud.

It told the story of Craig Hickman, who'd been a college-aged member of Pastor's L.A. church. He'd become suspicious of Pastor after beginning his own degree in psychology, because Pastor had claimed to have a degree that didn't exist. Digging deeper, Craig had discovered that church money was missing. That had eventually led to charges being leveled against Pastor.

And then Craig was beaten badly by a group of masked brutes brandishing baseball bats shortly after Pastor disappeared. A few weeks later, Craig's family home had been burned to the ground. The young man had disappeared soon after.

Some of this information Tom had found online. Some had been in a month-old report prepared by Jeff Bunker, the teenage journalism major who'd brought Cameron Cook to the field office on Wednesday morning. Jeff had started searching for Craig Hickman a month ago.

"I wonder what he's found," Tom murmured, and sent Jeff a text.

Any progress on locating Craig Hickman?

The reply was instantaneous. *Got sidetracked with finals, but they're done now. Will get back on it. The woman who mentored Hickman is a kickass reporter with the L.A. Times. Now mentoring me on research.* The text was followed by a gif of Kermit the Frog flailing excitedly.

Tom had to smile. He often forgot that Jeff was only sixteen. *LMK when you find something.*

A thumbs-up emoji from Jeff popped up seconds before Tom's phone screen was filled with an incoming call.

Raeburn. "This is Hunter."

"We have a situation. Texting you an address. Meet me there ASAP."

A text popped up with an address near the airport. "I'm on my way. Can you tell me what it's about?" Because his mind was spinning images of Mercy dead, of Gideon dead. Of Liza dead.

"SacPD got a call from one of its off-duty cops who was working a private security gig."

Tom's gut twisted. "Bowie Security?"

"Yes. I understand you hired them?"

"I did, yes. For Mercy Callahan's birthday party and out of my own pocket. No connection to the Bureau. What happened?"

Raeburn sighed. "You need to stop paying for things out of your own pocket, Tom."

Tom blinked, unaccustomed to hearing Raeburn address him by his first name. "That's fine, sir. Can you tell me what happened first?"

"A truck matching the description of the one on the office building security footage was following Bowie's SUV. The driver was a Bowie employee. Shotgun was the off-duty cop. When the SUV turned for the airport, the truck followed. SacPD was called. A cruiser tried to stop the truck, but it pushed it off the road and sped away. The two cops pursued. They were instructed to wait for backup, but did not. They were shot in the head. One of the bodies was missing his shirt, vest, and gun belt. The truck is still on the scene, along with the two bodies."

"Belmont," Tom said grimly. "And the cruiser? Did he steal it?"

"He did, but didn't take it far. It was found on the shoulder of Airport Boulevard with the body of a young woman in the back seat."

"Fucking hell," Tom whispered.

"You have all the information. I'll expect you to be at the scene as soon as you can."

Tom had bounded down the stairs and was already in his own vehicle. "Sir? Mercy's birthday party tomorrow is at the Sokolovs' house. If Belmont followed Bowie Security's SUV, he was in the Sokolovs' neighborhood."

"I'll tell them to cancel the party."

"I think it's too late for that. All of the guests were to have arrived by now. They're all in the Sokolovs' house. Rafe Sokolov hired the off-duty cops as security. Ten of them. I hired six more of Bowie's employees. I think we should have Bureau presence on the Sokolovs' perimeter. If Belmont tries again, we can find him."

"I'll arrange it," Raeburn promised.

Tom started his engine. "Do we have an ID on the victim left in the cruiser?"

"Not yet. Belmont destroyed her phone and she had no other ID. Midtwenties, Caucasian, and dead. That's all we know."

"Thank you, sir. I'll be there in thirty or less."

TWENTY-TWO

'm glad that you came today," Irina said, sitting on the sofa beside Liza. The Sokolov house was brimming with people, Mercy's party in full swing. "I feared you would not."

"I almost didn't," Liza admitted, watching Abigail play with Irina's grandchildren. Liza had retreated to one of the quieter corners. "But I didn't want to hurt Mercy's feelings."

"You have a good heart, *lubimaya*." Irina gestured to the children sitting in a circle on the floor playing a card game. Abigail was listening to the rules with the attention of someone learning the nuclear codes. "I'm so glad that she's having fun."

"She was nervous," Liza murmured. "Wanting to be 'normal.' She had a meltdown this morning. She'd insisted I put her hair in rollers overnight, but a few of them came out and her puppy stole them. One side of her hair was ringlets and the other was like cooked spaghetti."

"So you fixed it?" Irina asked fondly.

"I did. It didn't take long. Just took a curling iron and most of a can of hair spray."

"You spoil her."

Liza shrugged. "She's gone through so much upheaval in the last month. I think it's okay if she gets spoiled a little. Even her meltdown this morning was polite by normal-kid standards. It's awful good to see her with kids her own age. She spends too much time with adults."

"When this is over—" Irina began, then sighed. "I feel like I've been saying that a lot."

"Me too." Liza looked from the children to the living room doorway, her attention caught by a flash of gold—the light reflecting off Tom's hair. He looked as amazing in jeans and a T-shirt as he did in a suit and tie. Her gaze lingered, remembering how hard the muscle was under that shirt. Then she resolutely looked away, only to find Irina watching her.

"I thought as much," Irina murmured.

"Not his fault," Liza murmured back, not trying to hide it anymore. "He loves it here. Don't blame him. He'll pull back into his shell, and he needs this family."

"So do you."

"And I'll keep coming by. Don't worry."

"But I do. Did you get that job?"

"I did. I'm going to be working with a pediatric patient." Liza patted the older woman's knee. "Don't worry. I'll be fine."

"Do not tell me not to worry. It is what I do best."

Liza smiled at that. "I thought party hostessing was what you did best. I bet there are a ton of Mercy's family who would love to talk to you."

"You are a menace, Liza. But you are right. Do not hide here all afternoon," Irina chided, pushing to her feet. "Mingle with Mercy's family. They are good people."

"I know. I will." But there were so many of them and Liza was still raw from yesterday's argument with Tom, so she'd hide in the corner until she could make her excuses and escape.

"Well, hello." The Southern drawl belonged to Farrah Romero, a beautiful Black woman who was a brilliant biophysicist and Mercy's best friend. "Mind if I sit down?"

Liza patted the sofa cushion next to her with a smile. "Please do." She liked Farrah a lot. The woman was one hundred percent loyal to Mercy. "How was your trip?"

Farrah and her fiancé, André, had arrived from New Orleans the night before with a number of the Romero family. A few of her half siblings had also flown in.

"Worth every harrowing moment," Farrah said. "We were so nervous, worrying that Belmont would jump out from behind a luggage cart and shoot us, especially since André also shot him last month. But Rafe had it managed."

"He really did. I didn't understand why he'd hired so many security people, but now I get it." Mercy had said he'd hired six people, but Liza had counted at least a dozen. Some were posted around the house and others accompanied the drivers of the SUVs that had shuttled them back and forth from the Sokolovs' house.

"You knew there'd be security?" Farrah asked. "Rafe asked us to keep it a secret."

"I'd heard rumors" was all Liza would admit to. Mercy had played shocked and amazed very well. "It's hard to keep a secret around here. We had to get creative to keep Mercy off social media this weekend, just in case she saw a post from one of you about your flights."

"I'm glad you did," Farrah said fervently. "She does not need to know about those cops."

Liza's smile faded. "What cops?"

Farrah blinked. "The cops who got killed. Oh God, you didn't know, either?"

Liza felt like she was going to throw up. "No. We all stayed off phones and computers. Rafe was very firm about that. He wasn't even on his phone, just in case Mercy looked over his shoulder. Then Gideon and Daisy came over last night and made us put our phones in a box because we were playing a trivia game." She looked around to be sure no one was listening, then leaned closer to Farrah. "What happened?"

Farrah sighed. "The guy who was scheduled to pick us up was followed from this neighborhood to the airport. He'd just dropped off Mercy's sibs and was coming back for us because Mama, André, and I caught a later flight. A big truck followed him and made the driver and the off-duty cop with him twitchy. They called for backup and a cruiser tried to pull the truck over. It got away. The cops found the truck abandoned on a side road. When they began searching . . ."

"DJ killed them," Liza whispered. "Oh no. Does Rafe know?"

"I don't think so?" Farrah shook her head, uncertain. "André got the details from the people who eventually picked us up. There was . . . well, he killed a woman, too. To get her car."

"Rafe can't have known. He couldn't have gone on with this party had he known."

"I agree. We all made a pact not to mention it to Mercy, but I thought since you knew about the security and you're friends with Agent Hunter . . . I thought you knew."

"Poor Mercy," Liza murmured. "This has to end."

"I know. Mercy's gonna go off the deep end when she finds out. I'll be here till tomorrow if she needs me."

Liza winced. "She's going to be so angry with us for keeping this from her."

"But she gets her birthday with all of us here. I wasn't going to take that from her."

"I won't, either. It's just . . ." She trailed off, having no words to complete her thought.

"I know." Farrah straightened her spine and smiled, but it looked forced. "Gotta go back into the fray and mingle. My mama and Irina are comparing notes."

"Recipes, I hope?"

"I hope so." Farrah mock-shuddered. "If they start comparing notes on us, we're screwed." She started to walk away, then turned back. "Thank you."

"For what?"

"For being there for Mercy. I love her like a sister and it's been tearing me up not to be here for her. She told me that you've been supportive and I appreciate it."

Liza didn't deserve thanks. She didn't want it. "She's supported me, too."

Farrah just smiled, squared her shoulders, and reentered the party chaos.

Liza took out her phone and googled the shooting from the night before. The details were worse than she'd expected. Both of the fallen officers were family men who'd left wives and small children behind. There were photos of the scene and . . .

There, in the photos, was Tom. He and his partner, Ricki Croft, were talking to a uniformed officer. Everyone in the picture looked exhausted.

She found herself texting him a message of support before she remembered. They weren't friends right now, and that was on her. She felt small and petty. This was a big case and he probably needed someone to talk to.

She could do that. Just talk to him. Couldn't she?

Yes. She wasn't seventeen anymore. She was an adult. *Then act like one.* So she texted him.

Saw the story from last night online. You look tired. Call if you need to talk. Still want to be there for you if you want me to. That's what friends are for, right?

She hit send before she could change her mind, then watched Abigail play.

GRANITE BAY, CALIFORNIA
SUNDAY, MAY 28, 3:15 P.M.

Tom had been waiting for Rafe to leave Mercy's side for an hour. He needed to talk to the man, but this wasn't a conversation he wanted documented in any way.

He also didn't want to disclose any details that would be distressing, not yet. He especially didn't want to mention last night's murders. Tom had suggested that Rafe keep Mercy off social media until after her birthday party. He hadn't wanted her to know about the two dead cops and one dead civilian woman.

She deserved one day free of stress.

What he hadn't anticipated was that Rafe would also stay offline. The homicide detective had been in communication with his off-duty cop friends and the Bowie security guys, but Tom had instructed them not to mention the incident from the night before, either. It seemed that no one had said a word, and Rafe and Mercy were having one wonderful day.

Gideon knew, though. He'd seen the police report the night before. Tom was grateful the other agent had called him before calling Rafe or Mercy.

Together, Tom and Gideon had determined how to best protect the Sokolovs. Having called this house his second home since he was a teenager, Gideon had directed Raeburn's agents, placing them strategically around the perimeter. They'd personally knocked on neighborhood doors, advising the locals that security was heightened so that no one would inadvertently cross the perimeter and set off alarms.

Many of the neighbors were gone because of the holiday weekend. Tom was grateful for that. He didn't think any of them were in danger unless they got caught in the cross fire. He'd been personally patrolling the streets, making sure everyone was safe.

He needed to get back outside and was about to give up on talking to Rafe when the man left Mercy to cut her cake, retreating to the corner of the kitchen to watch her with a sappy smile.

Rafe gave Tom a nod as he approached. "What's up? Is Liza okay?"

Tom's jaw tightened. No, she wasn't. Anyone with eyes could see that she wasn't okay. But he just shrugged. "You'd have to ask her."

Rafe winced. "What did you want to talk to me about?"

Relieved that Rafe had changed the subject, Tom leaned a little closer to murmur, "I was wondering if you'd ever considered going into the private sector."

Rafe frowned, his confusion clear. "Like . . . what?"

"Like private investigating."

"Sure. Of course I have. But I've been advised not to make any huge career shifts for a little while longer. Why?"

"Because I have need of a PI."

Rafe turned from Mercy to give Tom his full attention. "Is it Eden?"

Tom laughed bitterly. "What else might it be?"

"Did you find them?"

"Not yet, but we're close. If you're interested in hearing more, we can meet tomorrow. Somewhere quiet."

"And Mercy?"

"Don't mention it to her for now. I don't expect you'll keep it quiet forever, but for now keep it to yourself. Let her enjoy her birthday."

Something in his tone must have given his anxiety away, because Rafe frowned. "Is she in danger?"

Tom took that to mean Rafe was asking if she was in any *new* danger. Which, given the sheer number of security they had around this house, she wasn't. "Not to my knowledge. Tomorrow?"

Rafe's eyes narrowed. "Send me a time and place. I'll be there."

"Thanks." And because Rafe appeared ready to push for more information, Tom took a step back. "I'm going to get some cake." He walked back to the kitchen table and kissed Mercy's cheek. "Happy birthday."

Mercy studied him with eyes that saw way too much. "Thank you. She hasn't left yet."

Not pretending to misunderstand, Tom nodded once, then headed for the front door, pausing at the living room. Liza sat with Irina, the two watching Abigail play. He almost went to her, but he had no idea what to say. Plus he had a job to do.

Leaving the house, he did a perimeter walk, working off the energy that had kept him edgy all day. A glance upward confirmed that the sniper Raeburn had sent was still in place. One of the neighbors had nearly died the month before when Ephraim was watching the Sokolovs' house. The old man had given them permission to use his home as a vantage point, telling them to "get the motherfuckers once and for all."

Tom was good with that.

"Seen anything?" he asked the agent leading the effort.

"Nope. Been quiet. Only a few of the families are even here. A few took off this morning." The man lifted a brow. "For their cabins in Tahoe. Must be nice."

"Must be," Tom agreed. "I expect the party to go on for another few hours. Bowie Security will shuttle some of the guests to the airport tonight for red-eyes back east. Everyone else will stay here overnight and leave throughout the day tomorrow."

"We'll be here. Shift change happens at six tonight, then again at six in the morning."

"Thanks. I'll stay until the party breaks up." Tom took another trip around the Sokolovs' property, paying attention to each bordering house, wondering where DJ Belmont was hiding. It had to be close. He wouldn't have been able to follow the Bowie SUV otherwise.

He wished they could search each house, but unfortunately they didn't have cause. It was frustrating as hell knowing that Belmont was close by. Maybe even watching him now. But so many of the houses were empty because of the holiday weekend. If he was hiding in one of the houses nearby, all he'd have to do would be to ignore their knock. Without a search warrant, they'd never know he was there.

It didn't have to be a direct line of sight, though. Not like Ephraim had achieved in the house across the street. It could be a block away. Two blocks, even. Probably no farther than that.

Grabbing a tactical helmet from the back of the Bureau van, Tom strapped it on and shrugged into a bulletproof vest.

"Going somewhere?" the agent asked him.

"For a walk. Belmont is here. I know it."

"Give me a second to gear up. I'll go with you."

The two of them walked the Sokolovs' neighborhood, eyes peeled for anything out of place. They still didn't have an ID on the woman Belmont had murdered the night before and they didn't know what kind of car had been stolen. But they were looking for anything out of place. Anything that caught their attention.

It didn't matter, though. There were no cars visible in driveways. All had been parked in the garages or had been driven out of town by the homes' occupants.

"I see nothing," the agent said when they'd walked two blocks in each direction.

Tom blew out a breath. "Me neither. Dammit, this is so frustrating. I *know* he's here."

"Maybe he's hiding somewhere else after last night."

"Maybe. But this is a prize that Belmont won't be able to easily ignore. Mercy is here and so is Gideon. He has to know that. He was watching last night. He knows that we had SUVs going back and forth to the airport. I can't see him walking away from this opportunity."

"If he makes a move, we'll be ready. If only we had search warrants for the neighborhood."

"I wish," Tom muttered as they started the walk back to the Sokolovs'. When they'd reached the van, he took off and stowed the tactical gear.

He needed to tell Rafe about the dead cops before he and Mercy were driven home. Rafe needed to be on full alert, even if he didn't share the reason with Mercy.

Tom entered the house, flinching at the roar of noise that assaulted him. The house was normally boisterous, but today . . . It was as loud as a home team crowd at the Garden.

Some days Tom missed playing basketball, but he did not miss that noise. Bracing himself, he walked toward the kitchen, pausing once again in the doorway of the living room. Liza was sitting on the sofa in the corner, just as she'd been when he'd left for his perimeter check.

She watched Abigail playing, her expression a mix of subdued contentment and grim determination. He knew what she was thinking about. On Tuesday she was walking into a nest of hardened criminals. For Mercy. And for the little girl who sat on the floor playing with Irina's grandchildren.

Liza might not walk out alive. But she was willing to take the risk. She'd done it before.

Please let her walk out whole and unhurt.

Rafe's angry voice snapped him to attention. "Dammit, Hunter, we need to talk."

Well, shit.

GRANITE BAY, CALIFORNIA
SUNDAY, MAY 28, 3:35 P.M.

DJ lowered his rifle and stepped away from Smythe's spare bedroom window. He'd wanted to pull the trigger so damn badly. But he hadn't. Because it would have been suicide.

The tall guy was a Fed. Special Agent Tom Hunter. DJ had seen him on the news coverage of the two dead cops and the still-unidentified female victim. Hunter had been at the crime scene the night before, with an Agent Croft, both looking serious.

Hunter and another man appeared to be on guard duty, dressed in tactical gear. DJ had seen them from his window and had felt a slight panic when they'd stopped, looking around them as if searching for something specific.

Me.

He'd grabbed his rifle out of habit and guessed he could thank his bum shoulder for keeping him from doing anything stupid. He'd felt the burn of pain when he'd lifted the rifle, which had broken the reflexive response that he'd built through hours of practice. Position, focus, fire. Kowalski had taught him how to use a rifle. DJ had perfected his skill, but this time he was glad he hadn't automatically pulled the trigger.

The Fed would be able to track the bullet's trajectory pretty damn quickly, and there was a small army protecting the Sokolovs' house today. He'd be surrounded before he could blink.

"Tomorrow, then," he murmured. "Or whenever your little party is over."

He had time. Pastor was going to be in rehab for weeks, after all. He'd fantasized about simply blowing the Sokolov house to smithereens with the party inside, but he didn't have the makings for a bomb. Not yet.

But Kowalski had explosives. DJ had seen him use them, and soon he'd have them, too.

He set the rifle aside and returned to his laptop. This, the photo on his screen, was where his focus needed to be today.

Because he'd finally found Kowalski. Or at least his kid.

A grinning six-year-old stared out from the screen. Little Tony Ward was in the first grade and played the piano. Kid was something of a virtuoso, in fact.

His mother was Angelina. His father was Anthony. It had taken a little digging, but DJ had found one photo featuring his former mentor. Roland Kowalski was Anthony Ward. A rich real estate developer who owned huge tracts of land.

So that's where he buried all of the people he had us kill for him. Good to know.

He'd first check Ward's home and loot whatever he could put his hands on. And if Kowalski had guards? DJ would kill them the way he'd killed those two cops. He'd go in under the cover of darkness, scope out a vantage point from which he could set up his rifle, and take out the guards one by one.

The way he wanted to kill the small army patrolling the Sokolov house. Difference was, the Sokolovs were expecting him, just like Kowalski had been when he'd set up the warehouse trap.

Kowalski wouldn't be expecting an attack on his home—and his thugs were a lot less likely to call the cops. Assuming the man didn't have a few of his own on payroll. DJ wouldn't have put it past him, nor would he let it stop him. Once he got his hands on Kowalski's weapons—and once the Sokolovs' party was over and the heavy security dispersed—he'd be able to tackle the Russian family's remaining guards single-handedly.

He hadn't expected to find Anthony Ward's address in the white pages but was still disappointed when it didn't show up at all—under any of his names or legit businesses. Damn these people and their corporations.

"That's a bust," he muttered and went back to staring at the photo of Tony Ward with his class the night of the recital.

And then noticed the caption: *Miss Stack's First Grade Spring Concert.*

The school's website had featured a list of staff. With their photos.

Thirty seconds later he had a full name: *Miss Stephanie Stack.*

A minute after that he had Miss Stephanie Stack's address, because *she* was a normal person.

Teachers had access to their students' personal information, like their birthdays and food allergies. And the names and addresses of their parents in case of emergency.

He stood and stretched. "Miss Stephanie, here I come."

GRANITE BAY, CALIFORNIA
SUNDAY, MAY 28, 3:40 P.M.

Tom turned his gaze from Liza to find Rafe clutching his cell and giving him a death glare. "So you read the news, huh?" Tom asked, surprised that Rafe hadn't cornered him already.

Rafe jerked his head toward a spare bedroom at the end of the hallway, setting off with an angry gait as he leaned on his cane. Tom followed with a sigh.

Rafe spun to face him as soon as he'd closed the door. "What the hell, Tom?" he hissed. "Belmont straight-up murdered an innocent woman and two cops, and you didn't tell me?"

"What would you have done differently had you known?" Tom asked wearily.

Rafe opened his mouth. Shut it. Then huffed out a sigh. "Probably canceled the party because Mercy would have felt too guilty."

"Which is why we didn't tell you. Mercy did nothing to feel guilty about and we—Gideon and I—wanted her to have a worry-free day. We wanted all of you to have a worry-free day."

"I guess now I know why Gideon and Daisy took our phones last night. They said that they didn't want us to cheat at trivia. They really wanted to make sure that we didn't hear about what happened." Rafe sagged against the door. "Mercy still doesn't know. I don't want to tell her."

"I'll tell her. And I'll tell her that I recommended we keep it a secret. She can be mad at me. At least she will have had this day."

Rafe swallowed. "Shit. Now I have to apologize for getting mad at you, don't I?"

"Nah. It's fine."

"Thank you," Rafe murmured. "Mercy needed this. We all did. She and I made a pact this morning that we weren't going to think about DJ Belmont until tomorrow. But you were acting weird, so I checked. The article said that you were at the scene."

"It wasn't good." That was all Tom could say.

"And the woman he killed?"

"Innocent bystander. Belmont stole her car. We still haven't ID'd her or her car."

Rafe frowned. "I thought he stole the cruiser."

"He did, along with one of the cops' shirts, his vest, and his gun belt. We assume he used the cruiser to pull her over. The woman's body was found in the back seat. He killed her there."

Rafe closed his eyes. "That woman died thinking she'd been killed by a cop."

"Yeah." Tom wasn't surprised that had been one of Rafe's first takeaways. It had been his, too, as soon as he'd seen the body. "Her phone was found on the shoulder. It appears that Belmont shot the phone and ran over it with her car. Once we get an ID on the victim, we'll try to track her car—if he still has it. Hopefully it'll lead us to where he's hiding."

"He's here, isn't he?" Rafe asked grimly. "Somewhere around here? In the neighborhood?"

"I think so. At least he was. But we're proceeding as if he still is, taking all the precautions we can. We've knocked on doors, done searches where we legally can. We have the neighbors who are here on alert, helping us watch for anything suspicious. In the meantime, Mercy's family will be safe. And then, tomorrow, we start looking again."

Rafe hung his head. "I'm sorry, Tom. I acted like an ass."

"I would have done the same. We're good."

"Thanks. Now, because you've done something for me, I'm going to return the favor." He found something on his phone, then held the screen so that Tom could see. "Look."

Tom reluctantly shifted his gaze to the phone's screen, then frowned. It was a photo of himself, his expression so incredibly vulnerable, so very sad, that he had to look away.

"Look," Rafe repeated. "I mean it, Tom. As your friend, I'm telling you to look."

I don't want to. But he did, cringing at the sight of himself looking like a kid who'd lost his puppy.

"You were watching her," Rafe murmured. "I was so damn mad at you, but I had to take a second out of being angry to take this picture. I need you to see."

Tom sighed, exhausted. "See what, Rafe?"

"You want her, but you don't want to. It's hurting you and it's hurting her. You both say that you're just friends, but that's bullshit. We can all see it. Why are you fighting this so hard?"

Wasn't that a damn good question?

Tom closed his eyes, childishly hoping that when he opened them, Rafe would be gone.

"I'm still here," Rafe said wryly.

"Of course you are." Tom looked up, met Rafe's piercing stare. "I don't know."

"You don't know why you're fighting it? Or you don't want to admit that you do know?"

Tom pinched the bridge of his nose. "Can't you just let this go?"

"I will, if that's what you really want. Except we both know you'd be lying if you said so. Pictures don't lie." He held out his phone again, the photo a slap to Tom's face.

The expression he wore was . . . longing. He swallowed hard as the admission took root in his mind. In his heart. "It's only been fourteen months," he whispered.

Fourteen months, twenty-three days, and seven hours.

"I get it," Rafe murmured. "I waited five years for Mercy to come along. I've wondered since we talked Wednesday—or didn't talk since you told me to leave your house—if I'd have been ready for Mercy if it had only been fourteen months since Bella."

"And?" The word grated on his throat, which was suddenly dry. Suddenly burning. As were his eyes and his nose. *Goddammit.*

"I don't know. But I also didn't have anyone I cared about like that back then. You do."

I do. It was no longer a question in his mind. *I'm so sorry, Tory, but I do.*

"Would Tory have wanted you to be alone? To feel like this?" Rafe waved his phone, Tom's photo still filling the screen.

"No." Of that he was certain. "She wouldn't have, but . . ." He closed his eyes, unable to look at his own face any longer. "She was pregnant. Only two months, but . . ."

"Oh my God," Rafe breathed. "I'm so sorry."

Tom was startled to realize that the searing pain had started to numb somewhat. "Me too."

Rafe was quiet for a moment. "I can't even imagine how much that hurts."

Tom shrugged uncomfortably. "I'm not sure that it changes what you've said. Tory still would have wanted me to move on. I'm not sure that it's possible now, though. I hurt Liza, without even meaning to. She left. I'm not even sure we'll be friends again."

Rafe sighed. "You want my opinion?"

Tom laughed, startling himself. "You're asking me now?"

Rafe grinned. "I'm my mother's son. I'm nosy, but polite about it." His grin faded. "I haven't known Liza long, but I'm a pretty good judge of character. Liza has a giving heart and she is *loyal*. Maybe even to a fault. Definitely at the risk to her own safety."

Tom's eyes flashed to Rafe's. Did he know about Sunnyside?

Rafe's eyes narrowed. "I'm coming back to that look on your face, Hunter. But first, I'm going to say that my money's on Liza forgiving your sorry ass. Now, what else do you know that I don't? This is what you wanted to tell me tomorrow, isn't it?"

Tom nodded. "You might want to sit down."

Rafe pulled up a chair. "Talk."

Tom did, telling him about Pastor and Sunnyside Oaks, and Liza getting a job there. When he finished, Rafe was equal parts stunned and furious. Which Tom had anticipated.

"You knew where he was and didn't tell us?"

Tom sighed. "What would you have done? Stormed the place? We know where Pastor is. According to his chart, he's supposed to be there for six weeks. We don't know where Belmont is and he's the biggest risk. But we're looking for him. I promise you that. But we're hoping to entice Pastor to tell us where Eden is, or at least to overhear him and DJ talking about it. Our goals are to find Eden, either use Pastor to lure DJ to the rehab center or wait for him to visit, then arrest them both."

Rafe was still angry. "What was the job you wanted to hire me for, as a PI?"

"Guard her."

"Liza?"

"Yes."

"Isn't that the FBI's job?" Rafe asked sarcastically.

"And they'll be there. They say she's a priority, but . . . I need more than that." The words were sharp, stealing his breath. He made himself breathe. "The Bureau's priority is the mission. I want to believe that they'd cover Liza even if it meant letting Pastor or DJ go, but I can't risk her life on that. Besides, everyone is all, 'Oh, Liza is a soldier. She can take care of herself.'"

"She can."

"But she *won't*," Tom said, panic rising to press on his chest. "You said it yourself. She is loyal at the risk to her own safety."

"She's doing this for Mercy, isn't she?"

"And for Abigail. Gideon and Amos, too."

"Does Gideon know?"

Tom shook his head. "No. And he'd be an awful choice to guard Liza even if he did. Pastor might recognize him. Belmont definitely would."

"They might also recognize me," Rafe pointed out.

"We can fix that. You've done undercover before. Gideon never has and I don't think he'd be good at it, but you were. You never could have stayed in your UC role after Bella was killed without being able to hide your emotions."

"True as well. So how are you going to get me in there? If I say yes, that is."

"I'm not sure yet. It may be as simple as smuggling you into the employee parking lot in the back of that SUV that your dad loaned her so you'll be close by in case everything goes to hell. Might be as complicated as getting you inside as an IT guy. We're working on giving them some network problems."

"When does she start?"

"Tuesday morning. So I have until then to figure something out."

Rafe stood, leaning on his cane. "Let me know. Either way, I'm in. She's charging into danger for Mercy. It's the least I can do."

Rafe left and Tom remained, wishing he could take a damn nap. He hadn't been so exhausted in a long time. Not since he'd been on the hunt for Tory's killer. It had sapped every bit of life from his soul.

He wondered if the loss of that life from his soul, that feeling of hope, had been permanent.

He wondered what he was going to do about Liza. He wondered if, when he figured it out, it would be too late.

And then he noticed a text on his personal cell phone. *Saw the story from last night online. You look tired. Call if you need to talk. Still want to be there for you if you want me to. That's what friends are for, right?*

His whole body relaxed and his eyes actually burned, so great was his relief.

Tom's hands shook as he typed his reply. *I want you to. Thx. Will call later.*

TWENTY-THREE

Well, I kind of figured that out a long time ago," Dana said. "Your feelings for Tom have never really been a secret."

Liza should have realized as much. Her Chicago "big sister," the woman who'd taken her in after Lindsay's murder, was insightful. This was one of the reasons she'd finally broken down and called her upon returning to her new apartment from Mercy's birthday party.

Dana Dupinsky Buchanan had known Liza for seven years and Tom for twenty—ever since he and his mother had escaped his abusive biological father. Dana's best friend was Tom's mother, and Dana's husband was Tom's hacking mentor.

Dana had both history and perspective, and Liza figured that she'd be able to give her good advice on keeping her relationship with Tom in the friend zone.

Right now Tom needed a friend and Liza was determined to be that for him, even if it hurt her that he didn't want more. "I'm not sure why I thought I'd be able to keep it from any of you," she said wearily.

"I'm completely confused by that myself. But it does explain Tom's behavior lately. He called his mom on Wednesday night and she said he seemed off. Caroline figured it had something to do with you."

Liza didn't have the energy to be annoyed. "You've been talking about us?"

"Duh." Dana paused, then asked warmly, "What do you need from me, Liza?"

"I wanted to come clean with you, I guess." About Tom. About Fritz. But the Fritz news, she held back. Learning that she'd kept that secret would hurt Dana the most. *I didn't even invite her to my wedding.* "And to ask for advice. Tom's in the middle of a really difficult case."

"We know. Ethan has alerts set up for news stories with his name. We saw him at the crime scene with the two dead police officers. There's more to it, I know, but we won't ask."

"I, um, offered to be here if he needed to talk. Any recommendations for keeping it in the friend zone? We share a lot of friends here. It's going to be hard for me to avoid him."

"That sucks, kiddo. I've never been in your shoes, but I have been in Tom's."

Liza was surprised at that. "Who?"

"I don't want to name names, because all that's in the past. Suffice it to say, someone I interacted with daily was in love with me for years and I never clued in. Everyone else knew."

"What happened?"

"I met Ethan and fell head over heels. Told this other guy all about Ethan, not even suspecting that I was basically stabbing him in the heart."

"I know how *that* feels. Tom told me about Tory the day he met her."

"Ouch." Dana's wince was audible. "That super sucks. What did you do?"

"Buried my hurt and asked him to tell me about her. What happened with this other guy?"

"After I met Ethan, he moved to another state. Met the sister of one of our friends at a wedding and they hit it off. Been married for years and they have a little boy."

"So he completely separated himself."

"For a while. Once he met his wife, he realized that he hadn't really loved me at all. Who knows? Maybe you'll meet someone in nursing school or while standing in a supermarket line. But you *will* meet someone." She hesitated. "What else is wrong, honey? I can hear it in your voice. Don't make me get on a plane to see you face-to-face," she added teasingly.

Liza wasn't so sure Dana was teasing and suddenly didn't want her to be. Maybe when she was no longer needed at Sunnyside Oaks, she could get a cheap flight to Chicago. For a hug.

Drawing a deep breath, she told Dana about Fritz. Dana didn't say a word until she was finished, and then the older woman sighed.

"I'm not going to say I'm not hurt, because I am. But only a little. I get why you avoided telling me. I'm mostly sad that you lost your Fritz. He sounds like he was amazing."

"He was. He deserved better than me."

"Do *not* say that," Dana said sharply. "He loved you and you cared for him. Would you have cheated on him?"

"*Never.*" Liza was shocked at the question. "You know I wouldn't have."

"Yes, I do know. Another question: *If* he'd lived and *if* Tom miraculously had fallen in love with you once you and Fritz had come home, would you have left Fritz?"

Liza considered carefully. "No," she said, relieved that she believed it with all of her heart. "We would have settled down and had a family. I loved him, even if it wasn't the way he loved me. I was . . . you know, attracted." Her face heated. "We would have been happy."

"Then you have nothing to be ashamed about," Dana said softly. "Stop punishing yourself. Were the months you had with Fritz happy ones?"

"Yes. They were. I mean, we were in a war zone, so it was a different kind of happy. But he made me feel special. And safe."

"Okay, last question. If Tom sees the light, will you believe him?"

Liza frowned. "What, are you asking if I'll believe he's serious?"

"That's exactly what I'm asking."

"I . . . I don't know."

"Then figure it out. Just in case."

Liza wasn't sure how to process those words. "In other words, don't give up hope?"

"Maybe. At least give him time to figure stuff out. He does care about you, of that I'm sure."

"Are you still friends with the man who thought he loved you?"

"Yes. He's one of the best men I know. If nothing else, I hope you'll have that with Tom."

Liza hadn't realized how much she'd needed that hope. "I love you. You know that, right?"

"I do. I also know that we are going to visit Fritz's family *together*, so I can meet them."

This time it was shame that heated Liza's cheeks. Not only had she denied Dana the opportunity to meet Fritz, she'd denied Fritz's family the opportunity to know hers. "They'd love that." Call waiting beeped in her ear. "I need to go. That's the security guard downstairs."

"Put me on hold. I need to know everything is okay. Especially because I know you're mixed up in this thing that's got Tom so worried."

"Yes, ma'am." Liza hit the hold button and answered the guard. "Yes? Can I help you?"

"Miss Barkley, there's a visitor for you here in the lobby. Says his name is Tom Hunter. He's got ID that says he's FBI." The guard lowered his voice to a whisper. "But he looks like a guy who used to play basketball."

Liza surged to her feet, the blood draining from her head making her dizzy. "Please send him up. Thank you." She hung up on the guard and said to Dana, "It's fine. It's Tom. I thought he'd call, but he's on his way up."

"Call me later. I want the details. Love you, Liza."

"Love you, too." Ending the call, Liza smoothed her clothing and dashed to the mirror to check her face. She'd cried when she'd first starting talking to Dana, but her eyes didn't look too bad. The knock at her door wasn't nearly as loud as the pounding in her ears.

Damn. He looked good even through the weird distortion of the peephole in her door.

Bracing herself, she opened the door. He stood there filling the space with his big body as he always did, but his head was lowered, his shoulders hunched. When he looked up, all she could see was utter exhaustion.

"Come on in. You look like shit," she said, stepping out of the way.

He laughed, a fraction of his weariness seeming to fade. "Thank you."

"Food?"

He winced. "Hell, no. Irina made me take a cooler full of food."

"Me too." It felt awkward between them, and she hated that. "Sit with me?"

He nodded gratefully, each of them taking the opposite end of the sofa in the living room. "This is a really nice place."

"It really is." She drew a breath. "Have you slept?"

He met her gaze. Held it. "Honestly? Not since you left."

She gaped for a moment. "Tom, no. You can't do that. You're going to get yourself killed."

"Croft said the same thing."

"Then listen to her." She started to rise. "I'll get the spare room ready for you."

He reached over and gently gripped her arm. "No. Please. I need to talk to you."

Slowly she sank back down to the sofa. That didn't sound positive, she thought, belatedly realizing that she'd allowed Dana's parting words to give her hope. *Serves me right.* "Okay."

He released her arm. "DJ Belmont has killed five people that we know of—a nurse, an elderly woman, a young woman whose car he stole, and two cops."

The tiny sliver of hope that remained circled the drain. This was only a continuation of the argument they'd had in Rafe's garage. "I know."

"That doesn't count the five federal agents he killed a month ago. And the owner of the truck he was driving last night, who he killed the same day as the agents. So all together, he's murdered eleven people in cold blood."

Liza's jaw tightened as she ground her teeth together. "I know. I can count, Tom."

"That's not what I meant. I meant that he's dangerous. You could come into contact with him at Sunnyside. If you are able to talk to Pastor and DJ finds out, or he finds you planting bugs . . . he'll kill you without a second thought."

He cares. It was all that kept her from showing him the door. "I knew that when I applied."

"I can't stop you from going through with this," he said, sounding as if he desperately wished to do exactly that.

"No, you can't." She rose this time, stepping back when he tried to grab her again. "Look, Tom, we've already danced to this song. If you want to talk about something else, I'm fine with that. But I'm not going to rehash this with you."

"I'm hiring a bodyguard for you," he blurted out.

Liza stared at him. "What?"

"A bodyguard. For you. If I can't keep you out of there, I'll make sure that you're safe while you're inside."

She sat back down, keeping to the edge of the cushion. "Your boss will have me covered."

"From outside the gates. If you sound the alarm, they'll have to force their way in, putting your safety and the mission in jeopardy. We don't know where DJ is. If he's managed to hide inside and he suspects you, then you're in danger *and* we're no closer to finding Eden."

"Your boss said they might have someone on the inside."

"Maybe. That's dependent on some other things that might not happen."

He wasn't lying. "You're afraid," she murmured.

"Terrified," he confessed hoarsely. "Aren't you?"

"Yes. But no more than I was every time I went into the field, and I did that more times than I want to remember."

Pride filled his eyes. "I know you did. I remember all of our Skype talks. You were afraid, yet you served. But this, having a bodyguard, is for me. Please."

Dammit. He knew how to play her heartstrings. "Who will my bodyguard be?"

He closed his eyes, his expression so relieved that her heart cracked. "Rafe."

"Wait. Rafe Sokolov?"

Opening his eyes, he narrowed them. "Just how many Rafes do you know?"

"Just the one. Okay, I'll bite. How are you going to get him inside?"

"I'm not sure, exactly. At the very minimum, I'm going to get him into the parking lot in the back of that SUV that Karl loaned you. We'll make a copy of the key card you get for access to the building and give it to Rafe."

"So Rafe will essentially be sitting outside in a black SUV, roasting in the sun while I work my shift on the off chance that I'll need him."

"Yes. Unless you can find a place where he can hide inside."

"It's not a horrible plan," she had to admit. "But there are cameras all over the place."

He pulled a pendant from his pocket with a grim smile. "You'll be wearing this. I can get control of their Wi-Fi cameras. The ones hard-wired to the server will have to be rerouted."

"You want *me* to do that?" she asked nervously.

"No. We'll hopefully get a network specialist in there, and that person can take care of it."

She held out her hand for the pendant. "Can I see it?"

He moved to the middle cushion before placing it on her palm and closing her fist around it. Then he covered her fist with his hand, warm and solid, and she wished this were real.

She tugged her hand free and let the pendant dangle on its pretty silver chain. The design was delicately done, but large enough to host a camera and microphone.

It was a rose. "It looks like my tattoo."

"I know. I was there when you got it, remember?"

"Of course I do. You were too chicken to get one yourself."

One corner of his mouth quirked up. "Still am."

She gave him back the pendant, wishing he'd move back to his side of the sofa. This close she could smell his aftershave, and she wanted to press her face against his neck and breathe him in, so she got up and dragged a wingback chair closer to the sofa.

When she sat down, his expression had grown carefully blank. That was his *I'm hurt* face, but she wasn't going to let him manipulate her. She'd be his friend, but on her own terms. That didn't include having to endure his amazing scent. And warmth. Because now she was cold.

"What happened last night?" she asked, changing the subject.

"You read the news story. We don't have a lead on the female victim. She was in the wrong place at the wrong time." He rubbed his palms on his thighs and she couldn't help but follow the motion, because he had spectacular legs. Thankfully, she'd averted her gaze by the time he looked up, his gaze uncertain. "What happened to Mike?"

"Mike?"

"Your friend. The one who came to see you on Wednesday." A muscle twitched in his cheek. "And who you went out on a date with on Tuesday night."

She shrugged. "We're just friends."

"He didn't seem to think so."

If she hadn't already had her hopes dashed, she'd think he was jealous. But she *had* had her hopes dashed, and she wasn't letting them get away from her again.

Which was a total lie. "He said the same about you."

"Why did you go out with him on Tuesday?"

She sighed, exasperated. "Because he asked me to. Can we not have this conversation?"

"That's fine," he said levelly. "But please answer the question first."

"Then it's not fine!" She stood up and spun to face the far wall. "I can't do this."

"Do what?" he asked, and she jumped because he was right behind her now, and she hadn't even heard him get up. "Can't do what?"

The timbre of his voice sent a shiver across her skin. She swore it had dropped an octave. His breath was warm on her neck, and her heart was racing faster now.

Hope sparkled in her chest and she shoved it back. "Don't," she whispered. "It's not fair."

The pressure at the base of her neck was a shock. It wasn't his forehead, like it had been on Thursday in his house. This pressure was soft and warm and mobile.

His lips. He was kissing the base of her neck. "What can't you do, Liza? I need to know."

She shook her head, angry arousal bubbling around the damn hope. "*No.* You don't get to do this. You don't get to tell me that you don't feel the same and then come in and do this. What do you want from me?"

The pressure of his mouth had disappeared with her first *no.* "I want you to tell me why you went out with Mike on Tuesday night."

"Fucking hell," she snarled. "You want me to tell you everything, but you don't tell me anything. Why did I marry Fritz? How long have I loved you? Now you want to know why I went out with some other man who doesn't even matter?" Guilt prickled, because Mike did matter. "He's a nice person. He liked me. He made me feel special. And when he asked me to go out with him, I said yes, because I am *not* a nice person. I used him to get your attention because I am *not a nice person*! Is that what you wanted to know?"

She was shouting now, desperately wishing for the sweet pressure of his mouth on her skin. "I wanted you to say, 'Hey, maybe *I* could ask her out. Maybe *I* could make her feel special.' I wanted you to wake the hell up, maybe even be jealous, but all you did was talk basketball." Her voice broke. "And give the man your fucking autograph. So the joke's on me, I guess."

"Will you see him again?" he asked quietly. So damn calmly.

She wanted to scream. "No. I told him that I wasn't ready. I told him about Fritz."

He drew a deep breath, but he must have taken a step back, because when he exhaled, she couldn't feel it. *For the best*, she thought. He must have been toying with her after all.

Except . . . *Tom isn't like that. He wouldn't humiliate me like that.*

For a brief moment she wondered if he was doing this to make her so angry that she'd quit Sunnyside. But Tom wasn't like that, either.

"Look," she said wearily. "I thought I could do this. I thought I could talk to you and be your friend and help you shoulder the burden for this case. But I can't. I'm sorry, but I can't."

"So Mike isn't coming back?"

He was about a foot behind her now. She was tempted to take a step forward, but that felt like retreat and she wasn't going to do that anymore, either.

"No. He's not coming back. *Why?*"

"Because he had flowers sent to you."

She stilled. "What?"

"I went home to walk Pebbles after the party and there were flowers on your doorstep. The card said they were from Mike."

Liza rubbed her temples. "I don't . . . I didn't . . ." She sighed. "What did you do with them?"

"I threw them in a dumpster," he said calmly.

Confused, she slowly turned to face him. He stood with his hands at his sides. Fists clenched. Jaw clenched. Body held ramrod straight.

He wasn't calm. Not at all. And that goddamn hope began to

sparkle again. "Why are you here, Tom? You could have called me about the bodyguard."

His throat worked as he tried to swallow. Finally he cleared his throat. "Am I too late?"

She took a small step closer. A tiny, tentative step. "Too late for what?" she whispered, afraid for the answer, but hoping, hoping, *hoping.*

The small step seemed to defuse his tension. He released his fists, his eyes fixed on hers.

"I don't want to lose you," he said, his voice low and gravelly. "I . . . I can't."

Okay. Not exactly what she'd wanted to hear. She dropped her chin, breaking eye contact. "You won't lose me as a friend. You don't have to force yourself to—"

Strong fingers gripped her chin and urged her to look up.

The breath caught in her chest and it was like all the oxygen in the room was sucked away.

His eyes were more intense than the bluest sky on the sunniest day. And he was close. She had to blink to bring him into focus, and then blink again as he came closer.

"Tell me to stop if this isn't what you want," he whispered, brushing his thumb over her bottom lip, sending new shivers all over her skin and rocketing her pulse into the stratosphere.

She laughed, a breathless, slightly manic sound. "I've wanted this for—"

She was silenced by his mouth taking hers, and it was gentle. So gentle.

Too gentle. She'd waited so long. She needed more.

He pulled away far too quickly, his breath coming in short, harsh pants. The hand that now cupped her face was trembling. This big man was trembling. *For me.*

The intensity in his gaze grew darker. Hotter. "I wanted to rip his hands off," he whispered.

She blinked. "What? Who?"

"Mike." He said the name like it was a curse. "For touching you. He touched you."

Her knees wobbled, relief making her dizzy. That she flattened her palms against his chest might have been for balance, but it wasn't. He felt so good. So hard. And sensitive, his muscles shifting and jumping under her touch. The fire in his eyes blazed.

He liked this. She closed her eyes, overcome. He *liked* this. He *wanted* this.

He wants me. She slid her hands higher until she could link them behind his neck, emboldened at the shudder that shook him. "I have one question," she whispered.

When she opened her eyes, she found he'd closed his, allowing her to look her fill. Tom Hunter was the most beautiful man she'd ever known. And he was holding her, hands on her sides, their bodies separate. Sweetly awkward, like a middle school dance. She wished he'd go higher or lower, but for now this was safe. For now this was enough.

He'd tensed again, though. Leaning up on her toes, she pressed a kiss to the hollow of his throat, making him swallow, his hands tightening their grip.

"What changed?" she asked. "I need to know that I didn't guilt you into this. I need to know that this is what you really want."

He yanked at her then, pulling her flush against him. The breath rushed out of her on a moan, because he was hard everywhere. *God, oh God.*

Everywhere. She tightened her hold around his neck, lifting on her toes again to perfect the fit. "Yeah," she breathed, "I guess this is what you really want."

"It is."

Please don't be a dream. But she didn't want to let him go long enough to pinch herself, so she wriggled closer, drawing a strangled groan from deep in his chest. Then his lips were on hers again, and this time there was no gentleness. Just raw want.

She could fall into this so easily. Too easily. But she pulled away, needing to know.

"What changed?" she whispered against his mouth.

"Everything and nothing. I wanted you. Wanted this."

"Then what—"

He interrupted her with another kiss, hard and fast. Then his lips curved. She could feel his smile and it lightened her spirit. "What changed was me. Someone helped me take a good look at myself," he murmured. "Showed me how I look at you." His hands were on her back, roaming up and down restlessly. "Someone made me realize that I was being a fool and paying more attention to a calendar than to my own heart."

Liza was going to bake that *someone* Dream Bars forever. "How do you look at me?"

"That's two questions."

"Indulge me. I'm . . ." *Needy. Fragile. Vulnerable as hell.* "I need to know."

He pulled back far enough to meet her gaze, and in his she saw the truth laid bare. "I look at you like you're the only thing I need to be happy. Is that enou—"

She pulled his head down and kissed him the way she'd always dreamed, hard and lush and a little indecent. Their mouths fit perfectly, their bodies aligning in just the right way.

Then his hands dipped lower, cupping her butt and lifting her off her toes like she weighed nothing at all. In three strides, he had her up against the wall, her legs wrapped around his hips.

He dropped his head to the curve of her shoulder and breathed her in. "Is this okay?"

She could feel him pulsing into her, and he was exactly how she'd fantasized. "Tell me this is real."

He straightened, resting his forehead on hers. "It's real. I promise."

She took a moment to absorb the rush of emotions, the thrum of lust. "Then it's better than okay. So much better." And then she kissed him again.

SACRAMENTO, CALIFORNIA
SUNDAY, MAY 28, 7:05 P.M.

It really shouldn't be this easy, DJ thought as he walked into Miss Stephanie Stack's kitchen. She'd left her door unlocked.

People really should be more careful. Especially since she was now living alone. Her Facebook status was "Single," and it was a new thing. An hour ago, she'd posted that she was planning to spend the evening "blissfully alone," watching the TV shows that her ex had sneered at, then taking a bath with a glass of wine.

The soft sound of a laugh track floated through the air as he crept to the doorway to the living room. She was sitting on her sofa, watching TV, her back to him. On the table beside her were a half-empty package of Oreo cookies, a mostly empty glass of white wine, and a half-empty wine bottle. It appeared Miss Stephanie was getting a head start on the booze portion of the evening.

She was playing a game on her laptop. That her laptop was on would make this easier still.

He assumed that she'd have her class roster somewhere on her computer. Depending on where it was stored, he might not need her involvement at all. If it was part of a password-protected school-owned software package, he'd need to keep her around. If her list was a simple Word document on her hard drive, her assistance would not be necessary.

He'd planned for this, planned to keep her alive in case he needed her password. He had precut lengths of duct tape fixed to his jeans and his silenced pistol in his gloved hand.

A bandana obscured his face, except for his eyes. One of Smythe's ball caps covered his newly bald head. He wasn't giving the cops any more photos of him. The carpeted floor quieted the sound of his footsteps as he approached.

Miss Stephanie cried out once when he put the barrel of his gun to her temple, but he stifled what would have been a scream by slapping one of the pieces of tape over her mouth.

"Get up," he said quietly.

She looked over her shoulder, eyes wide and petrified. She didn't move, frozen in place. She was young, maybe in her midtwenties, with strawberry blond hair piled atop her head.

With his left hand, he took her laptop from her, placing it on the cushion at the end of the sofa. "*Stand up.* I don't want to hurt you," he lied. "Do what I say and I won't."

She finally obeyed, her body shaking like a leaf, her pleas muffled by the tape. Stowing his gun under one arm, he quickly taped her wrists behind her back, then pushed her to sit and restrained her feet.

He took a seat at the end of the sofa, gun in hand once again. Her laptop was new and shiny and weighed next to nothing as he rested it on his knees and opened her hard drive.

From the corner of his eye, he saw her start to wiggle, like she was planning an escape.

Sorry, sweetheart. It wasn't her fault, of course. She was simply a teacher to the wrong kid. That wasn't going to stop him from using her to get what he needed, though.

What he needed was access to Kowalski's weapons stash, so what he needed was Kowalski's—*Excuse me, Anthony Ward's*—home address.

He pointed his gun at her face. "Don't even think about it."

She sagged, tears running down her cheeks and over the duct tape.

He typed *roster* into the laptop's search box, but got nothing. *Student* yielded too much, but *information* gave him the file that he needed.

"Ward, Ward, Ward," he muttered to himself. Anthony Ward Jr. was at the bottom.

Parents: Anthony (real estate developer) and Angelina (home-maker).
Allergies: None known.
Health concerns: None known.
Favorite color: Green.
Pets: Rottweiler named Lucky.

Well, that was particularly useful information. He needed to be prepared to drug the dog when he got there. Just in case.

And, finally, the pièce de résistance: Anthony Jr.'s home phone number and address.

DJ laughed, genuinely amused. "You can't make this shit up." He glanced at Miss Stephanie. "They live in Granite Bay, less than five miles from where I've been staying."

He took a photo of her screen with his phone, then closed the document and set the computer aside. Her nostrils flared as she watched him stand, hope flickering in her eyes.

"Sorry," he murmured. Because he really was. She hadn't spied on him like Mrs. Ellis had, or fought him like Mr. Smythe had. Or betrayed him like Nurse Gaynor had.

Or escaped and thrived like Gideon and Mercy had.

Stephanie Stack was just a first-grade teacher, who'd begun to shake her head, her "No, no, no" muffled by the tape.

At least he could make it quick. No need to make her suffer. He fired twice, checked her pulse, then went in search of something to drug Kowalski's guard dog. Five minutes later, he had a six-month-old bottle of oxycodone and a pound of hamburger.

Finally something had gone to plan.

TWENTY-FOUR

Tom ended the kiss and rested his cheek on the top of Liza's head. His heart was pounding like it would come out of his chest. He felt giddy with relief and tightened his arms around her. It was like he'd been underground for years and had finally emerged to breathe fresh air.

She shifted her hips, and he groaned because, most of all, he was horny as hell. His body had been in stasis for so long. He'd desired her many times since they'd moved to Sacramento, but not like this. Not with this clawing, desperate need, like a raging river after the collapse of a dam.

"I want you," he whispered and she made a noise so close to a whimper that his fingers flexed, digging into the firm muscles of her ass. "You have an amazing ass."

She laughed. "Thank you. I must admit to having ogled yours a time or two."

"Only a time or two?"

"A million times, or two," she murmured.

His lips curved and he kissed her hair. "There are things I want to do with you—" He groaned again when she shivered hard, her hips lifting so that she was pressing against his erection. "Wait. Just . . . wait. I need to think."

"No thinking. Time for doing." She released her hold on his neck, slipping her fingers between them and unbuttoning three buttons before his brain reconnected to his mouth.

He gave her a short, hard kiss before turning from the wall where they'd been leaning.

"First door on the left," she said huskily, then hummed when his feet stopped walking, his hips grinding against her of their own volition. "Mmm. You liked that."

Tom didn't think he was going to make it. "After," he choked out.

She looked up at him with a frown. And a little hurt. "After what?"

"I think we should talk. Don't you?"

Her lower lip poked out and he wanted to bite it. Just like he had every time she'd pouted since she was seventeen years old.

Now he could, so he did, tugging gently on her full lip with his teeth before following it up with a kiss that made her sigh dreamily. "You feel me," he whispered against her now-upturned lips. "You know I want you. That I want this. But I want to do this right."

She sighed again, put-upon. "Dudley Do-Right," she muttered. "Fine." She wriggled her hips again, trying to slide from his hold, but he was having none of that.

"Don't go." He punctuated his plea with another kiss. "Please."

He lowered them both to the sofa until he sat with his head back against the cushion and she straddled him on her knees, his hands rubbing up and down her thighs restlessly.

She smiled down at him, her expression wicked. "I could talk like this for a while."

He shook his head, unable to keep the smile from his face. "I need to say a few things. I need you to hear me."

She drew a breath and let it out, then sat back on his lap. "All right. I'm listening."

"You said that you've . . ." He felt his cheeks heat, and his eyes narrowed because she was grinning at him like the spitfire she was. "What?" he demanded.

She swept her thumbs over his cheeks. "You're blushing. It's sweet."

He rolled his eyes. "I am not sweet."

"Oh, okay. You are mean." She folded her hands in her lap, demurely waiting. Except for her eyes, which danced with an amusement that he hadn't seen in a very long time.

I love you. He startled, not sure when "wanting her" and "longing for her" had become "loving her." But the words were true. He knew it as well as he knew his own name. But he held the three words back. Not yet. He needed to say other things first. Important things.

"You said that you've loved me since you were seventeen."

She abruptly sobered, his intent finally seeming to register. "I did."

"I . . ."

She smiled ruefully. "You don't have to say it, Tom. I'd rather you wait until you know it's true than just say words back to me."

"But that's just it. I have loved you that long."

Her smile dropped away, her expression instantly wary. "But?"

"It wasn't like yours. Not then. Then, when I was twenty and you were seventeen, I knew I liked you. I knew I felt something for you." He huffed an awkward laugh. "I wanted you?"

A new smile bloomed. Sheer delight. "You did? Back then?"

"I did. But you were seventeen and you were grieving and I would never have taken advantage of you that way."

She traced his lower lip with her fingertip. "I know. But I have to say that knowing you wanted to is an ego boost."

He winced. "I never meant to make you feel . . . less."

"I know that, too." She drew a deep breath and braced her shoulders. "And then?"

"Then you joined the army and I was pissed off."

"I remember that."

"You were eighteen and I'd planned something . . ." He felt himself blushing again, his embarrassment made worse by the way she was watching him with wide eyes.

"Something?" she prompted. "Something . . . sexual?"

"God," he groaned. "Yes. I figured you were eighteen and I was still twenty and that I wasn't going to be a pervert if I made a move. But then you said you were going away. That you'd already signed up. You didn't tell me you were planning to do that."

That final sentence came out more accusingly than he'd wanted it to. She winced now. "I'm sorry. If I'd known . . ."

"Yeah, well," he grumbled. "I figured that you wouldn't have done that if you'd felt anything, so I stowed it. Told myself we were friends. That you were like my sister."

She looked horrified. "Shit."

He laughed. "I never managed to convince myself of the sister part."

"That's good, at least. But the friend part stuck, huh?"

"It did. When you'd come home on leave, it was hard. *I* was hard," he said ruefully. "I'd have to leave the room and go off by myself and say, 'Just a friend,' over and over until I was ready to come back out and be . . . well, presentable."

She grinned again, her gaze dropping to his groin, where he was still hard as a rock and raring to go. "Oh? And did those moments alone involve anything else? Like . . . y'know, relief? And are you almost done talking?"

"Behave, brat." He shook his head, but fondly. "When I was closer to twenty, yes, those little getaways sometimes involved me getting relief. As I got older, I got better at keeping you compartmentalized in the 'friend' box in my brain."

She was serious again. "You're good at compartmentalizing your emotions," she murmured. "That's how you survived an abusive father. I get that."

For a moment he could only stare. Then he chided himself for being so surprised. She'd always known him better than anyone else. "I think you're right."

"The distance didn't help. You graduated and got drafted to Boston and I was deployed."

"I worried about you all the time," he confessed. "Those Skype calls were some of the only times I thought I could breathe."

"And the other times?"

"When I was on the basketball court. In front of a crowd. Then everything else went away. But then, when you'd come home, I'd keep saying, *friend, friend, friend.* I knew it wasn't true deep down, but over time it became a kind of truth. You know?"

"I know." She hesitated. "And then you met Tory."

He nodded. "She was bright and happy and, well, there. *With* me."

"She made you happy," Liza said, without an iota of envy or anger.

"She really did."

Her fingertips brushed down his jawline. "I'm glad you had her. I'm glad she made you happy. I hope you can believe that I've *never* been glad that she died."

"I know," he said without hesitation. "You couldn't. It wouldn't be you."

Her smile was tremulous. "I must say, though, the day you met her was not my favorite day."

He remembered the flash of hurt in her eyes. How could he have missed it? How could he have compartmentalized his feelings to such a degree that he'd been so clueless? "I guess not."

"I got off the call with you and went to the PX and got an entire quart of ice cream and ate it all myself."

"Rocky road?"

She made a face. "No. It was mint chocolate chip. One of my friends found me eating it and weaseled some of the story out of me. She encouraged me to get serious with Fritz."

So they had arrived at act two of the program. "Fritz."

Her smile was sad. "Friedrich was his given name. His mom loved *Little Women*. Her favorite character was Jo, who ends up married to Friedrich, who she calls Fritz. He had such a nice family. My Fritz, not the book Fritz."

Tom swallowed, trying to loosen the clench of his jaw.

"He was my Fritz," she said quietly. "He was kind and I did love him."

Tom swallowed again. "I know."

"While I was with him, we were happy." She shrugged. "He was a good person."

"I'm glad you had him. I'm glad he made you happy."

She nodded, acknowledging the words that she'd said to him. She met his gaze squarely. "If he hadn't died, I wouldn't be with you. Even if you were alone."

"I know," he said again, and she visibly relaxed. "So now what?"

She lifted her brows. "That's a vague question. Be specific."

He looked around the classy apartment. "Will you stay here? Or will you come home?"

"Home," she said, and every tense muscle in his body let go. "On my side of the duplex. I'm not moving in with you yet."

His lips curved. "Not yet?"

"Nope. You're going to court me."

"I am?"

Rising on her knees so that she loomed above him, she kissed him hard. "You are. You're going to come over for meals and I'll come to your place for movies. We'll go out on dates. We'll continue to share Pebbles. And I will continue paying you rent for my side of the duplex."

"I donate it to the kids' charity in town, just so you know."

"I've always known that," she said. "You've got cash. I get that. I'm not rich, but I'm not poor, either. So I'll continue to pay rent, and you'll continue to donate it."

He grinned up at her. "And I'll court you."

She nodded sharply. "You will."

"Okay."

She frowned, a little line appearing between her crunched brows. "I have one more question. On Thursday night, when we were arguing about me going to work at Sunnyside Oaks, I thought you were going to kiss me."

"I was." He remembered that moment with excruciating clarity. The moment after even more so.

"But then you backed away like I had the plague and you looked appalled. I didn't expect that. Why did you do that?"

"Because I was still telling myself that you were my friend. I'd already fucked up and you'd moved out. I was afraid. I could see myself ruining what was left of our friendship." He hesitated. "And everyone kept telling me that you had deeper feelings for me, but I wasn't ready to let Tory go. I loved her. I really did. I don't know. Maybe I was afraid to move on."

"I get it," she assured him. "If you admit that you're open to moving on, you're also open to getting hurt, and that's scary, too."

"I'm sorry I hurt you," he whispered. "That night I knew I should let you go. I was about to text you, to say goodbye. But I couldn't make myself type it. I couldn't let you go."

"So you said good night," she whispered back. "I'm sorry I left without saying goodbye."

"I'll be careful with your heart. I might fuck up, but I won't hurt you on purpose."

"And I won't walk away without talking it out when you do." She rested her forehead on his. "Are we done talking for now?"

His hands began their restless journey up and down her thighs again. "Why?"

"Because I've dreamed of kissing you since I was seventeen years old and I haven't had nearly enough."

"Do I get to do what I dreamed of, too?" Because now that he'd broken down the compartment walls, he was remembering all of the fantasies he'd had to bury deep in his mind.

Bury deep. He shuddered at the images the words conjured, fantasies rushing to fill his mind.

It was like he was twenty years old again, and the feeling was intoxicating. *I can do* all *the things now. I don't have to pretend.*

She smiled against his lips. "That seems fair." Then she half laughed, half shrieked when he reared up and tumbled her to her back, coming to rest on top of her. Her legs parted for him and his body twitched, needing to thrust.

They'd do that, but for this moment, he'd feast on her mouth. She wanted to be courted. "I won't rush. We'll take this slow."

"Not too slow." Her fingers clenched in his shirt and jerked it free of his trousers before freeing the remaining buttons. She slid her palms up his torso, humming appreciatively. "Take it off. I've been waiting long enough."

Skin tingling everywhere she touched, he pushed to his knees and shrugged out of the shirt. He started to lower himself back onto her, but she sat up, hands reaching for him.

"Let me look," she whispered. "Just let me look."

She didn't only look, though. Her hands got busy, stroking his pecs and down his sides. He closed his eyes, tipping his head back, letting himself float as she touched every inch of his torso.

His eyes flew open and he sucked in a breath when she pressed her lips to his stomach, millimeters from his waistband. Every nerve in his body sang and his cock grew harder when he hadn't thought it possible.

She glanced up. "Ticklish?"

"No." He was breathing hard. "You make it hard to stay in control."

"Good." She kissed him again, but this time her tongue stole out to lick the skin she'd kissed.

He hissed. "Liza."

Another glance up, her brown eyes gone dark and needy. Then she shocked him by leaning forward, her mouth so close to his groin that

KAREN ROSE

he could feel her warm breath when she exhaled. "What if I don't want you to stay in control?"

"Liza," he warned. And then she inhaled, making a needy noise that severed whatever discipline he'd still possessed. "Fuck," he growled, pushing her to the sofa and following her down. He claimed her mouth, taking what he needed, and he wasn't gentle.

She shoved her fingers into his hair and pulled him closer, reminding him that his Liza was strong. He needed more, needed to touch her, needed to see her. Needed to be inside her.

He tugged her shirt up, feeling the silky skin of her stomach. She shivered, wriggling beneath him.

"Ticklish?" he asked, loving the way her cheeks were flushed, her eyes gone dark with lust.

"Yes." Her eyes narrowed. "And if you ever want to do any of those things you dreamed of, you won't take advantage of that confession."

Tom slid down her torso so that he could kiss the skin he'd bared. "Sorry," he murmured, brushing his lips over her ribs, then upward, taking his time, smiling as her skin pebbled. Until she made another needy whimpering sound.

His kisses became openmouthed and urgent, his hips rolling and thrusting against the sofa cushions when he really needed to be rolling and thrusting into *her*. He shoved the hem of her shirt higher, going stock-still when he uncovered her bra.

He looked up to meet her eyes. She was watching him, her torso still. She was holding her breath. "I want to see you," he said hoarsely. "Can I see you?"

"Yes. Please."

He might have chuckled at her politeness, but she reached behind her to unhook her bra, and then he couldn't breathe, either. Crossing her arms, she gripped the hem of her shirt and the bra together and pulled them off.

It took him a few heartbeats to find words. "You're beautiful."

Her lips curved self-consciously, but she said nothing.

He hung there, staring, torn between the urge to rush and take and taste and suck and the more overwhelming need to take his time. Carefully, reverently, he kissed the valley between her breasts and drew in her scent.

God. The delicate citrus of her bodywash was overpowered by the sweet, heady scent of her arousal. He was so hard that he hurt.

He kissed the underside of each breast. "I want you." He kissed the swells, avoiding her nipples, hard and erect. Humming in frustration, she palmed his cheeks and tried to pull his mouth closer.

Her whisper was barely audible. "Suck me."

Gently he grabbed her wrists, guiding them over her head and restraining them with one hand. "I only get this first time once," he told her. "I don't want to rush."

She tipped her head back. "Tom," she whined. "Don't distract me with being all romantic."

"Sorry."

"No, you're not."

"No," he agreed. "I'm not." He licked one nipple and her mouth fell open.

"You're a fucking tease," she growled. "I didn't expect—" She gasped when he closed his lips over the other nipple and sucked, her hips rocking up into him.

His brain and his cock were already ten steps ahead, planning what he'd do and how he'd do it, when a stark realization had him screeching to a halt. Lifting his head, he frowned. "I don't have anything. Condoms. I didn't bring any with me. I'm clean, but . . ."

She groaned. "So am I, and you know I trust you with my life, but I'm not on the pill."

He lowered his head, resting his forehead between her breasts. "I almost bought some, but I didn't want to assume what would happen when I got here."

She tugged one of her hands loose of his grip and stroked his hair. "Do you have some at your house?"

He looked up, his damn pulse rocketing. "No, but there are roughly sixty-two drugstores between here and there."

She brushed her fingertips over his cheek. "Let's go home, then."

God. Hearing her say "home," and knowing what they'd do when they got there . . . He drew in a breath and shuddered it out. "I'm going to need a few minutes."

She was back to stroking his hair, and it felt so good. "We have time."

Clarity cut through the haze in his mind. *Time.* She was going to Sunnyside Oaks in roughly thirty-six hours. If DJ Belmont caught wind of who she was . . .

Time wouldn't be something they had nearly enough of.

EDEN, CALIFORNIA
SUNDAY, MAY 28, 8:00 P.M.

"Hey." Graham stuck his head around the curtain separating Hayley's cubicle from the rest of Joshua's holdings. Which had grown, because he was now "in charge" and "deserved upgraded facilities."

It was insane. There was no upgrade to be had here. It was all horrible. *And my baby's going to born into this. My baby could die here. I could die here.*

Who would take care of Graham? Who would keep him from being "apprenticed"? Not their mother, for sure. *She* was the reason they were here. *She's the reason my baby's getting stolen if she lives. She's—*

Fingers pinched her chin. "*Hey,*" Graham repeated more firmly.

She looked up, surprised to see him kneeling in front of her.

"You were starting to panic," he said. "I could see it on your face."

She nodded, then slowly backed away from him, deliberately not breathing through her nose. He smelled like the toilets, but he was doing it for her, for them, to get them all out of here, so she wouldn't say a single word about it.

He grinned, unoffended. "I believe the word is 'pungent.' I think Joshua is torn between making someone else dump the pots while making me take a bath, and letting me continue because no one else wants to do it. And we don't have water for baths anyway. I brought you a snack," he added, reaching for the bowl of broth that he'd set on the floor.

Hayley took it gratefully. It was the fifth bowl of broth she'd had that day. Joshua made sure that she got food "for the baby," but it never seemed enough. Tamar had been slipping her extra too, but Hayley knew that she was taking the other woman's own rations.

She studied her brother as she sipped the broth. "What have you done?" she whispered, feeling a little of his good mood lighten hers.

Solar panels, he mouthed.

Hayley swallowed her gasp of delight. They were alone because Joshua had moved his other wives into quarters he'd claimed after declaring himself the acting pastor. It was temporary, he'd assured everyone, saying, *Magdalena will soon give birth and she needs privacy for that. I will relinquish this space when Pastor and Sister Coleen return.*

It had been then that Hayley had realized Joshua's expansion had been into Pastor's quarters. It hadn't sat well with the community, but Joshua reminded them that Pastor himself had left him in charge.

Graham said that tempers were short, and Hayley had heard shouting and fights all the way back in her little cubicle. She didn't leave her space except to go to the toilets. She didn't have the energy to even listen to the discord.

Graham and Tamar had become her windows to the world of Eden. Such as it was.

You got the solar panels hooked up? she mouthed back.

Graham nodded slowly, but his eyes were sparkling. *He's enjoying this.* Her little brother had developed a taste for disruption. *God help the world once we get back.*

"I'll hook up the computer tomorrow," he whispered. "I've been carrying it out in boxes that smell like shit. Because they once held shit."

"Makes sense, then," Hayley murmured, hope blossoming. "What can I do to help you?"

"Just stay here and stay safe." He patted her stomach. "Keep little Zit safe, too."

Hayley mock-scowled at him. "Her name is Jellybean."

"Forever to be known as Princess Zit." He rolled to his heels. "Gotta go. Curfew soon."

"You're respecting curfew?" Hayley asked. "Really?"

He winked. "My stepbrothers are offended by my bouquet." He mimed twisting a knife. "So I show up extra early."

"I love you," Hayley murmured. She never let him leave now without saying it. He was in constant danger. If someone found the solar panels or the computer, they'd beat him. Or worse.

But he was twelve years old and cockier than hell. "Ditto," he said. Then he was gone, leaving her with nothing to do but think. And maybe to hope. Just a little.

ROCKLIN, CALIFORNIA
SUNDAY, MAY 28, 8:30 P.M.

Liza dropped to her knees as soon as she entered Tom's kitchen, because Pebbles had rushed to greet her, tail wagging so hard that the dog should have fallen over. Wrapping her arms around Pebbles's neck, she nuzzled her cheek against the dog's fur. "Missed you, sweet girl."

Behind her, the door to the garage closed and Tom joined her, kneeling on one knee to scratch behind Pebbles's ears. "I'm right here," he said blandly. "Did you miss me, too?"

She pivoted on the floor, wrapping her arms around his neck. "I did. Every single one of the twenty minutes since I last saw you."

He ran his hands up her back and kissed her hard. "I was two feet away."

"You were in the front seat and I was in the back seat, on the floor and under a blanket."

He'd insisted, worried that someone might be watching outside the apartment building.

"To keep you safe." He searched her face, a frown on his. "You're nervous."

"A little. I mean, deciding we're having sex, then putting it off like this? Although I should be fine with it," she added lightly. "What's twenty minutes when I've waited seven years?"

She was babbling. Because she was nervous, and only part of it was the forced delay.

Most of it was worry that she'd forced him into this.

He tipped her chin up so that he could see her face. "Did you change your mind?" he asked quietly. "Because if you did, it's all right. We can wait until—"

She silenced him with a kiss, putting everything she had into it. It was lush and hot and channeled every erotic fantasy of him that she'd ever had. He groaned deep in his throat and palmed her butt, yanking her against him. She could feel him throbbing against her, and all she wanted was his hands on every inch of her skin.

He wrenched away, breathing hard, his eyes hungry. "Why are you nervous, then?"

"I don't want you to do this because I guilted you into it."

He shifted, pressing harder into her while tightening his hold on her ass. "I'm here because I don't want to be anywhere else. Do you believe me?"

She wanted to. She cupped his face and forced herself to answer honestly. "Mostly."

"Do you want to wait?" he asked, her nerves apparently catching.

Of that answer she was certain. "Not another minute."

He exhaled in a relieved rush. "Thank God. But if you change your mind—"

She pressed her finger to his lips. "I know. But I won't. Show me your bedroom, Tom."

He closed his eyes, drawing a breath. "I'm not going to make it that far."

"Then you'll come twice," she said, then laughed when he tugged her up the stairs and into his room.

He stopped short, drinking her in. "I've wished you were here."

She loved the look in his eyes. It made her feel desired and powerful. "You have?"

He nodded, hands lifting to unbutton his shirt. "I have." He toed off his shoes. "Usually when I was trying to sleep. I'd think of you all cozy in your blankets and I'd want to rip them off you and . . . make you scream my name."

Her mouth went dry when he took off the shirt. He was . . . wow. "You did?"

"I did." He pulled the belt from his jeans and freed the button. "I'd tell myself it was impossible. That I'd ruin our friendship."

"That was . . ." She forgot what she was going to say when he slid his zipper down.

"That was?" He shoved his jeans to his knees, revealing black boxer briefs that clung like a second skin. He was hard and big and she wanted him more than she wanted to breathe.

"Um." The sound came out a dry croak. His predatory grin made her heart race and her knees weak. She took a step back, lowering herself to sit on the bed. "What was the question?"

He kicked off his jeans and pulled off his socks, making even that movement look graceful and fluid. "I said I was afraid I'd ruin our friendship. You said, 'That was . . .' That was what?"

"I have absolutely no idea."

She heard his chuckle but didn't look up, unable to take her eyes off that bulge. She could *see* him pulsing and she itched to touch. He stepped closer, bringing that delicious bulge right in front of her face. She grabbed the hem of the briefs and yanked them down. His cock slapped against his stomach and she shuddered out a sigh before closing her fingers around him.

He hissed, his hands tunneling through her hair to lift her face to his gaze. "Do you believe me now?" he demanded.

She squeezed his cock, loving the dark pleasure that flashed in his eyes. "I think so. Still not sure." She was *so* sure. She licked her lower lip. "Maybe I should do some research."

Without waiting for him to reply, she took him in her mouth. His strangled cry was the sound she didn't know she needed, and she wanted to hear it over and over again.

"Wait," he ground out, his fingers tightening in her hair. She froze, looking up his body to his face. His jaw was so tight that his cheek twitched. "Just wait."

Carefully she pulled away, not licking him even though she wanted to. "What's wrong?"

"You're still dressed. I want you naked and I don't want to come until I'm inside you."

Liza shivered. "You want me naked?" She lifted her arms. "Then do it."

Her shirt was gone before she could blink, his mouth on hers as his fingers fumbled with the clasp on her bra. A second later it went sailing over his shoulder and he was pushing her down to the bed, her feet still on the floor. He gripped her wrists and pinned them over her head, his amazing body hovering just out of reach.

"Tom," she warned, writhing beneath him. "Don't tease me."

He gave her wrists a gentle squeeze. "Hands stay here." He let her go and lowered to his knees, parting her legs. He pulled off one of her boots and then the other, tossing them over his shoulders. They landed with dull thuds somewhere. She didn't care where.

Her body was on fire, her fingers flexing above her head, gripping handfuls of the bedspread.

"I need to—" She gasped when he dragged her pants down her legs, taking her panties with them. The clothing went the way of her boots. The air was cool on her heated skin, shivers racing over her like electric waves. "Please, Tom. Please."

Then the strangled cry was hers. His big hands parted her thighs and then his mouth was on her and . . . "Oh my God," she moaned. "Tom. Don't stop. Don't ever stop."

He didn't speak, humming against her instead. His mouth, his tongue . . . God, the man's tongue was criminal. She was instantly addicted.

She was in heaven. She was flying. She was almost there.

She stiffened, her body going taut as she arched, pressing her head back as the orgasm exploded and she heard herself cry out. He licked and sucked her through it, not stopping until she collapsed to her back, panting. "Ohmygod, ohmygod," she chanted.

He kissed his way up her body, lingering on the butterfly tattoo at her hip. And then he was kissing her and she could taste herself, which was way hotter than she'd thought it would be.

He pulled back far enough to meet her eyes. She blinked, feeling dazed.

"Do you believe me now?" he asked hoarsely.

"Yes."

"Good." He twisted, giving her a view of his flawless ass before turning back, a condom in his hand. "I'll stop if you—"

"I know, dammit," she interrupted, making him smile. "Hurry."

But he didn't hurry, taking his time as he slid the condom over his cock, which was bigger than it had been before. Longer and wider. She licked her lips, tasting herself once again.

"No fair. I wanted to come with you."

His smile became a wicked grin. "Then you'll come twice."

"I see what you did there," she muttered, then gasped when his hands closed over her ribs, lifting her up the bed. Carefully, as if she were made of glass.

His grin was gone, his expression serious and intense. *This is it*, she thought. What she'd wanted for so long. She reached for him, relieved when he settled his body over hers.

Finally. "Please," she whispered, pressing soft kisses to his mouth, his jaw, his chin.

He didn't make her wait, sliding into her in a single perfect stroke.

She'd wondered if it would hurt, because he was not a small man. It did not.

She'd wondered if it would feel awkward, once it finally happened. It did not.

She'd wondered if she'd resent his Tory in that moment. She did not, because he was looking down at her with a mixture of wonder and gratitude that she hadn't ever even dared to dream of.

I love you. The words burned her tongue, but she held them back. *Not yet. Not tonight. Soon.* "Perfect," she whispered instead. "Show me. Please."

And he did. And it was perfect. Every thrust, every cry, every touch. Every clench of his jaw as he tried to make it last.

And then he hit a spot inside her that she'd never known was there, making her cry out in shocked pleasure.

"There?" he asked, his voice so deep she could barely understand the single syllable.

She couldn't say anything, so she nodded and he thrust harder, faster, his glutes bunching under her palms as she clutched him closer.

"Open your eyes," he growled. "Look at me when I make you come."

She forced her eyes open, fixed her gaze on his, and let him see everything she was feeling. He groaned and thrust, holding himself deep, and she was frozen, teetering on the precipice.

"This . . . is . . . real," he panted, punctuating each word with a punch of his hips.

Her eyes filled with tears, because she believed him. "I know."

"Now," he demanded. Bracing himself on one elbow, he ran his palm over her belly, heading down until his thumb found her clitoris and he pressed hard.

She came on an overwhelmed sob. He came with a quiet roar, head thrown back, the muscles of his neck straining until he shuddered. Shaking, he lowered himself to his forearms, still careful not to hurt her.

He kissed the corners of her eyes. "Did I hurt you? I'm sor—"

"No. You didn't." She drew a breath, trying to get hold of her emotions. "It's . . . I wanted this for so long. And . . . here you are."

His lips curved. "Here *you* are. With me. Exactly where you're supposed to be."

She cupped his cheek, her hand trembling. "We're really going to do this."

"We are." He kissed her temple. "Give me a minute. I'll be right back. Don't move."

And then he was gone, taking his warmth with him. Liza thought she should climb under the covers, but she couldn't move. She felt boneless and utterly relaxed.

Finally. It was real. The happiness was real.

ROCKLIN, CALIFORNIA
SUNDAY, MAY 28, 9:30 P.M.

Tom got rid of the condom and braced his hands on the vanity, staring at his reflection. The man who stared back was familiar, but not. It was the eyes, Tom decided. His were calm.

He was . . . happy. Deep down, no faking it.

And he owed it to the woman in his bed who'd bared her soul, telling him her secrets—how long she'd wanted him. How she'd tried to forget about him. How she'd loved and lost.

He owed her the same honesty.

He turned off the bathroom light and hurried back to her, finding her in the same place he'd left her. He picked her up and tucked her in, earning him a dreamy sigh. "Love the way you can pick me up," she murmured.

And if that weren't a stroke to his ego.

He climbed in beside her, relaxing when she cuddled in close. She rested her head on his shoulder with a contented sigh. "Thank you."

"I feel like I should be saying that to you." He stroked her hair and she petted the hair on his chest. This was a perfect moment. Too nice to spoil.

Nope. Don't even think it. He needed to tell her a few things. He should have told her before. He didn't think what he had to say would make a difference, not to his Liza, but he should have given her a choice.

"I need to tell you something."

She stiffened, her breath hitching. "What?" she asked, the single word filled with a dread that hurt his heart. She thought he was going to say that he'd made a mistake.

"Nothing like that," he promised quickly. "This was everything I thought it would be. Better. Miles better. The only mistake I made was not getting over myself sooner."

"Okay." She relaxed a little. "What is it, then?"

"I did . . . something. Something not exactly . . ." He grimaced. "Not exactly right."

She lifted her head to meet his gaze, no judgment in hers. "Tory."

He nodded. "I found her killer. Online."

She tilted her head. "Did you kill him? Because I'd be okay with that."

He blinked up at her. "No, I didn't. Not exactly, anyway."

"Well, then, whatever you did do is all right."

He smiled. "I should have known you'd say that."

"You really should have," she said, mildly chastising. "Talk to me, Tom."

"I found him, in a chat room. He . . . bragged about killing women. And then he bragged about posing as a minister to give comfort to their families."

Her jaw clenched. "Sonofabitch. What did you do? I'm sure it wasn't nearly bad enough."

"I tracked him to Tory's parents' town. He was planning to 'comfort' them. I couldn't let him do that." He studied her face, watched her eyes flash with fury and sadness. And fierce acceptance. Yes, he should have known she'd understand. "I'd been in contact with the family of one of the other victims. I thought they'd want to see him arrested. For closure. I told them where he'd be. I thought they'd wait for the police."

"But they killed him before the cops got there."

"Yes. I wanted to kill him myself. I was so angry."

She kissed his jaw. "But you didn't. Why?"

"Because there were more victims. Their families deserved to see him convicted. There may have been other victims, and those families would never have answers."

Her smile was gentle. "I told you—you are not like your father. You never could be."

"But . . ." And this was the part that he'd worried about since the day Tory's killer had died. "I called the other victim's family first. Before I called the cops."

"You think that, deep down, you wanted them to kill the bastard?"

"Maybe? Did I use them? Did I really *not* want to do the right thing?"

She lifted a shoulder. "Ultimately, the choices the other family made were theirs, just like the choices you made were yours. You didn't kill him. You called the police. You waited. The other family could have, too." She sighed, moving closer until they were nose to nose. "You are not your father. I'll tell you every day for the rest of our lives if that's what you need to hear."

His heart eased. "Thank you."

She kissed him then, soft and sweet. "Is that it? All you needed to tell me?"

"Pretty much."

"Does your family know? I only ask so I know how to respond if anyone asks a question."

"They know everything except that I called the other family first."

She nodded once. "They'll never hear it from me." She settled back against him, her head on his shoulder. "You kept him from killing anyone else, Tom. I'm proud of you."

He shuddered out a breath, stunned by how much he'd needed those words. "Same. You scare me shitless, but I'm so damn proud of you."

She pressed a kiss to his chest. "We're going to be just fine."

"We're going to be perfect."

TWENTY-FIVE

Tom set the pizza box on the bed, not really caring what was inside, because Liza was in his bed, smiling up at him. "Pepperoni, extra cheese, green peppers, and mushrooms."

She sat cross-legged with the sheet tucked under her arms. All of the interesting parts were covered, but he figured he could persuade her to uncover again later. For now, she looked very happy and extremely relaxed and he felt a little thrill knowing he'd helped with that.

Pebbles trotted through the open bedroom door, her tail wagging.

"Did you bark at the evil pizza delivery man, Pebbles?" Liza crooned.

"She always does. This guy was smart, though." Tom set a six-pack of Coke on the nightstand. "He brought dog biscuits, probably hoping to buy some goodwill."

"But?"

"But Pebbles has already forgotten about him." Because as much as he loved the dog, she wasn't very smart.

"You're a fickle girl," she told Pebbles, who'd surprisingly bypassed the pizza, making a beeline for Liza, who'd leaned over to kiss the dog's muzzle.

Okay, so Pebbles was much smarter than he'd thought. Tom stripped off the jeans he'd put on to meet the delivery guy and got under the sheet with Liza, more than pleased with the way her gaze raked over his body.

"Do we have to eat?" But then her stomach growled, making her laugh. "I guess we do."

"We need fuel." He put a slice of pizza on a paper plate and passed it over to her. "Then we can go again."

She kissed his cheek. "A man with a plan," she teased, then moaned when she bit into the pizza. "This is so much better than what Rafe got over the weekend. That was like cardboard."

He stared at her, his food forgotten, the moan kick-starting his libido.

She saw him staring and laughed again. "Eat."

He shook his head, trying to clear it. "Which pizza place did Rafe call?" he asked after he'd devoured his first piece, because he'd been much hungrier than he'd thought. "I'll avoid them."

She studied the box with a slight frown. "It might have been this one," she said. "Maybe I just didn't have any appetite that night."

He sighed and started to apologize, but she shoved another slice of pizza in his mouth.

"Don't you dare say you're sorry," she scolded. "Maybe we had to go there to get here."

He swallowed the bite he'd been force-fed. "Maybe. I still hate that I made you sad."

"So make me happy again later," she said cheekily.

He ate another piece, then pulled her hair aside so that he could reexamine the tattoo on her back. He still had so many questions about the tattoo artist. "That guy Sergio Iglesias? He did an amazing job with this."

"He did. I'm really pleased with it."

"Do you have to go back to have it colored in?"

"I do. Probably next month. I thought I'd go before I start nursing school." Her eyes narrowed suspiciously. "Why?"

"Maybe I'd like to go with you."

She clearly wasn't satisfied with that answer. "Why?"

"Maybe I'd like a day to get away with you, to take a drive. To go to lunch after your session is over. Like we did with the first tattoo. I assume wherever you went had restaurants nearby." He nearly winced because he didn't entirely believe himself.

Neither did she, because her lips twitched. "Are you trying to get me to tell you where we went on Thursday?"

"Maybe."

"*Why*, Tom? Just tell me the truth."

He sighed. "Maybe I'm curious. Maybe I just like knowing about your day. And maybe I feel bad for the guy. You said the Bureau visit sent him into hiding."

"He thought they were ICE," she said, scowling. "He has a green card, but some entitled bitch wasn't satisfied with the tattoo he did, even though she signed off on the design. She threatened him. Even got some guys who claimed to be ICE to harass him."

It was his turn to scowl now. "That's wrong."

She chuckled, leaning sideways to kiss his biceps. "You are really cute, you know that? Such a Dudley Do-Right."

"Will you stop calling me that?"

She tilted her head. "Does it really bother you?"

He sighed again. "No, not really. It's fair enough."

"Well, I'll stop anyway. You are very earnest, though." She sobered. "It *is* wrong, and he's scared to death. It wouldn't be the first time someone got deported on made-up charges."

"I'll make some calls," he promised. "Let me see what I can do."

"Thank you."

"So . . . where *did* you go?"

She laughed so loudly that Pebbles ran in circles, barking. "Oh my

God. Okay." She wiped a tear from her eye. "Monterey. If Sergio says it's okay, you can come with me next time."

"I'll still make the calls."

"Because you are sincerely earnest. Nothing about you is an act." She smiled at him and he thought he'd never get tired of the sight. "You're a good man."

"Thank you. So how did you find him?"

"Instagram and Facebook. It wasn't hard. Any one of you Feds could have done it standing on your heads. Why didn't you?"

That was a damn good question. "Raeburn didn't think it was a lead worth pursuing. It wasn't like that person had been to Eden and could tell us where to find it."

"Well, he's not wrong about part of it. William Holly—a.k.a. Boaz Travis—can't lead you to Eden. He was only eleven years old when his mother got him out."

Tom hesitated. "He's also dead."

She gaped, shocked. "How do you know that?"

"We talked to DJ's relatives—his aunt and uncle. They owned the house where Pastor's wife and kids were living when Boaz Travis went to get the Eden tattoo. The aunt and uncle didn't know who Pastor's wife and kids were, but said that the elder Belmonts had grown fond of them while they rented. They said that 'William' committed suicide."

Liza sighed sadly. "Sergio said he knew that he was an unhappy young man." She sighed again. "Daisy and I were hoping that whoever we found could give us one of the more recent Eden sites. Amos said that they reused sites, so if we found other locations we might find Eden now."

Tom hid his wince. Liza and Daisy had gone to a lot of trouble because they hadn't known that the Bureau already knew all of the old sites. That was on him. Or on Raeburn, because he'd forbidden any information sharing.

He must not have hidden his wince well enough, though, because her eyes narrowed. "You know," she whispered. "You already know the locations of all of the old Eden sites."

He sighed. "I can't talk about it."

"How did you know?" she demanded, ignoring his reluctance.

"Ephraim left some notebooks in his safe-deposit box."

She drew a breath and let it out slowly. "He mapped out the old sites, but you didn't tell us."

"I'm not allowed to discuss the case with Gideon and Mercy," he said regretfully.

"I understand need-to-know. You'll make sure I know what *I* need to know, right?"

He tipped her chin up and kissed her. "If it keeps you safe, I'll tell you everything."

"I trust you," she whispered against his mouth, then jerked away with a gasp. "Pebbles, no!"

She leaped out of bed in all her naked glory and reached for Pebbles, who was headed out of the bedroom, Liza's boot in her mouth. Tail wagging, the dog thought it was a game and ran. Liza chased her around the bed, then stopped in the doorway.

Whirling around, fists on her hips, she glared at Tom. "A little help? She listens to you."

"Because I don't let her lick my face," Tom said dryly, then openly leered at her. "Plus I'm too busy looking at you."

She rolled her eyes, but she was pleased. "That shouldn't make me forgive you as easily as it does." She stomped out and he could hear her calling to Pebbles from down the hall.

And then he heard nothing.

He waited another beat, then jumped from the bed, closing the bedroom door before running to his office. Pebbles was half in and half out, her tail still wagging furiously. When he pushed by her, he could see the boot still in her mouth. "Drop it," he ordered.

She dropped it immediately and Tom bent to scoop it up. "Here it is," he said, but Liza didn't reply. She was standing at his bulletin board, staring at the photos he'd collected.

His first thought was to tell her they were classified, but she'd already either known or figured out nearly everything about the case. Still, he strode forward, tugging at her shoulder.

"Liza, honey, don't look at those. Some of these are intense. You don't want those images in your mind."

She looked over her shoulder, incredulous. "Tom, what part of 'I was a fucking combat medic' hasn't sunk into your thick skull yet?"

He grimaced. "Right. Sorry. Still. Come back to bed with me."

Ignoring him, she pointed to the photo of DJ Belmont as a child. "Where did you get this?"

Once again he considered telling her they were classified, but she was going into Sunnyside Oaks on Tuesday morning. She deserved all of the information he could give her.

Who knew what small detail might save her life if things went sideways?

He set her boot on his desk. "Waylon Belmont's sister-in-law let me take a photo of one of the pictures she had on the wall when Croft and I interviewed her. Interestingly enough, we were at their rental house when you called—the same address as was listed on William Holly's ID. We'd gone to check it first in the event that DJ remembered the house and went back there. He'd lived there with his mother at the time of their disappearance. Pastor's wife showed up with the kids four years later. Those photos are of DJ and his father at the same age."

"Whoa," she murmured. "So you were physically sitting in front of William Holly's old house when I called you about tracking him and his tattoo to Sergio?"

"Yes." Resting his chin on the top of her head, he wrapped his arms around her waist as he studied the photo of DJ Belmont, curious as to what she saw that had her so transfixed. "Why?"

She pointed to the grainy photo he'd pulled from the old newspaper article about Pastor's crimes against his old L.A. congregation, the embezzlement and fraud. "Bo and Bernice. Look at them. Now look at DJ. They're about the same age in these photos."

Tom did as she directed, then exhaled, far more stunned than he had any right to be. Because she'd immediately seen what he should have seen, but had not. "DJ and Waylon looked alike, but Bo and DJ could have been twins," he said quietly.

"Uh-huh. And who is the common denominator?"

"Waylon. That certainly would explain how Pastor's wife magically ended up in the Belmonts' rental house. Croft and I figured that Waylon had taken them there, but we weren't sure why." He tapped a document thumbtacked at the top of the bulletin board.

She lifted on her toes to examine it. "A marriage license? I didn't know that Waylon and Pastor's wife were married. Was this while he was in prison?"

"The day he was released. Dammit, I should have seen this before."

But he'd been distracted the day he'd fixed these photos to his board. By the woman who was now scrutinizing each and every document and photo he'd collected.

"What else did Waylon's brother tell you?"

"That Pastor's wife, Margo Holly, a.k.a. Marcia Travis, kept to herself, but the elder Belmonts—DJ's grandparents—kind of adopted her kids. Holidays, school events." He shook his head at his own thickness. "Because they were Bo and Bernie's grandparents, too. By blood."

"So . . ." Liza said slowly, "Waylon and Marcia marry and, I'm assuming, get divorced because she married Pastor six months later?" She'd found the copy of Marcia and Benton Travis's marriage license on his bulletin board. "Then what? They changed their names, cooked up fake backgrounds, and applied to work at a church in L.A.? And *nobody* checked up on their résumés?"

"Back then it was easier to fake an identity and a résumé," Tom said. "And I think that many congregations have a basic trust that whoever joins them in worship is one of them. Embezzlement from churches happens all the time *still*, and the churches are more likely to forgive the crime than a corporation would be. I can get you the statistics if you're interested."

"No, I believe you. That's doubly sad, you know? Assholes who steal from churches don't just steal money. They steal trust, too."

"Yes," Tom said simply. "I don't know how many of these cases are even reported—then and now. Religious organizations—whatever the denomination—are either more willing to forgive because it's ingrained in their beliefs or they're embarrassed to have been cheated."

"I imagine it's a little bit of both," she said thoughtfully. "I wonder if Pastor knew. That the kids weren't his, I mean."

"Good question. None of this helps us find Eden, but I'm kind of invested in the story now. Once we do find Eden, and Pastor and DJ are in custody, I'd like to find Marcia and ask her."

Liza leaned into him and he tightened his hold. "Do you know where she is?"

"Not exactly. I know where she went after she left Benicia, after her daughter graduated from college and her son killed himself. I know the daughter's name was Tracy and she got married and moved away. Merle's mother still gets postcards, but with no return address."

"Bernice is still hiding," Liza said sadly. "What about Margo or Marcia or Pastor's wife, whatever you call her?"

"She married an architect in Modesto, which was when she moved out of the house in Benicia. I can't find any architects in Modesto with a wife named Margo. Once it's safe, maybe you should do your Facebook magic and track her down."

"Don't make fun," she warned.

"I'm not," he promised. "I'm totally not. I'm serious."

"Then maybe I will." She turned to look up at him. "How did you know Pastor was at Sunnyside Oaks?"

"I was able to get into Eden's bank account by tracing transfers made to Ephraim's account. I set an alert for activity and it let me know that money had been transferred to Sunnyside Oaks."

"Who did the transfer?"

"I assume Pastor did."

"Not DJ?"

Tom frowned. "I don't have any proof one way or the other, but it seems that if DJ had access to the money, he'd have taken his share a long time ago."

"Pastor's holding on to the purse strings," she murmured. "Not a shock. He must do Internet transfers, since they have a computer."

"I figured as much. I haven't been able to trace the location of whoever's moving money around, though. We could subpoena the bank's records, but it's offshore and that would take a long time."

"And Pastor and DJ might find out and move Eden again. Plus, that young woman needs help now. The one who's pregnant."

"Hayley Gibbs. She's been on my mind," Tom admitted.

"No surprise. Just like I want to save Mercy and Abigail because I didn't save my sister, you want to make sure Hayley's baby is safe because—" She cut herself off. "I'm sorry."

His heart hurt, but she wasn't the cause. "No need to be sorry. I do want Hayley safe because I couldn't save Tory and our baby. You can say her name. You can mention the baby. It's okay. I know you care."

Her smile was tremulous, as was the kiss she pressed to his jaw before turning back to study the documents on his board. She tapped a finger on Eden's bank account summary, the minimal withdrawals and the hefty quarterly deposits. "The quarterly deposits are really big," she said. "Are they making that much money from selling mushrooms?"

"The guys in Forensic Accounting think that those are investment dividends, based on the rate of growth. Pastor and DJ may keep the cash from their drug sales for operating expenses."

"Wow. Well, whoever is managing their money is doing an amazing job."

"Pastor did time in the pen for bank fraud and forgery, among other things. He was a stockbroker who skimmed money from his clients. He was pretty good at making money for his clients, so they didn't suspect him for some time. He has the skills to manage money."

"I wonder how he did his banking back then. I mean, before the Internet."

Tom hadn't expected that question. "What?"

"Well, they've been nomadic for thirty years. The Internet's only been around for, what, twenty-five years or so? And online banking is newer than that. I guess Pastor had to visit an actual bank in person in the early days. Especially if he was setting up an offshore account. And someone had to manage his investments before the Internet unless he managed to leave the compound to do it himself."

Oh my God, she's right. Tom's thoughts began to percolate. "Amos said Pastor hasn't left the compound in more than ten years. Not until now—which Amos doesn't know about, so don't tell him." His heart began to beat faster as he mentally worked through the possibilities. "The money Pastor embezzled from his church in L.A. was never found. It's likely that he parked that offshore, too. He *had* to have had a banker on the outside at the beginning. What if he still does? Their money has grown incredibly and maybe Pastor's savvy enough to invest in all the right places, but . . . what if he's had help?"

"But you'd need to subpoena the offshore bank to find out who that is—or was, right?"

"Yeah, unless . . ." A puzzle piece dropped into place. "Unless I can find someone who knew him well enough to know who he'd trust with his money."

Liza turned in his arms, her eyes wide. "Someone like his wife?"

He smiled at her. "Exactly. I mean, *if* we find her and *if* she did know who helped him set up those accounts, it's unlikely that he's still working with that person after all this time. But it's a start. There should be some evidence, like paperwork transferred from one bank to the next." He cupped her face in his hands and kissed her hard. "You are a genius, Liza Barkley."

Her cheeks went pink, but she looked pleased. "But even if you find his banker, what does that tell you?"

"If he's communicated with Pastor recently—like to maybe transfer money to Sunnyside Oaks—we can get a warrant for his computer, or even his phone records. It might be another way to locate Eden. Especially if we aren't able to get the location from either Pastor or DJ. They may never discuss it inside Sunnyside's walls, and if we arrest them, they may not talk. We have to have alternate paths to getting the information we need."

"So you're going to keep looking for Pastor's wife?"

"Yes, but secondary to getting your protection set up. I need you safe on Tuesday, and every day after that you go into that place."

She nodded. "I'm not oblivious to the danger, Tom," she said seriously. "And I am afraid. But not so afraid that I'm going to back out."

"I know. I also know that you were incredibly brave the day your friends were killed. I know that you saved a lot of lives and got hurt yourself. Molina told me the whole story. She called your old CO, who was very complimentary. You never mentioned that you got a Purple Heart."

She shrugged dismissively. "I got shot in the hip, but it wasn't life-threatening."

He brushed his fingertips over the butterfly tattoo. "Here?"

"Yeah. Got that in Chicago, a few days after Christmas."

"Why didn't you tell me?"

She shook her head. "I didn't want you to know. I didn't want to remember that day."

"But you're okay with remembering it now." A statement, not a question.

"Yes. They deserve that much. For me to remember them."

"Will you tell me someday? About the Purple Heart?"

"Yes." Her voice trembled. "But not today, okay?"

"Okay. You want to go back and finish our supper?"

"That sounds perfect."

He led her back to the bedroom, grabbing her boot from his desk on the way out. As he expected, Pebbles sat at attention outside the bedroom door, sniffing the air.

He opened the door and told Pebbles, "Down." Immediately she dropped to her belly. "Good girl."

While Liza climbed back into bed, Tom dug his phone from the pocket of his trousers, hoping that he hadn't missed any messages. Raeburn had put them all on call, after all.

Thankfully there was nothing from Raeburn, but he did have a message. "Huh."

Liza paused, a slice of pizza an inch from her mouth. "What? Is something wrong?"

"No, it's a text from Jeff Bunker." He turned it so that she could see the message from the sixteen-year-old journalism major.

Got a promising lead on search for Craig Hickman. Expect news early in the am East Coast time. Will text when I know more.

"Who's Craig Hickman?" Liza asked.

"He was the college kid who first exposed Pastor's embezzlement from the church in L.A. He was beaten severely and then his parents' house was burned down. Pastor's followers were suspects. Craig disappeared shortly after that."

Her eyes widened. "He was killed?"

"No. One of Jeff's journalist mentors said he changed his name and moved away."

"That was probably smart," she murmured. "Why is Jeff looking for him?"

"I think he wants to write the story of his career when Eden's found. He's looking for all the background, and Craig Hickman is important because he started it all when he exposed Pastor's crimes.

He's keeping me up to date because I'm curious as well. Let me text him a quick thanks and then we can eat."

She smiled. "And then we can play."

GRANITE BAY, CALIFORNIA
MONDAY, MAY 29, 3:30 A.M.

Cop or Fed?

DJ studied the figure behind the wheel of the black sedan parked in front of Kowalski's house. The sedan had been there when he'd arrived hours before and hadn't moved. The driver wore a dark suit and tie. So probably a Fed. Possibly an undercover cop.

He thought of the trash he'd left in the can the day he'd packed his things and left the Yuba City house. Kowalski had touched a few of those cans. Maybe they'd gotten his prints, too.

That was a satisfying thought. But it could also be someone from a rival gang, out to end Kowalski, which wasn't a bad thought, either. Whoever it was, DJ needed to get rid of them before he made his own move.

The fence around Kowalski's—or Anthony Ward's—large estate was tall and likely electrified. However, the satellite view on Google Maps showed several large trees along the fence at the rear of the property. Depending on how old the satellite photos were, those trees could be even taller or possibly trimmed so that their limbs no longer hung over the fence. He was banking on the former, because that was how he planned to breach Kowalski's stronghold.

Kowalski had taught him that move, too. *He would be so proud.*

He'd thought a lot about Kowalski and had concluded that the man couldn't be convinced to back off. DJ needed to either kill him or get the weapons he was looking for, finish the job he'd started with Mercy and Gideon, then disappear.

It was possible that none of Kowalski's weapons were stored here, but DJ wasn't leaving until he'd found either enough firepower to take out the Sokolov house with Mercy Callahan in it or something to trade for what he needed. If he had to, he'd take Kowalski's kid.

DJ really didn't want to do that. Hostages were messy, but he needed as many weapons as he could get, and he wasn't naive enough to believe that Kowalski would just give him some. If Kowalski played ball, DJ would return the kid. Worst case, he could leave the kid at the Smythes' house and Mrs. Smythe would find him once she returned.

And if Mercy wasn't in the Sokolovs' house when he blew it sky-high? She'd show up to the funerals of whoever had been. DJ wasn't picky and didn't care if he killed the entire Sokolov family. He wanted Mercy and Gideon gone. Then he'd pick off Amos for stealing his truck and Daisy Dawson for shooting his shoulder.

Which, while not at a hundred percent, was far better than it had been a week ago. After a few nights in a soft bed, nightly soaks in Smythe's Jacuzzi tub, and doses of the painkillers he'd found in Smythe's medicine cabinet, his arm was steadily improving.

He still couldn't lift his rifle, so he now had it propped on the trunk of the Honda Civic he'd stolen from the woman near the airport.

It was time to get this show on the road. Kowalski's wife had finally turned out her bedroom light an hour before. He wasn't sure where the kid's bedroom was, but he had a decent idea. One of the windows had a very faint glow, like it might have been a night-light. He'd soon find out.

Centering the sedan's driver in his sight, DJ pulled the trigger. He wouldn't have a lot of time now, especially if the driver had been on his radio. His rifle had a damn good suppressor, but glass still made a shattering sound. And the driver would be unable to check in.

Someone could show up soon, so he slid the rifle to his back, adjusting the strap, then grabbed his nearly empty duffel bag. It was for carrying away any treats he came across. Hopefully lots and lots of rifles, piles of ammo, and a pound or two of explosives.

His handgun was holstered at his waist. In the duffel was the service weapon he'd taken from the cop he'd killed the night before, the drugged hamburger he'd taken from the schoolteacher, and zip ties that he'd taken from the dead cop's gun belt. He'd also brought rope, duct tape, and a can of black spray paint in case he encountered any security cameras.

Another of Kowalski's tricks.

He was sprinting from his car toward the house when a burly man came from a gate in the electric fence. The man approached the black sedan from the passenger side and peered in.

DJ dropped to a crouch behind a tree and slid his rifle from his shoulder, propping it on the ground. He slithered to his stomach and checked his scope.

Well, damn. He knew the burly guy. He'd met with him several times. He was Kowalski's right-hand man, responsible for the Chicos' security. DJ centered the crosshairs on the man's head and pulled the trigger.

The guy dropped like a rock.

DJ ran to Kowalski's security man and checked for a pulse. There was none, so he helped himself to the man's gun, phone, and keys, stowing everything but the keys in the duffel. The keys went into his own pocket.

He was relieved to find the tree near the back fence standing tall. The lowest limb was a little too high for him to easily reach, so he fashioned a pulley from the rope and a few minutes later was standing on the limb, looking into Kowalski's windows. The house was grand, of that there was no doubt. It had to be ten thousand square feet, the backyard enormous.

So far, so good. No lights in the house came on, so the wife and kid were still sleeping. There was no sign of the dog mentioned in the teacher's notes, which was a relief. It would take precious minutes for the drugs to incapacitate a Rottweiler. Plus, he liked dogs.

He heard the next security guard before he saw him, softly speaking into a walkie-talkie.

"Keating isn't answering. Be on alert and do not leave your post," the man commanded. Once he came into view, DJ realized he knew this guy, too. They'd done a drop-off a few years ago.

Drawing his handgun, DJ waited until the man was walking under the tree limb, then fired two quick shots into the man's head. He then jumped from the limb to the ground, landing in a crouch a few feet from the remains. He headed for the garage door, figuring the six-car garage was as good a place as any to store weapons, as the house appeared to have no basement.

He saw the third guy long before the guy saw him. Creeping along the back wall, the third security guy was definitely lower tier. He was young, maybe twenty years old, and scared.

DJ shoved his handgun to the back of the young man's head. "If you make a sound, I will kill you. Nod if you understand. Do not speak."

The man nodded frantically and did not speak.

DJ patted him down and found a knife and two guns. He added them to his duffel bag. "Good. I'm looking for weapons. Take me to them and I'll let you go."

The guy began walking toward the garage, where he unlocked an exterior door into the cavernous space. The entire wall was covered with cabinets and safes, and while the garage could easily hold six vehicles, the only ones inside were a van, a pickup, and a red Jaguar.

The young man made a grunting sound, and DJ realized that he was asking for permission to speak. "Go ahead. But if you scream, you're dead. I got nothing to lose."

"I don't know the combinations to the safes. I don't have keys for the cabinets, either."

DJ took the first guard's keys from his pocket. "Open all the cabinets." The safes would have to wait for another day.

The third guard complied and a few minutes later, all the cabinet doors were open. DJ was thunderstruck. There were enough guns here to stage a revolution.

DJ dumped the contents of his duffel bag on the passenger seat of the panel van, then handed the bag to the guard. "Three rifles. Ten boxes of ammo. Six handguns. Fill it."

The man sprang into action and a minute later returned with the bag mostly full. "Here," he said, his hands shaking.

"Explosives?"

The man swallowed. "There's some C-4, but it's in the safe. Dynamite is in the cabinets, though."

It would have to do. "Bring a box and put it in the back of the van."

The man complied, scurrying like a mouse. When he was done, DJ checked the contents of the bag before stowing it on the floorboard of the van. "Keys."

The man handed him the keys. "I did what you said. I'm gonna go now."

"You must be new," DJ said dryly.

"Real new. My first night was last week."

"Should have picked a different boss." DJ shot the man in the head, firing a second time before checking his pulse to be sure he was dead. He found the garage door opener in the van and hit the switch. When the door rose, he wasn't sure what he'd find, but he was pleasantly surprised to see no one there.

He drove down the driveway and past the black sedan to where he'd left the Honda Civic. Leaving the head of security's phone in the van, he transferred the box of dynamite and the duffel bag full of weapons from the van to the Civic, then slid behind its wheel. And drove away.

Two in the win column. If Kowalski had been home, he hadn't done a thing to save his men. Hell, the man probably had a panic room or some kind of a bunker he could hide in.

If he hadn't been home, he'd be hearing all about this from his missus.

Either way, DJ had gotten what he'd come for.

ROCKLIN, CALIFORNIA
MONDAY, MAY 29, 4:00 A.M.

Tom bolted upright in bed, waking Liza. Hearing the ringing of a phone, she propped up on her elbow to see him grabbing at all three of his cells, looking adorably confused.

"It's this one," she said, taking the other two from his hands. "The one that says 'Jeff Bunker' on the screen. You want to touch the button that says 'accept.'"

He gave her the stink-eye as he answered the call. "Jeff? . . . Well, yeah, I was asleep, but it's all right. What do you have?"

Liza sat up, giving him a stink-eye of her own. *Speaker*, she mouthed.

"Gonna put you on speaker, if that's okay?" He did so, then said, "Liza is here, just so you know."

Jeff was silent a moment, then cackled. "She's there? In your bed? Dammit, Liza."

"What?" Liza asked.

"I lost the bet. Shit. Zoya's going to make me pay, too. Thanks a lot, Liza."

She narrowed her eyes at the phone. "You bet on me and Tom?"

"What?" Tom burst out. "What the hell are you talking about?"

"Apparently Jeff has been betting on if we'd get together," Liza said dryly, then patted Tom's arm. "Are you awake now?"

"It wasn't *if*," Jeff said, still cackling. "It was *when*. I said it would be after Tom solved the case. Zoya figured before. I guess I don't mind paying up, though." He snickered. "Go, Liza."

Tom was shaking his head, utterly nonplussed. "You bet on me and Liza?"

"Keep up, honey," Liza said lightly.

Jeff laughed louder. "Oh my God. Am I the first to know? Oh, please say I can tell."

Liza met Tom's eyes. *Are we keeping this a secret?* she wanted to ask.

His eyes narrowed at her and then at the phone. "Of course you can tell. This isn't a secret."

"Good." Jeff sounded serious now. "I wouldn't have told if you'd said no. I'm getting better at not being an asshole."

"I know," Tom said gently, then yawned. "What do you have?"

"I found Craig Hickman."

Tom blinked. "I thought you were going to text me."

"I was, but this might be important. His new name is Zachary Goodman. He's a reporter for a local paper in Richmond, Virginia, and teaches English at the high school. I'm going to tell you how I found him first, because that explains what he knows."

Tom pulled his tablet to his lap, ready to take notes. "Whenever you're ready, kid."

"So. You remember that Hickman was beaten severely after he helped expose Pastor's crimes in his old L.A. church, right? That was after Pastor and his family disappeared. The L.A. church was left in shambles, with parishioners having screaming fights and flinging threats at each other."

"Those who wanted Pastor to stay versus those who wanted him gone," Tom said. "I know."

"Some of those were death threats, but Hickman kept digging. All of what I'm telling you came from Erica Mann. She's the L.A. reporter who wrote most of the newspaper articles back when the scandal first broke thirty years ago. The two have kept in touch all this time. I contacted her after we texted yesterday and asked her point-blank if she could get a message to Hickman. She was quiet for a long time, then said she'd forward him a message with my contact info but couldn't guarantee he'd answer it. But he did. He called me right before I called you."

"What did Mr. Hickman tell you?" Liza asked.

"That he'd been contacted twelve years ago by Erica Mann. She'd received an e-mail from a woman who wished to make him reparations. Hickman was interested only because he wanted to know who was looking for him. He's . . . really paranoid, even now. So he contacted the woman using an untraceable phone. He actually took the train to New York City to make the call because he didn't trust that they couldn't find him and he didn't want his family involved. He recognized her voice right away, even after all those years. It was Pastor's wife."

Tom glanced at Liza with a frown. "Why did she want to find him?"

"She said she felt terrible for the wrongs done to his family. I mean, this was twenty years later, so Hickman wasn't interested in her apologies and told her so. She said she understood, and that she wanted to offer him reparations in the amount of—wait for it—a million bucks."

Liza gasped. "Oh my God."

Tom whistled softly. "Wow. Did he take it?"

"No, but he didn't turn her down right away. He talked to his parents first. Hickman didn't want it for himself. He figured it was blood money, but his folks had lost everything, so he offered it to them. They didn't want it, either. So Hickman contacted her back and said no, but that if she was truly serious about reparations, she'd donate the cash to an L.A. charity for the homeless, for drug addicts, or for LGBTQ youth. All were groups that Pastor preached against."

"Did she?" Liza asked.

"She did. About three days later, there was an announcement that one of the LGBTQ youth shelters in L.A. had received an anonymous million-dollar donation. Hickman didn't know what had made her contact him or if she'd actually changed, but he was still suspicious. He knew that Pastor had left with some of the wealthiest of the congregation, all of whom had sold everything they owned, just like Amos did. Hickman figured a million bucks was a drop in the bucket to them and that if they really wanted to find him, they might donate the money as a trap."

"Ordinarily I'd say he was paranoid, but not in this case," Tom said.

"I know, right? He hired a private detective to trace her phone call," Jeff went on. "The call came from a Margo Kitson in Walnut Creek, California. You'll find her online."

Tom was already typing. "Oh my God, here she is. Margo Kitson. Married to Hugh Kitson. Here's her photo." He turned the tablet so that Liza could see.

A woman in a floor-length evening gown stood with a man in a tuxedo. When Tom zoomed in on the woman's face, Liza could see that it was an older version of the woman in the grainy photo with Pastor and the then-five-year-old twins on Tom's bulletin board.

"Is that the political fund-raiser from last year?" Jeff asked. "I found that one, too. Was going to send you the links. I have their address, too, if you're interested."

"I just found it," Tom said. "This is amazing. Thank you."

"If you can tell me where the million bucks came from without having to kill me, I'd really like to know," Jeff said. "I think Hickman would like to know what caused her to reach out to him in the first place. She wouldn't tell him when they talked years ago. That's all I got."

"That's a lot," Liza said warmly. "You did good, Jeff."

"Well," Jeff said, sounding embarrassed. "Least I can do for Mercy Callahan. If you can eliminate this threat to her and the others, I'll be glad. Are you going to Walnut Creek, Tom?"

"I am. I'd already put in for a personal day. I figured Rafe would need help getting the guests to and from the airport. But the security firm is doing a good job and there will be an FBI presence at the Sokolovs' for at least another day or two."

"I know. I'm here," Jeff said glumly. "It's like we're in prison. I hope it's over soon."

"Your mouth, God's ear." Tom held his finger over the end button. "We done?"

"Yep. I'd go to sleep, but I want to be the first one in the kitchen when Irina wakes up so I can tell her that she's out twenty bucks."

"She bet, too?" Tom asked, clearly affronted.

"Oh yeah. We had ten people in the pool."

Liza chuckled quietly, patting Tom's hand. "Who won?"

"Karl," Jeff grumbled. "He always wins. Zoya and I had a side bet that she won. But I get to announce it, so I'm good. Bye."

The call ended and Tom set the phone and his tablet aside. "We're going to Walnut Creek."

"We as in me and you?" Liza asked, hoping. "Or you and Croft?"

"I'll see if she wants to come with us."

Liza beamed up at him. "Thank you. It means a lot to me to help right now."

"I know." He kissed her lightly. "Will this be enough, though? Once we get Belmont in custody and the folks in Eden to safety, will your need to help be satisfied, or will I need to always worry that you're exposing yourself to danger?"

She wanted to frown at him for asking the question, but she supposed it was fair. She was trying to make amends for the people she hadn't saved. "It should be enough. By July I'll be in nursing school and can focus all that guilt on getting good grades and being a damn good nurse."

"The best." He shut off the bedside light and slid back down until he was under the sheets with her. "You wake up unfairly chipper."

"I was a soldier," Liza said, snuggling into him when he wrapped his arm around her. His chest was the nicest of pillows. "We learned to sleep with one eye open."

"I bet you'll go right back to sleep, won't you?"

"Why?"

"Because I'm awake now." He guided her hand to his erection. "What do you say?"

She wrapped her fingers around him and squeezed, his answering hiss like music. "Yes."

TWENTY-SIX

Tom reached for his coffee cup, frowning when he found it empty. He'd been looking for a way into Sunnyside's security network for the past few hours and had come up with nothing.

Liza had gone back to sleep after he'd made love to her for the second time, but he'd been unable to quiet his mind. All he'd been able to think was that she was going into a hostile situation from which she might not return. And that he'd lose her after just finding her.

So he'd crept from bed, kissing her forehead as she'd burrowed her cheek into his pillow, muttering for him to come back. He'd promised he was just getting a drink of water, but he'd returned to his office.

He had nothing for his trouble except a sleepless night.

A creak in the floorboards had him looking up a second before she appeared in the doorway, holding two cups of coffee.

"Did you sleep at all?" Liza asked.

"No. Is one of those for me?"

She placed the mug next to his keyboard. "You said you were getting up for some water."

"I couldn't sleep. I'm sorry."

She put her cup down and moved to stand at his back. "Lean forward."

He obeyed, then groaned when her hands did that magical thing to the muscles in his back.

"You're all tight."

He groaned again, for a much different reason. "I said that to you last night."

"Douchebag," she said fondly. "What are you doing?"

"Trying to get a toehold in Sunnyside's security network. I still don't have access to their cameras and alarms."

"I thought you did," she said, confused. "You saw the personnel records and patient records."

He folded his arms on his desk, letting his head fall forward. "They're on a different network, not connected to the rest. I got into the personnel and patient databases because one of the night nurses clicked on a link in a phishing e-mail. I honestly was shocked that it worked."

She worked her thumbs into the base of his neck, the way she knew that he liked. "Where did you get the e-mail address for the night nurse?"

"Guessed, mostly. Did an info-at with a bunch of different extensions."

"But the security network has been harder to breach."

"Yeah. I've sent e-mails to a few others on the list, like the facility accountant and network administrator. All the e-mails have links that will let me in, but nobody's opened them yet. Today's a damn holiday."

She gentled her touch, pressing a kiss to his neck. "Always wanted to do that when I was massaging you."

"Any time you want."

"The massage or the kiss?" she asked, amused.

"Either. Both. Just don't stop."

She leaned forward to kiss his cheek before returning to his back. "How did you know they were doing background checks on me if you couldn't see the security network?"

"I'm not going to be able to get anything past you, am I?"

"No, and answer the question."

"I embedded Trojans in the résumés you and the two FBI agents uploaded with your applications. When the HR manager clicked on your résumés, I got access to her computer. That's where I got the e-mail addresses for the accountant and network admin."

"I did not like the HR manager," Liza muttered. "She was smug, but I guess that's the least of their sins. You'll be able to get them for all the others, right?"

"I hope so. The problem is that the warrants only covered information on Pastor and/or DJ. Nothing else I see online or hear through your comm device is usable."

"What if *I* see stuff? You know, as a legitimately hired employee? Can I report any illegal activity that *I* see?"

He looked over his shoulder, his grin sharp. "Take lots of notes."

"Good. Are we going to Walnut Creek this morning?"

She was dressed, he noted. She'd even put on makeup, which she did not need. "Yes. I've been trying to reach Croft for the last hour, but—" His phone began to buzz with an incoming call from Croft. "Speak of the devil."

Liza stopped her massage, retreating to a chair in the corner. "I won't eavesdrop."

Her years in the army had taught her about classified information, and, other than the night when she'd listened in on his conversation with Raeburn, she'd always been hyper-respectful.

"Good morning," he said to Croft when he answered, keeping her off speaker.

"I saw your calls, but I was in the middle of a crime scene."

All of the stress that Liza had worked out returned in a blast. "What now?" he asked wearily.

Liza frowned but said nothing.

"I'm at Anthony Ward's compound in Granite Bay. We've got a dead Fed and three more bodies. All male, ranging in age from nineteen to forty-five. Angelina Ward and her children are gone. Their suitcases are gone and there's no sign of foul play inside the main house. The maid discovered the bodies this morning when she arrived for work."

"Who of ours?" Tom asked heavily.

"Wainright."

"Goddammit. He was a nice guy." The man had gone out of his way to be kind when Tom had first arrived in Sacramento in January. "When was he killed?"

"Sometime between three a.m. and six a.m. He'd made his last check-in at three. The maid arrived at six. His replacement was due at seven."

"I can be there in thirty minutes." He just needed to shower and change. Walnut Creek would need to wait for now.

"No, that's not necessary. Raeburn wants you to continue getting security ready for Liza's first day tomorrow. Plus, you're technically off the clock at the moment."

"We both know the second one means nothing."

"Raeburn said that, but Molina insisted you be given the time. She's worried about burnout."

"Yeah, I got a lecture."

"You mean the 'marathon, not a sprint' lecture? Because she gave me that one, too."

"That's the one. What else do you have from the scene?"

"The wife left her cell phone behind, along with all of her electronics. All in a neat pile on the spotless kitchen counter."

"She was afraid her husband was tracking her," Tom murmured. Liza's frown deepened, but she remained silent.

"I think so," Croft said. "Especially with the way she was glancing up at the camera when we talked to her on Friday. The maid said that the garage contained three vehicles when she left last night—a Jag, a pickup, and a white panel van. The van and the Jag were gone. We're looking for the Jag. We found the panel van a short distance away, empty. Next to it were tire treads that matched those left by the car Belmont stole on Saturday night."

"We still don't have an ID on the female victim?"

"Not yet. Her face wasn't . . . appropriate to share with the media."

"I remember," Tom said grimly. He'd see that woman's face in his mind for a long time.

"Yeah." Croft sighed. "The garage was lined with cabinets, and guess what they held?"

"I'm afraid to ask."

"Enough weapons to keep ballistics busy matching them to past crime scenes. Looks like there was also a box missing from the dynamite cabinet. The cabinets were all unlocked. There are a few safes too, but they weren't opened, and we haven't blown them yet. Bomb squad is afraid of what they'll find."

"*Fuck*." Possession of dynamite gave DJ an even greater range. "And Kowalski?"

"In the wind. He may have taken his wife and kids away, but I don't think so. Not with the way her devices were all stacked so neatly. It felt like a fuck-you."

Tom agreed. "I planned to make a small day trip today. I can cancel if I need to."

"Where?" Croft asked, drawing the word out to several syllables.

"I got a lead on Pastor's wife. I think she's living in Walnut Creek, married to an architect named Hugh Kitson. That's why I kept trying to reach you this morning. I thought you might join me. I want to know who set up Pastor's bank accounts thirty years ago. We can follow any handoffs over the years to discover whoever's helping him manage his money now."

"Huh." Croft was silent for a beat. "That makes sense. Where did you get the lead?"

"From Jeff Bunker, the journalism student who brought us Cameron Cook."

"You're an interesting partner, Hunter, I gotta say. I'll let Raeburn know where you are. He can call you if he wants you back here. Have you busted into Sunnyside's network yet?"

"No," he grunted. "Not for lack of trying. I'm just going to have to wait for one of those e-mails to play out. What about the three bodies found at the scene? Have you ID'd them?"

"No, but we think they were Kowalski's security. Keep me updated and I'll do the same."

Croft ended the call and he met Liza's gaze. "Nobody you know or need to know," he said.

"Okay."

He was surprised. "Okay?"

"If you thought I needed to know to keep me safe, you'd tell me."

He smiled at her and the words were suddenly there, needing to break free. "You know I love you, right?"

She sucked in a breath, her eyes growing bright with unshed tears. But she smiled back. "I think I figured that out. But it's awfully nice to hear."

He pushed away from his desk and knelt before her. "I love you, Liza Barkley."

She cupped his face in her hands. "I've been waiting to hear that for seven years."

He turned to kiss her palm. "And?"

She smiled down at him, her dimple popping. "Thank you?"

He poked her lightly in the ribs. "Say it."

She rested her forehead on his. "I love you, Tom Hunter. I always have."

He drew a breath. "You're right. It's awfully nice to hear."

They stayed there for a long moment, happy in their bubble. Then Tom sighed. "I need to get dressed, which is the exact opposite of what I want to do. But Raeburn could call me in, so if we're going to get to Walnut Creek, we'd better go now."

She sighed. "I'll walk Pebbles and put your coffee in a travel mug. Meet me downstairs."

DJ shifted in the driver's seat of the Civic. He'd been sitting in this same position outside Daisy Dawson's radio station since eight. Her car wasn't in the lot, but she was on the air.

The package DJ had addressed to her had been delivered, thanks to a college kid who looked so squeaky clean that nobody would have suspected him of wrongdoing. He'd seen the kid riding by on his bike and asked if he'd make a private delivery.

It's a peace offering for my girlfriend, DJ had explained earnestly. *I fucked up and hurt her feelings and she's not taking my calls. I got her a stuffed animal and chocolate. Think it'll work?*

In reality, the stuffed animal and chocolate had come from Smythe's house. The explosives were in the stuffed animal, a very rudimentary bomb, detonated with a common alarm clock.

He'd built two bombs, in fact. The first was a minute away from detonating inside the radio station, having been delivered by the random kid to whom he'd paid twenty bucks. It would be worth every penny.

It wouldn't be a big explosion. The box he'd taken from Kowalski's garage had been filled with a variety of stick sizes. DJ had chosen a quarter stick for Daisy Dawson's package, the size used in cherry bombs and fireworks.

He wanted the station evacuated so that he could finish what he'd started on Friday morning. Hopefully Gideon was in there, too. He'd kill them both and then he'd wait for Mercy to surface, either at their funeral or at the Sokolovs' house.

He'd driven by on his way out this morning, sticking to the street a block over. He'd spied no fewer than six guys patrolling, and that was just a two-second glimpse through the houses on the other side of the street. He wasn't getting close to the Sokolov house anytime soon.

So he'd arranged for their package to be delivered the following day by a private courier service. He'd drop it off as soon as he was finished here. Their package contained a significantly larger load. Four full sticks. If it didn't kill everyone in the Sokolov house, it would damage them severely. Hospitalize them at the very least.

Either way—whether at the hospital or at a funeral—he'd get close enough to Mercy to eliminate her. He needed to do it soon. Pastor was getting well enough to watch the news. He wanted Mercy's murder to have cleared the news cycle by then.

If it hadn't been for that bitch blocking his shot at the eye doctor last week, he'd have finished her off already. He'd put her on the list, too, just because.

DJ checked the time. "Three, two—" The explosion was audible from where he sat, the windows in his car rattling for a second before settling down. *Perfect.*

Except . . . He frowned. People were coming out the front doors of the building, but the two radio personalities kept talking as if nothing had happened.

Could the booth be that soundproofed? He hadn't expected that.

"—come out this weekend," the male show host was saying. "What do you think, Poppy? Will we have good weather for the festival? Poppy?"

"I'm sorry, Jake," Daisy Dawson replied, her tone having changed to one of concern. "I wasn't listening. There's been a small explosion at KZAU."

"*What?*" Jake exclaimed. "How? Why?"

"Nobody knows yet. They've evacuated the building," Daisy said. "If you're not sleeping in on this holiday morning and are out and about, you should avoid the area around the station."

"Come out," DJ growled. "Now."

Sirens were already blaring and the station employees were standing on the curb, wringing their hands. Smoke had started billowing already.

"We're broadcasting remotely," Daisy said, "so we're safe. Please, we're asking you to stay away from KZAU so that first responders can take care of our people and put out the fire."

DJ stared at his car radio in shock. "Remotely?" he whispered. Then his temper exploded. "Mother*fucking* sons of *bitches*." This had all been for nothing.

His attack on Gideon last week had done this. *You're a goddamn fool, Belmont.* He'd shot at Gideon and now Daisy was being guarded, her location kept secret.

Hands shaking with rage, he backed out of his parking space and drove past the fire truck speeding toward the station. Getting the second package to the Sokolovs was even more important now, but he'd have to be smarter. They'd be on their guard.

He had to think of another way to get the second package into the Sokolov home. "Fuck."

WALNUT CREEK, CALIFORNIA
MONDAY, MAY 29, 9:30 A.M.

The Kitson home was nice. Not as big as the Sokolovs' house, but fancier. "What if she slams the door in our faces?" Liza asked, nervous now that they were here. She'd driven while he'd continued to monitor the Sunnyside communications he could see.

"We'll get a subpoena to get her to tell us about Pastor's banker." Tom took her hand, giving it a squeeze as they walked to the door. "Let me talk for now," he murmured before he knocked.

The door was opened by the woman who'd worn the evening gown in the photo. Marcia Travis—a.k.a. Marcia Hampton, a.k.a. Margo

Kitson née Holly—smiled at them politely. "This neighborhood has an ordinance against soliciting." She started to close the door.

"I'm Special Agent Tom Hunter, FBI." He showed her his badge and the woman's face froze. "This is my associate, Miss Barkley. We'd like to talk to you."

After her initial shock, Marcia's eyes flickered with fear, then shame. "I . . ." She looked at her very expensive shoes. When she looked up, she was resigned. "I've been expecting you."

Liza *hadn't* been expecting that, but Tom was relaxed. "May we come in, ma'am?"

Marcia drew a breath and stepped back so that they could enter. "Please. Can I offer you something to drink? Coffee or tea?"

"No, ma'am," Tom said. "Can we sit and talk?"

"Of course." Marcia clasped her hands together as she led them into a sitting room.

Liza sat on a small sofa next to Tom while Marcia took the closest wingback chair.

"How did you find me?" she asked.

"Through a reporter who rejected your offer of reparations."

"Mr. Hickman," Marcia murmured. "I hope he's well."

Not responding to that, Tom studied her for so long that the woman began to shift uncomfortably. "How would you prefer to be addressed, ma'am? We have a number of names."

"Margo Kitson is who I've been for fourteen years. Or who I aspire to be. Call me Margo."

"All right, Margo." Tom looked around the room, his gaze pointedly pausing on the framed photographs lining the mantel over the fireplace. "Your daughter?"

"Yes. Tracy." Margo rose, retrieving a family photograph and handing it to Tom.

Margo and her husband Hugh stood with a younger blond woman. *Bernice*, Liza thought. Bo was missing from the family portrait, having killed himself.

A boy and a girl, both about eight years old, stood in front of Margo and Hugh. Two older children stood in front of Bernice and another man. They looked to be middle-school-aged.

Tom pointed to the children. "Your grandchildren?"

"The two oldest. They're Tracy's children. Chris is twelve and Robin is eleven."

"When you say Tracy, you mean Bernice," Tom said and she winced.

"Yes, but she no longer answers to that name. The younger children are mine, with Hugh."

Wow, Liza thought, busily doing the math. Margo had been thirty-three when she'd escaped L.A. and gone to Eden, thirty-eight when she'd escaped Eden and gone to Benicia. If those kids were eight years old, then Margo had conceived at age fifty-four.

Margo chuckled dryly. "I can see you figuring numbers in your head, Miss Barkley."

"I'm sorry," Liza said honestly. "I'm going to be a nurse. I can't help but think of how unusual your pregnancy must have been."

Margo lifted a slender shoulder. "Hugh loves my daughter and Tracy's babies were his grandchildren from day one. He did want babies of his own, though. So we tried." She shuddered. "Lots of fertility drugs. But it was worth it. It made him so happy."

Tom set the photo on the end table. "You said you were expecting us. Why?"

"Not you, per se. But I saw a news special a month ago, the one about the serial killer in Sacramento?"

"You saw the locket," Tom murmured. "The Eden locket."

Liza knew the news special Margo was talking about. She'd seen it as well. It was an account of the serial killer who'd murdered so many women. The reporter had briefly interviewed Daisy, who'd found the locket when she'd fought and escaped the killer.

Margo nodded. "The locket was only featured for a few seconds, but my heart nearly stopped. I've . . ." She blew out a breath. "I've been trying to figure out how to tell my husband. I wanted to go to law enforcement and tell them what I knew, but I couldn't blindside Hugh that way. Especially if I was held accountable for my part in Ben's scheme."

Ben. "Benton Travis," Liza said. The name Pastor had been given at birth.

"Yes. He stole a lot of money from our church, the one in L.A. I didn't know about it at first, but I didn't tell anyone when I did. I know that was wrong. Now I'm going to have to tell Hugh. He's going to be very disappointed in me, but he'll support me. I hope." She folded her hands in her lap. "What do you want to know?"

Liza thought Tom would begin with the banker but was stunned when he asked, "Did Pastor know that Waylon fathered your children?"

Margo's mouth fell open, her laugh brittle. "You certainly go straight to the hard questions, Agent Hunter. No. He never knew. I think . . . I don't know what he would have done."

"So you continued your relationship with Waylon after your divorce."

Margo nodded. "Waylon was my first love."

"Why did you divorce?" Tom asked.

She sighed. "It was this thing that Ben and Waylon cooked up between them. Ben figured they could start a church and get donations. Then he realized that if he became the minister of an established church—a wealthy one—he could have a steady income for not a lot of work."

"You were at the L.A. church for ten years," Tom said. "That's a long time."

"Ben found that he liked it. He always believed himself superior to everyone else. Being a pastor let him act out that role. Waylon had all the tattoos and looked big and bad, but he was sweet. Ben was the brains, but he was . . . what's the word the kids are using? A douchebag."

Liza had to swallow a startled laugh at hearing the word fall from this stylish woman's lips.

"He was a born swindler," Margo went on. "He and Waylon met in prison and . . . I guess Waylon was as snowed by Ben as everyone else. Me included, for a while. By the time we realized what a monster Ben was, it was too late."

"Waylon brought you to his parents when he helped you escape Eden," Tom said. "You lived in their house on Elvis Lane."

Margo nodded. "I was terrified that Ben would come looking for us. I didn't step foot from that house for years."

"Did Waylon's parents know that they were the children's grandparents?" Liza asked.

"They did. My William and Waylon's other son, DJ, resembled each other."

"Did you know that Waylon produced bodies that he found in a ravine and claimed they were yours?" Tom asked abruptly.

Margo gasped, all the color draining from her face. "What? No. That's impossible."

"That's why Pastor didn't come for you. He believed you were dead," Tom said. "No one is sure who those people were, but Waylon brought back the remains of a woman and two children."

"No." Margo shook her head violently. "*No.* Waylon would not do that."

"He did." Tom was insistent, but gently so. "He did again when Gideon Reynolds escaped eight years after you did."

"Gideon? I don't . . ." She looked away, thinking, then her gaze flashed back. "There was a little boy whose mother came to Eden, not long before we left. His name was Gideon."

Tom nodded. "His younger sister was Mercy. She was only a year old when you escaped. But if you saw that news program on the serial killer, you saw her, too. Mercy Callahan was thirteen when her mother got her out. Mercy was married to Ephraim Burton for a year."

Margo looked as if she'd be sick. "Not him."

Her reaction made Liza's stomach churn, thinking about what Mercy had suffered.

Margo twisted her fingers together, nerves on display. "That's why I ran. My daughter was going to be twelve. I *hated* that rule. I tried to get Ben to change it, but he wouldn't. I knew that my daughter was going to be given to one of those brutes and . . . I couldn't let that happen. Neither could Waylon. So he got us out."

"Who made the rule about twelve-year-olds being married?" Tom asked.

"Ben did, but it was because of Ephraim. He got several of the younger girls pregnant. Ben couldn't say Ephraim was a pedophile, because Founding Elders were important. They were church leaders. So Ben changed the rules so that Ephraim's raping of young women wasn't a crime. It was a . . . *sacrament*." She spat the word. "I couldn't stand it, but I also couldn't change it. Within a few years of being in Eden, it was like the men started believing that women were subhuman. I hadn't wanted to stay there, hadn't wanted to go there to begin with, but Ben had promised it would only be temporary. That we could leave when the scandal died down. Maybe six months. A year at the most. But he got used to the power. They all did, I think—the Founding Elders, I mean. Except for Waylon. The others *liked* having women subservient to them. I begged Ben to revoke the marriage law, not to marry Tracy off when she was still a child. He said he couldn't make exceptions, even for his own child." Her face grew hard and angry. "Maybe he did know that the kids weren't his. I don't know. I just knew we had to get out. Waylon made it happen."

"You didn't report Eden when you escaped," Liza said.

"Yes, I did!" she cried. "But when I told the police where to find them, they said there was no sign of anyone there. Waylon was angry when I told him. He asked if I wanted all of them to go jail. I did, except for Waylon. He was the only one of the Founding Elders who didn't have a standing warrant for his arrest. He'd served his time. He wouldn't have gone back to prison."

"Unless he'd killed another family to take your place," Tom said quietly.

Margo whimpered. "He wouldn't have."

Tom's tone remained mild. "At the very least Waylon was selling drugs grown in Eden."

"Growing a little pot is not the same as murder, Special Agent Hunter," Margo declared.

Liza frowned, Margo's words about standing warrants triggering a thought. "All of the Founders got new names. Ben was Herbert when he was the minister of the L.A. church, but he became Pastor in Eden. Edward McPhearson had been Aubrey Franklin, and Ephraim Burton was Harry Franklin. But Waylon kept his given name. Why?"

Tom turned to stare at her, pride in his eyes. "I didn't think of that."

Neither had Margo, from the look on her face. "I don't know," she murmured.

"Pastor made him the one to do supply runs," Liza went on. "Waylon sold the drugs. And he had the most recognizable face. He was covered in tattoos, right? Even on his face?"

"Right." She closed her eyes. "You think that Ben *wanted* him to get caught?"

Liza thought it was entirely possible. "Do you?"

"It makes sense, doesn't it? Ben knew I loved Waylon first. He hated that." Margo reached for a tissue, drying her eyes. "Waylon came to see us every weekend in that house in Benicia. Until one weekend he didn't show up, and that was it. I waited and waited, but he never came back. It devastated my children, Will especially. He loved Waylon."

"Did he know that Waylon was his father?" Liza asked.

She shook her head. "He'd always called him 'uncle.' But when Waylon never came back, Will felt abandoned. He'd always been an angry child, but he . . . Well, he took his own life."

"I'm so sorry for your loss," Liza murmured.

Margo's smile was small and sad. "Thank you. Eventually, I met Hugh and he offered me a better life. This is going to kill him. I assume that Waylon is dead?"

"He died seventeen years ago," Tom told her, then abruptly changed gears. "What made you offer Craig Hickman a million dollars?"

Margo jolted. "What?"

"A million dollars is a lot of money," Tom said. "Why did you offer it to him?"

She was quiet for a moment, struggling to regain her composure. "Waylon put it in an account for me when he helped me escape. I never spent it. I was afraid that Ben would know. When Tracy's first child was born, I offered her the money, for the baby. She was . . . appalled."

Margo grew pensive. "I didn't know that she understood what would have happened to her if she'd turned twelve in Eden, but of course she did. She knew I was scared and hurting, so she never said anything. When I offered her money, though . . . She said it was blood money. That I should give it to someone else, and suggested Hickman. When she'd started college, she'd looked up the whole sordid story of Ben's embezzlement. She told me to offer Hickman the money. I couldn't find him, so Tracy contacted that reporter. Erica Mann. She got me in touch with Mr. Hickman. He said he didn't want my money, that I should donate it. So I did."

"Where did Waylon get a million dollars?" Tom asked. "Did he steal it from Ben?"

"No, he said it was his share of the money. But Ben wouldn't have given it to him. He said he'd gotten it through Ben's financial manager. Ben called him his 'banker.'"

"Do you remember this man's name?" Tom asked, and Liza held her breath. This was what they'd come for.

"Of course. They were prison friends at Terminal Island. I knew him, too. His name was Daniel Park. He was in for securities fraud. Insider trading or something like that."

"Waylon had access to Mr. Park?" Tom asked.

"Yes. When we first started Eden, Waylon was the only one to leave—to get supplies. Ben would give him a code to use with Daniel, along with instructions on stock trades. That was how Ben and Daniel communicated. The code changed every time. Ben loved puzzles and he had a . . . what do you call it? The rule that tells how the code will change each time."

"A cipher?" Tom prompted.

"Yes, a cipher. Waylon figured out the pattern. Ben never did give him enough credit. Treated Waylon like he was dumb. I think Waylon would skim money from Ben's accounts and tell Daniel to invest it for him, pretending he was acting on Ben's instruction. Ben was very good with money. Waylon took his stock tips and was able to grow the money he skimmed. He told me that was where the million had come from."

Skimmed. Margo still was making excuses for the criminals in her life.

Margo looked away, then resolutely back at Tom. "Am I under arrest?"

"Not at this time," Tom replied.

She huffed out a breath. "I still have to tell Hugh. I hate this."

Not once, Liza realized, had this woman expressed sorrow for those who hadn't gotten out. She was only worried about herself.

Tom gave Margo one of his cards, then stood, holding a hand out for Liza. "We'll leave you to the rest of your day, ma'am," he said, and they walked out together to Tom's SUV.

"Well," Liza said once they were locked in and buckled up. "That was interesting."

"It was. I need to let Croft and Raeburn know about Daniel Park and then we can grab some lunch. Oh. Good timing," he said when his phone buzzed with an incoming call. "Hey, Croft. What's—" He stiffened. "Injuries?"

He pulled back to the curb, listening. He finally nodded. "I'm on my way. I'll use the flashers and get there faster." He paused again, looking over his shoulder at the Kitson home. "Yeah, we found her. I got a name to run. Daniel Park. He was in Terminal Island with Pastor and Waylon. He was a financial manager. Handled all of Pastor's accounts, so aiding and abetting at the very least. I'm hoping Pastor is still using him, but if not, we might be able to use him to find out who Pastor's financial advisor is now, and that person's communications might lead us to Eden." He listened a moment more. "See you soon." With that, he ended the call and pulled the car back onto the road, on the way to the freeway.

"What happened?" Liza asked.

"Explosion at KZAU. No serious injuries, except for the receptionist, who may have a concussion. Belmont stole some dynamite last night. The KZAU bomb was a small load, like a cherry bomb."

"So not to maim, but to get everyone out of the station," Liza said.

His brows went up. "You saw that in Afghanistan?"

"A few times, yes. Was Daisy there?"

"No. She and her cohost were broadcasting from their houses because of Gideon getting shot. They didn't mention that they weren't physically in the station until after the explosion."

Liza's stomach turned over. "He's still trying to get to Gideon so that he can get to Mercy."

"Yeah. We're gonna need to take a rain check on lunch."

"I couldn't eat a bite now anyway. Get us home."

TWENTY-SEVEN

om delivered Liza to the Sokolovs' house because that was where all of the security was. He was directed into the garage, where one of the bays stood empty for secure pickups and drop-offs. As soon as the garage doors were down, Irina burst from the house, Karl on her heels. They opened the passenger door and dragged Liza into their arms.

"Irina was worried," Karl said over Liza's head when Tom got out of the SUV. "The bombing at the radio station has us all upside down."

Karl owned the station, Tom remembered. "Your staff? They're all right?"

"All but our receptionist, but she'll be all right soon." Karl walked around the SUV and clapped Tom on the shoulder, his grin a little sly. "Thank you. I won two hundred bucks."

Tom rolled his eyes, his cheeks heating. "Yeah. Well. I need to go."

"Did you eat?" Irina asked.

"No," Liza said. "We came straight here. Now that I know everyone is okay, I can eat."

Irina pointed to Tom. "You cost me twenty dollars."

Liza laughed, the sound musical. "Take me to the food, Irina, and leave poor Tom alone."

Karl herded them through the laundry room and into the kitchen, which was bursting at the seams. Half of Karl and Irina's brood was here, as were Mercy's friends from New Orleans.

Irina shooed him toward the table. "I'll get you a plate. We had a late breakfast."

Tom pulled Liza's chair out for her and looked around. "Where's Jeff?"

"Asleep," Zoya said. "He was up all night doing something for you."

"He didn't tell you?" Tom asked, surprised.

"No," Zoya pouted. "I was annoyed, but he said he didn't have permission to share that. Just that you two were—" She waggled her brows. "You know."

Catcalls followed. Tom thought the seclusion was getting to them. They were a punchy crowd. "He helped us locate Pastor's wife," Tom said.

Silence descended as every eye met his. At least they weren't teasing him anymore.

Mercy exhaled unsteadily. "What?"

Tom sat next to Liza, nodding his thanks when Irina gave them each a plate full of eggs, bacon, and pancakes. "Jeff helped us locate Pastor's wife," he repeated.

"But . . ." Gideon swallowed hard and met his sister's gaze. "I guess she wasn't dead, either."

"I guess not," Mercy murmured.

Rafe scowled. "Jeff should have told us."

"No," Irina said, sitting down with her ever-present tea. "He did the right thing."

"Tell us about Marcia," Gideon said quietly. "What did she tell you?"

Tom glanced at Liza. "You can tell them. I need to eat and run."

Eating faster than his mother would have approved of, he listened as Liza shared what they'd learned. When she got to the part about the banker, he cleared his throat, and she glided past it so smoothly that he was certain she could read his mind.

"It doesn't sound like you cared for Pastor's wife," Daisy said to Liza.

Liza made a face. "She seemed selfish. She did report Eden once she'd gotten her kids out, but the community had already moved on to a different location. At least that's something."

"What's the next step, Tom?" Karl asked. "Do you have any leads on Belmont?"

"Nothing that you didn't find out the hard way," Tom said. "He stole a box of explosives from a business partner."

Irina abruptly set her cup on the table. "He has *more?*"

"Yes." Tom wasn't sure if that was classified, but this family needed to be aware. "Be very careful about anything that's delivered, even if it's something you ordered. Raeburn said that he'd keep FBI presence here at your house. Not as many as yesterday, but you'll still have protection." He stood. "I need to go now. Liza, a word please?"

She looked worried as she followed him into the laundry room. "What did I—"

He didn't let her finish, closing the door and then crushing her mouth with his. She hummed deep in her throat, her arms winding around his neck. As kisses went, it was pretty damn good.

She was panting when he backed away, and he was hard. "Keep yourself safe," he said roughly, as his phone began to buzz. "Hey, Croft. Did you find Daniel Park?"

"Not yet," Croft told him. "I'm texting you an address. Come there instead."

"What is it? Who lives there?"

Liza's eyes widened as she grew more alarmed. But she said nothing.

"Stephanie Stack," Croft answered. "She *was* Tony Ward's first grade teacher. Now she's dead. Two bullets to the head, like the nurse and the woman he killed Saturday night."

"Fuck. What was he looking for?" Then he knew. "Addresses. I'll be there as soon as I can." Tom ended the call, then kissed Liza one more time. "Stay here. I need you to be safe."

He could see that she wanted to ask more questions, but she nodded. "I will. I promise."

"Thank you." Tom waited until she was back in the kitchen before heading to the garage for his SUV. He'd left the Sokolovs' block when his cell buzzed again. He answered with his handsfree. "Special Agent Hunter."

"It's Raeburn. Where are you?"

"Leaving the Sokolovs' neighborhood."

"Good. Turn around." He gave Tom a new address, literally around the corner from Karl and Irina. "Belongs to a Mr. and Mrs. Nelson Smythe."

Tom instantly understood. "That's where Belmont's been hiding?"

"It appears so. We've identified the woman whose car was stolen. Kathy McGrail. She was supposed to return home from a business trip this morning, but she wasn't there when her husband woke up. He called her boss and learned that she'd come home early, wanting to surprise him."

"On Saturday night," Tom murmured.

"Exactly. That got him even more worried, of course, so he did a Find My Phone."

"But Belmont destroyed her phone."

"Yes, but she had an iPad in the car, and the app identified its last known location as of six this morning. After that the battery died. Get there ASAP. Rodriguez is right behind you."

Tom checked his rearview and, sure enough, Agent Rodriguez was following him. "Thank you. Do we have a warrant to search?"

"We have permission from the homeowner. The wife was out of town with her grandchildren, but is on her way home. Her husband wasn't answering her calls and she got worried because he'd texted that he'd been sick."

"Make and model of Mrs. McGrail's car?"

"Blue Honda Civic, three years old. Feed from the security cameras at the radio station show it parked down the block when the station blew. We put out a BOLO and got lucky. The car was spotted by SacPD, which is following now. Driver is wearing glasses and a wig, but is the same height and weight as Belmont. I've sent agents to back up SacPD, with instructions to intercept the car and take Belmont into custody ASAP."

Yes. Finally, Tom thought, his pulse thrumming. "Where is he?"

"About twenty minutes from you. I expect to have him in custody before he arrives. If we don't, do not engage Belmont without backup. I've sent more backup to your location."

"Yes, sir. I'm pulling up to the Smythes' house now. Will call you back soon."

He met Rodriguez at the front door. The other agent had a battering ram and together they broke the door in. The house was very quiet, but the scene in the dining room proved that Belmont had been there. Several sticks of dynamite lay on the dining room table, wires and detonation caps strewn about.

"Dammit," Tom said. He pointed to two sets of packaging. "He bought two alarm clocks."

"Two bombs," Rodriguez said. "My money's on the Sokolovs' house for the second."

"Mine too. They know not to accept any deliveries, but we need to alert them."

Rodriguez was already texting. "I sent a message to Raeburn and the agent he put in charge of guarding their house. They'll get a bomb squad out there to sweep the property to make sure he hasn't already managed to get a package into the house. Let's keep going. Keep your eyes open for the homeowner. I don't think he'll be in good shape, if he's still alive."

"Can you also let Raeburn know that we only found a few sticks here? And that he could have the box with him?" Tom had done a cursory search and saw no sign of the box DJ had stolen from Kowalski's garage. "If the box was full when he stole it, he could be carrying a fuckton of explosives."

They continued searching the house, Rodriguez checking the master bedroom and Tom heading to the side of the house that faced the street. He checked every room, in the closets and under the beds. Just in case.

He came to a halt when he saw the pink camera on the windowsill in a spare bedroom. "This window has a view of the Sokolovs' street," Tom called out. "He's got a camera set up. He's been sleeping in here. Printers are here, too, including a 3D printer."

Rodriguez joined him. "I found a lot of hair in the trash can. I think he shaved his hair off."

"We'll have to update the BOLO."

"Already done." Rodriguez grimaced at the view of the street. "He can't see the Sokolovs' front door from here, but he could see all the vehicular traffic."

"And the foot traffic." An unpleasant shiver ran down Tom's spine. "That spot, right there?" He pointed out to the street. "I was standing there yesterday with another agent. We were in tactical gear, but . . . damn. We were just standing there."

Rodriguez grunted. "You're charmed, kid. Either he didn't see you or he didn't want to risk shooting, knowing we were all there. Come on. Let's keep going."

They continued searching, ending up in the garage. Tom pointed to the hair dryer sitting atop a chest freezer. "What do you think?"

Rodriguez made a face. "That we need to open the freezer." He picked up the hair dryer and lifted the freezer's lid. "Fucking hell."

Tom stared down into the face of the homeowner. "Nelson Smythe." The body was covered in a blanket of ice—except for the face.

"What the hell?" Rodriguez asked. "His face is, like, *thawed*."

"The wife got a few texts from her husband's phone this weekend," Tom said. "I think he was using the man's face to unlock his phone."

"I thought you needed open eyes. Open and *alive* eyes."

"Not with all phones." Tom sighed. "I'll call the body in."

GRANITE BAY, CALIFORNIA
MONDAY, MAY 29, 12:05 P.M.

"Fuck." DJ gripped the Civic's wheel, yanking back into his lane after nearly veering into oncoming traffic. The loud blaring sound coming from his cell had scared him to death. It was one of those Amber Alert tones that made everyone race to silence their phones.

But a glance at the screen showed it was not an Amber Alert. It was an alert from the pink camera he'd set up in Smythe's spare bedroom.

Fucking hell. The camera had picked up audio nearby.

He hit the alert flag on his locked screen and held the phone to his face to unlock it. What he heard when he tapped the app icon made his blood run cold.

"This window has a view of the Sokolovs' street," a man called out. "He's got a camera set up. He's been sleeping in here. Printers are here, too, including a 3D printer."

Fuck. Fuck, fuck, fuck.

"I found a lot of hair in the trash can. I think he shaved his hair off," a second man answered.

"We'll have to update the BOLO," the first guy said.

"Already done." There was a slight pause before the second guy said, "He can't see the Sokolovs' front door from here, but he could see all the vehicular traffic."

"And the foot traffic. That spot, right there? I was standing there yesterday with another agent. We were in tactical gear, but . . . damn. We were just standing there."

The second guy grunted. "You're charmed, kid. Either he didn't see you or he didn't want to risk shooting, knowing we were all there. Come on. Let's keep going."

"Stay calm," DJ muttered. "Stay calm. Think."

He glanced in his rearview, his heart racing faster when he spied two cruisers behind him. They hadn't been there before. Neither had the two nondescript black sedans.

You got sloppy, he snarled to himself. *You stopped watching.*

Because he'd thought himself safe. Because he'd disabled the Civic's GPS.

How had they found him? A search of all the houses?

"Fuck." *Don't panic. Think.*

It didn't matter at this point how they'd found him. They had. He needed to ditch this car. He looked around, searching for a way out.

His gaze fell on the box on the floorboard of the passenger side. It still had a few sticks. He leaned sideways and grabbed four sticks. They were bigger than the stick he'd used in the radio station package, but smaller than the ones he'd used in the package he'd dropped off at the courier, bound for the Sokolov house first thing in the morning.

It would be enough to cause a panic, giving him time to ditch the Civic and find another ride.

If not . . . he'd have to shoot his way out. He patted his pocket, relieved to find he still carried Nelson Smythe's engraved lighter. He set the sticks upright in the cup holder and waited until he had the exact right moment.

He saw it a minute later when a city bus came to a lumbering stop in front of him. Just ahead was a strip mall.

Go, go, go. He floored the gas pedal, forcing a car out of his way so that he just slipped around the bus. He lit the first stick and started to count.

The fuse was two inches long, so he had five seconds.

He rolled the window down. *Four, three.*

He tossed the first stick out the window, unable to quell his grin when it exploded right on schedule.

People started screaming and cars came to screeching halts. Horns blared and the cruiser lights started flashing as they tried to get past the traffic jam.

It was chaos.

It was *perfect*.

He raced around the back of the strip mall before braking. He jumped from the car, grabbing the backpack he'd stuffed with his laptop, magnetic signs, and the license plates he'd created, then the duffel with the weapons he'd stolen from Kowalski. Everything else was replaceable.

Calm, calm, calm. Gun in hand, he ran the length of the strip mall, staying in the back.

Luck was still with him. A woman emerged from one of the stores, struggling with the big box she carried. He could see the key fob in her hand as she jostled the box, pointing the fob at a waiting minivan. A second later the side door slid open.

Not pausing, he ran up behind her and shoved her hard, knocking her down. She cried out, but he ignored her, grabbing her keys and shoving his duffel through the open side door. He glanced at her to see her scrambling away while pulling a cell phone from her purse.

Shit. He shot the phone, then fired once more, feeling a pang when her body went still.

Sorry, he thought as he climbed into the van, then wiped her from his mind as he drove away.

He'd ditch the van ASAP, but for now he was safe.

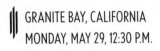

GRANITE BAY, CALIFORNIA
MONDAY, MAY 29, 12:30 P.M.

"What's happening?" Abigail asked in a small voice, clutching her puppy.

Sitting at Irina's kitchen table, Liza put her arm around the little girl and pulled her close. There was commotion in the foyer. "I don't know," she told Abigail. "But we won't leave you."

"Never," Mercy said.

"Never," Daisy echoed, her tone calm, but she petted poor Brutus with a frenetic energy. Brutus simply licked her hand, doing her job, helping Daisy keep her anxiety in check.

The word was repeated by everyone gathered around the table. It was still a decent-sized group, although most of Mercy's New Orleans friends had been taken to the airport. Farrah and her mother and fiancé remained, along with Irina, Karl, Zoya, Jeff Bunker, and his mom. Rafe and Gideon were at the front door, talking with the agents guarding them.

Amos, who'd gone to the front door with Rafe and Gideon, returned to the kitchen, his eyes turbulent. His smile was forced. "The federal agents are going to bring in some dogs."

Abigail brightened. "Dogs?"

"Not to play with," Amos said, taking the empty chair next to Abigail. "They're sniffing dogs. They're . . ." He looked at Liza helplessly.

"They're bomb dogs," Liza said quietly. "DJ is still out there and still wants to hurt people."

"He sent a bomb to Daisy's work," Abigail said, even more quietly.

Amos looked startled, then resigned. "I should have known you'd figure that out," he murmured. He opened his arms and Liza let Abigail go so that she could sit on her papa's lap. "Ask your questions, Abi-girl."

"Will he send a bomb here?"

"That's what the dogs are going to find out," Amos said. "They're trained to sniff out the stuff that bombs are made from."

"They have a job," Abigail said. "Like Brutus."

Amos kissed the top of her head. "Exactly. When they get here, we need to let them work."

"Okay, Papa." She sighed, a grown-up sound. "Why does he want to hurt us?"

Amos closed his eyes. "He's bad, baby. Just . . . evil. But Mr. Tom and all the other officers are looking for him. We just need to be brave a little longer."

Abigail nodded. "We could bake. Miss Irina always bakes when she's afraid. So do Liza and Mercy."

The three of them laughed. "You are far too smart, *lubimaya*," Irina said. "Come. We will bake. Mercy? Liza?"

"I am so in," Liza said, but her cell phone began to ring. It was Special Agent Raeburn. "But I need to answer this first. You get started and I'll help in a bit."

She went into the laundry room to take the call, shutting the door for privacy. So far, Mercy didn't know about her job at Sunnyside Oaks, and Liza aimed to keep it that way. Mercy had enough to worry about. "Hello?"

"Miss Barkley, this is Special Agent Raeburn. Are you well?"

"We're nervous," Liza said, knowing that he wasn't asking about her health. "But okay."

"Good. Very good. I'd wanted to bring you in for a briefing before you start at Sunnyside tomorrow morning, but it's better that you stay where you are."

"Has something new happened?"

"Things are . . . in play. For now, let's discuss your role. First and foremost, you are not to do anything that puts you in any additional danger. You will wear your wire."

"Yes, sir."

"Good. You will leave your personal phone with the agents manning the surveillance van. Agent Hunter will make sure you get a burner that you can use in an emergency."

"Because Sunnyside will break into my locker and search my phone. What's next?"

"We have custom shoes for you. They have a hollow sole in which you can conceal a small blade that we will also provide."

"How very James Bond."

He chuckled. "Isn't it, though? I assume they'll search you or maybe even have some kind of metal detector for you to pass through. The blade is ceramic and won't set off the detector."

"Yes, sir." Liza wondered if Tom had told him about recruiting Rafe and decided not to ask.

"Do you wear glasses?"

"Contacts, but I have glasses."

"Give your glasses to the agent on duty. He'll be around shortly for them. We're going to remove your lenses and replace them with non-prescription lenses. The frames will be fitted with a small camera. That way if something happens to the pendant Agent Hunter prepared for you, we'll still have a visual."

"I have my glasses with me, so that's no problem."

"Good. We still don't have access to the security network. This puts you at a higher risk."

"I understand. I'm still fully on board."

"I figured you would be. Do you have any questions for me?"

She drew a breath, then let it out, all while wondering how trustworthy this man was.

"Maybe I should rephrase," Raeburn said wryly. "Do you want me to transfer you to Special Agent in Charge Molina so you can ask her questions?"

She smiled at that. "No. I think Molina likes me too much for this. I'll ask you."

"I don't know if that's flattering or not."

"Not meant to be flattering, sir. Just honest. If something happens to me, well, I haven't updated my will since I was discharged. My beneficiary was my husband, but he's deceased. I signed a letter changing that and mailed it to myself. Please make sure someone checks for it."

Tom didn't need the money, so she'd left everything to Dana's halfway house for survivors of sexual assault. Dana would know how to make best use of whatever Liza left behind.

Raeburn cleared his throat. "You have my word."

"Thank you. That's all, sir."

"Until tomorrow, then."

He ended the call and Liza went to find her new glasses.

GRANITE BAY, CALIFORNIA
MONDAY, MAY 29, 7:45 P.M.

As soon as the Sokolovs' garage door lowered, Tom turned off the engine of his SUV and leaned his head on the steering wheel. He hadn't been so exhausted in a very long time.

He sat in the quiet, Pebbles's happy panting from the back seat the only sound. He must have fallen asleep, because the next thing he knew, the interior lights of his vehicle were on and Liza was sitting in the passenger seat, lightly squeezing his upper arm.

"Tom?"

He slowly lifted his head to blink at her blearily. "Sorry."

"Come on. You can have some supper and then a nap."

"With you?"

"Absolutely." She turned to the back seat with a sweet smile. "Hello, Pebbles. I missed you."

Pebbles was wriggling in her harness, trying to get to her favorite person.

"You had to come back to me," Tom said. "Pebbles would have been inconsolable."

Liza leaned over to kiss his cheek. "Come on. The kitchen is quiet. Everyone is watching a movie in the living room. You can eat in peace."

That sounded like heaven.

She released Pebbles from her harness, laughing when the dog licked her face. It was such a joyful sound, he couldn't find it in him to rebuke her tonight. He grabbed his briefcase and a bag of kibble and followed Liza into the kitchen. She took everything from his hands and set it aside before drawing him into a hug that he hadn't known he'd needed.

But he *had* needed it. So damn much.

"Baby, you're swaying on your feet." She led him to the table and pushed him into a chair. "What do you want to do first? Food or sleep?"

He patted his knee and she sat on his lap and kissed him. "That's all I could think about, all the way here," he murmured.

She kissed him again, then rested her head on his shoulder. "How bad was it? From the news reports, it looked awful."

"Nobody died," he said. "Which was a miracle. That fucking ass-hole threw fucking dynamite into fucking traffic." She pulled his tie free of his collar, the movement more caring than sexual. "Ten people were taken to the hospital. Three serious, one critical. The critical one wasn't in the blast. She was shot."

"The minivan owner."

"Yeah." Tom wasn't sure what the news had covered and what it hadn't. He'd been too busy at the scene and then in a marathon team meeting in Raeburn's conference room. "He was in too much of a hurry to double-tap her like he's done with his other victims."

She unfastened the top buttons of his shirt, allowing him to breathe. "At least you found her in time."

"True." Two of the cars tailing DJ Belmont had finally managed to get free of the traffic disaster, only to find DJ in the wind once again. He'd abandoned the Honda Civic that he'd stolen from Kathy McGrail on Saturday night and taken the woman's minivan.

"Do you know where he is?" she asked cautiously.

"No. He ditched the minivan for a laundry truck, then traded that for a really old pickup without GPS. He's in the wind. Again."

"He was so close," she murmured. "Just around the corner. Karl and Irina knew Mr. Smythe, but only to wave when they were out walking."

"His wife is angry."

"I can see why," she said.

"Not with DJ. Well, not only with DJ," he amended. "She's furious with Karl and Irina for welcoming 'troublemakers' into their home."

Liza immediately scowled. "What the hell?"

He shrugged wearily. "I know. It was a very unpleasant conversation. She arrived home when I was still at her house, before I got called to the scene of the blast. She was . . . incensed."

"She's in shock, I'm sure."

"Yeah, but I'm not looking forward to the interviews she's already threatening to give to the news. Karl and Irina don't deserve any of that."

"Should we warn them?"

"Raeburn will, so that it'll be official and on the record. He's supposed to call them tonight."

"I think he did already. Karl excused himself from the movie to take a call right about the same time that I heard you opening the garage door." She stroked his hair off his forehead, gentle little caresses. "There was also a report about a disturbance at another house nearby. A robbery with several homicides. The reports didn't say it was DJ, but it was, wasn't it? Was that the call you got from Croft this morning?"

He nodded. "The homeowner's a leader in the Chicos."

Her eyes widened. "DJ's tattoo that Abigail saw. Is that where DJ got the dynamite?"

"And several rifles and handguns and ammo." He sighed. "I didn't know the news was reporting that. Normally I'm on top of coverage, but today it's been one thing after another. What else are they saying?"

"Not that there was a gang connection, but they did say the homeowner and his family are missing. They speculated that it might be a ransom situation."

Tom thought about the way Angelina Ward had left her devices neatly stacked on the kitchen counter. "Unlikely. But I am concerned about his wife and kids."

"There was one more murder reported. A teacher at a private school here in Granite Bay."

He sighed again. "What did the media say about her?"

"At first only that her body was found. There was some talk from her friends that she'd had a bad breakup, and some thought that her ex could have done it. Later, though, when parents at the school heard about the 'disturbance' at the Wards' home, and that the family was missing, they put it together that one of the Ward children was in the dead teacher's class."

"Busy day for the media," Tom muttered.

"Did DJ kill her, too?"

"Croft is working that case. She thinks so." He stopped himself before he said his next words, which would have been *I do, too, because the man is a murderer and you're walking into Sunnyside tomorrow like a lamb to slaughter. Please don't do it.*

But he didn't, because she'd known DJ was a murderer when she'd agreed to the job. That he'd killed more people wasn't going to change her mind.

If anything, it would strengthen her resolve. So he bit the words back, even though he was screaming inside. "Can we not talk about this right now? I just want to hold you, okay?"

"More than okay."

She sat on his lap, giving him the closeness he'd needed—until his stomach growled loudly. She pushed to her feet. "Let me feed you."

Tom guessed that the food he ate was delicious, but he barely tasted it. It was as if all the sleepless nights had finally hit him like a freight train.

And he still hadn't gained access to Sunnyside's security network. He could shut down the network he had, but that was mostly e-mail and databases for employees and patients. He didn't want to damage the patient records. Patients included drug lords and their families, but there were also celebrities and their families—innocent people receiving care.

It was ingenious, really. Sunnyside Oaks was a legal, licensed facility where criminals had been successfully hidden among the legit patients who required discretion. Perhaps Sunnyside would even use the legit patients as a shield should they be discovered. The lives of those legit patients had to be protected.

They needed to proceed with extreme care.

So he'd convinced Raeburn to allow him to join the agents in the back of the surveillance van. Raeburn hadn't wanted him to, because he feared Tom was too close to the case now that Liza was involved. Tom hadn't let anyone at the Bureau office know that he and Liza were involved romantically as well. That would have gotten him tossed off the case for sure.

"I'll be in the surveillance van tomorrow morning," he told her after he'd eaten. "I can at least hack into their Wi-Fi cameras, but most, if not all, are probably hardwired. Until I can manufacture a network crisis, we can't touch the hardwired cameras or the alarm systems."

"It'll be okay," she told him. "Although I am relieved that you'll be close."

"So will Rafe. He's going to be in the SUV you're borrowing from Karl. I'm going to smuggle you back into the parking garage of your apartment in time for you two to switch vehicles and leave."

"Does Raeburn know?"

"No. I know I should tell him." He'd felt guilty about it all damn day. But not guilty enough to tell him. "Rafe knows that and he's still okay with helping. He's so grateful that you're doing this for Mercy."

"Mercy doesn't know," she murmured.

"Let's keep it that way."

"Agreed." She put his dishes in the dishwasher, then tugged him to his feet. "Come on. You need to sleep."

"I need *you*."

"I'll be right there with you." They walked up the stairs, Pebbles behind them. "This room is ours for tonight."

He stripped to his boxer briefs and slid between the sheets, happy when she stripped as well.

She noted him watching and winked. "I'm going to take care of you. On your stomach."

His libido flared, then waned. He grimaced, embarrassed. "I never thought I'd be too tired."

"Hush," she said again, surprising him when she straddled his upper thighs. "'Taking care of you' wasn't a euphemism for sex."

Then he groaned when she began massaging his back, long strokes that felt so damn good.

She chuckled. "Keep groaning like that and everyone will believe that's what we're doing."

"Like they don't already," he murmured, already relaxing. "They probably have a betting pool for that, too."

"Probably," she said and he could hear her smile.

This . . . This was good. Too good. Fear lanced his mind, making him tense up. *Please don't let her get hurt. Please just let me have this. Have her.*

"You're thinking," she chided quietly. "You went all tense just now. I guess I'm going to have to work harder."

She did, giving all the muscles in his back attention before scooting lower, tugging his boxers off to work on his buttocks.

"Hmmmm." His body was starting to wake up, but his brain wasn't cooperating now. He felt floaty.

"Let go, Tom," he heard her say. "Go to sleep. I'll be here when you wake up."

He must have needed the words, because they were the last ones he remembered hearing before sleep finally claimed him.

TWENTY-EIGHT

Nurse Innes met DJ when he came in through Sunnyside's employee entrance. Once again, she held a mask. This time he took it, wearing it without complaint.

"You get only one ambulance ride," she said as they walked to Pastor's suite. "You can say goodbye to your dad, but you can't stay here for long. The target on your back is too big."

His day had sucked, ending with his finally making a call to Nurse Innes when he got close to Sunnyside in the fourth of the vehicles he'd stolen that day. Afraid that Kowalski would be waiting for him in retaliation for the weapons he'd stolen and the men he'd killed, he'd asked the nurse for help getting into the facility unseen.

Innes had sent an ambulance for him and he'd had to ride in the back. But it had worked. If Kowalski had been waiting for him outside, he'd missed him. At least the Feds didn't know about this place. If they had, he'd never have risked it.

But they didn't know about Sunnyside, so it was the safest place for him at the moment. He'd changed vehicles four times after fleeing from the strip mall. He'd dumped the Civic for the minivan, then stolen a laundry truck before trading it for an old pickup.

The pickup had been too old to have GPS, but it was in bad shape and might not make it up the mountain when he got ready to return to Eden. But while driving it, he'd noticed an older Ford Explorer that looked rugged enough to handle the steep, curvy inclines. The Explorer had wandered in and out of its lane, its driver clearly drunk.

Finally, it had pulled behind a small church not too far from Sunnyside Oaks. The church's windows were dark, its parking lot deserted.

Curious, DJ had followed. And hit pay dirt. The driver had stumbled out of the vehicle, unzipping his pants and peeing on the grass at the edge of the parking lot. He'd stumbled again, slipped on the puddle of his own urine, and hit the pavement, passed out cold.

It had been entertaining, to say the least. And also the opportunity DJ had been waiting for. He'd disabled the Explorer's GPS, dragged the passed-out drunk into the woods behind the church, and rolled him into a creek, where he'd landed facedown.

Then he'd changed out the plates on the Explorer before driving it to a shopping center three and a half miles away. He'd parked behind an empty store up for lease, figuring that he'd come back for the vehicle when he was ready to drive to the mountain.

Then he'd called Innes, who'd told him he'd have to wait for the ambulance to be available.

He'd spent the entire hour that he'd waited cursing—first the Feds for finding him, then himself for being so complacent. He'd cursed Pastor for being so stingy with the access codes and Kowalski for trying to kill him. He'd cursed Mercy for being so well protected, Daisy Dawson for broadcasting remotely.

And he cursed the woman in the eye doctor's office, the one who'd spied him on the rooftop and told the other Fed. If it hadn't been for her, he would have had the perfect shot. *I should have just shot her.*

"Where will you go when you leave here?" Nurse Innes asked. "Back to your home?"

"Most likely, yes." *No.* Because Mercy and Gideon weren't dead yet. "When my father is ready to be discharged, will you transport him to a safe place where I can pick him up?"

"Of course. We've done that in the past. You can stay here tonight, but tomorrow you'll have to make other arrangements." She walked away, making notes on her cell phone.

DJ dropped his bags on the floor of Pastor's suite, next to the sofa in the sitting room. The couch was nowhere near as soft as the bed in Smythe's spare bedroom, but it wasn't awful. He figured that Coleen was either with Pastor or asleep. Either way, he'd deal with her later.

He was almost asleep when he heard a gasp. Bolting upright, his eyes narrowed when he saw Coleen standing in the door to her room.

"What are you doing here?" she asked him.

"I came to visit Pastor," he lied. "How is he?"

"Better. But his blood pressure is really high, so don't make him mad."

DJ rolled his eyes. "Why would I make him mad?"

"Because you're supposed to be in Eden."

"I was," he lied smoothly. "I left Brother Joshua in charge because the community wanted an update on Pastor's condition. I just got here."

She studied him for a long moment that became uncomfortable. "I saw you on the news. You've been here all day. You've been here all weekend. They say that you've killed people."

Fucking bitch. DJ's hands fisted. "I was protecting our investments."

She paled but was unconvinced. "Did you kill people?"

"Did Edward? Did Ephraim?"

Her lips thinned. "I'm not talking about them. I'm talking about you."

He suddenly realized he didn't know how she'd come to Eden. He knew *when* she'd joined—she'd been one of the original members. But he didn't know how or why. All the founders had been running from something. Pastor and Marcia had been running from fraud and embezzlement charges. Edward and Ephraim, bank robbery and a triple homicide.

Waylon was the only one who hadn't had a warrant against him at the time, and DJ still didn't know why his father had joined Pastor and the others. The same was true for Coleen.

"Have *you*? Killed someone, I mean?" he asked. "Answer me, Sister Coleen."

She went rigid. "Not your concern."

She has. How fascinating. "Then you have no room to talk. Has Pastor seen the news?"

"No. I'm trying to keep him from getting upset. Which is why you can't stay here. He left his room for the first time today. He got to go to the solarium, where the other patients gather. If someone sees you, they might mention the news, and he'll know. His health is very precarious."

Hell, that was the first good news he'd had all day. Not that Pastor was leaving his room, but that his survival was iffy. DJ could do a lot with iffy.

"I'll go tomorrow," he promised to shut her up. He'd leave when he was ready and not before.

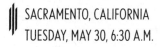

SACRAMENTO, CALIFORNIA
TUESDAY, MAY 30, 6:30 A.M.

"Mr. Saltrick," Nurse Innes said, "this is our newest employee, Miss Barkley. She's a nursing assistant and will be working pediatrics."

Liza smiled at the big man, but inside she was nervous. This was the guy whose computer Tom was trying to break into. "It's good to meet you, sir."

"You're the combat medic."

"Former, sir. I was honorably discharged."

"Well, thank you for your service. If you'll stand here, I'll take the photo for your badge."

Liza stood where he pointed and smiled when he said to. Three minutes later, she had her own entry badge.

"Wear this whenever you're on the property," he ordered. "Anyone not wearing a badge, especially new employees, will be considered hostile and dealt with accordingly."

"I understand," Liza said, thinking about Rafe hiding out in the SUV she'd ridden in this morning. Tom had woken her early and made love to her tenderly, and then they had left the Sokolovs' house with Liza and Rafe hunkered down on the floorboards in the back.

Just like she'd done the Wednesday before when Agent Rodriguez had gotten them out of the eye doctor's office.

Tom's hands had shaken when he'd said goodbye in the parking garage beneath Karl's apartment. His parting kiss had been hard and desperate and afraid, his "I love you" hoarse and broken. But he'd let her go without complaint, and for that she loved him even more.

Rafe had hidden in the very back of the SUV, where he'd stay until she needed him.

She worried about him. It was going to get up into the high nineties today, but Rafe had assured her that he'd done surveillance in black vehicles on hotter days than this. She'd left the windows cracked, and he had plenty of water and a battery-operated fan. The dark windows would block some of the sun's rays. She'd have to trust that he could keep himself safe.

She sat through a short security and privacy briefing during which she signed a number of forms, including an NDA. Afterward, she was instructed to follow Nurse Innes. "Come along, Miss Barkley," she said briskly. "I'll give you your tour and then introduce you to your patient."

Liza put on her special James Bond camera-fitted glasses and set off beside Nurse Innes.

The older woman eyed the hot pink rhinestone glasses with amusement. "Nobody will miss you in glasses like those," she said.

"A little girl in the eyeglass store helped me pick them out. I hope my patient will like them."

"I'm sure she will. Brooklyn loves bright colors."

The tour was short. Liza was shown the locker room and given a locker in which she stored her belongings, which had been carefully screened by Rafe and Tom. Rafe had been undercover for several years and had a good eye for anything that might give her away.

From the locker room they went to the break room and the gym. "You can use any of the equipment as long as you're off duty and none of the patients or their families ask to use it."

The supply closet was very well stocked. "We have everything a hospital has and, in some cases, more," Innes said. "Your patient will be undergoing chemotherapy next week. You'll be transporting her to and from treatments. Your supervising nurse will show you where."

"Miss Sinclair mentioned that the child is terminal when I had my interview. Is this correct?"

Innes frowned. "Did she explicitly say that?"

Liza had to think. "No. She asked if I could deal if the child was terminal. I assumed."

"That's good," Innes said, clearly relieved. "Brooklyn is not terminal, but her leukemia is advanced. She's responding well to treatments, so we continue to hope."

"That's good," Liza said, relieved for the child's sake.

"You don't speak to her about her mother or their home," Innes said. They'd turned a corner and were approaching a set of double doors over which was a sign that read *PEDIATRICS*. "Don't ask her questions about anything personal. Her mother has privacy concerns. Am I clear?"

"Yes, ma'am," Liza said. "I understand."

"See that you do. Her mother's travel schedule is busy. She isn't here often and Brooklyn gets lonely. Please accommodate her play requests whenever she makes them. Your supervisor is Nurse Williams. Come. I'll introduce you."

Liza entered the pediatrics ward, immediately charmed with the colors. Most of the rooms were empty, but all were very nice. This was not a normal hospital. Every room was a suite. Nurse Innes stopped at the third room from the end.

An older woman sat in a reclining chair, a book in her hand. She stood as soon as Liza and Nurse Innes entered.

"Good morning! You must be the new nursing assistant. I'm Nurse Williams."

"My name is Liza." She turned her gaze to the bed, where a tiny little girl sat up, a tray of oatmeal in front of her. The child was bald and did not smile. Until she saw Liza's glasses.

"Oh wow!" she exclaimed. "I like your glasses. I'm Brooklyn. Hi, Liza."

Liza looked to Nurse Williams. "May I?" she asked, gesturing to the chair next to the bed.

"Of course."

Liza sat next to the little girl and stuck out her hand. "It is very nice to meet you, Brooklyn."

Brooklyn smiled, showing a missing front tooth. Liza's heart cracked. She didn't bother telling herself not to get attached, because of course she would. She was already on her way.

"I hear you have treatments starting up soon, so let's get some play in beforehand. What would you like to do? We can read, play a game, watch a movie, whatever you'd like."

Brooklyn's eyes widened in surprise that Liza had been so up front about her treatments. Then the little girl's smile grew. "You'll play with me? And read to me?"

"Absolutely."

"Can you do voices?"

"You mean when I read to you?" Liza asked. "I'll do my best."

"Then I want you to read to me first. I have a Harry Potter book. And then we'll play with my dolls. And then Play-Doh. And . . ." She gasped. "Did you BeDazzle your glasses?"

Liza chuckled. "No. But if there's a BeDazzle kit anywhere in this hospital, we can BeDazzle some of your stuff and make you the sparkliest girl here." She looked over her shoulder to Nurse Innes. "Do we? Have a BeDazzle kit, I mean."

Nurse Innes smiled. "I'll send someone out for one."

"Yay!" Brooklyn cried, clapping her hands.

Yay indeed, Liza thought. *If I'm only here for a short time, I'm going to make sure I use it to help this little girl have some fun.* "I'll have to do chores in between play, like changing your bedding and stuff like that. But let's start this morning right. Where is your book?"

SACRAMENTO, CALIFORNIA
TUESDAY, MAY 30, 9:30 A.M.

"She's good with the kid," the surveillance tech said with a sad smile.

"She is," Tom agreed.

It was hotter than hell in the van, but he didn't want to be anywhere else. Watching Liza make a seriously sick kid smile was a beautiful thing. She'd read several chapters from the first Harry Potter book, doing "all the voices," and little Brooklyn had been delighted.

Then they'd taken a break to take the child's vitals and change her bedding. Now they were looking at photos of the stars and planets on the child's tablet.

Tom and the surveillance techs hadn't seen much of the inside of Sunnyside Oaks yet. They'd taken the tour along with Liza and Nurse Innes, who, according to what Irina had told Liza, was someone to watch.

After the tour, Liza had stayed in the child's room except for the few minutes she'd taken to deliver the soiled bedding to the facility's laundry. She'd walked slowly on the way back, making sure the cameras in her glasses and the pendant caught every nook and cranny.

He'd hacked the facility's cameras that were connected to Wi-Fi, and that had made him feel a bit better about her being alone inside. He'd thought they might see armed guards everywhere, but they hadn't. The only armed person seemed to be Saltrick, the security chief.

One was enough, though. Unfortunately, if there were cameras in the patient rooms, they were hardwired, because he hadn't been able to hack those, so they hadn't seen Pastor.

"Any luck on your phishing e-mails?" the tech asked.

"No. I'm worrying now that they're going to compare notes and realize someone is trying to break in." Because the Wi-Fi feed had shown the employees working on their computers, so it was likely that they'd seen his e-mails.

"We'll keep watch, but if any of the recipients go to the security office, we won't be able to see them."

Either the chief of security's office didn't have a camera or it was hardwired. Tom figured it was the former.

The tech chuckled. "The head nurse just told Brooklyn that she'll have her BeDazzling stuff in an hour."

Tom returned his attention to the monitor linked to the feed from Liza's pendant.

"Can we go to the sunny room to do our work?" Brooklyn asked.

"What's the sunny room?" Liza asked.

"The solarium," the nurse explained. "It's a common area and there are tables there where patients do puzzles and paint. BeDazzling would be a great use of the solarium, Brooklyn. We'll get a wheelchair for you."

Because the child was too weak to walk on her own.

"But first, you need to take a short nap," Liza told Brooklyn. "Those BeDazzler machines need some muscle, so you should rest."

Tom wondered who Brooklyn's mother was. Innes had only said that she traveled for business. She could be one of the legit clients. Tom hoped so.

He'd check the patient database, but he'd have to do so from his home system. The warrants only covered information specific to Pastor, so looking at Brooklyn's records on FBI time would make the Bureau in violation, and he wasn't going to do that.

The ringing of his work phone jerked his attention away from Brooklyn. It was Raeburn. He couldn't know about Rafe, but Tom still feared he'd sound guilty when he answered his boss.

"Special Agent Hunter."

"It's Raeburn. We need you back at the field office, ASAP."

Tom frowned. "Why? I thought I was assigned to surveillance today."

"We picked up Daniel Park, Pastor's banker. I want you and Croft in Interview with him. Now, Agent Hunter."

Tom wanted to argue, because panic was spiraling in his gut. But Rafe was in the employee lot, ready to assist should Liza need it. So he drew a breath and said, "Yes, sir. On my way."

SACRAMENTO, CALIFORNIA
TUESDAY, MAY 30, 11:30 A.M.

"Look, Liza, I did it! Isn't it pretty?" Brooklyn beamed.

She'd used a lot of her energy to push down on the BeDazzler tool, forcing the shiny rhinestone gem into an extra hospital gown. Her face was flushed from the exertion, the edges of the scarf she wore to cover her baldness damp from her perspiration.

"So pretty!" Liza held the cotton gown up. "This is going to be the awesomest thing."

They'd chosen a simple heart design. Brooklyn had wanted to do something elaborate, but Liza had convinced her that if they started small, they could be finished faster and she could wear the gown while she worked on the next project. In truth, Liza wasn't sure how long she'd be here and she didn't want to leave Brooklyn with nothing.

Still smiling, Brooklyn sagged into the wheelchair. "Can you do the next part? I'm tired."

"I can indeed. You just rest and tell me what to do."

Brooklyn grinned at that. "I'm the boss."

"So what color do we use next, boss?"

"Red."

Liza saluted. "Yes, ma'am." She reached for the red gem but froze when she saw a man entering the solarium. Frail-looking and about seventy, he wore round-rimmed glasses and his face seemed familiar. And then she knew.

Oh my God. It was him. It was Pastor.

She'd seen the photo tacked to the bulletin board in Tom's home office, the one taken of Pastor, his wife, and the twins shortly before he'd run to Eden thirty years ago. He was older now, of course, and looked terrible, his skin gray and his hair thinning, but it was him.

He was being pushed by one of the nurses, and following behind was a woman in her midfifties. Her hair was liberally streaked with gray and pulled off her head in a simple bun.

But it was the item she wore around her throat that had Liza's attention. A locket on a thick, heavy chain. An Eden locket. The nurse pushed Pastor to one of the tables by the window and covered his lap with a blanket. He leaned his head back, as if enjoying the sun on his face.

Belatedly aware she'd been staring, Liza jerked her attention back to the pile of red gems. But her hands were shaking so hard that she couldn't get the gem into the little plunger.

It was rage, she realized. Pure, unadulterated rage. She hadn't felt this *angry* in so long.

Not since she'd pushed Fritz's body off her own, grabbed her rifle, and started firing at the insurgents who'd attacked her unit. Who'd killed her friends.

Because that was what Pastor had done. He'd allowed people to be attacked and killed. She wanted to run over there. She wanted to break him. Hurt him. Kill him.

But she couldn't, of course. *So get it together, Liza.*

Carefully placing the gem on the table, she flattened her palms on her thighs, the soft cotton of her scrubs absorbing some of the clamminess. She drew a breath, remembering the relaxation techniques she'd learned to battle the anxiety of waking from a nightmare.

"Liza?" Brooklyn's voice had grown small and a little scared. "Are you all right?"

Her brain raced to think of something comforting to say, because the truth was not an option.

She lifted her head to smile at the little girl. "I'm okay. You ever have a nightmare, and then the next day you remember part of it and just, like, get a little scared again?"

Brooklyn nodded sagely. "Sometimes I dream that I die."

Liza sucked in a harsh breath. "Oh, honey. What an awful dream to have."

Brooklyn lifted a shoulder. "I know. I wake up and I'm afraid. The last nursing assistant wasn't very nice. She'd tell me to go back to sleep, even when I was crying."

Liza reached out, palm up. Brooklyn took her hand and squeezed. "I told my mom when she visited, and Mom told Nurse Williams to get another assistant. That's you."

"Well, I have nightmares, too. And they're scary, so I get it."

"Do you die?"

"No, but people I love get hurt, and that's scary, right?"

"Real scary. You don't have a mom to tell you that it's okay, because you're old."

Liza thought about her last nightmare and how Tom had run to her, holding her while she cried. Then Brooklyn's words sank in and her lips twitched. "I guess I am pretty old at that. But I learned some stuff that helps when I wake up scared. You want to know?"

Brooklyn sat up straighter. "Yes. Please."

"First is breathing." She demonstrated and within a minute, Brooklyn was mimicking the inhale-hold-exhale pattern. "Also, I cuddle my dog."

"You have a dog?"

"I do. She's big. Great Dane big."

Brooklyn's eyes widened. "She'd eat me."

"Nah, she's a softy. She might lick your face."

The child giggled. "That's dirty."

"True, but it does help to hug her. You can't have a dog here, but maybe a stuffed animal. Do you have one?"

"Not here. I had one at home, but I forgot it. Mom said she'd bring it to me, but she's working right now."

"Would you like me to ask Nurse Williams if I can get you one for now, until your mom brings yours?"

"Would you?"

"I would and I will. Now, the other thing you can do about bad dreams is to rewrite the ending. If I dream that my friends get hurt, then after I wake up, I close my eyes and picture them at a party instead, all healthy and happy. Just like the hurt never happened."

"So I could picture myself not dying? And doing a dance?"

"Exactly." Which wouldn't change Brooklyn's actual prognosis, but it might ease her fears along the way. "And then, the next day, you can wear this fashion statement." She held up the hospital gown again. "It says you are bada—" She clamped her lips shut and Brooklyn laughed. Such a lovely sound.

The little girl leaned forward and whispered, "Badass?"

Liza chuckled. "I need to watch my language. Let's get back to BeDazzling."

"That was very nice advice," a male voice said and Liza froze again. Pastor was two feet away, having been pushed to their table by his nurse. "May we join you?"

"Of course," Brooklyn chirped before Liza could speak. "I'm Brooklyn. You must be new."

She's done this before, Liza realized with a start. *She's been here for so long that she's accustomed to welcoming new patients.*

"I am," Pastor said, as the woman with the locket sat in a chair beside him. The nurse stepped back, watching with an eagle eye. "I just got here." He made a face. "I fell down. Broke some stuff. Hard when you're old like me. My name is Ben."

Liza noted the sudden tension in his companion's body.

He looked a little confused at the woman's reaction, then smiled. "People call me Pastor."

His companion swallowed. "It's a nickname," she said quietly.

Brooklyn just rolled with it. "Okay. We're BeDazzling. Wanna play with us?"

"Can I just watch?" he asked. "I like your scarf."

Brooklyn patted her head. "My mom brought it for me. It's from Switzerland." She turned to Liza. "Did you ever go to Switzerland?"

"Nope," Liza said. "I did go to Afghanistan, though. I saw some very pretty scarves there. They're called hijabs."

"I didn't catch your name," Pastor said, his eyes having flickered at *hijab*.

Liza had wondered if he would react. Amos had told them that Pastor was rabidly Islamophobic. "I'm Liza, Brooklyn's nursing assistant." Nervous and terrified that she'd show it, she busied her hands applying the next red gem.

"This is Sister Coleen," Pastor said. "She's kind of like a nursing assistant, too."

A puzzle piece dropped into place. *This is the healer. The one with the computer.*

Brooklyn's little forehead was furrowed. "Are you a nun? I knew a nun once. People called her Sister, too."

"Something like that," Coleen said. "Were you in the military, Liza? You said you were in Afghanistan."

"I was," Liza said. "But I probably shouldn't speak of it. Little pitchers, you know."

Coleen nodded. "I know. It's just that I've been . . . a little detached for the past few years. I've been catching up on news."

Liza supposed so, if *a few years* meant *thirty*.

"I watch the news," Brooklyn said. "On my tablet. Nurse Williams doesn't know." She lifted her brows, which looked a bit strange because she had no eyebrows. "Are you going to narc on me, Liza?"

Liza choked on a laugh. "*Narc* on you? Where on earth—" She cut herself off because she wasn't supposed to ask questions about Brooklyn's personal life. "I think I'll definitely be checking your tablet to see what you're reading. There are news outlets for kids. Otherwise you might see stuff that'll give you different nightmares."

Brooklyn had started to look defiant, but she nodded, her ire cooling. "That makes sense. But I'm not a baby, you know."

"No, you're not," Liza said.

"How old are you?" Pastor asked Brooklyn.

"Seven. Almost."

And then, as Liza worked the BeDazzler tool on the cotton gown, Brooklyn and Pastor proceeded to chat. It was the most surreal conversation Liza had ever heard.

The man was . . . sweet. There was no other word for it. He asked Brooklyn about her hobbies and the books she liked to read. He asked her about her schooling, nodding in approval when she said she was homeschooled.

And then he talked about his own children. Bo and Bernie. How he missed them. How they were angels in heaven now.

And Brooklyn comforted him, patting his gnarled hand with her small, bony one.

The two talked for an hour while Coleen quietly knitted a scarf and Liza finished the BeDazzled hospital gown. She tried to find a way to ask them where Eden was located, but every time she or Brooklyn brought up Pastor and Coleen's home, Coleen skillfully changed the subject. So Liza continued BeDazzling, working the red gems into a heart and adding Brooklyn's name underneath using smaller gems.

She lingered at the table as long as she could, aware that this was an opportunity for Tom and the FBI to study Pastor—his speech, his mannerisms, and the sheer charisma rolling off the man. Liza could now understand how he'd attracted his followers.

He honestly appeared to care.

Unless he was allowing twelve-year-old girls to be raped in the name of marriage or allowing thirteen-year-old boys to be raped in the name of apprenticeship. Or approving the murder of anyone who disagreed with him. Or making women into slaves. Or stealing the legacies and life savings of those who believed in his smiles and lies.

Finally, she stood and gathered Brooklyn's things. "I think it's time Miss Brooklyn had her lunch and a nap. Say goodbye to Pastor."

Brooklyn appeared ready to argue, but nodded. "I am tired. Can I see you tomorrow?"

"I'm here for at least six weeks," Pastor said.

"Me too," Brooklyn said glumly. "If I don't die first," she added matter-of-factly.

Coleen gasped softly, looking to Liza for confirmation.

"Your treatments are working," Liza said. "So I'm going to call horse hockey on that, okay?"

Brooklyn grinned impishly. "Is horse hockey like bullshit?"

Liza shook her head. "And on *that* note, we are going back to your room."

"Can we get a picture?" Brooklyn asked, clearly trying to delay their departure. "I like to show them to my mom when she visits." She patted her tablet, on which she'd been watching BeDazzler videos on YouTube. "Pleeeease?"

Coleen gave Pastor a nervous look. Pastor smiled. "Of course. Just for us, though, right?"

"Oh yes," Brooklyn said, genuinely serious. "There's hippo stuff."

Coleen looked confused. "Hippo stuff?"

"She means HIPAA," Liza explained. "It protects the privacy of patients."

"Oh." Coleen smiled thinly. "Of course."

"You get in the picture, too, Liza!" Brooklyn insisted.

Liza positioned herself behind the group, putting the tablet in selfie mode. "Say cheese!"

"Cheese!" Brooklyn belted out.

Liza snapped the photo, then put the tablet in Brooklyn's bag. She'd send a copy to Agent Raeburn ASAP. "All right. It's really time to go now. Say goodbye to Pastor, Brooklyn."

The child waved merrily at Pastor and Coleen. "Goodbye! See you tomorrow!"

See you in hell, Liza thought, but made herself smile. "Tomorrow."

She pushed Brooklyn back to her room, thinking that was all she'd see of Pastor for the day. She got Brooklyn's lunch and sat down with her tablet, as Brooklyn had access to the Internet. Liza didn't know who was monitoring usage and didn't want to get caught.

"Brooklyn, do you want to send this picture to your mom?"

"Yes, please. Her e-mail address is under Mom."

Liza found the contact and blind carbon copied herself before sending, then deleted the e-mail from the sent folder. She knew from Tom that a simple delete didn't permanently delete a file, but it would be gone at a cursory glance.

She was encouraging Brooklyn to eat her lunch when Nurse Innes arrived a half hour later.

"Miss Barkley? May I have a word? In private?"

Shit. What had she done? Had she been found out? Had they seen the e-mail she'd sent? "Of course. Brooklyn, I need you to stop playing with that food and actually eat some of it. You need your energy if we're going to BeDazzle again."

Brooklyn was rolling her eyes as Liza joined Nurse Innes in the hallway.

Innes pulled Brooklyn's door closed. "You've had a bit of an assignment change," the woman said. "You'll still be working with Brooklyn, but when she's sleeping, you're to report to Mr. Alcalde's room."

Liza got a bad feeling in her gut. "Of course, but who is Mr. Alcalde?"

Innes looked at her warily. "The man you just spent an hour talking to."

"Oh, I'm sorry. I don't think he said his last name, so I was confused. What will my duties be?"

"He wants you to read to him and talk to him. I think he likes your voice."

Liza made herself smile. "I'll be happy to."

"Meet him in the solarium in an hour. That'll give you time to get Brooklyn settled for the afternoon. Nurse Williams can take it from there. Mr. Alcalde has you until four."

"Yes, ma'am." Liza stood where she was as the woman walked away, then muttered quietly, hoping that Tom was listening, "I'll do my best to get him to talk about Eden."

TWENTY-NINE

hat's him?" Tom asked, joining Croft at the two-way window to the interview room.

Croft nodded. "Daniel Park. He owns a chain of hotels, one here in Sacramento."

Daniel Park was fit and looked far younger than his seventy years. He wore a bespoke suit that had to have cost a few thousand dollars. He appeared bored and was looking at his phone.

"How did you get him here?"

"A guest filed an assault complaint against one of his employees at the hotel here in the city. It was a while back but has gone uninvestigated. We asked that he meet us to discuss it. I'll make sure the actual complaint is followed up on. You okay? And your . . . friend, too?"

"I'm fine. Do I wish she weren't there? Of course. But she's capable of taking care of herself, or Molina and Raeburn wouldn't have put her in this role."

"Just checking. Mr. Park doesn't have a license to do financial transactions, because of his prior record, but I found a few recommendations from satisfied customers online, so he appears to be operating without one. He served five years for insider trading and tax fraud at Terminal Island. He was there with Pastor, Waylon, and Edward McPhearson."

"I want to get his cell phone records."

"What do you expect to find?" Croft asked.

"Pastor's wife said that back in the day, he'd give Waylon a onetime access code and instructions for Mr. Park, telling him what stock to buy. Waylon would make the call when he drove into town for supplies. The code was ever-changing and derived from a cipher that Pastor had developed. He's a numbers guy."

"You told us this in the debriefing yesterday evening. So why Park's cell phone records?"

"Because back when Waylon would contact Park, when Marcia was still in Eden, there were no cell phones. If Park is still doing business for Pastor—"

"That's a big 'if,'" Croft interrupted.

"Agreed," Tom allowed. "However, we know that Pastor has a cell phone now, because Amos saw him talking on it before he escaped Eden. If Park is still doing Pastor's bidding, I think Pastor would be making his own calls. Regardless, though, *someone* made two transfers from Eden's offshore accounts to pay for Pastor's care at Sunnyside."

"You're right. If Park's involved, he would have received the phone call sometime late Wednesday or early Thursday. But that's not going to be enough for a warrant."

"I'm hoping we can goad him into giving us enough for one. We know where Pastor is right now. So does Park. We can tell Park we have Pastor in custody and he's claiming that Park has been giving him financial advice without a license. That's an issue with the SEC."

"Especially since he's already served time. And if he has records of Pastor's offshore activity, we can charge him with perpetrating fraud on his congregation and illegally profiting from the sale of drugs. It's always the money, isn't it?"

"It's an adage for a reason," Tom said, "but I'm more interested in tracing his phone calls. If Pastor's called him recently, it could be a way to pinpoint Eden's current location."

"Even better. Okay, let's do this." She texted Raeburn to let him know they were getting started. "Raeburn's going to witness," she explained.

"Before we go in there, have you got any updates on Kowalski or his wife and kids?"

Croft sighed. "We found Angelina's Jag. It was valeted at San Francisco airport. She boarded a flight to Paris last night—her, Tony, the two-year-old, and their dog. Big Rottweiler named Lucky. Paris police put a cruiser outside the town house she's renting."

"But Kowalski didn't join her?"

"Nope. He's still in the wind. Part of me is glad that she's okay. Most of me thinks that she benefited financially from her husband's crimes and should be punished."

"I may be a little biased on that front," Tom admitted. "My father was a murderer, but my mom didn't know. She just wanted to get out because he was beating her—and me. She tried to tell people about the abuse, but no one believed her. So maybe, once we've closed this case against DJ and Pastor, we find out what Angelina knew."

"Raeburn's already got someone doing the digging, but you're right. We need to focus on Pastor and DJ right now."

Raeburn entered, quickly closing the door to keep the light out. "You two have a plan?"

"We do," Croft said.

"Then go."

Daniel Park looked up when they entered. "It's about time," he said impatiently. "I came when you asked. The least you can do is respect my time."

"Our apologies, sir," Croft said dutifully. "I'm working on getting an updated statement from the victim, so we're not ready to discuss the assault."

Park was furious. "You've got to be kidding me. I'll have your badge numbers. Now."

Tom just looked at him without saying anything for long seconds until Park's fury became discomfort. Then wariness.

"What's this about?" Park asked.

"Benton Travis," Tom said.

Park stiffened, fear flickering in his eyes. "I don't know who that is."

"It *has* been a while," Tom allowed. "Way back in your Terminal Island days."

Park scowled. "I served my time."

Tom smiled. "And you're still serving Benton Travis."

"This is ridiculous. You can't hold me here." He started to get up.

"He says differently," Tom said blandly, and Park blanched.

"That's a lie. He wouldn't."

"How would you know?" Croft asked curiously. "You don't remember him."

Park lowered himself back to his chair and crossed his arms over his chest. He said nothing.

"We talked to him this morning," Tom went on. "You know, at Sunnyside Oaks. Fancy place. He's getting good care there, by the way. In case you're interested."

Park had paled. "You're lying."

"Call him yourself and ask him," Tom challenged, knowing Park would do no such thing. To do so would be to admit that he was still in a business relationship with a wanted man.

"Have you arrested him yet?" Park demanded.

Tom chuckled at his expression. The man had realized he was damned if he did acknowledge Pastor and damned if he didn't, because Pastor had—allegedly—rolled on him.

"We will be arresting him," Tom promised. "We agreed to allow him to finish his convalescence at Sunnyside Oaks before we took him into custody if he gave us names. Yours was one of those names."

"I want a lawyer," Park said defiantly.

Tom nodded. "That's fine." They had enough right now to get a warrant for his phone records and maybe even his bank records.

"You're not charged yet, though. I mean, it might be as simple as aiding and abetting a fugitive of the law. Because he was charged back in L.A."

"That was thirty years ago," Park said. "Statute of limitations ran out decades ago."

"No statute of limitations on embezzlement," Tom said. "But you knew that. You're a money guy. When you talk to your lawyer, make sure he knows that we'll also be looking at all of your banking transactions. If you've accepted any payment from Benton Travis for any money management, then you've violated the SEC's rules. Considering you're a felon and all."

"There is a statute of limitations on that," Park said smugly. "Ten years."

"Not if it's been ongoing for thirty," Tom said. He glanced at Croft. "Is he free to go?"

"Of course. We can get to his phone and bank records, even if he flees. But if he flees, he's in even bigger trouble."

Park swallowed hard. "What are you offering?"

"*We* can't offer anything," Croft said. "We're just humble federal agents. But the federal attorneys will be chatting with you, if you have time to stick around. Sit tight." She rose, looking very badass. "Agent Hunter?"

They left Park in the interview room and found Raeburn in the viewing room, chuckling.

"'We're just humble federal agents,'" he repeated. "I really love watching you conduct an interview, Croft. It's like . . . art. And you also did well, Hunter. Nice job."

"Thank you, sir," Tom said, pleased. "I'll go start the warrant paperwork."

Croft settled into one of the folding chairs. "I'll watch Park while you do."

Tom was halfway to the door when he got an alert on his phone. He stopped dead in his tracks. "Cameron Cook just got an e-mail from Hayley."

He took the chair next to Croft, opening Cameron's e-mail account. "He gave me permission to view his account," Tom told Raeburn, who'd begun to pace.

"I know. Just read the damn e-mail."

"'Cameron, I hope you get this e-mail. We need your help, please. Hayley's ready to go into labor any minute and she's scared. There's a woman here, her name is Rebecca. She's first wife to Joshua, who's in charge because Pastor, DJ, and the healer are all gone to a hospital. Pastor's hurt and gets a hospital, but Hayley doesn't even have a doctor. Rebecca's been promised Hayley's baby and there isn't anything we can do about it. They're going to steal her baby because she got pregnant 'out of wedlock.' If Hayley even survives. We're in caves somewhere near Lassen, I think, because some of the rock is black and volcanic looking. It's cold and wet and people are getting sick. We're almost out of food. Water is scarce. I found the compound's sat dish and solar panels. Set up the computer outside. If it rains, the computer is fucked and I'll lose ability to communicate. Sending coordinates. Please help us.' It's signed, 'Graham.'"

"Where are the coordinates?" Raeburn demanded.

Tom sighed. "The middle of San Francisco Bay. This happened last time. They've got a proxy program hiding their location. They could be anywhere." He hit REPLY, speaking as he typed. "'Graham, this is Special Agent Hunter of the FBI. Cameron came to me for help. I'm sending you another e-mail ASAP. Click on the link. It'll let me control your computer. Your IP address is being hidden by a proxy program, so we can't find you.'"

Using his laptop, he found the Trojan he was looking for. He'd just hit SEND on the second e-mail when his phone buzzed with a call from Cameron Cook.

"They e-mailed again!" Cameron was practically shouting.

"I know. I've been monitoring your account. The coordinates are still hidden."

"What do we do now?"

"We wait for Graham to click on the link I sent him." Another call came through, this time from the surveillance tech in the van outside Sunnyside. Tom's gut twisted violently in knee-jerk fear for Liza. "I have another call coming in. I have to go, but I'll keep you up to date."

"Thank you," Cameron said fervently.

Tom took the surveillance tech's call and put it on speaker. "You're on speaker with Agents Raeburn and Croft. What's happening?"

"You are never gonna believe this," the tech said. "Liza took the little girl to the solarium to do a craft and who should sit down and talk to them? *Pastor.* He's even calling himself Pastor. I can patch you in so you can view the feed."

"Do it," Raeburn snapped as the feed appeared on Tom's laptop.

"Are you a nun?" a little girl asked.

"That's Liza's patient," Tom explained. "Brooklyn."

"I knew a nun once," Brooklyn went on. "People called her Sister, too."

Pastor sat in a wheelchair between the child and a middle-aged woman.

"Something like that," the woman said.

"Who's that?" Raeburn demanded.

"The healer," Tom said. "Graham said that the healer went to the hospital with Pastor. Her name is Coleen. Amos said she was there when he arrived in Eden."

"Let's go to my office," Raeburn said. "I want to see this on a bigger screen."

EDEN, CALIFORNIA
TUESDAY, MAY 30, 11:30 A.M.

"I'm *fine*," Hayley said through clenched teeth.

"No, you're *not.*" Sister Rebecca had been hovering for hours. She'd thrown Tamar out of Hayley's little cubicle, but Tamar had refused to leave, standing vigil at the curtain's edge.

Hayley glared up at Rebecca from her pallet on the cold stone floor. "I am *fine*." Which wasn't true. She'd been having mild contractions all morning and she was scared enough without the bitch making it worse. "You are making me tense and that isn't good for *my* baby."

Rebecca's eyes narrowed at the challenge. Her hand twitched like she was aching to use her fists. But of course she did not. She merely smiled cruelly. Hayley knew without a doubt that Rebecca would grab Jellybean as soon as the baby exited the womb.

From Tamar's pained expression, she knew it, too.

"I want you to stay as still as possible," Rebecca said. "I don't want you to go into labor until Sister Coleen returns. I want a healthy baby, so you will do everything in your power to delay labor. That includes staying put."

Hayley wanted to *kill* the bitch. *She* wanted a healthy baby? "If I promise to lie still, will you go? Because I'm really hating you right now."

One side of Rebecca's mouth lifted. "Don't worry. You won't have to expend your energy on hating me for much longer."

Tamar's eyes closed and Hayley knew she wasn't being paranoid in taking Rebecca's words as an obvious threat. There were so many things Hayley wanted to say to the woman. She wanted to threaten her back. But Rebecca held the power right now.

And the woman was right about one thing. She did want to delay labor for as long as possible, because Graham was so close to being able to call out for help. She hadn't mentioned the mild contractions to him. She hadn't wanted to break his concentration. He'd set up the last of the healer's computer equipment this morning and was using this latest trip to empty the pots to try to send out e-mails to the cops and Cameron.

Please, Graham. Please. Be careful. Be successful.

Her heart sank when there was a furor out in the common area. She could hear Joshua's voice. And Graham's. Neither sounded happy.

The curtain ripped back. Joshua had Graham by the collar and was shaking him. Bruises were forming on Graham's face and Hayley wanted to kill Joshua, too.

But all she could do was watch helplessly.

"Take him away," Rebecca cried, waving her hands. "He reeks."

"On purpose," Joshua growled. "He was up there, in the rocks . . . I'm still not sure what he was doing. He had a computer. He somehow smuggled a computer into the compound."

Rebecca's shock was genuine. "What? How?"

"It's not mine," Graham shouted. "I keep *telling* you. It's the *healer's*. It's *Pastor's*." Graham's voice was carrying and already the membership was gathering beyond the curtain. Which, Hayley figured, was Graham's intent, because Joshua was shaking him again, snarling at him to be quiet.

Graham was having none of it. There was desperation in his expression, in his voice, in the way he held his body rigid, fists clenched at his sides. He knew he was no physical match.

He was hoping for someone in the community to have the courage to stand with him.

"They hid this technology from you!" Graham continued to yell.

Joshua clamped a big hand over Graham's nose and mouth, and Hayley struggled to get up. The bastard wasn't trying to quiet Graham. He was trying to smother him.

"Get your fucking hands off him!" Hayley yelled. "He's telling the truth. I saw the computer in the healer's office at the last site. *Stop!* You're going to kill him!"

"*Brother Joshua.*" It was Isaac, their mother's husband. "You cannot kill this boy. If he has erred, it's Pastor's responsibility to decide his sentence."

Sentence? The hope that had speared Hayley's heart died. Isaac wasn't going to help them. Why would he? She was sure their mother had told him all kinds of lies about them.

"Pastor left me in charge," Joshua said in an ominous tone.

"Not to pass judgment." Isaac stepped up to Joshua and forcibly removed his hand from Graham's face. Then stared at him.

In challenge, Hayley realized. Isaac wasn't doing the right thing. He was vying for control.

Still, it was an intervention, and none too soon, because Graham was wheezing and coughing. Joshua would have killed him while she watched. The rage that had been on a constant simmer since they'd been dragged to this hell erupted.

"Do none of you care that your Pastor had a *computer*?" Hayley yelled. "Like you're pretending not to care that he went to a hospital when he let your loved ones die?"

The gathering crowd went silent for several long beats before the murmurs resumed. But this time they seemed to be agreeing. With that last statement, anyway.

"My baby died," one woman said loudly, even though her husband tried to shut her up.

"My wife died," a man said. "She was thirty-five. She might have lived if Pastor had allowed me to take her to a hospital, but he refused, no matter how I begged."

"And we can discuss that," Joshua said in his booming voice, trying to regain control. "For now, this boy has brought contraband into our community."

Graham pushed himself to stand at his full height. "Dude," he said, his voice hoarse from coughing, "I don't even have my phone. It was the size of a deck of cards and you confiscated it. Where would I have hidden a computer, for God's sake?" He staggered when the back of Joshua's hand connected with his mouth. Blood dripped from Graham's lip.

Joshua was breathing hard. "You will not take the name of our Lord God in vain."

"Fuck you," Hayley growled and struggled to get up.

Rebecca pushed her back down with ease. "You are a whore," she hissed in Hayley's ear. "If you don't shut up, I'll cut this baby from your body and make your brother watch."

"Lady, you'd better take your hands off me." Hayley was calm now.

"Or what?" Rebecca murmured.

Hayley ground her teeth impotently. Because Rebecca was right. She had no power here.

Graham wiped the blood from his mouth. "I repeat. Where would I have hidden a computer? *And* a set of solar panels? *And* a satellite dish? You're out of your fucking minds!"

Joshua's fist made a crunching sound as it struck Graham's jaw. "Be silent!" he roared. "If our healer possessed these things before you arrived, how is it that no one has seen them?"

Graham went down and Hayley tried to crawl to him, only for Rebecca to yank her back.

A single voice cut through the noise. "I have."

Again, silence reigned, the only sounds Graham's muted groans and Joshua's panting breaths. One of the oldest members pushed her way through to stand next to Joshua. Her nose wrinkled in distaste at Graham's smell, but she squared her shoulders to glare up at Joshua.

Joshua was a big man and this old woman was tiny. Her name was Sister Judith and she led the quilters. Hayley had never spoken with her in the weeks that she'd been here. Joshua turned his attention to the old woman, giving her a death glare that didn't seem to frighten her.

From the corner of Hayley's eye, she saw Tamar skirt the crowd to get to Graham, dropping to her knees to help him. Tamar gave Hayley a reassuring nod. Graham was okay.

Hayley returned her attention to the old woman, who'd lifted her chin.

"Will you hit me, too, Joshua?" she demanded. "Your own mother?"

Oh. Wow.

"Step down, woman," Joshua said quietly. "I don't want to have you removed."

"And you would, wouldn't you?" The woman turned to her fellow Edenites. "I saw the computer in Sister Coleen's office two moves ago. I wasn't sure what it was. Or, I knew what it was and didn't want to admit it to myself."

Joshua looked like she'd slapped him. "You didn't tell me."

"I was being a good member of the flock. But this—" She pointed to Graham. "You would have killed him, Joshua. His sentence is Pastor's job. He would have cast him out and let the wolves take care of him. You're wresting control because he is not here, and your father and I didn't raise you to do that."

Hayley shook her head, unable to believe this. The woman wasn't upset because Graham was right but because her son was usurping Pastor's authority.

"This boy did not bring a computer into Eden," the old woman continued. "Now, I'm not going to question Pastor. He must believe that we need this machine."

"Well, then," Graham said, still on the floor, his words slurred but his disgust still clear. "He'll be really angry when he comes back. Mr. Genius here broke the solar panels. Nothing works without a power source."

Oh no. Oh God. That was it, then. They were fucked. She looked to Graham, who held up one finger, then shrugged.

One e-mail? she mouthed.

Cameron, he mouthed back.

The murmurs had resumed and it seemed that the entire group took a giant step back, distancing themselves from Joshua.

"I didn't know the solar . . . *things* were his," Joshua said, sounding like a petulant child.

"I'm sure he'll understand that," his mother said. "But he won't if you usurp his authority. Put the boy in the box for now, Joshua. Get him out of your sight and cool your mind. Then, once Pastor returns, he can choose the boy's fate."

"Cast out," the group said, almost as one.

Hayley shuddered, because it was damn eerie. And then she gasped when the first real contraction gripped her, stealing her breath with its strength. *Shit.*

"Now look what you've done," Rebecca spat. "She's gone into labor. Go. Everyone go!"

SACRAMENTO, CALIFORNIA
TUESDAY, MAY 30, 1:30 P.M.

I need to get out of here. DJ had been pacing in Coleen's bedroom for hours, watching the news with mounting dread. The Feds now had his photo on every network, and for a brief time he'd been trending on Twitter. They even knew he was now bald.

At least they didn't know he was here. They didn't know anything about this place. So he was safe. *For now.*

But Gideon and Mercy had won. *For now.*

He'd retreat. *For now.* But he wasn't leaving here without Pastor— or at least Pastor's cash. He'd find his sunny island and pay someone else to take care of Gideon and Mercy. It wouldn't be as satisfying as putting a bullet in their heads himself, but the job would get done.

He consolidated the bags he'd brought with him, adding the fake license plates and magnetic signs to the weapons bag. The laptop didn't fit, but it didn't matter. This wasn't the first time he'd had to ditch a laptop. He'd bought a model with a removable hard drive for just this reason. He popped the drive and tossed it into the duffel.

He'd turned for the door when it opened, and Coleen entered the room. She closed the door behind her and leaned on it. And said nothing, simply watching him.

New dread coiled in DJ's gut. "Where is he?"

"Back in the solarium after his nap."

"What did he do while he was there?"

"He met a little girl earlier, and they chatted. He wanted to feel the sun on his face, so I took him back and left him with his nurse. I wanted to talk to you."

"What did they chat about? And who's with him now?"

"They chatted about all kinds of things. His kids, you know, his real kids. Bo and Bernie."

"That doesn't hurt me like you think it does," DJ said. "I never wanted to be his kid."

"He told the child his name was Ben."

DJ stared. "He *what*? Has he gone *senile*?"

"The nurse said it's probably an aftereffect of the anesthesia. That sometimes people get confused. I looked it up on the computer there—" She pointed to the computer the facility provided for the suite. "And it's true. But I also looked up all kinds of other things."

"Like what?"

"Like the news. Lots of stuff has happened in thirty years, you know? I kept up with medical news on the computer you gave me, but it seems most of the Internet wasn't available. I wonder why that is."

Because DJ had blocked their access. "Stop talking unless you have something to say."

Coleen tilted her head. "Mercy Callahan."

Fuck. "I don't know that name."

Coleen smiled. "Well, she went by Mercy Burton back then. She looks just like her mother. It's uncanny. Oh, and she's alive. Which you knew because you've been trying to kill her."

"I killed her thirteen years ago. I told you that."

"Either you were mistaken or you lied. Either way, you're trying to kill her now. And not doing such a good job of it."

He took a step closer, annoyed when she didn't flinch. "And how do you know this?"

"Because I saw a report this morning, before I took Pastor to the solarium. It was an interview with a lady whose husband's body was found in a freezer yesterday by the FBI. Who say you're the lead suspect. But you knew that, too."

DJ took another step closer. "That has nothing to do with Mercy Callahan."

"That's not what the man's widow is saying. She said that the family down the street is responsible. That they took in Mercy Callahan and Gideon Reynolds. Their photos popped up on the screen, and imagine my surprise. I thought Gideon was dead, too."

So had I. Thanks, Dad.

"Seems like your father also lied," Coleen said. "I wonder what Gideon's mother had over men. I mean, she was pretty, but not that pretty. But she had Amos and Ephraim and Waylon wrapped around her finger. And you, too, until you actually killed her."

"She did *not* have me wrapped around her finger," DJ spat. "I wanted to kill her when I let her stow away in my truck."

"Both Mercy and her mother were supposed to die then?"

At least Coleen saw the truth. "Yes. I wanted them to think they were getting away."

"So you took them to civilization, let them think they were getting their freedom, and then you killed them. Or tried to."

"I thought Mercy was dead. I didn't know until last month that she wasn't. Gideon either."

"I see."

He smiled tightly. "Good. Glad we had this chat."

"Well, maybe."

Coleen was playing him somehow. "Are you going to tell Pastor?" he asked.

She shook her head. "If I were going to tell him, I'd have done it already."

She was lying. He could see it in her eyes. He moved faster than she'd been expecting, trapping her against the door, pressing his forearm into her throat.

"What are you doing, Sister Coleen?" he asked in a low hiss.

"Nothing," Coleen rasped. "Just filling in the blanks. You're hurting me, DJ."

He used his free hand to pat her down, chuckling when he found the tablet concealed down the back of her shirt. It was Sunnyside's tablet and she'd figured out how to make it record audio. He hit the end button and dropped the tablet, crushing it with his boot.

Her eyes widening, she clawed at his arm as she fought to breathe.

"You were getting me to confess so that you could play it for Pastor." He smiled down at her, energized by her fear. "You thought you were smarter than me? You're just a woman."

He grabbed the chain around her throat and twisted hard, cutting off her air supply as he dragged her to the bed. He shoved her down and grabbed a pillow. Leaning close, he whispered, "This is how Waylon died. Just so you know."

He pressed the pillow to her face, putting all of his weight on it. She struggled. And then she was quiet. He remained another few minutes. Just to be sure.

Then he took her pulse, just to be very sure. She was dead. He took off her shoes and set them aside, then tucked her into bed, like she'd taken a nap.

He needed to get Pastor out of this place and back to Eden. Or at least partway to Eden. As far as it took to get him to cough up the codes. He'd have to steal a car to get out of the lot. And then he'd return to the Explorer he'd set aside. That would get him back up into the mountains.

Putting on the surgical mask, he slipped from the suite carrying his duffel. He met Nurse Innes on his way to the employee entrance.

"I'm glad you're leaving. I didn't want to have you escorted out."

Bitch. "My mother has everything covered. I'll call for an Uber," he lied, "but I want to stop and say goodbye to the old man on my way out."

"I'll walk with you."

He gritted his teeth. "You really want me out of here, don't you?"

Her smile was thin. "You've created quite a mess for yourself, Mr. Belmont. You are a security risk. If the authorities find you here, you'll put this facility in a very bad spot." They stopped at a door marked SOLARIUM. "Your father is inside. There, chatting with the nursing assistant."

DJ peered through the window. "That's not the assistant he was assigned." The nurse sitting nearby was the same, but not the assistant.

"She works in pediatrics. He met her this morning when she brought her patient to the solarium, and he demanded that she be assigned to him. We do our best to meet his needs."

There was something about the nursing assistant that bothered him. She was familiar. And then she turned her head and he saw her hot pink cat-eye glasses with sparkling rhinestones.

He'd seen those glasses before—in the scope of his rifle on that rooftop. She'd been with Mercy in the eye doctor's office. She'd blocked his shot.

She'd fucked everything up. And then the real truth descended.

She was with the FBI.

Fucking hell. He remembered Nurse Gaynor, the little bugs she'd been planting. Had she been hired by Kowalski or had she been with the FBI, too?

Either way, the Feds knew that he was here. They were probably waiting for him outside. Why hadn't they stormed the place? What were they waiting for?

Me. They're waiting for me. He'd snuck in via the ambulance the night before, so they didn't know. But they'd know now, because this woman was likely wired like Nurse Gaynor had been.

He needed to get out of here. But in a way they wouldn't suspect.

The ambulance they'd used last night would be perfect. Nobody would stop him from leaving, and any Fed waiting outside would assume he was legit.

All of this thinking took about ten seconds, and when he glanced back at Innes, she looked wryly amused.

"Miss Barkley is quite pretty," she said. "I think your father was charmed."

"How long has she been here?" he asked, keeping his tone casual.

He didn't succeed, because the nurse's eyes narrowed. "Today is her first day. Why?"

Because you are a fucking idiot and I don't trust you. "Introduce me," he said smoothly. "Maybe I'd like to be charmed, too."

Still wary, Innes opened the door, and DJ followed her into the bright room. It was hot, all the glass intensifying what was going to be a ninety-eight-degree day.

"Mr. Alcalde, excuse me for interrupting you," Innes said with forced cheer. "You've had a long outing today. It's time for you to return to your room. But before you do, your son came by. He says he's going on a trip and he wanted to say goodbye." She gave DJ a pointed look. "Say goodbye, Mr. Belmont."

Pastor stiffened in his wheelchair. "Why are you here?" he asked, his anger barely veiled.

As for the nursing assistant, she froze for a moment, and then her eyes flashed with such a vicious rage that he might have been cowed had she been a man. He'd definitely be killing her soon. But Innes first. Now he turned to the nurse and said, "I'll be going, but can I have a word with you first? Privately?"

Miss Barkley went still, eerily so. Not frozen, like before, but as if she were preparing. For what, he wasn't certain. Maybe to attack. Maybe to flee.

Nurse Innes picked up on the tension and nodded slowly. "Please stay here, Miss Barkley."

The Fed didn't blink. She didn't answer, either.

Nurse Innes led him to the door through which they'd come, into the hall and then into a supply closet. "What is wrong with Miss Barkley?"

He didn't answer her, just put down his duffel, drew his silenced gun and shot her in the head. When she fell, he shot her a second time.

Grabbing the duffel, he left the closet in time to see Miss Barkley halfway down the hall. He caught up to her and pressed the barrel of his gun to her back. "If you run, I'll kill you," he murmured. "Then I'll go into that solarium and kill every single patient. Not all of them are criminals. A couple of them are kids. You okay with them dying, too?"

She was ramrod stiff. "What do you want?"

He patted her down, finding no wires. Which made no sense. They'd have her wired somehow. Keeping the gun firmly at her back, he checked out her front. She flashed him a hate-filled glare, turning her body toward him in an awkwardly stiff way.

Her pendant caught the light and he abruptly realized that was where she'd hidden the camera, so he yanked it from her throat. She stiffened, but made no other noise. And because her glasses reminded him of his ruined shot at Mercy, he grabbed those and broke them in two.

DJ tossed the necklace and the glasses into a trash can, then answered her question. "I want you to come back to the solarium with me and push Pastor's wheelchair."

"And then?"

"Seconds are ticking, Miss Barkley. Or should I say *Agent* Barkley? Do as I say or I will kill everyone in that room and then blow up this whole building, including the little kids."

Her jaw tightened, but she nodded and turned back to the solarium.

As soon as they entered the room, he saw that Pastor was glaring. "What is the meaning of this? What are you doing here?"

DJ shoved his gun harder into Miss Barkley's back, hiding the movement with his duffel bag. "Move," he murmured. "And be casual. If anyone notices, everyone here is dead."

She obeyed, gripping the handles of the wheelchair so tightly that her knuckles whitened as she pushed Pastor into the hall.

"DJ!" Pastor snapped. "What is the meaning of this?"

"We're going for a ride, Pastor," DJ said. "The Feds have surrounded this place."

Pastor gasped. *"Hurry."*

Miss Barkley was a cool customer, DJ thought. She hadn't panicked. Wasn't crying. She was, in fact, acting like a real nurse.

"He shouldn't leave the facility," she said. "He's not ready medically."

"You can come with us and take care of me," Pastor said. "It'll be okay."

DJ pushed the woman to walk faster and, again, she obeyed. Pastor really was going senile. He hadn't put together that his nurse was one of those Feds.

DJ grabbed Barkley's badge and buzzed them out. *Perfect.* The ambulance was parked by the back door under an awning that shielded it from the rest of the lot. DJ opened the passenger door, surprised to see someone in the driver's seat.

"What the—" was all the man had time to get out before he slumped, a bullet in his head.

"Open the back," DJ told Miss Barkley. "Then get the stretcher."

She obeyed again, her muscles flexing under the strain. Keeping the gun on her, DJ helped Pastor onto the stretcher. "In you go."

The nursing assistant pushed the stretcher into the back of the ambulance.

"Sit tight, Pastor. I'm getting us out of here." DJ put his duffel in with Pastor, reached into the bag, and retrieved a zip tie. He used it to bind the woman's wrists together in front of her, then shoved her toward the passenger seat. "Get in. You're my insurance."

She lifted her chin. "No. I won't go."

He held up his phone. "You remember the explosion at the radio station yesterday? That was only a few little sticks. I planted a bomb in there with four of the big sticks." Which was a lie, but she didn't know that. "Filled the canister with nails and broken glass. It'll blow a hole in the wall and kill anyone in a forty-foot radius. And if they aren't blown to bits, they'll be human pincushions. You want that? All I need to do to detonate is make one phone call."

She swallowed hard and climbed into the ambulance.

He yanked the driver out, taking the man's badge before tossing his body to the ground. He got behind the wheel, relieved to see the keys in the ignition. He started the vehicle and headed toward the ambulance entrance, on the opposite side from the employee and family entrance.

Keeping his face averted from the security camera, he'd rolled down his window to slide the driver's badge through the card reader when he heard the roar of an engine. His side mirror showed an approaching SUV with heavily tinted windows.

Except for the driver's window, which was open, a gun visible. "Stop! Police!"

"Fucking hell," DJ growled. The gate was opening slowly, but he wasn't going to make it.

And then the SUV was T-boned by a dark sedan. The sedan hit the SUV on the back fender, forcing it into the fence. Saltrick, the security chief, got out, his gun drawn and pointed at the driver of the SUV.

Well, shit. Saltrick didn't know DJ was stealing the ambulance, intent instead on stopping the cop. *Things are going my way.*

The gate in front of DJ opened and he drove out. *Yes.*

Barkley was staring in her side mirror in annoyed frustration.

DJ smiled. "Not your day, huh?" She didn't respond and that annoyed *him*. "Aren't you going to say that I'm never getting away with that?"

She turned her head to stare at him with contempt.

No worry. He'd slap that look off her face at the first opportunity. They'd gotten away. For now.

THIRTY

It was like an episode of *The Twilight Zone*, Tom thought as he watched Liza and Pastor talk.

The man had been like a kindly grandfather with Liza's patient Brooklyn. And then again later, when Liza had been ordered back to socialize with him, he'd been kind and thoughtful. He'd asked questions about her time in Afghanistan and she'd answered him honestly.

If one didn't know her, they'd believe that she was having a lovely chat.

"Remarkable," Raeburn murmured. "He is an utter chameleon. He can torture, order killings, enable rape, and then talk to Liza like he's Mr. Rogers."

"I can see how people would follow him," Croft agreed. "They'd just trust him."

It was true. Then again, Tom had grown up with a monster, a murderous dirty cop whom everyone had liked and admired. "The best sociopaths can feign empathy. My biological father was the life of the party, the cop all the other cops looked up to. One of the guys on the force even named his kid after him. That was awkward, especially after he was killed in prison."

Croft sighed. "And all the time he was coming home to abuse you and your mother."

"Yeah. So I guess I'm a little cynical about people like Pastor."

"A little cynicism isn't a bad thing," Raeburn said. "Keeps you sharp."

Tom agreed with that, to a point. "But too much can make you bitter." His phone chimed and he grabbed it, hoping it was a notification of activity on Cameron Cook's account—maybe Graham telling him that he'd clicked on the link that would allow Tom to control his computer—because they'd heard nothing out of Eden. But it wasn't from Cameron Cook's account.

"Someone in the billing office finally clicked on my Trojan," he said, relief coursing through him. He'd be able to shut the security network down. Best case, they'd order in an outside contractor and the Bureau could get another person inside. Worst case, the security team would be so busy fixing their network that they wouldn't detect Liza's presence.

He had opened his laptop and begun to type when a strangled noise from Croft had him looking up at the monitor.

Tom's blood ran cold. "No, no, no," he whispered.

DJ Belmont had entered the solarium with Nurse Innes. The two left a moment later, but Tom had seen the look on Belmont's face. He knew. *Oh my God.* He knew.

Raeburn was already on the phone with the surveillance van. "Move," he ordered.

Federal agents, including a SWAT team that had been positioned near the surveillance van, rushed to cut off the exits.

"Run, Liza," he breathed. "Run."

Liza did, leaving Pastor where he sat and heading for the exit.

Tom fired off a text to Rafe, who was keeping watch from the employee lot. **Belmont in the facility. Liza headed to employee exit.**

Ready was Rafe's reply.

And then Liza stopped walking.

Tom's heart stopped at a man's murmur. "If you run, I'll kill you. Then I'll go into that solarium and kill every single patient. Not all of them are criminals. A couple of them are kids. You okay with them dying, too?"

"What do you want?" Liza asked, turning her body so that the pendant and her glasses caught DJ's face. He was bald and clean shaven, and a surgical mask dangled under his chin.

A moment later, the pendant was yanked from Liza's throat, followed by her glasses. And then all they could see was the inside of a trash can.

Tom stared at the monitor, trying to think of what he could do. None of the wireless cameras were picking her up, and he could only watch helplessly.

"They'll be searching for her soon," Raeburn said. "She'll be okay."

Croft squeezed Tom's shoulder. "Breathe," she ordered.

Tom realized he hadn't been, so he sucked in a breath that burned.

His cell began to buzz. It was Rafe. Tom snatched it up and answered. "Where is she?"

"In Sunnyside's ambulance. I'm in pursuit—"

A crash made Tom wince. "Rafe? Rafe?"

Both Raeburn and Croft turned to him with twin expressions of confusion. Raeburn caught on first. "What have you done, Hunter?"

Tom didn't answer. "Rafe?"

"Put the gun down!" a voice yelled.

"Police! *You* put *your* gun down," Rafe yelled back, then in a more normal voice, he recited the numbers on a license plate. "That's the plate on the ambulance he stole. Security just wrecked my SUV. I'm pinned against a rock wall. The ambulance is gone, but Belmont's in it, along with Liza and Pastor."

Tom had repeated the license plate numbers for Raeburn when a gun fired, followed quickly by a second shot. "Rafe?"

"I'm not hit," he said, a car door loudly groaning through the phone.

"Our people are in pursuit of the ambulance," Raeburn told Tom and Croft. "Are you talking to Rafe Sokolov?"

Tom nodded once. "Yes."

Through the phone they heard Rafe shout, "SacPD. Drop the gun, asshole! Hands where I can see them! Do not push me, buddy. On your stomach. *Do it. Now.*" After a pause, Tom could hear the click of handcuffs and another groan from Rafe. "His badge says Saltrick."

"He's the chief of security," Tom said dully.

"You hired your own muscle?" Raeburn demanded. "What the *fuck*, Hunter?"

Tom couldn't hear Raeburn, his boss's words not sinking in. "Rafe, are you all right?"

"Yeah," Rafe said, breathing hard. "Your guys just busted through the fence. Saltrick's restrained and he's the only one I saw leave. Dammit. I almost had them."

"You got us the ambulance's plate. Call if you need me." Tom stood, feeling Raeburn's barely restrained rage but unable to focus on anything but his own paralyzing fear.

"Where are you going, Agent Hunter?" Raeburn demanded as Tom turned for the door.

"To bring her back, sir."

Raeburn stood rigidly, shaking his head. Then gestured at Croft with a tilt of his head. "Go with him. Keep him from making this an even bigger clusterfuck."

"Yes, sir," Croft said respectfully.

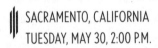

SACRAMENTO, CALIFORNIA
TUESDAY, MAY 30, 2:00 P.M.

"Where are we going?" Liza asked, proud that she didn't sound afraid even though she was. But she'd faced worse and knew that Tom was searching for her. She only hoped the FBI was no longer looking for the ambulance.

DJ had forced her from the vehicle, abandoning it behind what appeared to be a grocery store that had been closed for some time. He'd shoved her into a white Ford Explorer that had been parked, waiting for them.

He'd stolen this SUV the night before, or so he'd bragged to Pastor. He'd left it here, knowing he'd need something sturdier to get Pastor up the mountain roads.

He was probably telling the truth about going up into the mountains. They'd bypassed the interstates for a back road and were headed north.

"Eden," Pastor rasped from the back seat. DJ had moved Pastor from the ambulance to the back of the stolen Explorer with care. Whether it was genuine care or not, Liza couldn't be sure.

"We are," DJ said amiably. "And since the Feds cut Pastor's recovery short, you will be his nurse. I won't abide by him getting poor-quality care. He's too important to all of us."

In the back seat, Pastor beamed. That was, apparently, the right thing to say.

Liza didn't believe DJ, even if Pastor did. There was an oily quality to DJ's words. He did not have Pastor's charisma, for sure. It felt like he was pacifying Pastor. *But why?*

For the money, she realized. It almost always came down to money. Waylon had figured out Pastor's cipher system for the banking codes, but DJ didn't know it. If he had, she didn't think he'd have stuck around. He'd have stolen the money for himself.

She also didn't believe that DJ intended to have her care for Pastor. He'd likely kill her when he no longer needed a hostage. She wasn't going to make it easy for him, though.

She'd been thinking through the various scenarios and how she could best buy the time Tom needed to find her. Mercy and Gideon believed DJ had lied to Pastor to stay in his good graces so he could get the money. If that was true, pitting the two men against each other might be the best strategy. It might get her killed, but she figured that was in DJ's eventual playbook regardless of what she did.

"Then, as his nurse, I recommend you take him back. From what I've heard about Eden, it doesn't have a lot of conveniences. Not to mention medical resources."

DJ eyed her as they sped north on a rural route. "What do you know about Eden?"

Where to start? She sifted through all the information Margo Kitson had provided. "I know that it wasn't supposed to be permanent."

DJ laughed. "Who told you that?"

"She's right," Pastor said. "We were only going to hide there for a while."

"And everyone but your father was wanted by the Feds," she said. "So the founders stayed."

"And exactly how do you know that?" DJ asked silkily. Dangerously.

Liza considered telling them about finding Pastor's wife but decided to hold that card for later. "I have my sources," was all she'd say. "But they were very informative."

"Gideon and Mercy," DJ spat. "They know nothing."

"Gideon?" Pastor asked, confused. "And Mercy? They can't have said anything. They're dead. You know this, DJ. You took care of Mercy yourself."

Liza turned to look at Pastor. "Did he tell you that?"

"Yes. Of course."

Liza gave Pastor a pitying look. "Well, she's very much alive. I saw her just last night."

DJ's face turned so red that Liza was surprised steam wasn't blowing out his ears.

Pastor shook his head. "You're mistaken."

"She's lying," DJ stated flatly.

"She has a locket," Liza said. "I've seen it. Inside is a photo of her—a baby picture really. She's twelve and she's with this guy named Ephraim Burton. Maybe you've heard of him?"

Pastor's demeanor changed instantly from kindly grandfather to furious sociopath. "What are you talking about?"

"She's lying," DJ insisted. "And if she doesn't shut up, I'm going to shoot her in the head."

Liza drew a breath. *I'm sorry, Tom.* "I served in Afghanistan. I looked men in the eye who were a helluva lot scarier than you. You're going to kill me anyway. I might as well take you down with me. He lied to you, Mr. Travis. He told you that he killed Mercy, but she survived. Waylon Belmont said he killed Gideon, but he lied, too. Gideon is alive and well. And DJ here has been trying to kill them ever since, so that you won't find out."

She recoiled when DJ's fist connected with her temple. Pain exploded in her head and she breathed out a moan. *God, that hurts.* Still, she forced herself to continue.

"We know you have fifty million bucks in offshore accounts and that your banker is . . ." She glanced at DJ because he'd suddenly gone rigid. This made her smile through the pain. "I think that's something Mr. Belmont *doesn't* know. So that tidbit I'm going to keep to myself."

Playing them off one another might be the only way to keep herself alive until the cavalry arrived.

Pastor eyed her cannily. "You don't know, either."

"His initials are D.P."

Pastor's eyes flashed with anger and Liza hoped Tom was pursuing Daniel Park with everything he had. "What else do you know?" he demanded.

"Lots. I'd tell you, but he's going to kill me, so I'm not going to tell you anything more."

"Did you know this, DJ?" he asked calmly, which was somehow more frightening than his angry voice. "Did you know that the Feds know about us?"

"He did," Liza said, and then she frowned. "Where's the woman? Sister Coleen?"

Pastor tensed. "You left her behind, DJ. What were you thinking? She'll sing."

"No, she won't," DJ said grimly. And if looks could kill . . .

He didn't need evil looks, though. He had a gun. And possibly a bomb that he could detonate with his phone.

Pastor laid back, his shoulders sinking. "You killed her? Why?"

Liza remembered the woman mentioning the catching up she'd been doing. "All that news she was reading, probably. Did she see all the news reports on Mercy?" She shifted in her seat to meet Pastor's angry eyes. "There are many, many reports. All you need to do is look online."

"Who's going to be our healer now?" Pastor asked. Then he smiled cruelly. "How about you, Liza? We'd have to keep you subjugated, of course. Can't have you running your mouth to the community."

"We threaten a kid," DJ said. "She'll do anything to protect a kid. Won't you, Liza?"

Fuck. Divide and conquer just took a step back. "No. Many things, yes. Anything? No."

"Just take care of our people," Pastor said smugly. "And obey. And wear a locket." His eyes brightened. "And marry me. Since my wife is now gone."

Liza tried to think past the pounding in her head. This sucked. The thought of being Pastor's *anything* made her sick. But it bought her time and that would have to be good enough.

Tom would find her. And in the meantime, she could help that girl whose baby was due any minute. Hayley. Her name was Hayley.

She forced her lips to curve. "And they say chivalry is dead."

"She's lying," DJ hissed.

"About what?" Pastor asked mildly. "That she's willing to be our healer? My wife? Or that Mercy is alive when you said you'd killed her?"

"Yes." DJ's jaw was taut and a muscle in his cheek twitched. "All of that. Every word is a damn lie."

"Well. I don't think she's lying about Mercy, but you can easily fix that once we're all safely in Eden. And then we'll talk more." Pastor closed his eyes, clearly exhausted. "As for our new healer, she'll come to heel eventually. Get me home, DJ. I'm tired of all of this."

DJ shot her a venomous look and Liza swallowed hard. *Fantastic.* At least she was alive. *For now.*

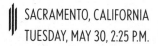

SACRAMENTO, CALIFORNIA
TUESDAY, MAY 30, 2:25 P.M.

"Where are we going?" Croft asked.

Tom clutched the wheel like a lifeline. Because it was. It was taking him to Liza. "Eden."

Motherfucking DJ Belmont. If he's touched one hair on her head . . .

"Okay," Croft said. "I'd question that, considering we don't know exactly where it is. But you're in a shitty headspace, so I'm gonna let it go. What will you do when we get there?"

Kill DJ Belmont. "I don't know."

"That's honest, at least. Let's plan some scenarios, shall we? Like we're professionals and not driving like crazy people up State Route 70 because Eden is 'somewhere up there.'"

The decision to take a back road had been Tom's. He didn't think DJ would risk sticking to the interstate. This road was the fastest way north other than I-5, and it cut through Yuba City, where DJ had owned a home. He'd be familiar with this road.

Tom wanted to snarl, but she was right. "Okay. Give me scenarios."

"I will. But first, be straight with me. Is Liza your 'friend' or more?"

"More." His voice broke and he had to clear his throat. "Everything."

"Honest again." Croft rubbed her temples. "You shouldn't be here, Tom. Why are we here?"

"Because I'd go all by myself anyway, and at least you're here with me to keep me from doing something stupid and clusterfuckish?"

"Fair enough. Scenario one: We can't find Eden."

No. His brain couldn't accept it as a possibility. But it was valid, nonetheless. "We keep looking. I keep looking."

She sighed. "You'll give up your career to keep looking? Because after this, you're not going to be allowed within a light-year of anything Eden."

"Yes. I might have already given up my career anyway."

"You're not wrong," Croft murmured. "Damn, kid. I was getting used to you, too."

He really didn't give a fuck, but he wasn't going to disrespect her. "What's scenario two?"

"I'll throw you a softball. You find Eden, and Liza is there, but DJ has dynamite."

"Attempt hostage negotiations. Protect the innocents. Bring snipers in to take him down."

"That's a good start. Scenario three: You get there and Liza's not there, but DJ is and he won't tell you where she is."

"But she's alive," Tom gritted out.

"Yes."

"Offer him the fifty mil. We could have taken it at any time. We didn't for the same reason that we never mentioned Eden to the media—they would have known we were after them."

"*What?* I mean, I knew you could have taken it, but you'd *give* it to him?"

"No. I'd *offer* it to him. There are lots of ways to do what appears to be a money transfer."

"Huh. That's actually not a horrible idea."

"Thank you," he said dryly, then braced himself. "And scenario four?"

"She's dead," Croft said quietly.

A wave of nausea hit him hard. *"No."*

"Then pull over, because you don't belong in this car."

Tom gripped the wheel tighter. "Then I retract my answer and take the Fifth."

She sighed. "That's what I thought. You should drive faster."

He was already driving twenty over the limit with his flashers going, but he sped up. "Which back roads will take us up to Lassen?" he asked. "And when do I have to choose a route?"

Croft checked her phone. "You've got till Oroville. Either you stay on this road and come at the caves from the west or cut across at Chico and approach from the east. Either way, there's no easy way to get there from anywhere, and the thought that we'll pass DJ on the way is like a fucking needle in a haystack."

"You'd take a different route?"

"No." She shook her head. "Carry on."

They'd driven in silence for another twenty minutes when he got a call on his burner. It was the same number Liza had called him from after visiting Sergio's tattoo studio. "Yeah?"

"It's Gideon. Am I on speaker?"

"No."

"Where are you?"

He didn't even consider lying. He'd probably tanked his career, so what the hell? "Going north on 70."

"Smart. Goes through Yuba City. He'll know that route."

"Exactly."

"We're going up I-5."

"Who's 'we'?"

"Mercy and me. And Daisy, of course. We're following the SWAT team. I tried to keep Mercy at home, but she insisted, so Daisy's locked and loaded. Mercy and Daisy are wearing all the tactical gear I could get my hands on."

Tom almost smiled. "Who gave you the tip?"

"Molina. I think we've corrupted her."

Tom had to blink hard. His eyes were burning. "I knew I liked her."

"This is our fight, Tom. Mine and Mercy's. If you find him, if you find Eden, we need to be there. The people are unlikely to believe you because you're the government. They'll believe us because we're not dead."

"How's Rafe?"

"Unhappy. Feds dragged him in for being where he shouldn't have been. He'll be okay, though."

"Good. Full disclosure, I don't know exactly where I'm going. Just north, toward Lassen."

"I figured," Gideon said. "We're hoping we picked the same route that DJ did, right?"

"Exactly. Contact me if you see anything." He ended the call and glanced at Croft.

She was shaking her head again. "Just tell the review board that you took that call when you stopped for gas and I was in the bathroom."

"Will do."

Tom drove for another twenty minutes before seeing a sign for Oroville. "Door A or B?"

"I don't know what to tell you, Tom."

"Can you check on the status of the warrant for Daniel Park's phone records?"

"Sure." She made the call to Raeburn's office while Tom drummed his fingers on the wheel. "Not yet," she said when she'd hung up. "Judge is evaluating."

Tom knew they had to follow due process, but he wished he'd hacked into the guy's phone himself. He was debating having Croft drive so that he could do exactly that when her cell rang. She listened for a moment, then breathed a sigh of relief, thanking the caller.

"The agent on duty at the Sokolovs' intercepted a package."

"Bomb?" Tom asked, praying that the family and their agents were all right.

"Big-ass bomb," she confirmed. "Bomb squad took care of it."

He was still shuddering out a relieved breath when his cell buzzed.

"We're fucking Grand Central Station here," Croft groused as she glanced at his phone's screen. "It's a 33 international calling code. Is that where I hope it is?"

"France," he murmured. "I think Angelina Ward taped my business card together." He answered, putting it on speaker. "This is Special Agent Hunter."

"This is Angelina Ward."

"Are you all right?" he asked.

"Yes, we are now. Thank you for asking. It was terrifying, honestly. I knew a cop was out there that night, but I knew Anthony wasn't coming home. He's good at anticipating trouble."

She didn't seem concerned that the agent had died. "You have a safe place?"

"Very safe." She laughed, but it was a brittle sound. "I have two French police officers sitting in front of my house. Hopefully they'll keep Anthony away if he decides to chase us."

"You taped my business card back together?"

"Of course. I think you knew I would. Anthony had cameras everywhere. Having that man, that DJ Belmont, jump the electric fence and murder the three men Anthony left on guard . . . I saw him kill one of the men. I've . . . I've never seen anyone die before."

Tom didn't think he believed that. "How can I help you, Mrs. Ward?" he asked.

"You can catch my husband and put him behind bars so that I can sleep again."

That he believed. "Can you tell me where he is?"

"Yes. Did you find my cell phone?"

Tom frowned. "Yes, ma'am. We found all your devices in a very neat stack."

"I wanted Anthony to know I'd left for good if he found the electronics first. I can give you the password to my cell phone. I wiped everything but the app I used to track him."

He shared a shocked glance with Croft. "You can track him?"

"Always have been able to. He never thought I was very smart. But I am. So do you want the password or not?"

"Of course I do. Please."

"9-3-5-5-6-9. Spells 'yellow.' That's also the password for the app."

Croft noted it and gave Tom a thumbs-up.

"Got it," he said. "Which app are you using? I'm not at the field office right now, so I don't have immediate access to your phone."

"FindMyCheatingSpouse dot com. User name is Angie W."

"Thank you."

"You're welcome. We're square now. You gave me a heads-up on Belmont. My kids slept in my bed that night. I kept the dog in my room, too, along with a small arsenal. I didn't sleep at all. I was terrified. If you put that sonofabitch I married away, I'll owe you another."

Tom didn't know what to say to that. "Have a safe day, ma'am."

She ended the call and Tom slid his phone back into his pocket.

"Oh. My. God," Croft breathed.

Tom glanced over to see her staring at her phone with huge grin. "What?"

She turned that grin his direction. "Guess where Kowalski is? You'll never guess, so I'll tell you. Here. On this road. About twenty minutes north."

Tom blinked. "What?"

"He's on this road. What'dya bet it's a coincidence?"

"No such thing," Tom murmured. "So Kowalski is following DJ?"

"He *does* have a score to settle."

"But how did Kowalski know . . . Never mind. We can ask when we find him."

"I'll contact Raeburn and let him know. You drive faster. We need to get there before they kill each other."

"And Liza." Tom floored the gas.

TWAIN, CALIFORNIA
TUESDAY, MAY 30, 3:45 P.M.

This is far enough, DJ thought once they were roughly an hour past the last big town on the way to Eden. This route was very remote and he hadn't seen another vehicle in at least a half an hour. There was a steep rock face to his left and a deep ravine to his right. There was also a pull-off with enough foliage to camouflage the SUV.

He rolled to a stop as close to the edge of the ravine as he dared. Edges sometimes crumbled, and he had no desire to go plummeting a hundred feet to his death.

Liza Barkley looked around, too alert for his liking. She'd served in the military, which meant she had fighting skills. She'd been silent ever since Pastor had informed her that she'd be their healer, seeming to accept that she wasn't going to be able to turn them against each other, but he wasn't going to take his eyes off her. She was trouble.

Of course, the damage was already done. Pastor had believed her about Mercy and the old man was unhappy.

Which doesn't matter. Because neither Pastor nor Liza would live to see Eden. When he was done with Pastor, the old man would be dead and DJ would be fifty million richer. And he wouldn't have to share it with the community or Coleen or Pastor's damn banker.

"Why are we stopping?" Pastor asked sleepily, having just woken.

So I can kill you. "So I can pee." He needed to get the lay of the land before he shot them. Dragging that drunk to the creek the night before had reinjured his shoulder. He needed to find a place to shoot them where he could just push them into the ravine.

And he really did need to pee, so there was that.

He was zipping up his jeans when he heard an approaching engine. "Shit," he muttered. He hunkered down, waiting for the vehicle to pass by.

But it didn't. It slowed down. And then it stopped.

Fuck, fuck. It was Kowalski's Jeep.

Motherfucking Kowalski. He followed me. How?

Both front doors opened and DJ recognized the passenger as another of Kowalski's minions. He and Kowalski strolled up to the Explorer like they owned it. The minion yanked Barkley from the front seat and Kowalski pulled Pastor from the back, holding the old man against his chest, a forearm pressed to Pastor's throat.

What the fucking hell?

"Where is DJ?" Kowalski demanded.

"He went up the rock face to get a cell signal," Pastor said weakly, and DJ was reluctantly impressed. Pastor didn't bat an eye as he lied. His face was sheet-white and he was putting his weight on his unbroken leg.

"Fine," Kowalski said. "I'll deal with him later, wherever he is. Who's the girl?"

"My nurse," Pastor replied. "I'm quite ill."

"I heard. You got hurt and DJ ran off to take care of you like a whipped pussy. He fucked up that night, Father."

"It's actually Pastor," Pastor said, gritting his teeth, but still showing no signs of fear. "I'm not Catholic."

Kowalski snorted. "Good one. He said you were his father. As in mother and father."

"Oh. Well, that's true. I had surgery, though, and you're going to pop my stitches."

"Oh, I'm sorry," Kowalski said sarcastically. "Let me be brief. I want you to contact your banker and have him transfer all your holdings into my account."

Fucking asshole, DJ thought furiously. *He's stealing* my *money.*

Pastor wheezed a chuckle. "You can't be serious."

"Oh, I'm very serious. So serious that you're really going to need that pretty nurse when I'm done—if you don't cooperate."

Pastor sobered. "You *are* serious. I'm just an old man. I have no money."

Kowalski laughed. "You had three hundred fifty thousand dollars to pay Sunnyside Oaks. You never even blinked at the amounts. So you have a lot more where that came from."

Oh, hell no. Who at Sunnyside had shared that information? DJ was going to find them and make them wish they'd never been born.

Pastor's expression went cold. "You know a lot about me. I don't even know your name."

"You can call me Kowalski." He drew a gun from his pocket. "I'm going to start shooting off your fingers and then your toes and then we'll get really serious."

"Can I have the girl?" the minion asked.

"I don't care. But find Belmont first. He's got a few things that belong to me."

"He *stole* from you?" Pastor asked, sounding aghast.

"Yeah. He stole from me, then killed three of my best security guards. Dominic, put the girl down and find Belmont. You can take her with you later."

"I'll put her in the car in case the bullets start flying. I like my women alive and breathing." Dominic grabbed a handful of Barkley's scrubs and forced her to the back seat of the Jeep. He shoved her in and slammed the door before returning to the Explorer. He studied the dirt, evidently finding DJ's boot prints, because he started walking his way.

DJ waited until he was close before dragging him behind the trees and shooting him twice in the head, ever grateful for his suppressor. He eased the body to the ground, then took the man's cap and shirt. Dominic was about his size, so the dead man's flannel button-up was a decent fit, the plaid pattern hiding the blood spatter. He'd snugged the cap on his head just as Kowalski called out.

"Where are you?"

"Comin'," DJ grunted. He jogged through the foliage and around the Explorer, stopping behind Kowalski. "Couldn't find him."

Kowalski went very still. Then he dropped Pastor and whirled on

DJ, gun drawn. "You bastard! You ungrateful little bastard. I taught you everything and you stole from me!"

TWAIN, CALIFORNIA
TUESDAY, MAY 30, 4:00 P.M.

Liza contorted her body so that she could reach her shoe. Raeburn had been good as his word, hiding that slick James Bond blade in the sole. Tom had made her practice retrieving it a few times that morning, and she was grateful for that now.

"You bastard!" a man shouted. "You ungrateful little bastard. I taught you everything and you stole from me!"

That would be the infamous Kowalski, she thought. Tom and Croft had been chasing him for nearly a week, and he'd just dropped into Liza's lap. *Lucky me.*

"You tried to kill me!" DJ roared back. "I went to Stockton. I *saw* you."

Yes, Liza thought triumphantly. She now held her shoe in her hands. She hoped her numb fingers could slide the blade free. DJ had pulled the zip tie really tight.

Two gunshots cracked the air, one after the other.

Luckily Dominic the Suave had given her cover. She assumed he was dead, having not returned from finding DJ. *Hopefully they'll kill each other.*

Ignoring them all, she focused on the task as she'd done in the field, treating injured soldiers while bullets flew and bombs exploded around her.

"Of course I wanted to kill you!" Kowalski yelled. "You led the cops to me, you moron. And then you steal from me?"

Liza exhaled when the blade slid from the sole of the shoe. *Thank you, Agent Raeburn. My own Q.* She flinched when a bullet penetrated the Jeep's windshield.

That was too close.

There had been no percussion before the windshield was hit. One of them had a silencer. Probably DJ. There'd been no audible shot when Dominic the Suave had gone looking for DJ and hadn't come back, nor had there been when DJ had shot the ambulance driver at Sunnyside.

Gripping the ceramic blade between her numb fingers, she sawed at the zip tie, stifling a whimper when the blade cut into her finger. Ignoring the pain, she redoubled her efforts. They were still shooting at each other, but their conversation had taken a different tone.

"I heard you trying to steal from my father. How dare you? How did you even find me?"

"You're a moron, Belmont. The rifles you stole were chipped. As soon as you left my house, I was on your tail."

Which seemed like a lie to Liza. If Kowalski had known, he would have killed DJ already.

"You're lying. You would have killed me already."

Ha! She sawed harder.

"And I will," Kowalski said. "Now that you've pulled your daddy out of Sunnyside."

Another gunshot cracked the air, followed a second later by a scream.

Fuck you, assholes, she thought. *Kill each other. Just don't kill me.*

The zip tie finally split, the pieces flying to the floor of the Jeep. Blood rushed into her hands and it was all she could do not to cry. *Crying is a waste of time. Think.*

She peeked into the front seat, her heart sinking when she saw that the keys were not in the ignition. She had three options: Hope they killed each other and didn't come for her, try to hot-wire the Jeep and escape, or run. She didn't trust that they'd kill each other and she didn't know how to hot-wire a car.

So I'll run. She tugged on the door handle, relieved when it opened. She'd been afraid that Dominic the Suave had locked her in. She hesitated. If they saw her, they'd shoot.

But they'd shoot anyway. Words she'd memorized in boot camp came flooding back. The Code of Conduct. *If I am captured I will continue to resist by all means available. I will make every effort to escape.*

"You will not harm my father!" DJ was screaming.

Another silenced bullet hit the windshield, shattering it.

Go.

She opened the door only far enough to slip out, then dropped to the ground and crawled to the rear of the Jeep. They'd come around a bend before stopping. She'd go back that way, and once she was hidden from sight, she could figure out which way was less likely to get her killed—up the rock face or down the ravine.

Her finger was bleeding, but it wasn't too bad. She gripped the blade in her other hand and crawled into the grass. DJ had hidden in the foliage when he relieved himself. She could hide there, too.

She finally exhaled when she was concealed behind the trees. *Go. Fast.*

Crouching as low as she could, she set off at a half jog, half crab walk.

Dammit, Tom, where are you?

THIRTY-ONE

Don't you dare touch him," DJ growled, crouching in front of Pastor.

It was actually over. He'd disarmed and disabled Kowalski quickly, because for all the man's bluster about teaching DJ everything, DJ was a better shot.

But he hadn't wanted Kowalski to die too easily. He'd played with him, shouting and shooting. DJ had wanted Pastor to hear him fighting "for him." Kowalski had been down several minutes before, and he'd screamed like a little girl. That had been satisfying.

Almost as satisfying as seeing his head burst like a melon from the kill shot.

"DJ," Pastor gasped. "Be careful."

Oh, yeah. This was exactly what he'd wanted. Pastor overwhelmed with concern and gratitude because DJ had protected him at the risk to his own life. It might be the "sacrifice" that Pastor needed to see to give him the bank codes. *Because I saved his life and everything.*

DJ shuddered out a sigh. "If I don't make it . . ." He pulled the sat phone from his pocket. "You can call for help." Pretending to brace himself, he lurched to his feet, firing over the hood of the Explorer five more times.

Every bullet hit Kowalski's corpse. *So satisfying.*

DJ turned, sinking to sit on the ground. He popped the empty magazine from his pistol, pulled a full one from his pocket, and reloaded. Then he sighed. "He's dead."

Pastor looked awful. His skin was gray, his face screwed up in pain, his body trembling. A new abrasion on his head was bleeding. "Good. What a disgusting man."

"Yeah, well. Listen . . . you could have died. *I* could have died. And with Coleen gone . . ."

"You'd have no way to let my banker know if I had died," Pastor said sadly.

His banker. Whose name Barkley had known. If Pastor didn't tell him soon, he'd make the bitch talk. "Exactly. It doesn't make sense for your banker to have no way of knowing that he should execute your will."

Pastor shook his head. "You really are a moron. If I die, I won't be calling my banker. In a week, he'll know. And if there is any hint that you killed me? He knows to revoke your inheritance. You don't fool anyone. You never returned to Eden. Coleen told me last night."

DJ sat motionless, seething. "She promised she wouldn't."

Pastor laughed. "You know what's funny? I didn't believe her. I told her I needed proof. You gave that to me just now."

Rage bubbled and flowed, red tingeing the edges of DJ's vision. "I could kill you now."

"But you won't," Pastor said confidently. "You're still that little boy whose daddy didn't love him enough. I didn't think Waylon would actually let me have you after my Bo and Bernie died, but he always surprised me. He was a doormat. He'd do what I said, so I'd up the ante, thinking surely he wouldn't keep obeying. I told him to divorce his wife so that I could marry her. And he did. He did everything I ever told him to do."

DJ stared at him. "Why? Why did you hate him?"

"Oh my. Of course I didn't hate him," Pastor said, making DJ feel like the question had no basis in logic whatsoever. "He was like a puppy. Making him dance to whatever tune I played?" He shrugged, grimacing in pain. "It was fun at first."

"But you were friends."

"No, he wasn't my friend. He was useful."

DJ wanted to strike back. Wanted to make this old man hurt. "Your wife loved him."

That was a direct hit. "But she married me. And she stayed with me."

"Until she left you."

The old man flinched. "She died," Pastor said defensively. "Waylon found their remains."

"Like he found Gideon's remains?"

"Gideon is dead."

"No, he's not. He's alive. He's an FBI agent. And he's looking for you."

Twin flags of red appeared on Pastor's pale cheeks as his breathing grew labored, and it occurred to DJ that he might not have to kill the old man after all. He might have a heart attack or a stroke, like Coleen had feared. "You're lying. Your father would never have lied to me."

DJ laughed. "I gave you my sat phone. It's got a signal. Look him up."

Hands shaking, Pastor did. His nostrils flared. "What is this?"

"My father absolutely lied to you. He got Gideon out. Don't feel bad. I didn't know until a month ago myself."

Pastor's jaw clenched. "And Mercy? Why help her escape?"

"I didn't mean for her to escape. I was playing with them, her and her whore mother. Made them think that they were getting out. Then I shot them, but someone came along and I had to leave Mercy there. She should have died from that gut wound. That's why I shoot people in the head now, when I can." Like he should have done to Gideon that day in the radio station parking lot. But he'd been operating on reflex and trauma. He hadn't been thinking. "Mercy was saved. She and Gideon reconnected. They're not going to rest until you're dead."

And me, too, but they'll have to catch me first.

One side of Pastor's mouth lifted. "I have to say I'm a little proud. Taunting Mercy and her mother that way. You learned that from me."

It burned to have to admit that the old man was right about that. "My point is that Waylon lied to you. Lied to all of us. He brought back a corpse and told us it was Gideon, because he let the little fucker go. Do you think he told the truth about your wife and kids?"

Pastor's half smile disappeared. "He helped them escape? They're alive?"

"It's possible, isn't it? I'd think probable, even. Your daughter was almost twelve and, as I recall, your wife didn't want her married off. So she ran. And my father helped her."

Pastor huffed a mirthless chuckle. "Your father was weak. And despite your best efforts, you're his son. Help me up. We need to get to Eden. I can't imagine what trouble they've caused after a few days without a firm hand. You'll clean up any messes they've made. And then you'll fix your own mistakes and take care of Gideon and Mercy. And then, if you're still alive, you'll find my wife and children and bring them to me."

"And if I do?"

Pastor's half smile returned. "We'll talk about access codes."

"You're lying to me."

"Maybe. But you'll do as I say. You always do as I say. I trained you myself. You've always done as I've said. After all, you went with Mc-Phearson when you could have said no. Gideon did. At least *he* fought back. *He* wasn't weak."

DJ stared, barely able to process the words past the pounding of his pulse in his ears. Years of McPhearson's abuse, the rape, the hurt . . . it all rushed back in a wave that left him numb.

Gideon wasn't weak? *And I was?*

Shock turned to fury and then to cold, brutal realization. Pastor wasn't going to give him the codes. He'd never planned to give him any of the money at all. It was a ploy, a carrot. A way to continue to control and manipulate him. *Like he's done for my whole life.*

Well, fuck this shit. He still had cash in his personal account. It wasn't fifty million, but it would have to be enough. He lifted the gun and pointed it at Pastor's head.

The old man's eyes widened, but then he smiled. "You won't. You can't."

"Watch me. Say goodbye, Pastor." He pulled the trigger, firing right between the eyes. Then he sat, watching the shock on Pastor's face. The betrayal. Then . . . nothing.

Pastor was dead.

And I'm free.

Euphoria had him pushing to his feet, but his legs wobbled like rubber and he dropped back to his knees, hard. *Fuck.* He stared at his hands. He was shaking. *This is bullshit. I am* not *weak. I am* not *going to let you win, old man.*

DJ shoved to his feet, bracing himself against the Explorer while he locked his knees and waited for the shakes to pass. Then he spat on Pastor's body. "I'll show you weak, old man."

But damn, he was tired. And he still needed to dispose of the bodies. He was going to have to drag him to the ravine. *No, I'll make Barkley drag him.* Then he'd shoot her, too.

He walked to Kowalski's Jeep and opened the back door. "Did you miss—"

He closed his eyes for a few seconds. Enough to regain control of his rage.

Liza Barkley was gone.

TWAIN, CALIFORNIA
TUESDAY, MAY 30, 4:25 P.M.

Liza had to stop running. The terrain had become too treacherous. One wrong step forward, one loose rock, and she'd plunge a hundred feet into the ravine. She could go back the way she'd come, but she'd surely run into DJ, and then what?

The rock face on the other side of the road was sheer. She might have been able to climb it, but that would have left her exposed. Her scrubs were dark blue. She'd have been the perfect target.

But DJ would be coming after her and she didn't know when Tom would arrive.

I'm on my own. She took inventory of her resources. She had the blade. She was strong, while DJ favored his left shoulder. She had the advantage of cover, for now.

She didn't have the strength to best DJ on a purely physical level. Even injured, he was stronger than she was. She'd been trained in hand-to-hand combat, but he might have been, too.

And he had a gun.

So, basically, she had a blade, no major injuries, and the advantage of being hidden in a thin copse of trees. He had a gun and she was trapped against the edge of a damn ravine. *Not amazing odds.*

She really wished she'd learned how to hot-wire cars. She'd be safe. *Safer*, at least.

Anytime now would be good, Tom.

She heard DJ's footsteps on the paved road before she saw him through the trees. She crouched low, using the cover of a bush that was no taller than her hip. She prepared to spring at him before he saw her, but he ran right by her. She silently exhaled. She could run back the way she'd come and steal Kowalski's Jeep, assuming he had the keys in his pocket.

That was better than standing here, waiting for him to find her.

Carefully, she backed out of the cover of the trees and ran as fast as she could, not bothering to hunker down. Speed was important now.

She made it back to the two shot-up vehicles and nearly cried with relief. Then grimaced when she saw Pastor's body, a bullet hole between his eyes.

No justice for Gideon and Mercy on that front. DJ must have finally had enough.

She checked DJ's stolen SUV first, but the keys were not in it.

She found Kowalski's body and dropped into a crouch to search for his keys.

He was in bad shape, over and above being very dead. His body, unlike Pastor's with that single shot between the eyes, was riddled with bullets. DJ must have emptied an entire magazine into the man.

He was still warm, his clothing soaked with blood. Which wasn't anything she hadn't seen before. She took the gun from his hand, checked the chamber, then ejected the magazine. It was empty. *Dammit.*

She tossed the gun into the trees so that DJ couldn't find it, then briskly patted Kowalski down, grimly triumphant when she pulled his keys from his pants pocket. She wiped his blood from her hands to the scrubs. Again, nothing she hadn't done before.

Keys in one hand, the ceramic blade in the other, she was sliding behind the wheel of the Jeep when cold metal burned the skin at the back of her neck. *Goddammit.*

"You're good," DJ murmured in her ear. "I'm better."

She spun the blade so that it was flat against the inside of her forearm. If she lost it, she'd be defenseless. "You're nothing."

"We'll have to agree to disagree. Get out." He jabbed the barrel hard against her neck and she winced. "Now."

"Or what? You'll kill me? I'm not helping you."

"I still have my phone. I can still detonate that bomb."

"I don't think you ever had one," Liza said flatly. And even if he had, the FBI would have swept the facility already, just like they'd swept the Sokolovs' house yesterday. Little Brooklyn and the other innocents wouldn't be harmed. "I think you're lying."

He grabbed the collar of her scrubs and yanked her from the Jeep, dragging her on the ground. "You do *not* get to disobey me."

She twisted out of his grip, catching his grimace. She'd hurt him. Good. She'd keep hurting him until either she killed him or he killed her.

"You do *not* get to tell me what to do," she fired back, distracting him with her words so that she could deliver a kick to his knees.

He grunted in pain, but he sidestepped out of her reach, his hand clenching the butt of his gun as he pointed it at her head. It was suppressed, just as she'd thought. When he fired, no one would hear. No one would come. She experienced a pang of regret, not that she'd volunteered for this assignment, but that Tom would probably be the one to find her body. He was on his way. She had no doubt of that.

I'm so sorry, Tom.

"Well?" she challenged as she stared up at him. "What are you waiting for?"

It was madness to taunt him. But he'd been raised in a community that viewed women as chattel, where women never talked back. Her best weapon now was his own fury.

He stared down, finger still on the trigger. "I'm imagining you with your very own locket."

"You're assuming you'll even have a community to oppress." She pointed at Pastor's body. "Without him, no one will want to stay. No one will follow you. Are you going to kill them all?"

His jaw tightened and she knew she'd hit a nerve. "Maybe. Maybe I'm not going back."

"I wouldn't. I've heard a lot about Eden's amenities and they're not great."

"Shut up and get up. Now. We're going for a walk to the ravine."

This would be it. Her only chance. She focused on his left shoulder, mentally rehearsing what she was going to do. Slowly she rolled to her knees, then rocked back on her heels.

Then she sprang, gripping her blade and thrusting it into his left shoulder, as hard as she could.

He screamed, dropping his pistol.

She scooped it up and backed away, holding him at gunpoint with hands that, miraculously, did not shake. He watched her with eyes filled with hatred. She'd seen those before, too. That day. That day when her friends had died. When Fritz had died.

"Don't move," she said quietly. "Or I will kill you."

"You won't," he said, and on the surface he sounded confident. Beneath there was doubt.

"I will. You're not the first person I've pointed a gun at. Nor the first I've killed."

But if you do, you'll never find Eden. With Pastor gone, no one else knows where it is.

Then shoot to maim.

But he snarled at her, lunging for her, stumbling to his knee, starting to rise again. She had her finger on the trigger, ready to pull—until they both heard it. An engine. A big one, from the sound of it. It was approaching quickly, coming around the bend. DJ froze, still on one knee. She saw the realization in his eyes at the same moment that she processed the sound.

They're here. They're finally here. Relief coursed through her and her legs went weak.

She glanced at the black SUV that was screeching to a halt. And that was the opening DJ Belmont had been waiting for. He lurched to his feet, grabbing her wrist and twisting until he could snatch the gun from her hand. In a practiced move, he jabbed the pistol into her temple, one fist clenching the neckline of her scrubs, cutting off her air.

Just as Tom burst from the passenger side of the SUV, gun drawn, screaming, "FBI! Drop your weapon."

TWAIN, CALIFORNIA
TUESDAY, MAY 30, 4:35 P.M.

Tom's emotions were a fucking roller coaster. He'd gone from abject fear as they'd approached, to pride and bone-wilting relief when he'd seen her holding a gun on DJ Belmont.

And then he'd seen the moment it had gone wrong. Her relief, her distraction.

DJ had made his move and now held her at gunpoint.

If the situation hadn't been so serious, Tom might have laughed at the look of frustrated annoyance on her face. At least she wasn't afraid.

His Liza had a spine of steel.

"Back off," DJ warned. "I will kill her. I have nothing to lose."

"What do you want?" Tom asked, grateful to Croft for making him practice the scenarios multiple times as they'd driven like a bat out of hell. She'd taken over the driving midway through so that he could pull out his laptop and check on the status at Sunnyside. Raeburn's team had everything under control there, and that—and seeing that Kowalski was still on the move, so DJ must have been, too—had helped him remain calm. But then Kowalski's vehicle had stopped and so had his heart. It hadn't beaten normally until he'd seen that Liza was still alive.

He could hear Croft getting out of the SUV. She'd been calling their location in to Raeburn, who was coordinating from the field office in Sacramento. Once they'd had Kowalski's signal to follow, Raeburn had redirected the SWAT team to veer off I-5 and head east.

He'd also put eyes in the air. There was a chopper not too far away.

All of this gave Tom a feeling of control that was just enough—barely enough—to allow him to think past the fear of seeing a gun at Liza's head.

"I *want* you to back off," DJ snarled. "Tell your partner to stop. Not another step forward. There are three bodies on the ground right now. None of them listened. Follow their lead and it'll be four."

Liza's gaze was locked on Tom's face and the trust in her eyes bolstered his spirit and ripped it apart, all at once.

"I've got something you want," Tom said.

DJ's eyes narrowed. "What?"

"Eden's bank account."

DJ went rigid. "You're lying."

"I'm not. How do you think we knew about Sunnyside? I saw the transfers from your account to theirs. I've had access to Eden's bank accounts for almost a month. We were just waiting for you to show up."

"You're lying," DJ said again, but this time he sounded less certain.

"First transfer on Thursday morning, one hundred thousand dollars. Second transfer, two hundred fifty thousand. We have Pastor's financial advisor in custody, so he can't take any more."

"What do you mean, any more?"

"He's been skimming for years. Just like your father skimmed when he had your job."

"How do you know about my father?" DJ's eyes gleamed, his greed apparent.

"Pastor's wife told us. Your father gave her a million bucks. Did you know that?"

DJ's face contorted into a scowl. "Of course he did," he muttered. "Bastard."

"Which is why you killed him."

"I killed him because he helped Gideon."

"I can see how that'd make you upset," Tom said mildly. "So. What do you want?"

"I want my money."

"Let her go and we'll talk."

"No. You're getting back in your SUV and driving away. You and your partner. You will transfer all the money to my account and then I'll let Miss Barkley go."

"Not gonna happen," Tom said. "Besides, we know where Eden is now. By the time you got there, you wouldn't have a home to return to."

Liza's eyes widened, her lips curving in a satisfied smile.

It wasn't true—yet. But it would be soon. Minutes before they'd come upon this scene, Raeburn had informed them that they'd gotten the warrant for Daniel Park's cell phone records and, sure enough, there were weekly calls from the same number, going back years. They were only interested in the calls over the last month. With any luck,

Raeburn would be calling them with a triangulated location within minutes.

"You're lying!" DJ spat.

"I told you. We have Pastor's financial advisor. And his phone records."

DJ paled.

Tom smiled. "I can see you understand where I'm going with this. So what's it going to be? We can talk money, but I hold the cards. You're not getting a penny until you let her go."

He watched the riot of emotions cross DJ's face, hoping he'd realize that it was time to fold. But, of course, he did not. He backed up a step, dragging Liza with him. She followed, her eyes locked on Tom's, her hands clenched into fists. She was waiting for instruction.

DJ was not going quietly. Nor was he willing to negotiate.

Tom and Croft hadn't really discussed this particular scenario, but Tom knew it would only end when DJ was locked away for the rest of his life. Or dead. Tom was okay with either.

Tom knew he should be a mess of nerves right now. But his mind, so accustomed to compartmentalizing, seemed to be doing okay.

From the corner of his eye, Tom saw Croft creeping around a shot-up Jeep. Presumably Kowalski's. They might not have discussed this scenario, but Tom had confidence in Croft's instincts. She'd do the right thing.

"Tell her to stop!" DJ shouted. "Your partner needs to back the fuck off." He yanked Liza back another step and then another until he was at the tail end of a white Ford Explorer. Pastor lay dead on the ground beside it.

Kowalski had to be dead. Pastor was dead. DJ said he'd killed three people here. The third wouldn't be Coleen, the healer. Her body had been found in her bed at Sunnyside. Best guess was asphyxiation. There was bruising on her neck in the pattern of the chain that held her locket. At some point, DJ had dragged her by it.

Like he was doing with the top of Liza's scrubs right now. Her mouth was open, her fingers clutching at the fabric pulled tight around her throat. And Tom remembered his mother doing the same as his father dragged her for some imagined infraction. Fury rose, but instead of clouding his mind, it made his focus singularly clear.

You are going to die, motherfucker.

"Back off!" DJ screamed. "I mean it." He dragged her toward the edge of the ravine, Tom and Croft matching him step for step.

Liza had been fairly docile, but that changed. She began to fight DJ, her gaze darting to her left. To the edge of the ravine, which was too damn close.

She couldn't breathe. Tom could see that she couldn't breathe.

She whipped her body to the right, away from the edge, and Tom saw something else. Something he hadn't seen as he'd driven up. A blade protruded from DJ's shoulder. Tom recognized it as the ceramic blade Raeburn had provided and now realized that this was how she'd gotten control of DJ's gun before they'd arrived.

His Liza was one hell of an amazing woman.

Tom moved so that he was in her line of sight and tapped his left shoulder. Twisting her weight that way was counterintuitive because it put her too close to the edge, but it was the only way to get DJ to let her go so they could get a clear shot.

Liza bobbed her head once in acknowledgment, then threw herself backward into DJ's left shoulder, shoving the protruding blade deeper.

DJ screamed, the sound wild and shrill. Like that of an animal.

His grip on Liza loosened and she dropped and rolled.

Tom's heart stopped. She'd rolled with the momentum of her leftward motion and was skidding toward the edge of the ravine. "*No.*"

From there, everything happened so slowly that it felt like a dream and so fast that he struggled to keep up. Tom dove for Liza, grabbing her ankle, stopping her momentum. She hung over the side, her head pointed straight down.

Croft fired and Tom heard DJ stagger and fall.

"Drop the gun," Croft ordered, but DJ ignored her.

Tom heard the pop of a suppressed bullet the moment that it hit him in the ribs. More correctly, it hit the Kevlar vest he wore beneath his suit.

"Fuck," he ground out, forcing his hand to grip Liza's ankle harder when his first reflex had been to let her go.

Behind him, Croft cried out in pain as she hit the ground.

Tom turned his head to see DJ crawling toward him, his expression filled with hate. "You thought you won?" DJ taunted. "You didn't." DJ went up on his knees, his gun pointed at Tom's head.

Liza was squirming, trying to lever herself back onto solid ground.

"Liza, *stop.*" She immediately stopped struggling. She trusted him that much.

Tom had dropped his gun when he'd reached for her, and it was trapped under his body. He could reach for it, but he'd have to let her go. Which wasn't going to happen.

He could hear Croft's quiet groans but didn't know if she was all right. From where he lay, prone on the ground, all he could see was Liza in front of him and DJ to his left.

And then, finally, the sound of helicopter blades filled the air.

DJ looked up for a second, but it was enough.

Tom rolled right, grabbed his gun with his left hand, and . . . hesitated. He was aiming for DJ's head, but that . . . That was rage and would deprive DJ's victims of their justice.

And that's not me. Adjusting his grip, Tom shot him in the right shoulder instead, firing three bullets in quick succession.

DJ dropped to his knees, screaming. Partly in pain, Tom thought. Mostly in fury. DJ had dropped his gun and dove for it now. When he twisted around, he held the gun in a two-handed grip and pointed it at Tom's hand, still clutching Liza's ankle. "She's going to die and you're—"

Tom fired again, striking DJ in the chest as another shot came from his right. *Croft.* DJ fell backward, blood spreading across his torso. And from the hole in his head.

He was finally still.

Tom sagged, letting his forehead rest on the ground for five hard beats of his heart. Then he reached for Liza's other ankle and began to tug.

Croft crawled to his side. "Let me help."

Together they pulled Liza back to solid ground and then the three of them collapsed, breathing like they'd each run a marathon.

"Are you all right?" Liza finally asked.

Croft's laugh was a little manic. "*You're* asking *us*?"

"Well, yeah. I'm the medic."

"We have vests," Tom said. "But hell. They tell you that it'll hurt, but . . ."

"They severely misrepresent the pain," Croft said, then groaned. "I think I busted a rib."

"But otherwise, you're all right?" Liza pressed.

Tom shoved up on his elbows. "You're covered in blood. Are *you* all right?" It was smeared on her thighs and he could see vague streaks that might have been from her fingers. Now that she was safe, he could think of everything else.

"It's Kowalski's. I'm fine."

"Good." Tom rolled to the side that didn't hurt like hell and pulled her close. She put her arms around his neck and he held her for a long moment while she shuddered against him. "You scared the hell out of me," he murmured. "Don't ever do that again."

She laughed, a slightly broken sound. "I wasn't afraid of heights before, but I am now."

"You're entitled." He tightened his arms, hissing in pain.

She scooted back, frowning. "You said you were all right."

"I've had broken ribs before," he assured her, "and this isn't broken. It's just bruised."

"But it sucks," Croft said woefully.

Grabbing her hand, Tom lowered himself back to his stomach, figuring he'd move later. He hadn't broken a rib, but he hadn't caught his breath yet, either. He kept seeing her sliding into a ravine and his breath would hitch all over again.

Liza sat up and ran her fingers though his hair. "I think the cavalry is here."

The helicopter landed behind them, the blades slowing to a stop. Then boots hit the ground. "Anyone need us to call for a medic?" a man called out.

Liza laughed. "No. How are you, ma'am?"

"Better than you," a familiar voice said dryly.

Tom rolled over to see Special Agent in Charge Molina striding toward them. He sat up, hiding his grimace. It was a point of pride. "Ma'am."

Croft didn't even bother, only managing to wave weakly.

"I thought you were recused, ma'am," Tom said, then winced because it sounded accusatory when he hadn't meant it to. "But I'm really glad you're here."

"Why?" Molina asked dryly. "You seem to have everything under control. Did you leave anything for us to do?"

Croft laughed, then moaned. "Hurts to laugh."

Molina looked around. "Report, please."

Tom exhaled. "We only know about Belmont. The others were already dead."

"Miss Barkley?" Molina asked.

"DJ pulled over, I think to kill me and toss me over the edge. But then Kowalski showed up and he and DJ got into it. Kowalski had come for Pastor's money."

"As so many do," Molina drawled. "Then?"

"I was in the back of the Jeep so I only heard them arguing. I assume DJ killed Kowalski first, then Pastor, but I didn't witness that myself."

"How did you end up holding a gun on DJ?" Croft asked, and Molina's brows lifted.

"I used the blade in my shoe to cut the zip tie and ran and hid. DJ ran past me, so I doubled back to take one of the vehicles, but he found me. DJ tried to get me to walk to the edge on my own, but I stabbed him, got his gun, and then lost it again when I got distracted by the arrival of Agents Hunter and Croft."

Molina was listening, a smile playing on her lips. "I see. And then?"

"Tom tried to negotiate with DJ, but he was a real dick. DJ. Not Tom."

Molina swallowed a smile. "I see."

"He was dragging her to the edge," Tom explained, then relayed how they'd taken DJ down.

Molina nodded, then walked toward the edge, keeping far enough back to be safe. "Who's this guy?" she called.

Tom exchanged a puzzled glance with Croft. "What guy?" he called back.

"Oh," Liza said. "That must be Dominic the Suave."

Tom snorted. "Who?"

Molina came back and crouched so that she was face level with Liza. "Dominic the Suave?"

"Kowalski's assistant," Liza said. "He thought I'd make a tasty snack and stuck me in the Jeep to save for later. That's where I was when I cut the zip tie."

Molina nodded again. "I see. Anything else?"

"Coleen is dead," Liza said. "DJ killed her. Probably Nurse Innes, too."

"We know," Tom told her. "We found both of their bodies. What happened to you at Sunnyside? We lost transmission."

"Yeah." Liza sighed. "I was trying to get away, but DJ said he'd kill everyone in the solarium. There were kids in there. He also claimed to have planted a dirty bomb that he could detonate with his cell phone. That's why I got in the ambulance with him. Is Rafe okay?"

Molina did not look pleased at that. "Yes. Did you hire him?"

Liza met Molina's gaze. And lied through her teeth. "Yes. Of course I did. Not like I didn't trust you, but . . . I'm not stupid, ma'am."

Damn, but Tom loved her.

Molina nodded. "I see."

Liza looked at her innocently. "I'm glad. Did you really find Eden?"

"We have coordinates now," Molina said. "We're sending transport vehicles to bring the members down from the mountain. But there is, apparently, a woman about to go into labor?"

Tom sat up straighter, ignoring the discomfort in his ribs. "Yes. Cameron Cook's girlfriend, Hayley."

Molina tilted her head at the helicopter. "Have you ever delivered a baby, Liza?"

Liza sucked in a breath. "Yes, ma'am."

The day her unit was mowed down, Tom remembered. *Please let her help*, he wordlessly asked Molina. *Please*.

Molina extended her hand. "Come. We've got medics en route, but it'll take them three hours to get there by car, two hours by air. We can get you there in under an hour."

Her smile radiant, Liza took Molina's hand and let the older woman help her to her feet. "Tom too?"

Molina met Tom's gaze with a small nod and he remembered that she'd talked to Liza's CO. She knew she'd delivered a baby that day, right before everything had gone to hell. "Of course he's coming, too. But Agent Croft, I only have room for two."

Croft waved them on. "I'll stay and wait for the crime scene techs and the ME. Y'all go. Text me later."

"I will," Tom promised, then followed Molina and Liza to the helicopter.

THIRTY-TWO

Liza's new fear of heights was put to the test an hour later when they arrived at the Eden coordinates derived from Daniel Park's cell phone. There was no place to land, so they were lowered by a pulley to an area just big enough for two, maybe three SUVs.

She and Tom looked up at the cave entrance. There was a short walk up a steep trail and they set off right away. Molina quickly caught up.

Molina had explained that she was there for the Eden rescue and had only recused herself from the DJ Belmont part of the investigation. When Tom had asked her what she would have done if DJ had still been threatening them when she arrived, she'd merely shrugged.

Tom had grinned. His boss was far more flexible than most people gave her credit for.

The three of them were the first wave of the Eden rescue, Tom carrying bags of food and water that Molina had brought, hoping the offer of sustenance would ease their way in. Mercy and Gideon were on their way. Amos would be arriving a few hours after that.

They'd anticipated resistance, but they hadn't anticipated a man guarding the cave entrance with a shotgun and a darkly forbidding expression.

"Hello," Liza called. "I'm a medic." She no longer wore Sunnyside Oaks's scrubs, as they'd been soiled by mud and blood—both Kowalski's and Belmont's. Luckily one of the helicopter pilots had had a pair of sweats in his duffel, and she'd changed while they'd been in the air. It was a good thing she was tall. The sweats were baggy, but she'd only had to roll up the sleeves. Far better than walking up to the Eden compound covered in blood. "Do you have need of emergency services?"

They'd agreed that Liza should be the first to speak, as the community had been brainwashed to distrust the government.

"No," the man said. "Take your helicopter and go."

But a scream met their ears.

"Hayley," Tom murmured. "Call her Magdalena." To the man he said, "Please lower your weapon. We're a rescue party."

"We don't need to be rescued," the man bit out. "Go away or I will shoot your heads off. You're trespassing."

Technically, the man was trespassing, but Liza wasn't going to escalate things by pointing that out. She took a step closer, her hands up in surrender. "My name is Liza. I was sent by your healer, Sister Coleen. I work at the hospital where Pastor has been recuperating. She was busy caring for Pastor, but asked me to come and help. She's worried about the young woman who's about to give birth. Magdalena."

The man hesitated. "Sister Coleen sent you?"

"She did. She was afraid the baby would be born breech and that she wouldn't be able to get back in time for the birth."

"Who are they?"

"Tara is my assistant," Liza said, pointing to Molina. They'd agreed that this would be a less precarious mission if Tom and Molina didn't scare them by identifying as FBI right away. "And Tom is here with food and water. Sister Coleen also said you were low on supplies."

The man looked torn. "Can you prove what you say?"

Liza smiled at him. "Sister Coleen thought you might say that. Can I show you a photo of us together?" She took Tom's phone from her pocket and the man eyed it suspiciously. "Here we are, just this morning."

She showed him the photo that she'd taken at Brooklyn's request—*bless her*—and had accessed from her e-mail using Tom's phone. Molina had assured her that Brooklyn was well after the raid, which had soothed her mind enough to focus on this next task.

The man frowned at the photo. "Pastor looks awful."

"He was hurt badly. But his recovery was going well when I left today." Which was true. Pastor's recovery hadn't tanked until DJ had killed him.

"Who's the bald kid?" he asked gruffly.

"That's my patient. She's got a kind of cancer." Another scream echoed through the caves. "May I please come in? Magdalena sounds like she needs assistance."

The man made his reluctance clear, but he lowered the shotgun and stepped back so that they could enter. "You have to leave after."

"Of course." Liza couldn't help but stare as they were led through the compound. "These caves are beautiful."

"They're cold and wet," the man grumbled. "Some of our people are sick."

"I'd be happy to help them as well," Liza told him. "I didn't get your name, sir."

"Brother Joshua."

Liza recognized his name. Joshua was Amos's guess for who would take Ephraim's place.

Joshua continued to look uncomfortable. The people they passed met them with shock and downright animosity. But they also watched Tom with interest, whispering that he carried two big bags filled with food.

Liza just smiled and waved, making sure the first-aid kit she'd taken from the helicopter was prominently displayed. The red cross was a symbol most people recognized. Even those who'd been hiding for thirty years.

They followed Joshua through a maze of rooms, many partitioned off with curtains. Some were legit curtains and others were clotheslines with drying laundry.

The young woman screamed again and this time it was closer. Joshua pushed the curtain aside and three shocked pairs of eyes met theirs.

Hayley—Liza refused to call her Magdalena in her own mind—lay on a pallet on the floor, sobbing. Two women kneeled next to her. One was older and had a harsh face. The other was much younger and exuded an air of gentleness.

The older woman rose, shock quickly morphing to outrage. "What is the meaning of this?"

Liza met Hayley's wide eyes and gave her a small wink.

"They were sent by Sister Coleen," Joshua said. "Two healers, and the man carries food and water. You may return to your own quarters, Tamar."

"No," Hayley cried. "Tamar can stay. Make Rebecca go."

The older woman's face darkened. "You will be silent, Magdalena."

Liza left the politics to Molina and Tom, dropping to her knees next to Hayley. "I'm Liza," she said for everyone to hear, then lowered her voice. "Graham got through."

Hayley grabbed her hand and squeezed so hard that Liza thought her bones would crack. "He's in the box. Get him out. Please."

The box. Liza knew what that was because Gideon had been put there for a whole week. It was where rule-breakers were confined and given only the most basic rations of food and water.

Liza looked up at Tom and he gave her a nod, his promise to take care of it.

"I want my brother here for my baby's birth. Please," Hayley begged.

"He stays in the box," Rebecca declared. "Pastor can determine his fate when he returns."

"That might be a while," Liza commented. "He could be hospitalized for up to six weeks."

A collective gasp rose from behind them and Liza realized that a crowd had gathered. Tamar dipped a cloth in a bowl of water and dabbed at Hayley's forehead, leaning in to whisper in her ear something that Liza couldn't hear.

Hayley nodded pitifully. "Thank you," she whispered to the woman.

Tamar patted Liza's shoulder. "I'll be back later."

Behind them, Molina and Tom were telling Joshua about the supplies they'd brought, so Liza leaned in close. "We're here to get you out," she whispered, then raised her voice. "I'd like to examine Magdalena. Can we give the patient some privacy?"

Tom and Molina instantly stepped from the room, as did everyone else except for Rebecca. Liza turned to her with a polite smile. "Are you a trained nurse, ma'am?"

"No. But I have children."

"She's barren," Hayley spat. "Her children were birthed by other women. She wants to take my baby as soon as she's born, and I won't let her."

Liza continued to smile even though she wanted to beat Rebecca to a bloody pulp. "There are so many supplies. Perhaps you can aid with distributing them."

The woman shook her head. "I'm staying."

Hayley screamed again with another contraction. When it was over, Liza pushed aside the curtain. "Tara, can you come back, please?"

Molina promptly returned. "Yes?"

"This woman is a danger to my patient. Can you remove her?"

Molina took the woman's arm and forcibly removed her from the room. But Rebecca's irate shouts grew abruptly quiet as the two headed for the entrance. Liza briefly wondered what Molina had said to shut her up.

Liza grinned. "Let's have a baby, Hayley."

Hayley's eyes filled with new tears. "Say it again, please. My name."

"Hayley," Liza said gently and brushed Hayley's damp hair from her face. "Now I'm going to have a look at your baby. We don't have any equipment so I'm gonna have to go old school."

"Have you delivered a baby before?" Hayley asked as she nervously watched Liza pull on a pair of gloves and sanitize her hands.

"I have. In a war zone, no less. A little village in Afghanistan."

"You're in the army?"

"I was until recently."

"And the baby was okay?"

"Yes. The baby was breech and the mom was scared. Her husband saw us distributing food to the village and asked me to help. We had no medicine and no special equipment. The mother and baby were fine."

"Who are you now?" Hayley whispered.

"Just a nursing assistant," Liza told her, then leaned in again. "The other two are FBI. They've been looking for Eden for a very long time."

"Thank God," Hayley breathed. "Is Cameron okay?"

"Cameron is fine. Just worried about you. How far apart are your—"

Hayley screamed again, her stomach rippling from the contraction.

"That answers that question. Three minutes. Let me see how dilated you are. Oh!" she said a minute later. "I see the head. You're about to meet your baby. I understand she's a little girl?"

"Yes. Jellybean."

Liza grinned. "All right, then. On the next contraction, I want you to push."

She moaned at the next contraction, but pushed like a champ. The contraction passed, and Hayley panted in silence, readying for the next.

The curtain parted and Tamar returned. "Everyone is getting food. They are so happy."

"And Graham?" Hayley asked.

"The lady, Tara? She's taking care of him. He's dehydrated and hungry, but she said that Liza should stay here and that she would handle it."

"Tamar, can you sit behind Hayley? Help her remember to breathe during the contractions."

Fifteen minutes and five giant pushes later, Liza held a beautiful baby girl with a pair of very strong lungs. Liza had to do some deep breathing of her own, but her eyes still filled and tears still fell. "She's perfect," she said to Hayley. "Beautiful. Ten fingers and toes."

"Let me help you wash her," Tamar said. From a box she retrieved a clean towel and filled a bowl with water and cleaned the baby with such tenderness that Liza cried some more.

"You're almost done," Liza told Hayley as Tamar put the baby in her mother's arms. "One more giant push."

She was dealing with the placenta when the curtain was ripped aside. Liza smelled the boy before she saw him. "Holy God," she coughed. "What did you fall into?"

"Don't worry, I'll stay over here," the boy said, his voice squeaky high and raspy at the same time. "God, Hayley. You did it. You really did it. She's okay?"

Hayley looked up from her baby and smiled. "She's perfect."

The boy grinned, his face dirty and tear-streaked. "Hey there, Zit."

Hayley shot him a mock glare. "One more time, Graham, and I swear."

"Do you have a name picked out?" Liza asked.

"I have one in mind," Hayley said. "I want to check with Cameron first."

Liza sat back on her heels. "You could have done this without me, Hayley. This was as simple a delivery as they come. But I need to get you out of here, so I'm going to tell them that you need a hospital, okay? For now, just lie here and relax. You earned it. And Uncle Graham, if you can wash up—I mean squeaky clean with soap and water—you can hold your niece."

"He volunteered to empty the toilet pots," Tamar said quietly. "He stunk so bad that the leaders didn't bother him. That's how he set up the computer."

Liza looked over her shoulder at the empty doorway. Graham was gone, the curtain drawn. "Oh. Now I feel bad. I mean, he can't come around the baby that dirty, but . . ."

"It's okay," Tamar said. "He's a good boy, and smart. He knows about germs." She hesitated. "Will you take everyone who wants to leave?"

"Transport is on its way," Liza replied, and Tamar nodded but didn't look as happy as Liza expected. "Do you want to leave?"

"Yes, but . . ."

Hayley looked up at Liza. "She doesn't want to leave her son. Rebecca stole him. She stole Tamar's baby. Don't let Joshua tell you that it's hers."

Liza's gaze shot to Tamar's, horrified. "You have my promise."

"Thank you," Tamar whispered.

"What's your real name, honey?"

"Tiffany."

"You have my promise, Tiffany. We'll make sure your baby is returned to you. The authorities will probably require a DNA test—that's a blood test," she added, not knowing how long the woman had been in Eden. "That'll prove the baby is yours, but I know people who can make that happen."

Tiffany wiped tears from her face. "Thank you. Is it really going to be six weeks before Pastor and Coleen come back?"

"At least," Liza said grimly. "At the very minimum."

Tiffany's lips curved. "Are they in jail?"

Liza didn't say a word and Tiffany's eyes widened when the truth sank in. "Did you do it?"

Liza shook her head. "DJ."

"And *he's* in jail?" Tiffany pressed.

Liza shook her head.

The two younger women shared a knowing glance. "Good," they said.

 EDEN, CALIFORNIA
TUESDAY, MAY 30, 7:30 P.M.

Tom found Liza in Hayley's room holding the baby an hour and a half later and his heart . . . hurt. Some of it was sad hurt, because he couldn't help but think about what Tory would have looked like holding their baby. He didn't think Liza would fault him for that.

But most of it was good hurt because she looked beautiful holding that tiny bundle. She was standing, rocking the baby while she hummed a lullaby off tune.

She looked up and her expression filled with concern. She walked over to him, and he could see that the baby was sound asleep. "You okay?"

"Yeah. I was just thinking that if we ever have kids, they'll never sing in a choir."

She chuckled. "We don't have the best musical genes, do we?"

He relaxed then, her simple acceptance that they'd have a family a balm to his soul.

"Of course," she added, "if we adopt kids, we could get the next Beyoncé. They'd make us a mint and we could retire young. Or we could just adopt normal kids and make them happy."

She'd chosen her words with such care, and he loved her for it. Yes, they'd try for kids biologically. And if they were successful, that would be great. But even if they were, there were kids out there who needed a home, and they'd provide that, too.

"How's Hayley?" he asked. The girl was curled up on the pallet, her head in Tamar's lap while Tamar knitted what looked like a baby blanket. "Is she all right?"

"Asleep," Liza murmured. "She was really far along by the time we got here, so Jellybean came fast."

Tom brushed his finger over the baby's soft cheek. "Hi, Jellybean. It's gonna be okay."

Liza frowned at him. "Are your hands clean?"

"Like I'd touch a baby with dirty hands," he scoffed. "I just washed them with soap and hot water. I had to after helping Graham get clean. Oh my God." He shuddered.

"I know. But you know why he did it, right?"

Tom nodded, still touched by the boy's love for his sister. "Yes. He really is a kid genius. He set up the dish and the solar panels and hooked it all up to the computer. The solar panels are trash because of Joshua, but at least Graham got out that one message."

"He's a hero." She met his eyes. "You want to hold her?"

Tom nodded, his eyes burning when she put the baby in his arms. "You're a lucky little girl, Jellybean. Your parents love you. Your daddy cannot wait to meet you."

The baby yawned, looking too damn cute.

Liza sighed. "Will you bring charges against Hayley and Graham's mom?"

"I don't know. Molina is making notes of all the infractions. Which reminds me of why I'm here. Gideon and Mercy arrived, along with several agents. Things are getting tense. Rebecca was yelling that Molina is denying her rights."

"Molina can charge her with kidnapping. She stole Tamar's baby."

Tom was floored. "What the hell is wrong with these people?"

"I wish I knew."

"Well, at least Joshua isn't carrying his shotgun anymore," Tom said. "I convinced him to put it away. It was confiscated by the ATF agent who arrived in the second wave."

"That's good. Oh, and Tamar is really Tiffany and I promised her that she could leave and we'd take her baby and pending DNA testing she'd get him back."

"I'll make sure Molina knows."

"Thank you. Did you say there was hot water?"

"Yes. We've had two helicopter drops—both included tanks of water and a gas-powered water heater. Does Jellybean need a bath? We're going to need baby seats, too, for the transport vehicles." The logistics of this transport were daunting. "Oh, I also need you to come with me. There are a number of people who need medical attention."

"Why didn't you say that right off?"

"Because you were holding the baby and my brain circuits fried."

She patted his cheek gently, then turned to Tiffany. "I'm going to take the baby with me," she said. "Can you stay with Hayley in case she wakes up? Until Rebecca is confined, I don't want to leave Jellybean here, and I don't want Hayley thinking the baby's been stolen."

They heard the shouting as they drew close to the entrance. Tom gave the baby to Liza and rushed to help. As expected, Joshua was in Gideon's face, calling him a liar and a fraud, sent by the government to take away their First, Second, and Fourth Amendment rights. Molina stood next to Gideon and there were four federal agents behind her.

Mercy stood to the side, looking anxious. She'd known that coming back here would resurrect a lot of bad ghosts, but she'd done it anyway because she'd wanted to help.

Graham sidled up to Liza. "I'm clean. And sanitized. Can I hold my niece now?"

Tom rejoined them, watching the gathered crowd from the sidelines as Liza put the baby in Graham's arms. The boy began to cry, the sight sweet and at stark odds with the angry Joshua.

Gideon remained calm, ignoring Joshua's rant and talking to the members of Eden who stood silently gawking at him. "If you want to leave, we will transport you. My sister Mercy and I came back to let you know that there is life after Eden. We will help you find a place to live and integrate back into the community at whatever level you wish.

If you've suffered at the hands of a husband or as an apprentice like we did, there are resources to help."

That seemed to strike a chord. Many of the members nodded and whispered to each other.

"And if we don't want to leave?" Joshua demanded.

"Do you really want to stay?" Gideon countered. "You don't have fresh water or food. You don't have sanitary toilet facilities or real medical help. Sister Coleen did her best, but many of you need trained doctors, not merely a person who wants to be helpful but gets all of her medical know-how from books and the computer."

"When is she coming back?" Joshua demanded.

Tom thought they should tell the truth, but Molina had been afraid of a riot. Apparently, she had changed her mind. Probably because of the agents standing behind her.

"She's not," Molina said, and the murmurs grew to irate cries.

"You've arrested her?" Joshua shouted, and the tension ratcheted up tenfold.

Many of these people had been brainwashed as to the evils of the government for thirty years. Tom marveled that Amos had adjusted so well.

"No," Molina said, holding up a hand for order. "She was killed by DJ Belmont."

"That's a lie!" Joshua cried. "Why would he do that?"

Mercy stepped forward, her face drawn and pale. "Probably because Coleen found out about me. That I survived. That DJ lied when he said I'd died trying to escape. He shot my mother in cold blood. She did die. But he was interrupted when he was trying to kill me."

"That. Is. A. Lie," Joshua repeated.

"Listen to it with your own ears," Molina said. She produced a cell phone and one of the agents hooked it up to a speaker. "The hospital where Pastor was staying provided computer devices to all the patients and their families. They can be used as cameras and tape recorders. We think Coleen was recording Mr. Belmont in an attempt to prove to Pastor what she'd learned. She was suffocated and there were bruises around her neck where Mr. Belmont grabbed her locket chain and twisted."

Tom noticed several women in the gathered crowd put their hands to their throats, their expressions indicating that they had also been controlled by their locket chain.

Molina tapped her phone and DJ's voice could be heard.

"Where is he?"

"Back in the solarium after his nap," Coleen replied.

"What did he do while he was there?"

"He met a little girl earlier, and they chatted. He wanted to feel the sun on his face, so I took him back and left him with his nurse. I wanted to talk to you."

"What did they chat about? And who's with him now?"

"They chatted about all kinds of things. His kids, you know, his real kids. Bo and Bernie."

"That doesn't hurt me like you think it does," DJ said. *"I never wanted to be his kid."*

That drew a gasp from the crowd.

"How did they get that tape?" Liza asked Tom in a whisper.

"Someone in billing finally clicked on the link in my e-mail. I got into the security network and downloaded this file while Croft and I were driving to you. Sunnyside uploaded everything the patients and families did on the devices."

Coleen went on to accuse DJ of deceit when it came to Mercy. Tom watched the crowd as DJ admitted it all. This was making a difference. And then . . .

"Are you going to tell Pastor?" DJ asked.

"If I were going to tell him, I'd have done it already."

"What are you doing, Sister Coleen?" he asked, his voice suddenly louder.

"Nothing." Coleen's voice was hoarse, like she couldn't breathe. *"Just filling in the blanks. You're hurting me, DJ."*

The recording abruptly ended and the crowd was absolutely silent. Even Joshua had ceased his ranting.

"Sister Coleen was found a few hours later, dead in her bed," Molina said.

Joshua stepped back, shaken. "No. That's a fake. Like the moon landing." He spun around and addressed the membership. "Don't listen to her. She's lying. She probably has Sister Coleen in a cell somewhere." Then he spied Graham holding the baby and started for him, a foul look on his face. "Don't you touch my wife's baby."

Graham's eyes widened and he turned, showing Joshua his back and protecting the baby with his own body. He didn't have to.

Tom stepped in front of Graham, never so glad to be six-six with heavy muscle. Joshua wasn't a small man, but he had to look way up.

"You will not put your hands on him," Tom said quietly. "Or the baby. Or her mother."

Fear crossed the man's eyes and he turned to the crowd. "This is how it starts. They come in and tell us what to do. How to live. How to worship. Pastor will fix this when he comes back."

Molina cleared her throat. "Pastor is also dead. DJ killed him, too."

A collective wail rose from the group, many of the members falling to their knees in grief.

"Why?" Joshua demanded. "Why would Brother DJ kill Pastor? That makes no sense."

"Agent Hunter?" Molina said. "Please tell them why."

Tom raised his voice. "Because he wanted Pastor's money. Pastor's bank account had fifty million dollars in it."

Once again there was silence, broken by muted weeping. Joshua laughed harshly. "Fifty million dollars? You are insane. Look at us. We don't have anything."

"How much did you donate to Eden when you joined?" Tom asked Joshua.

Joshua frowned. "We sold our home and donated the profits. It was about three hundred thousand dollars."

Tom pointed at another man about Joshua's age. "And you, sir?"

"Four hundred thousand," the man said, clearly troubled.

Tom pointed to various members, and after five people, the total was already over two million dollars. "He invested well and supplemented with sales of the drugs you grew and harvested."

One of the men shook his head. "We never sold drugs."

"Tell them to look in the cave room where the tools and schoolbooks were stored," Graham said. "There's a box marked *Smithy Tools*. It's filled with cocaine and pot. Full disclosure," he added, "I took a brick of the coke to try to blackmail Brother DJ into letting my sister go to the hospital. Like Pastor was able to. The coke is hidden under a rock near the computer. The package is unopened." He pointed a finger at Joshua. "And before you can claim I smuggled it, remember that Isaac, the head of our household, thoroughly searched us. Those drugs belong to DJ."

A man stepped forward. "I'll check. One of your policemen may come with me."

Tom exhaled slowly. He'd thought they'd ask who killed DJ and he wasn't sure how to answer that. He'd had to surrender his weapon and badge to Molina on the way to the caves. It was standard procedure when one fired their service weapon. He'd probably have to undergo counseling before he was reinstated.

Molina clapped her hands to regain the group's attention. "While they are checking Graham's claim, we can transport anyone who wants to go now. If you'd like to talk to Gideon and Mercy first, they will be here. Amos Terrill will also be here in a few hours."

A middle-aged woman stepped forward. "Amos is all right? And Abigail? I've been so worried. She's my daughter's best friend."

"They are very much all right," Molina said kindly. "Amos realizes that many of you may want more proof, and he will tell you what he saw that drove him to run from Eden. If you'd like to leave, the first transport will depart in two hours. I'll stay here to answer any questions."

"And if we choose to stay?" Joshua asked, still belligerent.

"I can't make you come with us," she said, "unless you're suspected of a crime. Like kidnapping or child endangerment."

Joshua's jaw tightened. "And for those of us who are innocent of wrongdoing?"

"I can't make you come with us, but you can't stay here. This is private property."

Two hours later, the first transport departed, Tiffany and her little boy on board, and there wasn't an empty seat.

And, after Amos arrived and talked to the remaining members, the next transport was also filled.

Finally, an ambulance arrived with two paramedics. Hayley and her baby were loaded in with Graham riding in the back with them.

Tom waved as they drove away, headed to Sacramento, where Hayley would be checked out at UC Davis. Arm tightly around Liza's waist, Tom turned to Gideon, Mercy, and Amos, who'd stayed to help the members understand the new world.

"We did it," Tom said, feeling both satisfied and oddly unsettled. "We found them."

"*You* found them," Mercy corrected with a smile. "You and Liza. Thank you."

Amos nodded. "Yes. Thank you both. For me and for Abigail and every person who felt trapped and too afraid to escape."

Tom didn't want the gratitude. He was doing his job. He knew Liza felt the same way.

"Did you notice that no one asked about DJ?" Liza asked, redirecting the conversation. "I think everyone knew that he was capable of everything we told them."

"I agree," Mercy said. "And I for one am not sorry at all. Pastor, Ephraim, and DJ are all gone. We can live our lives and not worry that they're coming to kill us."

Amos put his arm around Mercy's shoulders. "Abigail never has to worry about what happens when she turns twelve. You all have done a good thing. I'm proud of you."

"It feels . . . unfinished," Tom murmured. "I mean, there's still the fifty million to figure out, but over a hundred people have to start new lives."

Amos sighed. "They'll have to learn technology and how to function in a real community. They'll have to unlearn all the fiction they've been taught as fact. Some of them might even choose to continue living in isolation, but they'll still need support. Land and supplies. Medical care and guidance on how to rebuild legally. It's not going to be easy."

Gideon nodded. "The hard work has just begun."

EPILOGUE

GRANITE BAY, CALIFORNIA
TUESDAY, JULY 4, 2:30 P.M.

How was your first day at nursing school, *lubimaya*?" Irina asked, settling into the lawn chair next to Liza's.

Liza thought this might have been the first time Irina had sat down in days. The Sokolovs were hosting a barbecue and Irina had been in overdrive. The kitchen was filled with food, the house filled with people, and, because no one was shooting at them, the backyard was crowded as well.

The day was a scorcher, well over a hundred degrees, but awnings shaded and fans blew and children ran through the sprinklers. So many children, including a few from Chicago.

Karl and Irina had invited Liza and Tom's family to join them, and they had. It had been a huge surprise—for both Liza and Tom. Apparently Irina, Tom's mother Caroline, and Liza's adopted big sister Dana had been burning up the phone lines, setting all this up.

It was heaven.

"Surreal," Liza answered. "I mean, I'd wished so long to get there. I'd served my tour and gotten my undergrad degree, all while hoping to be accepted at UC Davis. I was seriously just happy to be there. But then I went to orientation last week and everyone knew my name."

"You are a hero," Irina commented with a smile. "Again."

Liza rolled her eyes, still embarrassed. The news had been saturated with their discovery of Eden and the defeat of DJ Belmont and Pastor. Gideon, Mercy, and Amos had become the poster children of cult survivors, and Hayley and her baby had been showered with Internet affection and real-life gifts.

Baby Liza Tiffany was the most pampered infant in the city. And grown-up Liza still got a lump in her throat every time she thought of Hayley naming the baby after her.

"I did what anyone would," Liza murmured. It was her stock answer and she held to that belief with both hands.

"Anyone with a good heart and a healthy amount of courage," Irina said.

"I had good role models."

"Here one of them comes," Irina commented as Dana Dupinsky Buchanan approached, a tray of cold drinks in her hands.

"Absolutely." Liza squeezed Irina's hand. "And another one is sitting right here."

"Ach." Irina fanned her face with her free hand. "You make me cry."

"Liza." Dana took the chair on her other side, passing them the drinks. "Why are you making this nice lady cry?"

Liza began to defend herself until she saw that Dana was teasing. "You're terrible."

"So I've been told. Regularly." She reached across Liza to tap her glass to Irina's. "To all the terrible people who love you."

"Hear, hear." Irina sighed happily. "Everyone is having a good time, yes?"

Liza smiled, completely content. "A very good time. I think Tom's sister has adopted Abigail." Nine-year-old Grace had taken the younger girl under her wing, and Abigail had followed her all afternoon like an imprinted duckling. They'd tasked themselves with making sure the "little kids" were staying out of trouble. "And Karl is on a cloud talking basketball with two ex-pros." Tom and his stepfather Max had indulged Karl's excitement, telling him stories about players they'd known. "He is too cute."

"He is," Irina said fondly, watching her husband talk animatedly while flipping burgers on the grill. "I think I'll keep him."

"And that kid from Eden—Graham?" Dana chuckled. "He's been following Ethan around ever since he learned that Tom was a hacker and Ethan taught him everything he knows."

"Hopefully Graham will keep using his brain for good and not evil," Liza said wryly. "He'd gotten in with a bad crowd before their mother took them to Eden."

"But he's in a better home environment now?" Dana asked, concerned. She was always concerned about kids in abusive homes.

Liza nodded. "His mother lost custody of Graham, and Hayley's nearly eighteen. The two of them moved in with Cameron Cook's family, and it seems to be good for all of them."

"And I got to hold that precious baby," Irina said, then grinned. "And when she needed a diaper change, I got to give her back."

"That's the best part of grandparenting, right?" Dana eyed Liza. "Or aunting? I mean, I am an amazing aunt."

"Not for a while," Liza said. "Tom and I talked about it. No kids until I'm done with nursing school."

"Time will fly," Irina said wisely. "Which reminds me, I have a cake in the oven and it's almost done." She started to rise, then changed her mind. "I meant to ask. How is Brooklyn? The little girl Liza met at Sunnyside Oaks," Irina explained to Dana.

"Keepin' on." Liza had so much respect for this tiny little girl, whose mother had rushed home as soon as she heard the news, transferring her to UC Davis's pediatric cancer ward as Sunnyside had been shut down while under criminal investigation. All of its patients had been transferred to hospitals all over the area. "Her mother is spending more time with her now because she's finished shooting her film. She's an actress, a single mother who had no one to help her with Brooklyn. She didn't want her daughter harassed by photographers, so she put her in Sunnyside based on the recommendation of a friend. Tom, Abigail, and I visited her at the hospital this morning." Abigail and Brooklyn had become fast friends. "She's got another round of chemo, but the doctors are hopeful it'll be her last. She said thank you for the cookies, Irina."

Irina smiled. "The least I can do. I missed my visit this past week because of all of this." She gestured to the people filling the yard. "But I'll see her in a few days." She stood up. "I have to pull that cake from the oven. If it burns, I will have revolution."

Dana chuckled as Irina hurried away. "I like her."

"I knew you would." Liza looked around, grinning at Tom, who was sneaking up behind his mother with a Super Soaker. Caroline would not be pleased. "He's just a big kid."

"And happier than I've seen him in a while. Which makes Caroline and me happy, too. We always wondered if anything would happen between you two."

"They had a betting pool here," Liza grumbled. "Karl won two hundred bucks."

Dana clapped her hands, a delighted expression on her face. "We had one, too!"

"Who won?"

Dana preened. "I did. And everyone said I cheated because I told you to keep your heart open if he changed his mind, but I took the cash anyway. The girls at the shelter had an ice cream party. They said to thank you."

Liza laughed. "Karl donated his to Tom's charity here in town. It's a sports program for kids from abusive homes."

Dana leaned into Liza's shoulder companionably. "It's like we came full circle, you know?"

Shrieks from across the yard had them looking up. Caroline was dripping wet and had wrested the Super Soaker from Tom because he was laughing too hard to stop her.

"He's gonna pay for that," Dana said fondly.

And he did. He didn't even run, taking his punishment like a man.

"I feel like . . ." Liza sighed. "Is it stupid to worry that things are too good?"

"No. It's normal. I struggled with that for years. Still do." Dana met her eyes, serious now. "You've earned every bit of happiness. If another shoe falls, you'll deal. You're not alone."

"I know." And she wasn't, the object of her affection striding across the lawn, dripping wet and looking like every fantasy she'd ever had. Every carved muscle was on display. "Wow."

Dana snorted. "Stop it. I knew him when he was seven."

"He's sure as hell not seven anymore."

Dana shook her head. "I'm going to leave you to your drool. I'll see you later."

Tom tried to hug Dana as they passed, but she shoved him, still shaking her head.

Tom dropped into the chair she'd vacated. "You okay?"

"More than." Liza gave him a peck on the lips. "How are your lips cold? It's hotter than hell out here."

"I filled the Super Soaker with ice water."

"Oh, your mom is gonna get you back. I mean, this"—she gestured to his wet T-shirt—"was just the first wave of attack. Although I do like the outcome."

He grinned wickedly, sending her libido on a roller coaster. "Really?"

"You know it. How long before we can go home?"

"Too long. My mom told me not to even think about sneaking off for 'private time.'"

"They did come an awful long way to see us."

His grin softened to a sweet smile. "They did. We're pretty lucky, you know that?"

"We are." She linked their fingers together. Kissed his knuckles. "Love you."

"Love you, too."

Her head resting on his shoulder, they enjoyed the little bubble of quiet.

Which was promptly popped by the clearing of a throat.

Liza looked up with a smile of welcome. "Hello, Tara."

Tom made a strangled sound in his throat, his reaction every time she called his boss by her first name. She'd done so for the first time the day they were in Eden, and she said it didn't make sense to go back to formalities. Tom disagreed.

"Ma'am," he said, standing at attention. Liza wanted to hug him hard and drag him to bed.

Molina's lips twitched. "Agent Hunter. I wanted to thank you for inviting me and let you know that I'm headed out. I had a nice time talking with your mother."

Tom made another strangled sound. "I'm glad, ma'am."

"Now you're just being mean, Tara," Liza said with a chuckle. "I'm glad you could come. I might not see you again for a while with school taking off. Thank you for the commendation, by the way." The special agent in charge had written a letter praising Liza for delivering Hayley's baby under conditions that were less than ideal. "My advisor put it in my file."

"You deserved it. Now I have to get back to the office. We're preparing for preliminary hearings on Joshua and his wife."

The two had been charged with kidnapping, along with several Edenites who'd engaged in the sexual assault of minors. Liza had already been given permission to miss class for the hearing. She'd promised Hayley and Tiffany that she'd be in the courtroom to lend moral support as they testified.

"I talked to Tiffany a few days ago," Liza said. "She's doing well. Cameron Cook's family is renting her the apartment over their garage. She starts training to be a nursing assistant in a few weeks. For now, she's reconnecting with her little boy." Prompt DNA testing had proven that the child was hers. It was one more nail in Joshua and Rebecca's coffin.

More serious charges were pending the results of autopsies of the women who'd died in childbirth, their bodies exhumed from the graveyard at one of the previous Eden sites. Their families believed that Rebecca had killed them after the babies were born so that she could claim the children, but the families had had no power to accuse her back in Eden.

They were accusing her now.

"Give Tiffany my best regards," Molina said. "Make sure she knows to send me any address updates. The money recovered from Eden's accounts is going to be awarded to the members who aren't guilty of any crimes. It might take a while, but she should get a sizable sum to live on while she attends school."

"I will," Liza promised. "She'll be so grateful."

Tom sank back into the chair once Molina was gone. "She and my mom were talking? Why is this my life?"

Liza laughed. "You just said how lucky we are."

"And I am. I have you. And you'll protect me when my mom and my boss join forces."

She kissed his mouth, no longer cold. His lips were warm and pliable and made her want to forsake their visitors and head for home. "Pebbles needs to be walked."

"She does. We could go home, walk her, have time for a quickie, and come back here later."

She grinned against his lips. "They wouldn't even know we were gone." Which was total bullshit, but she didn't care. They wouldn't be gone long.

He lurched to his feet, tugging her to hers. "Let's go."

ACKNOWLEDGMENTS

The Starfish—Christine, Brian, Cheryl, Kathie, and Sheila—for the plotting and everything else.

Hope Blaess for all the information on army medics, university education while deployed, and, most of all, for your service. Thank you.

Caitlin Ellis for all you do to keep the business going while I'm in the cave.

Sarah Hafer and Beth Miller for all the editing and proofreading. Your keen eyes and attention to detail are invaluable.

Sonie Lasker for your help with the Russian translations, the military detail, and for your service. I'm so proud of you, sister mine.

James "Egypt" Lee for the network guidance, DEFCON stories, and hacking theory.

Claire Zion, Jen Doyle, and Robin Rue for all your support as I wrote this, my twenty-fifth novel.